S0-ARK-946

MISCHIEF

Also by Ben Travers

Novels

THE COLLECTION TODAY
THE DIPPERS
VALE OF LAUGHTER

Plays

A BIT OF A TEST
BANANA RIDGE
THE BED BEFORE YESTERDAY
CHASTITY MY BROTHER
CORKER'S END
A CUCKOO IN THE NEST
A CUP OF KINDNESS
THE DIPPERS
DIRTY WORK
MISCHIEF
A NIGHT LIKE THIS
NUN'S VEILING
OUTRAGEOUS FORTUNE
PLUNDER
ROOKERY NOOK
SHE FOLLOWS ME ABOUT
SPOTTED DICK
THARK
TURKEY TIME
WILD HORSES

MISCHIEF

by Ben Travers

Including *Mischief*, *Rookery Nook*, and *A Cuckoo in the Nest*

HARPER & ROW, PUBLISHERS

New York, Hagerstown, San Francisco, London

 For information address Harper & Row, Publishers, Inc., 10 East 53rd Street, New York, N.Y. 10022.

FIRST EDITION

Library of Congress Cataloging in Publication Data

Travers, Ben, 1886-
Mischief.
CONTENTS: Mischief.—Rookery nook.—A cuckoo in the nest.
I. Title.
PR6039.R3M5 1978 823'.9'12 78-4746
ISBN 0-06-014347-9

---

78 79 80 81 82 10 9 8 7 6 5 4 3 2 1

Contents

MISCHIEF

Ben Travers

'Why, the news is that Cuckoldom in folio is newly printed; and Matrimony in quarto is just going into the press. Will you buy any books, Mademoiselle?'

The Provoked Wife
Vanbrugh

PART ONE
Morning of Mischief

CHAPTER I

Prelude to Mischief

One night Mr and Mrs Reginald Bingham went to Ciro's. They had been married only about six months. Mr Bingham had never been to Ciro's before in his life. His surprise, therefore, upon seeing his wife there was considerable.

She was dancing with Algy Richardson Gascoyne.

Mr Bingham had left home only that evening, intending to go to Yorkshire on business. His first night away from home since his marriage. And here she was. The moment his back was turned. Algy Richardson Gascoyne.

Her behaviour gave her rather pompous bridegroom of fifty furiously to think, and even yet more furiously to imagine. He retaliated by leaving Ciro's without giving her the chance of seeing him, and by returning to their house in Prince's Gate in good time to witness the manner of her home-coming. She kept him waiting such a devil of a time that he began to think she must be out for the whole night, which gave him to imagine more furiously than ever; but at length, from an upper window, he saw her arrive in a taxi; and after kissing Algy Richardson Gascoyne good-night, she came, still dancing, indoors and up to her bedroom, where, erect in the bed, with the brow of Jupiter for some nonsense of Juno's, and with as much dignity as can possibly be assumed by a middle-aged gentleman in Swan-stripe pyjamas, he confronted her.

She was startled, certainly, but not so impressed by his challenge as he had hoped. Indeed, she laughed aloud, and told him that if he only knew how supremely ridiculous he looked, sitting up there in his pyjamas and doing a strong silent act, he would pull the blankets over his head and keep them there. After which, she proceeded, very flippantly, to continue to dance while disrobing; so that the scene suggested not so much the first breach of the married peace, as the spectacle of an Oriental potentate being wooed from his ennui in the approved method.

'Stop that now. Come! Tell me at once, where have you been spending the night?' demanded Mr Bingham.

'I've been to Ciro's with Algy Gascoyne,' she replied. 'And – (*I wanna go way home to Wagon-Wheel-Gap – tew Wagon-Wheel-Gap with yew*) – And what have you been up to, I should like to know. Yorkshire, indeed!'

'As a matter of fact, I was at this Ciro's myself, and saw you there,' announced the husband, secretly a trifle peeved at the frankness of her confession.

'*Were* you? I never saw you there. And if you saw me, why ask where I was? And who were you at Ciro's with, you old Yorkshire pudding?'

Mr Bingham, unfortunately, had a perfectly straightforward, above-board and business-like reason for having been to this place, Ciro's. Simply the man with whom he had hoped to conduct business in Yorkshire had arrived in London, and had met Mr Bingham at King's Cross while the latter was waiting for the train. So Mr Bingham had returned with this man to Piccadilly, had dressed at his club, had dined and conversed with this man, and (this man being rather a nob) had subsequently agreed to accompany this nob to this place, Ciro's. At Ciro's, glancing down from the gallery at the dancers below, he had beheld his wife, who could have no such good excuse for being there, especially with Algy Richardson Gascoyne.

Mr Bingham had with difficulty succeeded in keeping his sorry secret from the nob. If truth be told, he had been subjected to the poisonous ordeal of listening to the comments of the nob concerning his wife, whose appearance happened to make a decided hit with the nob. Mr Bingham did not, however, repeat this detail to Mrs Bingham,rightly judging that it would only appeal to her vanity and make her more obstinate and troublesome and matters worse generally.

'So that is how I happened to be there,' he concluded. 'As for you, will you kindly stop all this humming and buzzing and swaying about, and put on your nightgown and oblige me with an explanation of what you mean by it? Come!'

Mrs Bingham, who was very young and pretty, and who had becomingly shingled hair and a retroussé nose and jade earrings, and who was by this time in a condition calculated to drive the most case-hardened Oriental potentate from his ennui, responded by seating herself casually on the foot of the bed, and giving her husband her candid, if somewhat involved, views on how to be happy though married, when respectively fifty and twenty-six. He was slow to succumb to her pretty arguments and her patently innocent admissions. Why had she not informed him of her intentions for the night, before he set out? Because, dear old fathead, the intentions had never occurred to her until after her lonely dinner. This youth, though – Algy Richardson Gascoyne? . . .

'Well?' she asked sharply, exhibiting for the first time, and, despite her condition, a certain warmth. 'What have you got against him anyway?'

'You allowed him to kiss you in the cab.'

'Yes. I've known Algy for years.'

'That's no excuse now you're married.'

'He was at school with my sister.'

'Your sister?'

'I mean I was at school with his sister. It's all the same thing. A kiss in a taxi – good heavens! If every taxi told!'

'There's no need to be festive about it. I'm very put out. In fact, I won't stand it. This, after six months! You're behaving like a fast woman.'

'Well, I've had to behave like a very slow one for the six months,' said Mrs Bingham, leaving the bed.

He continued rigorously, 'I should raise no unreasonable objection to your going out to a dance, but I dislike these underhand methods.'

'So do I,' she cried. 'You saw me there, and sneaked home and watched me arrive and spied on me generally. Now, look here, Reggy. We've been very happy so far, but this is the way to begin spoiling things.'

Mr Bingham wormed himself with difficulty (he was stout) into a recumbent attitude. 'We'll discuss this in the morning. If you must have amusement, I'll take you to amusement. But you'll give me an undertaking to see no more of this young man.'

Mrs Bingham, who was in front of her mirror and threatening to resume dancing, declared that she would do nothing of the sort.

'Oh, won't you! We shall see,' said the husband, raising his head without moving his shoulders. 'Stop that, will you, at once, and get into bed.'

He turned on his side, and continued to mutter to himself in the sheets, 'Idle young gadabout! Do-nothing of a fellow! I'll teach him to kiss you in taxis.'

'He learnt that years ago,' commented the wife.

The Reverend Stanley Hipgrave does not participate in the events hereinafter chronicled, for he has left these shores and is now in Australia. But may his deanery be plagued by rabbits, and may he never again hold the ashes, for what he did before he started.

For he married her to Reginald Bingham – gay, elegant, fascinating Eleanor – he married her to this pomposity of fifty. Any discriminating clergyman, taking but one look at the couple as they presented themselves for wedlock, would have turned and bolted himself into the vestry until after the hours prescribed (for some reason) for the ministers of God to perform this line of their business. But Hipgrave merely gulped, read, joined, blessed, pocketed his fee, and went to Australia.

But the luck of this man Reginald Bingham, his outrageous success! He seemed to spend his life in observing the ambitions of his fellow-men, and in swooping in upon them and cutting them out. Hitherto he had confined his activities to business, which he conducted on the lines of a modern and commercial equivalent to some snorting mediaeval swashbuckler – discovering rivals with interests in timber forests and options on coalfields, and cutting them out and bashing them on one side with great sweeping drafts on banks, and enormous thudding great batches of preference shares, even as his earlier prototype swung the foes from his path with his searing steel.

Reginald Bingham's only reason for going down to Hutton Court, Henley, as the guest of Sir Somebody Duddingbury for the week-end, was that he understood that Sir Somebody was about to interest himself in some oil-wells, or something; and Mr Bingham made up his mind that he would discover what it was all about, and, if there was anything in it, that he would cut Sir Somebody clean out of the business. And down at Hutton Court, also for the week-end, was this delightful creature, Eleanor.

He found her surrounded by fatuous and sandwich-handing and cushion-thumping young penniless men in flannel bags. Was diverted for the first time from stern commerce to more romantic adventure. Swooped in and utterly routed the open-mouthed flannel-bagged brigade, and cut them out and carried off this delicious woman and bore her away and upped his banns and Hipgrave-ho before she had time to recover her breath, so it appeared. But, as a matter of fact, she had never lost her breath at all.

She submitted with cynical readiness to this pounding fellow. She admired him for his cool supremacy, rather as one admires a good-natured policeman on point duty. He was very kind and very liberal. He had no sense of humour, but – oh, why make excuses for her? She made none for herself. Money! Money, money, money! The frailty of such women is half their charm; and, if Eleanor had never exhibited frailty more culpable than this bargain, the fact makes her only the more tantalising.

They met in September – early in October were married. He bought her a magnificent house in Prince's Gate, and she had everything she wanted, except fun. For no young men in flannel bags came to Prince's Gate. When Reginald entertained he entertained bald elderly men, whom he invited to dine in the Borgia spirit, in order that he might 'feed them champagne' and cut them out and buy them off and do them down. At these dinners Eleanor vice-presided in the most admirable manner; but afterwards she would often go upstairs to her bedroom and lie awake for hours and hours, until all the guests were half tipsy and completely cut out, and Reginald would come thudding upstairs, clapping his great hands together and saying, 'Ha! a good night's work! Are you asleep?'

This Reginald Bingham was naturally, with all his success, a man of considerable authority of manner. His voice was sonorous, and he had a habit of pulling his nose about with his thumb and forefinger, and of then extending the forefinger, quivering to command attention. He seldom questioned: he stated, dictated. To his relatives, to men at his club, to the stranger within his railway carriage – they all 'got the finger', as his brother Henry put it.

Reginald was clean-shaven. He would pronounce an edict, and then let his face sink to his chest with his eyes upturned to study the effect on you; and there would roll up, round his mouth and cheeks, chin upon chin – waves of chin.

In body, he swelled in an arc of a circle from top waistcoat-button to middle trouser-button. In demeanour, grave; deprecating mirth as sheer waste of time, suspecting levity often where none was intended. He employed a special little vocabulary of terms for the rebuking and cutting short of levity. Thus, to his clerk: 'Very well, then; put it in the correspondence file A, where it should go. And see here, you – don't you try any of your flounce with me, or you'll go clean out.' To his stockbroker: 'Come now! I called you up for a quotation. If I require any bubble and squeak, I know where to go for it.' Even to his caddie: 'My jigger? Very well, then, hand me my jigger. And when I happen to want any festivity from you, I'll let you know.'

This was the man whose marriage bed our Eleanor had elected (still venting a faint echo of her desire to emigrate to Wagon-Wheel-Gap) to share. Many blamed her for it, but she never blamed herself as yet. The scene which had just taken place in the bedroom was the first of its kind. Never before had he spoken a cross word to her, nor she a callous, aggressive word to him.

Eleanor – an elegant name: an elegant woman. Vivacious, but of great tact and charm, and, to Reginald at any rate, more fascinating even in her repose than in her vivacity, as is often the way with elegant women. But she had a quick turn of the head for anything that promised a new excitement, a new interest. As a result, her interests did not last very long. She was wont to snap up a pleasure, as a lizard snaps up a fly and swallows it immediately and undigested, so as to be ready to snap up the next.

Very good company; with an intimate, whispering delight for the funnily improper. Natural, laughing, worldly. Oh, and her style and her looks! Not daring in her dress, but always right, and always confident of her rightness. Not merely a very attractive and presumably frail woman for your banter and hints. She had amused, knowledgeable eyes that would take stock of you with cool reserve from behind their long lashes, and you would pretty soon discover that if you were to win her friendship it would be of her choice, and not yours. Reginald pulled his nose about with the sheer triumph of possessing her. And may Hipgrave be held up by bushrangers, and have his last damper destroyed by kangaroos.

In the morning they woke to peace and goodwill. Eleanor kissed her husband and said she was sorry she had been out to Ciro's if he didn't like it, and still more sorry that she had been rude to him about it. All of which he acknowledged with a pat and a rather exasperating air of ascendency. He admitted, though, that he had been perhaps unnecessarily put out, and secretly reflected with some vexation that, had he been a trifle less impetuous, he might have remained at Ciro's a little longer and soaked the nob really thoroughly while he was about it.

Thus, the incident appeared to be closed. Reginald made no further reference to Algy Richardson Gascoyne. Eleanor noted the omission, but resolved to be sporting about it, and not to invite Algy to the house, or to go out of her way to see him. Absurd, of course; but she wanted to be strictly loyal to Reggy, even in his absurdities, until she had cured him of them.

But what about the sportmanship of Reggy?

That very morning, he rang up his sister, Louise, from his office, and told her that he would come and see her at teatime. He required some information concerning someone. He would prefer to see her alone, so perhaps she would arrange for her husband to be elsewhere at the time of his visit.

Louise, who was the wife of Colonel Piper, arranged this without difficulty, and at five o'clock her brother presented himself at her flat in Gloucester Road. Louise did not feel very certain of Reggy these days. So long as he had kept his success to himself, well and good. But when one's brother Reggy suddenly decides to share his success with an Eleanor, ah, then is one tested.

If Reggy had been a normal brother, like Henry was, one might have made bold to comment. But Reggy was so successful and phenomenal, and, in his most relaxed moments, so condescending to one, and, in his more superior moments, so much richer than one and so contemptuous of one, that Louise had never been able to speak her mind. Once, more stung than courageous,she had said, 'I hope, Reggy, she isn't fast.' At which up went the forefinger. 'That'll do, Louise. I know. Jealous. Because she is young and is to have a house in Prince's Gate. Oh, don't tell me. Fast, indeed! She is to be my wife, isn't she? Very well, then. Stop that.'

And all the time Eleanor was fast, and Louise knew she was fast. A woman's instinct. And one day Reggy would find it out for himself.

Of course, mind you, she *liked* Eleanor. She said so herself. 'Of course, mind you, I *like* her, poor girl.'

'My dear Reggy,' said Louise, 'one so seldom sees you nowadays. And how are you? And Eleanor? I saw her only two days ago in her car outside Harrod's. I don't think she noticed me. Have you had tea?'

'Yes, yes, thank you. Never mind about all that. I've called to ask you a question, haven't I? Very well, then. Now.'

He seated himself, faced his sister, brought his hands to his knees. 'Algernon Richardson Gascoyne,' he said, and let his face sink to his chest. Chins, chins appeared.

The dawn of suspicion glimmered in the expression of Louise. 'Why do you ask about *him*?'

Reginald forefingered her away from suspicion.

'He is trying to interest himself in a certain – ah – proposition, of which I – ah – happen to know something. You know a good deal about him, I fancy. Well?'

'I don't,' said Louise. 'Let me see. He lives in a flat in Half Moon Street, doesn't he?'

Reginald heaved.

'Oh, do not make statements and then turn them into questions. Does he, or does he not, live in a flat in Half Moon Street?'

'Yes.'

'Yes. He lives in a flat in Half Moon Street. Well?'

'I don't know much about him. I should think he's unquestionably a bad lot. He seems very well off. He does no work anyhow, and he has a noisy little car. I don't mean rattly. I mean the rich sort of popping noisiness. He's just one of those sort of young men about town, as they used to call them when there were any. Of course the chief thing against him is his aunt.'

'His aunt?'

'Yes. Mrs Krabbe. I don't know much about *him*, but his aunt is known to be a most dreadful character. He has a sister too. I don't know much about the sister.'

'Your knowledge,' said Reginald, 'appears to be rather limited all round.'

'Well, why come to me, if you want to find out about the Gascoynes?'

'I only want to know about the young man.'

'Well, there's someone much nearer home who can tell you all about *him*,' said Louise.

'Who do you mean?'

'Eleanor, of course.'

'Eleanor? Does she know him?'

'Oh, Reggy!'

'What?'

Louise, for once tremendously daring, rose and openly sneered at Reggy. It was not intended for a sneer. It was intended for a confidential smile of perspicacity.

'You may be clever,' she said, 'but really . . .'

'What are you talking about, and grimacing about? What is all this toshpail?'

'Why did you want to see me alone without Willy? You must think I'm very dense. As if Algy Richardson Gascoyne had any interests in one of your business concerns! As if you didn't know he was one of Eleanor's set before she married! Really, Reggy . . .'

Reginald made elaborate chewing movements, frowning very deeply.

'Louise,' he said, after a few moments of this, 'if you imagine that there's any trouble at home, you're mistaken.'

She began to protest. He cut her short. 'Stop that. *But* – Yes. He – this young Gascoyne man – has been trying to associate with Eleanor on the sly, and I don't like it.'

'Quite right. Oh, he's a horrid lot. I'm sure of it. In fact, I *know*.'

'Mind you,' continued Reginald, speaking deliberately and very seriously, 'Eleanor is young, and susceptible to flattery and flapdoodle. I cannot always be with her. So perhaps it's as well that you should know of this. So that *next* time I'm called away on business and have to leave her alone . . .'

'What!' cried Louise, scarce able to contain herself, 'has something actually taken place, then?'

'Certainly not,' he replied sternly. 'Only I may require you, from time to time, to – ah – keep Eleanor company if I have to be away from home. There!' He rose. 'Will you do so?'

'Yes, of course I will. Only, Reggy, if there is anything – up – I mean, it's only fair that I should know *all*. Then I can keep my eye open.'

'Thank you; I don't require you to keep your eye open,' he answered with dignity from the doorway. 'Nothing is – up – as you put it. There is no hanky-panky in *my* home. She knows exactly what I think about things. I don't believe in married couples having secrets from each other.'

'No, nor do I,' said Louise, 'but . . .'

'Very well, then. There you are. Good-bye. Oh, by the way, you needn't mention any of this to your husband.'

He went home for tea, and exchanged very hearty greetings with Eleanor.

He offered to take her to a theatre that night. This surprised her, for she had made him go to one or two plays soon after they married, and had discovered that he had a strong dislike for the drama. Then she saw what this meant. It was a reflection on last night. It would have been more gracious of him not to have suggested the theatre, but rather to have ignored last night completely, as though it had never occurred. This was rubbing last night in. This was a metaphorical fore-fingering over last night.

'All right,' she thought. 'When in doubt, be natural. I like theatres; he doesn't. But it won't do him any harm to be unselfish, so we'll jolly well go.'

They jolly well went to a revue *intime*, of her rather wilful choice, entitled 'Hi!' Eleanor would have enjoyed it more if she could have laughed without feeling all the time that he was surprised at her and impatient with her for desiring to laugh at 'Hi!' He himself sat positively stupefied at the festivity of 'Hi!' But when she glanced at him he always smiled and nodded, as though to say, 'Go on; laugh if you find it amusing. Don't mind me.'

She longed suddenly, in the middle of 'Hi!' for one of two men. She longed for the man who would lie back in his stall and 'laugh like a closet', as Algy would say. She longed, alternatively, for the man who would say, 'I can't stick this tripe. Do you mind if I go and get a drink?' Now, at this moment, there dawned on her for the first time (and only six months after her marriage) the full force of what she had incurred – the first gleam of realisation of what his money was going to cost her.

Oh, fearsome thought! She was tired, perhaps, and worried by his bringing her here at all as the result of last night, pointing the moral tale, so to speak. She really was fond of him. She really didn't feel that little shrinking feeling as she looked at the other men in the stalls and compared them to him. She told herself she didn't. She couldn't, because if she did – after only six months of it . . .

Then another thought. 'You knew it all the time. You knew it, subconsciously, the whole time from the moment you accepted him. And you swore to yourself you'd never let yourself regret. And six months of it, and here you are. Go on. Go on with your job. Go on laughing at 'Hi!' and let him smile indulgently at you for being such a fool, and pull his nose about with satisfaction at having rubbed it well into you about last night.'

Thought fearsome! The car was waiting for them outside, to take them home after the show – a magnificent two-thousand-guinea affair. She caught sight of it, standing outside there, with misgiving, almost shrinking from it, as though she were ashamed of it, and ashamed of being the owner of it. Why? She didn't know why, at the time; only was conscious of that vague uneasiness about the car. It was only later that she realised it was discontent; not discontent with the car itself, but discontent that the car was all she could get with his money. And she wanted more – infinitely more. Or infinitely less, was it?

When they got in he had to sit up and do some work which he had put off, rather pointedly, in order to gratify her craving for amusement. She turned to go upstairs, then followed him into his study. This wouldn't do. The air must be cleared – by a storm, if necessary, but cleared.

She told him in her own natural way that next time he was angry with her, and when she had said she was sorry, then let them forget it and go on as if nothing had arisen. No more of these stratagems and coals of fire.

He said, 'You're over-tired, I think.' Then he lost his patience. 'Confound it, you ask to be amused, and I do my best. I take you out to amuse you. You choose your own form of entertainment – this thing, "Ho!" I postpone my work to take you out. What more can I do?'

'It wasn't you and I,' she said. 'That's the whole secret of a man and woman getting on together, I believe, – to be "you and I". We can get on very well, I believe, so long as you are you – to yourself as well as to me – and I am allowed to be I, and not the wife out of "The Problems of Matrimony" by Doctor Virginia Creeper.'

He looked quite alarmed. 'What in the devil's name are you talking about?'

'Can't you understand?' she said. 'I don't promise I shall

never do anything to make you angry, but when I do ...'

'You make me angry now,' he cried, and obviously told the truth, for he went on to speak his real mind. 'A nice evening's entertainment this has been! I suppose you prefer dancing on the sly with your Algys, but I can tell you, you'd better try to find my company amusing enough for you, because, by Christopher, it's the only company you'll get.'

'That's better,' said Eleanor, perceptibly brightening. 'That does me more good than fifty theatres.'

But, even then, he pretended he didn't understand her.

This was in April.

At the end of June Reginald had to go to France on business which would keep him abroad for a fortnight or more, and would entail a good deal of travelling. He might have to go to Holland, and possibly Sweden. His plans were very unsettled. It would be better, he thought, if Eleanor remained behind. It wasn't as though there was any pleasure to be got out of it. What did she say?

She was quite willing to fall in with his wishes in the matter. Of course she liked to be with him, but on a business visit of this sort ... Later on, he should take her to Pourville for a real holiday.

So she said she would stay at home by herself, and in private made an honest and quite unsuccessful attempt not to feel pleased.

But, two evenings before Reginald was due to leave, along to Prince's Gate came Louise. With a slightly exaggerated heartiness of manner and rapidity of speech which smacked of prearrangement, she sprung her invitation. Would Eleanor come and stay at the flat in Gloucester Buildings for the fortnight while Reggy was abroad? Reggy, while Eleanor yet hesitated and eyed him plaintively for help, brought his hands together just as he was accustomed to do when he came up to bed after feeding and freezing out a victim.

'Excellent! Now, that is really most satisfactory. My one misgiving was that you might feel lonely all by yourself here, my dear.'

Eleanor, who read the symptoms of the rapidity of speech and falsity of smile in Louise, as a doctor reads your measle-spots, immediately, and with the best of grace, accepted. She would come along to Gloucester Road on the day following Reggy's departure.

'I shall be leaving by the day-boat train, you know – quite early,' said Reggy, stretching himself aimlessly.

'Yes, why not come the same day?' said Louise.

'Very well, then,' said Eleanor at once, 'the same day. Thank you most awfully, Louise. Topping of you.'

She felt the indignation in her like a physical pain, nagging and being aggravated and telling of danger. And, because she knew that to rebel now would be his justification, she fought it. She did not analyse her feelings, but she decided that, in some way, she owed it to her own pride to ignore this insult. Ah, but this couldn't go on. This wasn't *her*. This wasn't 'you and I'. Then the thought came to her, 'He can never be "you and I"; he hasn't got it in him.' And her conscience said, 'It's your own doing – it was your own choice.' And she said, 'I know; but I thought I might be able to make him "you and I".'

Patting and smiling, off went Reginald to his boat-train, and, within half an hour, Louise was at Prince's Gate for her. She thought, 'Oh, I know where the brink of catastrophe is, well enough, without being lugged to it and shown it'; but she only said, 'How kind of you to come along so soon. I haven't even packed anything yet.'

She went upstairs and packed things, pride laughing nervously in her throat and fighting that pain of anger.

But she was right, and oh, how dangerous a thing it is to drag a young woman like this – capricious, but battling with her caprice; impatient, but wearing patience like a penitent's sackcloth – how dangerous a thing it is to drag such a woman to the brink of catastrophe and to say, 'Look at what we are holding you back from.' Because the prospect beyond is not by any means repellent. On the contrary, it is a very dazzling prospect, and an enticing one.

Why, you, madam, who perhaps have yourself been to the brink and had a look, you know very well how difficult it is to avoid making just another little sneaking visit, for another little peep at that tantalising prospect beyond. It is such a seductive experience. The devil himself employed it as one of his temptations in the wilderness.

CHAPTER II

A Skirmish with Mischief

The three little brothers Twigg were dentists; L. Twigg, D. Twigg, O. Twigg. They practised in Kensington and partnership. Each had his own torture-chamber, whizzing drill, patients, small talk. They participated in profits, a waiting-room, an attendant and the habit of completely gagging a victim and then saying, 'Now, tell me when this hurts.'

Into the waiting-room of the three Mr Twiggs there came one Monday morning Mrs Piper and her sister-in-law, Mrs Bingham. The attendant soon showed Mrs Piper into the L. torture-chamber and informed Mrs Bingham that Mr D. would be disengaged shortly. The attendant then handed Mrs Bingham an excellent, if somewhat superannuated, volume entitled *King Albert's Book*, and withdrew.

At 11.30, a gentleman arrived to fulfil an appointment with Mr O. The attendant ushered him into the company of Mrs Bingham, gave him *Sea-Pie*, and left him there.

At the moment of this visitor's entrance Mrs Bingham was busily engaged in searching in a handbag for a handkerchief. This found, she replaced the handbag on the table, and glanced at her fellow-victim, who was standing looking at her and grinning very broadly.

'Golly!' said Eleanor. 'Did you come on purpose?'

'How do you mean exactly "on purpose"?' replied Algy Richardson Gascoyne, 'I didn't come on purpose to see you, but I did come on purpose to see O. Twigg. However, I shall be only too pleased to see you instead, because I'd much rather see you then anyone else, and I'd much rather see anyone else than O.'

'Algy,' said Eleanor, both her hands in his, by this time, 'what a fluke! You were the one person I felt I ought to see, and the one person I was trying not to. Can you understand what I mean?'

'Yes,' he said, 'because, as a matter of fact, that's almost exactly the state of affairs between myself and O. Twigg.'

'Never mind O. Twigg. Do you know why I haven't been near you or written to you or rung you up for the last two months?'

'No, I do not.'

'You're not hurt about it, are you?'

'Oh, dear no,' said Algy. 'I supposed that, when wanted, I should be sent for again. Meanwhile, a little goes a long way. You nearly laid me out last time. I love to dance, but oh, my feet! Why haven't you?'

'Because Reggy, my husband, saw you dancing with me at Ciro's, and kissing with me in a taxi,' she replied.

'That's really very second-sighted and magical of him,' said Algy, 'considering he was spending the night down a coal-mine in Yorkshire. Did he rub his lamp, or something?'

'He didn't go. He stayed in London and came home. He was at Ciro's and saw me dancing, and he was at home and saw me kissing.'

'He sounds like the flying squad of the Purity League,' said Algy.

'I found him in bed.'

'Ah! I must say, I wondered where you found him.'

'He's a dear,' said Eleanor, quickly on the defensive, 'and I'm always anxious to please him. And he said he didn't like my going out with you and kissing you in taxis.'

'Oh, the spoilsport!' remarked Algy, indignantly.

'So that's why you haven't heard of me since.'

'Where is this man now?' asked Algy. 'With any luck he might object to my being here, and I'm longing to find an excuse to foil O.'

'He's in Paris,' said Eleanor. 'And if only you knew the trouble you've caused, you'd never kiss a girl in a taxi again.'

'Don't tell me then,' said Algy.

She seated herself, and recounted the sequel to their last meeting. She was very flattering to Reggy. She mentioned the visit to 'Hi!' but only as proof of Reggy's genuine desire to gratify her. She laughed over the sweet, well-meaning care which had inspired his sending her now to Louise while he was on the Continent. Only because he was afraid she might feel lonely. Algy needn't think it was because Reggy couldn't trust his wife.

'You said just now it was the direct result of my having kissed you in the taxi,' said Algy.

'Yes, and so it is of course,' she admitted candidly. 'Only, can't you see I'm doing my best to be loyal?'

Algy nodded. 'Quite right too. So that what it boils down to is that there aren't to be any more nights at Ciro's because Reggy doesn't like it, and you're not going to do anything Reggy doesn't like. Is that it?'

She did not reply for a moment; sat intertwining her fingers, examined them, looked up at him suddenly and laughed.

'I don't know,' she said. 'Silly, isn't it?'

'No,' said Algy. 'No; if that's the reason, it's a very good one. That's all right, Elly.' He caught her wistful look, and laughed back at her. 'Only, if it's just because you're afraid Louise would find out and report it on your husband's return – if *that's* your reason, what time do we meet?'

'Oh lord, I'm not afraid of Louise,' said Eleanor. 'Besides, she doesn't know that there's been any trouble over you.'

'I bet she does.'

'I bet she doesn't,' said Eleanor almost vehemently. 'I hope Reggy's got a bit more self-respect than to go and repeat a thing like that to his sister.'

'Well, then, if Louise doesn't know I'm undesirable, your reason must be that you know your husband is against our spending the evening together, so we won't do it. As I say, I think you've been very sensible.'

'I've been very dull,' said Eleanor, toying with this situation. In very much the same way a child toys with a china ornament, and it is the liability of the china ornament to fly into a thousand fragments at any moment that constitutes its peculiar charm as a plaything.

'Yes, I've been very dull. Why must "sensible" be another word for "dull"? It never has been before with me. At Louise's – my hat, it is dull, Algy! After dinner at Louise's!'

'How long have you been there?'

'Three days. I've got another ten days of it – ten nights.'

'Who is there?'

'Louise and Willy. You don't know them, do you?'

'No. I know Louise by hearsay. Who is Willy – Louise's little boy?'

'Her husband. He's rather a dear in his way, but it isn't a very exciting way. Still, I believe I might have some fun with him if Louise wasn't there. He's an old retired colonel.'

'The only way to have fun with old retired colonels is to tread on their feet,' said Algy. 'And even that palls after a time.'

'Then there's Henry,' continued Eleanor. 'He's been in once to make a four at bridge.'

'Who is Henry?'

'Reggy's brother. He's just come home on leave from some job in the East. He's quite human too. He's younger than Reggy. I like Henry.'

'Well, dash it, why can't Henry take you out and make a fuss of you?'

'Oh, I don't want to be taken out,' she said impetuously. That little pain of annoyance was still with her, and she seemed to feel a nasty twinge of it just at this moment. 'I only want to be myself. My husband can't go away for ten days without leaving me to be guarded like a fallen housemaid in a rescue home. This woman's jealous of me, and she loves the job, revels in it, gloats over it. I can't go out alone for five minutes to a post-office. Why, she's here now – with Mr L.'

'My God! I wish I was L.' said Algy.

'I tell you, Algy,' went on Eleanor, and her fingers beat a little tattoo on the table, 'there's only one thing that keeps me from plunging off the deep end and shocking them all to blazes.'

He said quite coolly and sincerely, 'Well, Elly, if he's a good old thing at heart, and you're fond of him, you're quite right to stick it.'

'Fond of him! If I were as fond of him as all that I'd be in Paris with him, wouldn't I?'

'What is it, then?'

'I could dodge Louise in ten seconds,' said Eleanor. 'Or I

could snap my fingers in her face and go off home on my own, and go off elsewhere on my own too. And the only reason why I don't do it is because that's just what they're asking me to do and challenging me to do and egging me on to do. "You can't be trusted, so while I'm away you go to Louise." That's what I was told. He went to Louise without asking me and fixed it up. Retaliate – good heavens, I could retaliate quick enough. That's the very reason why I don't – because it seems so easy and – cheap. It seems more dignified to let him be a—' She checked herself, was silent for a moment; then looked up at Algy again and laughed. Quite a jolly laugh; no bitterness in it. Only, in it, in the laugh, just the faintest note of a query.

Algy didn't laugh. He merely said, 'Well, I'm awfully sorry it's turned out like this, Elly.'

'Oh, it hasn't,' she replied. 'I didn't mean to say things against him. He's all right. Only, I do get so bored and irritated sometimes. It's all up to me. It's my doing. Only it isn't quite "us" just yet, you understand?'

'Yes,' said Algy. 'And you'd better not ask my advice. Because, personally, I wouldn't stay at Louise's another day.'

'Ten,' she said. 'Ten more.'

Algy raised his head suddenly and stood with his mouth open, as though listening.

'Hold on,' he said, 'I've got an idea.'

'Oh, I've got plenty of ideas,' said Eleanor. 'But—'

'Wait a moment. You know Diana?'

'Oh, Diana, yes. How is she? I forgot to ask. It's years since—'

'Diana is at the moment all on her own in a cottage.'

'In a cottage? Where and why?'

'Old Hole.'

'Old Hole? Is that the name of the cottage?'

'No, old Hole is my uncle. Benbow Hole.'

'Your uncle?'

'Yes, my uncle. *Mon oncle*. The old gentleman who has the *parapluie*. You have *not* heard of him?'

'I've heard of your aunt,' said Eleanor.

'Oh, no; she's quite different. She has *la plume*. She is my father's sister, and old Hole is my mother's brother, so they don't pair off at all. Though I should think it's quite possible that Auntie may be the original cause of Uncle Benbow Hole being a woman-hater.'

'A woman-hater?'

'Yes. He lives all by himself in a cottage miles from anywhere, hating women. All except Diana. Diana is the sort of girl that can get on with every man and can't get off with any of them.'

'But you said just now that Diana was alone in the cottage.'

'She is. You see, the uncle got suddenly taken worse, and was vetted and sent cursing to a cure at Harrogate. So Diana had to go down and look after the cottage while he was away. Poor little devil, I imagine she's pretty lonely, as it's a most out-of-the-way spot and she couldn't get anyone to go with her at such short notice.'

'Why didn't you go with her yourself?'

'What? Why should I? She's only my sister. On the other hand, why don't you take it on for a week?'

'Me?'

'Yes,' said Algy. 'It would get you out of Louise gracefully and yet without detriment to your rather involved sense of dignity. Moreover, I would come down and stay hard by and take you for runs in the car with Diana as chaperon. Not even your husband could object to our meeting under the eye of Diana. And lastly, and frankly leastly, you would be doing Diana a very good turn.'

Eleanor did not reply, but sat digging her finger into the pretty point of her chin. Algy, who was a loose-limbed young man of thirty, rested his behind against the table and watched her, smoothing his hair. He had a long mouth set to a smile, but his large and rather surprised eyes saved his expression from any suggestion of malice. While she deliberated he continued to talk, not persuasively, but in the languid tone of one who has plenty of time to play with.

'It seems to me to fit in all round. Your husband doesn't want you to see me alone in taxis and Ciro's and places. You want to do your best to please him, but rather resent being looked upon as unable to take care of yourself, or unwilling to, as the case may be. For you to meet me under circumstances beyond suspicion, namely, with Diana in the offing a very fair compromise. You'll be having your own way, and your husband will be having half his own way, which is half more than his share as a husband. You will escape from Louise and Siddy, or whatever his name is, and, though I don't suppose you care much about going to a Somerset cottage for a week in June in the ordinary course, it'll be very kind to Diana. You say that Louise doesn't know about the little dust-up at home over me and you and the taxi and Ciro, so she can't possibly suspect you of ulterior motives. In any case, the motives are not ulterior. I daresay I ought to confess quite openly that my inclinations are strongly ulterior, but even if I wanted to misbehave myself I shouldn't suggest bringing Diana into it, partly because she's my sister and partly because I know she wouldn't stand for it. So there we are, and if you agree I'll wire Diana and tell her you're joining her tomorrow.'

'Where is this place?' asked Eleanor. 'Is it fearfully countrified?'

'Cows in the bathroom,' said Algy. 'Chool is its name. April Cottage, Chool. I'm afraid it must be an absolutely one-horse place. In fact, I should think it was no-horse; because my uncle dislikes his fellow-man and simply loathes his fellow-woman.'

'Where would *you* stay?'

'There must be a town not far away. And where there is a country town there is a choice of pubs.'

Eleanor breathed deeply and dubiously.

'I daresay I should get on with Diana all right for a week,' she said. 'But, you know, I'm afraid it isn't so much for her sake that I'm inclined to go. Only it *would* be an opportunity for showing my people that I'll stay where I like. It wouldn't be like packing up and going home, which would be asking for ructions which I want to avoid. Yes, I think I'll go.'

'Righto,' said Algy casually. 'When?'

'Tomorrow.'

'I'll wire Diana to meet you. Better make it the day after

tomorrow, then she can write you all about it by tonight's post.'

'All right,' said Eleanor. 'The day after tomorrow. Wednesday.'

'And as for me,' said Algy, 'I won't come down at all unless you like.'

'Oh, don't take any notice of all that tommy-rot,' said Eleanor. 'Of course you can come down.'

'Mr D. Twigg is ready now, madam,' said the attendant from the doorway.

The attendant was masculine; a monotonous, melancholy man, as who would not be, after a course of years misspent in the occupation of piloting victims to the rack? He held the door open for Mrs Bingham, who obeyed his summons and went her way as promptly and gallantly as a grand duchess facing the inquisitors. In passing, she said to Algy, 'I shall hear from your sister tomorrow then.' He nodded and she nodded back with a smile.

The attendant consoled Mr Richardson Gascoyne with the information that Mr O. would soon be ready for him, and was, in fact, only waiting for the gentleman who was going to administer the gas. He then followed Mrs Bingham into the hall and closed the waiting-room door.

Algy had not been alone thirty seconds before his pleasant countenance once more was illumined with inspiration. Of course! Fool! Why hadn't he arranged to motor Eleanor down to this unexplored retreat? In justice it must be stated that, whatever his declared inclinations, he only thought to render Eleanor a purely practical service. Indeed, it came as a shock to him to realise that, if he did motor her down, he couldn't prudently call at Louise's for her. What narrow-minded humbug! Poor old Elly! Why in Heaven's name had she gone and married into this state of affairs?

Algy, being like most of the young generation today very outspoken, was no worse than he appeared on the surface. On the surface he appeared to be a very fortunate and idle young man who differed from the majority of well-to-do young men in finding life very amusing. It cannot be said that he displayed any of the qualifications of the heroic, unless a sense of humour may be urged as the saving grace in so lamentable a case. But Algy did not concern himself very deeply with the subject of heroism. He was well off but not pretentious; he was idle but not vicious – the right women liked him, a good sign. The right men liked him, a better. He knew the difference between escapade and dishonour, and was good at cricket. Stand Eton, Oxford and the Empire Promenade where they did?

He decided immediately to invite Eleanor to be motored down to this place, Chool, because he had a completely comfortable conscience in the matter. Unfortunately, he couldn't communicate his idea to Eleanor at the moment, for by the time she was through with D. he would be in the grip of O., while Louise, having survived L., would be back in the waiting-room. He must therefore write to Eleanor. What was Louise's address?

A telephone directory stood on the writing-table in the window, and he crossed the room and was instinctively turning the pages before he discovered that he had no idea of Louise's surname. He had probably heard it, but had forgotten it. He hadn't even really met Louise at all.

Well, never mind; he must write to Eleanor at her own house at Prince's Gate, with 'Please forward' on the envelope. Only, dash it, he must wire Diana to do the same. A silly situation, considering that in this very building were both the lady whose address he wanted and the lady the address belonged to.

Then a very simple solution occurred to him.

On the centre table lay the vanity-bag. Eleanor had pushed it on one side as she looked up and saw him first, and there it remained. He opened it and glanced at the contents. A small purse; her little complexion-and-lips outfit complete with small mirror – no more. She had retained the handkerchief.

He quickly scribbled a note on the Twiggs' note-paper

Darling Old Elly,

Look here. I'll have my car ready on Wednesday next and off we'll go to this place by road. I won't call for you, in case Louise is nosing about, but come early to my rooms in a taxi and we'll push off from there. Ring me up if you can. My best times are before 12 noon and after 4 a.m. I'll send that wire off today. Love.

Algy.

He popped this note into the handbag, which he had scarcely closed before the grim sentinel reappeared in the doorway and conducted him from the sunshine of dalliance into the gloom of gas and torment, where Mr O. and his sinister accomplice welcomed him, pinioned him, and prepared their fell balloon.

'Tell me if I hurt you,' said Mr D.

'It's all right,' said Eleanor. 'I only want to blow my nose.'

She took the handkerchief from the ready-made, feminine pocket at her bosom. Rather fortunate that she had retained the handkerchief. She had really meant to put it back in the bag.

On her way out Mrs Piper inquired of the attendant whether he thought Mrs Bingham was likely to be long.

'Some time yet, madam,' he replied, not without a certain savage satisfaction. 'She's only been gone in five minutes or so.'

'Oh. Well, will you please tell her that I have gone on to High Street to do some shopping, but that I shall be back at my house in about half an hour, if she will come straight there, please?'

The attendant bowed his compliance with these instructions; and Mrs Piper, stepping into the waiting-room, picked up her handbag and left the house busily.

CHAPTER III

Out of the Bag

The young man in the District train rose suddenly from his seat and passed right down the car. Once before he had assisted a female in the Underground to have an epileptic fit and had got misunderstood about it by his young lady.

Already slightly flushed by the heat, the business of taking the train and the recent ordeal of dentistry, Louise had opened her handbag half-way between Gloucester Road and High Street in order to powder her nose. She was perhaps on the mature side to perform this popular public feature of the feminine toilet, but she very wisely decided that it was preferable to powder in the District than to feel that other women, quite as old as she, were looking with interest at the condition of her features.

But Louise did not powder.

The note was on a folded piece of dental paper, unaddressed and unenveloped. Louise, who was near-sighted, held it close to her face. The handbag slipped from her lap to the floor of the car, and she made disinterested guessing efforts to pick it up with the left hand while still completely absorbed in Algy's missive.

When the young man opposite her looked up from his paper she had just finished reading the note. She was staring vacantly into space, flushed now to a rich shade of beetroot and with the veins of her neck distended. It was then that the young man passed right down the car.

At High Street Louise did not proceed to shop as she had intended, but stood upon a kerb, performing violent air-stabbing work with a purple parasol. A willing taxi bore her to her home address, and she sat upright upon the jolting seat, now freely powdering, re-reading and very audibly overcome with warmth and agitation.

Louise was a short woman with a good, big, old-fashioned,

high, Victorian bust and no nonsense about it. She closely resembled one of the more aggressively protuberant types of domestic pigeon. She suffered consequently in a minor degree from the malady known to the patent medicine vendor as 'quick breath'. She blew a good deal.

She was not an ill-intentioned woman, but somehow it is very difficult for a lady of this shape to be at once forty-eight and pacific. She was very religious, but her devotions, emotional and high-church, did not appear to be bringing her very lasting consolation; while her bodily ailments, chiefly imaginary, caused her to rely a good deal upon material physic as well. Her bedroom cupboards were full of little ominous doses. Above the mantelpiece hung a crucifix, and immediately below it on the ledge stood a small and horrid yellow bottle bearing the chemist's label – 'Mrs Piper. Liver.'

But this was the best medicine for Louise – action; action prompted by some scandal or mischief. Then she could move with the fleetest. Then the bottle of liver-mixture was readily forgotten. So, for the matter of that, was the crucifix.

Algy left the Twiggs' in company with the gas-specialist. He hesitated, as the attendant opened the front door for them. His operation had not lasted long. Eleanor might still be here. But if so, Louise would assuredly be waiting for her. He rather shrank from questioning the attendant as to the movements of the two ladies, so contented himself with a quick glance into the waiting-room as he passed. Ah, Eleanor had evidently departed. The handbag had disappeared. Algy offered the gasman a lift, and a few seconds later, Eleanor, gaining the front doorstep, caught a fugitive glimpse of the back of Algy's head being borne rapidly away in a taxi.

When Louise reached her home, which was a flat near Bailey's Hotel, she found her husband, Willy Piper, standing looking out of the dining-room window with his hands in his pockets and the general air of a man who is trying hard to think of something to say he wants to do before his wife can say she wants him to do something he doesn't. He was a quiet, grey man of sixty. His life was one long yielding protest.

She cried, 'Willy! Willy!' and he turned.

'Hallo! What? Hallo, I say, what the deuce is the matter?'

She flourished the dental love-note. Panting, she made her revelation.

'I found this – in my bag when I – left – Twiggses. It is meant for – Eleanor. It is from – that young man.'

'What young man?'

'Algy Rich-ardson Gas-Gascoyne. He's the cause of her being here – while Reggy's away – if you only knew – which you don't.'

'No, I certainly don't,' said Willy. 'I say, steady yourself, Louise. What *is* all this?'

'I left this bag in the waiting-room at Twiggses. When I came out this was in it. It's a love-letter.'

'For *you*?' exclaimed Willy, incredulously.

'No, I tell you. For Eleanor.'

'Oh, I see. Yes, that, of course, sounds more – I mean, go on. A love-letter from—?'

'Algy Richardson Gascoyne. Eleanor must have seen him there. She's encouraging him to go off with her.'

'Go off?'

'Yes.'

'Oh, go on, go off,' said Willy. 'What d'you mean? Do a bunk? No. Go on.'

'She's arranging to run away with him, I tell you. In a car. And stay somewhere together.'

'Oh, rot!'

'What's rot? You haven't read the letter.'

'Nor has Eleanor, I don't suppose,' said Willy. 'And if you're so certain it's meant for her I don't think you ought to have read it.'

'I had to read it in order to make so certain it was meant for Eleanor, didn't I?' Louise asked defiantly.

'Oh, lord, it's no use arguing,' said Willy. 'What's he say?'

'You can read it for yourself.'

'I don't want to. All right, I'll have a squint at it.'

Louise handed him the note with a gesture intended to convey its dramatic importance. 'This is no squinting matter,' she declared.

He took the note with the indulgent reserve of an elderly gentleman for anything improper.

'Read it aloud,' said Louise.

He read it aloud. She had recovered her breath, but drew in a further supply in a satisfied hiss.

'There you are, you see. You can tell the sort of thing that Eleanor says about me to total strangers. Not that I care about *that*. Only Reggy has caught her spooning with this young man before. The point is what's to be done about it.'

Willy handed back the note and tapped pince-nez against his thumbnail.

'I don't see what you can do,' he mumbled.

'What?'

'M?'

'What did you say?'

'I said, "What are you going to do?" '

'What do you suppose?'

'M? Show her the note, I should, and say how you came to get it. You can explain. After all, it wasn't your fault.'

Louise, at this, peered at her husband's face as though she had suddenly discovered a blemish thereon.

'Oh,' she said, witheringly, 'and surely I ought to apologise to her for having discovered that she is off on the loose and deceiving Reggy and apparently preparing to shatter the seventh commandment with this young man that Reggy has forbidden her to see and that he has sent her here to us to avoid her seeing?'

'Oh, lord!' said Willy. 'I say, Louise, don't start making some appalling row and raising old Harry. Tell her she mustn't do it, if you like. That's the straightforward thing to do.'

'That's what you'd do, is it?'

'Of course. At least, if I did anything that's what I'd do. If you think it's your duty—'

'And what about my duty to Reggy?'

'Well, dash my wig,' cried Willy, raising his voice in despair rather than in argument, 'what better turn can you do Reggy than to stop his wife buzzing off in a car with this blighter?'

'Yes, and make her doubly careful next time.'

'I don't think, myself, that there's as much in it as you make out. I don't believe Eleanor's—'

'That she's what?'

'I don't believe she's hot stuff like that.'

'I'm sorry I consulted you at all about this,' said Louise.

'You haven't. So you needn't worry about that,' said Willy. 'Well, what's your idea, then?'

'I shall say nothing. I shall wait and hear what Eleanor's excuse is for leaving here on Wednesday. She's bound to tell me where she's going.'

'Why should she?'

'Because she's doing it all in a thoroughly underhand and hole-in-the-corner sort of way, and she wouldn't leave a false address, because she'll want her letters to know what Reggy's movements are. You see, you don't *think*, do you? So I shall just wait and see and lay my plans accordingly. I may have to wire Reggy.'

'Hell!' said Willy. 'Well, it's nothing to do with me, mind. I refuse to take any part in it.'

'That's just as well, I expect,' said Louise.

When a pair yoked in the double harness of matrimony succeeds in jogging along the highroad of life without mishap, it is generally taken for granted that they are evenly matched in speed and temperament. But there are, truth to tell, a great number of tandem teams upon the road; the mare setting the pace, her partner either pulled or propelled in distressed accordance, while that exacting female driver, Mrs Public Opinion, is ever ready to display her impartial proficiency by severely curbing the one and heartily flogging the other. Ah, many and many a tandem on the road. And here was one of them.

Eleanor returned to the flat in Gloucester Buildings light-hearted as a schoolgirl within sight of the holidays. It was all so pleasant. She was delighted now at her decision to get out of the flat. She could gently score off Louise and provide Reggy with a tactful little object-lesson. She disliked the idea of staying in a cottage, and was not confident of being able to appreciate the depths of the country for a week with

Diana Richardson Gascoyne, but these were objections easily outweighed. She would be free to be herself anyhow, and to show them that she fully intended to be herself what was more. And yet it was all so pleasant. And she felt that the more pleasant she made it the more complete would be her little triumph over Louise.

In less care-free mood she would have observed that there was something up at the flat. Willy was self-conscious, spoke even less than usual and buried himself beneath the folds of a *Times* which he had already practically learnt by heart. Louise was aggressively sociable, assuring and buoyant as a cork on the ocean. After lunch Willy was sent to Lord's. The two women repaired to the drawing-room, rather aimlessly, as women do after lunch.

'What are your plans for the afternoon?' asked Louise.

'Yours,' replied Eleanor, sweetly. 'But I think I'd better write some letters.'

'Now?'

'Yes.'

'I see. Let me think,' said Louise. 'Tomorrow is Tuesday, isn't it? I thought on Wednesday we might go off somewhere for the day. Would you care to?'

'Yes,' said Eleanor. 'I should.'

'You don't mind using your car? It would be rather nice to get out into the country.'

'Yes, wouldn't it?' said Eleanor.

'M'h'm. Very well then. I'll leave you to write your letters now. Reggy is still in Paris, isn't he?'

'Yes, he's staying there longer than he expected. He's at the *Roi Edouard Sept* until Thursday or Friday.'

'Oh, yes? My love to him,' said Louise.

She left the room, exasperated by the coolness of this wanton. Why no mention of her departure on Wednesday? Was she going to try and keep it dark and make a bolt for it? Or perhaps she hadn't thought of a good enough excuse yet.

No mention all that day of the impending parting. Louise got quite restive about it. All sorts of doubts arose. Why was the note in the handbag at all? Surely Eleanor must have seen the young man and made some tentative arrangement of which the note was the outcome? In the evening a light was thrown by Eleanor returning the handkerchief with apologies and thanks. Louise laughed skittishly. 'Not at all, dear. That's quite all right. But what a good thing nobody saw you taking it. They might have thought you were pilfering.'

This drew no reply and Louise had to content herself with speculations.

Next morning out it all came. A letter was brought by hand from Prince's Gate, having arrived there by the first post. Eleanor read it at breakfast before the eyes of Louise. Then looked up blandly.

'I say, Louise. I've got to go.'

'To go?'

'Yes.'

'To Reggy? To Paris?'

'No. I've just heard from a girl friend who wants me.'

'What, dear? A girl friend? Wants you? Where?'

'A girl called Diana Richardson Gascoyne. An old friend. We were at school together.'

'Oh-h, yes,' said Louise. 'I think I've heard the name. What is the matter with you, Willy?'

'What? Nothing. Coffee-grounds in my throat. Why can't this cook—?'

'And is she ill or something?' continued Louise.

'No, but she's all alone in a cottage at a place in Somerset and she's fearfully lonely and she's just heard that Reggy's away and so she wants me to go and keep her company for a week. So, naturally, I will. It's only kind, isn't it?'

'I see. And when do you think you'll go?'

'Tomorrow,' said Eleanor, definitely. 'I hope you don't mind. It's been awfully good of you to look after me as you have.'

'H'm. How are you going down there? Are you taking the car?'

'Oh, no. You can use the car while I'm away, if you like. No, I shall go by train. She tells me the train to come by. Leave Paddington 11.15, change at Bristol, and go on to a place called South Ditherton.'

'Well,' said Louise. 'I suppose I can't prevent your going.'

Eleanor laughed fondly. 'It's very sweet of you to want to,' she said.

'What sort of a place is she at then?' asked Louise.

'A tiny cottage, apparently. She's looking after it for a sick uncle.'

'Nothing infectious, I hope?'

'I hope not,' said Eleanor. 'Because I'm going to sleep in his bed, it appears.'

'I beg your pardon, dear?'

'The uncle's bed. Oh, he isn't there. That's why Diana's there. She says here, "There's only one bedroom; in fact, there's only one bed at present, but I'll get another." '

'Good gracious,' said Louise. 'Well, I suppose you know your own mind?'

'Oh, intimately,' said Eleanor.

'Tomorrow you say you're going?'

'Yes. I shall have to go home and get some country things.'

'When? This morning?'

'Yes.'

'I'll come with you.'

'Do.'

'Will you wire Reggy?'

'Reggy? Oh, no,' said Eleanor. 'I'll write him. You can forward any letters that come here for me. I'll give you the address.'

'I'd better write it down now, while we remember,' said Louise.

She rose and made for the writing-table. As she passed Willy he grimaced and whispered something below his breath about washing his hands of it. Louise nudged him violently to caution, but even when she was at the writing-table the idiot continued to perform foolish pantomimic gestures indicative of the washing of hands. Eleanor, however, was looking through her letter again.

'April Cottage, Chool, near South Ditherton, Somerset,' she said, glancing up at Louise, who inscribed, repeating.

Presently, the two proceeded together on foot to Prince's Gate.

'I never knew,' said Louise as they went, 'that you were such a great friend of this Miss Richardson Gascoyne's.'

'No? Oh, yes,' said Eleanor.

'Let me see – hasn't she a brother?'

'Yes. Algy.'

'Is that his name? You know him too?'

'Better than I know Diana, if anything,' said Eleanor.

'Indeed? Then you've seen him lately?'

'Oh, sort of on and off, you know – like one *does* see the friends that are such friends that you don't have to worry whether you see them or not.'

'Indeed, yes. No, I'd no idea. And then isn't there an aunt with rather a shaky reputation?'

Eleanor laughed.

'Shaky is rather an apt description of her,' she said.

'Why? Has she got palsy or something?'

'No. She gambles.'

'Gambles?' echoed Louise.

'Yes, gambles. I don't mean that she leaps about in a field. I mean she sits at a table and plays roulette.'

'Good gracious!' said Louise. 'At Monte Carlo and that sort of place?'

'That sort of place,' said Eleanor. 'Only you don't have to go to Monte, you know.'

'But Eleanor, dear. Are these people respectable?'

'Well, they're very much the same sort of people as I am,' said Eleanor, heartily. 'So you can judge for yourself!'

'I hope you don't gamble?'

Eleanor made an elaborate gesture with the parasol which she carried, almost pinking Louise on the nose.

'After all, everything's a bit of a gamble, isn't it?' she replied. 'What about marriage? Willy, I suppose, was more or less a safe spec., but I call Reggy a positive plunge. Still, the more you plunge the more you stand to win, don't you? And I only gamble at games of skill, you know.'

'I'm afraid I can't quite follow you when you talk in that deep and whatsaname sort of way,' said Louise. 'But I think you were fortunate to marry Reggy.'

'The fortune was all on one side, I suppose?'

'Oh, Eleanor! No, I don't say that.'

'You mean you won't again? That's all right then.'

'Here's Prince's Gate,' said Louise.

'Yes, I know,' said Eleanor.

Just after Eleanor had left Gloucester Buildings with Louise, Algy rang up, having ascertained her address from her housemaid at Prince's Gate. He only succeeded in getting somewhat confused in conversation with Willy, who was an indifferent performer on the telephone. Algy extricated himself by pretending to be cut off and decided to wire. Thus on her return to the flat with Louise and a striking assortment of ladies' summer wear (country), Eleanor found a telegram awaiting her.

> Mrs Bingham 6 Gloucester Buildings SW7.
>
> What about motoring down tomorrow told Diana I should probably motor you but have heard from her you are going by train oh why do this wire whether you decided go with me in car also where meet and what time all eager for fray
>
> Algy.

Eleanor, who was alone in the hall of the flat, Louise having failed to observe the telegram and slipped into her room to take a Dr Murger's Digestive Tablet before lunch, gave vent to a little exclamation of tolerant reproach. Why hadn't he mentioned this before? So like Algy to spring a suggestion of this sort on her at the last moment! It would have been delightful to drive down. She disliked the prospect of a long and tedious railway journey broken by a change at Bristol. But she had left it too late now. Louise had stated her intention of coming to Paddington to see her off. And if Louise discovered that Algy was to be at Chool she would only go and write to Reggy about it. Eleanor preferred to tell Reggy about it herself and at her own time and in her own way.

She went out while she had the chance and crossed the road to the post-office, where she despatched her reply.

Richardson Gascoyne 14a Half Moon Street W1.

Must go by train you had better motor down alone and come cottage thursday love

Eleanor.

'I hear you had a telegram?' said Louise, who was washed, shrived, medicated and awaiting lunch when Eleanor got back.

'Yes. I've just been replying to it.'

'From the friend you're going to see at this cottage, I suppose?'

'Yes,' said Eleanor.

CHAPTER IV

Rural

Early on the Wednesday afternoon Diana Richardson Gascoyne locked the front door of April Cottage and set off at a busy walk up a winding road which led through a wood to the superior road above. The June day was hot and very still. There was thunder in the air, Diana thought. And she was quite right. There was.

After walking for nearly an hour she arrived at South Ditherton, a typical Bathstone town, cut across and across by two great main roads, like swords sparing not an old and quiet breast in the greed of conquest. The one road ran due North and South, the other due East and West; and at the point of intersection was the market square of South Ditherton and the War Memorial, round which were gathered all the chief institutions of the town – the best shops, the Town Hall, the Masonic Rooms, the Parish Church, the Methodist Church, the Presbyterian Church, the Congregational Chapel, the Baptist Chapel and the *Ring o' Bells* Public House.

The railway station lay not far from the market square, and, after a glance at the Town Hall clock, Diana increased her pace and her already considerable heat. This did not detract, however, from her appearance, for in the most adverse circumstances she could not fail to look nice. She was graceful, though she had none of her brother's length of limb. But neat and pretty and very bright-looking in her brown country coat and skirt and her yellow jumper.

The kind of girl who attends bazaars and keeps up with superannuated governesses. Eminently nice. Many, finding her reserved and undemonstrative, said she was dull; but the observant discovered in the depths of her brown eyes possibilities – possibilities. But the depths were deep.

On arriving at the railway station Diana found, to her

relief, that the Town Hall clock was fast. Fast too, for South Ditherton, was young Pawley, of Pawley's motor, who was already waiting at the station by Diana's appointment.

Pawley's motor was an institution. It remained, after many years, the only automobile plying for hire at South Ditherton, which was perhaps fortunate for Pawley. Pawley, on this occasion, was asleep in the tap-room of the *Ring o' Bells*, and the motor was in charge of young Pawley.

The latter was a red-headed youth with a drooping eyelid. And when you see a young man with a red head and a drooping eyelid in charge of a car, that car will shift. Young Pawley used his drooping eyelid to accentuate the expression of extreme cynicism with which he regarded the fine old-world traditions of South Ditherton. In his hands, Pawley's motor became a pounding Juggernaut, an emblem of the disrespectful and headlong callousness of the younger generation. This incurred the fierce resentment of some of the older folk. They would protest sometimes to old Pawley. 'That old mowerr of yours, Mr Pawley, that lad o' yours 'e don't 'alf burrst the guts of she.'

But the indulgent parent took a pride in young Pawley and in the headlong modern propensities of young Pawley, and would himself sometimes sit alongside the driver's seat and would bare his toothless gums and jerk his head at young Pawley for the benefit of the natives, as the old motor flashed past them at a bouncing seventeen miles an hour – like some old pioneer of a modern craze who could still turn out and show 'em he could take a turn with the best.

Diana said to young Pawley, 'Oh. Before you take me and the friend who is coming by this train out to April Cottage, I want you to call at the furniture shop. I ordered a bed to be sent out to the cottage today and they've never sent it.'

Young Pawley removed a cigarette, and shot some stray remnants of tobacco from his lips by an abbreviated and dry spitting process. He then said,

'Early closin'.'

'Won't the shop be open?' asked Diana.

'Na,' replied young Pawley. 'Na, it won't and o' that neither.'

'Oh, dear. Well, I don't want to hang about trying to attract their attention and that sort of thing, because I expect my friend will want to get straight out to the cottage after her journey. Is there time to run round to the shop now, before the train comes in?'

'Ther's time,' said young Pawley, in a non-committal manner. 'But it be gorrn closin'.'

'Take me round there anyhow,' said Diana firmly, getting into Pawley's motor.

The furniture shop presented the appearance of an elaborate monument erected to the memory of some dead undertaker. It was locked and barred. The contents were thickly veiled from public view. There was no bell.

'It looks hopeless, doesn't it?' said Diana.

'Ah, it do, and o' that also,' said young Pawley.

'What a nuisance,' said Diana. 'I wanted that bed. Take me back to the station, please.'

She returned to the station discomfited. Eleanor was not perhaps the best person for little trifling disarrangements to happen to. Now Eleanor would have to sleep in the one bed and Diana would have to sleep in a chair or something. It didn't really matter; only she wanted everything to be as nice as possible for Eleanor. Eleanor would have a sort of surprised smile for the place if things were wrong.

The train arrived and Eleanor descended; but not before Diana had seen her looking inquiringly out of her carriage window. She was easily spotted, being alone in the firsts. Her face was not the face of one who says, 'Hurrah! Here I am,' but the face of one saying 'Great Scot! Is *this* the place I've chosen to come to?' But she exchanged with Diana greetings hearty, if a trifle sobered by the heat. Even in her exclusive first she had found the journey rather an ordeal. It had left her with a pain which gripped her across the brow. The jolting monotony of the slow train on from Bristol had given her an unpleasant pulpy feeling all over her body, as though her flesh was not properly attached to her bones, and the heavy mineral smell of the railway lingered in her nostrils.

Worst of all the effects of the journey was the little devil who had arrived and taken possession of her nerves, urging her to be short-tempered and pricking her to be curt. The little devil showed her Pawley's motor and said, 'Look at your conveyance. Say something sarcastic about it.' The little devil said of Diana, 'Look at Diana. She's being affable. Tell her that you can't stick her being vicar's-daughterish like that.' Eleanor held her lips together and nodded and tried to look glad. But the little devil stayed with her.

'This is South Ditherton,' it said. 'Dull? My dear, this is Piccadilly compared with what you are going to. For a week. It's your own fault. It's only your lack of spirit. You talk so much about being yourself. If you'd stuck to being yourself you'd have told Louise to go to hell, and you'd have been at Ciro's tonight.' Nag, nag, the little devil, nagging at her nerves. In her forehead, thud, thud. She had to shift her feet about in the car for some reason. It helped her to control herself.

She was duly deposited at April Cottage with Diana, and there for the moment she should be left; for the homeward trek of Pawley's motor is not without pertinent adventure.

Pawley's motor swung round into the main road and crashed upon her homeward course, undermined features of her mechanism twanging and vibrating within her protesting belly. She bounced through the outskirts of South Ditherton into the market square, which, on early closing day, was unlikely to contain any material reason for caution. But in the vicinity of the market square was the doctor's wife. And where the doctor's wife was were dogs.

If the doctor's wife was engrossed in conversation, the subject was a foregone conclusion. She could have engaged in a viva voce competition with the editor of *The Dog World* and knocked him sideways. She knew the points, pedigrees and prices of Hamways Humbug, Bellamy Bluepeter and Condescension of Crosstown. Her life was one tangled turmoil of leashes, litters and Lactol. By this time she had got to be rather like a dog herself.

The doctor's wife was talking to the vicar. The vicar was deaf, and the whole market re-echoed with the pleasantries combined with information uttered for his benefit. Even old Mr Moody, sitting on the bench outside the *Ring o' Bells*, heard them and was somewhat intrigued by shrill female cries of 'Dam' and 'Bitch', until his companion, Mr Jewell, informed him that it was only the doctor's wife talking to the vicar.

But young Pawley did not hear the doctor's wife; and though the doctor's wife could not fail to hear young Pawley, she did not realise that Fifi was in the middle of the market square, labouring under a misapprehension as to the functions of the War Memorial.

Fifi finished, as dogs always do, just as young Pawley hurled Pawley's motor into the market square. The result was that young Pawley missed Fifi and hit the War Memorial.

Fifi escaped with a fright, young Pawley with a shock and the War Memorial with a chip. But Pawley's motor remained propped against the War Memorial, her already overwrought vitals rent asunder and water pouring, as from the rock of Moses, from her riven radiator into the market square.

Young Pawley naturally blamed Fifi; old Mr Moody blamed the doctor's wife; the doctor's wife was inclined to blame the vicar; and Mr Jewell, who was an advanced Socialist, made a rather sneaking attempt to blame the War Memorial.

But no matter who was to blame. The fact remained that Pawley's motor was presently lugged from the scene, like the trunk of some veteran beast, once the pride of the herd, vanquished at last and slain in the unremitting war of Progress.

And South Ditherton was without a hireable car.

From the main road, as it runs eastward from South Ditherton, fork modest tributaries, wandering like wanton children from their mother road and getting dreadfully involved in marsh and meadow land; skirting this village, wheeling hopefully round that boundary, swerving to ask their way of a venerable knoll, and, as often as not, expiring contentedly at the heavy gate of a hospitable farm.

But not all expire. Some struggle through to connect scattered hamlets; hamlets that are the youngest offsprings of a town, even as their road is the youngest offspring of the great main thoroughfare – places of ten cottages apiece. Alongside most of the cottages is a trim plantation of cider-apple trees; and at the door of most of the cottages is a gaunt housewife, thin as a lath to the waist, and full with the unremedied results of much progeneration below, reprimanding, in an accent too soft for wrath, the children who are in the roadway, engaged in the delightful pastime of 'scaaring they pooltry'.

Around these hamlets as far as eye can reach, are meadows; the richest grazing in England is here. Hard by the hamlets the little roads give birth in their turn to rutty paths. You may turn down one of these, and dally by the rough meadow gates of an evening, and along the path there will come to you, like an enchanted memory of your childhood's realm of Caldecott, a stumping, funnily-hatted old man with a collie and a three-legged stool and the tinkling of cans; and the cows will cluster with sedate pleasure to meet him at the gate; and presently there will steal upon your senses the warm, seductive scent of new milk.

The firstborn of the main thoroughfare from South Ditherton branches off very confidently to the north soon after you leave the town. Not all the country in this direction is meadow-land. Harking back to the west you will find hills and, clinging to their sides, deep, still woods.

In the cup of one such hill-side, guarded by a towering grove in the background, facing a green strip of valley, fed by an adventurous grandchild road that came zigzagging down through the glade to join the dell; early and brightly in the sunshine, quickly and deeply in the shadow – was April Cottage.

From the upper road you would never have guessed its existence. Not even the thin blue ribbon of smoke from its kitchen chimney rose above the tops of the trees that skirted the plateau above. You might even follow the zigzagging road down for a steeply declining hundred yards before you would come suddenly upon April Cottage, as the adventuring hero comes upon the unexpected and hazardous cottage of the fairy tale.

Here normally lived alone – and happier so – old Hole, the uncle who was now at Harrogate. He lived the life of a recluse, withered, disgruntled, content only in displeasure. He saw scarcely a soul, conversed chiefly with his hens, and with them in no very amicable terms. Here, in spasms of calculating resentment, he penned a prodigious manuscript – a life-work on the subject of the evil wrought by womankind on the history of the world. He tolerated, however, Mrs Easy, who came from the neighbouring hamlet of Chool and described herself confidently as a help. She came of a morning and cooked Mr Hole's one meal and performed strange hissing and thumping operations in Mr Hole's one bedroom.

One morning Mrs Easy sent little Easy into South Ditherton to find the doctor and to tell him to come out and inspect old Mr Hole. This mission little Easy, though hampered by chronic adenoids and his elder brother's boots, duly performed. He arrived at the doctor's gate, was bitten by an Alsatian wolf-hound, was told through the window by the doctor's wife not to be afraid, delivered his message and was brought back to April Cottage by the doctor himself in his car.

The result of the doctor's visit was that old Mr Hole was ordered to Harrogate. Very reluctantly, and after making dreadful blowing noises through his nose at little Easy for having brought the doctor at all, he consented to go. The question immediately arose as to who should look after the cottage for three weeks during his absence. He refused to have strangers in the place. He would not even have Mrs Easy, unless that lady agreed to sever herself from her offensive progeny. So he was driven to fall back once more upon the best of the diabolical sex, and Diana came.

Chool, as a place, was a mere myth. With the exception of the two or three cottages which housed Mrs Easy and her neighbours, and which were themselves a considerable distance from April Cottage, there was no sign of a village of Chool. There was a ruin which might conceivably in the days of Alfred the Great have been Chool Church. But there was no post-office; there was no village shop. There was not even a village inn. The most remarkable feature of Chool was its non-existence.

Diana silently decided that she must have company here; company intimate enough to share Mr Hole's one bedroom and to harmonise in Mr Hole's one sitting-room. She thought it wiser not to raise the question of the company to Mr Hole; but in the interval of time between her summons and her accession she busily canvassed her girl friends, who all with one accord began to make excuse.

Thus Diana arrived alone, and, being a practical young woman, made the best of things. But, being a practical young woman, she was not slow to incur the hostility of Mrs Easy, who regarded the cottage as her perquisite, and resented the first hint of authority from this makeshift.

Mrs Easy was an import from the artisan environs of Bristol; a beetle-browed, hostile woman with a caustically flexible nose and enormous hands and feet; sudden and loud in her methods, seeking refreshment in grievances. She was always quite ready to pour scorn upon Mr Hole. She would often return to her cottage snarling like a cat, vowing that she was through with it. 'Today, for the last time, have I crossed his door. Never no more of it, not me.' But she was always there next morning and Mr Hole, pondering over his incensed manuscript in his sitting-room, would frown quickly upwards at the sound of the familiar clang of china in the bedroom above; until by degrees Mr Hole and Mrs Easy became, as it were, acclimatised to each other in wrath.

But this young woman at the cottage—

Mrs Easy's attendance on Diana had already become irregular when, one morning she did not put in an appearance at all. Next day she came, but merely stood with arms akimbo in the doorway of the kitchen, watching Diana cook.

'Oh, that's you, is it?' said Diana without looking up from her saucepan. 'If you can't come regularly, you'd better not come at all.'

'I shall come when I please and when I can manage it,' replied Mrs Easy. 'I am the mother of seven. I also have a husband.'

'So I should hope,' said Diana, stirring.

'And let me tell you,' continued Mrs Easy, 'that I 'ave noticed several goings-on which would not please Mr 'Ole. You 'ave changed round the furniture in his sitting-room in a manner which he would abore. And as for straightening his bookshelves, if he knew it he'd be borne off in a fit.'

'Do your work and don't talk about it or keep away,' said Diana.

At which Mrs Easy returned to her cottage, where the unpopularity of Diana with little Easy showed a very marked increase.

It was extremely lonely at the cottage. Diana had been there almost a week before she received her first visitor. Her first visitor arrived early on a Monday afternoon on a red bicycle. A telegraph boy.

Diana received the telegram with excitement which rapidly changed to quick suspicion. Algy was the author, and the elaborate programme set forth in the telegram could not have been devoted solely, or even mainly, for her benefit. This from a sister's experience.

Richardson Gascoyne April Cottage Chool South Ditherton Smst.

Eleanor Delaney now Bingham at large her husband abroad would like come stay with you for week on Wednesday if can do write her Princes Gate please forward shall probably bring her down in car.

Algy.

Eleanor? No. Diana's first instinct was antagonistic. She wanted company but Eleanor wasn't right. Not for the cottage.

Their girlhood friendship had waned. Even when they did meet nowadays they had very little in common. Except a soft spot for Algy.

Diana had half expected Eleanor to marry Algy. She wouldn't have minded that. Eleanor was Algy's sort and they would probably be very happy. So Diana had heard of Eleanor's engagement with disappointment for Algy and with great, great disappointment in Eleanor. A fat, pedantic man of fifty. There could be only one reason for this. A house in Prince's Gate? Yes, she thought so. A Rolls Royce? What a pity. Oh, what a pity.

Eleanor in this cottage? She wouldn't like it. She liked lots of gaiety and people. Diana could remember feeling hot-cheeked at Eleanor's supreme confidence in public. She would never endure this cottage. And why in the world was Algy the instigator of this queer business?

Still, Diana couldn't very well refuse. Sitting in Uncle Benbow Hole's parlour and biting his penholder a good deal Diana wrote the necessary letters—

To Eleanor: her pleasure at hearing from Algy that she cared to come down for a week. But it was frightfully quiet and dull and the tiniest cottage in the weirdest spot, and she must be prepared to rough it. Own cooking and housework. And so on. But if Eleanor really meant it, she would meet her on Wednesday at South Ditherton station. The best train, etc.

To Algy, simply:

Dear Old Algy.

I have written to Eleanor and told her to come if she likes. I hope she won't be terribly bored. There's no room for you. I've told E. to come by train. Much love.

Diana.

The only reply from either party was another wire – from Eleanor this time.

Arriving Wednesday Ditherton 3.8. Love

Eleanor.

And here was Wednesday, and here was Eleanor at the cottage, looking already rather incongruous in her smart travelling costume. Young Pawley had dumped her portmanteau on the front step and departed, so Eleanor had to help Diana carry the portmanteau upstairs. The dressing-case was light, so Diana could get that upstairs alone.

Diana, laughing, but with a touch of anxiety in the laughter, showed Eleanor the cottage. Eleanor did not seem to take very much interest in the cottage. She did not say, 'Oh, what a sweet cottage!' She did not even say, 'Oh, what a beastly little cottage!' She just seemed to take the cottage for granted, and said she had a headache after her journey and might she have tea? 'Oh, sorry, old dear,' said Diana. 'Of course you shall have tea. Come down to the parlour again.'

The parlour! The little devil went down to the parlour with Eleanor. She felt a sudden whelming desire for space and rest – elaborate and untroubled rest; unrestricted, expensive space. Tea and cushions and a long cool terrace to herself. 'One bedroom for the two – one bed, in fact!' laughed the little devil. 'Not even a hanging cupboard. Three of the five drawers in the chest of drawers! If you want to hang your things up, you've got to hang them on a hook behind the door. Carrying portmanteaux upstairs! This for a week! You're going from bad to worse, you know. Why didn't you listen to me in London? Why hadn't you got the spirit to strike? You'd have brought Reggy to heel. Look where he's brought you!'

'I'll go to the kitchen and put the kettle on,' said Diana.

Put the kettle on! Oh, for a cooling, starched maid with the tea all ready!

Not very sympathetic you find her? Unless you, who read, happen to have a good old train headache at the moment. In which case you will say to her, 'Go on. *I* know. Hit Diana over the head with her confounded kettle. Burn down the cottage. I'm with you.'

Diana, in the kitchen, bit her lip over the kettle. Just as she had foretold. She had wanted a friend, a convivial spirit; someone who would have a good laugh at the cottage and the bed and the chest of drawers and the hangers behind the door. Someone who would rough it, and help with the cooking, and wash up, and feed the chickens, and Vim the sink. That was the company she wanted. Instead of which—

Eleanor made an effort after tea and apologised to Diana, who laughed it off good-naturedly enough. So far there had been no mention of Algy. But Diana seemed to find in Eleanor's change of mood a cue for Algy. But she should have waded diplomatically into the subject. Whereas with pent-up determination, and therefore obviously, she plunged into Algy.

'Now, tell me; what is Algy up to?'

'Algy?'

'Yes. What is all this, Eleanor?'

'All what?'

'Why did he send you down here? Was it only because he wanted to bring you in his car?'

'No, of course not,' said Eleanor. 'He never thought of bringing me in his car until afterwards. Why do you ask in that tone of voice, as if his car was his bed? You're as bad as Reggy.'

'Oh!' Diana took this up quickly. 'Has *he* been inquisitive about Algy and you then?'

Eleanor laughed shrilly. 'Diana, do you suppose for one moment that anything ever has happened or ever will happen between me and Algy?'

'I don't say it has. I only—'

'If you think Algy's like that, it shows you're a pretty bad judge,' said Eleanor. Then she felt the pain again at her head and the little devil at her nerves. 'Good God!' she cried. 'Can't I keep my friends just because I'm married? I'm sick of all this puritanical humbug. And there's quite enough of it from my own relations without any from his.'

Diana flushed. But in indignation, not in humiliation.

'If I married a man,' she said speaking hurriedly and against her own judgment, 'and he had to go abroad, do you think he'd go alone? I don't want to interfere in your private affairs; only why does Algy crop up just now? That's what I want to know.'

Eleanor drew breath for something pretty tart; but resisted and relapsed.

'Oh, don't be a fool, Diana,' she said in an altered key.

'All right,' said Diana, relapsing too. 'Sorry. Only if things aren't all they might be at home, Elly, don't let Algy go and take advantage of it.'

'He's not that sort,' said Eleanor.

'Well, don't entice him to be.'

Eleanor laughed again. 'Every bachelor is a Lothario to his sister,' she said. 'Let's change the conversation. Have you seen Edyth Pye since she married?'

That concluded Algy for the evening. Eleanor supposed she must let Diana know that he was going to turn up next day, but she awaited a more propitious moment. Diana still subconsciously fretted. Why was Eleanor here? Because Algy had sent her. Why had he sent her? Algy might have conceived some intrigue involving this visit. But why had Eleanor consented? She was hating it. Diana could see her hating it. Hating it, even when she calmed down and said her head was quite all right now, and changed the subject, and laughed and devastated the good repute of poor Edyth Pye.

They strolled out presently across the dell; returned and had a meal at seven. Diana explained about the bed to Eleanor and told her to occupy the bedroom, and that she herself would sleep in a chair in the parlour. They went early to bed. Intermittently, they engaged in rather aimless conversation, embracing many subjects. But not embracing Algy.

So here is a cottage in the depths of a Somerset vale, with four rooms and one bed, and with two women as its only occupants. And the Chinese, those kite-flying, sign-writing philosophers, have designed a character to depict in their etymology the word 'discord', a character which is nothing more nor less than the drawing of two women alone in a little house. No fools they.

CHAPTER V

Urban

Louise, returning from Paddington, found her husband doing absolutely nothing, like some patiently tethered beast; tethered to the morning-room by his *Times.* He cocked a wary eye up at her. She looked as if she might be in a pretty busy sort of frame of mind. She confirmed this impression.

'Now! I've seen her off. He wasn't there or in the train. He'll no doubt be going down by car. I should like to keep him under observation, but I can't do everything by myself, and I've had an invitation to go out this afternoon, and I don't see how I can refuse. However, it's quite obvious what the game is. He'll be down after her today. The sister is either in it or being used as a sort of decoy. I don't mean decoy. I mean the other thing – pretext. Now!'

Willy rose with a noise, half a groan and half a grunt, like that which issues from a tired dog.

'It's all very well to say "Now!" You've left it too late to do anything now. She's gone and the harm's done. And if she's such hot stuff as all that there probably isn't a sister in the cottage at all.'

'She got a letter from the sister and I saw the postmark,' said Louise, with a superior smile for this Watson of a colleague. 'As for it being too late, it isn't too late at all. Only I didn't take any really serious steps until they were absolutely called for.'

'Oh, good lord,' said Willy. 'What do you intend doing?'

'The first thing I'm going to do is to wire Reggy.'

'To wire Reggy?'

'Certainly.'

'Louise, this is asking for the most appalling and howling row. What can you—?'

'I meant to send the wire on my way back here, but I forgot. You'd better sit down and write it out for me.'

'I absolutely refuse to be mixed up in this.'

'You're not being mixed up. Writing a telegram out for me doesn't mix you up. Sit down and write. It will get to Reggy by this afternoon and he can catch the night boat if he wants to. I rather wish I hadn't said I'd go out this afternoon; still, nothing very much can happen just at the moment. Are you ready to take down?'

Willy was not ready to take down. He remained standing in front of the writing-table pulling the lobe of his ear.

'Even suppose a feller does go to see a girl who's staying with his sister,' he said slowly, 'it doesn't necessarily follow that he's going to – that they're going to—'

'To what?'

'What?'

'Yes.'

'What?'

'Oh, sit down and write.'

Willy essayed one last excuse.

'Aha!' he said, 'you don't know Reggy's address.'

'Aha, my aunt!' said Louise, vigorously. 'I got it from Eleanor herself.'

'Oh, what's the use?' soliloquised Willy, and sat.

'Now, take this down,' said Louise. 'Bingham. Roi—'

'What? He's in France somewhere, isn't he?'

'That's just what I say, Roi—'

'What?'

'Err-oo-ah—'

'You mean "Roo", don't you? French for "street"?'

'I mean what I say. Bingham, Err-oo-ah Ed-oo-ar—'

'Here, hold on. What's all this – erroo, erroo? I don't get this.'

'Err-oo-ah – "King!" Err—'

'King? Oh, you mean "Wah".'

'King Edward the Seventh Hotel. Err-oo-ah Ed-oo-ar Sept Hotel.'

'Oh, righto. I see now. Wah Edward the Set. Yes?'

'Pareeee,' said Louise.

'All right. Yes?'

'Now. "Sorry to have to report Gascoyne turned up again and after Eleanor who—" '

'Hi, hi, hi. Boil it down, dash it. It's expensive.'

'Begin again,' said Louise. 'From the beginning – "Gascoyne again attentive Eleanor who responds. Think it my duty wire and report. She gone his sister cottage Somerset today—" Have you got that?'

'What? No. I thought you were just sort of practising. Besides, you can't go and send a wire like that.'

'If you think you can send a better one, go on.'

'I absolutely refuse to have anything to do with sending a wire at all. If I *had* to wire I'd simply say, – er – "Better come home, serious news Eleanor." '

'Oh. Then he would immediately think some serious accident had happened to his wife.'

'H'm. Well, so it may have by the time he gets back,' said Willy philosophically.

'Begin again,' said Louise.

Eventually the telegram was completed. Willy was bidden to rehearse it. He made his dog noise again and sat round; but rather spoilt the effect of the telegram by interspersed commentaries of his own.

'Bingham. Wah Edward Set Hotel, Paris. Sorry inform you Gascoyne – I don't believe you ought to mention names really – back and attentive Eleanor. Have definite proof – you haven't – she not averse – I absolutely wash my hands of this. They have arranged meeting cottage Somerset – that's pure guesswork too, and for all you know the sister is a very respectable woman and wouldn't countenance it even if they did intend to – return at once to prevent. Louise. There you are; and if you choose to push stuff like that about all over the telegraph wires in two countries you can do it on your own responsibility.'

'Give it to me,' said Louise. 'I will go and send it at once.'

She went at once and sent it.

In the afternoon Willy went again to Lord's, where he was bored but at least independent.

And Louise took a small Nux Vomica and crossed herself and went to play Mah-Jongg with Mrs Strathbean.

Algy was as yet in two minds as to whether he should make South Ditherton that day or an early start the next. At noon he proceeded to a garage in Jermyn Street and tentatively tuned up his merry carburetor. He returned to his rooms after lunching at his club. At the sound of his latchkey his servant, Lemon, hurried to the door and met him with a confidentially hushed announcement. Captain Dumfoil was in the sitting-room.

'The dashing Guardee,' said Algy to himself. 'What does *he* want, I wonder. All right, Lemon.'

Algy had now occupied these rooms for several years. A narrow passage ran the length of them, and from this three doors gave access to his respective apartments, sitting-room, bedroom, bathroom. There was only one door on the other side of the passage, and this, at the end farthest from the main entrance, led to a small room which served as a butler's pantry. Here Lemon ironed trousers and pessimistically studied form.

Lemon was a recently-married ex-soldier, willing but depressed. He went home to sleep; home being a couple of rooms above some mews off Curzon Street. None of Algy's meals, except breakfast, for which Lemon and a gas-ring were jointly responsible, were taken on the premises.

Algy found his present visitor stolidly awaiting him in the sitting-room, an unwonted and, apparently, rather unwanted guest. Algy pulled a little grimace on the threshold, but greeted Captain Dumfoil cordially enough.

'Hallo, Dumfoil!'

'Hallo, young man!'

'What brings you here?' asked Algy. 'Have a drink?'

'Oh, no, thank yer,' said Captain Dumfoil.

'Oh, all right. Cigars, cigarettes, chocolates?'

'No, no.'

'Matches, magazines, cup of coffee, lemonade, chewing gum? No? You seem in merry mood. What's up?'

Captain Dumfoil stretched himself into an attitude suggestive of a desire to impress. He was a stuffy, hairy man of forty. Tradition dogged him. A generation ago the Captain Dumfoils of their day had lounged, literally propped up by soirées. Into the frills of their shirt-fronts whiskers magnificently wept. Around them curvetted the coyly frisking crinolines. In the field of Mars almost ridiculously brave; quite ridiculously supine in the courts of Venus. The natural successor of these yawning bravos was Captain Dumfoil.

Fashion had long since, of course, removed the whiskers and also, in its turn, the supercessor of the whiskers, the moustache enormous. Captain Dumfoil contented himself with a square-cut continuation of the hair in his nostrils. In speech he was handicapped by a tongue too large for his mouth. His 's's' were splutters; his diphthongs a sheer mess.

'I haven't much time to spare,' said Captain Dumfoil. 'But I thought I'd just drop in and give you a gentle hint about something. And if you take my advice you'll listen.'

'What's the matter with you? Have you come to deliver a moral lecture or something?' asked Algy.

'Now, listen, young feller-me-lad. It's about that place at Richmond.'

This, in Captain Dumfoil's phraseology, was 'Ripsmond.' Algy looked puzzled for a second; then enlightenment spread over his countenance.

'Oh, Richmond? Oh, you mean Shady Nook?'

'Shady Nook, yes. And well named. I strongly advise both you and your aunt to give it up.'

'Why?' expostulated Algy, taking his leisurely seat on the sofa. 'It's all right. It's just like any other casino or gambling hell, whichever you choose to call it, according to the state of your luck.'

'It isn't,' rejoined Captain Dumfoil. 'It's a rotten hole. And the old merchant that runs it is a crook.'

'Who? Phonk? What if he is? He can't defraud a whole roomful of people in broad nightlight.'

'Can't he!'

'You've been stung,' said Algy.

Captain Dumfoil shifted impatiently in his chair.

'You chuck it,' he repeated. 'Of course, I know what the matter is with you. You're under the influence of your aunt.'

'Very good influence, too,' said Algy. 'Don't you, of all people, start saying things against my aunt. Who was it called the Publican names?'

'What publican?'

'The Publican and the Pharisee. Oh, I suppose you won't have heard of them. About the only publican you've never struck, I should think.'

'Ha!' said Captain Dumfoil. 'I should think that even the Publican would have derived a little cold consolation from Mrs Krabbe.'

'What have you got against my aunt?'

'Nothing, nothing. But she gambles rather indiscriminately,' said Captain Dumfoil, patronisingly.

'I know she gambles,' said Algy. 'She gambles like a film tenderfoot. What of it? So do you.'

'Not at Shady Nook,' said Captain Dumfoil. 'Now, look here. If I tell you something, can I trust you to keep it absolutely dark?'

Algy made faces. 'Well, I don't know,' he replied. 'You say it's something that concerns my aunt?'

'Yes, it does, in a way.'

'Well, if it's a secret that concerns Auntie,' said Algy, 'you'd better not tell me, because I should naturally repeat it to her. What do you think?'

Dumfoil rose with the deliberate self-importance of a stage lawyer.

'In that case,' he said, 'I shall merely content myself with repeating – steer clear of Shady Nook.'

Algy rose too.

'Well, I'm sorry if you've let 'em do you down, Dumfoil,' he said. 'But I think Auntie and I can look after ourselves.'

Captain Dumfoil tossed his head with a blunt laugh. He stood in the sitting-room doorway and massaged a Malacca cane with his wash-leather glove.

'From one who knows,' he said. 'That's all. Later on, perhaps, I may be able to be a little more talkative about it.'

'Oh, perish the thought,' said Algy.

This concluded the interview.

Lemon was hovering in the passage to let the visitor out. Algy called him into the sitting-room.

'Are my things packed, Lemon?'

'No, sir. You said—'

'I know. That's all right. I think I shall probably push off this afternoon. I shall just pop over and say good-bye to Mrs Krabbe first. I shall be away for about a week, I expect. So you'll be able to be at home most of the time. That'll be convenient for you just now, won't it?'

'Yes, sir,' assented Lemon, gloomily.

'By the way, how is your wife keeping?'

'Thank you, sir,' said Lemon, 'very patient, she is. The event is imminent, as the saying goes.'

'Well, you can be there most of the time; only just look in occasionally, you understand?'

'Oh, yes, sir.'

'Righto, then. Now, just get my things packed, and I'll go and see Mrs Krabbe.'

Mrs Krabbe though partaking of a late luncheon, was not in the dining-room of her house in Hertford Street, but in her bedroom. She was, in point of fact, in the bed, a massive Jacobean affair, furnished with such a wealth of mattresses that Mrs Krabbe appeared to be quite high in the air. Pillows not only supported her at the back but propped her up at the flanks. Her wig rested candidly on a stand near the window; but she was wearing a boudoir cap, tilted at a coquettish angle over her prominent Roman nose. She was eating salmon fish cakes and reading the *Morning Post* through an eyeglass.

To her came Denise, the discreet and dexterous, a French maid with as many secrets at the back of her head as there were pins at the back of her dainty apron. To her came Denise, knocked, stood and awaited the august attention.

This was granted presently in the form of what can only be described as an eating stare.

Mr Algy was below and desired audience. Mrs Krabbe nodded, pushed her boudoir cap a trifle further over her nose, and resumed her reading.

'Hallo, darling!' said Algy, arriving cheerfully and stick-swingingly upon the scene.

He advanced to the bed and kissed his aunt, who received the salute unemotionally.

'Sorry not to have seen much of you for the last few days,' he said. 'And not to be going to for the next few.'

'Why? Where are you off to?' demanded Mrs Krabbe, in her singular voice which was a sort of trilling croak, not altogether unlike the sound of an old gentleman gargling.

'I'm driving down to the country for a day or two.'

'Oh,' said Mrs Krabbe. 'Love affair?'

'No. At least – no, not exactly.'

'Oh, rubbish! What kind of a love affair? Speckled or plain? Kensington Gardens or the Metropole, Brighton?'

'Nothing, Auntie. Simply I've sent someone down to keep Diana company, and I'm going down there too.'

'Sent her to Diana!' said Mrs Krabbe, in puzzled tones. 'What on earth have you done that for? Are you afraid of going too far, or something?'

'No, Auntie. It's quite a Platonic affair.'

'M'yes,' said Mrs Krabbe, doubtfully. 'I don't believe in that stuff. Who is she?'

'Eleanor Bingham,' said Algy.

Mrs Krabbe performed elaborate research work at the back of her teeth with a forefinger.

'Damn these fish balls,' she said. 'And who's she?'

'You know. Eleanor Delaney.'

'Oh. She's married.'

'Yes.'

'Only just married.'

'Yes. Last autumn.'

'Where's her husband?'

'Abroad.'

'H'm.'

'But as I tell you, Auntie, it's nothing – like that. She's going to keep Diana company, and I—'

'Keep off it,' said Mrs Krabbe. 'You don't want to trot about with young married women. It isn't sporting and it's very seldom sincere.'

'But, I tell you, it's not that sort of thing.'

'Then it's poodlefaking, which is worse,' said Mrs Krabbe. 'Oh, don't tell me. You may not intend to trip up. And then one day there you are together and the opportunity is there and you think – "Oh, well—" and something happens just like an accident and then you're sorry. I know what I'm talking about. I've done it myself before now.'

Algy shook his head.

'Not in this case,' he said. 'Besides the opportunity *won't* be there, and I wouldn't take advantage of it if it was. Diana and she are going to be together at old Benbow's cottage.'

'And where are you going to be?'

'I don't know yet.'

'Don't you go, boy,' said Mrs Krabbe.

'I must. I've promised. Besides, I want to.'

'Who have you promised? Diana?'

'No. I tell you, Eleanor's an absolutely straight girl.'

'Married a fat man, didn't she?'

'What? Well, yes, she—'

'With a lot of money?'

'Yes.'

'Don't go,' said Mrs Krabbe.

'I'm going, Auntie. I'm sorry.'

'I never knew you were such a fool, Algy.'

'I'm not a fool. Nor's she.'

'All right, then. You don't often require advice. I suppose that's why you won't take it when you get it. It's a mug's game. It's worse than that; it's a mean game. You'd better clear out now. I want to get up.'

'You don't understand, Auntie—'

'There's nothing,' said Mrs Krabbe, 'connected with, or suggestive of, any form of impropriety that I don't understand from A to Z. Now then. Do you want to see me in my bath?'

'Not in the least,' said Algy.

'Very well, then. Get out, there's a good boy.'

'Half a second. There was something else I wanted to tell you. What was it? Oh, yes. What's today? Wednesday?'

'Yes. Why?'

'Tomorrow's Thursday. You'll be going to the Nook tomorrow night, I suppose?'

'I daresay. Why?'

'Nothing particular. But I've just had rather a queer visit from Dumfoil. He came about the Nook.'

'Dumfoil? The Nook? What's *his* trouble? He never goes there now.'

'I know. And as for what his trouble is, I'm afraid I can't quite tell you. He's an insidious sort of bird. He's the kind of man who can never tell you anything without tapping your waistcoat buttons with his cigarette-holder. But I rather think that he was hinting at the play at the Nook being crooked.'

'Much obliged to him,' said Mrs Krabbe. 'I wasn't born yesterday.'

'He said that old Phonk is a crook.'

'Well, who does Captain Dumfoil expect to find running a gambling joint? The Archbishop of Canterbury?'

'Phonk has never tried to take any advantage of *you* has he?'

'Advantage of *me?*' croaked Mrs Krabbe, in a subdued, incredulous voice. 'Advantage of *me?* He'd better try. He'd be sorry for it.'

'Well, but with all said and done, Auntie, what could one do?' asked Algy, who appeared grudgingly to share to a certain extent Captain Dumfoil's views on Mr Phonk.

'I know what *I'd* do,' replied Mrs Krabbe, promptly. 'I'd make his life a misery for him, and he knows it. Why, I could have him kicked out of every indecent club in London.'

'Seriously, though?'

'I am serious. No gaming-house keeper can afford to play crooked, and your Captain Dumfoil would know that if he had half my experience.'

'You mean, he'd get shown up?'

'Of course, he would. Why, if this Phonk tried any dirty business with me, I'd show him up myself. My goodness, I should jolly well think so. The first sign of any jiggery-pokery there and I'd bring down the walls of his Shady Nook on him in a style that would make Joshua look like a cornet solo on a charabanc.'

'All right, then,' said Algy. 'So long as you're satisfied it's all on the level.'

'Of course, it's on the level. Captain Dumfoil's a bad loser, that's all.'

'That's what I told him. Well, good-bye, Auntie.'

'You're going now, are you?'

'Yes.'

'With this Mrs Chance-it, or whatever her name is nowadays?'

'Yes. She's not the kind of girl you think. Just because she married that stiff. So don't start that again.'

'Well, I'd stop you if I could,' said Mrs Krabbe. 'I tell you that straight. Go away then.'

Algy went away in a mood rather aggressive for so amiable a youth. He went straight to Jermyn Street, and brought his car round to his rooms. Half an hour later, the two-seater was drinking Bath Road like wine.

Denise came over to Half Moon Street presently. Mrs Krabbe had no note of Miss Richardson Gascoyne's address. Mr Lemon would, no doubt, supply this. Mr Lemon was, however, out. He returned to the rooms later in the evening, and again left them. Soon after he had again left them, back came Denise. Discovered Mr Lemon's home address from the hall-porter. Mr Lemon was not there. Mrs Lemon, on the verge of great expectations, was there and glared with undisguised hostility at a young foreign woman coming and asking for her husband in this manner, especially at so tactless a moment. Could give no information.

Denise went back once more to Half Moon Street. Left a message with the hall-porter. Mr Lemon was to ring up Mrs Krabbe. Lemon reappeared in Half Moon Street at six. Rang up Mrs Krabbe. Mrs Krabbe was out. So was Denise. Only the cook was in. Knew nothing of the matter regarding which the person on the telephone was talking of. It was past eight o'clock before Mrs Krabbe got Diana's address.

During the afternoon a telegraph boy came swinging and whistling up to the Pipers' flat. So that when Willy came back from Lord's he found the telegram propped against the stand for hat-brushes on the hall table, took it up doubtfully, as one takes up a bee presumably dead, glanced at the contents and said, 'Oh, utter hell!'

So that when Louise came in, all fatigued and heated from harbouring red dragons and punging her opponent's wind, she triumphantly closed down upon Willy and flourished the telegram in his face. It was from Paris.

Piper 6 Gloucester Buildings London Angleterre.

Cannot possibly return until tomorrow till then you have my authority take all measures you consider necessary

Reginald.

'I know,' said Willy. 'I've read it. Look here, that has gone and done quite enough harm without your doing any more.'

Louise disregarded him entirely. She stood in the dining-room doorway and eyed the telephone speculatively.

'I must find out whether that young man's left,' she mused. 'What's the time now? Six. Ye-es—'

She advanced into the dining-room and took up the telephone directory. Willy could not be said to stand and watch her, for his eyes were on the ceiling.

She called up Algy's number. A male voice answered.

'Oh. Is that Mr Richardson Gascoyne?'

'No, this is his manservant speaking.'

'Oh. Erm – yes. I'm – er – Oh, has he gone yet?'

'Pardon?'

'Mr Richardson Gascoyne told me he was leaving town today for the country. I'm a friend of his. I – er – only wanted to know whether he'd gone.'

'Yes, he's gone, madam.'

'Oh, he *has?*'

'Yes, madam.'

'Oh. Yes. I see. Yes. Thank you. What time did he go?'

'Early this afternoon. Excuse me – that's not Mrs Krabbe, is it?'

'I beg your pardon?'

'Mrs Krabbe'

'Missed his cab?'

'No, 'm. Is that – are you Mrs Krabbe?'

'Oh. No, no. No. No, I'm – no.'

'Oh, I beg pardon.'

'Not at all. All right, thank you. Good-bye.'

'Here, I say, you know; this is absolute barefaced lying,' said Willy.

'Nonsense,' said Louise. 'It is diplomacy. One had to meet guile with guile.'

'What's the next bit of guile on the programme?' asked Willy.

'I'm going out.'

'Where to?'

'I thought you said you didn't want to be mixed up in this?'

'I don't.'

'Then you'd better let me do things my own way without asking questions. I've got an idea. I'll tell you afterwards what I've done very likely. I shall probably be back in time for dinner. I may be a little late.'

'Oh-h! What *are* you going to perpetrate now? All right. I'll go out myself to the club for an hour.'

A few minutes later Willy descended from the Tube at Down Street and walked into Piccadilly towards his club. Just as he was about to turn up the club steps he found himself face to face with another man; a plump, bronzed man of about forty-five with a neat moustache and a lingering smile of amused tolerance for the whirl of a world in which he seemed, in some indefinite way, a novice. Willy brightened up at the sight of him.

'Hallo!' cried Willy. 'Henry!'

Henry. The youngest Bingham. Louise's inconsiderable young brother. Reginald's alleged, but really utterly futile and negligible, younger brother. Yet here, in a sudden apparition, you found all the qualities of which you had thought the Binghams devoid. All Reginald's share – all Louise's share. Good humour, generosity, the ability to laugh, irresolution, incompetence, non-success – all epitomised in sleepily gentle eyes and in a lazy smile.

Willy clapped a hand to this Henry's shoulder and drew him into the club. And lugged him into the plot.

CHAPTER VI

The Telegram in the Bosom

Very early on Thursday morning Eleanor sprang into a startled sitting attitude, wildly awakened, violently jerked from sleep into baffling surroundings; her mind half benumbed, half horribly alert. So may the soul of a sinner awaken to the frightening surprises of Hades.

Who was she and where? Then sleep fell from her brain. She returned to life. She was Eleanor Bingham. And she was in Mr Hole's bed.

But part of the horror remained. What fiend had shrieked her into consciousness? The fiend shrieked again, and Eleanor relapsed, her panic giving place swiftly to wrath; while Mr Hole's rooster continued conceitedly to challenge the first glimmer of our important Thursday.

Bird accursed! Why hadn't Diana warned her? It was what o'clock? Eleanor took a watch from the chair beside her bed and peered into it. A quarter to four. Further sleep was, she knew, impossible. A quarter to four – five – six – seven – eight; four hours until normal and reasonable daytime. Four hours. And she would lie awake and cocks would crow and birds would twitter and cows would moo. Every morning for a week. No. No, no.

She had fallen asleep with mischief on her pillow. The little devil was still there. His insinuations now took a humorous turn; embittered humour was in her heart. The joke was at her own expense. She, who had made such a to-do about being herself and about being natural and about refusing to let her in-laws have their own way, had struck a blow for liberty and for her self-esteem. And this was where she had, in that good cause, arrived. This! It was really funny. Bitterly funny.

She would go back to town that day. That really was sensible; that really was herself. She would leave this place,

Chool, this day, Thursday. It might hurt Diana's feelings, but she'd been a jolly sight too considerate about people's feelings. She would up and be herself, and if she grieved and startled and shocked people's feelings they could lump it. Oh, yes, the rooster could crow. Go on. Crow, you brute! It was the last time he'd keep *her* awake at four in the morning.

She'd wait until Algy came down and then she'd get him to take her back to town in his car. She'd go home. And stay home. That is to say she would make her own home her base, during a short, glorious, personally-misconducted tour of good old London. The little devil simply chortled at this. 'Even if you go a bit beyond the limit, you've been driven to it. You can always feel that. Think of what you've tried to put up with. Reggy sneaking round to Louise and getting you tied up there. Louise's, after dinner. This little effort of your own to extricate yourself with the best intentions! This cottage! Diana! The rooster! Oh, be damned! Off you go, my dear, and be really yourself and let it all rip. After all, this is only what's been in the back of your mind ever since you married.'

She thought over her marriage, humorously still; smiling to herself as she lay in bed with her hands clasped behind her head. She compared her marriage mentally to taking a flight in an aeroplane. To a sedate and ordered citizen suddenly making up his mind to have a dart at it, just to see what it was like. And being up there, finding himself up there, clinging and wondering whether he could keep his breath and being hurtled along in the wind, and all before he had really quite definitely made up his mind whether he'd go up or not. But the aeroplane flight didn't last long; couldn't. The citizen returned and resumed his hat and his normal citizenship. Or crashed.

Something wrong there though. Because if she climbed out of the aeroplane and went off on her own again, that would mean a crash. So it didn't quite pan out somehow. What did it matter? She was half asleep anyhow, and would be quite asleep if it hadn't been for that confounded cock, so if the analogy didn't come quite right, what the dickens did that matter?

Anyhow, one thing was certain. London today. Real London. No Louise. No Diana. Go on, you – crow away!

She fell asleep again from time to time, but it was fitful sleep between jerking, startled awakenings. Every time she opened her eyes they grew brighter at the thought of buzzing away in that little car. How intolerably slowly the hours passed. She got out of bed and wandered about the room; sat for five minutes in a senseless chair; up again and to the window, through which the light of a dull, inhospitable day was now fully illuminating the deeply rural surroundings.

At seven Diana woke up in Mr Hole's sitting-room chair. She made tea and crept upstairs. Eleanor had got back into bed and was, apparently, asleep, but she jumped at the creak of the door.

'Sorry to wake you up so early,' said Diana. 'It's only seven. Here's some tea. Sleep as long as you like.'

'Don't worry,' said Eleanor. 'I woke at a quarter to four. Doesn't that cock crowing disturb you in the mornings? Or at night, rather?'

'I didn't know it did crow,' said Diana.

'Never mind,' said Eleanor. 'It doesn't matter now. It might have been worse, I suppose. I was expecting cows to moo, but they haven't. I suppose they don't do it in the early morning.'

'Well, have your tea,' said Diana. 'And if you like to get up fairly soon I'll hot the water up. I shan't make it awfully hot, but good enough for a bath this weather.'

Eleanor felt frozen to the marrow and was tempted to say so, but restrained herself. It wasn't for much longer.

There were exactly four rooms in April Cottage. As you entered, the sitting-room or parlour was on the left, and this, like the bedroom above it, ran the whole length of the building. On the right of the front porch was the combined kitchen, pantry and scullery. Between parlour and kitchen ran a passage ending in a back door, where a plot scarcely broad enough to accommodate a dustbin separated the cottage from the bank of the towering grove in the rear of the establishment. Half-way along the passage the staircase shot upwards like a ladder, and the greater portion of the space above the kitchen was required for a landing. There was, however, a small room, used undesignedly as a bathroom, across the landing from the bedroom.

The parlour and bedroom were of quite reasonable size; but, while the bedroom was furnished with frugal severity, the parlour possessed many of the properties of a storeroom. The walls were lined with books, many of them very dull and nearly all of them very dilapidated. Mr Hole's own contribution to literature was represented by reams of manuscript which had been stuffed into the lower shelves of one of the book-cases – sheaves of foolscap, scored and underlined and blotted and, in places, disfigured by the attentions of a critical mouse.

The room had a large open fireplace with a fire ready built, for April Cottage became very chill after sunset in the hollow of the hill, and Mr Hole was no Spartan. In the centre of the parlour was a round table on which he partook of his one meal every day, before and after which occasion the round table became submerged in literature.

The aged, long-suffering armchair in leather formerly red, which had been Diana's bed on this occasion. Two stern fiddle-back wooden chairs. A great solid writing-table in the window. An old black oak sideboard. The rest – books. Rows of fat, uniform, worm-eaten books with the labels peeled from their bindings, standing stolid in outraged dignity, like a line of aldermen in disgrace and stripped of their insignia. Books without any bindings at all, or with the bindings held hazardously around them by string, as the trousers are held round a tramp. Books in prose, in poetry. Books in Latin. And below them the longest book of them all, not yet a book and never to be a book, colossal and furious work of a mistaken lifetime.

Diana had declared a war of cleanliness on the parlour, thereby incurring the deep suspicion and animosity of Mrs Easy. Many of the books had fallen to pieces in her hand, but she had persevered, and the room now wore quite a cheerful aspect with flowers in a jam-pot and a dainty check tablecloth. Oil lamps and candles were, of course, the only means of lighting the cottage, but fortunately at this time of year daylight lasted throughout the waking hours. A well in the front garden supplied the water. In the front garden also was a small coal-shed. These, the fowl-run and an intricate liaison of grass and flower-bed formed the grounds of April Cottage, which were bordered by a privet hedge. At the angle of the privet hedge the little road from above joined the grassy lane which bounded the dell.

A gate, green with moss, connected the side-road with the short gravel path to the porch. Away to the other side of the cottage was a long tract of spongy meadow with ferns revelling in the marsh-land in the cup of the hill. There were queer birds-eggs to be had for the asking within fifty yards of April Cottage. For a couple of cigarette cards little Easy would show you a dozen likely places.

Little Easy's mother, leaving her cottage at about nine o'clock on this Thursday morning, looked up and worked her elastic nose at the heavens. She then re-entered her cottage and again emerged, armed with an heirloom in the shape of one of those umbrellas employed by commissionaires at wet receptions. She proceeded along the upper road towards South Ditherton, gaining the corner of the little road down to April Cottage just in time to see Pitcher's motor-van rounding the bend and steering down through the trees. Mrs Easy halted and her nostrils played like those of a terrier. Pitcher's, the South Ditherton furniture shop? What could *they* be delivering in a van to April Cottage?

Mrs Easy was sorely tempted to follow and investigate. She had cast the dust of the cottage from her elastic-sideds – but only because of this young woman. Not because of Mr Hole. She reckoned she still owed it to Mr Hole to keep an eye on things. He had left his address at Harrogate with her in case of emergencies. Suppose she discovered some outrage in course of perpetration at April Cottage! She would not hesitate to let Mr Hole know. It was her plain duty. She had already felt very inclined to report the matter of the tidying-up of the parlour.

She walked on to the corner and stood deliberating. The van had disappeared round the bend of the hill. Then there came from the rear the sound of one whistling – not with the lips, but through the teeth. Mrs Easy swung round. A telegraph boy, aimlessly stunting on a red bicycle, extended one confident hand to a handle-bar to avoid collision. But did not stop whistling.

'Here!' said Mrs Easy, sharply.

The telegraph boy slithered a boot upon the road and turned.

'Where are you going?' asked Mrs Easy.

'Cottidge,' replied the telegraph boy, and jerked his head in that direction.

''Ave you got a telegraph then?' said Mrs Easy.

'That's ri',' said the telegraph boy, producing a telegram from his wallet and studying the address with caution.

'Oo is it addressed to?' demanded Mrs Easy.

The telegraph boy had another look. 'Dinah Robinson Crusoe,' he replied.

'Let me see,' said Mrs Easy, advancing and appropriating the telegram.

'Richardson Gascoyne – that's that young woman that's there. H'm. Fer her, is it? H'm.'

Very grudgingly she restored the telegram to the boy.

'Very well, then, take it and give it to her and do yer work sharp and proper,' she said. 'Don't stop and hang about here.'

The telegraph boy, hardened by many dealings with the young ladies in post-offices, ignored this taunt and went his way.

But this settled Mrs Easy. She followed.

A thunderstorm was apparently brewing in the sky. A minor thunderstorm was, Eleanor thought, very likely brewing in the cottage. She shrank from offending Diana. But her mind was quite made up. It was rather difficult, all the same, to come out with the information that she was going back to London forthwith. She thought it over during breakfast and decided to postpone the announcement. It might even be propitious to wait until Algy turned up.

She was very agreeable to Diana and by way of showing, in advance, that there was no ill-feeling, she entered gladly into the morning housewifery. She said she would wash up the breakfast things while Diana made the bed.

Eleanor was accordingly in the kitchen when Pitcher's van drew up at the gate. She glanced out and saw the elderly driver descend and begin heaving something off the back of the van. What was this? Oh, dear! The other bed. The other bed would not be wanted now. She ought to tell Diana before Diana accepted, assembled and made the bed, that the bed would be untenanted. It was very awkward. Diana had already come running excitedly downstairs and was at the gate. Eleanor could not follow her out and begin wrangling with her in the baffled company of Pitcher's driver. Better let it be. Eleanor withdrew into the kitchen and hid her face in the washing-up.

Pitcher's driver was very, very like a toad. He suffered from a chronic affliction of the throat which made all he said appear very confidential. He put his face close to Diana's, and said,

'I've brought ye yer bed.'

'Good!' said Diana. 'Bring it in, please.'

'Ah!' whispered Pitcher's driver. 'Signal-arnded, I don't know that I can manage she.'

'Oh, is it heavy? I'll help you,' said Diana.

'Thank'ee,' said Pitcher's driver.

'Oh, but I don't want a double bed. A single one I said.'

'This bed,' said the driver, placing his hand upon the corpse of the bed, dismembered and swathed within the van, 'she be the only bed in the shop. For hire, that be. That's what she be. The only one.'

'But I haven't room for a double bed. Let me think, now. One moment! You'd better come with me, and I'll consult my friend.'

She went indoors to the kitchen. The driver, stooping and very toad-like, followed and cocked an appreciative eye on Eleanor from the kitchen doorway.

'Eleanor, they've only got a double bed on hire—'

'Oh, if the bed won't do—' began Eleanor, readily.

She caught the driver's eye. No, she really couldn't make this the opportunity for her revelation. 'Do what you think best, dear,' she said.

'Well, we'd better take it, I suppose,' said Diana. 'There's room for it.'

'Is there? I shouldn't have thought there was – for another large bed. The room isn't as big as all that.'

'I tell you what we might do,' said Diana. 'If it's the only bed we can get, we might share it, and send the single bed to be stored. That would make enough room.'

'Er – yes, but – All right. Just as you think.'

'Of course, I've only got single sheets though,' continued Diana. 'I don't know what to do about that.'

'You can 'ire 'er clothes for 'er,' said the driver.

'Thanks, I don't care much about hired bed-clothes; do you, Eleanor?'

'What? No. I—'

'You can 'ire new material at the shop,' said the driver.

'Are you sure?'

'Ah,' said the driver, 'new material.'

'Well,' said Diana, 'bring the bed upstairs. And I'll take the single one back to be stored. I'll go on your van. Then I can see about the sheets and things, and you can bring me out again. You don't mind, do you, Eleanor?'

'No,' said Eleanor. 'I think you'd much better go and see about it. Of course, really, I—'

'What?' asked Diana, pausing in the doorway. The driver also paused and peered inquisitively.

'Nothing,' said Eleanor.

Diana returned with the driver to the front gate and the van and the bed. Here they were greeted by teeth-whistling. The telegraph boy remained on his bicycle, supporting himself by the van.

Diana took the telegram; a little frown gathering. Algy, no doubt.

Diana Richardson Gascoyne April Cottage Chool near South Ditherton Som.

Do your best to stop any funny business between Algy

and that woman stopping with you he says platonic I know better so dont put up with any hokey pokey

Auntie.

She gave a little introspective nod to herself over this; a little tightening of the eyes. 'No answer,' she told the telegraph boy, who pushed himself off from the van, performed a stunting half-circuit and laboured off up the hill. Diana placed the telegram in her bosom and turned to assist Pitcher's driver with the bed.

From the cover of a convenient bush by the roadside Mrs Easy took astonished stock of what followed. She saw the young woman and Pitcher's driver carry into the cottage the component parts of a large brass bedstead and a voluminous roll of mattress. After a considerable time had elapsed, the driver brought from the cottage the outraged segments of Mr Hole's bedstead and, in a haphazard cone of desecration, Mr Hole's mattress.

A double bed. A double bed taken into the cottage and the single bed removed. And a telegram. This young woman was expecting company. Did Mr Hole know of this? Would Mr Hole have given consent to company at his cottage? Very unlike him if he had. Did he, in any case, know of this bed-shifting business? Preposterous! Never in this world would he have consented to such a thing. And, even if the young woman was expecting company and had obtained leave to have company, why so pointedly and with such careful preparation a double bed in lieu of an extra single? Who was she going to share the double bed with?

Pitcher's driver placed the single bed aboard the van, climbed into the driver's seat and waited. Mrs Easy waited too, wide-eyed and nose-working in the thicket.

Diana put her hat on thoughtfully in the bedroom. So her suspicions were well-founded. Even Auntie, who was no stickler in such matters, had been moved to protest. The question was should she go straight to Eleanor and have it all out now? After all, there was no sign of Algy here. She had been rather hot-headed in the matter of Algy last night, and Eleanor had been very resentful and difficult. It was rather asking for it to launch an accusation before there were any grounds for it. Wiser to wait, at least, until she returned from South Ditherton with the bedding.

Eleanor, as we know, was not without her quandary. She was in the parlour now. Diana looked in on her way down.

'I shan't be long,' she said. 'Will you be all right?'

'Yes, of course. Rather.'

'Anything you want?'

'No. Oh, you might bring some papers out.'

'Yes, I will. Oh, and, by the way, what do you like to drink? I haven't anything here; but I'll get some wine ordered if you'll tell me what sort.'

'No, thanks,' said Eleanor. 'Don't you go ordering wine.'

'I may as well. I'm going to the shop, in any case. I want to get some brandy. I've always forgotten it up to now. But they say you should always have brandy in the house. Besides, it's useful for cooking.'

'Well, don't go ordering things for me.'

'You've only got to say the word,' said Diana, turning.

'Have I? Well, then – Diana—'

'Yes?'

'Er – is that man still waiting to drive you in the van?'

'Yes. Why?'

'It's all right. Nothing.'

'No, but what?'

'Would you get me some cigarettes?'

'Yes. Is that all you wanted to say?'

'That's all.'

Diana fidgeted for a moment in the narrow hall. Her fingers went to her bosom. She drew the telegram forth, then put it back. When she came back would do. Besides, she had no evidence of anything.

'Well, good-bye,' she called, and went.

From her hiding-place Mrs Easy saw her close the gate and climb into the van. Oh, so she'd locked up the cottage, had she, and was going off to South Ditherton, was she? Probably to meet the double-bedded friend. Very well, then. But Mrs Easy would come and have another look at this later on. If the young woman thought she could make this sort of use of Mr Hole's cottage without his getting to know, she'd never made a greater mistake in her life. Never a greater.

The van climbed past the ambush and went its way. Mrs Easy regained the roadway and ascended the hill again. She proceeded towards South Ditherton at a steady pace. Her walk was stiff and rather crouched, like that of some beast of prey, cautious lest it should forewarn an artless victim. Half-way to South Ditherton the threatened thunderstorm broke, and her appearance became even more extraordinary beneath her commissionaire's umbrella.

The garage of the *Ring o' Bells* was situated alongside that hotel. Algy, having slept and breakfasted late, had actually started his car running when the first warning clap of thunder sounded above his head. He said, 'Oh, curse this!' and went indoors to get his mackintosh. A second or two later the furniture van thudded slowly past the *Ring o' Bells*, and, by the time Algy emerged and set off with his nose towards Chool, Diana was in Pitcher's.

CHAPTER VII

Maiden Shame

Puck finds his comedies ready-made; a haphazard, extempore producer he. He does not even select his company, but presses into bewildered service any unfortunate who may chance to cross his path. An imperious little Titania may find herself thus wildly intrigued; a stately, disconsolate Helena. You may observe querulous Lysander protesting in the toils. Even old, egregious Bully Bottom may presently blunder in upon the scene and – bless him – be translated.

In the club on Wedneday evening, while Willy related his sorry tale, Henry Bingham filled a very deliberate pipe, lit it, let it out, failed to notice for some time that it was out, re-lit it, let it out again and knocked it out thinking that he had smoked it. All the while he listened and nodded and perpetually smiled. He appeared extremely inert. The very sight of him would have irritated Reginald like a flea.

'Yes,' he said, at length. 'I sympathise.'

'Thanks,' said Willy.

'Not with you, old man,' said Henry. 'At least, my sympathies with you are more or less permanent. No, I'm sorry for her.'

'For Eleanor.'

'Yes.' He mused and began systematically to refill his pipe. 'I rather like Eleanor,' he added.

'So do I,' said Willy furtively and through closed lips.

'She's a man's woman, I suppose,' continued Henry. 'Only at the moment it doesn't seem quite clear which man's.'

'Don't know about that,' said Willy. 'Looks clear enough to me.'

Henry stretched for a match; took one. Seemed to be struck by a thought just before striking the match, but at last struck it.

'This blighter's gone after her already, eh?' he asked.

'Yes. Louise discovered he pushed off in his car to-day.'

'This sister? She's in it, you think? Seems a bit thick for a sister.'

Willy shrugged.

'Society people, I suppose,' he said, airily. 'They'll do anything, won't they?'

'Sounds like it,' admitted Henry, lighting his pipe.

'Mind you,' he went on, after a good deal of puffing and of prodding the burning tobacco with his finger, 'mind you, I think if Eleanor knew Reggy was on the scent she'd chuck it. Not for her own sake; for his. She didn't seem to me to be the kind of girl who'd go out of her way to be cruel to Reggy.'

'She would have known if I'd had my way,' said Willy. 'Heaven knows what Louise is up to now. Women are damned unsporting, some of 'em.'

'What I should like to see,' said Henry, 'is Louise utterly scored off and getting it full in the neck from Reggy for bringing him home. I should love to see him arriving to-morrow, all fuming and sea-sick, only to find he'd been made a fool of.'

'You wouldn't say that if you had to be left with Louise afterwards.'

'I wouldn't say it if I didn't think Eleanor deserved a chance. But all this conspiracy— If only she got to know—'

'If she got to know what Louise had done,' said Willy, 'it would only get her back up, and then the worst would happen in any case.'

Henry examined his pipe-stem doggedly. 'She ought to be given the chance,' he repeated. 'By all the laws of fair play. If all this ended in a bust-up for her and Reggy and nobody had done a hand's turn to prevent it, I should feel very guilty.' He paused. 'What do you say the name of this place is, again?'

'April Cottage, South Ditherton. Why? You're not going to wire or anything?'

'N-no,' said Henry. 'A wire might only make things worse, unless it was frightfully carefully worded.'

'Well, it's no good writing,' said Willy. 'By the time a letter got there it would either be too late or totally unnecessary. You follow my example, old man, and keep out of it. I must go home now. I shall be late for dinner. I'll let you know what happens.'

'Righto,' said Henry. 'I say, don't let Louise know you've told me about this.'

'No fear,' said Henry. 'And don't you tell her I told you. So long.'

Henry returned to his hotel on foot and very deep in thought. On entering the hotel he stood and looked at the hall-porter as though he were trying to make up his mind to break some devastating news to that individual. He then requested the loan of an A.B.C. time-table.

Though late for dinner, Willy was home before Louise. She arrived soon after eight. She made no reference to what she had been doing. Indeed, she did not return to the subject of Eleanor at all. Willy found small comfort in this. Louise was keen-eyed and complacent. She entertained her husband throughout dinner with little bright snatches of piffling conversation. When she remained silent she seemed lost in faraway reflections of the most gratifying kind.

Willy drooped moodily over the table, occasionally shooting a glance upwards at her, as a cribbing schoolboy eyes the master's desk. What hate had she been committing now?

This state of affairs continued all the evening. When Louise had dined and taken a Dobbson's Settling Lozenge, she joined Willy in the drawing-room, where she sat on the sofa, officially knitting; but every time he looked up from his Patience it was to find her gazing at the wall opposite to her with an expression of determined rapture worthy of some virgin of the Salvation Army.

Thus, until his bedtime, she baited him. At his bedtime he asked bluntly. 'Tell me. What have you done about Eleanor?' And she replied, 'I would rather say nothing at the moment. I have arranged something, but I've got to see how it pans out. It is very stuffy to-night, but don't forget to draw your dressing-room blinds. I saw that girl opposite you watching you last night while you undressed.'

Like Charity, Willy suffered long, enduring all things. There were one or two foibles in Louise which he endured with difficulty. He overlooked her habit of dosing herself with all manner of quack muck. At any rate it meant that she had to keep pretty well, if only to justify the qualities of the muck. As for her religious practices, he regarded these with grave bewilderment, but he was the last man in the world to disparage Christianity in any form. Born of Louise's religious principles, however, was a habit that Willy detested. She cultivated certain outlandish and impossible acquaintances who were connected with the church at which she worshipped.

The church itself was not a good straightforward old Church of England such as Willy understood; where you go right ahead through the regular service with the psalms and the lessons and 'Brief Life is here our portion' and – dash it, if he'd known that he wouldn't have come – the Litany, and the sermon about Martha and Mary, and 'Hark, Hark, my Soul', and that's that. Oh, no. This church of Louise's was a very different concern. He had been there with her once, and never in his life had he felt so self-conscious and unnatural. To begin with he was separated from Louise, the sexes being kept strictly apart. There was a good deal of incense. It was very difficult to tell who were clergy and who weren't – even the choir-boys wore fancy dress. Some of the service was in Latin. The limit was reached when a feller came down the middle and loosed a positive gas attack of incense, at which Willy murmured aloud, 'Whew!' and stood up when he ought to have knelt, and felt altogether extremely conspicuous and out of place. To this day he couldn't have told you whether he had been to Morning Service or what. Still, if Louise liked it, let her go by all means. But these friends—

There were two or three of them and they weren't gentlefolk. It was difficult to determine exactly what sort of people they were, and Louise herself was reticent about them. She visited them at their homes, wherever they may have been, and occasionally one or another of them came to the flat. They weren't like the poor people that Willy's mother and sisters used to district-visit in the old days; they were middle-class, confident people. Wth them, apparently Louise held a sort of spiritual intercourse blended with tea and chatter. Sometimes she went out with them, but as far as Willy could see it was a toss-up whether they went to a *matinée* or to confession.

He protested once. 'I say, Louise; who is that youth with the rabbit-teeth? I've caught him here once or twice before, and he always looks as if you've told him that I live here too but he isn't to take any notice. He looks rather a cad to me. Who is he?'

Louise had said, 'He? Oh, a nice boy. He's a sacristan at St Phipp's.' (She and her friends always employed this diminutive for St Philip's. They were on very familiar terms with the twelve apostles.)

'What's his name?' asked Willy.

'His name? His name's Berty Pitts. I've rather taken him up. He's reading for the church.'

'Oh, I see,' said Willy. 'I suppose you're helping him read.'

And as he pulled down his blinds and started to undress himself on this particular evening, Willy pondered over some of the rather difficult and obscure traits in Louise. His own simple mind found it difficult to reconcile her very intense religious exercises with the spiteful and insidious methods she was employing over this miserable affair of Eleanor. Not that it was any use protesting. But she was like that over all sorts of things – over her health; over what she had been doing on any given day; over these damned friends of hers – always rather cautious and enigmatic at the best of times. This feller, Pitts. Willy didn't care a straw really; but all the same—

Transmission of thought this, perhaps. For in the next room Louise was thinking of her young friend Berty Pitts at that very moment. She had been thinking of him all the evening, of him and of her own subtle little strategy for the morrow. And she had, as we have seen, found these reflections very satisfactory.

Eleven o'clock the next morning found Louise for the second day in succession on Number 1 Platform at Paddington. The 11.15 giant was again about to run a rejoicing course westward. Louise stood on the platform at the open window of a third-class carriage and exhorted its inmate.

'You quite understand, now, don't you? I want you to avoid asking questions or doing anything that might look suspicious. Only don't fail to find out who is there – whether these two people are there and whether the sister is there too. You know more or less what to expect and you can soon find out what's going on. And, in any case, mind you ring me up as soon as you possibly can when you've found out. By tea-time you ought to be back at this place, South Ditherton, and there's sure to be a telephone there. The porters are coming along shutting doors now, so I won't wait. Good-bye. You've got that money and everything else you want? That's right. Good-bye.'

She quitted the platform and the station with the hurried gait of relief at a ticklish job accomplished unobserved.

She would not have been unobserved, however, had her brother Henry been true to his traditions. But for once he had caught his train and had left London for South Ditherton nearly two hours earlier, by the 9.35.

There was a golden rule for pedestrians on the Chool Road. Mrs Easy, though town-bred, had learnt to observe it. At the sound of the approaching car she sought the ditch, and stood in it behind an indignant rampart of umbrella.

To her surprise the car hove to. She raised the umbrella cautiously. From beneath the hood of the car there peered the face of a young man who regarded Mrs Easy with the air of critical hesitancy. For the fraction of a second Mrs Easy flattered herself with apprehension as to his intentions.

'Can you please tell me the way to April Cottage?'

Mrs Easy disciplined her features. So *this* was the visitor! Much as she had supposed – a young man. Ah, and what a type! A regular road-scorching, idle lover of disgracefulness. A typical liver in shame. And proud of it. Not hiding his iniquity under a bushel, as the scriptural saying went, but all blarsy and boasting of it. An undoer of women. A News-of-the-Worlder.

The double-bed, eh? Yes, and that proud cat at the cottage. Mrs Easy wasn't surprised a bit. She knew the sort. All – 'don't you dare to talk to me; I'm a lady, I am. I share beds with young men, but I remain a perfect lady, and don't you forget it.' That sort. Oh, Mrs Easy had known all along that this kind of thing was on the cards. All along.

She replied to Algy in the most disarming way, however.

'Yes, I can tell you. The first to the left and you'll find it at the foot of the 'ill.'

'Oh, good! Thanks.'

'It's Mr 'Ole's cottage you mean, isn't it?'

'That's right.'

'But Mr 'Ole is not there, 'imself, jest now, you know.'

'No, I know. That's quite all right, thanks,' said the young man in a tone of, Mrs Easy thought, complete satisfaction.

'There's a young lady there these days, looking after the place, so I believe,' said Mrs Easy.

'Yes, so do I,' said Algy. 'Good morning. Wet, isn't it?'

Off he shot, leaving Mrs Easy piqued. She had been anxious to inform him that the young lady was out, in order to study the effect of this news upon him. He had evidently arrived earlier than she expected. She had gone into South Ditherton to meet him, and, as luck would have it, they had missed each other. On second thoughts, it was perhaps as well that she shouldn't appear too knowing. It might only put them on the alert. Because now, Mrs Easy was absolutely decided as to her course of action.

One thing she could bank on with certainty. Mr Hole had no knowledge of these goings-on. He would disapprove, and his disapproval would be expressed immediately and violently. When she got to South Ditherton she would send him a telegram, informing him that his cottage was being rebedded and transformed into a house of ill-fame.

She saw Diana in South Ditherton; saw her, moreover, in circumstances which only served to supply fresh and damning evidence of her guilty designs. Pitcher's van was still in attendance. It was drawn up outside Stagg's, the wine merchant's. The young woman was coming out of Stagg's, carrying two bottles of Hennessy's Three-Star Brandy, and a flagon of Australian Burgundy. Under her arm was a large box of expensive cigarettes.

Mrs Easy visualised with difficulty the scene of reckless abandon to be enacted beneath the modest roof of April Cottage that night. Fortunately, she had once witnessed a cinema film of an at-home in New York, at which young women in bathing costumes (one-piece) disported themselves in a swimming-bath filled from a fountain with champagne. She was thus able to appreciate at least the spirit prompting the prospective orgy of Chool. She almost ran to the post-office.

Pitcher's van rounded the last bend of the downward zigzag. 'Ah!' exclaimed Diana. 'Oo!' echoed the toad, and applied a shrieking brake. A very trim but very wet two-seater stood outside the gate of April Cottage in the rain.

'Thank you,' said Diana. 'I'll get down. You can get past and turn, can't you? You needn't wait. I'll manage my parcels.'

She gathered together her bed-clothes, her brandy, her Burgundy, her cigarettes, some newspapers and a parcel of assorted groceries. The toad made ear-splitting noises with gears and manoeuvred into departure. Diana turned at the gate to look again at the two-seater.

The aperture in its rear was open, and into it had been stuck one end of the portmanteau which she had helped to carry upstairs, the night before. That, somehow, was the crowning injury. Diana recalled the fag of hoisting that portmanteau up the ladder of April Cottage, herself doing all the lifting and pulling while Eleanor trailed after her. Eleanor's end of the portmanteau had been on the stair-but-one below most of the time. And here the portmanteau was – repacked and back in Algy's car.

So Algy had turned up. And they had decided that they had better make a clean breast of what they were up to, and go off together. They must have come to this decision pretty quickly. In fact, Eleanor must have run upstairs and packed directly Diana left the cottage. Evidently she had known all the time that Algy was about to arrive. She might have let Diana know, before the latter had gone to the trouble of getting beds and Burgundies. It was really rather surprising that they hadn't gone off already, merely leaving a note.

All this in a throb of indignation sharp as a sting. And the venom of the sting was the sight of that jutting and already saturated portmanteau – dumb lump of informative insolence.

They were waiting for Diana in the parlour, all ready mackintoshed, standing, Eleanor toe-tapping in impatience. There was an air of nervous, Gretna Green surrender about her, Diana thought. Her very attitude was a confirmation of Auntie's misgivings.

Diana entered the room without a word and put down her parcels. Eleanor began to gabble some apology, heedlessly and taking the wrong intervals for breathing, like a schoolboy who knows his repetition.

'Oh, I don't mind your not staying,' said Diana. 'It doesn't hurt my feelings at all. I thought you wouldn't like this place. I don't myself. I'm only so sorry you had to come all this way for the sake of kidding your sister-in-law.'

'I didn't, Diana; I fully inten—'

'Oh, and I don't mind your kidding your sister-in-law. She sounds rather the sort of person I should enjoy kidding too. That's not the point.'

'Well, what is the point, may I ask?'

'All right,' said Diana, 'let's get right to it. I'm awfully sorry if your marriage hasn't turned out a success, Eleanor; but I'm blowed if you're going to lug Algy into it.'

'Diana!'

'Oh, tripe!' said Algy. 'Don't pay any—'

'I'm blowed if you're going to,' cried Diana. 'And if he is a big enough poop to allow himself to be lugged, then he's jolly well got to have someone to stand out and catch hold of the seat of his pants and lug him back again.'

They stared at her, quite startled. She was erect and quivering. Hot spots were in her cheeks. Her eyes were ablaze.

'You look rather attractive in a state of fury, Diana,' said Algy. 'You ought to cultivate it. Only do try and find a reasonable cause for fury. There are plenty about.'

Eleanor glanced out of the window at the rain and tucked up her mackintosh collar.

'Well, I'm sorry to have to go like this, and I've tried to say so, but you won't let me. And as for all this hot air about me and Algy – if you think—'

'I think the worst,' said Diana. 'There you are. That's flat.'

'Flat,' said Algy, 'is a mild description of it, believe me.'

'If you want to know,' said Eleanor, 'I'm going back to my own home at Prince's Gate.'

'Go where you like,' said Diana, 'and do what you like, and do what your husband doesn't like. Only don't let him find out.'

'I'm going to tell him exactly what I've been doing directly he gets back,' said Eleanor.

'Oh,' said Diana. 'That's a nice prospect for you to look forward to, Algy.'

'If you aren't a good enough sport—' began Algy.

'Oh, a sport!' cried Diana. 'You're a couple of sports, aren't you? Motoring about in the rain on a sneaking little so-called love affair, and keeping well off the high road in case the sister-in-law should pop her head out of the hedge.' She swung round on Eleanor. She was like a live torch being beaten out; words flew out of her like hot sparks.

'London to Chool one day with a great deal of fuss and preparation and advertisement. Chool back to London the next day in an oiling little secret two-seater. And I'm to be a sport. A sport! If you were a sport and were really in the least fond of Algy, you'd chuck it for his sake. And if you were really fond of your husband you'd chuck it for *his*. There's only one person you're fond of, Eleanor.' She turned to Algy, flaming. He flinched as from some stinging beast. 'You'll find that out for yourself before long,' she cried. 'You miserable, misled little pipsqueak.'

Eleanor stood looking past Diana's head, tight-lipped. She slowly turned and said something in a quiet conversational tone to Algy about starting the car up. Soon, and without another word, they went.

CHAPTER VIII

Cats and Dogs

They retrieved Algy's suit-case from the *Ring o'Bells* and were soon splashing along the main road eastward. All the morning it rained without cessation. Occasionally, with the almost incredible onslaught of the thunder-shower, it poured. Algy thought they'd better stop and shelter, but Eleanor turned this down. 'Not until luncheon, anyhow. I want to get back to London,' she said, 'back to town.' Her eyes were bright from her own reflections. Algy, steering in mild obedience through water-holes, glanced at her now and then, as though slightly in doubt as to what sort of mood she was really in. She was rather silent and looked ahead through the rain – beyond the rain. Alas, dear Diana; the surest way of driving certain of your fellow-women into transgression is to accuse them of it in advance.

'This is poor going,' said Algy. 'You ought to have seen how she ran yesterday. Why wouldn't you be driven down yesterday? I can't make that out.'

'Well, you never asked me. And I didn't think of it.'

'What? But what about my note? In the bag?'

'What note, in what bag?'

'My note in your hand-bag at Twiggs'. You know. You left it on the waiting-room table. I put a note in it.'

'You put a note in that vanity-bag?'

'Yes. Saying I'd motor you down. Don't say you didn't see it?'

'It was Louise's bag, you priceless chump,' said Eleanor.

Algy skidded.

'What did you say in the note?' added Eleanor.

'I don't know. Nothing much. Louise never said anything about it?'

'No. Perhaps she didn't know it was meant for me.'

'She couldn't have thought it was meant for her,' said

Algy. 'If she had, she'd have bought a pair of motor goggles and come to my flat yesterday. Besides, I addressed the note pointedly to you.'

'But there was nothing suspicious in your asking me to be motored down. As I told you before, Louise didn't know that Reggy had deep-ended about you.'

'Louise would suspect a curate left alone in a cathedral with a pew-opener,' said Algy. 'I bet you she's up to some dirty work about it.'

Eleanor jerked back in her seat with a sudden cry of exasperation. 'Oh, all these people! I don't care a hang. Let's get back to town.'

'Louise has probably sent the note to Reggy,' said Algy.

'I expect so. I don't care.'

She gazed straight before her at the drenched and untransparent wind-screen.

'Reggy – Louise – Diana—' she said. 'They're asking for it, these people.'

'My aunt, too,' said Algy. 'I'm disappointed in Auntie. Still, she, of course, judges only by her own experience which one knows to have been mottled in the extreme. It's so silly really, because it would be quite easy to prove all these people wrong, if one could be bothered. You've been with one or another of them all the time. You were five nights with Louise and one with Diana.'

'Yes,' said Eleanor, slowly. 'But it's tonight they'll want to know about. I think we'll get them guessing rather about tonight, shall we?'

At South Ditheron Mrs Easy, having dispatched her telegram to Mr Hole, secured a lift in a cart conveying milk-cans. This took the high road and put her down at a point from which she could gain her cottage by doing some wading through fields. Had the milk-can cart proceeded along the Chool Road Mrs Easy might have been rather baffled. She would have met first the little car, containing the double-bedding roué, a completely strange woman and a portmanteau, and at a later stage Diana on foot; all hurrying through the rain from the cottage of profligacy. It was well for little Easy that his mother undertook her detour, for she arrived home very wet but so grimly satisfied with her morning's endeavour and so pleasantly preoccupied with anticipations of further research work during the afternoon, that little Easy enjoyed quite an unusually harmonious dinner-time.

It was a quarter past twelve when Diana once more found herself in the lake which, on a dry day, was the market square. She had left the cottage hard in the wake of the two-seater and covered four miles to the post-office without a halt. Her shoes and stockings were wringing wet. She was still angry and miserable and weary with that irksome weariness which follows a long walk in the rain on a hot day.

Her feelings were not soothed by the attitude of Miss Frisby, who presided over the post-office. The moment Diana entered Miss Frisby ceased to count insurance stamps for an old lady, and glared at Diana rather as a bishop might (in company) inspect an indecent photograph. Miss Frisby was a tousled virgin of some thirty-five wet summers. She provided lively support for the theory that the Postmaster-General employs a touring press-gang for the purpose of discovering all the most forbidding young females and installing them behind the cages of post-offices.

Diana returned the silent challenge and went to the telegraph desk. The telegraph desk proved that Miss Frisby, however displeasing in aspect, was at least thorough in her post-official superintendence. The metal pencil-case attached by a heavy chain to the telegraph desk had a pencil in it. Right in it. The pencil indeed had been so much appreciated and used that it had been worn right down until it was embedded in the pencil case, with its point on a dead level with the top of the metal. This was all thanks to Miss Frisby. Most of the metal cases chained to telegraph desks have no pencils in them at all.

The pencil was just another little annoyance. Everything this morning was hostile to Diana. Eleanor – her smart, supercilious selfishness; quite apart from what she was up to. Algy, the grinning, misled fool. The weather – the clammy fatigue of the long walk in the heat; the sloppy misery of the long walk in the wet. The staring, unspoken challenge of the post-office woman. Right down to the little irritating obstruction of the post-office pencil – everything hostile. A miserable day.

Diana battled with the pencil rather than put her uncertain patience to the test of words with Miss Frisby. Her telegram was brief and to the point. 'They have both returned London today together in car. Diana.' Miss Frisby could not disguise her disappointment at so meatless a meal.

For, less than two hours before, Miss Frisby had transmitted something much juicier concerning the young occupant of April Cottage. Quite a long time after Mrs Easy had handed it in and stamped it with an eye-flicker of self-important reserve for Miss Frisby, the latter lady had remained pondering the telegram's contents and tapping her front teeth with a pen-holder. Finally, staunch in her duties, she had carried it to an inner chamber and commanded some unseen agent within to consign it to the wires.

Diana, from the post-office, went to Pawley's. She would take Pawley's motor back to the cottage, change her clothes and get some food. Depressing enough in any case seemed the prospect of April Cottage out there, damp and deserted, for many more days yet. Another long foot-slog out to it in squelching shoes – no. Pawley.

Pawley's yard contained Pawley's motor, looking not unlike one of those nauseating coloured charts of the human entrails. It also contained young Pawley, who was sitting with one of the removed entrails across his knee and hitting it with a hammer.

'Is the car out of order?' gasped Diana.

'Ay,' replied young Pawley. 'That she be an o' that thorough.'

Diana went to the South Ditherton Drapery Mart and bought a pair of stockings. These she carried to the *Ring o' Bells*, where she assumed them and ordered lunch.

Algy and Eleanor lunched at Bristol. Rather than deviate from their course into the centre of the city, they stopped at a minor hostelry near the Great Western station. Inside the Great Western station on the down platform waited one Herbert Harrowing Pitts. Before they had finished their lunch and continued their run from South Ditherton to London, he had achieved his connection and was continuing his run from London to South Ditherton.

Henry was nearly there. His train was due at South Ditherton at 1.50, and about time too. He had left London in the morning sunshine and had brought neither coat nor umbrella. Apart from the prospect of getting obviously soaked to the skin and of having to sit in that condition for at least four and a half hours in some undetermined return train, he was really not at all certain of what lay before him. Somehow he must find this April Cottage and warn Eleanor and this fool boy that Reggy was on his way home. They might thank him; they might flout him. But he would at least have the satisfaction of knowing that he had done his best in the family cause.

Henry had not yet lunched. Alone of our protagonists he had not yet lunched; and 'twere well to catch a glimpse of each, ere we plunge into the imbroglio of this Thursday afternoon. At Bristol then, as we know, with a dangerous light in her eyes, the siren Eleanor. Handing her familiarly the mustard and chatting to her undesignedly enough, but not unaware nor heedless of that gleam of unrevealed caprice, the squire Algy.

In their respective trains, the shadowy agent, Pitts; and, fore-ordained victim-in-chief of the whole affair, well-intentioned to get most deeply involved in its meshes, unprotected to get wettest in its rain, the fortuitous Henry. At South Ditherton, Diana; her normal sunny nature rapidly dispersing the clouds of distress under the influence of the *Ring o' Bells* cold pork and stone ginger. At Chool, her every munch a silent anticipatory threat, Mrs Easy.

Willy, scenting upheaval, had gone out early and had dug himself well in for the day at his club, where now he chewed a tough and apprehensive cutlet. Louise, at home, pecked at something cold, did table devotions, took a tablet, popped in and out of the rooms, glancing at clocks, drumming on window-panes, behaving like a lively bull-finch in a cage. Her tendency to 'quick breath' was particularly marked this day. She got a telegram from Reggy in the course of the afternoon, and hopped about more than ever.

Mrs Krabbe got a telegram too. Denise brought it to the bedroom with the luncheon. She rubbed her eye-glass along it and drew her Roman nostrils up into a great sniff. Then threw the telegram in a ball to the floor and turned inquiringly to her meal. 'All right; leave the telegram where it is. What in the world have I got hold of here? Trotters or something?'

The luncheon of Captain Dumfoil in the Carlton Grill, though attended by an experienced chorus lady (the term 'dashing' as applied to Guardees being associated almost entirely nowadays with this line of business), was a dull and rather morose proceeding unenlivened by telegraphy. But Lemon got a telegram with his. The hall-porter from Algy's block of flats brought it along, thinking it might be urgent. Lemon, whose wife's mother had been sent for in a hurry, and was in a rather overwrought state all round, received it with a groan. It announced his young master's immediate return to London. 'Oh, well,' said Lemon, 'I don't object. Anything to distract the mind.'

And away up at Harrogate, plodding in from his morning exercise, with the rain dripping from features plum-coloured in exertion, bent, blowing, scowling horribly, falling foul of a bell-boy, came old Mr Hole to *his* telegram.

> Hole Belvedere Htl. H'gate.
>
> Cottage all upside down now young man joined her double bed got in yours out also wine bought disgraceful behaviour undoubted easy.

Mr Hole turned in the hotel bureau and brought down his walking-stick with a thud of annoyance on the foot of an elderly gout patient at his side.

'My bill,' he cried. 'My bill. Understand? My – my – bill – bill. My bill. This comes of having women in these places. You tell them a thing five times and then they only look at you. What? Going? Yes, of course, I'm going. You! A train-bill. You hear? A train-bill. A train – train – bill – bill. A train-bill. Oh-h-h-h-h-h!'

There remains but one of our principals – the last but by no means the least. His progress on this fateful Thursday may be traced to a somewhat later stage in the proceedings, until, as the evening draws on, we shall call for him again, nor find him laggard.

He, too, may first be observed in the bureau of an hotel, proposing settlement and furious excursion. This earlier in the forenoon. And in this case notice of departure had already been given. Even as Reginald in heated haste entered the bureau, the clerk dived for a pigeon-hole.

'Now then,' said Reginald, 'erm – l'addition, s'il vous plait. Mon addition pour la visite totale.'

'You beell for the 'ole tahm,' said the clerk. 'All right, sir. I 'ave it ready for you.'

'Oh,' said Reginald, in a somewhat resentful tone. 'Oh – then – vite.'

'Here you are, sir. You return to England?'

'What business is that—? Oh, I see – yes. Pour les lettres. Pour advancer. Oui. Vous avez mon address dans votre livre des visiteurs. Voici votre argent. Donnez le receipt.'

'Certainly, sir. You wish for a taxi?'

'I know perfectly well what I wish for, thank you. I wish for my receipt. And if I wish to go and see any clowns, I can find my own way.'

Very forebodingly and with a brow deeply furrowed in anger he was borne to the coast; glaring through the windows of his railway carriage with gloomy contempt for the sunny land, some of whose inhabitants he might this very day have skinned and bought out and cleaned up but for this untimely contingency at home.

This, our luncheon hour, he spent still in the Paris–Calais boat-train. He was *à déjeuner* in the – ah – *wagon de diner*. A Frenchman opposite to him consumed celery by the method of placing the end of a stalk in his fist on the table and working down to it with his mouth. Reginald would have protested, but the Frenchman had no English, and

Reginald could not at the moment recall the French word for 'of, or belonging to, the jungle'.

At Calais that crotchety old gentleman Neptune responded to Reginald's mood by preparing a heavy ground swell. A solicitous steward predicted 'a bit of a roll' and advised Reginald to arm himself in advance with a pillow. He was told that he would be sent for as and when required, and that meanwhile he needn't trouble himself to be cocky.

If Reginald boarded the boat in an ill-temper, the experiences of the brief voyage did not serve to appease it. The boat, for some preposterous reason, waited for an abnormal and overdue train, which, when it arrived, flooded the already well-patronised vessel with a gang of touring outsiders. Reginald was literally hemmed in, in his carefully selected chair on deck. On his left sat one of those females to whom the mere sight of a line of boats drawn up on a dry beach brings a faint qualm of nausea. On his right sat an elderly voyager with a grey beard and an ulster, who started very confidently and conversationally, but finished up a good second to the faint heart on the left, and who, handicapped as he was by beard and ulster, became particularly untidy and disagreeable.

Reginald landed at Dover, beneath a leaden sky, unimpaired physically but full of fury. He vented his spleen upon a customs' man and gained the railway platform, only to be informed that the first train due out was already full, and that he had better hurry if he wanted a seat in the second. This the reward for his dignity in refusing to compete with a vulgar crowd of elbowing Goths on the landing stage. He secured an inferior seat in the second train, in a carriage containing five obnoxious and inflamingly festive men.

It boded ill for anyone who should obstruct him at the other end of his journey. Before the second train left (the first was scandalously dilatory) he sent a wire warning Louise of his impending descent upon the capital.

Was that rain he heard upon the station roof? Oh, yes, sir, the guard informed him. It had started to rain pretty hard, and looked likely to continue. A good job too. The crops needed it. Reginald seemed to take this as a serious personal affront. 'Do they indeed! Well, I don't happen to be a crop.'

But the guard was right and the rain did continue. Throughout the journey to London it thrashed the carriage windows in a vehement crescendo. And when at last – impatient beyond expression at the tardiness of his traffic and the undesirability of his fellow-travellers; chafing, almost beyond the ability to sit still, at the upheaval of his business affairs no less than at the unspeakable cause of that upheaval; fatigued in limb but in will relentless; sickened in stomach but in visage unsparing; – when at five o'clock p.m. at last he shook his forefinger at a taxi man and threaded his way through the congestion of Victoria into the streets, the heavens were still pouring down upon him their tears – vain tears – for the frailties of woman; while above them grumbled intermittently the appropriate voices of the male gods, in an ominous mutter of resentment.

PART TWO
Noon of Mischief

CHAPTER IX

He Dallies at Ditherton

Flourishing stolidly among the temples of Nonconformity in the market square, the *Ring o' Bells* worthily upheld traditions as well-recognised and certainly as popular as any of theirs. It was not an inn; it was an hotel. The distinction was the same as that which makes a sunny, spectacled and big-lapped dame with grey hair, whatever her class, not an old woman but an old lady.

A cobbled courtyard fronted the hotel, with the signboard in its midst. Beneath the windows on either side of the porch were those seats in which we have discovered Mr Moody and Mr Jewell over their ale and gossips on the afternoon of Wednesday, when Pawley's motor spent her last breath. The windows themselves appertained respectively to dining-room and tap-room, as might be gleaned from a very close inspection of the faded white inscriptions beneath the black wire blinds. The dining-room inscription was diffuse and catholic in its range of appeal. You could evidently obtain wines from the wood and (philosophical sequence) good stabling to follow, while that special accommodation which is always apparently demanded by cyclists was not forgotten. The tap-room window held its own with the one bold, comprehensive, monosyllabic exhortation – 'Beer'.

It might be thought that Henry Bingham, that hesitant man, would have paused to make inquiries at South Ditherton station. Not he. He thrust his ticket into the velveteen waistcoat of a porter and struck forth into the rain instinctively. He had scarcely had time to get wet before he was in the dining-room of the *Ring o' Bells*.

The room was unoccupied. The relics of somebody's luncheon remained on the long centre table, but the consumer of the luncheon had departed. Henry looked in vain for a bell, so rapped with his fellow patron's knife on the table and waited.

The dining-room was not rich in the fulfilment of those promises held out to the favoured cyclists or even to the mere itinerant wayfarer. Its furniture was limited to some very thickset wooden chairs and a fireside bench, whose seat was so copiously studded with brass-headed nails that it resembled some mild form of mediaeval torture. Above it hung a photograph, which appeared at first sight to constitute an awful warning in the form of a group of victims who had incurred the penalty of the bench, but which, on careful inspection, turned out to be a portrait of the South Ditherton and District Cricket Team of 1899.

After considerable knife-rapping Henry walked to the dining-room doorway and called: 'Hi! I say.' At which, from the mysteries of a kitchen passage came a woman with a dish-cloth.

'Oh!' said Henry. 'Hallo! Good morning, or afternoon, or whatever it is. Look here. Can I—?'

'Muriel!' exclaimed the woman with the dish-cloth, completely and instantaneously disappearing.

Henry returned to the dining-room where his patience was rewarded by the appearance of an apple-cheeked damsel with hefty red forearms and a smile like a searchlight, as broad-beamed and buxom a wench as only the West Country can produce.

'Did you want summat to eat, sir?' she inquired.

'I did,' said Henry. 'I don't mind much what it is, but I want whatever it is badly.'

'Ther's some coold porrk,' said Muriel. Henry rubbed his hands together.

'Oh, rather,' he said. 'Cold pork and beer. That's the stuff to give the Turks. When will it be ready?'

'It's ready now, sir,' said Muriel, and exit.

Ten minutes later, to the squeaking of boots which might have been the dying protest of the pork, it came. Henry was by this time past his patience, but the sight of Muriel and the pork in combination was so elevating that he stifled his remonstrance. He attacked the pork, while Muriel stood by the window, held, apparently, by an irresistible delight in watching him deal with crackling. Beer, in a blue china mug, romantically enhanced the rural atmosphere of the pleasant meal.

'Now,' said Henry, having taken the edge off his appetite, 'can you tell me the way to April Cottage?'

This had rather a startling effect on Muriel. Her whole countenance seemed to open like a box.

'Why,' she said, 'but the young leddy from April Cottage has jest gorrn.'

Gorrn! Ah, this was the sister. But why gorrn? In what spirit gorrn! Gorrn in hostility, indignant at finding herself being cuckoldised without option into the illicit affairs of her brother? Gorrn amicably and by pre-arrangement, as to leave them free for their naughty date at the cottage? Gorrn, anyhow, the sister; which meant that they were alone there together and that he must hurry to them with his warning. His chief motive was to warn; but at the same time he would do well to arrive in time to anticipate any regrettable action on their part. After all, there they were in a sequestered cottage; and one must find something to do on a wet afternoon like this.

'So she has gone, has she?' he said. 'I'm not surprised. I hardly expected to be in time to see her. But – do you happen to know anything of anybody else at the cottage at the moment?'

'Why,' said the ready girl, 'there was a young gent stayed here last night and went ther' this mornin'.'

'Ah! He stayed *here* last night? And only went to the cottage this morning? Right. That's just as well.'

'Well, sir,' said Muriel, 'he went th' this mornin' and then coom back here and get his bag.'

'Aha,' said Henry. 'Aha! I see. He came here, slept here, went out to the cottage this morning, had a look see, and back he comes for his bag. Aha! And then?'

'He had a moterr. And when he coom back ther' was a leddy in it with him. A strange leddy.'

Yes, yes. This all tallied. The sister gorrn. The brother goes out to the cottage, finds his Eleanor, and they come joy-riding back to the hotel to get his bag and return to the cottage together. Yes. yes.

'Yes, yes,' said Henry. 'And when the young gentleman had got his bag, off he went again in the motor to the cottage with the strange lady? Yes?'

'That might be,' said Muriel. 'They went in that direction. But they'll be harrd put to it if they be to stay ther'.'

'They will,' said Henry. 'But why do you say so?'

'I've heard tell ther' be oonly one bedroom in that cottage,' said Muriel.

'Yes, so have I,' said Henry. 'Still, I don't suppose that's altogether escaped their notice. Besides, in any case, I shouldn't think they'll be going to bed just yet, should you?'

'Maybe the young gent intends to coom back here again for tonight,' said Muriel.

'No. I think I can safely say he doesn't intend to do that,' replied Henry, sagely. 'Tell me, how long ago was it when he and this strange lady went back together to the cottage in the car?'

'Oh, soom hours ago now,' said Muriel.

'M'yes,' said Henry. He deliberated for a moment, stroking his moustache; then abruptly rose.

'I should like some cheese,' he said, 'and I should love some more beer; but I don't think I'd better hang about too long.'

'I'll get your bill, sir,' said Muriel.

'Oh, well, if you're going to wait and get bills, perhaps I've just got time for— Bring me my bill in the bar, will you?'

Mr Plum, the landlord of the *Ring o' Bells,* was himself presiding over the tap room, a short, rosy, conversational man with no collar. The inveterate Messrs Moody and Jewell were in attendance.

'A beer, please,' said Henry. 'And can you tell me how far it is to April Cottage?'

'April Cottage?' repeated Mr Plum. 'Ther' aren't no April Cottage in Dither'n.'

' 'Oole's,' exclaimed Mr Jewell.

'Ay, 'Oole's,' echoed Mr Moody.

'Oo! Ah! 'Oole's?' said Mr Plum. ' 'Oole's cottage?'

'What? April Cottage is the name,' said Henry.

'Ah! But belonging to Mr 'Oole,' said Mr Jewell.

' 'Oole,' echoed Mr Moody.

'That's right,' said Mr Plum. ' 'Oole be the name of the owner.'

'Oh,' said Henry. 'I don't know. I daresay. But Mr Oole is not there now. At least, I hope not.'

'Noo,' said Mr Jewell. 'E aren't ther'.'

'Noo,' said Mr Moody. 'Not 'ee.'

'You see, sir?' said Mr Plum ' 'E aren't ther'.'

'No, I *know* he's not,' said Henry. 'We're all quite agreed about – oh, my beer; thanks. We're all quite agreed about Mr Oole. He's not there. But his cottage is there, isn't it?'

'Ay,' said Mr Plum.

'Yes. Well, where is it?'

Mr Plum raised his eyebrows and glanced at his associates as though requesting their indulgence for this poor soul.

'Wher' is it? Why, wher' you jest said, sir,' he replied. 'You say, "The cottage be still ther'. Wher' is it?" Why, wher' you said.'

'Yes, but—'

'Ah, don't you see, Burrt,' said Mr Jewell. 'The ge'm'n don't know wher' he be.'

'Noo, that be right,' agreed Mr Moody. 'That's wher' his trouble lie. 'E don't know wher' he be.'

'Yes, I do, thank you,' said Henry. 'I know where I am all right. But I don't know where the cottage is.'

'Ah, that's jest what I say, mister,' said Mr Jewell. 'You don't know wher' he be.'

'Who?'

'Why, the cottage to be sure,' said Mr Jewell.

'Ah-h-h!' said Mr Moody. 'That be the trouble. You don't know wher' he be.'

Henry took a brief fortifier of beer and turned again to Mr Plum.

'How far and where is April Cottage?' he asked.

'Ah!' said Mr Plum 'Wull, do you know Chool?'

'Chool? Who's he? You mean Oole? Please don't start about Oole again. What I want—'

'No, not 'Oole – Chool,' said Mr Plum.

'Chool,' said Mr Jewell.

'Chool,' said Mr Moody.

'Chool,' said Mr Plum.

'Chool, mister,' said Mr Jewell.

'Ah!' said Mr Moody with the composing finality of one speaking the tag of a Victorian farce. 'Chool.'

Henry had some more beer.

'Yer see what it is,' said Mr Moody, in a confidential aside, 'it ain't no good fer to tell 'im Chool; because 'e don't know wher' he be.'

Mr Jewell scratched his head.

'If 'e don't know wher' Chool be, how be he going for to find out wher' the cottage be?' he asked.

'Well, damn it, he isn't at this rate,' said Henry. 'I may tell you I'm in a very great hurry to get to this cottage. I only allowed myself the time to come and have this glass of beer because I was waiting for my bill for lunch. Unless I can get to April Cottage quite soon something rather serious may happen.'

Unfortunately, Mr Jewell interpreted this as a threat. He had already gazed at Henry very menacingly for several seconds, and placed his beer-mug on the floor beside him, when Muriel entered with the bill.

'Ah!' said Henry. 'Good girl. How far is this place, and how do I get there?'

'Main road east, first to the left and first to the left again, sir. About four miles,' said Muriel.

Henry turned, quite indignantly for him, on the tap-room sages.

'There, you see! I ask her, and she tells me almost quicker than I can take it in. And you, with all your Ooling and Chooling—!' He again looked at Muriel, and briefly pondered. 'Four miles, though, by Jove! I must buck up. Where can I hire a car?'

'Pawley's—' Began Muriel, from force of habit, only to be drowned by a chorus of revengeful ridicule.

'Pawley's mowerr – noo— Burrst. Ay, burrst— Noo, burrst yesterday— Noo, she burrst she wer'— Aye, and thorough.

Ther'll be no 'iring no Pawley's mowerr not today ther' will. Ay, that ther' won't— Ay – Noo— Burrrrst!'

Henry turned again to Muriel.

'The car you mentioned appears to have exploded,' he said. 'Where can I hire another? Quick, now.'

'Ther' aren't another,' said Mr Plum.

'You mean to tell me that in a place this size there is only one car?'

'Ay,' said Mr Plum.

'Ay,' said Mr Moody.

'And she's burrst,' said Mr Jewell.

'Ay,' agreed Mr Moody, 'and she's burrst.'

Henry finished his beer quickly. 'Come with me,' he said to Muriel.

'Oh, sir – where?' said Muriel. 'To April Cottage?'

'No, girl, no. Don't you start being silly now. I want you in the passage. I can't stick this.'

' 'Old on, sir, 'old on,' said Mr Plum. 'Ther' be more ways left of getting around Dither'n, if so be you want to get around. Ther' be Pillbutton's 'ackney.'

'Ah,' said Mr Moody. 'The 'ackney.'

'You can 'ire a bi-cycle from Mrs Leake,' said Mr Jewell.

'I'm not going to ride a bicycle for four miles through this rain,' said Henry. 'What about this hackney?'

'Pillbutton be the proprietor of her,' said Mr Plum.

'Pillb—' began Mr Moody.

'All right, thank you,' said Henry. 'Where is Pillbutton?'

'Three yarrds down the road, he be,' said Mr Plum.

'Three yards?' repeated Henry, incredulously.

'Ay,' said Mr Plum, 'three yarrds.'

'Three yarrds,' said Mr Moody.

'Three yarrds,' said Mr Jewell.

'The third yard you come to on your left, sir,' said Muriel.

'Oh! I see. Yes, thanks. Good girl. Come into the passage. How much is the beer?'

'Now,' said Henry, as he gained the porch of the hotel, accompanied by Muriel. 'The third yard on the left. Is Mr Pillbutton anything like those other gentlemen? If so, you'd better come, too. Never mind. I expect I can manage. Only it's awfully wet. I suppose you haven't got such a thing as an umbrella?'

'No, sir,' said Muriel. 'But I might be able to borrow one for you, if you care to wait.'

'I simply can't wait any longer. I've probably waited too long as it is. I'll go without. Thank you; you're a very good girl. Here, that's for yourself. Now – this yard? The third on the right?'

'Left, sir.'

'Left? Right. And April Cottage? First to the right and first to the right again?'

'Left, sir.'

'Left? Right. Good girl. Good-bye.'

Already sadly perplexed by the entanglements of the taproom, disagreeably surprised by the distance to April Cottage, subconsciously funky of the reception which awaited him when he did get there, yet regardful of the need for haste, he plunged forth into the rain, which was at this moment falling with hellish intensity. By the time he reached Pillbutton's yard he was very wet. In Pillbutton's yard was an overgrown boy with a squint, sitting beneath the leaking roof of an open shed on an upturned box and scratching the ear of a collie dog with a straw; and in a stable opposite an old, bald man cleaning the metal on some harness with saliva.

'Ah!' cried Henry, hurrying into the shelter of the stable. 'Here we are. Are you Mr – what is it? Button-hook or something – Pillbutton, that's it. Are you Mr Pillbutton?'

'Me, sur?' replied the old man. 'Noo – nay – noo – nay – noo – nay. Nay. Me? Noo.'

'Well, I don't care a damn,' said Henry, who was wearing his summer pants and could already feel the damp through the knees of his trousers; who had not yet begun to attack the four miles to April Cottage; who had, in fact, travelled a considerable distance in the opposite direction in order to find Pillbutton's yard and was, in consequence, later than ever in getting off the mark; who was determined to stand no further procrastination from these blasted natives. 'If you're not Mr Pillbutton, you must be connected with his establishment. Otherwise you wouldn't be standing there spitting on his saddles. Come on, now. Buck up. I want to go to April Cottage in the hackney.'

The old man laid aside the saddle and started massaging himself instead. He then walked to the door of the stable and stood regarding the overgrown boy doubtfully.

'It might so be that I could get him to harness the punch,' he said at length.

'The punch?'

'Ah. The oonly horse in the stable at this here present moment be the punch. It might so be I could get him to harness the punch. He drive the punch, he do.'

'Oh, does he? That's all right. I'll tell him to harness the punch at once.'

'Steady, mister,' said the old man, laying a hand on Henry's arm. 'You have to be careful with he, if you want for to get him to do anything.'

'Why?' demanded Henry.

'Because he's half sharp,' said the old man. 'You leave him to I.'

He crossed the yard to where the boy was sitting. Henry, groaning aloud with impatience, followed and took shelter beneath the eaves of the leaking roof.

'Pete,' began the old man, very deliberately. 'If I was to say to you as how it would be impossible for to harness the punch to the hackney and take 'un out on the road, you'd 'ave to say as I was right.'

'Garn,' said the boy, looking up defiantly. 'Easy.'

The old man shook his head.

'Not in this 'ere rain,' he said. 'The punch wouldn't goo.'

'Garn,' said the boy. 'He would easy.'

'Also, moreover,' said the old man, 'the 'ackney would get so spockled up in the rain and mud and all, you'd never be able to cleanse her free.'

'Yah,' said the boy. 'I've unspockled 'er o' wurrse.'

'Oh, I say, really, confound this—' began Henry, but the old man turned upon him with violent gesticulations.

'Go easy, sur,' he said. 'It be coming on foine.' He drew a

step nearer Henry and proceeded very confidentially to explain.

'You see, sur,' he said, 'this be the oonly method o' getting Pete to do ought. You got to so to speak challenge 'im; to as it wer' make out to 'im that 'e can't do what you want 'im to so as to get 'im to do 'un. That be the oonly way with 'im, be reason of his being half sharp.'

'Good heavens!' cried Henry. 'And when you get to the place you're aiming at, I suppose you've got to bet him a bob he can't stop the punch? No damn fear! I'll walk.'

At this moment a choked waste-pipe in the eaves overflowed in a waterspout, full on to Henry's Trilby hat.

'Oh, curse this place!' he cried, springing too late to one side. 'Why was I ever such a misguided fool as to – I don't care. I'll go through with it. Pete! You can no more get that punch out of that stable and put it in the hackney and drive me to April Corrage than I can jump from here to the moon.'

Pete was on his feet in two seconds and across to hitherto uninspected stable buildings in five, the collie barking and curveting at his side. Henry, attempting to dry his shoulders and knees with a handkerchief, watched his progress keenly. Pete entered the stables and reappeared, dragging a light governess cart.

'Great Scot!' exclaimed Henry. 'Is that the hackney?'

'Ah,' replied the old man. 'That she be.'

Henry surveyed the pitiless heavens.

'I shall have to be diplomatic with this Algy,' he soliloquised. 'You can't walk into a house and tick a man off and then borrow a pair of his bags.'

CHAPTER X

And Looks Like Dallying at Chool

Plodding, plodding along a Chool Road which was a seething pond (she began by trying to pick her way, but there was soon no way to pick); gaining, at the end of it, a zigzag decline down which the water was running in rivulets as from a spring; her rain-proof coat proved under-proof; her dear little Donegal tweed hat a sponge; but with her anger mollified now into the helpless amusement of philosophical affliction, Diana at last reached April Cottage.

It was now a quarter to three. She had taken well over the normal hour to walk from South Ditherton.

She wrung the Donegal hat out in the porch. Her shoes made water-squeezing noises in the passage. She entered the parlour and removed her rain-proof, testing various portions of herself underneath. Not so bad. The exteriors could do with attention. She would change her coat and skirt and her new stockings. Ran upstairs and did. Brought the wet things down again to the kitchen to dry them before the fire.

The kitchen fire was out.

Suddenly almost as a blow, and for the first time since she had been an exile, Diana felt the whole burden of her loneliness. Somehow the fatigue of having to rebuild and rekindle that fire would have been far less a fatigue with someone to stand by and watch her doing it. But why? Last night she had had someone standing by. Had that been much solace? Then as she stood, clasping her wet raiment, her morning's anger turned to something near despair, she realised the cause of the depression.

Beat, beat, beat, the rain on the roof. Swish, swish, the rain running down the pipes into the lushed gutters, Ssssss – in the trees above the cottage. That was it. That unceasing, inexorable visitation of the skies. She had never known till then that, more than in darkness, more than in suffering, more even perhaps than in death, one must have company in rain.

('Half a tick! Let's see – first to the left, yes. Pete! You can't turn to the left to save your life.')

Well, well. If the company was hard to find on ordinary days it was out of the question this afternoon. She had laid aside her wet things and was at the kitchen fire place with a brush, when she remembered something. To be sure. In the parlour was a fire all ready laid, needing only a match. Besides, a fire in the parlour would be pleasant today.

So she lit the fire in the parlour.

The punch was practically amphibious. It revelled in Chool Road. Great spurts of water came kicking up into the hackney. Attacked by the elements from above and below, Henry remained in a state of sodden bewilderment, on a seat of which the only dry spot was that occupied by the only dry spot on his clothing. He could no longer complain, however, that his time was being wasted. Pete, even if half sharp, was no mean Jehu.

The punch appreciated Pete a good deal more than did the majority of the latter's acquaintances. It entered fully into the Pete method. When Pete said 'Whoa!' the punch leapt forward as though stung. To stop the punch all standing, almost within its own length, Pete said 'Hup!' He had not said this yet with Henry.

The corner of the zigzag was obscured by trees, and though Henry was watchful, he was so blinded by water and carried away by the speed of the punch that the hackney had passed this next objective before the passenger was able to shout. When he did shout he shouted: 'Oh, hi! (First to the left again.) Stop! That is – er – I bet you can't stop.'

'Hup!' said Pete, and the punch skated and came to rest.

'Now – one moment – yes. You can't go down that road, you know,' said Henry. 'The punch simply couldn't do it. It's too steep.'

'Right ahead,' said Pete to the punch, who obediently turned.

But at the sight of the zigzag and of the perilous decline of the zigzag and the rivulets. Henry's eyes widened. He had rashly incited Pete. It *was* too steep. Henry clutched the rail of the hackney and attempted to adjust his mind quickly, so as to be able to challenge Pete out of this desperate essay. In his nervous excitement he went to the lengths of betting Pete half-a-crown that he couldn't turn the punch on so difficult a level and stop again at the top corner. Whereupon Pete laughed aloud at such incredulity in the powers of the punch, and told the punch once more to go right ahead and hup; and Henry climbed, thanking God, from the hackney, richly rewarded Pete and set off on foot down the zigzag. After all, April Cottage couldn't be far away. He must have been pretty nearly Muriel's four miles already.

And Pete drove back to Pillbutton's yard and unharnessed the punch and pushed in the hackney and tethered the punch and fed the punch. And presently, the punch being a very little punch, Pete sat down in his favourite spot in the stable, with his head resting against the punch's belly, and went to sleep. And after a little while the collie came in, too, and lay down beside him and licked his hand.

The sound in Diana's ears was no longer the sound of rain. That was drowned, or forgotten. She only heard a roar – an ominous, awe-inspiring, joyous roar like laughter. The most terrible laughter in the world. The laughter of fire.

Only in the chimney, but frightening enough. There was good food for the flame clotted all the way up the wall, and the flame seethed delightedly up and feasted.

Feasted, roaring; increasingly roaring. Great fragments of the meal half-devoured, great blazing masses of soot, came hurtling down into the grate. Smoke filled the parlour.

Diana ran out into the rain and looked up. A black cloud, poured forth from the chimney, was hanging in the still air, dissipating reluctantly and ever massing in volume. While she watched, flame was in the cloud, and soon a fiery wisp of danger, flung up from the chimney, fell on to the slope of the tiled roof, expiring into powder in the rain. Another, bigger, more threatening wisp, burning on this time as it clung to the sloping roof for a few moment before sizzling out. Diana was frankly frightened. Forgot she was lonely, but remembered she was alone. Forgot she wanted company, but knew she wanted help.

She ran back into the parlour. The roar had increased. Smoke was pouring through cracks in the brickwork of the fireplace right up to the ceiling. She put her hand to the bricks and had to withdraw it quickly.

Nothing dangerous really, she told herself. Only a chimney on fire. Still, frightening. She didn't like those burning masses of stuff blowing from the chimney. Not that there was any chance of the house catching fire, was there? It would burn itself out soon in the chimney. It roared louder than ever at this, and a blazing chunk of rubbish was thrown right out of the grate on to the worn carpet of the parlour. She beat it out with her wet coat. The mess the parlour was getting into! Not that that seemed to matter now. She raked at the fire with a poker and took fuming lumps of coal away in the tongs, filling the grate with risky, clotted, red-hot stuff that belched smoke into the parlour.

Suddenly she remembered – salt. That was the recognised household remedy for a fire in the chimney. It might be an old wives' tale, but there was no harm in trying. It so happened that among that parcel of groceries she had brought back from South Ditherton that morning had been a cylindrical tin of salt in far too great a quantity for her requirements. The young man at the shop had harangued her into accepting it while she had been preoccupied with thoughts of Eleanor. It was in the kitchen. She ran and found it.

When she got back to the parlour she found a piece of cinder merrily burning a hole in the carpet. She flung salt on the fire and, shielding her face with her hand, stooped and tried the rather futile experiment of shooting salt from the tin up the chimney from below. The roar did not diminish. If only she could get on the roof and pour the salt down the chimney—

She hurried out into the rain again. Perhaps by getting on to the bank behind the cottage she could scramble on to the roof. She ran round behind and investigated. She might be able to do it. The cottage was scarcely a yard from the bank, which rose almost sheer. Then she noticed a small curl of smoke issue from a cranny between two tiles in the roof, and for a moment her heart stood still. Was the cottage on fire?

She must have one more look at the parlour before she dared attempt her gymnastic feat from the bank. She once more skipped round the house (the back door was still locked) and glanced into the parlour. So far as she could see for smoke, the parlour was not on fire. Out again through the front porch – and full into the waistcoat of Henry.

She uttered a little cry, but quickly recovered herself. A man. Who? Never mind who. She thrust the tin of salt into his hand.

'Quick!' she said. 'Scramble on to the roof from the bank at the back and pour salt down the chimney.'

Henry had visited many strange dwelling-places, but was quite unable to recall any reception so staggering. He stood, saturated and foolish, blinking alternately at the tin and at Diana. She was in no mood for discussion. She caught his sleeve and pulled him round the cottage before he managed to utter a syllable.

'Come up here on this bank,' she said. 'Quick! You can soon see what's the matter.'

She grasped a tree-trunk and pulled herself up on the bank. Henry attempted to follow, slithered and sat heavily at the foot of the bank.

'Oh, look, look!' cried Diana. 'More smoke from more places! Do, do, please get up and come up here and look, and scramble up and pour salt.'

'Righto,' said Henry rising. 'It doesn't much matter what I do now. But why pour salt? As a matter of fact, I've just poured some into my eye.'

'Never mind,' said Diana. 'There's plenty left in the tin. Here, take my hand and I'll help you up.'

He complied, conscious even in so practical a moment of a brief, passing sense of felicity at the touch of her neat fingers.

'Now,' she went on, hastily, 'do you think you can get up on to the roof and sort of haul yourself up the tiles to the chimney? I'm sure you can. Perhaps if I stood here and sort of – pushed you from behind—'

'Yes,' he said. 'I think you might do that. But why, exactly, are we doing this?'

'Well, good heavens, can't you see the chimney's on fire? What do you suppose I'm doing? Birdnesting? And trying to climb up and put the salt on the tails of the birds? Up you go, there's a – do, please, will you?'

'Oh, I see. Now I'm beginning to get the idea. But why salt?'

'It does it, it does it – it puts it out,' cried Diana, gesticulating wildly. 'Oh, do please scramble and try.'

'*Does* it?' said Henry, with interest. 'How very queer of salt. I never knew that. I wonder why it is. Righto. I'll try.'

He tried. By clinging to a hazardous rain-pipe and lurching violently upwards with one knee, even a man stout and out of training might easily accomplish the feat. Henry, however, lurched tentatively once and returned to the bank.

'I think it would be easier if I didn't have the salt to carry,' he said.

'I'm afraid there's no object in going without it,' replied Diana, rather curtly. 'The whole idea in going up there is to put the fire out with the salt.'

'I might take off my coat and wring it down the chimney,' said Henry. 'It would probably flood the room underneath the chimney, but that is up to you to choose.'

'Can you put the salt in your pocket?'

'I don't think so. My pocket is so wet, you see. By the time I took the salt out again it would probably be like a sort of bun. Which, I suppose, would not have the same effect on the fire. As a matter of fact, it's news to me that salt "does it", as you say, in any state.'

'Oh, I say, really, something must be done quickly. It's still blazing. Look!'

'Yes. Righto. I suppose you could hold the tin of salt and hurl it up to me when once I'm there?'

'The top's off the tin,' said Diana. 'Carry it in your mouth, holding the tin at the edge between your teeth. Can you do that?'

Henry tried. 'I can,' he said, 'but it cuts the top of my nose most dreadfully and simply pours salt into my nose and moustache. However, as you said, there's plenty. Righto. I'll try again.'

With the tin in his mouth he gripped the water-pipe and lurched with the knee. In this attitude he perilously hovered, turning to utter weird and salted incitements to Diana to push as arranged. At considerable risk she too leant her weight against the gallant water-pipe and pushed. Eventually he half climbed, half rolled on to the sloping roof. Throughout the proceedings water continued to pour down unceasingly from above; fire and smoke to pour up unceasingly from below.

Henry's progress was not facile. The angle of the roof was steep and the tiles were very slippery with the rain. The tin by this time, and thanks in a great measure to his attempts at conversation, was cutting the bridge of his nose so infernally that he removed it and stuck it in the front of his coat. Cautiously on all fours he clambered onwards to the chimney.

He stretched a hand upwards to clasp the chimney. 'Don't touch the bricks,' shouted Diana; but she was too late. Ar'ch!' he cried, and waggled his scorched fingers. Then slipped on the greasy tiles and staggered to recover his balance.

The tin fell from his coat and rolled down the slope, leaving a salt-water canal to mark its route. Henry clutched at it, missed it, overbalanced, took seat on the tiles and with the whoop of an uncontrolled tobogganist, followed it.

Diana's hand went to her heart. For a brief second she closed her eyes; then jumped from her bank to where he lay. He had fallen on his feet, but his legs had given way under him. He sat, almost blocking up the narrow space between the cottage and the bank, clasping his left foot. His face was screwed into an expression of extreme agony.

'May I swear?' he whispered hoarsely.

'Rather,' replied Diana. 'I'm only so thankful you can.'

He managed to rise with her help and, with his arm round her shoulders, to hop round April Cottage to the porch. The parlour was out of the question. Diana propped him on a kitchen chair. She went on her knees and took off his shoe and his sock. He sat back with closed eyes, groaning a word of thanks, his hands tightly clutching the arms of the wooden chair, while he drew in every breath between closed teeth in a faint whistle of pain.

'I – I'm sorry,' he managed to say after a little while. 'It's no good my trying to pretend it's nothing and – oo – that it'll – soon be all right and – oo – that sort of thing, because it hurts too much to – be brave about.'

'P'raps you've broken your ankle,' said Diana. 'Now, does that hurt? When I do that?'

He kept his mouth shut for ten seconds and then said gently:

'Don't run the risk of my being rude to you after you have been so very kind – hitherto – to me.'

'I wonder if it would be any good if I bathed it in hot water,' said Diana.

'It's very sweet of you to think of it,' he replied. 'I shouldn't think it would be the least good.'

'Are you sure?' said Diana. 'Because I can easily – oh, no, I can't.'

She glanced at the cold kitchen grate, and sighed.

'I should have to make up another fire and light it,' she added, 'and then heat the water up. But I'll do it like a shot if you think it would help.'

'For God's sake,' said Henry, '—excuse my expressing myself rather firmly – but for God's sake, light no more fires in this place today. I am through with salting them.'

'Well, there's only one thing to be done,' said Diana. 'I must go into South Ditherton and get the doctor. I'll put my room ready for you upstairs and you can lie on the bed till the doctor comes.'

Henry sat cautiously upright and regarded her with interest, while still grimacing frequently from pain.

'Are you the sister?' he asked.

"I'm Diana Richardson Gascoyne.'

'Oh. This is very strange. I thought you'd gorrn.'

'What?'

'Muriel told me you'd gorrn.'

'I don't understand. Who is Muriel? Who are you, if it comes to that?'

'Muriel is a girl in a pub at that place, Blither – what's-its-name. Oh, bl – excuse me – may I? Thanks. Oh, blast this agony!'

'Poor thing. I wish I could do more for you. Who are you?'

'I'm Henry Bingham. Eleanor's brother-in-law. I came down because I thought there was something – ar'ch – going on down here between her and your brother and I wanted to warn them. Where are they?'

'They've gone,' said Diana, briefly rising. 'One half moment. I'll just see whether the house is on fire and then I'll—'

'Gorrn?' exclaimed Henry. 'They've gorrn and you haven't gorrn? Muriel is almost as bad as those three gentlemen in the bar.'

'What?'

'Never mind. I've been misinformed. You'd better trot along and see about the fire. We mustn't fiddle while Rome is burning. Then come back and we'll go deeper into this problem.'

She went and returned immediately. The fire in the chimney was subsiding. He needn't really have gone on the roof at all. This was small consolation. She found him still grimacing and chair-gripping in his pain. His plump cheeks were quite pale.

'Wait there a little while longer,' she said, with busy sympathy. 'The first thing to do is to get that room upstairs straight and help you up there. It may be a tiny bit less agonising when you lie down. We can tell each other all about Eleanor and Algy later on. They don't matter now.'

'I can't lie on a bed,' murmured Henry.

'Why not?'

'Because I'm wet through. Nor merely wet, but through.'

'Oh,' pondered Diana. 'Yes, that's going to be rather troublesome.'

'It's been it for some time already,' said Henry.

'I don't know quite what's to be done about that,' said Diana. 'I've no spare things except my own, and my uncle has locked up all his. Do you think you could put on a crêpe-de-Chine nightgown with your foot?'

'It doesn't sound very easy. But if I'm going to lie up on a bed I think I'd better try.'

'You'll have to take your things off, in any case, if you're going to sit or lie about here for long, or you'll catch pneumonia. It doesn't matter my being wet, because I'm going out again. Stay where you are for a minute or two, and I'll have the bed made and the room ready for you.'

He looked up at her, nodded, and managed to smile his pleasant smile. For a moment his appreciation overcame even the suffering which he was fighting to endure.

'Thank you immensely,' he said, 'You entirely charming person. If I'd known that this Algy had a sister like you I need never have troubled to come down here at all.'

A spasm of pain overtook him and he winced, but recovered and regained his smile.

'But I would have,' he added. 'I would have.'

Diana smiled back at him for a few eloquently silent seconds. Then, with a little business-like jerk of the head, turned and plunged into her unexpected domestic business.

The parlour was like some spent Gehenna of soot and smoke. She closed the door upon it. The whole cottage was filled with the fumes of the chimney blaze. What did that matter? A shrug for that. The rain which had so depressed her was still hammering remorselessly upon the roof. She only heard it now between her bustling labours of tucking the new sheets and blanket on to the double bed and of sweeping her own articles of clothing from here and there about the room into the chest of drawers; and heeded it not at all.

Henry, in the kitchen, found some material solace in his pipe, the stem of which received a pretty severe testing in his spasms. He found it difficult to think of anything except the pain, but he was sick about Eleanor. If only he could have delivered his warning and driven the two delinquents back into a condition of artificial respectability for the reception of

Reggy – if only he could have achieved this and *then* have found that he had to stay at this cottage with the sister – that would have been ideal. As it was, there seemed no hope of rescuing Eleanor now. Apart from that it might be worse. That is to say, the foot could not possibly be worse. But the sister might be lots worse – lots. He couldn't, in fact, remember ever having encountered anybody's sister who could be much better. This, in little pranks of thought between bouts of agony soul-twisting, unendurable.

Diana soon finished and was down in the kitchen again.

'Come on,' she said. 'I'll take you upstairs now. The bed's all ready.'

He smiled and levered himself up on to his sound foot. He again placed his arm round Diana's shoulders and, with her assistance, he staggered to the staircase.

Meanwhile neither of them spoke another word, much to the disappointment of Mrs Easy, who had just arrived outside the kitchen window, where in horrified but unflinching absorption she vainly waited for more.

The one sentence she had heard was, it must be admitted, a bit of an appetiser.

CHAPTER XI

The Threepenny Hero

At a quarter past three, the *Ring o' Bells* was given the chance to justify itself. A keen cyclist arrived.

He did not arrive cycling, nor sought he accommodation. But, when Muriel, her face opening like a box again, only more widely than ever, told him that the only possible way for anyone to get out to April Cottage now, unless one walked, was to hire a cycle from Mrs Leake and ride it through the rain, the visitor, without hesitation, agreed to do this. A keen cyclist, evidently.

Muriel, her tongue itching with rumour and question, took stock of this latest April Cottager, and restrained herself. She wasn't sure that she liked the look of him, and idle talk might only go and put difficulties in the way of the former stout gentleman, who had gone out to the cottage in Pill-button's hackney. And, rather than offend the former stout gentleman, Muriel would die, For with him he had carried away, undreamt-of as the cup in the sack of Benjamin, a large portion of Muriel's heart.

Mr Herbert Harrowing Pitts presented himself, therefore, at the cycle shop of Mrs Leake, a queenly, bulbous figure, with a black satin dress which had swept the floor for well-nigh a generation. She supplied him with a rather angular machine, of the late Victorian model, with racing handle-bars and metal grooves on the pedals for the reception of the toes.

Mr Pitts was not, by nature, the sort of young man who rides a push-bicycle from Mrs Leake's to April Cottage in a deluge without some pretty stern motive. Louise Piper supplied the motive for almost every disagreeable action which this unfortunate satellite performed. He did not love Mrs Piper, though he sometimes thought he detected on her part a coy little flutter of half-naughtiness, as he handed her into a taxi or touched her inadvertently at a tea-table. But he enjoyed from Mrs Piper a patronage so hearty, that he was often tempted to attribute it to some cause beyond the purely religious.

A year ago he had been in a drapery establishment, but, impressionably responding to the combined advances of Mrs Piper and St Phipp, he had (and very creditably) invested a modest inheritance in the prospect of holy orders. Meanwhile, Mrs Piper called him 'dear boy', and took him to *matinées*.

She did more than this. With little smiling hints, she corrected his occasional lapses in deportment, teaching him to acquire that ease of manner – that confidence, bordering on supreme indifference to everything and studied insolence to everybody – which the best people always regard as so estimable a characteristic of the high-church clergy.

Berty Pitts, schooled in that verbally punctilious line of commerce in which a waistcoat is a vest, and a vest is – 'Vest, sir? Oh, you mean gent's singlets? Yes, certainly. Mr Feeny! Singlets!' preserved, like a secret sin, a failing for nice attire. At the moment, he fortunately wore a mackintosh, or shower-skin; but, by the time he had gained the Chool Road, the rain had penetrated his vest to his shirting, while both his singlet and summer panting were feeling the effects of unwonted exercise from within. His beaverine head-joy was, of course, sodden. His foot-felicity and half-hose had been wet before he started.

But he toiled on through the morass of muddy water. Even his precious raiment must be sacrificed at the dictates of Mrs Piper.

He had got to please Mrs Piper this day, in fashion most peculiar. At this cottage, a couple were contemplating, if not yet actually performing, the act of mortal sin. Mrs Piper had thus herself described their occupation, dropping her voice and blinking her distaste at having to mention such a subject to one who would, of course, embrace celibacy. But Berty's job was not in any way to interfere with the course of mortal sin. He was simply to spy, unobserved, round the cottage, discover who was there, take notes of anything he chanced to overhear, and report immediately by telephone from South Ditherton. If caught, he was to excuse himself by saying he was picnicking, and wanted some water. He recalled this instruction just as he entered the largest puddle on the Chool Road, and decided that it was lacking in subtlety.

Though intimidated by the hazards of the commission, he had, of course, given way without much demur. He had to. 'For your sake, dear soul,' he said, 'it shall be done.' (Louise herself had told him to call her 'dear soul', but, slightly tainted by a Cockney accent, it didn't sound as beatific and Phippian as she had hoped.)

So here he was, at it – in the puddles. He had had about enough of Mrs Leake's bicycle by the time he got to the corner. He dismounted, removed his beaverine, flung back his long forelock by a jerk of the head, and wheeled his bicycle cautiously down the zigzag.

Diana knocked at the bedroom door, and listened. The response was an effortful groan, like an exaggerated sigh. She decided that her first duties were those of the nurse. The proprieties could take care of themselves. She therefore walked into the room, fully intending to undress him and put him into his crêpe-de-Chine nightgown, if he were unable to complete this office for himself. Thank God, for so practical and sensible a young woman.

He proved, however, to be so far into his nightgown that he was already half-way out again. He had tried to button the neck, with the result that the button had burst, like a stone from a catapult, and lay upon the floor. Also, upon the floor lay his discarded clothes (cast aside haphapazard in the strain of the disrobing operation) and one or two patches of damp from the same.

He was not thoroughly on the bed, but was propped in a very uncomfortable position, with his injured foot up, and one hand levering against the seat of a chair at his side. The effort of undressing had evidently been very arduous. He was still biting into the stem of his now cold pipe. He made an apologetic effort to hold his nightgown together at the bosom with his disengaged hand. He was grey with anguish.

Diana was supporting him in a moment, grasping him tightly round the shoulders, and helping him into position for reasonable comfort. Her cheek brushed his, and the crêpe-de-Chine nightgown could not have been pressing more closely to her had she been wearing it herself. Bad luck on Mrs Easy that the bedroom wasn't downstairs.

She said, 'Of course, on thinking it over, I believe it's cold water you ought to have on your foot.'

He murmured with closed eyes, 'Don't trouble. I've had quite enough water, hot or cold, for one day.'

'Oh, I know!' she exclaimed, then. 'I ought to have thought of it before. Would you like some brandy?'

He opened his eyes.

'Stupid of me to forget it,' she went on. 'I'll bring you up a glass.'

'Thanks,' he said. 'I could do with a bottle.'

'I've got two bottles in the house.'

'Oh, good! That'll keep me going till the doctor comes, anyhow.'

'And some Australian Burgundy.'

'Yes? I think the brandy would go best.'

'I'll bring both bottles up,' said Diana. 'Then you can keep them here. I expect you'll be here for some time.'

'I hope so,' said Henry, and tried to smile; but even that was an effort now.

Diana busied herself.

With her flexible nose in the crack of the front-door Mrs Easy watched her come downstairs. She carried a gentleman's entire outfit, down to his very socks. She entered the kitchen, where she left the clothes, and reappeared with a bottle of brandy in either hand. With these bottles she again quickly ascended the stairs to the bedroom. The orgy was unquestionably about to commence.

Very tantalising. It was impossible to obtain a view of the interior of the bedroom through the window. Mrs Easy bit her lip, and decided to go round to the back. She might be able to observe something from the back, through the small window on the landing at the bend of the stairs.

At the angle of the cottage, she halted, backed to the porch, outward from the porch on to a border, and eventually, by skilful and neck-straining backing, into the coal-shed.

The young man deposited his bicycle in some bushes at the side of the road, and advanced very cautiously, peering at the cottage through the privet hedge, testing the latch of the gate before operating it, avoiding the gravel path; dithered half-heartedly and with protruding teeth half-way between the gate and the cottage; then stealthily pursued his shrinking but conscientious advance. There were already a little note-book and a pencil somewhere in his cuff. Mrs Easy, wide-eyed in the coal-shed, sensed an ally.

'Does it seem to do you any good?' asked Diana.

'Rather,' said Henry, whose colour was returning. 'Lots of good. I think I shall carry on with the treatment for a bit, if you don't mind.'

'I certainly should,' said Diana. 'I should drink as much as you possibly can.'

'Thanks,' said Henry. 'There are two bottles, aren't there? I'm not a heavy drinker, as a rule, by any means, but if only you knew the extremity of – never mind about that. But it helps, so I really think I shall go steadily at it, neat. I shall, at the worst, remain quite pleasant. I've been told I am really at my best on the very exceptional occasions when I fall slightly under the influence of fire-water.'

'That's all right,' said Diana. 'I've the satisfaction of knowing that you won't be able to chase me about the cottage in any case. Now, I'd better go and get the doctor.'

'Before you go,' said Henry, 'let's talk a little. I want to know what's happened about Eleanor, and all sorts of things.'

'Yes, and I want to know about you. But—'

'And I about you. That's it. Let's talk.'

'But I must get the doctor to you.'

'No hurry. What can he do? He'll only start hauling my foot about and hurting me like nothing on earth.'

'He may give you something to soothe it.'

'I've got that,' said Henry. 'By the time the doctor arrives, I shall probably be so soothed that I shall mistake him for an annual meeting of the Royal College of Surgeons. Let's just talk for a few minutes.'

Diana looked at him with her head on one side. For the second time that day, she was very wet and ought to keep on the move. Moreover, her reason for being in the room was to nurse him. Her duty as a nurse was, as she knew from experience, to say, 'Well, I must love you and leave you,' and to go for the doctor without further delay. But . . .

'Just for a few minutes,' he repeated. 'It really won't make any difference to the foot – nothing could.'

He had awfully nice eyes. Rather like a spaniel. After all, nurses were surely always instructed to humour their patients, if possible. She sat on the foot of the bed.

She told him her experiences of the morning – briefly, and not without bitterness against Eleanor. He seemed very regretful about Eleanor, and the tiniest bit regretful that Eleanor's behaviour should arouse in Diana wrath, rather than pity. When she concluded, he shifted his foot with a little 'Ow!' of painful effort, then returned readily to the subject of the runagates.

'Do you know my brother?' was his first question.

'No.'

'It would be easier for you to understand what I was driving at in coming here, if you know Reggy.'

'Why?'

'Because I don't believe Eleanor's the kind of girl who'd smash up a man's home if she thought twice about it; and unless she's warned about this, the home will go wallop this very evening. That's why I came – to warn her. My brother's coming home today.'

'What! Then he knows already?'

'He knows nothing definitely. If he got home and found her on the drawing-room sofa doing crochet work, he couldn't accuse her of anything.'

'I see,' said Diana. 'Then you sympathize with Eleanor sufficiently to try and pick her up and bung her on the sofa just in time, as it were?'

'Don't you?'

'No,' said Diana, slowly. 'I think she's behaved rottenly to everybody, including herself.'

'I believe she's fond enough of my brother to pull up in time.'

'Then that's worse than going ahead, and being openly and defiantly false to him,' said Diana.

'M'yes. But there's provocation, mind. My brother is more like a brilliantly accomplished performing elephant than anything else I can think of at the moment. Listen. I am not an habitual bibber of Three Star brandy. Eleanor is not at heart a sinful person. I am driven to drink brandy by an insufferable pain in my foot. Eleanor is driven to have a fling by a husband who, believe me, is very nearly as good an excuse for her fling as my foot is for my brandy. She's only up to a bit of mischief. She doesn't get any mischief at home.'

This failed to cut any ice with Diana.

'Whatever your brother's like, she married him, knowing what he was like. I don't see that she—'

'She married him for his money. I grant you that. And now she's disillusioned and reckless. But if only she could get going properly, she could be a happy woman even with Reggy. She could be happy with anybody. I can see that in her. Only she must have sympathy. That's why she's got mine.'

Diana blinked. 'She appeals to you very strongly, it appears.'

'All her sex appeal to me very strongly,' said Henry. 'You see, I travel along the extreme edge of the straight and narrow, so most of the ladies I run up against are like myself – on the right track, but only just, and liable to wobble off. Awfully nice people you know.'

Diana smiled with tight lips.

'Don't you think that if you went along the middle of the road you'd meet nicer ones still?' she asked.

'Oh, nicer, I suppose, yes,' said Henry, with a little sigh, 'but for good company, give me the edge.'

Diana got up.

'Well, I suppose it's too late to help Eleanor now, in any case,' she said.

He nodded disconsolately. 'I wouldn't abandon all hope even now,' he said, 'only I'm afraid I'm incapacitated for further action.'

'Yes; I'll be off for the doctor. I ought not to have hung about so long.'

'Righto,' said Henry, 'I'm very sorry you've got to go.'

'Oh, I don't mind going.'

'No, but I shall miss your company.'

'I shouldn't have thought you would. I'm one of the people who stick to the middle of the road.'

'No, you're not. I know what you are. You're one of the people from the middle, who come to the side in the cause of charity – to help the wobblers.'

She laughed. 'I think that's exactly what you are,' she said. 'Look here, I must be off.'

'Righto,' he repeated. 'Don't let the doctor bring any ghastly-looking apparatus for repairing torn ligaments or putting limbs back. I know what these doctors are – hearty, tormenting blighters. "Ha! Put your ankle out, have you? Right. I'll just put it back again." He won't.'

'Good-bye,' said Diana; 'drink plenty of brandy.'

'I will.'

'Can you read?'

'At present I can.'

'You'd better have something to read to try and distract your mind. There are some books downstairs. They'll all be covered with soot, but still— Oh, *I* know. I expect my uncle's views on the female sex would interest you. I'll bring you selections from his manuscript.'

'Is he for or against the sex?' asked Henry.

'Strongly against.'

'Oh, well, nothing like a counter-irritation to help me along with this ankle. Bring me Uncle on Woman.'

She ran down to the parlour, and fought her way through the smoke to the window, which had remained closed since last she had left the cottage. She retrieved and dusted a ream or two of Uncle from the foot of the bookcase. She stood for a moment contemplating the sorry condition of the room. Later in the evening she must tackle it – a polluting business.

She carried the manuscript upstairs. Henry was in an agonising position half out of bed, trying to retrieve his tobacco pouch from a small table just out of his reach. She closed the door, and went once more to his assistance.

Berty Pitts, hovering just beyond the porch, heard someone come downstairs. By straining forward he could have caught sight of the someone, but he instinctively drew back and remained in an upright, evasive attitude against the wall of the cottage. The someone entered a room on the ground floor, remained there a few moments and again went upstairs. Berty heard the upstairs door close with, he thought, the decisive slam of a door which is intended to remain closed. He gained sufficient confidence from this to creep round through the porch, and even into the cottage. The kitchen door stood open. The room was unoccupied. From the parlour came no sounds of life, but in a room upstairs were voices. He raised his head and listened. Then, very stealthily, his teeth protruding abnormally, he stole upwards to the little landing at the bend of the stairs. Here he again paused, his heart throbbing, his fingers nervously clutching his pencil and his nasty note-book.

From the room ahead of him, on the right, he could hear the voices plainly now. He could hear what they were saying. He heard one or two sentences; his eyes widened and he licked his pencil.

All of which Mrs Easy, who had emerged from the coal-shed, and negotiated the bank behind the little landing window, with thrilling relish witnessed.

Diana propped Henry back on to the bed, handed him his pouch and some matches, gently reprimanded him. 'I do hope I can trust you to take care of yourself while I'm away.'

'I wish you hadn't got to go,' he replied. 'While you stay here and talk, I forget the pain.'

She laughed, and crossed the room to the dressing-table, where she started rearranging her hat, as ladies do, before setting out on an urgent mission through country in which they are unlikely to meet a soul. She wouldn't be long, she said. The doctor would motor her back.

He sighed.

'Really, I mean it,' he said. 'When you sit on the bed and talk, I don't feel the pain. If I don't feel the pain, why go for the doctor?'

She completed her toilet and returned to the bedside. By this time Berty Pitts was on the landing.

'We mustn't go on any longer like this,' were the first words that fell upon the ear of the stairway detective. 'I'm beginning to blame myself for being here with you now. Think of the injury I may be doing you.'

'The injury's done now; and it's very sweet of you to bother so much about me. After all, it's rather a poisonous prospect for you, too.'

'Oh, I don't mind. At first I thought it was awful to have to go so far. But now I do it regularly, and I'm getting hardened to it.'

Passages even more unblushing followed – passages which held Berty scribbling incriminations he could scarcely credit. From Mrs Bingham – 'Anyhow, I can't stop now and you mustn't ask me to. It's for your own sake.' From the man – Gascoyne, or whatever Mrs Piper had said his name was – '*I* don't want to let you go a bit.' And, 'You make me forget my troubles,' and, 'If we're parted now, it'll only drive me to the bottle.' Then she, 'Are you comfy?' And the man, 'To tell you the truth, I'm not very. I wish I could get a little higher in the bed. Thanks, that's better. If you could just put your arm under me there – *thaat's* better. Look out! you're on my foot.' 'Oh, I'm so sorry.' 'No, it's all right; only don't rest your weight . . .'

Berty felt encouraged (either by the remarkable success that was attending his efforts on Mrs Piper's behalf, or by personal curiosity, in which considerations of the dear soul were, for once, forgotten) to extend his researches to the heroic hazard of a keyhole reconnaissance. He advanced an adventurous foot. A loose stairboard creaked loudly, and fear, like an electric current, thrilled the nerves of his scalp.

He slapped an ungoverned hand to the banister, and dropped his note-book into the hall.

He cared not how quickly, how noisily his descent was accomplished. He used the banisters as sloping parallel bars, down which he slid. He snapped up the note-book as an urchin snaps up a misdirected golf-ball, and scooted for the porch, for the gate, for the bush, for the bicycle.

Mrs Easy, who had occasionally taken brief superintendence of the literature enjoyed by little Easy, had long since decided what Berty Pitts was doing there. Mr Hole had received her wire, and had immediately despatched a detective to the cottage. Quick work, but, as Mrs Easy had gathered from the career of Bloodhound Baxter – Sleuth, and other heroes of little Easy's threepenny library, them detectives possessed an extraordinary gift for being on the spot at the right time. But, even so, did he know all? Did he know of the double bed, of the brandy, of the stripping? She might be able to put an extra note or two in his book for him.

As Berty Pitts snatched his bicycle into the road and gripped the low handle-bars, he saw a woman hurrying after him through the trees above the cottage, and violently gesticulating. Assailed by more electric head-treatment, Berty thrust his cycle at the slope of the zigzag, and essayed a hopping, panic-stricken get-away. Mrs Easy retained, however, the presence of mind requisite in one's dealings with sleuths. She gained the edge of the steep bank beside the roadway, and shouted after him, 'Hold on; I speak as a friend.'

Berty hesitated.

'If you come back here,' said Mrs Easy, 'I can likely tell you more than what you know.'

Berty retraced a few paces, still guardedly heading his cycle in the direction of escape.

'I don't think I'd better wait,' he said. 'I'm in rather a hurry to go.'

'Yes, so I noticed,' said Mrs Easy, from the bank. 'Oh, I was watching you, with all your clever ways. I speak as a friend,' she repeated hastily.

'Well, what is it you want to say? I can't wait.'

'I know,' said Mrs. Easy, 'one or two things which not

even you may 'ave yet found out as regarding what is going on inside that cottage.'

'I think I know enough,' said Berty.

'Ah! But do you know all? Do you know as 'ow the single bed was removed from that room this morning, and a double subsistuated?'

'A double bed?'

'Ah! You see – with all your knowing ways. And at the bedside two bottles o' brandy specially got in. Oh, not for ordinary mealtime drinking – for boozing there in the bed. Two bottles!'

'Really? Good gracious! No, I—'

'Ah! You see? You'd start peddling off with only 'alf the worst known. And *that's* not all.'

'Really? Still – that's all right, thanks. I think I'll be—'

'Do you know,' continued Mrs. Easy, indomitably, 'that that young man is lying upon that there bed without a stitch of clothing upon his person?'

'What? How do you know? Is there anywhere where you can see into the room from?' asked Berty, with a tentative movement of the front wheel of his bicycle.

'No,' said Mrs Easy. 'But you can put it down in your little book and take it from me. And there may be one or two more things I can think of if—'

'Thanks,' said Berty. 'That'll do, thanks. Oh – yes. There is one thing. The other lady, where is she?'

'What other lady?'

'The sister?'

'Whose sister?'

'Er – his sister.'

'Go on!' said Mrs Easy, contemptuously. 'His sister!'

'Oh; then they are alone here together? No other lady here at all?'

'Not likely,' replied Mrs Easy. 'Did they *sound* to you as if they was hoping to see their sisters?'

'I see,' said Berty. 'Many thanks. Only, I say, don't tell anyone you saw me here, will you?'

'I said I spoke as a friend, didn't I?' said Mrs Easy. 'Let that suffice. What I speaks as, I acts as.'

'Good!' said Berty. 'Many thanks – good-bye!'

He willingly attacked the upward slush of the zigzag, well satisfied. This woman, whoever she was, would not give him away. And she had confirmed his impressions, and added to his store of information. It was not really at all surprising about the sister. The dear soul had had her doubts about the sister still being there. With lightened heart, Berty faced the ravages of rain and fatigue upon his homeward way.

Well satisfied was Mrs Easy, too. Her work of vengeance was well-nigh completed. Just one more peep through the landing window, and she could return home to change her wet clothes and cheerfully await the inevitable and devastating visitation of the morrow upon the deserving victims of her proficient indignation.

She manoeuvred back through the trees and down the slope, to her landing window. In so doing, she missed seeing Diana, who quitted the cottage at the same time and passed through the gate unheard. By the time Mrs Easy was back at the foot of the bank, twitching her nose through the window, Diana was half-way up the hill, on her innocent and unsuspecting mission; while Berty Pitts, his head lowered over his racing bars, in his breast pocket verbatim evidence so startling as to necessitate paraphrase on the telephone, churned the Chool Road.

Mrs Easy, with a final sniff of triumph, turned and went home, leaving the cottage a deserted, a begrimed, a dripping prison, wherein languished one solitary sufferer, methodically fortifying himself with his only material solace, and apathetically turning the virulent pages of Hole on Woman.

CHAPTER XII

Patients

For many minutes after Diana had left the cottage, Henry lay suffering very severely. He had no thought for anything except his foot – his accursed foot – ache – ache. He got that deadly sensation which sometimes will attack the mind during pain, or while one is performing some finicky task – that oppression of the present. Presumably, some time in the future, the pain will have gone, the task will be completed. But here it is now – the pain is here now – now – the task is not done yet – not yet.

Then the fingers stiffen in exasperation at the task – the nerves concentrate to the pain – one's whole system seems near some maddened point of breakage. Henry felt goaded to move, knowing full well that to move meant a spasm of pain. Actually, he did move, rather than lie still and have his nerves goaded by that fiend of the present tense. Pain shot from his foot and knifed his whole system. Even in that, there was a cruel, paradoxical feeling of relief.

Dismal – solitary. If he shouted aloud, there was none to hear. He felt goaded to shout, too, as a sort of aimless change. The spasm of pain passed, and he lay back exhausted, and feeling the cold of the sweat on his forehead.

He put out a hand, and grasped the neck of the bottle at his elbow, as some poor wretch, blinded with agony, may turn and grasp the weapon to end it.

Then, with an effort, he mastered his thoughts, and forbade them to dwell on the ache. It was not easy to do this, or to enforce it. There wasn't much else to think about. Absolute desolation. Rain on the roof. Hole on Woman.

That girl – a sweet, natural girl. A sweet face. He admired that type. And not only in looks attractive, but in the bright, confident, self-possession of her nature. She had brushed his cheek with hers, as she helped him on to the bed, but she hadn't remarked on it at all. So many girls would have glared, as if it had been his fault; or giggled, as if it had been their intention. But she hadn't. She must have noticed it, though. P'raps she had rather enjoyed it.

Hallo! He had forgotten his foot for a whole minute. It was better – the ache was really better. Ar'ch! But he must keep his mind off it.

Woman. Now, what was all this trouble of Uncle's? Woman in Five Parts. Part Four. Woman of the Orient. Section One: Traditional. Section Two: Historical. Section Three: Philosophical. Section One: Traditional:

> As we duly noted in that portion of this survey devoted to the Old Testament (*vide* Part I. Sec. II. Preface. P. 34. Footnote on Rachel) it is to be the Orient that we must turn for the purest conception and the most rational and logical observance of the prerogative of the female sex. Here the mind of man, untainted by the false doctrines of modernism, and still uncontaminated with the sphacelus of scientific quackery, has ever derived inspiration, direct and unadulterated, from the Divine fount of Wisdom.

Here, steady on, Uncle! Come to the point, you old poop. They know how to treat 'em in the East? Well, why not say so, instead of tying yourself up in great knots of lingo? No; pages of that sort of thing. Stop a bit; what was this?

> From the queen of the *beau monde* to the trull of the gutter, the Western woman sways a vile and unchartered ascendency over her natural despot, schooled by traditions loathsome to the simpler and more saintly Orient mind. Her natural and patent duties are performed at a bargain. We dumbfoundedly witness the astounding sentiment of 'give and take' being applied even to marriage. In the Eastern world, despite the high-flown and erotic rhapsodies of certain romanticists and poets, a woman is born

not only exclusively to give, but to give by choice. All that she takes, she takes at her master's indulgence. The only bargain she obtains is the bargain of the whip.

Henry laid the manuscript aside with a smile.

'I wonder what the girl did to Uncle,' was his reflective comment.

Berty Pitts, in a condition closely resembling that of a dog exhausted by swimming, pulled up at the *Ring o' Bells*, and propped his offensive vehicle in the yard. Muriel, repressing her curiosity, informed him that he could telephone from the private room used as an office, and conducted him thither. Telephony in the West Country is still almost invariably conducted by means of those instruments upon which one has to press firmly while grinding a little handle in order to awaken the soporific damsel who presides at the exchange, while subsequent conversation can only, for some remarkable scientific reason, be effected on the receiver. Berty, after some delay, issued his trunk call to a distant lady, who received it as though making a note of an unimportant engagement six weeks ahead. Berty sighed, sadly contemplated his outraged attire, and asked Muriel for tea while he waited for the call to come through.

He was still waiting when Diana passed the hotel. For a girl who had walked about eleven miles, and driven eight, in the course of the wet day, she seemed splendidly fresh. She had found it necessary to keep to the side of the Chool Road and, in this connection, had recalled her conversation with the kindly soul she had left at the cottage. And when she got to South Ditherton her first objective was not the doctor's house. She went to the post-office.

She might yet be in time to warn Eleanor. She sent another wire to Mrs Krabbe— 'Have heard husband returning unexpectedly today inform them if possible – Diana.'

This was soul-satisfying all round. It was her practical duty to rescue her brother from a scrape if she could. It was her moral duty to consider the wishes of the unfortunate would-be preserver at the cottage. And it afforded a pleasing feeling of immense superiority over Eleanor – Eleanor, the slipping wayfarer at the side of the road; Diana's, the hand of rescue, stretched from the moral middle.

Diana's ring at the doctor's door-bell was the signal for canine uproar from apparently every quarter of the house. After a few moments the doctor's wife put a worried head through the open window of a front room, and thus addressed the visitor:

'Do you want the doctor? Quiet, Shrimp! Excuse me not coming to the door, but I can't very well, because several of the dogs are loose in the hall, and I've got a bitch who is just going to begin whelping in here, because the stable roof has sprung a leak and if I opened this door some of the other dogs might get in and upset her. I'm afraid the doctor's out.'

'Oh, dear!' said Diana. 'It's something very important.'

'I can take a message. Shrimp, dear, lie down again. Missus will come back to you in one second. Perhaps, if you could tell me through the window— Shrimpy, dulling! do stay on your nice whelping-board. It's so very important that you should, you know. Now?'

'April Cottage, Chool,' shouted Diana, against the belling in the hall. 'A man with, very likely, a broken ankle.'

'Oh, yes?' said the doctor's wife, calmly. 'All right. Thank you. Rip! Will you not make such a noise out there! You're disturbing Shrimp. I'm afraid I don't know exactly what time he'll be back, but I'll tell him when he comes.'

'Yes, but – you understand, it's terribly important,' cried Diana. 'The accident happened nearly two hours ago. The man's in agony. I must find a doctor at once for him. Is there a doctor at the next place – Filcombe, isn't it called? I simply must—'

'He won't be long, I'm sure. I'll see that he's told. There's nobody at Filcombe at all. It's a most dead and alive place. My husband attends all the people there.'

'Well, I'd better wait,' said Diana.

'Just as you please. I'm afraid I can't ask you in, or, of course, I would. This is the consulting-room, and there's another bitch in the drawing-room. She's coming on, and I have to keep her apart from the others, too. Of course, she *would* choose this time. She's always inconvenient in her little arrangements. There, Shrimpy! *Do* do what Missus tells you, dulling!'

'Well, I simply don't know what I'd better do. You see—'

'I know what it is,' said the doctor's wife, sympathetically. 'These things always happen like that. I had a Great Dane that got injured just when the vet was away at a meet. We had to have him destroyed.'

'I'm afraid I can't very well go back and destroy my friend,' said Diana, who was getting steadily deafened and irritated. 'But will you promise to send the doctor out directly he comes back?'

'Oh, yes. I promise you that.'

'There'll be no delay, will there?'

'No, no. Oh, no. The moment he— R-rip!'

The doctor's wife withdrew her head from the window. Diana clenched her teeth in her annoyance. She glanced at her wrist-watch. It was half past five. She would stand on the doorstep in the rain until the doctor returned.

The Alsatian wolf-hound that had bitten little Easy put its head round a corner of a conservatory, and growled. The doctor's wife returned to the window. From all parts of the house still resounded baying and yelps of challenge. Incited, no doubt, by these, the Alsatian wolf-hound slowly rounded the conservatory and advanced snarling.

'Oh, my goodness!' said the doctor's wife. 'I didn't know Wotan was loose. What a nuisance! He'll get wet. I don't know how he got out. He must have got through the dining-room window. Don't be afraid. He doesn't mean any harm; only he's rather savage.'

Diana, who was but human, closed the front gate only just in time. From the house came a frenzied, cataphonic paean to the glory of Wotan.

The doctor's wife, a conscientious woman, experienced a good deal of difficulty in fulfilling her first duty. She must make a note of this call on her husband's services, or it would slip her memory. Her first duty, though, was, of course, to pacify poor Shrimpy in the face of this unnerving liveliness.

After several minutes, she succeeded in enticing her favourite into a position of wheezing recumbency on the whelping-board. The doctor's wife then turned to the writing-table.

Oh, but Wotan must be called in before he got too wet. He made such a terrific mess of the house when he was wet, and it was difficult enough to keep servants in any case. In order to get Wotan into the dining-room through the hall it was necessary temporarily to remove his *bête noire*, Tango, from the precincts of the hall, and, with Nina monopolising the drawing-room, and the cat being in the kitchen, the only possible thing to do with Tango was to put him in the lavatory.

Tango, being disobedient and displaying a marked aversion to the lavatory, enabled Rip to get into the consulting-room and to frighten Shrimpy off her whelping-board; while Wotan, having successfully expelled the female client, was now triumphantly uprooting a bone from beneath some budding geraniums in the front-garden; and Nina, resenting her drawing-room Coventry, had managed to scramble on to the window-ledge, where there were some vases. Upstairs, Fifi and Rascal had, to judge from their sounds, discovered some unexpected ratting in the spare bedroom.

'Children, children!' said the doctor's wife. 'You really are rather a handful sometimes.' She was single-handed. The cook had gone to see why the man hadn't come to mend the stable roof. The housemaid had left, abandoning a fortnight's wages, by the first train that morning. It was thus some time before the doctor's wife found the opportunity to return to the writing-table and make her note, while the details were still fresh in her memory.

'Something Cottage, Filcombe. Man with broken arm. Forget name of cottage. Anybody in Filcombe sure to know.'

Now, with perplexity, came to Diana exhaustion. As she stood dismally in the roadway, she realised the weariness of her bones, the heaviness of her feet. If only the doctor would sail round the corner in his car! Just as she was beginning to feel inclined to fling herself down on the wet bank at the roadside, and to give way to despair, she heard the sound of a motor approaching. It turned the corner and came towards her. A sense of bitter disappointment overtook her. It was not the doctor's car. It was only a van – but it was Pitcher's van.

Diana hailed the toad. He drew up and came into neutral with a shriek of tortured metal.

'Are you going towards April cottage?' called Diana.

'What, you again?' replied Pitcher's driver. 'Noo; I ain't goin' past along o' Chool. That way I do be goin', but be the main road.'

'You can go through Chool, and drop me, can't you?'

'It be a long way round. I got to get back to the shop before he closes. Was you goin' straight ther'?'

'Well – I wanted to call at the chemist's; and also, if possible, at somewhere where I could ring up the doctor's wife from, to remind her of something I've just told her.'

The driver shook his head.

'I darn't bide,' he said.

'All right,' said Diana; 'I'll take the lift and chance it.'

Without further invitation, she clambered into the van. The toad changed gears with strange, corresponding changes of facial expression, and jerked into progress.

'I dar'n't let meself to think,' said the toad, with no little sense of his own benevolence, 'what they would say at the shop to my goin' all around be way of Chool, if they was to know that I was goin' via he.'

Diana plucked up her spirits. She had misgivings about the doctor's wife, but the latter was probably more reliable than she appeared during the ordeal of Shrimpy's whelping. As for the chemist, probably no chemist could supply anything that would improve the foot. What the Downblotton chemist, Bather, might prescribe, would almost certainly do more harm than good. The chemist was better left alone till the doctor called.

Besides, this Mr Bingham kept telling her that it was her company which brought him the greatest relief, and sounded as if he meant it. So the sooner she got back to the cottage, the better. And it was a quarter to six. Tea-time was long overdue.

A quarter to six. At a quarter to six our old friend, Mr Benbow Hole, of Hole on Woman, was glaring from a railway carriage at the town of Peterborough. Peterborough, though by no means as wet as Chool, can seldom have been much wetter in June. A parson with spectacles, sitting opposite Mr Hole, noticed the old gentleman's expression as he surveyed Peterborough, and remarked:

'Wet, isn't it?'

Mr Hole transferred his glare to the parson.

'Yes,' he replied, deliberately; 'at a guess I should say that there must be just about one drop of rain to every damn fool in the world.'

The conversation then languished, and before very long the parson pretended to go along the corridor to search for a late tea, and changed his carriage.

At the Harrogate booking-office, Mr Hole had inquired for the first train to Bristol. The booking-clerk had scratched his head.

'To Bristol?' he repeated dubiously.

'To Bristol,' said Mr Hole. 'To Bristol To – to – Bristol – Bristol— To Bristol.'

The clerk, after some research, informed him. By attempting to travel in a direct route across-country to Bristol, he would arrive at that city at the hour of three minutes to one a.m.

'Really!' said Mr Hole. 'I infer that the directors of the railway companies, being born owls, are anxious to impose the habits of owls upon the general public. I can get to Bristol earlier by going to London, I believe. Can I not?'

Further investigation proved that this was the case. By arriving at King's Cross at 7.10 and leaving Paddington at eight, Mr Hole could make Bristol by 10.20. This he decided to do, and here he is at 5.45, scowling at Peterborough.

But, by this time, certain other events had taken place elsewhere. A modest tinkle from the homely office-parlour of the *Ring o' Bells* at length summoned Berty Pitts from his tea to his duty. At the other end of the line Louise was already twittering excitedly.

And even as she 'hallo'd' to greet the far-away voice of her faithful steward, there sounded from heaven a crash of thunder, and through her dining-room doorway strode, like Vengeance, the massive figure of Reginald.

CHAPTER XIII

Sound and Fury

He slapped his umbrella to the dining-room table, with an instinctive 'Stop that; I am here.'

Louise, from the telephone on the writing-table, eyed him, smiled and continued to nod reassuringly, while yet straining her ears for Berty.

'Hallo?' came the solicitous voice of the latter, while yet a great way off.

'Hallo!' cried Louise. 'Is that you? Hold the line. My brother is here.'

Reginald drew himself up – all nostrils. 'To whom are you speaking of me? What concern is it of that person—?'

Violent nods, smiles and agitated whispering aside by Louise.

'I'll tell you in a moment. Just one moment, and I'll expl—Hallo!'

'Hallo?'

'Hallo, Berty. Listen. My brother is here—'

'Berty?' cried Reginald, advancing upon the writing-table. 'What is this? Put that receiver down this instant, and speak to me.'

'All right. In one moment,' said Louise. 'If one doesn't continue to gabble the whole time, the people on the exchange think you've finished and cut you off. They always do that. Hallo! Berty? Hallo!'

'Hallo?' came accents like the last despairing farewell of a departing soul.

'Can you hear me?'

'Hallo?' said Berty, just audible, and now, apparently, at the actual moment of passing into the Beyond.

'Oh, dear! Hallo!'

'Stop that, I tell you. Berty? Who and what—?'

'One moment. Hallo!'

'Hallo?' from Hades.

'Hold the line.'

'What?'

'Hallo?'

'Is that you, dear soul?' implored Berty.

'Don't be impertinent,' said the lady at the exchange, 'I'll put you through in a minute.'

'I'll explain the whole thing,' said Louise. 'Only I must just – Hallo! Hallo, *Exchange*!'

'Put the thing down and stop that, do you hear me?' roared Reginald. 'Listen to me – to *me*.' He beat himself savagely on the chest. He was in small humour, you will remember, for bubble and squeak. While Louise still vainly cooed and nodded and frowned and blinked and 'hallo'ed', he bellowed above her, his fists quivering aloft. 'Do you think I have abandoned a couple of big business deals and returned from Paris in order to listen to you talking some tingle-tangle on the telephone? Put it down, I say; or, by Christopher I'll—'

'You're thrrrough now,' said the lady on the exchange.

'Oh! Hallo!'

'Ah! Hallo?'

'Hallo! That's better.'

'Hallo!

'Hallo?'

'Now—'

'Yes.'

'Hallo!'

'Yes. That's better.'

'Listen. Berty! Hold the line.'

'What?'

'Hold the line.'

'I am.'

'Yes, but my brother's just arrived.'

'What?'

'My brother. Mr Bingham. Her wife. I mean, his w— I mean her husband. He's arrived. I want to— Hallo?'

'What?'

'Hold the line a moment.'

'I am.'

'Yes, but—'

'Do you want to drive me to assault?' asked Reginald.

'One moment. It's all to do with you, Reggy. Hallo, Berty?'

'Yes?'

'Hold the line.'

Louise turned, still cramming the receiver to the side of her head. To Reginald she discharged a breathless *résumé* of her tactics and measures. Reggy had told her to act as she thought best. She had done so. She gave a brief outline of Berty Pitts. Berty Pitts, during this interval, retired again to Hades, whence he continued to 'Hallo' in a plaintive pianissimo.

'A boy?' fumed Reginald. 'A boy?'

'Well, a young man,' said Louise. 'I—'

'Investigating my private affairs? Have you taken leave of your senses? What bumble-puppy, in heaven's name, have you been up to?'

He seized the receiver, and dragged it away from her. His neck bulged, swollen and crimson, above a collar sagging in exhaustion.

All the while Berty continued, 'Hallo? Hal-*lo*? *Hal*-lo? Hal-*lo*?'

'Your time is up. Do you want another thrrrree minutes,' said the lady at the exchange.

'Oh, but I haven't spoken at all yet,' said Berty.

'Excuse *me*.'

'Well – but, I mean – I have spoken, but—'

'Then you shouldn't say you haven't. I will put you through for another thrrrree minutes.'

'Now!' said Reginald. 'Are you there?'

'Hallo?'

'Don't you hallo me. Are you—?'

Louise managed to squeeze her face into speaking range.

'It's my brother – Mrs Bingham's husband. You may tell him all.'

Reginald shouldered her into oblivion. The voice of Berty replied in a melancholy tenor.

'But, oh, dear soul, if you but knew—'

'Stop that,' shouted Reginald. 'I know where to go if I wish to listen to ballads, thank you. Now! What have you been up to? Come!'

'Hallo?'

'Will you stop hallo-ing at me, blast it! Am I hunting? Tell me what you have been up to.'

'Oh. What? Well— I – I 've been to the place. I – er – are you there?'

'You may think yourself pretty lucky that I am not where *you* are. Go on.'

'Oh! Well – er – I went there – er—'

'Will you kindly tell me in so many plain words what you have been up to! Without repeating everything three times. If I want to listen to anthems I know where to go and listen to anthems. I have not come all the way from Paris, leaving some most important business deals, to listen to anthems. If you are capable of understanding six consecutive words of simple, grammatical Anglo-Saxon, what – have – you – been – up – to?'

'Are you speaking?' asked the lady at the exchange.

'Don't *you* begin,' snorted Reginald. 'Once and for all, now. You take my advice and stop that, or you'll be sorry. Now, you! Your report. Come!'

'Hallo?' said Berty, who had been in the unknown again, for a brief season.

Reginald turned, fuming, bubbling with fury, to Louise.

'Who is this doodle that you have employed? Eh? Where did you get him from? Where did you find him? A barn-yard? A barn-yard?'

'Hallo?' said Berty.

'Speak up, London,' said the exchange lady.

Reginald crashed heavy, beringed fingers on to the writing-table.

'Stop your clacking, will you!'

'Do you want to go on speaking?'

'I do. That is precisely what I do want. And if, on the other hand, I happen to want monkeys, I am quite capable of—'

'Hallo?' said Berty.

'Now! You! Well?'

'Oh! I – er – got cut off, I think.'

'You will be,' replied Reginald, 'if I have any more of this diddling. Now! Your report!'

'Oh. Well, sir, as I say, I went – er – to this place. There was no one there. I mean, I didn't— Hallo?'

'Prrrress the receiver, Downblotton,' said the exchange lady.

'Hallo? Well, as I say, I went to this place, and there was no one there. At least, I mean, there was, but I didn't see anyone. At least, that is to say, I saw a woman.'

'Where did you find this ullage? Where, in God's name? A scullery? A pig-house?'

'And she told me they were upstairs together in the bedroom.'

'Who?'

'This other woman.'

'The other woman was upstairs?'

'No, no. She—'

'The other woman is the sister,' interposed Louise.

'Stop that, will you? You! Who told you who was upstairs in the bedroom?'

Louise pricked up her ears.

'Mrs Bingham was upstairs – with him. They were together in the bedroom. In fact, I'm afraid they – they – they were—'

'They were what?'

'In bed.'

'Oh, the devil!' muttered Reginald.

'What?' asked Louise, unable to contain herself. 'What does he say?'

'Oh, stop that, I tell you. You! Go on.'

'I hardly like—'

'Go on, I say.'

'Well, they – er – as I say, they were in bed.'

'How do you know?'

'I heard.'

'How can you hear whether a person or persons is or are in bed?'

'What?' asked Louise, goggling.

'Stop that. You! How do you know, I repeat?'

'I beg your pardon? Oh, I – well, I heard what they were saying.'

'And what were they saying?'

'I – I've got it written down, but I can't very well read it.'

'You can't read your own writing?'

'Yes, but – oh, first of all, they had a double bed brought in on purpose.'

'On purpose?'

'I beg pardon? Oh, well, anyhow, they had a double bed brought in. There was a single bed, and they had it taken out, and a double one brought in and some brandy – two bottles – in the room—'

'What, what, what?'

'Brandy. Two bott—'

'Brandy? What for?'

'Erm – I don't know quite. I suppose . . .'

'You suppose what?'

'I beg pardon? Well – I don't know quite, but I suppose the idea was to sort of – drink and – I don't know; anyhow, they, they had it there with them. Oh, and there was another thing.'

'What?'

'Well, I – on the telephone, sir, and all – it's not very— Besides, I was only told this by the other woman.'

'What other woman, you—?'

'The sister,' said Louise.

'For the last time, will you stop that? You! The other woman. Who was she?'

'I don't know exactly. I met her outside. I think she was a sort of caretaker. She told me—'

'But you said you heard for yourself?'

'Er – yes, but . . .'

'What did you hear?'

'Oh, but I can't – really, I mean – on the teleph—'

'What – did – you – hear, I ask.'

'What they were saying in the bedroom, but—'

'And what did they say? Do you want to drive me to

frenzy? Can you remember what you heard them say?'

'Yes, I – I noted it down, but—'

'Then read it.'

'The man had taken off all his clothes,' he said.

'What! Did you hear him say so?'

'No, but – the other woman told me that. Oh, and the sister wasn't there at all. Mrs Piper said she might not be. She'd gone. At least, if she'd been there at all, she'd gone. But—'

'You have notes?'

'Yes, sir, but—'

'You have eyes?'

'I beg pardon? Yes, but—'

'You have a mouth?'

'I beg pardon?'

'Read your notes of what they said.'

'Oh-h! Well, first of all, so far as I heard, he said to her— No; first of all she said to him—'

'Your time is up,' said the exchange lady.

'More,' said Reginald.

'I'm sorry. But you've had six minutes, and the line—'

Reginald fisted a pen-tray.

'I've quite enough to contend with as it is. If I have any miouwing from you, by Christopher, I'll have you kicked clean out. You be careful who you're dealing with.'

'Don't be cross with him,' said Louise. 'He's doing his best I'm sure.'

Reginald shot out a forefinger.

'Out of this room with you, into the passage, until I've finished, or I'll put you there, you flickering poll-parrot.'

'Reggy!'

'Now! You! Hallo, there! Connect me, will you!' Bang, bang, bang, bang, with his fingers on the telephone lever. 'You, I say! At the exchange!'

From the bowels of the telephone system, echoed sounds appalling and ear-splitting. Then a lusty masculine voice,

'Hallo, Billy, old bean! That you?'

He was near the end of his tether – his collar was no longer a collar. His face was purple. Even Louise shrank towards the doorway. He gathered himself for a final effort. The fist which held the receiver to his ear shook with passion.

'You! Woman at the exchange! Remove this howling cad.'

To him, by some mechanical fluke, replied the voice of Berty gabbling the dire secrets of the note-book. Reginald cut him short and bade the palsied youth begin again.

A deadly silencing malignity seemed to quell him now, as he listened, crouched, attentive, like some gigantic beast of prey in that most menacing moment before the deadly plunge. His breath came in long, whistling snuffles through his enlarged nostrils. His eyes bulged. Throbs shook his pendulous multiplicity of chin. Occasionally he said, 'Go on!' in a voice which vibrated with arduous restraint.

Berty concluded. 'That's all, sir, as far as I heard.'

Still exercising great restraint, Reginald managed to put a few further questions. This woman – the caretaker woman? Would she give the alarm? Oh, no. She seemed quite averse to the whole thing. The couple sounded as though it was their intention to remain at the cottage for the present? Oh, most decidedly. They seemed to be there for – well, some time. They would hardly have gone to bed otherwise. Then followed orders, issued in a tone which brooked no disobedience. Berty was to stay where he was. Where was he? At the what – the Ring of Bells Hotel, South Ditherton. Very well, then. He was to remain there, and to await the arrival of the speaker who would proceed down immediately by road. Berty sighed deeply to hear this, but did himself more harm than good by sighing.

'Well, there? Hallo, I say! Do you hear me?'

'Yes, sir, I—'

'And you will do what I tell you?'

'Yes; oh, yes. Very well.'

'Then say so. Don't make flute noises at me, but say so.'

'Yes, yes. Very well, sir. All right.'

'H'm. Then see to it.'

He crashed home the receiver, and turned.

Then burst the storm. A poor minor effort still rumbled in

the heavens. He put it to shame. He pounded the table with his fist. The pen-tray leapt into the air. He flung to his feet, overturning his chair. Fury, like an evil spirit, possessed and flooded him.

'What have I married?' he shouted. 'My saints, what thing have I married? A common baggage? An everyday, how-de-do, afternoon tart, my soul?' He beat the air with his raised fists.

'Reggy! Reggy, dear . . .'

'Don't speak to me. Get your hat; you shall come with me to this place.'

'Yes, but what—?'

'Your hat!'

She fluttered to the doorway and hopped out of the room, like a bird escaping from captivity. He remained in the dining-room, terrible; a man in the full power of passion; destructive: the wrath throbbing and seething in him as the boiling water throbs and seethes in a cauldron. He snatched up his umbrella and threw it aside. Some papers lay on the dining-room table. He swept them to the floor with a fling of the arm. A little Pomeranian dog with a blue bow and a running nose – a perquisite of the cook's, who refused to remain in any situation without it – came, following the scent of strange boots, into the dining-room, and queried Reginald's feet. He shot a glance down at it, closed his eyes and took a wild kick at the dog, missed it and caught the leg of the table. He blundered fiercely round the room, pushing chairs aside; his fingers twitching at the ornaments.

Then, relieved at finding something to handle, he returned to the telephone. Called up his house at Prince's Gate. Infuriating delay and lever-banging. Then the voice of the cook.

'Well?'

'Don't you well me, or I'll send you neck and crop out of the house. It is Mr Bingham speaking.'

'Mr Bingham?' This was a startler for cook, but patently the truth.

'Yes; your master. And don't you forget it.'

He ordered the car to be ready and waiting for him within

five minutes. Was Wimble, the chauffeur, there? He was about the place. Lucky for Wimble. In five minutes. Outside the house. Flogged down the receiver again.

Willy, who had relied on the boat-train being punctual, chose this ill-timed moment to return to the flat. He heard his brother-in-law on the telephone in the dining-room. From his wife's room came the sound of drawers being busily exercised in their sockets. Thither, still in his dripping mackintosh, Willy proceeded.

'What's happened?' he asked.

'I'm going down to the place where Eleanor is. Reggy is going. He is furious. It's just as well I should go.'

'But – what information have you got?'

'Oh, don't you start worrying me with questions now.'

'No, but, dash it – if there's going to be a row—'

'Oh, there's going to be a row, all right,' replied Louise with a cold laugh for the excess of her triumph.

'Yes. Well, I don't see why you should be lugged into it. I won't have it. Dash it. I've stood a good deal—'

'I've no time to waste in arguing.'

'All very well. This may lead to devilish trouble. It's all pure surmise.'

'Indeed, it is no such thing. Do you think I haven't made sure?'

'How have you made sure?'

'I sent down and found out.'

'What? Sent down? Sent who down?'

'I took what steps I thought fit. Don't you begin—'

'Who did you send? Come on, now. This is going to lead to an infernal family rumpus, and I jolly well intend to know what's been going on.'

'If you want to know what's going on, you'd better ask Reggy. He's just been told on the telephone.'

'Who by?'

'The person I sent.'

'Who?'

'I sent Berty Pitts.'

'What!'

'Oh, don't stand in the way. I'm in a hurry.'

'You needn't hurry,' said Willy. 'You're not going.'

'I am going.'

'Are you! I've put up with a good deal. You're not going. You've done harm enough. You mean to tell me you actually sent that—'

'Louise!' bawled Reginald from the dining-room. 'Will you hurry yourself!'

'I'm coming now.'

'You're not,' said Willy. 'By gosh, I've stuck a good deal. I'm going to see that you—'

She hurried past him down the passage and into the dining-room, Willy at her heels. The latter gained the front door. Next moment Reginald came sailing down upon him from the dining-room, his hat crushed upon his head, his umbrella gripped by its middle. Willy stood firm.

'Look here, Reggy; I've just heard what Louise has been doing and I object. I won't have her drawn any further into this, and I won't have her go down with you. So you can—'

Reginald heaved back his mountain of chest.

'Out of my road, you blot!' he roared; and seizing Willy by the arm, he flung him into the umbrella stand.

Next moment the door was hurled back on its hinges. Louise scuttled past and through; then Reginald. Bang! the door. By the time Willy had picked himself up and opened it again, they were downstairs.

The injured husband hurried to the dining-room window just in time to see a taxi splashing away from the front door through the rain.

'Oh very well, then,' said Willy, undefeated.

He turned to the devastated writing-table, and from a leather rack pulled out a Bradshaw's Guide. From beneath the sanctuary of the sideboard, the little dog, still quivering like a released spring, watched him with rolling eyes.

CHAPTER XIV

Another Telegram in Another Bosom

Eleanor's guardian angel lay stunned and derelict somewhere on the Bath Road. She had decided that his services would not be required this evening. Indeed, she was taking good care to see that he did not press them upon her.

This was one of the occasions on which she meant to go full tilt for folly and hang the consequences! She looked as though she had experienced this mood before. We, who have credited her with having come in innocence to Reginald's arms – without actual previous inquiry into those things that Mother knows – might glance at her now, and wonder whether we had not been flattering her.

Have we, in this surmise, flattered her? Of course, we know that she leant instinctively toward honour for the most part; but even this she did spasmodically rather – a creature of impulse, whatever the motive, good or bad. Her girlhood had been an orphaned, inefficiently guarded, indefinite, shadowy period. Some of these continental finishing schools, my hat! She finished her education pretty wise, I'll warrant.

Then there is that quick turn of her head towards excitement; that keen appetite for the new experience, the new plaything. That had been in her nature from the first; nor rested content, surely, with the latest style in shingling and Paris models? We know the fascination she held for the subservient sex. Reginald himself had to swim through a sea of flannel bags to get at her.

Suppose then that she had, in her time, ventured to the tree of the knowledge of good and evil, and plucked an apple or two. Did she steal there, with guilt thumping in her bosom and with eyes side-to-side in conscience-stricken care? Not she. She would have been caught up in a whirl of recklessness, into a mood of devil-may-care (and he did, I expect) jubilant folly. Knowing what she did to be wrong, but feeling that somehow it didn't matter if it was wrong, because she was not her ordinary good self and hadn't to worry whether it was wrong or not. A sort of abandoned holiday of the soul.

And she was, all the time, a woman who had strong, eager moments of resistance and regret. But not for one of these lapses. She'd look back at them with bewilderment at herself, but not with remorse. Any little act of unkindness or ill-temper would bring her twice as much mortification. I daresay that you yourself have had a bite at the fruit of the tree now and again, and can understand.

If then, she had erred (which is only guesswork) she had done so in this mood, and this was the mood that was with her now. She was full tilt for the tree. In high spirits, and with only a laugh for the rain and the discomforts of her drive. And looking her best – weather-nipped in the cheeks.

They arrived at Algy's rooms at five-thirty.

Algy said he had better take the car along and garage it. He had been warned not to leave it knocking about in Half Moon Street, and he had good reason to avoid being taken an interest in by the police force. So the hall-porter removed Eleanor's luggage and showed her upstairs, where Lemon, in body, if not in spirit, hovered in the passage.

Algy sent up a message that tea was to be made, and that he himself would purchase eatables. So Lemon made tea in his pantry, and Eleanor went into the bedroom and removed her top coat and powdered her nose and pulled about the side bits of her hair.

A cheerfully masculine bedroom. Plain, serviceable furniture and accessories; nothing dainty or trifling. No pictures of the Kirchner school, or young ladies stripped to the waist in order to stroke cats ('Puss-Puss') or to eat cherries ('Cherry Ripe'). Instead, school groups – 'Myself when young,' Algy would say, 'eagerly frequenting.' Cricket gear in the corner. The pyjamas on the bed expensive silk pyjamas, but made for the sake of comfort, rather than for the sake of art. The very toothbrush on the glass ledge of the washing-stand was a big, male toothbrush.

A door led direct from the bedroom to the sitting-room,

whither Eleanor repaired. Another eminently manly room very modern; not overfilled with furniture. A Chesterfield sofa, turned from the fireplace to a more sociable angle during the summer months – an ample sideboard for a room in which breakfast was the only meal usually partaken of. Book-cases – pipe-racks. The pictures – a drawing of the Grand National, and a portrait study of the interior of the National Sporting Club during a bout. Some Bateman proofs and some caricatures of celebrities of the sporting world and the musical comedy stage. Golf clubs lying on the top of one of the book-cases – a man's rooms.

Eleanor sat on the sofa, very settled in attitude, but with just a thought of speculation in her bright eyes as they looked around her.

Too manly? Too – too cricketing? He had his common lapses, of course; she knew that. But to her in this, her mood of danger (and welcoming the danger and ready to court any trouble) would he say, 'No, dash it, Eleanor – we may be pretty wild people at times, but don't lose your head, old Elly, you funny old darling.' A nod from him, and she was lost, and she craved the nod just now. Full tilt. Constraint and heed were like the thunder murmuring away up there – a great way off; off the earth. But he—?

He had approached the subject sometimes himself – with a look of bland mischief in those big surprised eyes of his. That morning in the Twiggs', for instance, he had approached the subject, but only in chaff, it seemed. *Was* it only chaff? Diana had accused him flatly; there could be no two constructions put upon what she was driving at. But he had taken her insults with a 'pooh' – as though they were just preposterous, sisterly stuff and not worth denying.

Thus, speculation in the eyes of Eleanor; but not slow, amused speculation; animated, provocative. He might begin to talk about consequences. Well, she wasn't reckoning the consequence, but anyhow, she'd stand the racket. It should be her funeral – not his. There would be no publicity about it in any case. Reggy was not the man to advertise his own inefficiency and failure as a husband. Algy might argue, 'But you don't love me.' Oh, love! Whom did she love? She'd cut herself adrift from love when she married. Regret? She'd feel no regret at all. She'd resisted, and with what results? Here was her husband in heavy mistrust, consigning her to Louise – Louise longing, plotting, to drive her into indiscretion. She held back, just to spite Louise, only to find Diana branding and scolding already, and this aunt of Algy's snorting at her foregone conclusions. Well, confound it, if she were going to be stoned, in any case, she might as well have her fling too. Convenient argument! Oh, but what mattered reasons and arguments and counter-accusations now? And resistance and pride? Full tilt and be hanged to them!

Lemon floated in and out of the room with his tea-cloth and crockery. Eleanor had learnt of his cause for anxiety from Algy in the course of casual conversation. She made inquiries in the always rather diffident tone with which the unmotherly woman approaches the subject of birth. Lemon thanked her in a hushed melancholy.

'Thank you, madam. Very patient. Her mother is with her – a knowing one, she is. Tonight, if not sooner, is her forecast. It's certainly a very trying time for the husband.'

When Algy came in, Lemon caught him in the passage while he was removing his mackintosh. Mrs Krabbe had twice rung up to know whether he had arrived back yet. She requested that he would telephone her directly he came in.

'Oho!' said Algy. 'How did she know I was coming back today? You didn't tell her, Lemon?'

'Oh, no, sir.'

'Ah, I see. Righto. I may ring through. Don't worry any more about that. Here, take this tea-fodder.'

He entered the sitting-room, and was greeted by Eleanor's brightest smile. She looked very much at home.

'Diana's been busy,' he said, 'wiring Auntie all about us.'

'I don't mind who she wires or what she wires,' said Eleanor.

'Silly little ass,' said Algy, drawing a chair up to the tea-table. 'Well, what's the programme, old thing?'

She raised her eyebrows. 'I don't mind. I shall take my luggage back home by-and-by, and dress. I've only country stuff with me. Besides, I should love Louise to find out I'm back in town, and I expect since collaring that note she's bribed my maids to hand on any information they get. Kind of thing she would do. Anyhow, then I'll join you again here, and we'll dine and dance. Oh, I'm going to get 'em guessing; I told you. If I were sure Louise knew I was back, I'd stay out all night.'

'I'm blowed if I'd worry about Louise any more.'

'I'm only worrying about galling her. How about your wise old aunt?'

'Poor old Auntie,' said Algy. 'She's generally pretty shrewd over these affairs, too.'

'Is she still inclined to butt in?'

He nodded.

Eleanor stretched back complacently on the sofa.

'If she's going to keep me from enjoying myself tonight, she's got her work cut out,' she said.

'Not knowing you properly,' said Algy, 'she very likely misjudges your range of enjoyment.'

'P'raps she doesn't,' replied Eleanor, not looking at him.

'What?'

'P'raps she's seen Reggy once or twice. It wouldn't take a very experienced woman to predict what'll happen to Reggy's wife in the end.'

Algy glanced at her without making any comment on this. She met his eyes, and smiled quickly. Lemon entered with the tea, which she welcomed with a little exclamation of gratitude. She left the sofa and took a chair beside Algy at the table. When Lemon departed, Algy made no attempt to return to the former conversation. She noticed that. She noticed, too, that her remark had not been lost on him. He was, for once, during the meal a trifle self-conscious with her, talking his nonsense with a suggestion of artificiality. A young man entertaining a girl to tea at his rooms, as it were. Not quite Algy and Elly. And it only wanted a nod from him – and—

But before they had progressed very far with their tea, there came a ring at the electric bell of the front door.

'Hallo!' said Algy. 'Who's this, I wonder?'

'I don't care,' said Eleanor, in the sing-song monotone in which people do not care.

'It's either Auntie or a summons for Lemon.'

The ring was repeated before Lemon (and he was not slow to respond) could, by any physical possibility, make more than three yards of passage.

'It's Auntie, then,' added Algy.

It was Auntie. She made no inquiries of Lemon. She came and inserted a Roman nose into the sitting-room.

'M'hm,' she said, as though confirming a suspicion, and advanced. She had braved the rain in a black-and-white striped georgette frock, and a hat trimmed with roses. She drew after her by a leader a very miniature and tinkling Skye terrier.

'I suppose you don't mind my bringing Beckett,' she said.

'He'll be quite safe,' said Algy. 'We have no mice. May I—?'

'And so this is Mrs Thing,' said Mrs Krabbe, with a nod at Eleanor. 'Yes, I believe I've seen you before.'

As a rule Eleanor might have been rather amused by the unlikely experience of finding herself a mere impression of a former meeting, but, in her present mood, Mrs Krabbe was asking for it.

'Yes,' replied Eleanor. 'And now that you've heard I'm going to the devil, I suppose you'll have to make up your mind to see me pretty frequently.'

Mrs Krabbe sat on the sofa in a manner which suggested that to do so strained her amidships, which it did. She spoke in a modulated tone of hoarse nonchalance.

'I don't care a gnats' fleabite where *you* go,' she began, but Algy chimed in.

'Oh, I say, this is a nice matey little greeting. Let sisterly love continue, girls. This is not Louis Wain's Almanac, or anything of that sort.'

'I've come, if you want to know, on a most friendly mission,' said Mrs Krabbe.

'Well, break the news gently,' said Algy. 'I didn't even have time to begin to say, "Mrs Krabbe – Mrs Bingham," before you flew at her like an angry ginger tom and bitter end.'

'To be candid with myself as well as with you,' proceeded Mrs Krabbe, addressing Eleanor, 'I was rather jealous of your friendship with Algy, but he tells me it's quite a Platonic affair, so now I don't mind. You see, I rather count on his going out with me on certain evenings, and tonight happens to be one of them. And now, of course, as it's purely a Platonic business, he will be able to come out with me.'

'Indeed?' said Eleanor. 'Well, well. I suppose it's more difficult to remain Platonic after dark, especially in the summer time. In fact, it may be impossible. But we can let you know definitely tomorrow morning.'

'To which,' said Algy, 'Auntie, arching her back, and twitching her whiskers, replies—?'

'You don't quite see what I'm driving at,' said Mrs Krabbe. 'There'll be no competition for Algy tonight.'

'I know there won't,' put in Eleanor.

'Because, if you're merely a nice, kind, Platonic, married friend,' went on Mrs Krabbe, 'you'll be out of that chair and on your way home directly you've finished your tea, if not sooner.'

'Well, presently, yes; I know I shall. To dress for tonight.'

'Oh, no,' said Mrs Krabbe. 'To meet your husband. He's coming back from abroad today.'

Eleanor looked at her suddenly – startled. It was possible; that was why she jumped. It was almost likely, if Louise had forwarded that note. But how on earth should this old woman know?

Algy pushed his cup across the table for more tea.

'Auntie, darling,' he said, 'you lie in your teeth, which I shouldn't do, because they must be awfully uncomfortable to lie in. I've seen them in the tumbler.'

Mrs Krabbe's reply was to crush her chin to her chest and, gazing downwards, to fumble in the folds of her bosom. She, at length, produced a creased telegram, which she unfolded with a good deal of blowing at the edges. She then ferreted in her vanity-bag for her eyeglass.

' "Have heard husband returning unexpectedly today –

inform them if possible – Diana,"' she read, and exhibited the telegram aloft like an auctioneer.

'Diana,' exclaimed Eleanor. 'Where can she have heard that?'

Algy frowned in silence at the waving danger signal; then at Eleanor; then at his Aunt, who made an elaborate Gallic gesture of incomprehension.

'I don't know how she found out,' she said, 'but Diana wouldn't tell a lie.'

'She hasn't got the brain to invent this one, anyhow; that's the point,' said Algy.

Eleanor had recovered her composure and was pouring out his tea.

'Probably Diana got a wire addressed to me, and opened it—'

'A wire, who from?' said Algy.

'From her husband, I suppose,' said Mrs Krabbe, readily. 'After all, if a husband comes home unexpectedly from abroad, he usually wires his wife, doesn't he?'

This was received in silence. Mrs Krabbe rose from the sofa. 'Especially,' she added, casually, 'when the wife is a good-natured, Platonic sort of person, who is very likely being kind to someone else while the husband isn't there for her to make a fuss of.'

She retired towards the door, in a stately and deliberately sweeping movement like that of a sailing vessel, with Beckett, a small rowing-boat, in tow.

'Well, I've got a taxi waiting,' she said. 'I'll call for you at the usual time,' she added to Algy, who rose.

'No!' This was Eleanor. Mrs Krabbe hove to and tacked. 'If that news is true,' said Eleanor with animation, 'it decides me. I was going home before. Now I'm not.'

'I suppose,' said Mrs Krabbe, musingly, 'that no one in this world has had his name taken in vain more systematically than this poor devil, Plato. Whoever *he* was.'

'You don't understand. My sister-in-law has been trying to make mischief about me and Algy. That's the meaning of my husband coming home. All right, then they shall jolly well have a run for their money.'

'I see,' said Mrs Krabbe. 'And what does Algy stand to win?'

'If Algy wasn't keen on my society, he'd say so.'

'So it's really only a bit of husband-baiting?'

'No. I'm going out with Algy, because I like going out with Algy. If my husband chooses to dash about to and fro the Continent to try and stop it, that's his concern.'

'But the fact remains, that you're giving, and trying to give, the impression of being naughty, and getting all the discredit for being naughty, without actually enjoying the pleasure of the naughtiness. Well, I've heard of a few mug's games, but I think this returns the penny.'

She turned again to the doorway, but once more veered.

'And, in any case,' she added, 'whether that's the game or the other thing, you might show a little more consideration for Algy. I don't like to see young men spending their time in a manner calculated to rob them of their self-respect; so you'd better leave him to me. *I'm* only going to take him to a gambling hell.'

'If I'm the blighter with the apple,' said Algy, 'Venus wins on this occasion. Sorry, Auntie.'

'Am I Venus?' asked Mrs Krabbe.

'No,' said Algy.

'I thought not,' said Mrs Krabbe. 'Well, if Venus's husband calls round and takes her home, I shall be going to Shady Nook at about tenish. I've ordered a car.'

She departed.

Algy smiled and waved her off the premises, and returned to Eleanor.

'Poor old Auntie,' he said. 'She's got a good chance. By golly, though, how damned mean – all this sneaking home after you, and trying to catch you unawares. Unless I'm doing the gentleman an injustice and he's wired you at Diana's to come home, and that's how Diana found out. That may be it. But think of it, anyhow. Louise sending on that note to him. He, instead of telling her to go to hell, as any decent husband would do, comes crawling back without a word to you. My word, poor old Elly, you *have* struck it rich. I thought you were out for a bit of fun and couldn't get any at home, but – you certainly have got some provocation if this is the sort of stuff you're up against. Of course he *may* have wired to the cottage. Still, in any case, fancy coming home on the word of a nasty sister who pinches notes in the wrong hand-bag. My golly, what people! I suppose Diana *didn't* get an inspiration and invent his home-coming to suit her own ends. Oh, no. That's altogether too Machiavellian for Diana. Still, who the deuce can she have heard from?'

Eleanor let him babble on, while not insensible of his more lively sympathy. She sat with her eyes fixed on the book-case behind Algy, and her lips held in an introspective smile. After a little while, she aroused herself and returned to the sofa. Algy stretched himself, and glanced at his watch.

'I suppose you mean that – when you said you weren't going home?' he asked.

'I'm not going home to find him there,' said Eleanor. 'He's got to leave home to find me now.'

He nodded. 'And as for all that chat about me, and doing me an injustice, and all that nitrogen of Auntie's and Diana's you needn't—'

'If I thought that was true, I *would* go home,' she said.

'It isn't true,' said Algy. 'It isn't true – there! Only what are we going to do about your evening things? You'd better ring up for them to be sent here, or send Lemon for them.'

'No. Don't you see, if it's true that Reggy's home, it alters things. I wouldn't have minded Louise finding out that I was back in town, and in your rooms – that would have been great. But if Reggy knew, he'd come round here and spoil our fun. And I've got a very pretty evening frock with me that I took to Diana's. Not the one I wanted to wear, but never mind, it'll do. And my jewellery.'

'Well, there you are then. You can dress here, of course. But he's bound to find out you're in town before long, and he'll know where to find you, so we must be prepared for him to come steaming in.'

'If he does,' said Eleanor, 'I'll make a point of being half-dressed in your bedroom at the time. But, if you ask me, I think he's much more likely to dash off down to April Cottage.'

'Oh, what a glorious thought! But it looks as though Diana has let on that we're not there.'

'Oh, I don't know and I don't care,' cried Eleanor. 'I'm not going home till I'm taken home. And home and my husband and all that aren't my first consideration at all just now.'

She paused for a moment, then turned to him very earnestly.

'Algy, you know me. You know I wouldn't chuck a home where I could be happy, or a husband who was reasonably fond of me. But – oh, I don't know. I suppose I'm one of those bad characters who can only find happiness in enjoyment. I told you a lie just now, Algy.'

'What?'

'I said if I didn't think it was fair to you I'd go home. I was only thinking of myself. I felt as if something said, "You've got a chance of happiness. You're always saying you can't get the happiness you want. Well, here you are. Don't let it go." But it *isn't* fair to you. I know it isn't. I know in my heart it isn't. Unless you – unless you . . .'

He caught her hand quickly. She looked up, right into his eyes; not pleadingly, not enticingly, but as a woman looks at a man when they are of one mind and trying to make a decision.

'Do you mean it, Elly?' he asked.

'Do you? Do you?' she answered.

A nod and she was . . .

He nodded; so slight a nod that it was scarcely more than a smile.

'Kiss me,' she said.

He kissed her.

CHAPTER XV

Burden on Two Strings

Muriel, daughter of rumour, gave a sustained performance of that facial feat, which was so like the opening of a box, as she lingered in the passage of the *Ring o' Bells,* and happened to overhear a good deal of what Mr Berty Pitts had to say on the telephone. She remained close to the door of the office-parlour, held by attentive and eye-contracting suspicion.

This person had been to the cottage, and was now repeating information which might refer to her stout gentleman. If so, it was hardly credible that the information was the truth. It might, of course, refer to the first, sporty, younger gent who had stayed at the *Ring o' Bells* the night before. If so, what of the stout one? No mention of him that Muriel could hear, and she didn't miss much.

If her stout one had been followed and spied on, and was now being lied about, Muriel decided that it would be acting dishonourably to stand there, and listen without following up this advantage by further investigations. Perhaps, if Muriel had searched her heart, she would have discovered that her prevailing prompting was a mild attack of jealousy. It could not, it could not be true that her stout one had parted from her company, only to share the bed of the cottage lady. Never! His questions had not pointed to any such intention. It couldn't be him that this telephoning person was after telling of.

Still – she must investigate.

It so happened that, just as Muriel ceased to happen to catch what the person was saying on the telephone, Mr Plum came into the passage from the bar. He had a letter for the evening post, and Muriel had better run along to the post-office with it. Incidentally, for the first time at South Ditherton since about ten clock that morning, it had stopped raining.

Muriel took charge of the letter, but waited until Berty had finished his conversation before she set out. She offered to return his bicycle for him to Mrs Leake's. He readily accepted, and, informing her that he would be at the hotel for dinner, if not for the whole night, wearily took the hint furnished by a sketch of an unproportionate hand with the nails thickly outlined in black, which pointed upwards from the wall at the foot of the staircase with the legend beneath it, 'To Lounge.'

As a daughter of rumour, Muriel naturally knew the ropes with regard to the dissemination of local news. Mrs Leake was not a daughter of rumour. She was the mother of rumour.

Mrs Leake's cycle shop was next door but one to the post-office, and on occasions when lack of custom made it unnecessary for her to mind her own business, she would often just pop in to see her friend, Miss Frisby, and to mind other people's. Today, under skies depositing rain upon the earth as from a bucket, there had been no very marked activity in the world of cycling; but the same cause had prevented Mrs Leake from undertaking a pop. Now, at least, that the rain held off, she popped in no time.

Now, Heaven defend the fair name of Miss Frisby, but no one could deny that Mrs Leake possessed an amazing gift of divination concerning current local happenings. Particularly did this apply to matters important enough to warrant the reception or despatch of telegrams. She made no secret of her powers. Having popped into the post-office and sensed the day's news, she was always willing to hand it on to the less visionary world at large. On one occasion, Miss Huddle, leaving the cycle shop with an inflated tyre, had paused to congratulate old Mr Body on the birth of a grandchild, long before the telegraph boy had stunted his red bicycle to the bewildered old gentleman's cottage.

This evening, Chool provided an unusual field for the clairvoyance of Mrs Leake. She 'obtained' a remarkable message which had been sent off much earlier in the day by Mrs Easy to Mr Hole. So many hours had elapsed since its sending, that the spirits were naturally inclined to be a little bit vague as to detail, but the message undoubtedly attributed the most shameless conduct to the young lady who had taken over the cottage. She, herself, had been in and sent off a wire or two; the latest only half-an-hour or so ago. But her messages had been comparatively trivial and pointless, and were not considered to be worth Mrs Leake's while to get into communication about.

Mrs Leake returned to her cycle shop sorely vexed that she had not held a séance before the young man with the rabbit teeth had called and hired his bicycle to go to the cottage. He must be in it, whatever it was. Was he the lover expected? He had no luggage, but perhaps he had sent that in advance. Probably this evening, he had said, he would return the bicycle. That didn't sound like a very thorough – er – well, visit.

Just inside the cycle-shop she found Muriel with the bicycle. With a regal beam of welcome she bundled the girl into her private room, and sat her down. There, head to head, they exchanged their respective solid facts and electro-biology.

'She wer' in the town half-an-hour ago?' exclaimed Muriel, presently. 'Oh, but that can't well be, Mrs Leake. Not if what he said on that ther' phoon wer' the truth. She'd never have had the time. It can't be her he spoke of.'

'There was another woman come to the cottage yesterday,' returned Mrs Leake. 'It was driving back from driving her there that young Pawley drove into the War Memorium.'

'Ah, I toold you, Mrs Leake. That wer' the one that the sporty one drove back to the hotel this mornin'. And then, this new one say on the 'phoon that ther' was oonly the two at the cottage in bed, with another that I take him to mean to be Mrs Easy also ther'; but not in with 'em.'

Mrs Leake screwed her face into an expression suggestive of necromancy, but was much too far from the post-office to hope to get any definite results.

'This new one's lying, and that's my opinion,' said Muriel, not without heat. 'And if she wer' in the town oonly half-an-hour ago, that proves it. And no one ain't got no right for to poke their noses and tell lies about it over so nice a gent as the fatty one I spoke of. I have a mind to see further into it, I have. Mrs Leake, if I could get leave for to go out for a while tonight, would you lend me a bicycle?'

'You shall have the *Sunbeam*,' said Mrs Leake, 'the *Sunbeam*, you shall have. Only mind you bring it back directly you've heard what's what. You may take it with you now.'

'Thank you,' said Muriel. 'If I can manage, I shall get out to Chool, and speak to Mrs Easy. I'll take it in a minute, Mrs Leake. I've just got a letter to poost.'

'Very well, then,' said Mrs Leake. 'If you see Miss Frisby, you needn't go telling her that I've told you I know what was in Mrs Easy's telegram. I like to have facts cut and dried before I make mention of things. Otherwise it's mere gossip, which I dislike and will never consent to be a party to it.'

Out at Chool, Mrs Easy heard the sound of prodigious motoring, and ran to her cottage door. She caught sight of the vehicle as it thumped away in an easterly direction. Pitcher's van! But why on the Chool Road? She knew where the van was bound for – Marchant's farm. Mrs Marchant had bought some things at an auction, and was expecting delivery. But Marchant's farm was on the upper main road. Did this mean more luxuries from Pitcher's for April Cottage? H'm. If so, a nice condition the occupants would have been in to receive them.

Mrs Easy's attention was distracted from the problem of Pitcher's van by little Easy, who had been unable to resist the undoubtedly pressing temptation of venturing into the road and indulging in the priceless sport of puddle-kicking. Mrs Easy regained him, gave him one for himself, and put him to bed to avoid the trouble of changing his footgear.

But even as the steam from the sodden vale arose with the evening, and floated before the portals of April Cottage, so from the mind of Mrs Easy there continued to arise and float in the same direction the mists of sullen conjecture and still inquisitive derision. Already, perhaps, Mr Hole would have received the detective's report. Oh, if only the orgy might in blissful ignorance be continued until the devastating old gentleman himself arrived like a cleansing sheet of flame to purge his corrupted premises! And oh, that Mrs Easy might be there to see!

All the way from Harrogate to Peterborough, and from Peterborough to London, the mind of the avenger himself kept returning to this scarcely conceivable behaviour on the part of his one trusted niece. It only proved what he had always contended – that there was not one woman in the world, not one, from Caesar's wife downwards, who was really above suspicion. Most people who express themselves chiefly in superlatives are poseurs; and the most bigoted poseur is the one who relies, for preference, upon his own company. Deep in the heart of old Mr Hole there was a little tender spot for our Diana.

But either she or Mrs Easy was up to mischief. And mischief at April Cottage – it was only a question of how quickly he could get there. Two or three times in the course of his journey he worried, like a terrier at a hole, at his pockets, and re-read Mrs Easy's telegram. A young man – a double bed – wine? Diana? incredible! By all the bachelors of threescore, if Mrs Easy had lied ... The official promenading the train for tickets, discovered Mr Hole in the act of imagining what might happen to Mrs Easy if she had lied, and told the guard he had better have an eye to him from time to time.

This of Diana! Incredible! He might have believed it readily enough of any other woman – But Diana ...

Wait! This blasted train got to London at what time? Seven-ten. The Bristol train left Paddington at eight. Fifty minutes. He must wire for a car to meet him at Bristol to drive him to Chool. Apart from sending the wire, he would have ample time, provided the confounded train was punctual, to make any investigations that might assist him to form a definite idea of what was going on at April Cottage. That young fool, Diana's brother, lived within calling distance. He might know something. What was his address?

Ah, that could be discovered from a telephone directory. Even if it were true, and Diana were up to some inconceivable mischief at the cottage, it would be too late for her brother to issue a warning. On the other hand, some gleam of enlightenment might be forthcoming, even from so utter a young beetlehead as this Algy. Yes; he'd call at his rooms.

From London to South Ditherton was already coursing that magnificent car which had been bought to gratify Eleanor. It was progressing along the slippery roads at a pace too fast to please Louise, who had forgotten, in the haste of departure, to bring any Busby's Nerve Pills, of which it looked as if she might require a good many by the time she got home again. The pace of the car was, however, too cautious for Reginald, who shifted impatiently in his seat every time it unavoidably slackened. His passion had given place to a dour, heavy, glaring churlishness.

Between little jerks and gasps of apprehension for her safety, Louise gave him a detailed and somewhat self-defensive account of what had occurred in his absence. He commented but little, and then, for the most part, in muttered apostrophe:

'Common rampant intrigue! This goat; I'll settle his hash. Shameless, scheming skit – by Christopher – we shall see!'

Only when Louise unwisely overdid the self-justification did he flare once more into open rage.

'Blame you! Of course I blame you. Undoubtedly. I put her under your charge, didn't I? Not out of your sight, I said. And here's the sequel. I come home to find her gutting in some stew-house of her own with this fish. Not your fault, indeed – you gull! You'd better stop that.'

'I don't know how you imagine I was going to keep her in sight, while I sat in a dentist's chair . . .'

'That'll do. If you think I'm in the mood for pantaloonery, you'd better think twice.'

'You're in a very disagreeable mood, anyhow,' said Louise.

'Thank you,' said Reginald. 'If you came with me, expecting to hear me give a Christy minstrel entertainment on the way down to this cottage, I'm afraid you'll be very disappointed.'

She made bold, however, to insist on their halting for food by-and-by. He, frowning at his watch and blowing through his nose, consented. Truth to tell, he was very spent. For a record of the meal one should apply to a certain whiskered waiter at a roadside hotel, to whom its details will ever remain graven upon the memory.

Their far objective, the *Ring o' Bells* at South Ditherton, pursued the even tenor of its evening way, untroubled by the impending visitation. Apart from the tap-room, from which there came, like the sound of the sea on shingle, the continuous vibration of Somersetshire debate, the hotel had only one visitor. The lounge was not rich in comfort or interest, especially when the occupant is condemned to remain therein for several hours, at the end of which time the change from monotony will probably be even more unpleasant than the monotony itself. Berty found little pleasure in sitting and gazing at a stuffed owl in a glass case on the mantelpiece, and a brilliantly-coloured portrait of Queen Victoria above it. He noticed that it had stopped raining, but was too weary to undertake further exercise. Fortunately, the lounge contained one or two books – some the property of the hotel, others evidently left behind by vanished patrons. The former were almost entirely religious, which, as we know, was extremely appropriate of them, in Berty's case. At the foot of the book-case, however, between 'Stepping-stones to Grace' and 'The Heaven of the Heart,' he discovered a coverless and derelict copy of 'The Confessions of Maria Monk,' and resought the hard horsehair of the lounge sofa, a trifle uplifted in spirit.

'Are you better?' asked Diana, looking in at the bedroom on her return.

Henry turned a sleepy smile in her direction.

'Oh, much better You know, I don't think I've really broken anything. I think it's just a sprain. Is the doctor coming?'

'I hope so.' Diana crossed instinctively to the dressing-table and had a look at herself. Then she came back to the bed, sat and recounted the episode of Wotan. 'But I told the old driver to call at the doctor's again to make sure,' she concluded. 'So he's sure to come along soon. I think I'll wait and let him come before I start on the parlour. Besides, I haven't had any tea yet, nor have you.'

'I've managed without tea,' he said. 'I never knew I could drink so much brandy without showing it. But if you want tea, bring it up here and talk to me while you drink it. It's seemed a long, long time since you went away.'

'Well, I won't leave you again. I think I'll do without tea; it's so late. I shall have to light the kitchen fire, and get some dinner ready soon.'

'I'd rather have your company than your cooking,' he said. 'I've missed you, you know. Did you get wet?'

'Oh, I'm dry again by this time,' said Diana.

'Well, anyhow, I insist on your resting a little before dashing off into further domesticity. You can talk to me till the doctor comes.'

So she sat and talked with him, and once having commenced to sit and talk, sat and talked on for an unconsciously long time. He told her of his life in the East, of his many strange experiences and acquaintances. And, between the lines, he told her of his philosophical and charitable nature, of his readiness to understand and to help anyone who needed help, from an Eleanor to a little Easy. He did not appear to regard his willingness to assist his fellow-creatures as a virtue. He sighed over his reminiscences, as though such a trait had always been a weakness, and certainly a very great handicap. But in that hour he won Diana's heart; though, when at last she roused herself and went down to the kitchen, he lay and wondered fearfully whether he had bored her.

Meanwhile, what of the doctor?

Pitcher's driver, having delivered the goods bought at auction by Mrs Marchant (Mrs Easy was quite right), laboured back to South Ditherton and garaged the van. Pitcher's being closed by this time, he proceeded on foot to the doctor's and braved the canine citadel. He gained the front door in safety, and the cook, having by this time returned from the roof-mender's, interrogated him through a crack of the same, while keeping one or two dogs at bay in the hall with her feet.

' 'E be wanted,' said the driver, 'out at April Cottage o' Chool. The leddy ther' inform me that the gent ther' 'as hurrt his foot severe. She say she's ben 'ere once a'ready.'

The cook shook her head.

'Not to my knowledge. The doctor 'as been in and gorrn again. He had an important call to go off to Filcombe.'

The driver removed his cap and scratched his head with the hand that held it.

'Wull, all I can say is, when 'e coom back, tell he.'

'Very good, then,' said the cook. 'You'd better move off. I can't hold this dog back much longer.'

Diana lit her fire and did her cooking. The labour seemed light enough now, even to one who had had an arduous day and no tea. She took the meal upstairs, and they had their dinner together. Henry, though still in severe pain, was unable to recollect any meal so near his heart's desire.

Many hours of the long June daylight yet remained; but already, beneath the heavy skies, the spirit of evening seemed to hover over the valley. Diana's remaining duties threatened to outlast the daylight. She had to wash up the dinner things, to receive the doctor, possibly to arrange to receive and administer whatever the doctor prescribed for the foot, to clean out the parlour, and, for the second night in succession, to prepare her own bed in the parlour chair. But she didn't hurry away from the bedroom after dinner. Together they sat and talked on, and Henry, having now satisfied himself definitely that she was not bored, became quite open about the extraordinary attraction which he found in her.

She did not gainsay him; and when she was alone again in her kitchen-scullery, she found herself paying small heed to the washing-up.

'If Eleanor only loved Algy,' she thought, 'really *loved* him – would I have blamed her? Blamed her? I'd have helped her. No, I wouldn't; not this morning. But this evening I might have.

'If this man – this darling man – were married and unhappy, wouldn't I chuck all my principles and love him? No. I know what it is. You don't have to chuck your principles to get happiness; because, if you stick to your principles, happiness will come along all right one day.'

She began to sing over her washing-up. Henry heard her, and smiled in the throes of a foot-spasm. But Diana scarcely heard herself; was scarcely aware that she was singing.

Look here, upon this picture, and on this. Our Diana progressing through life down the middle of the road; a nice girl, dull in the opinion of many. Uninitiated until now in the universal theories of love and romance, but constant to their cause. And here is at last the one proverbial man, like a modern Lohengrin amazingly consummated, borne suddenly into her life and established, apparently more or less permanently, but without a hint of dishonour, in her bedroom.

Our Eleanor, dancing down the side of the road; a delightful girl, bright in the opinion of all. A cheerful infidel regarding the theories of love and romance. With no partner established in her bedroom, but herself surrendering to the first partner to hand and gaily established in his.

Even by their consorts you may know them – the orthodox, big-hearted Henry; the pleasurable, unstable Algy. And by their prosecutors – the one descending in the stern discipline of the uncle; the other in the jealous vengeance of the husband. True, both are at the moment consuming hot miles of pursuit towards the two places respectively occupied by each other's quarry; but this is Puck's contribution to our June day's work.

Diana – losing count of her plates, washing one twice, another not at all. Singing almost unconsciously, her pure heart full of this new and wonderful emotion of a happiness long dreamt-of, now rapturously fulfilled.

Eleanor – with one hand through the door of a young man's bedroom in the midst of her laughing toilet, and with the lips of the young man to the hand in the sitting-room.

Chool and Piccadilly. Two women. The only two there are.

PART THREE
Night of Mischief

CHAPTER XVI

Peregrinations of an Unwanted Man

Br-rr-rr – the electric bell of Algy's rooms, and the heart of Lemon leapt. He was just going to nip round home in any case, to see how things were going. But here was crisis brought to him.

He hurried to the door and presented a white face to the purple ditto of Mr Hole, whom Harrogate had failed to restore to a state of health conducive to stair-climbing.

'Is this where young Mr Gascoyne lives?'

'Yes, sir,' said Lemon.

'Is he here now?'

'No, sir.'

Mr Hole growled like a dog.

'He's jest this minute gone out to dinner,' said Lemon.

'What do you mean by just this minute?'

'Well, about five minutes ago, sir.'

'Then what the hell do you mean by saying just this minute? You don't say "My grandmother's cat is just this minute having kittens under my bed last Tuesday," do yer?'

'No sir—'

'No. However – he is in London?'

'Yes, sir.'

' 'M. You know who I am?'

'No, sir.'

'No. Well, I'm Mr Hole.'

'Mr—?'

'Mr Hole. Mister – mister – Hole – Hole. Mr Hole. His uncle.'

'Oh. Yes, sir.'

'Oh, yes. Now, look you here, do you know anything about April Cottage?'

'I beg pardon, sir?'

'Oh, my patience! Do – do – you – you—?'

'No, sir; I don't,' said Lemon.

'You know nothing about April Cottage?'

'No, sir.'

'You don't know who is there?'

'No, sir.'

'You know that my niece, Mr Gascoyne's sister, is there?'

'Yes, sir.'

'Then why did you say—?'

'Oh, I didn't—'

'You did.'

'Yes, sir – but – apart from Miss Richardson Gascoyne being there, I don't know anything about it.'

Mr Hole lowered his head, and fixed Lemon with a dreadful eye. He then consulted his watch.

'Oh, well,' he muttered, turning resignedly. 'I'm not surprised to hear that you don't. From the look of you I should think you know sweet salvation nothing about any damned thing on earth.'

Lemon was only too pleased to allow this disgruntled old gentleman to express any opinion of his capabilities he chose, so long as he cleared out. Quite enough to contend with apart from him. He felt instinctively that it would be courting trouble to admit that young Mr Richardson Gascoyne had returned from April Cottage that very afternoon, bringing with him another gentleman's wife. Better far to be called a fool and see the Uncle stumping away baffled down the staircase.

Quite enough to contend with. His young master had openly hinted that there was a possibility of the gentleman the lady belonged to arriving upon the scene. Mrs Krabbe, persistent in her inquisitions, would be certain to blow in again before long. Before long, too, unless he himself plucked up courage to creep round home and whisper awed inquiries of his mother-in-law, might come the boy from the mews below home, breathless in unnerving report.

So Lemon took a melancholy bowler hat and left the rooms. Just outside the house he encountered Denise, the maid of Mrs Krabbe, who assailed him like a hurricane. Madame was still uncertain as to whether she was to look for escort that night. Was Mr Gascoyne now at liberty? Oh, what, Mr Lemon, was this affair? Never before had Madame and Mr Gascoyne had a how-do-you-say tiff. She had been sent to obtain definite information regarding the operations of Mr Gascoyne. There was, Denise understood, another lady in the case; but by this time Madame was of the opinion that the other lady would have discovered that her goose had been cooked, to use the droll phrase of Madame.

'Well, if you take my advice, though don't say I said so,' replied Lemon, 'you'll tell the old lady that 'e's already gone out to dinner and is best left to his own intentions. So she'd best not send, call, nor 'phone any more to-night.'

Denise performed semaphore in Half Moon Street.

' 'Ere, don't start that,' said Lemon. 'People will think we're having words. You'd best run back and say there's no one in the rooms, and that's all you know. I've troubles enough of my own without none of yours.'

He went his way, peering anxiously ahead when he got to the corner, as though he half expected to see an open-air crèche set out in the middle of Curzon Street.

At the Marble Arch end of Park Lane the road was up. Mr Hole's taxi found itself, towards the conclusion of the rush hour, wedged three-quarters of the way down one of the longest queues of traffic that had ever been seen in that vicinity. Mr Hole extended his head through the window.

'Why didn't you go through the Park?'

The taxi-driver gradually inclined his ear.

'Eh?'

'Why – why – didn't – didn't—'

'I didn't know the road was up.'

'Of course it's up. Any fool could have told you that. Busiest time of the year, isn't it? No earthly reason for the road to be up, is there? No, then very well – up it goes. I've kept as clear of this blasted city all my life as I can, but I've learnt that much. And when they've got it down again they'll wait for another really busy season and then tar it. And if you don't get me to Paddington in time to catch the eight o'clock train, by Satan, I'll tar *you*.'

Outrageous state of affairs! He had wasted valuable time

in going all the way to that young booby's flat to interview a gaping and futile manservant. He had yet to send off a wire to Bristol for a car to meet him – good God! and it wouldn't be delivered now if he did send it. All he could do to catch the train, in any case. This mile of stinking motor 'buses! In maddening, jerking stages he progressed, finally to gain the foremost place in the queue and be held up by the fool policeman on duty, who seemed neither to know the urgency of Mr Hole's case, nor to be able to grasp it when informed.

By the time he reached Paddington Mr Hole was half-way through the window of the taxi, and shouting at any other vehicle or individual that appeared likely to thwart his progress. The big hand of the clock which faces the drive down to the station was quivering at the hour.

The name of Lemon's mother-in-law was Mrs Frush. Like serpents, such ladies may generally be classified with either the large, ponderous squashers or the nimble, poisonous stingers. Mrs Frush was a squasher.

Lemon found her in his living-room with an elbow on the table, reading the account of a murder in the evening paper. She exhibited a contented and confident inaction which drove the mild man almost to tears of rebuke. Mrs Lemon was in her room, into which he thrust an expression of terror-stricken inquiry.

'It isn't yet, Stan,' she murmured. 'You shall be sent for.'

Lemon returned to Mrs Frush in awful, confidential challenge.

' 'Ere,' he said. 'Is this all right?'

Mrs Frush took a brief reinforcement of stout.

' 'Usbands!' she soliloquized. 'Always the same the first time.'

'Well, when—?'

'It hasn't started, not proper yet. In about a couple of hours I shall look for it to be going nice. And the sooner the least seen of you, believe me, the better. I 'ave midwifed a dozen, to say nothink of bearing me own. You'd better get back to your valliting. You shall be let known.'

Ten minutes later Lemon was again holding his despondent head in his pantry.

The thunderstorm, moving in a sulky circle, had returned to London. Its ominous rumble could be heard in the far distance and at long intervals. The air was oppressive and very still.

Lemon presently held an inspection of his master's bedroom. Here was an ample opportunity for valliting. Both Eleanor and Algy had dressed therein in turn, and, apparently, in the carnival spirit in which one casts aside one's garments like cares and dons one's festival array. The bedroom was about as tidy as the bedroom of a couple of children who have just undressed for sea-bathing.

Lemon hesitated, however, to tidy the bedroom. So pointed a reminder of his chaperonage might be tactless. Shortly after he had cleared away the tea, he had been instructed to reclaim Mrs. Bingham's luggage from Dawkins, the hall porter, and he himself had assisted Algy to carry the portmanteau into the bedroom, where now it lay, open and ransacked. But there had been something in his master's manner which had suggested that Lemon had better consider himself, metaphorically, blindfolded during the portmanteau-to-bedroom-carrying episode. 'No,' reflected Lemon. 'I think this here bedroom had better remain a closed book to me.' The sitting-room was different. He removed the glasses and replaced the cocktail-shaker in the sideboard cupboard.

They dined at the Savoy. Never before had Eleanor looked so bewitched with pleasure. The evening costume designed for wear at Chool may have been a secondary effort, but would have supplied the cows and chickens with an experience very novel in the realm of Mr Hole; a beautifully-modelled gown of delphinium blue. Her pearl drop-earrings. And eyes that seemed to catch the lights and to shine back their revelry into Algy's. Which spake again.

If during tea they had not been quite Eleanor and Algy, they were not the old Eleanor and Algy now. Not so much easy conversation. None of Algy's precocities; and as for her, who would have believed that she had been restlessly awake in the early hours of this very morning in the megrims of discontent? Eagerly contented now. Her eyes were on his nearly all the time, laughing into his, but half-hidden by her long lashes. So peeps an expectant girl through her curtained window to greet her lover.

The band discoursed appropriately; not swaying, yearning strains, but the mettlesome infection of ragtime. Champagne went with this and went well; a clever vintage with just an added hint of frivolity in its bouquet. Moët.

They sat there until after nine o'clock, held by the transcendent fascination of the near future.

'What shall we do now?' said Algy. 'Stay here? Go on somewhere? It's still broad daylight. Somehow it seems too early to go to Ciro's yet. If we go there at all. Shall we pop round to the rooms and see whether there's any news and then go on somewhere?'

'All right,' said Eleanor. 'But I don't care whether there's any news or not.'

'I expect Lemon will be knocking around. I'll push him off and tell him he'd better stay at home tomorrow morning in the midst of his anxieties. Considerate, what? Besides, though as you say we don't care, it would be interesting to hear whether there have been any inquiries for you.'

'It's going to thunder and rain again,' said Eleanor, as they got into a taxi.

'That doesn't matter,' said Algy.

'Nothing matters,' she said, sitting erect and looking straight in front of her, but stretching a hand out to him. 'Nothing matters.'

Lemon heard the sound of Algy's key in the front door with a gape of apprehension. Back already? What was the etiquette of menservants in such a situation? Graceful and unbidden retirement? Or should he wait and put his master and himself to the embarrassment of respectively slinging and being slung from the scene?

Algy relieved his doubts – very tactfully, Lemon thought.

'Hallo, you still here, Lemon? Oh, well, Mrs Bingham and I are going out to dance directly; and we shall be late back, so, of course, you needn't stay. By the way, has anybody called here?'

'Your uncle, sir.'

'What!'

'Yes, sir. Soon after you'd gone.'

'My uncle? Are you sure?'

'He said so, sir. An elderly gentleman. Rather a – well, a trifle abrupt, sir.'

'That's he. But in London? What did he want?'

'He seemed to think there was something going on amiss at April Cottage, sir.'

'What! Who had he heard from?'

'I don't know, sir. But I think he's gone down there. Dawkins told me he had a taxi with luggage and told the man to drive to Paddington.'

Algy followed Eleanor into the sitting-room.

'You hear this? Uncle has been putting his ear to the ground too. Goodness knows how he discovered that we'd been using his cottage as a trysting-depot. We appear to be in the grip of the hidden hand. Anyhow, he's hiked off. There's that to be thankful for.'

'Strikes me that he'll walk into his cottage tonight and discover your sister entertaining my husband,' said Eleanor.

'By golly, it's Reggy's Waterloo, if he does,' predicted Algy. 'But how can this old man have smelt out trouble at the cottage? Tell me that.'

'Who knew his address?'

'Only Diana.'

'Well, there you are.'

'You don't mean to say that Diana has actually tried to rope in Uncle to stop us meeting?'

'I don't see why not. All the other members of both our families seem to be at the game. Perhaps Diana thought it was a shame that poor old Uncle should be left out.'

'Well, they've dished it up between them anyhow,' said Algy, returning to the passage. 'Lemon! Nobody else called?'

'Mrs Krabbe's maid, sir. I understand Mrs Krabbe still hopes that you may be able to go with her tonight. But I took the liberty of informing the maid that I thought most decidedly not, sir.'

'Oh, poor old lady,' sighed Algy. 'I'm afraid she's rather upset with me for once. She's perfectly certain to call in again herself. In fact, she said she would, at about ten. I think we'd better be out of the way by then. I tell you what, Lemon. You might wait here till she's called; and tell her that I have gone out dancing, and that I shan't be back till – oh – the early hours of the morning.'

'Very well, sir.'

'And then you can be off, if you like, Lemon. There'll be no need for you to be here. I shall be very late, and I can manage Mrs Bingham's luggage for her. And I expect there'll be plenty for you to do at home, so you needn't hurry here in the morning. I'll see to my own breakfast. Right you are then. Good luck, Lemon.'

He turned again to the sitting-room.

'I forgot,' he said. 'Auntie will be poking her nose in here again at any moment. We don't want any more fur flying. I think we'd better push off again right away.'

He glanced out into the passage. Lemon had retired to the pantry.

'Shall we?' he added. 'Just for a bit? The night is yet young. In fact, it hasn't started yet.'

She assented with a shrug and a smile.

'All right,' she said. 'Just for a bit.'

'Is Dawkins down there, Lemon?' called Algy.

'I don't know, sir. Shall I call you a taxi, sir?'

'Yes, please.'

They followed Lemon down. He was rather a long time getting the taxi, but at length as they waited in the doorway of the house a car drove up outside and they moved instinctively forward. The face of Mrs Krabbe peered at them from the interior of a hired limousine.

'Well?' she inquired through the open window. 'Was the telegram true?'

'I don't know,' said Eleanor.

'You needn't have called, Auntie, dear,' said Algy. 'I told you I was going dancing. Later on, when we've finished dancing, she'll be going home; so she'll be able to let you know tomorrow whether the telegram was true or not, if you're really as curious as all that.'

'Well, I call it very foolish tactics, that's all, and whatever you're up to,' said Mrs Krabbe. 'When my husband went abroad there was no knowing what I did. But I was always on the mat when he got home.'

'We're going to Ciro's,' said Eleanor. 'Perhaps he'll be there. He was last time.'

'H'm. Well, you know where *I'm* going,' said Mrs Krabbe.

'Yes,' replied Algy, with a turn of the eye at the immobile driver. 'I hope you'll have a very pleasant soirée. My kind regards to the vicar.'

At this moment Lemon arrived, clinging to a taxi. It pulled up in front of Mrs Krabbe's car, and they got in.

'Ciro's,' called Algy. 'It's all right now, Lemon. Good night, Auntie.'

The taxi frisked away, the limousine gliding condescendingly in its wake. Lemon plodded upstairs again for his bowler hat. The thunder was still rumbling in the distance.

'You again!' exlaimed Mrs Frush. 'I thought I told you to keep away until such time as you were told. There's the boy from the mews waiting to be sent for you directly we can do with you in 'ere.'

' 'As it started?' moaned Lemon.

'Yes, it 'as.'

'Well – Lord love us – how long does it take?'

'Sometimes forty-eight hours, and sometimes less,' replied Mrs Frush, with relish. She propelled Lemon firmly by the waistcoat until he was out of range of his own doorway. 'You won't 'ear nothing yet. In two hours' time you may call back again; just in case things are quicker than what I foresee.'

Lemon descended and for an hour roamed the streets like one in a dream, scarce noticing where he went; his hands thrust in his trousers pockets; his pathetic bowler on the back of his head. The thunder intermittently growled, but towards the conclusion of the hour its sound increased in volume. Lightning flashed forth, and upon the bowler hat drummed the first heavy, hot spots of the rain.

At this moment (he had been wandering in an unconscious circle) he found himself in Half Moon Street. Oh, well; if they weren't going to be back till two he might as well go up and wait in his pantry for the next hour. He dare not brave Mrs Frush before the stipulated time-limit. And to go back and hang about in the mews seemed somehow harrowing. Almost within sound – no, no.

The street door was locked, but Lemon had his key. Wiping his bowler with his coat sleeve he once more climbed the weary stairs. He unlocked the door of the flat and turned to close it. Suddenly he paused and shot his head round towards the sitting-room. Someone there! They were back again. He was wanted little enough anywhere that night, it seemed; but nowhere less than here.

Then he heard his name called quickly, agitatedly: 'Lemon! Lemon!'

He swung the front door to, and hastened to the sitting-room.

CHAPTER XVII

Doors

The doctor, whom Diana ushered into the bedroom of April Cottage at about nine o'clock, proved to be rather a jolly soul.

'I'm very, very sorry to have kept you waiting so long,' he said. 'I've been searching the wrong place for a man who wasn't there with an arm he hadn't broken. Comic affair.'

'Oh, intensely humorous,' said Henry.

The doctor inspected the crêpe-de-Chine nightgown with some interest.

'Going to a fancy-dress ball when it happened?' he inquired.

'I may tell you I came here with no luggage, no overcoat, no umbrella, and in Pillbutton's hackney,' replied Henry.

'The bedclothes hadn't been properly aired, in any case,' added Diana. 'But I didn't think we need *insist* on his catching pneumonia. So I lent him a nightgown.'

'Ah, I see,' said the doctor. 'A bit tight across the shoulders, but any port in a storm.'

'And while discussing trivialities,' said Henry, 'I have, in bed with me, what a few hours ago was a foot.'

'I suppose I'd better go,' said Diana.

'Certainly not,' said Henry. 'I shall want you to stand by and hold my hand. I know what this medical research work is. I'm not quite sure about the limitations of the nightgown, but you can untuck the bedclothes at the foot of the bed and work upwards.'

She gently exposed the foot; then stood beside Henry and held his hand like a child's. The doctor stooped to his inquisition, and the grip on her hand tightened, and hers in response.

'Hum!' said the doctor. 'What on earth have you been trying to kick?'

'Earth itself,' replied Henry. 'I took a flying leap from heaven and punted the globe.'

'He went on the roof to put a chimney out,' said Diana.

'He's put out more than a chimney,' said the doctor.

'I told you so,' said Henry. 'He's going to put it in again. Hold tight.'

'Is the ankle broken?' asked Diana.

'It's out of joint, and the little toe's out of joint, and muscles and ligaments – I wish I'd known about this before. I'd have had you taken to the Cottage Hospital at Downblotton. As it is – I've only my two-seater. I don't think we could manage very easily. Pawley's motor has crashed. I don't quite—'

'His clothes are still wet,' said Diana.

'And if,' concluded Henry, 'you think that I am going to be driven half across Somerset on a wet evening in a crêpe-de-Chine nightgown by Pete in Pillbutton's hackney, I don't.'

'Then I suppose the only thing to do is to try and fix you up for the night and leave you where you are.'

'Of course,' said Diana.

'Well, I'll be as gentle as I can. Hang on to something.'

Diana, without hesitation, drew nearer and put her arm round his shoulders. He clung to her in a close embrace, clung as a martyr, racked by the pains of hell, clings to the faith of heaven.

'What's this gentleman's name?' asked the doctor of Diana, as she conducted him downstairs again.

'Mr Bingham,' she told him.

'Oh, erm – you're all right here? I mean – you can manage and that sort of thing?'

'Oh rather,' said Diana.

'That's all right then,' said the doctor quickly. 'Only I understand you didn't expect to have to put him up here, and I'll make arrangements to have him shifted tomorrow morning, if you like.'

'I suppose you advise it?'

'Oh, yes; unquestionably. I wouldn't have left him here tonight; only I know what the Downblotton ambulance is. It would probably be tomorrow, in any case, before it arrived on the scene. I'll have it sent for first thing; and I'll come and look you up in good time. I suppose I'd better bring one or two pairs of pyjamas along, hadn't I?'

'Thanks,' said Diana. 'I went into South Ditherton myself this evening, but I never thought of the pyjamas. I had other things to worry about. And really I don't think that a doctor ought to keep Wotan.'

The doctor sighed.

'I'd already insisted on his being got rid of,' he said, 'only at the last moment he scared the life out of a rate-collector. So I reprieved him until after next quarter-day.'

He went out to his car, and Diana back to the bedroom to acquaint Henry with the distressing prospect of the Downblotton ambulance.

'Of course,' he said. 'That's quite right. I can't stay here indefinitely. But the moment I can put foot to ground I shall come and see you again.'

'I may not be here then,' said Diana.

'Wherever you are,' said Henry.

She laughed. 'Well – are you feeling better?'

'Yes.'

'Have you had some more brandy?'

'Yes.'

'I've got to go and clear up the parlour now.'

'Oh, don't run away.'

'I must. The room's like a coal-yard and I've got to sleep there.'

Henry reached out for the open manuscript of Hole on Woman and harangued her from its pages:

In the wisely-ordered *ménage* of the Orient the woman presents her society to her lord only at the latter's express desire; but so long as he displays partiality for her consociation, at his side she will spontaneously remain. This is her first commandment. No other delight is she permitted to esteem as commensurate with this duty; no other duty as commensurate with this delight.

'There!' said Henry. 'What have you got to say to that?'

'I think it's absolute tosh,' said Diana.

'Well, I don't,' said Henry.

Berty Pitts did not obtain his dinner at the *Ring o' Bells* until well after eight o'clock, and even then it was not so rich in luscious viands as a student of the window-inscription might have anticipated. Muriel served him in a manner very different to that displayed for Henry's lunch. She developed a chronic sniff, which was particularly noticeable during the handing of dishes. She originated no conversation. Her mistrust of her client appeared to deepen with the slow setting of the sun.

Berty himself was not communicative. He ate sparingly of a stew which might well have been the sequel to the death of a local goat, followed by Spotted Dick, according to Muriel's blunt reply to what was, after all, a very reasonable question. After having eaten this as a child eats raspberry jam, suspecting Gregory Powder, he inquired pessimistically whether there was anything going on in South Ditherton. The reply was in the negative. It appeared that there was dancing on the green on the night of the annual Flower Show, and a demonstration of local musical talent every Boxing-night; but that the present was neither of the occasions in question.

Berty turned again dully to the lounge, and Muriel, having bustled through such duties as lay before her, sought Mr Plum.

'Be it all right for me to go out for a while, Mr Plum?'

'Wull, I dunno,' replied Mr Plum. 'That dinner for one – be he a-goin' to bide?'

'He don't seem to know,' said Muriel. 'But if he be, I'll be back for to make his bed.'

'You'd best make her now,' said Mr Plum. 'If he wait all the even' in the lounge a-uncerr'n as to whether or no he be a-goin' to bide, it seem best for me to provide for he to bide. You'd best make her now.'

More delay thus. It was nearly half past nine before Muriel mounted the Sunbeam. Judiciously she went first to Mrs Leake and equipped herself with a lamp.

She found Mrs Leake in a state of intensified curiosity. She had held Miss Frisby in conversation as the latter left the post-office, and had achieved a belated vision of a further telegram (now the spirits came to think of it) received that morning and addressed to Miss Gascoyne. Something about someone stopping someone else from carrying on with somebody – the manifestations were very hazy. All additional reason though for Muriel to hurry up and get out to see Mrs Easy, and to restore the Sunbeam first thing on her return.

By the time Muriel finally set out the doctor was back in South Ditherton. And less than a minute after she had turned the corner and parted company from the main road, there came pounding along the latter, on the last lap of its greedy course, the magnificent if mud-stained chariot of wrath, in which, sitting forward with an eye for every building, his lips moving in some inarticulate and hypothetical hymn of hate, came down the Assyrian like a wolf on the quiet fold of the *Ring o' Bells*.

It splashed into South Ditherton. 'Halt!' bellowed Reginald, in a voice which rang round the market square and shook the War Memorial. 'This is the place. Toot; go on – blow your hooter. Wake 'em up. By Christopher, I'll jolt these people.'

'Don't frighten them, Reggy,' protested Louise. 'It isn't their fault. Besides, you don't want it to get about that you're here.'

He paused on the step of the car and turned to forefinger an ultimatum to her.

'From now onwards the less you talk the better. Understand that. Especially if you're going to talk toshpail.'

Mr Plum's ripe complexion was by this time adorning the entrance to the hotel. Reginald crossed the courtyard in a manner which caused him to withdraw a pace or two and to grasp the inner handle of the door.

From Reginald's nose the forefinger shot forth at Mr Plum.

'You! Are you the landlord?'

'Why shouldn't I be?' asked Mr Plum, cautiously.

'Are you, I say?'

'Ay.'

'Yes. You. Are you?'

'Ay.'

'Yes, you. Are you the landlord?'

'Ay.'

Reginald smote the ledge of the porch with his clenched fist.

'Stop that Mic and Mac. I won't have it. Are you the landlord?'

'I told you so fowerr times,' said Mr Plum. 'Ay, ay, ay, ay.'

'Ho,' said Reginald. 'Well, you needn't think I've come here to hold a conversation with a sailor. Now then! There is a young man waiting at this hotel for me to arrive. Kindly send him to me.'

Mr Plum cogitated for a brief while behind his half-closed door. There could be scarcely any question that the new visitor intended to dot, if not to murder, the dinner for one. He could not countenance assault in the precincts of the *Ring o' Bells*. He himself had occasionally dotted a drunk in the tap-room; but that was different.

'Come!' cried Reginald. 'Stop that shuttling. Go and bring him along, or, by thunder, I'll come and fetch him.'

Mr Plum's indecision was somewhat relieved at this point by the sudden appearance of a bosom, which thrust itself into the aperture of the doorway.

'I will find him,' said the bosom. 'You stay here, or just inside somewhere.'

Both parties accepted this intervention. Mr Plum directed Louise to the lounge and Reginald to the dining-room. Berty Pitts, warned by the hooting of Wimble, had parted company with Maria Monk and was biting his nails at the window.

'My dear!' said Louise.

'Oh, my dear soul, at last!' replied Berty. 'But, I say, this is a shocking business. I—'

'I thought it might be when I sent you,' said Louise.

'Never mind. Come downstairs with me and tell my brother about it. He's naturally rather upset and impatient, but not with you, of course.'

'But I've told him all I know. What does he want me to do now?'

'Simply to tell him how to get to this place, I suppose. He's going there at once.'

'Oh. He won't want me to go with him, will he?'

'No, no. I shouldn't think so.'

'Is he there?' resounded from below. 'Hallo, there, you upstairs! Are you there, you?'

'Oh, Reggy,' said Louise affably, as she descended the stairs. 'This is my friend, Mr Pitts. He—'

'Ha!' cried Reginald, swooping forward from the dining-room doorway and assisting Berty down the last six stairs. 'Come! My car is waiting. Direct the chauffeur and in you get.'

'Oh, but—'

'Stop that. Don't you start butting me or I'll but you. Direct the chauffeur. Louise, will you stir yourself! You! Wimble! Listen.'

He bore Berty across the courtyard and exhibited him to Wimble, shaking the instructions out of him as a master shakes the guilt out of a schoolboy. 'There! You are clear, Wimble? Very well, then. See to it. You, Louise, get in. Now you!'

'Oh, but I don't think I ought – I should really have thought—'

'No, thank you,' said Reginald. 'No poetry just now. Into the car with you.'

Mr Plum's face peered from above the wire blind of the tap-room. A singular affair. The dinner for one had been decoyed downstairs by the bosom, and was now apparently being allowed to choose where he would be driven to, in order to be done in.

Diana soon discovered that the cleansing of the parlour could not possibly be accomplished before dark. She did her best with it, but even so, the room could not be slept in. She only succeeded in getting very heated and begrimed, but not disheartened. She even faced the prospect of getting what sleep she could later on by calling into service the only remaining bed in the cottage, namely, the kitchen table, with a heedless laugh. First, though, she would jolly well have a hot bath. The kitchen fire was still in.

She had festooned the range with Henry's articles of apparel, and these were now dry enough to collect and carry upstairs. She took them to the bedroom and placed them neatly on a chair. At the same time, she collected her own essentials for encampment in the kitchen. Informed Henry that she was heating the water for her bath, and that he could wash if he liked. He liked. Her own preparations for ablution and retirement were thus delayed until that inopportune moment in which, bearing down upon April Cottage from South Ditherton, Reginald halted Wimble at the corner of the zigzag, and stepped out of the car into a puddle; and, bearing down upon April Cottage from Chool, Mrs Easy and Muriel left the road and took a foot-soaking short cut through the steep plantation.

Diana tested the water in the bath with her toe. Just right; cool enough to get into by tentative stages; hot enough to bask in and soak away the toils and impairments of the busy day. She stepped into the bath; gingerly sat; luxuriously lay.

One cannot lie in bed for several hours, even in pain, without courting at least the curiosity of Morpheus. And the more neat spirits one consumes during this prostrate period, the more pressing become the attentions of the old colleague of Bacchus. Henry, having obediently washed and having been tucked up for the night which was still gradually dimming day, settled his head upon the pillow and closed his eyes.

Then for the first time he became supinely aware of the effects of the brandy on his afflicted system. His head felt heavy; a little leaden weight pressed upon his temples. Soon before his closed eyes appeared the manuscript of Hole on Woman, but in the distressing form of a gigantic tee-totum, spinning unceasingly and with the lines blurred and illegible. Here and there a word would advance in letters of increasing size to the edge of the tee-totum, then retreat into the general blur. At length, however, the vile tee-totum ceased to spin and slowly faded from his vision, leaving in its place a spacious Oriental interior, where, surrounded by acres of rich carpet, he reclined upon the April Cottage double bed. Seated on the floor beside him, Diana amused herself by throwing bottles of Hennessy's brandy at the old man from Pillbutton's yard, who caught them dexterously and juggled with them. Right at the end of the hall, across the acres of carpet, was something indefinitely disagreeable, something connected to him by an electric wire, along which a current of pain was occasionally shot into his otherwise lordly and comfortable substance.

' 'Ush!' said Mrs Easy to Muriel in a strained whisper, as they gained the porch. 'You foller me. Then we shall see what's what and who's clever.'

The front door was open. Mrs Easy crept into the cottage, Muriel faint-heartedly at her heels. The kitchen was deserted. 'You'd best wait in there a moment while I eggsplore,' whispered Mrs Easy. Muriel waited in the kitchen. Mrs Easy put an ear to the parlour door. Gave a series of six little double sniffs. Opened the parlour door.

Oh, for Mr Hole at this moment! The sacred parlour of April Cottage, lately her especial charge. In her reign never interfered with. Now not only interfered with, but violated by some wanton rite of riot and burning. Mrs Easy withdrew from the parlour a face such as one only sees in pictorial representations of the French Revolution.

Leaving Muriel, infirm of purpose but coerced, in the kitchen, Mrs Easy ascended the stairs.

Muriel, practical even in the midst of alarms, had wet feet; the kitchen a bright fire. She instinctively crossed the room, sat down on a chair which grated along the stone floor, and, raising the sole of one boot to the blaze, knocked over a shovel.

'Ssssh!' from the staircase.

Diana, lying becalmed in the silent delectation of the bath heard the shovel. Heard the 'ssssh!' which, like most feminine ssssshes, was louder than the noise it sought to quell. Sat up, with her hands to the rims of the bath. Then sprang from the bath and, pulling open the bathroom door, thrust out an inquiring head.

It was nearly dark now. She saw the figure of, she thought, a woman, turn on the little landing at the bend of the stairs and skedaddle. Stung with a sudden resentment stronger than either alarm or modesty, Diana whipped up a bath-towel, flung it over her shoulders, and followed.

She gained the bend of the stairs in time to see the kitchen door closed from within. Without hesitation down she went, grasped the handle of the door. It was held against her. She opened her mouth to challenge the intruder. At the same moment something obliterated the light of day from the porch. Turned her head quickly. A young, strange man. A startled cry, a violent hoisting of the bath towel, and upstairs she went again. The face of Reginald, looming in the porch, whither Berty had guided it, underwent a quick change. He arrived and glared into the cottage only to see a pair of female legs, briefly shrouded by a flapping towel, scurrying upwards out of view.

Diana, on the top landing, hesitated a moment, really alarmed now. Through her brain flashed the thought that here was aggression. That door held against her; the attitude of the man in the doorway, peering, waiting. Danger! She glanced quickly from left to right – at the bathroom door, at the bedroom door. Then came a muffled, masculine word of command from below and stealthy footsteps on the stairs. Diana felt her heart throbbing. A cry died in a choke at her throat. Protection! Even the protection of a crippled ally. She darted at the bedroom door. Closed it behind her quickly, with just a side-glance for the bed, from which came no responding movement.

There was no key to the door. She held to the handle only to feel it turned in her grasp. The bath-towel was slipping from her left shoulder. She released the handle, clutched at the towel, was swept backwards into the room. She shouted something – she didn't know what.

Henry also shouted something; but it is unlikely that he knew what he said either; for his challenge was issued in the rambling tone of dreams, and in terms extravagant.

'Who calls,' he demanded, 'upon the Wazeer?'

Reginald stood in the doorway, turned to stone, staggered past the ability to move a muscle. Equally transfixed, but in a more uncomfortable attitude of straining amazement, stared from the landing, Louise. At the head of the stairs Berty Pitts stood biting his nails with ravenous nervousness. Reginald's eye slowly rolled from the utterly strange young woman standing behind the bed-post and doing her best to hide the fact that she was attired only in a towel, to where, behind a screen of brandy-bottles, forehead-furrowed and one-eyed, gazed at him from the pillow the foolish face of his younger brother. At the foot of the stairs at nudging attention stood Mrs Easy, performing nose-twisting unprecedented, and Muriel, her face a bigger box and a more widely-open box than ever before. And, from the gate-post of April Cottage, Puck turned a delighted somersault, and ten minutes later was in Piccadilly.

Was in Piccadilly just as a taxi, returning from Ciro's even before the theatres were out, turned down Half Moon Street. Inside it were a couple sitting close together and conversing in intimacies very subdued. They unclasped hands and got out of the taxi nonchalantly enough. Mr Dawkins was not in the hall, and they proceeded upstairs unobserved and in silence.

In the sitting-room he took her and held her in his arms. 'I love you, you know,' he said. 'I've only been waiting to love you, all my life.'

'I love you too,' she said. 'I do now. More than I ever thought I could love anybody.'

Five minutes of this. He holding her to him tightly, stooping to kiss her; she a little pale, dreamy-eyed and dreamily smiling, trembling rather. At last he released her, but her hand came back into his. She stood for a moment at arm's length from him, her eyes gazing into his. Then she held out her other hand to him.

B'rrrrr—

Still holding her hands he turned with a quick frown.

'Who the devil can that be? It can't be for Lemon; he's gone.'

Eleanor did not move; spoke very calmly.

'Reggy,' she said. Then with a curt laugh, 'He's too late. I'm not here, see? And if he forces his way in and finds me here, I'm here for good. Is that a bet, Algy?'

He shook her hands. 'Absolutely,' he said. He jerked his head towards the bedroom door. 'But I suppose you'd better – while I just see—'

She nodded. He dropped her hands and she left him. He walked quickly to the door which led to the passage, and stood listening.

B'rrrrr—

With the long strides of exasperation he went and pulled back the latch. Swung open the door with a glare of defiance for the invader.

It was Captain Dumfoil.

CHAPTER XVIII

Exasperating Efficiency of an Angel

'Oh, you *are* here then?' said Captain Dumfoil.

'Yes?'

'You alone?'

'What? Yes.'

'You are alone?'

'Yes. Why?'

'Oh; well, I can spare you a minute or two,' said Captain Dumfoil, entering.

'I've got to go out in about one minute, myself,' said Algy.

Captain Dumfoil laughed in a caustic monosyllable. 'Ha!' He inspected Algy rather patronizingly. 'I don't think so,' he added, and led the way uninvited to the sitting-room.

'As a matter of fact, I can't stay long myself either,' he proceeded. 'Still, I thought I'd look you up.'

'Well, here I am,' said Algy, following his visitor with but little of his customary affability. 'What is it?'

'Yes, good job you are here,' said Captain Dumfoil, seating himself ponderously on the sofa. 'I know where you were just going. You were going to pick up your aunt and push out to Richmond.'

'Oh, don't start that again,' began Algy; but the other cut him short.

'You wait a minute, young feller-me-lad. I couldn't make myself sufficiently explicit yesterday morning. I could only warn you to keep clear of the place. I didn't know at the time that the advice was so expedient.'

Algy shifted restlessly. 'Oh, get it off your chest, Dumfoil.'

'All right, all right.' Captain Dumfoil raised a quelling palm. He then pulled down his dress waistcoat, examined his front stud, struck a telling attitude and continued.

'When I saw you yesterday morning I was trying my best to convey to your rather limited intelligence that this place,

Shady Nook, was about to receive the attentions of the police.'

'What!' Algy's hand gripped the back of a chair. 'The police! You never said so.'

'You wouldn't let me,' said Captain Dumfoil, placing his thumbs in his armholes and leaning back on the sofa complacently. 'Of course, I ought not really to have told you as much as I did.'

'You didn't tell me anything.'

'I told you enough to put you on the qui vive if you had any sense. Only you said you repeat everything to your blessed aunt, and I couldn't trust her.'

'Do you mean to say that the place is going to be raided?' asked Algy.

Captain Dumfoil nodded in the midst of a yawn.

'When?'

'Tonight, I believe. Give me a cigarette, will you?'

Algy handed him the silver box impatiently.

'But how d'you know?' he demanded. 'Has someone given information to the police about it?'

'Years,' replied Captain Dumfoil, selecting a cigarette and tapping it on the back of his hand. 'I have.'

'You have?'

'Years,' said Captain Dumfoil. He paused to light the cigarette; then returned to his contented attitude on the sofa. 'I laid the information about a month ago,' he continued. 'Since then they've been keeping the place under observation; been fixing things up. Took 'em rather a time, because they had to plant someone as one of the clients, and that meant they had to find a new policeman and give him time to win the confidence of the management. I thought it would be soon; but I only heard an hour or so ago that they hoped to bring it off tonight. I've just been along to young Jack Molyneux – stopped him going. Thought I'd do the same for you. Only fair to warn the few decent people who patronise the filthy hole. Frankly, I wouldn't have minded whether your aunt had been copped or not.'

'Funny!' said Algy, thoughtfully. 'My aunt was saying only yesterday that she—'

'That she what?' asked Captain Dumfoil, suspiciously.

'That she'd treat any crooked place the same way as you've done. Only she swore the Nook wasn't crooked.'

'Pooh! Stiff with crooks,' said Captain Dumfoil, airily. 'Warren of 'em. Phonk, Great Scott! I've watched him at it. He'll be sorry he ever chose me for a victim.'

'Well I'm much obliged for the information,' said Algy. 'I suppose I'd better let my aunt know.'

'Let her know you're not going to take her tonight. Don't let her know why. She holds a brief for Phonk and I don't trust her, and that's that. She'll find out why soon enough.'

'But, dash it, I must warn her.'

'No need to warn her at all. Simply tell her you're not going to take her. If she chooses to go down there on her own, that's her look out.'

'But be reasonable, Dumfoil. Suppose I found out that she – that she'd failed to take the hint and had gone down there—?'

'You do what I tell you. Tell her not to go – say you're not going to take her and she'd better stay at home.'

'But she'd want to know the reason.'

'Yes, and then if you tell her the reason she'll try and warn Phonk.'

'I'll swear to you that Phonk shall not be warned. There!'

Captain Dumfoil grunted querulously.

'Oh, what's the good?' he said. 'She's an incorrigible old gambler. She's been bound over twice already. If she chooses to make pals of crooks, she doesn't deserve to be considered.'

Algy paraded the room restlessly, then halted at the table.

'Look here, Dumfoil,' he said, 'whether you're right or wrong about Phonk, the fact remains that you've taken the trouble to call here and put me wise. I may not agree with your methods but, by all the rules of the game, I can't warn Phonk, even if I wanted to. And if I tell my aunt, I'll guarantee the same thing holds good.'

Captain Dumfoil shook his head.

'I know women's ideas of sportsmanship,' he said. 'I've had some. She'd say I'd done the dirty, and she'd pretend she was justified. Always some wriggle. I know women.'

'She shall not tell a soul. I give you my word. Is that good enough?'

'You swear that?'

'I swear it.'

'I suppose you'll hop off straight away now, and tell her?'

'Yes,' said Algy.

Captain Dumfoil rose; knocked an irresolute ash into a silver tray on the table.

'Then she'll give you a promise and break it.'

'No, she won't,' said Algy. 'What time is this – round-up due to begin?'

'Why?'

'Because I shall probably remain with her until then.'

'Oh, I see. Yes, you'd better. Though, as a matter of fact, I don't know when it's coming off. Of course, it may not come off at all tonight. If it doesn't . . .'

'If it doesn't my guarantee holds good,' said Algy quickly.

Captain Dumfoil laughed bluntly.

'You've got a dashed sight more confidence in the other sex than I have,' he said.

'Yes,' said Algy. 'Perhaps I've been luckier.'

'H'm! Well – I'm away.'

'Righto,' said Algy, agreeably. 'Many thanks. Very friendly of you to come.'

'That's all right,' said Captain Dumfoil, as he walked to the door. 'It isn't you we're after. So long.'

He turned in the passage. 'Now, don't forget. Keep an eye on that aunt.'

'Oh, I will,' said Algy.

He returned from seeing Captain Dumfoil off the premises and stood for a brief, irresolute space in the sitting-room doorway. He glanced towards the bedroom, then at the gathering night through the window. Swore curtly, but with a wealth of feeling. The bedroom door opened cautiously.

He hurried to Eleanor.

'Elly! Did you hear?'

'Not very much. Who was it, and what did he want?'

'There's a raid on the Nook.'

'Raid? The Nook?'

'Shady Nook. The place at Richmond where Auntie goes. The place where Auntie's gone. They're going to raid it. The police are going to raid Auntie.'

Eleanor looked at him inquiringly. She seemed on the point of expressing gratification at these tidings, but his worried frown checked her, and she bit her lip.

'Does that matter?' she asked.

'Matter!' he cried. 'Elly, it means I must go.'

'Where?'

'To Richmond, my dear. I must go down there, don't you see?'

'To get raided, too?'

'To lug Auntie out of it. Mustn't I? I must. Elly, I must.'

She intertwined her fingers.

'Now?' she asked.

He sighed, but made no answer. He seemed to be waiting for her decision. 'Yes,' she went on, in a quick, practical tone, 'I suppose it's the right thing to do, isn't it?'

'Well, I can't get to hear of her being in a thing like this and leave her to it, can I?' said Algy, gloomily.

'How long will you be?'

'I'll nip round and get my car and run down there. I know how to get into the place, even if they're watching it. I'll have her out of it and push her off home, and come straight back here. I don't know – an hour?'

'Will it be exciting? Any danger? I'll come too, if you like,' said Eleanor.

'That's out of the question. You'll have to wait here. There won't be any excitement at all, especially if I go at once.'

'But if they catch you?'

'They won't catch me. I shall be too early. And even if they do catch me, I expect I can wangle out of it. They won't start shooting, you know, or anything like that. It isn't America. They might have to put the bracelets on Auntie. But I can get away with it before any of the fun starts if only I dash off at once.'

'Your aunt won't want to come back here?'

'I won't let her. One good turn deserves another. She can jolly well go home to her bed and not be inquisitive.'

'I'm to wait here alone?'

'Not for long. I'll be back in an hour; it's hardly dark, yet.'

She pouted prettily. 'I know; but . . .'

'I know, too,' he said, and caught her to him. 'Only an hour, Elly; only an hour, old darling.'

At this point came the first flash of lightning, a more admonitory clap of thunder, and soon afterwards, as we know, Lemon's key in the lock of the front door.

'It's all right,' said Algy; 'it's only Lemon, It must be he. He's the only person who's got a key. Lemon! Lemon!'

He released Eleanor, and buttonholed Lemon, as the latter blundered agape into the sitting-room.

'Lemon, look here. I've got to chase out. Mrs Krabbe has gone to Richmond, and I've just heard that the cops are out and beating her up. So I must go down and have her out of it. See?'

'Dear me, how awkward, sir,' said Lemon.

'Yes. Mrs Bingham will be waiting here till I get back. You'd better stay, too.'

'Yes, sir,' said Lemon. 'But how long? . . .'

Algy passed him and removed his mackintosh from the rack in the passage.

'How the devil do I know?' he replied. 'Here, give me a hand into this. I'll take my cap. Where is it?'

'There, sir, on the end peg. But I might be wanting to get home again, sir. Things are getting a move on.'

'Well, the sooner I go, the sooner I'll be back.' He scrambled into the mackintosh, whipped the cap from the peg, and ran back to the sitting-room doorway to kiss his hand to Eleanor.

'I'll be here,' she said. 'Don't be long.'

'You bet I won't. Good-bye, old thing.'

'It's starting to rain heavy, sir,' said Lemon; 'also to lightning.'

'That's right. Keep cheerful,' replied Algy, and was gone.

Lemon, apparently a little vague as to what was expected of him, returned solicitously to the sitting-room. Eleanor was at the window, drumming her fingers on the ledge.

'You know all about this, then?' she said.

'Er . . .?'

'You know all about this gambling business?'

'Oh. Yes, madam. He's confided to me in confidence about it,' replied Lemon.

'What happens to you if you get caught?'

'Well, I don't exactly know, madam. As far as the gambling goes, it's generally only a caution, I believe, or, at the worst, a fine. But . . .'

'But what?'

'Well, madam,' continued Lemon with misgiving, 'of course interfering with the police in the execution of their duty, that's more serious.'

'Is that what he's doing?' asked Eleanor casually.

'If he's caught, it is,' replied Lemon judiciously. 'I know a feller that got a month for it, madam.'

'Dear, dear,' remarked Eleanor, window-ledge drumming. 'I don't want to have to wait here for a month.'

Lemon made no comment on this, but asked whether there was anything he could do for her. She replied, 'No,' with many thanks. She would stay where she was, and watch the storm. It was rather fascinating. Very vivid lightning. He'd better close the window, though. The rain was coming in.

He crossed the room and closed the window for her. The storm did not serve to relieve his settled melancholy. In fact, he dimly seemed to recollect some dismal legend concerning the grievous effects of thunder and lightning upon women at childbed. He felt almost bound to remonstrate politely with his visitor's heedless relish for the hostilities of heaven.

'Excuse me, madam, but I think you want to be careful with lightning – how you go too near it and that. A feller I knew had his brother struck.'

'Really?' replied Eleanor. 'Your friends seem to have had rather a thin time, one way and another. Oh, did you see that flash?'

'Yes, indeed I did, madam.'

'Right across the sky.'

'Yes, madam. Almost like electricity,' said Lemon.

A tremendous, culminating roll of thunder; then, in a

brief, intense torrent, the rain. It spent its violence against the window, where Eleanor remained alone, for Lemon had withdrawn into his hermitage pantry. The full lashing anger of the storm was soon over, and, to the accompaniment of the thunder as it boomed away into the distance, the rain relapsed into a steady downpour.

Eleanor stood there for a long while, then slowly turned from the window. Her storm was over, too – her heart-storm, her passion. While she had been waiting in that other room – while that man had been talking to Algy – she had felt vexation pricking her; and had known even then in her heart that it was not merely the vexation of being interrupted. It was the vexation of realising that this was a love which could not weather interruption.

She had keyed herself up to a mad moment – all through the day – to this crisis. Every minute of pleasure she had enjoyed that evening, in her short round of gaiety, had been merely a preliminary, a titillation. Then, just as she raised her hand to pluck the fruit, circumstance had caught her by the wrist. The moment of crisis had come and gone. The wild mood passed from her as the storm raged and passed, leaving only the steady drizzle of normal life, normal affections. The thunder was scarcely audible now. The spell was broken.

She confessed to herself how effortful had been the weaving of that spell. Difficult enough at times to defer to a guardian angel; more difficult yet to get rid of him for long.

She returned to the sofa, and sat there in the darkness, and half in tears. But, even then, the tears were the very human tears of disappointment at having failed in her wanton caprice, rather than the tears of self-reproach at having submitted to it. Of all our mortifications the most teasing is to be baulked of a peccadillo.

Presently she rose and had another look at the weather. Still raining persistently. She wouldn't be able to get a taxi just now for love or money. All the same, the rain wouldn't last for ever, and the theatre crowds would disperse before long. She switched up the light, and went to the writing-table.

Dearest old Algy,

I know I said I'd be here when you came back, but – somehow – that interruption and all – *you* know. I expect you feel the same really, and I don't believe it will ever be quite like that again. I don't think it was really going to be happiness – just a sort of reckless fit. All my doing – I know I'm frightfully impulsive and weird. Help me to be just your old pal Elly again. I'm going home. I expect I can make it up with Reggy, only there aren't going to be any sackcloth and ashes, and we'll meet again soon. Understand me, won't you? With love. Elly.

P.S. – Hope you rescued Mrs K. I know you had to go. Don't think for a moment that I was against your going. This doesn't sound affectionate, but oh, you dear old thing, I daresay we shall really go on being fonder of each other than we ever could have if – you know.

She enclosed the note in an envelope, stuck it, and scribbled his name. Left the envelope on the writing-table. Again to the window. No; rain, rain. Should she ring up Prince's Gate for the car? No. A few hours before, she was willing almost to court gossip and belowstairs speculation. Now she only desired to return to her home dignified and unexplained. She would repack her portmanteau, and get Lemon to try and get her a taxi.

Then, once more, *b'rrrr* – the electric bell, and the sound of Lemon scuttling from his retreat. She stood, her hand on the centre table, upright, listening; catching her breath in a little nervous laugh. Oh, perversity of fate! If this were Reggy now!

Lemon pushed a haunted face into the room as he passed.

'It's for me, I feel sure,' he whispered. 'Still, I'd better keep this door closed, madam, while I make sure.'

She nodded.

'Yes, all right.'

He closed the door, but she nipped off the light, and opened it again. Stood intently, holding it just ajar.

Dawkins' voice. 'There's a gentlem'n here asking for Mr Gascoyne . . .'

Lemon's agitated reply. ' 'E's not 'ere; 'e's not 'ere.'

'Well, I told 'im I thought not, but . . .'

Then the sound of one arriving upon the scene, evidently out of breath and of temper.

'I don't care a damn whether he's out or in. I've been to every hotel in this infernal city looking for a bed, and I'll go no further.'

Lemon again. 'Good heavens, it's you, sir!'

'Yes, it is. Get out of the way. I'm coming in here.'

'What, did you miss your train then, sir?'

'Do I look as if I'd caught it? I wish to God I'd come straight back here, instead of trying about fifty pestilential hotels and getting caught in the rain.'

'Yes, sir, but . . .'

'I left my luggage at Paddington. You'll have to find me some things. I don't care where I sleep, so long as I sleep in the dry. Take that umbrella. Shut that door.'

Eleanor took the hint and shut hers. A moment later gently shut the door of the bedroom.

'Well, come along; where do I go?' demanded Mr Hole.

'Er – the – er – sitting-room is in here, sir; but – er – one moment, sir, and I'll jest – see if it's – straight.'

'I don't care whether it's straight or crooked, so long as it's dry,' said Mr Hole.

Lemon fumbled with the sitting-room door-handle; turned it, directed an agonised glance into the room. Then, temporarily relieved, entered and switched on the light. Mr Hole followed, shaking the wetness from his garments.

'You can take my coat and waistcoat and dry 'em,' he said, removing the articles in question. 'What's in there? His bed-room?'

'Er – yes, sir; but . . .'

'All right, then. I'll go in there in a moment, and take my trousers off.'

Lemon could not recall having ever been faced with a predicament so distressing. He saw now that he had made a diplomatic slip at the outset. If only he had said, 'A lady is here, sir, waiting for Mr Gascoyne to take her out dancing,' all might have been saved. His silence now definitely pointed the guilt of his master and of Mrs Bingham. He was a very conscientious servant. It did not occur to him that they had only themselves to blame.

He sailed into the strategic fray, snatching at inspiration as he went.

'You must have some whisky, sir. I can see you shivering. If you'll take a seat on that sofa, sir, I'll help you off with your boots, and get you a nice warm dressing-gown and a drink of whisky.'

Weariness overcame the normal truculence of Mr Hole. He sat upon the sofa in his shirt and trousers and agreed to imbibe whisky.

'That's right, sir,' said Lemon, assiduously at the sideboard. 'Half-and-half, sir, or neat?'

'Neat,' said Mr Hole. 'But I'd rather take brandy – the young rip! All right; give me some brandy.'

'There, sir,' said Lemon, handing him a goodly measure. 'And now you'll want the dressing-gown.'

Mr Hole repeated a muffled threat concerning his trousers; but Lemon succeeded in gaining the bedroom, very much in the manner of a lion-tamer making his exit from the cage at the conclusion of a performance.

'Oh, madam,' whispered the harassed man, 'it is the master's uncle. He talks of staying here for the night. He may come in this room at any moment.'

'Is it the old gentleman the cottage belongs to? Mr Hole, the woman-hater?' asked Eleanor.

'Yes, madam. But you see there's this other door leading out from this room into the passage, if you . . .'

'If I what? I can't spend the night flitting from one room to another and hiding. Why shouldn't he know I was here?'

'Oh, madam, I – don't please think I am going beyond what I ought to say, but I don't think it would do the master any good if the old gent found you here.'

This seemed to impress Eleanor. She took thought, glanced around at the disorder of the bedroom, then comforted Lemon with a nod.

'Well, I *was* just going when he arrived. So keep him in that room, and I'll put my things together and go. I can call for my luggage in the morning. I'll leave it under the bed.'

'Thank you, madam. And he won't hear you packing, will he?'

Eleanor waved the pessimist away. 'Not if you go and keep him busy in the sitting-room.'

But circumstances were against Lemon. No sooner had he regained the sitting-room, edging through the doorway with a Jaeger dressing-gown, and a transparently forced grin of blandishment for Mr Hole, who, by this time, had his boots off and was squeezing the slack of his trousers analytically, than – *b'rrrr* once more, and this favourite butt for the pranks of Puck had to down the Jaeger on the centre table, gasp an apology, and make for the door again like a scared spider.

'Oh, excuse me, sir; that's for me, I think. I'm expecting a call from 'ome. My wife – excuse me, sir, jest a moment. Oh, deary me! . . .' He did not wait for the inevitably caustic comment from the sofa.

Yes – right this time. Mr Dawkins at the door. 'Ho, Mr Lemon, there's a message for you. They can do with you at 'ome now, as soon as you can get round.'

'Oh, my Gawd! Any news? Anything definite?'

'No, that's all that was said. A boy from the mews brought the message. 'E's 'opped it.'

'Oh, all right, Mr Dawkins.'

Back to the sitting-room.

'Yes, it's what I thought, sir. It's my wife. She's having a baby. I feel I ought to go. But . . .'

'Then go. I don't want you.'

'No, sir, but . . . Yes, sir, but . . .'

'Go! I'm not keeping you. Go, go!'

'Oh, lawd! Yes, sir, I . . .' He dithered, unable to resist a glance of sidelong apprehension at the bedroom door. 'I dessay I ought to stay, but I feel I must do my duty to my wife.'

'You appear to have done that,' said Mr Hole; 'get out!'

'Oh – but . . .'

'Get out! Get – get – out – out! Get out.'

'Oh lawd!' repeated Lemon, below his breath, and got out.

He sneaked into the bedroom from the passage.

Eleanor was folding stockings with preposterous care and indifference to danger.

'All right,' she whispered. 'I heard. Run along.'

'Madam, if you'd like to leave your things as they are, and let me see you out now . . .'

'Then he'll only come in here and find my things knocking about the room. Just as bad as finding me. Rather worse. I'll finish and find my way out all right.'

Lemon bowed to Fate, hurried to his pantry, assumed his foolish bowler, closed the front door of the rooms behind him and pelted downstairs. Threw from his bent back the weight of other people's troubles, and coursed out into the darkness and rain to shoulder his own.

During Mr Hole's perambulations in search of hotel accommodation, a young person (a woman, of course) had run out from the cover of a building to get into a waiting taxi, and had stepped in a puddle, thereby wetting Mr Hole's trousers. He could still feel that particular patch of damp just above the right knee, and thought he detected a responsive ache in the limb below. In his state of health, to remain there, sitting on a sofa with wet trousers, was ridiculous. He arose and crossed the room in his socks to the bedroom door, making no sound.

Forewarned as she was, Eleanor was quite startled.

CHAPTER XIX

So Much for Berty Pitts

This should satisfy Puck on his midsummer night. Two ladies discovered in respective bedrooms. The one in affrighted innocence; the other culpable in her original intention, and innocent only through the chance intervention of Captain Dumfoil, followed hotly by the resuscitated guardian angel.

But the blameless lady in the company of a gentleman who is wearing one of her nightgowns, sustained by brandy, and in her bed. The culpable lady unattended. The blameless lady clad only in a bath-towel; the culpable lady in full evening dress. The blameless lady damned at a glance; the culpable lady armed with the cool alibi of the errant swain somewhere half-way between Richmond and Vine Street. The blameless lady shrinking in towel-hoisting indignation from the flabbergasted pursuer of the culpable. The culpable lady archly greeting the empurpling inquisitor of the blameless.

Of the surprised quartette in the April Cottage room, Diana first found tongue, with Louise a good second – trust the women.

'Who are you, and how dare you come in here like this?'

'And who are *you*; and how dare you be here with him, of all people in the world, and in this state?'

Reginald then partially recovered.

'Silence, you!' Out went the forefinger at the bed. 'You! Where is my wife? What the devil are you doing here, lying lushed in a bed? With this person in a towel? How under heaven did you get here? Where is my wife?'

Henry awkwardly raised his head from the pillow, but continued to keep one eye closed, which gave a woeful impression.

'Clear out of this room, you blundering great poop,' he

retaliated. 'How dare you come bursting into buildings, and frightening young ladies out of their baths?'

'Don't you dare try and bounce me,' roared Reginald. 'You are spiced. Why are you here at all? Where is my wife and that other blackguard of a fellow? There's no need to ask what's going on here, but where is my wife? Do you think I've come posting home from the Continent and down to this place to look at you lying tanked in a bedroom? You, madam – in the towel. If he can't answer, perhaps you can. Where is my wife?'

'I shan't tell you anything,' said Diana, 'while you're cad enough to stand there and I'm in this state.'

'Don't you worry,' said Henry. 'Trot back to your bath. I'll fix this. I know how to deal with this stiff. He's my brother. Get out of the way, you great hulking tough, and let her go back to her bath.'

Reginald moved to one side, chiefly in order to emphasise his questions with his fist on the washing-stand, and Diana, seizing this opportunity, made a dash for the door. She was by no means dry yet, and Louise backed instinctively. Berty Pitts, on the landing, came to attention like a ranker. The bathroom door closed with a bang.

'And who is that woman, and what is all this?' demanded Louise, re-entering the bedroom, but Reginald silenced her with one crash of the soap-dish.

'Stop that.' To Henry – 'You! Where are they?'

Henry again sought the pillow in the most intolerably lackadaisical manner.

'Gone to town, of course,' he said, sleepily. 'What do you suppose? There's barely room in this cottage for the two of us. A foursome would be quite out of the question.'

'Wake up now!' pursued Reginald. 'I want the details of this degraded affair. You may be sostenuto, but you can talk. Wake up, or by Christopher, I'll come and knock what I want out of you.'

This threat had no effect on Henry, who remained impassive, but was, truth to tell, engaging in acute mental exercise on the pillow. Louise was his trouble. How was he to account for his presence without giving Willy away? By the time Reginald had advanced from the washing-stand, drawing himself up and apparently contemplating assault, Diana, now shrouded in night-gown and dressing-gown, had emerged from the bathroom, and, with a quick stare of undisguised hostility for Berty Pitts on the landing, came once more to face the invasion of the bedroom. The sight of her brought Henry his inspiration. He again grunted into an awkward attitude on one elbow.

'If you want to know why I'm here and in these – circumstances and bed and nightgown and so on,' he said, 'I don't mind telling you, though it's no business of yours.'

'I want to know where my wife is,' shouted Reginald.

'That's all part of it. Listen, and don't interrupt. And don't stick out your finger at me, or I'll throw a bottle of brandy at it. I am in this bed because I've had a very bad fall and crippled myself. I'm in this nightgown because I got wet through coming here. And I'm here at all, because I was sent for.'

'Who by?' asked Louise.

'By Miss Richardson Gascoyne,' replied Henry, with a blink of assurance at Diana. 'This is Miss Richardson Gascoyne. This lady, whose hospitality you have so modestly and deferentially accepted.'

Reginald snorted with impatience. 'Will – you—?'

'Stop that,' said Henry with authority. 'I am telling the tale. And if I want any ventriloquism, I'll send you a postcard.'

He settled himself more comfortably on the elbow. Just as he was about to plunge into his revelations, he decided that he could do with a little drop more brandy. Reginald began to parade the narrow space between the bed and the washing-stand like an infuriated sea-captain on his bridge. Henry then filled and ignited a deliberate pipe.

Eventually, he began, with a good deal of puffng, to relate his version of the day's events. Eleanor came to stay at this cottage, the property of Mr Hole, a noted authority on Woman. Diana's brother Algy, who also, for some groundless reason, appeared to some of them to be an ardent student of the same subject, followed his friend Eleanor down to the cottage – and why not? However, this Diana, Miss Richardson Gascoyne – but it would save time to refer to her as Diana if she didn't mind – being a lady of such an extraordinary nature that she was able to combine successfully exceptional beauty with the most transparent and admirable sense of virtue – a rare combination, owing to the considerable difficulty which a lady naturally finds in being both very pretty and very good – and Louise needn't look like that, because she had never had to face the difficulty and didn't know – anyhow, this Miss Diana had felt just a trifle restless about Eleanor and Algy. She had quite expected Algy to blow in on the heels of Eleanor, and wasn't entirely satisfied in her own peerless mind that it was all quite nice. So she had asked him, Henry, to come down, too, to support her, and to confirm the impressions that he had always held, and still continued to hold with regard to the perfect innocence and justification of Eleanor's friendship with Algy.

Well, down comes Eleanor and down comes Algy sure enough. And Diana (or Miss Diana, or, better still perhaps, the goddess Diana, Diana being the goddess of radiant maidenhood, in addition to hunting and sleeping in the moon) allows, perhaps, just for once, her inherent virtue to become a trifle too transparent; and directly Algy shows up, she is unable to prevent Eleanor from spotting that she has her suspicions. Poor Eleanor, innocent of any improper design as a babe unborn, discovers with horror that her dear friend thinks she is working the Potipher's wife stuff on Algy, who, with all his excellent qualities, is no Joseph. This naturally gets Eleanor's goat. There is a brief display of fireworks, and off she bungs with Algy in pique and a twelve-cylinder Woolworth; but even more in innocence than ever, her very bunging off in this manner being a demonstration of disgust at being doubted. He, Henry, arrived too late to do any good, and had definitely decided not to apply for a job with the Fire Brigade.

'That'll do,' cried Reginald. 'Where did they go? Where?' He swung round on Diana. 'You, pray? You were here when they went – where did they go?'

'To London, naturally,' replied Diana. 'That's where they live, isn't it?'

He stared past her with wide eyes, visualising the now inevitable results of this fatiguing tragedy of misdirected effort and inflaming muddling. He slowly turned, his fingers twitching. Glanced at Henry, who was now attempting to rest his head upon the pillow and to smoke at the same time. Useless to waste good wrath on this despicable and half-pickled noodle. A better victim was near at hand. Louise flinched as she met his eye.

Berty Pitts had drawn nearer to the door, held in compelling horror, like a serpent-haunted rabbit, by the narration of Henry. He shifted his position a little, on hearing the first trend of Reginald's latest outburst.

'You! You see what you've done? Plotting with some flap-eared spy and getting hold of the dirty end of the stick! . . .'

An unwholesome atmosphere. Berty decided that he would feel more comfortable in the garden. The landing, and indeed the whole interior of April Cottage, was by this time very dark. Berty stole, sideways and still listening, towards the staircase.

At the head of the staircase, he pulled up with an involuntary cry of surprise. Some unexpected sentinel gripped him by the arm. Muriel, hearing the voice of her beloved stout one, had made bold to ascend.

'No you don't,' whispered Muriel. 'Not yet.'

'Who's that out there?' asked Diana, sharply.

The whole bitterness of failure swelled up and burst from Louise in a wave of recrimination.

'If they weren't here this afternoon, you were. And I know what went on in this room, because it was heard.'

Henry cocked up an eye from the pillow.

'What's that?'

'Yes,' cried Louise. 'Heard! A friend of mine came and heard everything. He thought it was Eleanor in the room, but it's none the less true of whoever *was* here . . .'

'What friend of yours?' demanded Diana. 'No one came here. And if anybody did, there was nothing . . .'

She broke off and made for the door, but an unexpected

champion stayed her, pushed back his sleeves, pulled down his coat, pulled back his shoulders, tweaked his nose, and made for the door instead.

'Leave him to me,' said Reginald. 'I'm the best person to deal with him.' He heaved out into the landing. 'Now then, where is this hop?'

'Here he be, sur,' said Muriel.

It all happened so quickly that Mrs Easy, who, after starting much more confidently than Muriel, had refused to budge from the hall, was taken by surprise. All she knew was that a body was hurled violently from the darkness aloft. When she knew anything else, she knew she was sitting in the hall. Near at hand and in a similar attitude, but holding his head, was the detective. From the bend of the stairs came a satisfied valediction. 'There! So much for you and your bo-peep.'

The detective remained where he was, but Mrs Easy struggled to her feet, rehearsing threats of vengeance dire, when Mr Hole should return to his polluted home. Before she could give due utterance to these, she was once more made the victim of sudden collision, Louise having indignantly pushed past her brother on the staircase, and hastened down to the assistance of Berty. Mrs Easy lost her balance, and so did Louise. The floor of the darkened hall gave a passing impression of being occupied by some reveller returning intoxicated from representing an octopus at a carnival.

On the landing, Diana peered curiously into the face of Muriel.

'I coom, miss,' the latter made haste to explain, 'for to back up like the stout gentleman. I 'eard lies being spook of him on the 'phoon at the hotel.'

Diana, calmly prepared for almost any development of this nightmare, led the girl to the bedroom.

'Come in here,' she said, 'and explain what you mean.'

She struck a match and lit a candle which stood on the chimney-piece. Muriel remained in the doorway, breathing deeply and regarding her wounded hero with a fatuous and yearning smile.

Henry blinked his perplexity. 'Is that girl in the flesh,' he asked, 'or was Reggy right about me?'

At this point Reginald strode back into the room, somewhat appeased for the moment.

'I have got rid of that sneaking mess,' he informed Diana. 'Kicked him downstairs. I – ah – must apologise . . .'

'Not at all,' said Henry. 'Go and kick yourself downstairs too.'

'I – ah . . .' continued Reginald, disregarding this, 'I know that you may have thought that I acted rather – hallo! Who is this young woman?'

'You leave her alone,' said Henry. 'I don't know in the least why she's here, but the place seems stiff with people, so I daresay it's all right.'

'H'm,' said Reginald. 'How came she in here, listening to my private affairs?'

'Well, my goodness,' said Diana, 'you're pretty cool, I must say. You didn't exactly break the front-door bell yourself, did you?'

Reginald lowered his face and multiplied his chins.

'I was entirely misinformed,' he said, 'by that sister of mine and that greaser. Never mind. I kicked him down the stairs. Now I must go back at once to London. There'll be some more kicking downstairs before I've finished my night's work, I can promise you.'

'Oh, hell!' said Henry. 'Only too pleased to get rid of you, but where are you going thumping and roaring off to now, you great thundergutted boob?'

'Thank you,' replied Reginald. 'I know where to go, well enough. I feel I must once more apologise in a measure to you, Miss – ah—'

'Oh, get out,' said Henry, 'and take Louise with you. Also the gentleman who is now at the foot of the stairs, and anybody else that you happen to find strolling about the premises.'

Louise and Berty had by this time disentangled themselves from the morass of struggling humanity in the hall, and had dragged themselves into the porch, where Mrs Easy stood, waving her great hands in their faces and prophesying. At the approach of Reginald, she withdrew to the right-hand corner of the cottage, but continued to prophesy.

'Reggy!' exclaimed Louise. 'It is monstrous, your treatment of Berty. After all he has gone through for you today, to be assaulted and kicked . . .'

'If he stands there within range of me, by Christopher, I'll kick him again,' replied Reginald.

'Tomorrer 'e'll be back,' said Mrs Easy. 'Tomorrer. Then we shall see what some of you get. You little know.'

'What! Who is that man? Stop that, will you?'

'You must apologise at once,' said Louise.

'You lost your temper and behaved like a – like a bull. I can only say . . .'

'Silence!' said Reginald. 'You, you miserable little sneaking, lying . . .'

'Those who are staying there, and, likewise, those who have come there and helped to mess the place up. All in it. And all will get it likewise. You little know. I do.'

'I am going to London,' said Reginald, with a sniff of disgust for the corner of the house. 'You will come with me at once. Attend, will you! Don't take any notice of that person. Some beer-sodden peasant.'

'I will come when you have apologised to Berty, and not before. How do you expect us to come back to town with you, when he is still bruised by your brutal boots?'

'I don't. I don't! There's no question of *his* coming back, so you needn't think it.'

'I shall get to know 'oo's 'oo,' said Mrs Easy, 'and when I do, woe betide 'em.'

'I shall certainly not take him back to London,' said Reginald. 'Why should I? After he's had the effrontery . . .'

'I don't want to go back,' said Berty. 'I don't think you're safe. You've no control over yourself, sir. I don't suppose you know now what you've done.'

'To poke his nose into my private domestic affairs,' continued Reginald. 'And, with your help . . .'

'You wait till Mr Hole gets the names of those who has been and come and disgraced his cottage,' cried Mrs Easy, who was even more annoyed at being ignored than at having been mishandled, and, like many another dame in a temper, was inclined to become uncontrolled and fantastic in her threats. 'Blotted out, that's what they'll get – like some of them bad mockers in the 'Oly Bible.'

'And, with your help, to botch the whole business up for me,' proceeded Reginald.

'I shall not come home with you unless you apologise and take him too,' said Louise.

'I am not going home, and I don't want you with me in the least. So, as regards that . . .'

'Then what do you suppose we are going to do?' asked Louise.

'We can go back to that hotel,' whispered Berty.

'You can go to the devil,' said Reginald.

'You must take us there,' said Louise.

'I'm going the other way. I've no time to waste. Oh, very well – to get rid of you, I will drive you to the hotel. Only he must sit in front with Wimble. I cannot stand him in with me.'

'I'd rather be outside,' said Berty.

'Sodom and Gomorrow,' said Mrs Easy, soaring upon the wings of simile, in her neglected wrath, 'will be nothing to it – nothing. A game of spillikings to it will it be.' With which Parthian shot, she withdrew into the bushes.

A few minutes later, Diana bade Muriel a pleasant good-night, and thanked her for her good intentions. The girl rather wistfully replied that she would gladly do more than that for so kind a gentleman, and, when she reached the porch, lingered one-footed for a moment, then turned with a last pleading effort.

'Oh, miss! Can you manage single? Would you allow me for to stay and be his nurse for the night?'

'No, thank you,' replied Diana, gently, and closed the door of April Cottage upon the eventful evening.

Muriel found her bicycle in the hedge outside the tightly bolted and unilluminated abode of Mrs Easy. She had no matches, but the moon was doing her best to struggle through the heavy clouds.

In the car Louise began silently to waver. She had always

known it was impossible to dictate to Reggy, and she began to regret having tried to do so on this occasion. It would be most inconvenient to stay the night at this hotel. She had nothing to sleep in, or to wash herself with or to comb herself with, or to clean her teeth with. She had left at home all these requisites, all her other toilet accessories, her much-needed medicines and her crucifix. She was chagrined at the failure of her promised and sweeping personal victory over Eleanor. She was considerably shaken and bruised by her collision with Mrs Easy, and her participation in the shambles of the hall floor. But she stuck to her point.

'I would come home with you, if you would apologise. You may leave him here if you like, but I insist upon your apologising.'

Unfortunately, Reginald stuck to his.

'I am not going home. Where I am going, I prefer to go alone.'

The car drew up before the darkened portal of the *Ring o' Bells*.

Louise eyed her brother. 'Well – leave him here,' she said, 'and I'll come with you. I daresay, when you think it over, you'll agree to apologise.'

Reginald was no longer in furious mood, but calculating again, heavy-browed and mouth-working. He turned to Louise with an air of long-suffering finality.

'Open the door and get out!'

'Well, Reggy, I think I'll . . .'

'Open the door and get out. You, in front! Get off the box.'

Louise flared. 'I think your behaviour is simply disgraceful,' she said.

'Thank you. The less you interfere in my affairs for the future, the better they may progress.'

'Interfere! When you came to me yourself, and . . .'

'Did I come and ask you to make a howling mess of a simple commission? With your nosing outsiders? Get out of my car, and stay out of my car. You! Wimble!'

Wimble, one of those well-trained chauffeurs who only hear remarks addressed to themselves, descended, and came to the door of the car.

'Help Mrs Piper out of the car; then drive back.'

'Where to, sir?'

'To London.'

'Reggy! This is . . .'

'T'ch'ach!' said Reginald, in a hoarse whisper. 'In front of the man! Kindly get out of the car.' He helped her on her way with a push. She bridled and got out.

'To London, sir?' repeated Wimble, incredulously.

'Yes – to London.'

'Excuse me, sir; it'll take all night, I'm afraid.'

'I'm quite aware of that.'

'Very good, sir.'

'I know it's very good, thank you. If it wasn't very good, I wouldn't go. Come along. Up you get. Move!'

Mr Plum received his guests with a dazed tolerance. He had always anticipated that the dinner for one would, if spared, return to bide; but that the bosom should also turn up again and demand a bed was a complete surprise. She might have a bed, but she'd have to wait for it. Muriel was still out. He himself could not make beds. The barman was unlikely to be able to make much of a bed. Mother could make beds, but had rheumatism, and had herself sought the downy. (Mother was Mrs Plum. She it was who, on Henry's arrival, swam briefly into our ken with a dish-cloth, called Muriel, and swam out again.) So the lady must wait for her bed, unless she took the dinner for one's bed, and he waited. Neither of them had any luggage, or seemed, even now, fully prepared to bide.

They said they would wait and go to bed when both beds were ready. Together they limped upstairs to the lounge to wait. Mr Plum went to the tap-room, and had a beer and let 'em be. Muriel progressed to their aid very slowly, cautiously and peeringly in the fickle moonlight.

'Dear boy,' cried Louise, the moment they were alone in the lounge, 'how can I tell you how sorry I am for the way you've been treated. I shall never forgive my brother. I'm not surprised that his wife has run away from him.'

Berty moaned on the sofa.

'The fierce brute! He knocked me about terribly. I wasn't

prepared for him, or – ohh! I believe I've ricked my spine.'

She hastened to his side.

'Where, my poor boy? All for my sake. If only I'd known! Where are you hurt?'

'Just here. Just above the lower part of the back.'

'I wish I had some of my embrocation with me. I'd rub you. Perhaps they have some sort of embrocation here. I'll find that man and ask. And I'll give you a good massage, you poor, dear thing.'

Mr Plum, called from the bar, had some stuff they used for horses. He'd see whether he could put his hand on it in a few minutes. For the moment, he was busy. He waited until the lady had returned to the lounge, then had another beer, and did one or two other jobs in the tap-room. He kept nodding to himself significantly. So the dinner for one *had* been dotted. He thought he was going to be.

It was getting late when Muriel reached South Ditherton, but she was mindful of her promise, and proceeded first to Mrs Leake, who was still up, and came wrestling excitedly with the bolts of her shop door. Muriel ran the Sunbeam into its rack, and turned bursting with narrative.

Half-way through the tangled tale, shadowy figures hovered outside the plate-glass windows of the cycle shop. Two men. Mrs Leake muttered an interjection, and swept to the door.

One of the two men was Dan, the railway porter. The other an elderly stranger.

'Oo, Mrs Leake,' said Dan, 'this gen'm'n 'e coom be the laate train.'

'Well, why bring 'im 'ere?'

'Wull,' replied Dan, 'ther' ain't no conveyance around these days, ye see; not since Pawley's mowerr be 'ad a mishap to. So I bring 'im 'ere, for to see whether or no you could assist 'un.'

'Where did you want to go, sir?' asked Mrs Leake.

'April Cottage,' said the gentleman.

Cue, this, for Muriel. She hastened to the doorway. Who was this, then? What information did he require about April Cottage? By a long process of cross-interrogation, to which

Mrs Leake and the porter contributed, Muriel at last ascertained that the gentleman was after the stout lady who had accompanied the furious, shouting gent; while Willy groaned at the information that she had quitted the cottage for a destination unknown. He asked many other questions, which Mrs Leake answered, only to be corrected by Muriel; and finally chafing at this promiscuous method of enlightenment, he tipped the porter and dismissed him; thanked Mrs Leake, and decided not to trouble her for a bicycle that night, and requested Muriel to show him the way to a respectable hostel.

'I'm going ther' myself, sir,' said Muriel, readily. 'I worrk ther'.'

'Good heavens!' said Willy. 'You seem to be an extraordinarily convenient sort of girl to run up against at night, in a strange town. Come along, then.'

Mr Plum opened rather an irritable front door for Muriel.

'Coom along, coom along with yer. Yer late, and ther's company. That dinner fer one, 'e'es coom back, and a lady with 'e. Coom in.'

Muriel indicated Willy. 'Another of the parrty,' she said; and, in an eager aside, to Willy, 'They be here, sir.'

'Who?'

'The leddy you want, and the younger gentlem'n.'

'What? Where are they?'

'They was in the lounge,' said Mr Plum, 'but I fancy he be gorrn to 'is room.'

'Number fowerr,' added Muriel.

'That's all right,' said Willy. 'I don't want him. Where is the lounge?'

'Oop ther', sir,' said Muriel, and he hurried past the landlord, who waited to attack his handmaiden with a volley of querulous demands for enlightenment.

The lounge was unoccupied. Willy reappeared at the top of the first flight of stairs.

'Where's the lady's room?' he asked.

And Mr Plum called testily back, 'She aren't got one yet.'

'Gosh!' muttered Willy to himself, staggered by his own half-formed suspicions. He paused to glance at the doors on the first floor. Number 2. Number 3 . . . Yes, Four. He tried the door. It was unlocked. He went in.

Berty's spine had been duly embrocated, but he had neglected to replace his shirting, which hung in a dissolute fringe round his trousers. Louise had discovered a stiffness in her right knee, as a result of the embroilment of April Cottage, and this she was permitting Berty to inspect, it being difficult for one of her figure to determine for herself whether the joint was swollen.

Berty, a trifle preoccupied perhaps, found himself taken firmly by the ear and conveyed to the staircase, while Louise, overtaken by not the least of her night's surprises, and handicapped by the fact that one stocking had been pulled over one shoe, followed, as best she could and venting wild protest, in the rear of the procession.

At the foot of the stairs Willy transferred his grip from the ear to the collar and turned to address his wife.

'Go back to that room, and shut up. I'll be up there again in a minute.'

'But Willy – how dare you! How dare you follow me down here like this and behave like this? I'll . . .'

'You don't underst— Let me expl—' said Berty.

' 'Ere, 'ere, 'ere!' cried Mr Plum, 'I don't want to 'ave no trouble 'ere, ye know.'

'And I damn well don't intend to,' said Willy. 'Open that door.'

'But, look 'ere, sir . . .'

'Willy! That boy has already—'

'Here! Give me a chance, it's all a mist—'

'Open that door,' repeated Willy.

'Oh, he's best away,' said Muriel, and opened the door.

'Wull, by Jeremy,' said Mr Plum. ' 'E don't seem very popular to me. What's 'e done?'

Willy did not reply. Louise was still shouting. Berty was still protesting. Mr Plum was helplessly questioning. Muriel was holding the door open.

Berty was hurtled forth in his flapping shirting. The door was slammed. He crept away – goodness knows where – into the unsympathetic night. His mission was over.

A somewhat pathetic, defenceless figure; but the weak are born to suffer in this hard world. His indignities were many; his one consolation, the fact that Willy's boot had landed rather below the bruised portion of his back.

But Berty Pitts had another consolation, out of this strenuous day's training for the church militant, in the long run. As he stood and tucked in his shirt in the courtyard of the *Ring o' Bells*, he decided finally and definitely that his friendship with the dear soul must cease. She was nice, but not nice enough to counter-balance the extreme nastiness of her male relations. And, after all, he reflected, he had never been really so fearfully keen on her as she on him. No. He was through.

He kept his vow. The first action that Louise performed on her return to London was to call at his address. He was out. She called again. He remained out. She wrote. He summoned up all his courage, and made no reply to her. She inserted a paragraph in the personal column of *The Times*. 'Dear Soul wants her boy back – not her fault.' He didn't read *The Times*.

He even gave up attending St Phipp's. The last he ever saw of Louise was her right knee.

CHAPTER XX

Shadow of a Fairy Wing

'A woman!' shouted Mr Hole. 'A woman!'

There are not a few old gentlemen who, in Mr Hole's case, would have uttered this exclamation rather as a shipwrecked mariner utters his exultant, 'A sail! A sail!' Mr Hole's tone was, however, more suggestive of the panic-stricken householder's 'Fire! Fire!'

'I wish you wouldn't come creeping in like that,' said Eleanor. 'You gave me quite a jump.'

'What are you doing here?' demanded Mr Hole.

'Minding my own business.'

'Ah! That's just precisely what I thought,' said Mr Hole, and flung back into the sitting-room.

This young rip of a nephew with a woman in his rooms! A good-looking strumpet – of course, that was to be expected. But to remain here, a butt for her cheek – unthinkable. And he could still hear the rain, and he was in poor health and already damp. And where the devil was he to go? Oh, blast this!

To his intense annoyance Phryne strolled after him into the sitting-room.

'You needn't go,' she said, 'I'm not staying here, of course. You can use that room, if you want to.'

'Thank you. You don't suppose I'm staying here, either, do you?'

'Why not?'

'That'li do,' he rapped out, seating himself on the sofa and seizing a boot.

'Don't be so ridiculous,' said Eleanor. 'I don't think really we can either of us go out in this weather, so you'd better make the best of it.'

He glared at her with red-rimmed eyes from the sofa.

'I would rather go out and walk through the rain than stay here with a woman,' he said.

'What an extraordinary sentiment!' she replied. 'Most men I know would gladly walk through the rain in order to get here.'

'Oh, I daresay,' said Mr Hole.

'But then, of course, you're different, aren't you? I've heard of you. You're Algy's uncle, the woman-hater.'

Mr Hole, who was about to begin putting on his boot, paused and looked up again sharply.

'I am not a woman-hater,' he said. 'Nothing of the kind. I will not allow anybody to say that of me, because it gives an entirely false impression, and shows that the – that the person who says it hasn't got the gumption to make proper distinctions.'

'You run women down, anyhow.'

'Yes, and why? Because, in this God-forsaken community of ours today, a woman is neither educated up to the fulfilment of her prerogatives, nor would be content with them if she were.'

He subsided with a grunt, annoyed with himself at having been decoyed into discussion with this mistress. 'But I've no desire to continue the subject, thank yer,' he added.

'Oh, but I have,' she said; 'it's very interesting. What are a woman's prerogatives?'

'I'm not going to start arguing with you. The very fact of my finding you here like this—'

'You're trying to put the left boot on the right foot,' said Eleanor, as, indeed he was.

'Kindly do not speak to me,' he said. 'I don't like it.'

He placed one unsteady foot over a knee, and was in the throes of pulling on his sodden boot, when, in the most barefaced manner, this cool witch stepped forward and, before he could believe his eyes, glided back again towards the bedroom with his other boot. For a moment he could only stare; then attempted to master his anger and to speak with stern authority.

'None of those tricks with me! Give me my boot.'

'If you think,' she replied, with a slight assertive swaying of the head, 'that you're going to come in here, to think the worst of Algy, to say the worst of me, and then to pop out again, you're very much mistaken, Mr Hole.'

'The boot!' he cried.

'I suppose you've never been about very much, since those stupid and immoral days when it was supposed to be improper for a girl to visit a friend in his rooms—'

'Will you give me the boot?'

'Presently,' said Eleanor. 'It's quite against a woman's principles to give a gentleman the boot while she's still got any use for him!'

She stood swinging the boot by the laces as she talked. The tormented old gentleman had perforce to sit with his hands on his knees, inattentive and snorting, but in her subjection.

'You'd better listen,' she said, 'because until I'm quite satisfied that you see the mistake you've made, I can't possibly give you the boot. I owe it to Algy as well as to myself; or rather, you do.'

She told him her name – Mrs Bingham. She was a friend of Algy's, and had been dancing with him, thus fulfilling one at least of a woman's prerogatives – it being quite preposterous to suggest that men ought only to dance with each other. She had dressed – just as Mr Hole had been hoping to undress – in Algy's room; and had now returned to collect her belongings before going home. Algy had gone on elsewhere, on receiving an urgent summons from a male friend. Some mission of charity, she understood. Would Mr Hole now apologise and retract his insulting presumptions?

'My boot!' said Mr Hole.

'I'm sure it would do you good to apologise for once in your life,' said Eleanor. 'There's no harm, I assure you, in a young man having a friend who is a married woman. It's only when a woman's married that she begins to be able to appreciate the difficulties that beset a young man.'

She heard the voice of the guardian angel in her ear: 'Oh, I say! Not that old chestnut. I don't think you can serve that up even to him.' But this only made her rather more defiant. She raised her voice at Mr Hole.

'You've entirely misunderstood me, and I resent it very much. I'm not only a friend of Algy's—'

'I can quite believe that,' said Mr Hole. 'My boot!'

'I'm a friend of Diana's too.'

'Eh?' said Mr Hole, sharply.

'Yes. In fact, if you care to know, I've just returned from seeing Diana at your cottage. I slept last night in your bed. So how do you like your eggs boiled now?'

'What! Who gave you permission to go to my cottage?'

'I went on my own. I heard Diana was lonely, and I'm not surprised, now I've seen the place.'

Mr Hole jumped up from the sofa.

'What has been going on at my cottage, then?' he cried. 'Tell me. I demand to know.'

'Going on? I should think it must be difficult to think of any place on earth where less is going on – except your nasty rooster. He goes on.'

Mr Hole stood before her, doing Zulu-dancing movements of disquietude.

'Answer my question. Something outrageous has been going on down there. I've been warned. Now, tell me at once.'

'Warned?'

'Yes. You'd better tell me the whole truth. You've admitted you were there. When did you leave there?'

'This morning.'

'Well? . . .' Mr Hole fumbled at the dressing-gown. 'Oh, d— Where did that quivering idiot of a man put my coat? Ah!' He snatched his coat from the back of the chair, where Lemon had placed it. From the breast pocket produced his dilapidated telegram.

'Kindly explain that to me,' he said. 'And you may just as well tell me the truth at once.'

Eleanor dropped her boot gingerly, and took the telegram with a smile of curiosity. She read it aloud with increasing bewilderment and excusably faulty punctuation.

' "Cottage all upside down – now." Now. Oh, I see – upside down now. "Young man joined her double bed; got in yours. Out." Got in yours? Out? "Also." Oh, out also – I don't – Oh! "Also wine bought. Disgraceful behaviour undoubted easy." '

She looked up, her brows knitted in perplexity. 'Except for the last sentence, which seems to be a sort of general truism, the whole thing appears to me to be absolutely gibberish,' she said. 'Is it in a code or something?'

'Easy,' explained Mr Hole, watching her closely for any symptoms of masquerade, 'is a name. The name of the sender; as you know, if you've been to the cottage.'

'Oh! Yes. The charwoman that Diana sacked.'

'What!'

'One moment, let's try again. "Young man joined her." Joined who, does that mean?'

'My niece, of course. You needn't try to—'

'Oh,' said Eleanor. 'I think I see daylight of sorts. "Double bed got in – yours out" – yes. Easy, with her back up and trying to make mischief.'

'Come on. What has she been doing, this niece of mine, tell me that,' repeated Mr Hole. 'Who is this young man that has been to see her? It's no good shuffling. I shall find everything out.'

'The young man was Algy.'

'What? You needn't think that'll wash. Double bed?'

'I assure you Algy has been there. Diana, myself and Algy.'

'At my cottage?'

'Yes.'

'In one double bed?'

'Algy didn't sleep there. I slept there one night in your bed and the double one came this morning.'

'Oh, tell me the truth, girl!' cried Mr Hole, almost beseechingly, in his weary anxiety.

Eleanor looked at him steadily, and with a faint smile.

'I've a good mind to tell you the whole story,' she said.

'What? What?'

She turned to the sofa. 'Come and sit down here again. You can take that other half boot off. You won't be going yet. You'd better take your socks off, too, if they're wet. I'll get you Algy's bedroom slippers.'

'Certainly not! Leave me alone. I wish to hear—'

'You shall hear everything. Take off your socks.'

'I don't want slippers.'

'You do want slippers,' said Eleanor. 'I daresay one could always tell a despiser of women by his feet.'

She went into the bedroom, and returned in a minute with woolly footgear. Strange to say, Mr Hole was awaiting her barefoot. She collected his boots and socks and laid them neatly aside.

'Thank you,' he muttered, briefly. Then, Zuluing again on the sofa, 'Now, the facts about my cottage?'

Eleanor came and sat beside him on the sofa. Her face was like that of a woman gazing into a mirror, and knowing that somewhere below that reflection lay her true self. She did not speak for a time, and the old man began almost to whine. 'I'll tell you all about myself,' she began, at last, only to be interrupted at the outset.

'I don't want to know about you. I want to know about the cottage and Diana.'

'Diana and the cottage come in,' said Eleanor. 'I'll tell you everything in its turn. I don't suppose an ordinary person would sympathise much, but as you are like I am, rather a weird sort of being, it's just possible that you may understand me. It's rather a long story.'

'Oh, go on, for God's sake,' said Mr Hole.

'Are you warm?'

'Yes, yes.'

'Are you dry? I mean your exterior.'

'Yes, yes. Will you—?'

'Then listen,' said Eleanor.

She told him everything – everything to this queer old, petulant, inaffable, intolerant man – a strange confessor to choose. She was as frank and unbiassed as possible. She showed him herself – changeable, restless, pleasure-loving; a choice target for his vituperation. Her Reggy, on the other hand, must surely have impressed him as an ideal overlord. She told him of her marriage – Reggy got her, that was all, as he would get a hat. 'Yes, I'll take that – how much?' And she was a willing purchase. No hint of Diana or April Cottage yet, but Mr Hole sat scowling and listening rather intently.

Reggy's suspicions of her friendship for Algy – quite without foundation at the time. (Mr Hole's eyes widened a trifle at this qualification.) Then, the whole story of this latest episode – this first episode – in her married life. Her motives, as she had found them, now good, now bad, during the last twenty-four hours. A regular shuttlecock between the devil (a smashing wielder of the battledore) and the guardian angel (a neat placer) with Puck calling the score. That's what she had been, until the guardian angel had slipped one over out of the devil's reach, and that exponent of the game had thundered and retired in defeat. But would probably want another game before long.

Every detail she told – Diana, right in her surmise from the outset, if a bit previous in coming out with it, was completely justified. In fact, the only exaggeration that Eleanor was guilty of all through was a slight tendency to emphasise her eulogy of Diana. The whole story – she even told him where Algy had gone now. She felt a little glow of confidence, almost of tenderness radiating, as it were, from this funny, gruff old man. He said nothing, only occasionally gave her a frowning attentive nod. She liked the way he listened – felt him warming to her, though his expression never lost its severity.

Finally, she rose and brought her note from the writing-table, opened it and handed it to him. He frowned quickly through it; returned it to her. She took it back, and wrote another envelope for it, leaving it where it was before.

She sat again at his side on the sofa, as though awaiting his verdict. They remained thus in silence for quite a time. His first words were:

'My bed. Is at Pitcher's. She shouldn't have done that.'

'Don't you worry,' said Eleanor. 'You'll find your cottage much straighter than you left it, I expect.'

He growled away. 'I don't want it straight. I—'

Having pondered for another minute, and arrived at the conclusion that his affairs were not, after all, so disorganised as he had feared, he worked his eyebrows round at Eleanor.

'Why have you told me all this about yourself?'

She did not reply, but sat with clasped hands.

'Why?' he repeated, but not roughly.

'Well, I had to put Diana right with you, but – there was another reason besides.'

'What was it?'

She shook her head. Her voice sank to a whisper. He saw tears mount to her eyes and her pretty throat quiver.

'Because – I don't know – I wanted to tell someone. I'm all – I'm all muddled in my life and unhappy and wrong, and – I don't know – I can't steer clear of mischief; and I don't think I want to.'

'Mischief,' repeated Mr Holes, definitely; 'yes. You're very young yet, I suppose.'

'I believe it's the time of year, as much as anything else,' said Eleanor, recovering her natural manner.

'The time of year my foot!' replied Mr Hole. 'That's no excuse.'

'I don't want an excuse half the time,' she said, 'and that half is always the most enjoyable. I mean it though. I think it's much easier to fall into mischief at midsummer than at ordinary times. Don't you?'

'No,' said Mr Hole. 'Fiddle!'

'Oh, I don't know,' cried Eleanor. 'June and Piccadilly, and the sort of thrill of summer days and nights.'

'Yes; a nice summer day we've had today,' said Mr Hole.

'Ah, but don't you feel the sort of spirit of midsummer in your heart?'

'No, I do not,' said Mr Hole, 'and I hate the heat.'

'I know I nearly lost my head and went too far,' said Eleanor, 'but there is a good sort of mischief, too. Isn't there? Jolly, happy mischief. You must know that. Come on. You haven't been a grousing old misogynist all your life.'

'Come on? What do you mean "Come on"?' asked Mr Hole, with a trace of alarm.

'I don't believe I'm really inclined to be a bad character. I believe the fairies have come out for their annual midsummer school-treat, and have been having a bit of a game with me. And now it's over, and I'm going home to my husband – by the skin of my teeth – but there it is.'

'Oh, stuff!' said Mr Hole. 'You're simply a woman who is, I suppose, very attractive in the eyes of the average simpleton. Thanks to your social conditions, you've been given the opportunity to go astray, and you've very nearly taken it. You have thought better of it, I'll grant you that. But your behaviour throughout has been very dangerous and reprehensible. And it is outrageous bunkum to try and lay the blame on a fairy.'

'I'm happier now, anyway,' said Eleanor. 'Telling you all about it has made me happier, you very grumpy and rather dear old thing.'

'That'll do,' said Mr Hole, with a sniff, not entirely, perhaps, of distaste.

'Only I do want to be happy always – as happy as I can be with my nature – and with my husband's. They seem so different. But perhaps you say that a wife has no right to a nature of her own.'

'Well, a husband must be reasonable,' said Mr Hole. 'I've never denied that. Your gentleman sounds to me as if he could do with a lesson or two.'

'Nobody can teach Reggy a lesson,' said Eleanor.

'Then he must be a pig-headed fool!' cried Mr Hole, flaring for the moment into his customary wrath. 'There's no man on earth who can't afford to modify his opinions on occasion.'

'Well, we all want a little sunshine as well as the rain, don't we?'

'What?'

'A little laughter with our tears,' said Eleanor. 'Rain is very disagreeable, but very efficacious – so are tears. But, dash it, one must have some sunshine as well. My husband has no sunshine.'

'Then give him some,' said Mr Hole.

She thought over this difficult task for a moment, then turned to him, lightly.

'I shouldn't think *you* enjoy an awful lot of sunshine,' she said. 'Shall I practise on you?'

'No, thank you. I don't require any more sunshine than I get.'

'April Cottage,' remarked Eleanor – 'rather a wet April, I'm afraid.'

'So much the better. More likely to be left to myself.'

'I expect I could supply just the kind of sunshine you want. Do you know what I'm going to do?'

'Good heavens, what? Now, look here—'

'Don't be alarmed. I'm going home. I shall leave my things here till the morning, and call for them. And before I go, I'm going to exercise a woman's prerogative. I'm going to tuck you up on this sofa, and send you off to sleep.'

'Now, look here. I absolutely forbid—'

'A pillow,' said Eleanor, and was up and in the bedroom before Mr Hole could struggle to his feet. He stood and argued, protested, threatened, while she, with deft, long fingers, arranged his bed.

'That's it,' she said. 'Now, take your collar off and lie down.'

He grudgingly ceased to refuse her and gave way. Confound her. He was quite ready to admit he was sleepy, but . . .

She again returned from the bedroom with a blanket, and Mr Hole, of Hole on Woman, muttering an incoherent blend of gratitude and malediction, was tucked up.

'Now, just a nightcap,' said Eleanor.

'No, I tell you; I don't want—'

'Yes, you do. A tiny liqueur brandy to send you to sleep feeling all cosy inside.'

'I can't go to sleep yet. This young gambling rogue is at large, and may come dashing in with a dozen confounded policemen at his heels . . .'

'Oh, don't you worry about him.'

'I'm not. I'm worrying about myself.'

'You won't be doing that for long,' said Eleanor. 'Now, take this.'

'Oh – thank you. I don't suppose a little drop more will do any harm. I wish to goodness you wouldn't go on with this fussing and folly. Thank you. But it's ridiculous. I can't go to sleep yet.'

'Well, you can read for a little while.'

'Read! What is there fit to read in this feller's book-case? Besides, I can't see to read. It tries my eyes.'

'Oh, then I shall have to read to you,' said Eleanor.

'I absolutely decline—'

'Ssh. I'll turn this reading-lamp on and switch the other off.' She busied herself about the room. 'There! It's got a nice red shade. How restful! Now, what would you like me to read?'

'Nothing,' said Mr Hole.

'He's got all sorts of nice books tucked away here. Poetry. I'll read you some poetry.'

'You will do nothing of the sort. I dislike poetry very much.'

'Shakespeare?'

'No. Poof!'

'Oh, well – Byron?'

'No. H'ngh!'

'Mrs Hemans?'

'Oh, God!'

'Shelley?'

'H'm?'

'Lie down,' said Eleanor.

'Oh, woman, I will not be bullied and commanded and read to.'

'Lie down.'

He growled a last remonstrance, and closed his eyes, nor opened them again that night. He felt, from the sound, that she must be sitting on the floor at his feet, and he thought he detected the gentle pressure of her head against the bottom of the sofa. But as soon, almost, as he allowed himself to court slumber, slumber clasped him into her tender arms.

Soon there came to him the sound of a voice sweetly speaking words he used very dearly to love in younger, calmer days. He was conscious of them; unconscious; heard them in fitful murmurs; floated away on the wings of sleep to the sound of them.

'I love tranquil solitude,
And such society
As is quiet, wise and good;
Between thee and me
What difference? but thou dost possess
The things I seek, not love them less.

'I love Love – though he has wings,
And like light can flee.
But above all other things,
Spirit, I love thee—
Thou art Love and Life . . .'

She stopped reading, and looked up from the page; turned slightly – just a sidelong tilt of her chin – towards the head on the sofa. You would pray for her not to laugh at this, her latest, quaintest conquest; for what could her laughter be now but derision, and the hard irony of the courtesan at her curtain?

But in her laughter there was a little tremble of the lip; and into the brightness of her eyes stole the tears again. Soft rain to kiss the sunshine.

CHAPTER XXI

The Sunny Morning

The rain had ceased by the time Algy got back to his rooms; so indeed had the night. The indigo blue of a new and fairer dawn was in the sky. It was roughly the hour between sparrow-twitter and milk-clang.

He crept in very silently. Poor dear! What a vigil had been hers. Probably she had gone to sleep. He opened the sitting-room door without a sound. The red standard-lamp was burning. Yes, poor darling, she was curled up and asleep on the sofa.

He whispered affectionately, as he tiptoed forward,

'Oh, my—'

Mr Hole grunted loudly, and made a half-bouncing movement, as though sitting in a dream upon a pin. But he did not regain consciousness, possibly because the stifled cry of surprise which burst from Algy was exactly simultaneous with his own grunt.

Algy stood for some seconds, staring at his uncle in desperate bewilderment; then gaped at the bedroom door. It was ajar – Uncle must have been in there, or she – But where was she? He stole into the bedroom. The curtains had not been drawn, and he could see at a glance that she was not there. What the devil had happened? Lemon? Was he about? He stealthily explored. Lemon was not about.

He took another furtive glance at Uncle, who had now rid himself of the dream-pin and was slumbering lustily. Presently, in the bedroom, Algy found Eleanor's luggage. She had packed her things, but left them. Her portmanteau and dressing-case were beside his own, still unopened, bag. Had she managed to get out without Uncle finding her? That might be it. She had heard him come in, had quickly put away her belongings, and had crept out of the rooms. On the other hand, she might have left in tears of wrath, after a furious encounter. Well, he must wait till the old nuisance woke up. He'd soon learn the truth then.

Miserable sequel, anyhow, to a depressing experience. He had made his objective in good time, in spite of the storm. He had had to put his car up at a garage, and to walk to Shady Nook through the rain. Having arrived, he had found Mrs Krabbe in winning vein, and she not only declined to leave the tables and come down and speak to him in the hall, but even when he went up to see her, could not be persuaded tc grant him a few moments' privacy until her luck turned. She merely remarked aloud, 'Oh, I suppose the husband turned up then?' and played on. She enjoyed a success which suggested that, however sinister had been the host's methods in dealing with Captain Dumfoil, he certainly lacked the courage to apply them in the case of Mrs Krabbe. And she was playing baccarat with Mr Phonk at the time.

When, at length, Algy succeeded in imparting his secret warning, she merely said, 'Bless my life, is *that* all? Good of you to trouble to come, my dear; and I won't break faith with you, after what you promised that rotten stool-pigeon, but they won't be here till twelve at the earliest. I'll just have another dip or two and then come along.'

In vain Algy had reasoned. He was just on the point of leaving her to her fate, when Mr Morris, of the Metropolitan Police Force, pulled up the blind in the lavatory, and it was too late.

The proceedings had been very protracted and irksome. Algy had succeeded in persuading them that he was not playing, and had escaped with a kindly Cockney lecture from an inspector; but Mrs Krabbe had returned home with an appointment. 'This has been a lesson to me,' had been her parting words to Algy. 'Never again. In future I shall have nothing to do with anything of that sort. I only went there out of patronage to Phonk, who backed a bill once for me when I was hard hit. But I've finished with that sort of business now. In future, I shall only go to one of those good-class places in Piccadilly.'

Very weary was Algy, but he had no thought of sleep. He went to Lemon's pantry and boiled the ample kettle. Three kettles full, and he had quite a good hot bath in the making, though the making took a good deal of time. The hour of five was striking as he got into it.

Immediately – *B'rrrr!*

But he needn't have got out. He heard a raucous challenge from the sitting-room.

'Who goes there?'

Before the ring had been repeated, or Algy had dried his legs, there was a sound of blanket-entangled upheaval and egress. 'Oh, wait a moment – confound this thing all round my feet. Who are you, blast you, at this hour? Hold on.'

Mr Dawkins, in makeshift *déshabillé* and no melting mood, had left Reginald to it, and gone downstairs again to air his grievances. The traveller returned, though his journeys had been accomplished in a very expensive and commodious car, was feeling, and showing, the effects. He had attempted to sleep in the car, and had awakened with a stiff neck. His collar had been like limp paper before he started, and he had covered well over two hundred and fifty miles since then.

He pulled his nose at Mr Hole.

'You are the man here, what? Is your master here? Come.'

Greek and Greek. Mr Hole's back seemed to arch ominously. Algy remained, straining his ears, in the bathroom and the nude.

'Who the hell are you?' asked Mr Hole.

'Stop that. You can't cockadoodle me. I know what I want.'

'So do I,' replied Mr Hole, side-glancing furtively at a walking-stick.

'Stand aside,' said Reginald. 'I'll look for myself.'

'You'll look for yourself in the gutter,' said Mr Hole. 'I asked you a question. Who the hell are you? Who the hell are you? Who – who – the hell – the hell—'

Reginald nosed the passage from the front-door.

'I intend to come in,' he said. 'I advise you not to try and stop me. I've come five hundred miles to do it, and—'

'Oho,' cried Mr Hole. 'Damn my eyes, it's the husband.'

Reginald's forefinger went up, like a terrier's ear.

'There you are. Out of your own mouth. They're here. Let me by.'

'They're *not* here. I'm alone in the place. Oh, you can come in. You'd better. I've been hearing about you.'

'What? Where is my wife? Who are you?'

'I'm this boy's uncle. I had the pleasure of spending part of the night with your wife. Then she tucked me up to sleep and went home.'

'*You* here with her? Tucked! Explain yourself, sir. I insist on—'

'Don't stand and gobble there. Come in. I'm not going to stand repeating myself on a blasted doormat. I tell you, your wife has been here alone with me. And very attractive I found her. And I'm not partial to 'em as a rule. In you come.'

He piloted the baffled Reginald into the sitting-room. Algy, robbed of his dressing-gown, girt up his loins as best he could and advanced very cautiously into the bed-room.

Mr Hole stumped to the writing-table.

'Now then, you see this letter?' he held it up. 'Recognise the writing?'

'Give it to me,' said Reginald.

'Certainly not,' said Mr Hole. 'It isn't addressed to you. You notice who it is addressed to? Yes. Now I'll tell you something.'

He placed the letter in the pocket of the dressing-gown, and sat deliberately on the sofa.

'That letter,' he went on, 'is a letter of renunciation. She told me all about it. At the start, she only wanted to have what these young people look on as a bit of fun. Dancing, and such-like. She seems to get a fat lot of fun out of you! Don't you interrupt now. You can talk when I've done, if you want to.'

He paused to yawn. Reginald was standing in a tense attitude, and now firmly gripping the end of his nose, as though he found that, while of compelling interest, Mr Hole smelt.

'Before long,' continued the latter, 'she found herself being driven into danger. It may not be for me to say who seems to have done most of the driving. But when she got to the danger, she stopped in time. Not an easy thing for a woman to do, I think. A damned unusual thing, anyhow. It's easy enough to repent, but it's a tough job to stop in time, even for a man. But she did – she stopped. This boy has been out somewhere else all the night – gone to look after his aunt who's in trouble. So she stayed here with me for a bit, and then went home. And she wrote him that letter; she showed it to me. A simple, natural letter, offering to keep up her friendship with him, but only her friendship. I can't altogether blame the boy for being dangerously attracted. Even I was young once, and she's – well, she's the wife of a singularly lucky husband, I consider.'

'You,' said Reginald, 'you stopped this, I can see.'

'Nothing of the sort. She stopped herself. That letter was written before I ever saw her. She was just off home when I came in here. Only waiting for the rain to stop. And if you're a sensible man, you'll follow her very shortly. However, I don't wish to dictate what you should do, but it may interest you to know that I, who have written a work of rather more than one million, five hundred thousand words on the subject of Woman, am very deeply impressed by her – qualities.'

Reginald heaved out his great chest. He seemed to be on the point of challenging the right of any man to pay compliments to his wife. After a moment's reflection, he contented himself with a nod and a curt acknowledgment.

'Thank you. Yes. I shall go home at once.'

'Well, find your own way out, will yer? I want to go to sleep again,' said Mr Hole.

Beautiful dawned the day at South Ditherton. The sun was streaming in through the window of Number four bedroom when Muriel climbed the staircase of the *Ring o' Bells* with the eight o'clock tea. At her knock, Louise sat up with a little cry, and instinctively elbowed Willy.

'The girl with the tea. Get up and unlock the door, but don't go and say "Come in", before you've got back into bed.'

'Hallo! What?' asked Willy, raising a sleepy head.

'Don't forget you have no pyjamas with you, and have taken your trousers off.'

A new light seemed to dawn with increasing consciousness over Willy's expression,

'Now then; not so much of it,' he replied, suddenly. 'You can get out and open the door yourself. You've got your petticoat on.'

'Oh,' said Louise, gently. And she, too, seemed to recollect something. 'Very well, dear; yes. I'll see to it.'

She began to climb out of bed.

'Oh, be blowed to all that,' cried Willy. 'It's all right, old girl. I'll get out.'

Louise got back with a demure little, 'Very well. Only, if you meant what you said last night . . .'

'No, no, no; that's all right,' said Willy, and plunged happily out of bed and into subjection again.

Sunshine, too, at April Cottage. A gentle rap on the bedroom door and anxious enquiries.

'Come in,' said Henry. 'Good morning, good morning. What a lovely day! Did you sleep?'

'Did you?'

'Not so bad. Oh, tea! That *is* kind. I can do with some tea. I've got a slight throat this morning, but I don't think it's anything much, and I'm going to an infirmary in any case. I wish you were going, too. At least – you know what I mean?'

'I expect my uncle will be coming back soon,' said Diana. 'I might come and look you up at Downblotton. Shall I?'

She was handing him his tea. A sentimental smile beamed on his round face. He took and held her hand, instead of the cup.

'It will save me a journey if you do,' he replied. 'Oh, curse! I beg your pardon, but I've spilt some hot tea on my hand.'

But before this – before Louise and Willy and Henry and Diana and Muriel fluttered an eylid between them.

Eleanor, having silently stolen back into her own house with her own key, and sighed with relief to discover that Reginald's return had resulted in sedulous sheets on the bed in her room in case, laid herself therein and remained, very tired but drowsily watchful, until long after daybreak. Then she fell asleep, but not for long. For she awoke again at half-past five, to sit up in bed suddenly with a little 'Oh!'

Reginald remained stationary at the foot of the bed. His chins were in evidence.

'Hallo, Reggy!' she said. 'I— Oh, I am so glad. I heard you'd come home.'

'You,' he said, 'have also done that apparently.'

'Well, of course. I don't want to be anywhere else now you're back again. Oh, Reggy! I'm so glad to see you again. Why should I want to be anywhere else?'

Reginald, the pompous extremist, overdid it, of course.

'You shall go,' he said, 'where you like, when you like, and with whom you like.'

Eleanor slowly opened her eyes. This sounded unexpectedly propitious for Reggy.

'You have absolute liberty to do whatever you desire, with my full consent, and not only with my full consent, but also with my full approval and confidence, because I know that you will only do the things that are right. And if Louise ever attempts to make mischief between us again, by Christopher, I'll—'

'Oh, it wasn't Louise's fault.'

'Yes, it was. Of course, I am ready to admit that, to a certain extent, I was rather to blame . . .'

'What about me?' said Eleanor.

'You? No. Not at all. You might have been, but you – you stopped.'

'What?'

'Oh, yes; I've heard all about it.'

'Oh-h!' It dawned on Eleanor. 'Have you been along to Half Moon Street?'

'Yes. I – ah— I know I ought to have had greater faith in you.' He cut this short. He found apology very uncongenial.

'Oh, that's all right,' answered Eleanor. 'I didn't deserve

much faith in me. I very nearly— You met the uncle I suppose?'

'I did.'

'I see,' said Eleanor. 'Oh, well, Reggy – it's over – all over, and no harm done. I disobeyed you, and you distrusted me. If you're prepared to call it quits . . .'

He assaulted a bed-post.

'Sto— Don't, please, talk like that. I did not come here for bargaining and inquests. I came here for complete reconcilation and – ah – a fresh start.'

'Righto,' said Eleanor. 'And a little more ordinary common-or-garden humanity, Reggy darling. Just the teeniest bit less solemnity and self-importance. And now, come and give me a kiss.'

He obeyed – a hearty, resounding, slovenly business, which she did her best to appreciate.

'I know I'm not like other men,' he said.

'That's the last thing I want you to be,' said Eleanor.

He pulled his nose.

'Yes,' he added. 'For one thing, I rather think I can claim to be more successful than the herd.'

'Yes, but there's one thing you want that you haven't had enough of up to the present. I'll try and see that you get it in future.'

'H'm? What?'

'Chaff,' said Eleanor.

He took it kindly, with arched eyebrows and an unctuous, wrinkling smile.

'Ho! Will you, indeed?'

Pinched her cheek and went to put on his pyjamas.

Mr Hole, quite his old self, snarling, eyebrow-working, choleric, completed a savage verbal onslaught which failed to have any marked effect on Algy, who suffered it with a pertly waving cigarette, as he sat at his table. His uncle was erect on the sofa, but still involved in blanket about the legs.

'All very well, Uncle,' remarked Algy, 'but I'm not sure you haven't had a bit of a reminder yourself.'

'I? What do you mean?'

'Oh, I know you're very clever and prejudiced and self-reliant and all that, but you know, there's something no man can really get along without.'

'What the devil are you talking about, boy? What thing?'

'Why—'

Algy broke off, and turned his head sharply.

'What thing?' repeated Mr Hole. 'Come along, now. What is it?'

There was a confused scuffling sound in the passage outside. Then Lemon, heated, dishevelled, but triumphantly beaming, burst into the room, carrying his bowler hat.

'Oh, sir!' he cried. 'Oh, sir!'

'Hallo, Lemon! What is it?'

'It's a girl,' said Lemon.

THE END

ROOKERY NOOK

CHAPTER I

Augustus – A Preliminary Compendium

'The Principle of Archimedes,' said 'Gimlet' Prosser, folding his great hands inside his gown and addressing the Lower Remove Science Class in a wearied monotone, 'was established by him while in the bath. He entered the water and immediately leapt out again. Why did he suddenly leap out again, Dudson?'

'Please, sir,' said Dudson, 'it was hot.'

'O God!' murmured 'Gimlet' below his breath and, utterly ignoring Dudson, continued: 'He then ran through the streets, forgetting even to put on his clothes (the only point of the story which some of you boys seem able to remember) and shouting "Eureka, Eureka! I have found out, I have found out!" What had he found out, Graves? Longhampton, bring me what you are eating.'

'I have practically finished it, sir,' said Longhampton.

'I do not desire to investigate what you are actually masticating. But there is more in the bag. Bring the bag to me.'

To eat successfully in 'Gimlet's' Stinks class was a feat rarely accomplished and, for this reason no doubt, perennially attempted. Indeed he was more eaten at (as Graves put it) than any other master, unless, of course, you count poor old Stubbs, the half-blind instructor of drawing. 'Gimlet' knew by intuition when the most crafty and surreptitious eater was at it. More, he possessed the power to detect ('by sheer gift of smell', as Graves would say) the actual form of diet upon which the eater was engaged. He 'openly flaunted' (Graves again) this peculiar and useful faculty. Thus:

'When a body is immersed in fluid – not necessarily water

– it is buoyed up by – Andrews, I think you are eating gum-prunes. Bring them here, please.'

Or:

'Apply the nozzle of the pipette to the spirits of wine in the beaker and draw in gently with the mouth – all except Compston, who is unable to do so; his mouth being already full of chocolate-nougat.'

Longhampton shuffled uneasily towards the master, swallowing desperately as he went. 'Gimlet' inspected the contents of a miserably dishevelled and unclean little paper bag with a curiosity amounting almost to research. He then turned and delivered judgment, smacking the back of the culprit's head mechanically and rhythmically as he did so.

'White, creamy ones, you beastly little boy! You will stuff – stuff – stuff – all through your childhood, until you become a white – fat – flabby – man, whose whole constitution has been undermined by sickly – white – creamy – beastliness. Disgusting and repulsive! Write out the Principle of Archimedes two hundred times in extra school, you foul – fat – clout.'

Sniggers from the form, headed by Graves, who was hoping to escape defining the Principle of Archimedes through this diversion, but in vain.

Prediction remarkable! The good-hearted 'Gimlet' recites his prophecy and vanishes from our ken, pluming himself, hands in gown, upon his prescience. And behold Augustus Longhampton at twenty-eight!

But do not let his appearance tell against him too heavily. Remember that even in the days of his cloutish youth he had in him the saving grace of mischief.

About fatness there are no half degrees. In the bad man who is fat his fatness is his final damning knavery. On the other hand fatness may uplift the good-natured fool into the ranks of the lovable.

At twenty-eight Augustus was not outrageously fat. He was merely a little too fat, especially about the face. He was rather like a reformed edition of that Augustus of the Strewwelpeter family, the chubby lad who refused soup and perished miserably. But somehow the taint of the white creamy ones lingered yet over his whole personality. How 'Gimlet' (now with God) would have snorted in self-satisfaction and swung his gown!

Augustus had eyes that were beady and yet retained a look of helpless interrogation. He had a very short-clipped, nostril moustache. He had a way of blowing out his cheeks in perplexity and relaxing them into a smile at his own expense. His general attitude towards life reflected the surprised obedience of the newly-married orphan.

The marriage of Augustus took place but six months prior to the events more pertinent to this chronicle; and, seeing that it was the sole cause of these events taking place, and of the embarrassment to Augustus contingent on these events, the ceremony may be glimpsed in passing. Here, the best authority will be one Clive FitzWatters, cousin and best-man, whom we may quote verbatim, as he sits at the marriage feast and rehearses the romantic details for the benefit of an attendant dowager fresh from the continent.

'She? Clara? A Miss Posset, as you know. My dear lady, the Possets – *the* Possets. You'll find them on every hoarding that's big enough—

' "Posset's Jams in Jar and Tin:
Return your Jar and you're twopence in" –

'Yes, those people. Oh, very well off indeed. No, there is no longer any father. Only Mrs and a sister, a Mrs Twine. Yes, it was clever of Augustus, wasn't it? An aunt of ours smelt her out at a week-end house party and grabbed her like a trumped ace and then got hold of Augustus in the other hand and flung them together into a punt.

'There! That is Mrs Posset, the mother, over there. Observe the wedding garment. Looks rather as if she's been wedged into it by a high-class plumber and left for the day. A trifle asthmatic in the "h's"; but a kind heart. She looks to me at the moment exactly like a lavatory attendant at the old Brighton Aquarium who has won a guessing competition in *Answers* and is blowing the proceeds.

'Mrs Twine? Now, let me see. Ah yes; there she is, over there among the wedding presents like a fowl whose run has just been dug up. That is her husband, Twine, behind her; the short man in the enormous wedding trousers. Oh, yes, Mrs Twine is a good deal older than Clara. The Twines? In the jam business? Oh, no. They live on part of the dividends somewhere in Somerset. I've tried to be pleasant to the Twines, but whenever I talk to Twine I feel he's rather a worm, and whenever I talk to Mrs Twine I feel I am.

'Well, well. I suppose it's all for the best. Augustus had to do something for himself – had to be preserved in fact. Hence, one might almost say, the black currant situation.'

Thus the rather cynical youth Clive. And there was certainly no exaggeration in his statement regarding his cousin's need of the nutritive powers of jam.

The Longhamptons were of Irish descent. Not for many generations, however, had the family set foot upon the estates which remained nominally its due. In the massacres of 1641, the Longhampton of the period, whose name had become associated with the partisans of Strafford, had been driven forth and his lands laid waste by the Catholics. Following Cromwell's Act of Union, the estates were rescued from the Catholics and appropriated by the Protestants. During the Civil War of 1689 the property passed into the hands of the Freebooters. Upon King William asserting himself, the Freebooters were exterminated and the estates confiscated by the Desperadoes. The latter appear to have enjoyed a fairly long innings, but in the rebellion of 1798 they were ejected and forced to surrender the territory to an overwhelmingly superior force of Moonlighters.

During the potato disease of 1845, the Moonlighters were compelled by starvation to negotiate with the Corn Law Free Traders, who, however, yielded their claims to the property almost immediately to the Protectionists. Two years later the Protectionists gave way to the Young Irelanders, who, in 1858, were in their turn worsted by the Fenians.

From the time of the defeat of the first Home Rule Bill it had never been easy to determine the actual tenants of the Longhampton estates. But, as lately as 1905, a feud had been reported, owing to the shooting of an agent by a party whose right to exercise this authority was contested by the other local inhabitants.

Some one had once suggested to Augustus that he should, himself, visit his property in Ireland. He replied modestly that he had already been to one war, and there the matter dropped. Instead, like a wise youth, he married Clara Posset, of Posset's Jams, and speeded away to a perpetual honeymoon in a Rolls Royce. And Mrs Posset, who had always, as she herself confessed, 'sensed at least a lord for Clara,' went back rather wistfully to her home in Sutton, and Mrs Twine took Mr Twine back to Chumpton in Somerset and Clive FitzWatters went to Ciro's. All of which, a generation ago, would have appeared to constitute not only an impossible beginning for any romance but a definite end of all romance.

But during this generation all sorts of dreadful changes have overtaken Romance. She has been kidnapped by Realism, thoroughly outraged, and thrown into various shameful conditions. She has been lugged into the streets; she has been flung on to the screen. She has been exhibited in her half-forgotten modesty, a Godiva of today, to a populace of which every member is a Peeping Tom. She has been driven into the slums, into the factories, into the offices, into the Night Clubs, into the Ladies' Illustrated Weekly Supplement.

Yet, in the process, she has gained rather than lost her wondrous glamour, her wild, speculative attraction for mankind. How many a Winter's Tragedy have we seen gently disburdened by her sweet presence! Shall she not be bidden to come tripping and lend her merriment to the Comedy of Summer?

And even if she be not a guest at the nuptial ceremony of Augustus Longhampton, be sure she is watching it from no great distance, and marking down that puffy, complacent personality of his with eyes that sparkle with brooding mischief.

CHAPTER II

Excursion

One morning in mid-August found Clara at full buzz. Augustus always mentally likened her to a bee. There was none of the Malaprop affectation of the new rich about Clara. A dark little, buzzing, working bee was she, to whom the seductive lure of Life's honeysuckle was a secondary consideration; her first, the ordered routine and exhaustive housewifery of the hive.

The male bee, inclined to be torpid, and already somewhat saturated with the juice of the honeysuckle, led a conscientious but slightly puzzled existence in the hive, from which he found himself at frequent intervals firmly but quite kindly buzzed forth. But the simile ill fits Augustus, for they say that without a sting no bee can live. In Clara's case it grows even more apt; for, though never yet displayed, her latent powers of sting were indubitable.

Having honeymooned (or 'jam-mooned', as Clive sardonically suggested) well into the London season, the Longhamptons were taking their summer holiday rather late. The moors (a closed book to Clara) did not claim them. Their destination was that quiet sea-side resort, Chumpton in Somerset, at which Clara's sister Mrs Twine and brother-in-law, Twine, resided. Clara had taken a furnished house at Chumpton for a month, and Clara had furthermore arranged that Clara's mother, Mrs Posset, should go and spend the said month with Clara at the furnished house that Clara had taken. Augustus was going too.

Considerable buzzing therefore on this London morning in mid-August.

'Gussy!'

'Yes, dear?'

'Have you finished packing?'

'Yes.'

'Then come down.'

'Half a tick. I'm just trying to do the lid.'

'The what?'

'The lid, dear. The lid of the box. It's rather difficult to manage.'

'What are you trying to do?'

'The lid.'

'What?'

'Darling, my lid. I can't quite—'

'I thought you said you had finished?'

'I said I'd finished packing. I have. I've put the things into the box. The whole trouble is I've packed too thoroughly. Too keenly. The box won't shut.'

'Well, hurry up; because Abbot is going to take all the luggage and send it off by the 11.15 from Paddington.'

'All right. It isn't far to Paddington.'

'It's ten.'

'Ten? Ten what? Millimetres or something? It can't be ten anything in English. Don't be decimal, darling.'

'It's ten o'clock. The train goes at 11.15.'

'Oh, I see. All right.'

'It isn't all right, Gussy. You've got to drive Abbott and the luggage to the station in the car.'

'I know. I will. Where is Abbott now?'

'He's out. Getting labels.'

'Then Cook. Isn't Cook in?'

'Why don't you take some of the things out of the portmanteau and pack a smaller bag as well?'

'I believe if Cook could be got to sit on this lid—'

At this point Abbott, a bony, panting man, with a nose chronological of the seasons, made an obviously unwilling reappearance with labels.

'Oh, Abbott, have you secured the labels?'

'Not yet, madam.'

'What? Hadn't the shop got any?'

'Yes, madam.'

'Then why didn't you buy some?'

'I did, madam.'

'Then why did you say you didn't?'

'Pardon me, madam, I didn't think I did.'

'Have you or have you not got labels?'

'I have, madam. I thought you meant stuck them on.'

'I wish you would say what you mean and not waste time. You'll have a lot to do at Paddington and it's ten. Go upstairs and sit on the master's lid.'

'I beg your pardon, madam?'

'Gussy!'

'Yes, dear?'

'I am sending Abbott.'

'I know. You told me.'

'I mean to you, now.'

'Oh! Good!'

'One moment. Give me the labels, Abbott.'

'Give you what, dear?'

'I am speaking to Abbott.'

'Come on, Abbott.'

'Yes, sir.'

'Abbott! The labels.'

'Oh. Yes, madam.'

'Abbott!'

'Coming, sir.'

'I said red ones, Abbott.'

Considerable buzzing, you see.

'Now, Abbott; take a run from the door and land full on the lid.'

'O – h. Yes, sir.'

At this moment – *b'r'r'r'r* – the electric house-door bell below.

'Abbott!'

'Now, Abbott, try and leap so that you land full on the top of the lid.'

'Abbott!'

'Take a good run and take off from about two yards. I mean to settle this box.'

'Abbott!'

B'r'r'r'r.

'Abbott! The front door bell!'

'Half a tick, darling. Leap, Abbott!'

'Abbott, do you hear the bell?'

'No, madam.'

B'r'r'r'r.

'What?'

'Oh. Yes, madam, but—'

'Half just one moment, darling. Abbott is practically in mid air. Now, Abbott—'

'I can't go and answer the bell myself; I'm writing labels. Abbott can help you when—'

Crash! 'Ow!'

'Look out, Abbott!'

'Abbott! Do you hear me?'

B'r'r'r'r.

'Yes, madam. I'll come. O – h!'

'What's the matter? Have you hurt yourself?'

'Thank you, madam. My foot, slightly.'

'Have you incapacitated yourself?'

'Not to speak of, madam.'

'Then go and answer the bell.'

'I say, Abbott—'

'Sir?'

'Come up again directly you've done that.'

'Yes, sir.'

'And next time you'd better try standing on a chair and leaping downwards on to the lid.'

'Oh – h! Yes, sir.'

B'r'r'r'r.

'Hurry up, Abbott. Do.'

At the front door stood a telegraph boy. An added moan burst involuntarily from Abbott.

Immutable, unemotional witness of the drama of Life, delivering joys and sorrows to the home with an unconcern which we, who take too much thought for our morrows, would do wisely to study. With snatches of superannuated but hard-dying melody enlivening his duties and giving expression to his indifference. Still, after all these years, keeping the home fires burning; and even so, how necessary! Unremittingly and habitually still for ever blowing bubbles; and, even so, how apt!

In and out of our pages he will pop unnoticed, with a variety of strange tidings; from his red bicycle will vault, slithering his long-suffering soles upon the pavement and upon the gravel; heeding our fevered protagonists not a jot; detached and callous spirit of the outside world. For ever blowing bubbles. Cupid's naughty brother. At the front door stood a telegraph boy.

His appearance at this juncture could mean nothing but an additional spasm to the anguish of the departure. Abbott bore the yellow envelope up to the morning room pessimistically enough. Clara was at her writing table engaged with punctilious labels. From the room above echoed a lingering combination of heat and despair.

'Oh, a telegram! Gussy, a telegram! Give it to me, Abbott. Tell the boy to wait. It may be from the people whose house we've taken or something. Gussy, a telegram!'

'All right, dear. Open it and shout out what it is. I'm just having a final—'

'Gussy! It's from Mother.'

'Oh?'

'Gussy! She can't come. She's been taken ill.'

'Hurrah!'

'What?'

'I've done my lid. I had to leave out some of my thick pants, but I don't suppose it will get cold while we're there. At the moment the very sight of thick pants is enough to make me burst my blood-vessels.'

'Gussy, did you hear what I said? Mother isn't well and can't come with us. Come down here.'

Down he came, mopping an undignified brow. Clara handed him the telegram with a little shrug of resignation. Augustus read the message aloud, frowning and blundering not a little over its unpunctuated context.

Mrs Longhampton 49 Collington Terrace London

Too unwell travel today no need alarm not one my usual fits doctor says thinks only stomach will travel later join you there tell gertrude not worry no dizziness or quick breath like when have fits sorry mother

'Oh dear!' said Clara. 'Isn't it an upset?'

'That's all she seems to think it is,' replied Augustus reassuringly.

'I mean an upset about her not being able to motor down with us today. What had we better do?'

'Go without her, I suppose,' said Augustus in an ill-contrived tone of regret.

'We mustn't be inconsiderate about Mother.'

'I'm not being. I'm awfully sorry both about and for your mother. But what I mean is we must go today. You've let this elegant home to some American citizens who are coming here tomorrow morning. Meanwhile we've taken the house at Chumpton and are all ready to start, down to lids and labels.'

'We could go to an hotel and wait till Mother gets better,' suggested Clara.

'It seems a pity, when the house at Chumpton is all ready for us.'

Clara deliberated.

'Yes,' she said, 'I don't want to disappoint Gertrude, after all the trouble she's taken.'

'Exactly. She's fussed around and got things ready for us there, and has engaged a daily woman, whatever that means, as from today. The only thing to do is to push off at twelve o'clock in the car, just as we intended.'

Clara turned away from him, as though she preferred to

ponder the matter without his valueless assistance. She often did this. It was one of those little habits he had learnt to endure in unprotesting patience. In fact, it was Clara's signal for silence. Gertrude did it to Twine too.

'I don't like leaving Mother to follow us all by herself,' said Clara at length, rattling her fingers on the edge of the writing table. 'It's a long journey and she's not well. But then, of course, you could come up again from Somerset and bring her down in the car, couldn't you?'

'Oh,' said Augustus, in a voice of forced filial piety which would have discredited a curate, 'but how much quicker for her by train; and, for one in doubtful health, how much more dependable!'

'But, I tell you, I don't like Mother going about in trains by herself.'

'She could get into a carriage with ladies.'

'And, if she is suddenly taken ill in the train, do you suppose I should like her to have to fall back on some imaginary lady?'

'Well, no,' murmured Augustus. 'I don't suppose it would be an extraordinarily popular move with any of the interested parties.'

Clara flared up at this.

'Don't try and be funny. Especially about Mother. How would you like to have fits?'

'This is stomach,' protested Augustus gently. 'It says so in her wire – where are we? – "stomach will travel later" – no – "doctor says thinks only stomach".'

'All the same,' said Clara with decision, 'she is not going to travel down by train alone.'

'Very well, then,' said Augustus. 'We will go to an hotel and wait till she's all right again.'

'No, we won't. You shall motor to Chumpton by yourself.'

'What?'

'Yes. That's what we'll do. I will go to Mother and stay with her till she's well, and then bring her down to Chumpton by train. You shall take the car down there today. I will take all my luggage and you can take your boxes in the car. That will save Abbott going to Paddington and all the bother and excess and everything.'

'Excess?' echoed Augustus curiously.

'Yes. Some of the luggage would be overweight.'

'But no one was going to travel with the luggage. It was simply going as goods by passenger—'

'Darling, do not stand and talk and argue and waste time. Just listen to what I tell you. Directly Mother can manage the journey we will join you. Meanwhile you will be able to get the house all ready for us. The woman that Gertrude has engaged to come in by the day will be there waiting when you arrive this evening, so you won't have any trouble. Besides, Gertrude herself will look in tonight to see that you've got all you want. She will see that you're properly looked after until I come.'

'Oh!' agreed Augustus in a minor key. He nursed his own secret opinion of Gertrude.

'I think,' said Clara, 'that I had better wire Gertrude. But first of all I must wire Mother.'

'Yes, let us wire your mother. How dreadful that sounds! Like a Chinese crime.'

'Is that telegraph boy still there? Abbott!'

'Yes, madam.'

'I will go down and see to everything,' said Clara.

Briskly she went; in a few minutes, buzzing reappeared. 'I have looked up a train for myself to get to Mother's. Victoria, 11.18. Oh, dear! What an upset! I hope you will manage to look after yourself all right. I am sorry we shall be parted for a day or two, but there it is. Now I must write some fresh labels for myself. You won't be lonely, will you, Gussy?'

'I shall miss you, you know. Come as soon as you can.'

'Directly Mother's capable of travelling.'

'Yes, but if she doesn't get capable. I – I suppose, in that case, she wouldn't come at all?'

'If she's as bad as all that I may have to stay with her all the time.'

'Oh, but you don't anticipate my being a month all alone at Chumpton?'

'You wouldn't be alone. You'd have Gertrude and Harold.'

Harold was Mr Twine. Fortunately only Abbott, who happened to be passing the open doorway at this moment, noticed the facial expression of Augustus.

'By the way,' added Clara, 'I must wire Gertrude.'

'Again? You've just wired her once, haven't you? If you don't look out she'll fuse or something.'

'I haven't wired Gertrude. I've only wired Mother. I'll wire Gertrude and tell her what's happened and that she is to keep a careful eye on you at Chumpton.'

'I don't think you need put it quite like that,' said Augustus.

She glanced at him resentfully. She then crossed the room and closed the door; an unnecessary precaution, for Abbott could be heard on the floor above, transporting his master's portmanteau in brief and thudding spasms.

'Gussy. I do think that, just when we've got to be separated for a day or two, you might avoid making inferences of that sort.'

'Great Scot! I'm not making inferences.'

'Yes, you are.'

'No, darling. All I meant was – pick your words to Gertrude. Because I know perfectly well that Gertrude doesn't think I'm quite all I should be.'

'Oh. And are you?'

'Nowadays – certainly. But it was Gertrude who took the trouble to nose out that perfectly reasonable little episode of my bachelor days and to report it to you and to your mother.'

'Well, I told Gertrude and Mother that it was all past and done with and that I was quite prepared to forget it.'

'Exactly. That's just the very reason why I don't want you to go and give Gertrude the impression that I'm not to be trusted in future.'

Clara executed her little turning-away movement.

'You're very susceptible,' she said.

'I am no longer in the least susceptible,' replied Augustus firmly.

'I mean susceptible in thinking that I was thinking about that sort of horrid thing when I wasn't thinking about it in the least.'

'Oh, hell!' ejaculated Augustus, suddenly and unwontedly unconstrained. 'Let's cut all this out and go together to Chumpton and call back for Mother later on.'

'Mother comes first,' replied Clara, unappeased, snappy.

'That's news to me,' said Augustus.

She did not reply. She merely gave her dark tresses a little shake, seated herself at her writing table and buzzed into composition of the telegram to Gertrude. He watched her in silence, his animation subsiding as the bubbles subside on water taken off the boil. Outside, a passing cloud obscured the bright August sunshine.

Clara was a member of the species whose defining quality is the indefinite. Of appearance we speak now. She could be definite enough in practice, Heaven knows. She was on the short side, on the full side, on the sallow side. Probably even her mother, who had, as we know, 'sensed a lord' for Clara was conscious that all the purple and perfumes of Arabia could never have transformed Clara into a credible lord's lady. That self-contained matrimonial agency, the aunt of Augustus, had pretended to disagree. 'Quite a nice-looking girl. Her complexion may be nothing to write sonnets about, but it's her own, which is more than mine is. Presentable? Of course she's presentable. Jolly sight more presentable than most of the people she'll be presented to.'

By the time Clara swung round in her chair, Augustus was once more the willing hound, scolded out of his egregious growl. She too was her busy, buzzing, natural self. She read her completed effort to Gertrude aloud for her husband's benefit.

'Oh – h!' he said. 'Yes, very well. All right, dear.'

Clara rose briskly.

'Dear Gussy! I'm sorry we had a tiny—'

'Oh, no, no. That's all right, darling. We were both talking rot.'

'I can't say I remember talking rot.'

'I mean, I was.'

They embraced fondly.

'It's horrid parting from you,' said Clara. 'You will be as happy as you can without me, won't you?'

'Never so happy as with you, darling.'

Blissful moment! Outside, the cloud passed by, and forth again blazed the glad sunshine. Then – buzz, buzz – back to duty. 'Now I must rewrite the labels for myself' – buzz – 'I wish Abbott had bought red ones. I told him red' – buzz – 'Gussy, will you go and see that all my luggage is put in a separate pile in the hall?' – buzz – 'Abbott will help you. Abbott!'

Buzzed Abbott to the morning room. Buzzed Augustus and Abbott down from the morning room to the hall. Presently buzzed herself into a taxi and buzzed the taxi to Victoria Station. Buzzed off the telegram to Gertrude. Buzzed the 11.18 train from Victoria to Mother at a rate of record punctuality. Improved each shining hour.

Augustus partook of beer and a brief nap. Awoke, with a guilty eye for the clock, at noon. Ambled forth and got his car from the garage. Ambled presently down through Hounslow to the Bath Road. Behind him his replete portmanteau and a set of golf clubs. Before him, had he but known it, embarrassment dire, catastrophe romantic, entangled travesty of a holiday.

Had he but known it! Had he but glimpsed a vision of the adventure to come, would he have advanced or retired, which? Foot-brake or accelerator, which would it have been? In any case, he glimpsed no vision at all; so on he went, nodding, sleepily still, over his wheel, as he absorbed the smoothly fleeting miles of Bath Road; the gentle pulsation of his engine humming a lullaby of restful pleasure; the generous summer sun smiling down upon him from a sky whose clouds were but little fleecy clouds, innocuous as sheep in a meadow.

Very nearly asleep, drove this nice, plump fool of a fellow on towards Chumpton.

CHAPTER III

The Nook Gained

This Chumpton, situated on Bridgwater Bay and not to be confused with Chumpton Chedzoy forty miles inland, is remote from the busy thoroughfare of Life, facing as it does on three sides a lengthy expanse of pasture land, and on the fourth, at some distance, America.

Rejoicing in this isolation, Chumpton retains the manners and customs of bygone years. Its natives are in many cases insolubly connected with the maintenance of cattle and swine, and have, by long association perhaps, absorbed something of their charges' dispassionate nature.

Chumpton's industries are Chumpton's institutions. To exemplify: there is a coastguard station and a lifeboat. But it can only be presumed that, should the coastguard ever happen to sight, from the back parlour of 'The Boar and Litter,' a ship in distress off Chumpton, then the gallant lifeboatmen would carry their providential craft over the mile of mud which forms the foreshore, and would plunge it with a rousing cheer into the ripples which the trained eye can sometimes detect on the horizon nearest America.

But no ships pass off Chumpton. The coastguard and the Customs Officer, instituted by some ultra-cautious government in days of old and officially overlooked ever since, serenely slumber on, and the lifeboat reposes in dry dock, a time-honoured playground of youthful pirates.

Chumpton possesses, however, a railway station, from which small trains, laboriously fuming, disconnect with main line trains at a junction some miles distant. It is an accepted fact that the departure of outgoing trains from Chumpton is regulated by the movements of the station bus. The train is there for the purpose of bearing away the freight deposited at the station by the bus; to leave without the freight would be patently ridiculous. And the bus, being apparently a relic of the mid-Georgian coaching era, is a trifle uncertain in time-table, though commanded by a local Goliath with an optimism calculated to defy the flight of days and moments. ('Laate? Noo. Two minutes maybe. Who cares fer a couple o' minutes?') Thus the small trains disconnect.

Like Gaul, all Chumpton into three parts divided is – Chumpton Town – Swallow Road – Swallow. Swallow is the quarter where lies the golf links, and is in itself a little sunlit hamlet, nestling among the sand-dunes, its industries caddying and laundry work. Between Swallow and Chumpton Town lies Swallow Road. Swallow Road.

Swallow Road is the aristocratic and refined portion of Chumpton. Here stand the residences of the rusticated but patrimonially genteel and utterly nice residential ladies who dwell at Chumpton and adorn its township; of the retired but still bellicose and Morning-Post-shaking sons of Mars who settle at Chumpton and thrash its links. Here stands Swallow Lodge, the home of Admiral Juddy and here Swallow Dene (the Misses Creepe) and Alcasar (Mrs Moon) and Frascati (Mr and Mrs Twine); and many other well-appointed and utterly nice residences, containing many other desirable and perfectly-appointed residents, stand in Swallow Road. So desirable are the residents that each is a little better than the other, but all observe the first of a neighbour's obligations, and arrive, as in duty bound, at the tea-table and at the Bridge-table, bubbling with little murmuring currents of gossip or pregnant with great bursting thunderclouds of rumour.

Here, too, like little busy balls of quicksilver on a plate, are little cliques, running together, amalgamating, separating and running together again into another little ball. Here are the Ladies' Golf Club and the Ladies' Croquet Club and the Ladies' Bridge Club, with Mrs X of the Golf Committee and Mrs Y of the Bridge Committee secretly criticising Mrs

Z for the futile manner in which she acts as a member of the Croquet Committee; and with Mrs Y and Mrs Z mutually vilifying Mrs X for the preposterous resolutions she sees fit to recommend to the Golf Committee; and indeed with all three ladies agreeing over an utterly amicable teapot, as to the absolute impossibility of catering for the critical and sneery tastes of some of the less enlightened and, in fact, 'not quite quite' residents of the less desirable and more poorly-appointed residences of Swallow Road.

Inland off Swallow Road lay (and still lies) Lighthouse Road, declining steeply to the boundary of the prairie of pasture land aforesaid. In Lighthouse Road stood (and still stands) Rookery Nook, the home of Mr and Mrs Mantle Ham. Lighthouse Road contained no lighthouse, nor any sort nor kind of any condition or hint or innuendo or legend of, concerning, about, or, in any possible way, vaguely suggestive of a lighthouse. The lighthouse was miles away, the other side of the Ladies' Golf Club. However.

Rookery Nook was at the Swallow Road corner of Lighthouse Road, and was in consequence not involved in the steep decline of the latter. Indeed it stood in a very lofty and eminent position at the corner there, and raised its head considerably above the heads of some of the residences on the opposite side of Swallow Road; so that, as viewed from the sea-shore, Rookery Nook had rather the appearance of a very upright dowager, seated in the second row at a children's matinée.

Among all the well-appointed residences of Swallow Road, Rookery Nook enjoyed a reputation of its own for appointment. The modesty of its name was due to the fact that the Mantle Hams regarded it as a mere country retreat in comparison to the mansion which should have been theirs if they had decided to burden themselves with a mansion nowadays. But the neighbours who were fortunate enough to be invited to Rookery Nook (and how many a visionary battle had been fought, how many eyes torn metaphorically from their sockets over those contentious invitations!) stated without hesitation that Rookery Nook's interior did full justice to the eminence of its position. It was practically the only house in Lighthouse Road.

As a matter of fact there was another house in Lighthouse Road; but so sharply declined Lighthouse Road, that, whereas Rookery Nook stood proud and pre-eminent and white and clean and high and dry, the house below it appeared to huddle forlornly in a dell, shadow-swept by the plantation of elm trees which screened Rookery Nook from a neighbour so undesirable.

In the mists of morning and evening, which began only at that dell and which saturated and depressed only that dell, squatted the melancholy little house down the decline; the tall, regular line of elms blocking the view, as the fan of a horrified matron blocks out a vision obscene. Hopelessly situated little house, no doubt badly-appointed little house, there it huddled in the mists, not unlike some cold and outcast paddling child, paddling too late, alone and entirely without enjoyment.

And whereas no resident raised her head more imposingly or basked in the sunshine of Swallow Road esteem and of Swallow Road consultation more absolutely and more beamingly than Mrs Mantle Ham, so there hung over the occupants of the small house in the dell a mist of rumourous suspicion and of strange, intangible secrecy.

The man who lived there was undoubtedly very foreign – German, Dutch, or Swede – his nationality had never been clearly established. But with him lived a daughter who was unquestionably pure English. A good-looking girl, in a way; but – well, really – as if she could really be his daughter. No, thank you.

'No, thank you,' said Mrs Mantle Ham. 'No, thank you,' echoed Mrs Twine, of Frascati, Swallow Road. 'No, thank you,' chorused the readily responsive community. Some of the husbands, sneakingly discussing the 'daughter' in the sanctuary of the Country Club, had come to know her by the title of 'Miss No Thank You'.

Once, an unguarded resident of Swallow Road had spoken to Mrs Mantle Ham of 'the house next door', and had been severely bitten. As if a house like that, containing such shameless people, could be even mentally regarded as 'next door' to Rookery Nook!

They had been there for over a year now, the foreigner and the 'daughter'. Nobody called of course. The Rector had originally made a tentative effort and that had sufficed.

For the Rector had returned to the sunlight of Swallow Road with gills working and eyebrows raised. Over his experience tea-cakes had grown cold and trumps uncounted. At the gate of the little house he had conducted persuasive but sceptical overtures with a bull-terrier of the type whose sniff is worse than his bark. Gaining the front door, the Rector had been confronted by a horny and hostile maidservant of middle age. At the head of the staircase had hovered a fleeting vision of a daughter in, the Rector thought, deshabille.

The horny maid, leaving the Rector on the doorstep, repaired to an inner chamber, whence issued the sound of one challenging syllable:

'Who?'

The comparatively measured tone of the maid had been heard to explain. Then followed this remarkable comment:

'He shall go. I do not care for him. I do not agree with his beliefs. Tell him that I worship only the Gods of Wine and of Fire.'

On the delivery of this message the Rector stated mildly that he had not called necessarily in the cause of the True Faith, but primarily to extend a neighbourly greeting to one who had recently taken up his abode in the parish. This declaration received a more practical, but no less menacing, response, overheard from the inner room.

'Tell him that if he fails to go immediately, I myself will come and run him out.'

Lingered and thickened therefore the mists overhanging the little house in the dell. No attempt was made to alter the rather inappropriate name with which former tenants had endowed it. 'Pixiecot' (in one word) it remained. From the transactions of the horny maid, who performed the shopping for the household, it was ascertained that the name of the gentleman now in possession was Putz.

With the advent of an important golf-meeting, accompanied by a protracted and embittered Bridge squabble, Swallow Road soon lost interest in the Putzes. Then, suddenly, in the spring of the year with which we deal, the interest was reawakened and intensified by a very singular happening.

Mr Mantle Ham had gone out one evening to attend a committee meeting of the Country Club. Mrs Mantle Ham retired at eleven o'clock. At eleven-thirty Mr Mantle Ham entered her room, labouring under strange excitement and tangibly heated about the brow. Mrs Mantle Ham, sitting up in bed and regarding him with a cooling wonder, demanded the reason of this unusual condition in her husband.

'I have just seen a most amazing and inexplicable thing,' said Mr Mantle Ham.

'Bonsor,' said his wife (his name was Bonsor), 'are you quite sure?'

'How the devil could I have seen it if I wasn't sure I'd seen it?'

'Who was at the meeting?' put in Mrs Mantle Ham, who kept a black list of her husband's acquaintainces.

'Never mind about the meeting. This didn't happen at the meeting. It happened next door.'

'What!' cried Mrs Mantle Ham, sitting up further in bed.

'I mean, down the road.'

'Down this road?'

'Yes. Do you think I meant down the Old Kent Road?'

'You mean at that dirty little house?'

'Yes.'

'What happened? What have you been poking your nose in there for? How came you to go anywhere near that disreputable little shameful, shameless house?'

'Well, I'll tell you if you'll only—'

'Tell me then – spluttering there!' said Mrs Mantle Ham.

'I was coming home, and just as I got to this gate I heard sounds coming from that house.'

'What sort of sounds?'

'Sounds of a sort of row.'

'Well, if there were sounds, I suppose there was a row. I wish you'd—'

'I don't mean a row, a noise. I mean a row. A row going on.'

'A quarrel?'

'Yes, I thought so. Anyhow I heard a row, a noise. So I went down to the elms and had a squint.'

'A squint?'

'Yes. To see if I could see what the row was.'

Mrs Mantle Ham heaved in bed, but was too interested to be punctilious.

'I looked through one of the elms,' continued Mr Mantle Ham, 'and what do you think I saw?'

Mrs Mantle Ham violently adjusted her boudoir cap but said nothing.

'I saw,' said her husband, dropping his voice mysteriously and illustrating his story with a wealth of gesture, 'the man come out of the house. He had his pyjamas on.'

'So I should hope. Well?'

'In his arms he carried the woman. Like this. In his arms.'

Mrs Mantle Ham heaved up a mountain of bedclothes with a knee.

'Go on, go on,' she said. 'I don't imagine he was carrying her on his head.'

'As a matter of fact, he was practically. He had her head over one shoulder and one arm slung over one arm and he held one hand in one hand and, as far as I could see, the sort of under part of one thigh in the other.'

'You seem to have looked very closely. Go on.'

'Well, naturally I was interested. She had pyjamas on too.'

'How do you know?'

'Well, dash it, I could see. The moon is quite bright and there was a light from the house shining right on to her.'

'And presumably on to him too, if they were in this peculiar attitude?'

'Yes, I suppose so. Well—'

'You don't seem to have noticed him much. Go on.'

'I have just told you. He was holding—'

'Go on.'

'Well, I stood and watched. Naturally, I mean to say, one doesn't often run up against this sort of thing and I was keen to see exactly what was going to happen.'

'H'm. Well?'

'Well. He carried her, in the way I've told you, out into the front garden and put her down in a sort of sitting attitude in a sort of bird bath.'

'In a bird bath?'

'Yes.'

'With water in it?'

'No, so far as I could see, there wasn't any water in it.'

'Then how could it be a bath?'

Mr Mantle Ham, who was a short, stout man with a bald head and blue veins on his face, apostrophised the ceiling.

'Is there any water in your bath in the morning before you turn it on? Is your bath any less a bath because—'

'Never mind, never mind. The man carried the woman out into the garden in her pyjamas and sat her down in a dry bird bath. What then?'

'Well, I suppose you'll admit that was pretty extraordinary for a start. As a matter of fact I'm not positive it was a bird bath, but it was a sort of stand thing, something like a sun-dial standing about three feet from the ground. He sat her on it and moved about two or three yards away.'

'And she continued to sit?'

'Yes. Her attitude puzzled me. I couldn't make it out.'

'You mean the way she sat? Why did you find that so interesting?'

'I do not mean the way she sat. I mean her mental attitude. She turned her face away from him in a devil-may-care sort of way. Sort of longwooer.'

'What?'

'She didn't seem to care.'

'Was that so very peculiar?'

Mr Mantle Ham apostrophised.

'If I carried you out into the garden in your nightdress, and sat you down on a stone bird bath, would you treat it with longwooer?'

'Thank you. If you wish to draw comparisons between me and this low woman and in whom you seem so interested—'

'Well, aren't you interested?'

'Not in the very least. Go on. What happened then?'

'The man began gesticulating at her and talking.'

'What did he say?'

'I couldn't quite catch. He was talking some foreign language I think.'

'I suppose you mean you caught, but couldn't understand.'

'He sort of declaimed, like this—'

'Don't do that,' cried Mrs Mantle Ham. 'You'll wake the servants.'

'He kept it up for about two or three minutes; then he sort of dashed at her and picked her up again and sort of strolled about with her as if he was sort of looking for another place to put her.'

'And then?'

'Well, I sort of craned, I suppose, and must have made a noise; because the dog—'

'What dog?'

'They have a dog. An ugly looking brute. It was with them. It must have heard me, because it came in my direction. Still, I think I'd seen all there was to be seen.'

'Did you run away from the dog?'

'Oh no. I think it was quite friendly. But I'd seen enough.'

'Did the dog go for you?'

'No. Poor devil, I expect it gets ill-treated and was looking for a friend. It came behind me almost up to our front door, sort of whining.'

'Yes, I heard you slam the door in a great hurry.'

'Did I? I didn't mean to. Anyhow, that was what happened. Don't you think it was most extraordinarily queer?'

'I really refuse to interest myself in the doings of such impossible and degraded people. Especially at this time of night. Don't make a noise undressing. Remember to switch off your light.'

Nevertheless, Mrs Mantle Ham found the story of sufficient interest to retail it to Mrs Wintle on the following morning. Mrs Wintle ate it ravenously and hurried down the Swallow Road. Immediately the wildest rumours spouted forth like waters from a geyser. The daughter [*sic*] had been seen posing in Nature's state on a pedestal in the garden, while Mr Putz poured libations at her feet and cried aloud upon the names of his heathen deities.

But no more was heard of the strange occurrence, and from any inquisitive eyes Pixiecot seemed to shrink even more deeply into the mists of secrecy. Then came that priceless row, when Mrs Fludyear removed the croquet hoops in order to prevent Miss E. Creepe from playing before the lawn was in fit condition, and once more the Putzes dwindled into temporary oblivion.

Chumpton Town evinced no interest in the Pixiecot ménage. The horny maid settled the tradesmen's accounts regularly, and, for the rest, if they were folk who preferred a quiet life and to keep theirselves to theirselves, why, let 'un bide. Once only had the eccentric behaviour of Mr Putz invited comment during the evening dissertations at 'The Boar and Litter'.

Behind Pixiecot was a meadow used for the occasional and primitive cricket matches extemporised by Chumpton. One afternoon, a swarthy townsman – no other indeed than the station 'bus driver – on going in to bat, inquired, with much whetting of the palms and twirling of the willow, how many runs were allowed for a hit out of the ground. On being told six, he proceeded to hit the first ball he received for this number. The ball cleared the hedge and fell, with a distant sound of crashing glass, somewhere in Pixiecot. Long-on, a somewhat reluctant small boy, was commissioned to retrieve it. At the boundary he was confronted by Mr Putz, who, with flashing eyes, was holding the ball aloft, like a Pagan victor returning with a trophy of the fray. The small boy began to stammer an apology, but this was cut short.

'It is good,' said Mr Putz. 'Tell him with the club that, yes, it is good. It is like battle and bullets and great red balls bursting through my house. More.'

The batsman did his best to oblige Mr Putz, but, after two inglorious attempts, had his wickets shattered; whereupon Mr Putz, who had been watching from the hedge, made an extravagant gesture of dismay, and retiring into Pixiecot, reappeared not again.

His action was attributed, in 'The Boar and Litter', to the fact that he was 'a bit furren'. This explained anything he might do, comprehensively and finally. And Chumpton Town thereafter paid little heed to Mr Putz or to his household.

The summer months passed dreamily by. Mrs Twine negotiated for a month's lease of Rookery Nook on behalf of her sister, Mrs Longhampton, and obtained the boon together with a gush of social self-satisfaction which an obvious undercurrent of jealous Swallow Road comment served only to increase. And in Chumpton Town a few misguided holiday-makers were collected by the straggling little trains and emptied into the station bus. A few chars-a-bancs, loaded with trippers from the Welsh coast, came pounding into the neighbourhood to be held up and regarded with slow fear by wayside cows. And the Chumpton natives, reflecting as usual the emotions of the cows, themselves gazed with slow fear at these Juggernaut emblems of the rapid and noisy world beyond Chumpton, and studied with sadly shaking heads the mile of mud which alone offered further egress from that rapacious and progressive world.

And in Swallow Road Mrs Stagg threatened to resign from the Bridge Club, and Barbara Uphill won the Croquet Tournament, receiving six bisques (her mother being on the handicapping committee), and other less important events took place. And finally, in mid-August, Mr and Mrs Mantle Ham packed up and went to stay for a month in Scotland; and people realised that this definitely signalised the conclusion of the Summer Season, and that, within a few weeks, they could settle down to the ordered and traditional routine of Autumn.

And into this ordered and traditional routine of Chumpton Town and of Swallow Road came, very late one evening, open-mouthed in inquiry, urged by gesticulating thumbs, impeded by kine, in trouble with changing gears, the stout and smiling Augustus Longhampton, and landed his car, with much out-cheek-blowing of satisfaction, in the well-appointed garage of Rookery Nook.

CHAPTER IV

The Nook Invaded

Upon the very threshold of Rookery Nook occurred a portent.

Augustus, having stowed his car in the garage, tried to enter the house by a side door, which, however, he found to be locked. So, leaving his portmanteau in the car, he walked round to the front door.

The front door strangely opened at his approach, like the front door in a fairy tale. At this a wiser man might have hesitated to proceed, fairy tales being notoriously dangerous ground for recently married gentlemen of under thirty. But Augustus was not wise to portents.

The automatically-opening door was, in point of fact, readily accounted for. On gaining the portal Augustus found himself face to face with the daily woman.

The daily woman was short and round. She had no neck and, as a result of this deficiency, her head appeared to be straining out of the morass of Tartan costume which adorned her person, as the head of an indifferent swimmer strains upwards to avoid the ocean. Very inflamed was her face, owing perhaps to the continual effort to remain above her body, but, more probably on this occasion, owing to wrath.

'At last!' were her first words. 'And about time too, if I may say so.'

'Sorry!' said Augustus. 'I had a punct—'

'Well, now you 'ave come, will you kindly come in and mind the cat,' said the daily woman.

This rather nettled Augustus. Had he, dash it, just completed a long and trying journey for no better purpose than to sit and mind a cat? A disgruntled yowl from his feet interpreted the true significance of the daily woman's stricture.

'You are treading on its tile at this moment,' she pointed out.

'Oh, so I am,' said Augustus, investigating. 'What a nice ca—'

'Get off, get off!' said the daily woman.

Augustus side-stepped gingerly, and the cat shot like an electric streak into the pantry.

'You see, I didn't expect to find cats here,' said Augustus. 'You, I take it, are the daily woman?'

'Me name is Mrs Leverett,' was the somewhat pertinent reply. 'Engaged be Mrs Twine. Mrs Twine, she informed me that you would be coming alone without the lady and tells me to wait 'ere until you arrives. Whom 'owever, I should not have consented to do so, 'ad I not thought that you would 'ave been 'ere at a Christian hour.'

'I'm awfully sorry,' said Augustus. 'My paths were with thorns beset and that sort of thing.'

'Mrs Twine, she also stated that when you come, I was to go over to 'er 'ouse and tell 'er so.'

Here Mrs Leverett was unconsciously happy in her phraseology. It was indeed the custom of Mrs Twine to 'state' prospective events.

'Whom 'owever,' continued Mrs Leverett, 'I cannot do. I am a working wife and mother, and there at 'ome, waiting for me at this moment, is my children and cetera, not to mention my 'usband and what not.'

'By Jove!' remarked Augustus pleasantly. 'I wonder you can find time to be daily. All right. I'll let Mrs Twine know I'm here. Don't you wait. I'll find my way about. Only you might let me know where the food is kept.'

'Mrs Twine, she 'as sent in some 'am and two eggs, which I 'ave laid in the dining-room,' said Mrs Leverett. 'The eggs is already 'ard-boiled. Also bread, butter and cetera.'

'That's fine,' said Augustus. 'I'll look after myself. You'll be back here again in the morning, I suppose?'

'At eight,' said Mrs. Leverett. 'Earlier, I cannot be.'

'Righto. Give me a call at eight.'

'Your bed is prepared in the large room.'

'Righto. I'll find it.'

'I 'ave the key of the side door and can let meself in. Will you wish for tea in the early morning?'

'Er – well, I do rather wish for it as a rule,' said Augustus.

'Very well. And 'ow long will it be, sir, before your lady come down 'ere?'

'I've no idea,' said Augustus.

'Mrs Twine, she will be 'aving the ordering of things in the meantime. Is that it?'

'That's it. Mrs Twine is pretty good at it.'

'Good night to you then,' said Mrs Leverett.

'Goodnight to you, Mrs Swiveller,' said Augustus.

Half-an-hour later found Augustus refreshed and well-liking. He had located the dining-room, the ham, the eggs. He had repaired to the garage, where, aided by the well-appointed lighting arrangements, he had propped his portmanteau up in the car, unlocked it and, with considerable dislocation of a variety of wearing apparel, had extracted from it a bottle of whisky, which he had borne in triumph to the feast, leaving the problem of how again to close the portmanteau in order to lug it indoors to be decided upon a full stomach.

In careless enjoyment of a post-prandial cigarette, he presently emerged from the dining-room and took stock of Rookery Nook.

O eminently desirable, the modest mansion of Mrs Mantle Ham! O for the hand of a house-agent, that we might obtain our bearings with seemly deference!

The front door gives entrance to spacious hall, suited to additional living room and containing fine old open fireplace in Jacobean style with rich oak overmantel. Parquet flooring, valuable Turkey matting, oak-panelled walling and mullioned windowing.

The hall furniture comprises large Chesterfield, one, situated near fireplace; chairs, one set of six after Chippendale, massive hall table and other accessories. At the far end of the hall the servants' quarters and another small passage, curtained off and leading to recess for gents' hatting and a foregone conclusion for usual offices.

On the right, winding sharply, the staircase (oak). On your left, as you stand with your back to the entrance, the dining-room and, beyond it, the study. The drawing-room door on your right, between the fireplace and the staircase.

Stately and decorous dining-room, with oil paintings of the only two Mantle Hams who had rashly submitted to the ordeal of portraiture: to wit, Mr Mantle Ham's father, a three-bottle man, surprised by the painter in a mood of glassy-eyed challenge just after the third, and Mr Mantle Ham himself at twenty odd, in the guise of a very erect and self-conscious huntsman. Overcrowded, perishable, perilous drawing-room; full of things. Full of a cold pale-grey stretch of carpet; carpet calculated to magnify one promiscuous drop of spilled tea into an eye-smiting puddle of blemish; carpet upon which one unstudied footfall would stand forth in damning imprint, like Friday's upon the desert strand. Full of things. Full of garish cretonnes, stuffed out with bulging pieces of furniture, like the wives of profiteers in gala array. Full of great, soft, yielding sofa and receptive, sitter-engulfing chairs. Full of little tables that could be propped up by disentangling little, spindly legs, some of which could be shot out to one side in order to support a hovering flap. Full of china-cupboards, full of shepherdesses, staring in timorous fragility, awaiting but a sneeze to fly into a thousand bashful fragments. A full room. Full of pictures, not in water-colour but, even more delicately, in the faintest tinted chalk, the coyness of their workmanship emphasised by the elaborate gilt of their frames. A room too precious and perishable for Bridge. Those shepherdesses were incongruous with a doubled spade. For Bridge, the hall, where Mrs Mantle Ham could really let herself go, and where her partner could hold none of her trump-suit and fail to take her out without detriment to the brittle drawing-room mirror or to the ormolu clock whose very beat was but a lingering threat of expiration.

Beyond the dining-room, the study; sanctum of Mr Mantle Ham. A very orderly room; nothing in it of pipe-racks or of stray golf-clubs. A stiff room. All the books were not only in all their bookshelves, but were all in perfect order, sized like a squad for drill, leather to leather, buckram to buckram. On one of the bookcases a bust, unidentified but bearing a remarkable resemblance to Dan Leno in plaintive mood. On the walls prints of Old Testament subjects; of the patriarchs and prophets, with beards flowing to the weather and togas tactfully adrift in exertion, engaged upon the more remarkable of their several historical performances. But, apart from the energy of the prophets and patriarchs, the study was a very stiff room.

On the ground floor then – the dining-room, stately; the drawing-room, full; the study, stiff; the hall, rich. Augustus, a trifle awestruck, glanced up the stairs, wondered how the devil he was going to manage about his portmanteau, and, operating promiscuous but profuse first-floor lights from the hall, crept aloft, feeling not unlike Ali Baba in the treasure-houses of the piratical forty.

Facing you upstairs, swamping you upstairs, practically constituting upstairs, was the bedroom of Mrs Mantle Ham. It was two-bedded. The lady having elaborately planted herself out for the night in the great centre bed, Mr Mantle Ham was wont to creep in and pot himself out in a poor little minor bed, like the weakly and neglected offspring of the parent bed alongside.

Formerly there had been seven bedrooms in Rookery Nook. Now there were but five. Mrs Mantle Ham, being without issue, had adjudicated two small rooms for the maids, a slightly larger room to the occasional visitor and a very angular little room to Mr Mantle Ham for his dressing-room. The remainder of upstairs had been appropriated for and flung into the already existing bedroom of Mrs Mantle Ham.

The whole of the upper portion of that wing of Rookery Nook which overlooked Swallow Road was accordingly bedroom. At either end of the bedroom was a recess, where had stood the two smaller rooms since demolished and enwombed into the bedroom. This architectural essay had rendered possible the housing of Mrs Mantle Ham's bedroom furniture, which was of considerable bulk. A huge chest of drawers, a washstand whose marble top and sides might have been hewn from the slabs of some Babylonian temples, a dressing-table with massive carved legs bulging at symmetrical intervals into swollen dumplings, a Gargantuan wardrobe – these were Mrs Mantle Ham's 'bits', as she herself described them. There were, in addition, a built-in cupboard, probably about the size of a small ship but, during the Longhampton occupation, locked, and a lesser but spacious cupboard with hangers and shelves. A big room. The only really small thing about it was Mr Mantle Ham's bed.

One of the two amalgamated smaller rooms still bore the appearance of an annex and was used as a boudoir, though undivided from the remainder of the bedroom. There were, owing to the amalgamation, windows on three sides. The decorative scheme was bold; the wallpaper depicting the ace of clubs sprouting from a basket of vinery like an Indian conjuring trick. Few pictures, two fireplaces. A big room. Augustus scratched his neck and went downstairs again.

The front door remained open to the still, hot night. Augustus seated himself on the hall Chesterfield, yawned and decided to smoke another cigarette before dealing with his accursed portmanteau.

Oh lord! He had promised to go over and report his arrival to Mrs Twine. Well, he was dashed if he started forth to seek out Frascati and renew his acquaintance with his sister-in-law. She would come nosing over in the morning. That would be time enough. It was too late to go now. He hadn't even unpacked.

Presently he bestirred himself with a very deep sigh and strolled to the front door. All was silence. Darkness had fallen now. Beyond the sweep of the gravel drive he could discern the tall colony of elms silhouetted against the sky.

He pirouetted upon the doormat and once more surveyed the interior of the rich hall. He felt very lonely in this luxurious haven. An indefinite sensation of unrest seemed to possess his mind. He would have laid him down to rest in some cosy cottage oblivious to strange surroundings, if, indeed, a cosy cottage can ever be strange. But this house, this eminent residence, these rooms, rich, stately, stiff, full, big – these confines undetermined, these surroundings shrouded by the deepening gloom of night depressed and bewildered him.

Well, well. His lamentable portmanteau must be tackled anyhow.

He returned to the garage. The portmanteau presented a sadly dissipated appearance, propped up on the rear seat, widely agape; a strange plethora of wearing apparel and other personal effects hanging from its jaws. Augustus, flinging himself upon it, succeeded in fastening the left-hand front strap, but this only widened the breach on the right and seemed to add to the portmanteau's general aspect of obstinate intoxication. He released the left-hand strap and the lid shot upward, jerking him severely on the point of the jaw.

With an oath which would have done credit to an offended bos'un, Augustus threw back the lid and proceeded to gather all the articles which lay within the circumference of an elaborate embrace. The lid fell heavily forward again upon his arms. He jerked it back and dragged forth his catch. This time the falling lid caught his wrists and hurt rather.

He carried the fruits of his unlucky dip back through the front door into the hall and flung them on to the table of Mrs Mantle Ham. A purple silk sock remained coyly on the mat, and somewhere round the corner of the gravel drive were a tobacco-jar (probably smashed), a pair of braces, and a little sponge, in a rubber case, for cleaning golf balls.

Augustus took another breather on the front step. It was growing late, and his arrangements for the oncoming night had been fraught with disorganisation rather than progress. He had still to shut the blasted portmanteau, to heave it off the car, to lug it indoors and, goodness knew how, up the stairs. Should he unpack it by a series of these embraces in the car, and dump the contents on the hall table? Boring prospect – fatiguing! Already he could feel beads of perspiration affecting the upper portions of his person. He would stand in the doorway and cool down, before committing himself to further exertion.

So in the porch of Rookery Nook he aimlessly stood. A ripple of night breeze fanned the tops of the line of elms, like a ripple of mischief running through a class of maidens in school. From Chumpton Town sounded the notes of the church clock booming forth the hour of eleven. Then, suddenly, like the expectant, prearranged signal for the commencement of some festivity – bang!

Bang! Not a sharp, exciting bang, as of a firearm, but a dull, sullen bang, as of a door. Very slowly Augustus turned his face to the right and blinked.

Nothing further happened. Near at hand a grandfather clock ticked disinterestedly on. When it had ticked for five minutes uninterrupted, Augustus yawned, blew out his cheeks at the conclusion of the yawn and went heavily back to the garage.

Ten minutes later, progressing sideways, like a crab with some overpowering booty, he returned round the sweep of gravel, his portmanteau carving an extensive weal in his wake. At the front door he let his end of the portmanteau fall and stooped to manoeuvre the burden into line with his altered course. Then, with a moan of persevering effort, he hauled it up the short flight of steps.

He gained the mat, again let the portmanteau fall, and raised his left hand to rub his working arm.

The left hand gripped the right biceps and remained motionless. Indeed the only portion of his anatomy which did not remain motionless was his mouth. This by stages widened.

Seated on the table, surrounded by derelict boots and stray collars, was a young woman with a mass of blonde hair flowing down over her shoulders and wearing pink pyjamas. Her attitude was nonchalant, but she met Augustus's gaze with a smile of wistful appeal.

If his first sensation was one of unutterable amazement, it quickly passed. The instinctive shock of finding a strange girl in pyjamas on the hall table must have visited him, but he heeded it not. For from the moment in which his eyes rested on her face all other considerations died like sound.

She was a symphony of the countryside; she was an idyll of the bower. She was the rose of summer, full and sweet and beautiful, dominating all the dainty flowers of cultivation, all the exuberant blossoms of Nature. Every woman is a flower, is she not? Think of any woman you know – does not each one of them typify a flower? Here a soulful iris; there a rampageous poppy. Think of the post-war rhododendrons. Do you not know Miss Tulip of Purley and little Mrs Foxglove of Beckenham?

Rose of Summer!

She was not pretty, she was beautiful. She was not bewitching, she was enthralling.

Enthralled stood Augustus.

CHAPTER V

Sanctuary

Enthralled stood Augustus and, smiling wistfully back, sat the beautiful girl for a space of time which seemed longer than was actually the case. Then she said:

'You've just come here, haven't you?'

'To tell you the truth, I thought it was you who had done that,' replied Augustus.

'I mean, you have only arrived this evening, and are a stranger to the place?'

'Yes,' said Augustus, his eyes not yet leaving her face. 'Why? Is it a place where this kind of – I mean where rather unusual sorts of things generally happen?'

'No. Oh, no. It's a very quiet sort of place.'

'I should think it has to be,' said Augustus.

'I heard you had just arrived from my woman.'

'Oh-h,' said Augustus, leaping at conclusions. 'Is my daily woman your woman too?'

'No,' said the beautiful girl. 'Nutts.'

'Nuts?'

'My woman's name is Nutts.'

'Oh. What a remarkable name.'

'My name is Rhoda Marley. I live next door with my father. His name is Putz.'

'Poots?'

'Yes. P-u-t-z. He's my step-father. We live next door.'

'Is your father ill? Or is your house on fire, or anything urgent?'

'Well, nothing exactly urgent. But I shouldn't have come here like this in the ordinary way, should I?'

'Oh. Then something extraordinary has, in point of fact, occurred?'

'Yes. Shall I tell you exactly all about it?'

'Yes please,' said Augustus.

The girl's voice was as charming as her appearance, with a rather melancholy ring in it, very clear, but not high or shrill. She placed the palms of her hands on the table and shifted her sitting position gracefully, no easy feat. She moved the loofah, on which she had been sitting, a few inches further down the table.

'It was pricking me rather,' she explained apologetically.

'Wouldn't you like to sit on the sofa?' queried Augustus, rather uncertain as to the social procedure demanded by the circumstances.

'No thanks,' said Rhoda Marley. 'My feet will dry more quickly if I swing them. There's rather a heavy dew outside.'

The eyes of Augustus stole downwards to the coral toes.

'I say. They *are* wet,' he exclaimed. 'So are the ends of your – yes, what a dew there must be. Sign of fine weather though, isn't it?'

'I had to walk through some rather long grass to get here. I'm so sorry I had to come at all; but I don't quite see what else I could do. I hope you don't mind?'

'Not at all,' said Augustus vaguely. 'Would you like a dressing-gown or anything?'

'Thank you,' she said.

Augustus took a rapid inventory of the rest of the table.

'There's one in my portmanteau,' he said. 'I'd better get it out for you at once.'

'Thank you. All right then; I won't start explaining till you've got it out.'

Augustus closed the front door and bent to unstrap his portmanteau. Delving within it he discovered the dressing-gown; discovered also, incidentally, a flask, and pressed spirits upon the beautiful Miss Marley. She declined with thanks. She never touched spirits.

'As medicine,' he urged. 'You mustn't go and develop pneumonia in here. That really might be very awkward.'

'For me. Yes.'

'Yes, and for me too.'

She laughed.

'I'm awfully sorry,' she repeated. 'But I really don't see what else I could have done.'

'I'll hear all about it in a minute. Just wait until I've pulled this dressing-gown out,' said Augustus.

All the while his brain was awhirl. Astounding episode. And doubly astounding in that she was so exceptionally lovely. For a brief moment he had thought himself dreaming. The notion had even crossed his mind that he had very suddenly died and that this, contrary to all anticipation, was the first thing that took place on the other side. It was just at this point that the beautiful girl had found herself to be sitting on the loofah; and Augustus decided that this visitation, however abnormal, was at least terrestrial.

Another queer little impression occurred to him as he groped for the dressing-gown. Of this disquieting situation of her own creation, the girl herself seemed to be the one unambiguous and reassuring element. Her personality appeared to radiate integrity and to count upon it in return. There was no hint of indelicacy about her. There was an unassumed honesty and natural charm in her voice and manner that rendered her egregious circumstances free from all suspicion. Her almost dangerous beauty she seemed to employ as a first line of defence against misunderstanding and reproach.

'Many thanks,' she said. 'What a nice Jaeger one! I say?'

'If you don't mind standing on the floor for a moment, I'll help you into it.'

'I say?'

'Yes?'

'I wonder whether you would be still more kind?'

'I should think it's quite likely. What?'

'Well, as a matter of fact, these pyjamas of mine *are* very much affected by the dew and the long grass. Do you think you could let me go into one of these rooms and put on a pair of yours?'

'Er – certainly,' said Augustus. 'If you anticipate being here long enough to make it worth while.'

'I think when you've heard my story you'll keep me for the present. I mean, you won't turn me out again. I hope you won't anyhow.'

'But don't you think it would be better to give me some sort of glimmering of an idea as to why you came here? Now, that is. Before you put on my pyjamas.'

She hesitated.

'Well, you see, if I once start, I'm sure you won't want me to stop and go off and change my trousers. And I really think I'd better wait and tell you everything later.'

Augustus nodded.

'Close to you, on your right,' he said, 'you will find the nether portion of a gent's slumber suiting. It is new and guaranteed silk.'

'Thank you. They'll do beautifully. Where can I go and put them on?'

'Anywhere except the drawing-room,' said Augustus judiciously.

'And could you possibly lend me a comb? Then I really should feel happier. I suppose you haven't got anything that I could tie my hair up with?'

'I can raise a comb,' said Augustus, turning to the portmanteau. 'Have a look on the table, and if it's not there – oh, here it is. About the tying, I don't seem to see anything that suggests itself. I suppose sock-suspenders would hardly – or a bootlace—?'

'You haven't got anything with tapes in it, by any chance?'

'Tapes? Yes, I think, if I took cover behind my box-lid for a moment I might be able to reappear with a tape.'

'I didn't mean anything you're wearing now,' said Miss Marley hastily.

'That's all right. I didn't either. But I've thought of something with a tape. The ones with the best tape are my thick ones, which unfortunately, I had to leave at home. But I believe the thin ones have fairly decent tapes. Now, half a moment – where?'

'Oh, please don't damage your thin ones for my sake.'

'That's all right. They can easily be retaped. I have a wife, you know.'

'Your wife isn't here now though, is she?'

'Here? No. My God, no, she is not,' said Augustus.

'What a pity,' said Rhoda Marley. 'Do you know of any lady in the place who might be able to help me?'

'I've got a sister-in-law here, a Mrs Twine. Do you know her?'

'No. I don't know anyone.'

'I think Mrs Twine is better where she is for the moment,' said Augustus with decision. 'Oh, look what I've found. A bundle of handkerchiefs tied up with ribbon. That's better than any tape.'

'Excellent!' said Rhoda. 'The hair-ribbon I had to leave at home came off handkerchiefs.'

Augustus crossed the hall and switched on the study light. She followed him with a smile of gratitude.

'You can't even give me some faint, preliminary idea of why you are here?' he asked.

'I'd rather wait and tell you fully,' she replied. 'I shan't be a minute.'

She bore the dressing-gown, the pyjama trousers, the comb and the ribbon into the furious company of the patriarchs and closed the door. Augustus returned to his littered hall, very stupidly blew out his cheeks and flipped them with his forefingers.

That bang of a distant door! That was it. She had suddenly bolted from her home in pink pyjamas; not stealthily, but violently. She had slammed the door behind her, but not in anger, not even, it seemed, in remorse; but in some strange caprice. The step-father, she had hinted, was there. Why did he not follow her, even if powerless to prevent her from dashing into the night? The woman, oddly named Nutts – what was her function? And why, why should this beautiful fugitive choose this haven on this particular occasion? Interesting decidedly, but—

And yet she was so genuine. That was the most amazing feature of what might otherwise have been a bold piece of roguery. Even so, he must be guarded. What was he letting himself in for? What had she let herself in for?

And so beautiful! Perfect in feature; soft and delicate of cheek. Probably of average height, but, in her night attire and with her hair flinging over her shoulders, conveying the rather engaging impression of being littler than herself, as a woman always does in these intimate circumstances.

No no, dash it all though – quite apart from what the girl herself might be like to look at – this was very wild work. Had she been in the habit of strolling in like this and sitting herself down on the hall table and chatting to the Mantle Hams? Incredible. People with a drawing-room like that—

No no. This might be very embarrassing. It was fortunately improbable that anyone would blow in at such an hour, but supposing that Gertrude, by some devilish means, discovered what was going on in Rookery Nook. Would any power on earth persuade her of the innocent truth? None. Should he send over to Frascati and court her aid? How could he, until he had ascertained the motive of Rhoda. Something in coming to him? Not that, in any case, he was likely to invite the co-operation of the Twines in this matter. Oh, altogether, how irrational, perplexing, piquant, hazardously thrilling, disturbingly pleasurable, the unexplained incursion of this fugitive Venus!

Like a Venus swathed in a rough extemporary mantle by the herdsman Paris, she reappeared, enveloped in Jaeger. Her hair, secured by handkerchief ribbon, had been coiled about her head and held in place by some dexterous feminine touch. The alteration did not detract from her appearance but it added a suggestion of the conventional; and she seemed aware of this, for she smiled with a deference more bashful than she had exhibited while yet untired and in pink pyjamas.

Beautiful girl! Adventure dreadfully provocative! Augustus bowed her to the Chesterfield; himself took an adjacent chair and toyed with it rather than sat in it, wobbling upon the edge.

'Now,' she said. 'I think I had better tell you first what has taken place tonight, and then go back and try to explain how it came to happen.'

Augustus assented silently.

'What happened tonight,' she went on, 'can be told in one short sentence. My step-father has run me out.'

'Run you out?'

'Yes. That's his own expression for it. He just picked me up and ran me out – *phit* – like that.'

'You mean to tell me that your step-father has turned you out of the house next door into the night – *phit*?'

'Yes. He's threatened to do it before. He's even pretended to do it; but I never thought he really would.'

'Good God!' exclaimed Augustus. 'He must be very hard to please. But I suppose he had certain reasons?'

'Yes. I took the risk. As a matter of fact, what I did was nothing wrong, except that it was in direct disobedience to his orders. He wouldn't have found out though; only Nutts split.'

'Nutts split!'

'She informed against me.'

'I see. She is on his side, she.'

'Yes. Oh, she's simply his abject slave.'

'But may I ask what you did – this forbidden thing?'

'I ate wurts.'

'You did *what*, in Heaven's name?'

'I ate wurts. Wurtleberries. A local fruit.'

'You ate wurts and Nutts split. What a vegetable tragedy! But you don't seriously mean to tell me that your step-father ran you out for eating wurts?'

'Yes. He'd forbidden me to eat them. He dislikes wurts.'

'I should jolly well say he does,' remarked Augustus. 'But I don't see that he's justified in disliking them as much as all that. The blighter wasn't asked to eat any wurts himself.'

'They leave a black dye, like ink, on the lips and tongue. He saw me once before, just after I'd been eating some, and he told me that if he caught me eating wurts again he would punish me.'

'Your step-father talks to you like that?'

'He talks to everybody like that. I'm fed up with it,' said Rhoda.

'I suppose,' suggested Augustus, 'that the real truth is that this affair of the wurts led up to other things, and there was a bit of a dust-up, and finally he lost his head and took you and ran you out in your pyjamas?'

'More or less,' said Rhoda. 'But he really ran me out almost straight away and because of the wurts.'

'Well, surely your best course is to walk in again?'

She shook her head. Her lip quivered but she spoke with calm deliberation.

'No,' she said. 'You wouldn't advise me to do that if you knew how I was liable to be treated. I'm through with it.'

'Then what are you going to do?' asked Augustus in monotonous inquiry.

'I don't know,' said Rhoda.

'Do you know anyone here you can go to?'

'No.' Again the quivering lip. But she pulled herself together, sat up a little and continued without any animosity in her pretty, deep voice.

'I'm a social outcast here. I know nobody.'

'I don't suppose you've missed much,' said the brother-in-law of Gertrude Twine.

'My father is half a German, you see.'

'He sounds two-thirds a Prussian to me.'

'He is Prussian in principles.'

'And, until now, you've been living alone there in that house with this man?'

'Yes. And Nutts.'

'Why?' cried Augustus, his mouth remaining open at the conclusion of the syllable.

'My mother died eighteen months ago, and I promised her I would stick to my step-father.'

'Rather a hard thing to do if he runs you out.'

'Yes, he's a very queer man and an odd mixture. I'm not sure myself even now what his exact nationality is. My mother met him on the Continent when she was paying a visit to a foreign countess she knew. He practically commanded my mother to marry him. She was a very beautiful woman—'

'I can quite believe that,' murmured Augustus.

'So she did marry him. He is a very masterful sort of person. My mother said he was more like a man is intended to be than other men are. She was very devoted to him.'

'And he to her?'

'Well, yes, in his curious way. You see, the way his mind seems to work is this. He decides what is best for anyone he's fond of and orders it to be done. It's all for the benefit of the person he orders, at least, so he thinks. For instance, about these wurts. He thought it was a pity that I should disfigure my mouth, so he commanded me to give them up. I have known him whip a hat off my mother's head and throw it on the fire and then make her go and buy another hat at three times the cost of the burnt hat. A sort of queer combination of devotion and discipline, if you can understand.'

'I suppose you've satisfied yourself with regard to his sanity?' asked Augustus circumspectly.

'Oh yes. But of course he doesn't care for me as he cared for my mother. In her case the devotion was so great that the discipline was more insistence on her accepting favours than anything else. With me it's just the other way about. I'm sure I was never intended to go through what I've had to go through for the last eighteen months, and tonight he's reached the limit. I'm not going back to be treated like that again.'

Her eyes filled with tears. All her insouciance had melted in confession. She was a very pathetic figure. Augustus was completely won. However remarkable, her story was unquestionably genuine. Falsehood could never appear in a guise so simple and appealing.

'Poor dear – in your pyjamas and all,' was his heartfelt comment.

'I hope I haven't done wrong in coming here. What else could I do?'

'Of course you couldn't wander about outside all night.'

'And I'm certainly not going back, wherever I have to go,' added Rhoda, with determination flashing through her tears.

Augustus shifted a little nervously on the edge of his chair. How could he counsel this lovely creature to return to a home of tyranny? On the other hand—

'I knew the Ham people had gone away; and Nutts told me she had seen a gentleman arrive here alone in a car, so I thought I could count on getting shelter anyway,' said Rhoda with complete ingenuousness.

'Ye-es,' said Augustus. 'Though if you refuse to go back – quite naturally, mind you; I'm not disputing that at all – but if you won't go home and haven't any clothes, I don't quite see what's going to happen.'

'I don't want to embarrass you in any way,' she said quickly.

'Oh, you don't embarrass me – so far as I am concerned personally. But you see – I've no clothes for you. Of course there's that sister-in-law I spoke of; but – to be quite honest – she would go out of her way to put a wrong construction on things, and she would absolutely refuse to believe your story.'

Rhoda nodded readily.

'I don't suppose one woman in a thousand would believe it,' she said.

Augustus performed smoothing movements of the hair with his right hand.

'Mind you,' he said, 'if I went round to her house and sort of confessed, as it were, that you were here, it might spike her guns, so to speak, but I can't see myself doing it and I don't think it would bring us any material assistance.'

'Why would it be so very terrible if she found out and *didn't* choose to believe us?'

'Oh, it wouldn't be very terrible,' replied Augustus casually. 'Only she'd try and make mischief with my wife.'

'Oh!' cried Rhoda and jumped up from the Chesterfield. 'I didn't realise what you were driving at. I'll go at once.'

'No, no, no,' said Augustus. 'You can't go. You've nowhere to go to. Sit down, do.'

Rhoda glanced at him, sighed and again sunk upon the Chesterfield.

'Now let's just face the facts,' he continued. 'Here am I, a married man, in this house all alone. You blow in, in a condition which makes it quite impossible for you to push on elsewhere. You refuse to go back home and I don't blame you. But do let us decide quite calmly what we're going to do about it.'

Rhoda turned upon him a pleading gaze, faintly illuminated by the ghost of a smile, and gave a little heave of the dressing-gown preliminary to replying.

'Don't misunderstand me,' protested Augustus. 'I'm only too willing to help you – absolutely only too. But I can't quite see where this is going to stop – I mean about your not having any clothes and so on. I don't see that you'll be any better off, however long you stay here, unless we can wangle some of your clothes from Nutts. Do you think we could do that? Even then, where are you going? Meanwhile someone's pretty certain to find out. My sister-in-law is the kind of woman that goes about with one ear to the ground, like a Kaffir rumour-merchant. Not that I'm only thinking of myself. I know there's you to consider too. But this seems rather like asking for trouble all round.'

'Directly I can get some of my things, I shall go to London. I have friends there,' said Rhoda.

'You have a friend here too,' said Augustus gently.

'Yes, I think you are being a perfect darling to me,' said Rhoda. 'And I quite see that it is a little bit imposs. for you. I won't stay a moment longer than I can help.'

'But you can't go to London tonight, can you?'

'No. I meant tomorrow morning.'

'Oh-h,' said Augustus.

For a few moments they faced each other without saying more. The little hint of a smile still lingered about her lips. Unconsciously perhaps, he encouraged it. But she, from the first, had remained innocent of the smallest inkling of cajolery.

'If your step-father knew you were here with me alone, what do you suppose he'd do?' asked Augustus at length.

'I don't know,' said Rhoda. 'You see, he's never actually run me out before.'

'Perhaps he's waiting for you to go back and say you're sorry.'

'He'll have a long wait then,' said Rhoda.

'How would it be if I went and told him you were here alone with me? I don't feel that I ought to put you up for the night without making some effort to straighten things out.'

'You must do what you think best of course. I don't think it's likely to do very much good.'

'Couldn't you return just for tonight and pretend to be sorry? Then you could hop it for London in the morning. Besides, by this means you could get some clothes.'

'If he saw I wanted to go, he'd probably take good care I didn't.'

'He should have thought of that before he ran you out.'

'Yes, but I warned him, just as he picked me up, that if he ran me out I should never come back. I've got a will of my own just as much as he has.'

'You certainly have,' said Augustus blankly.

He rose and turned towards the door, stretched himself, scratched his neck.

'Anyhow, I'll go and see him,' he said.

'I think you're splendid,' said Rhoda. 'I know it will be quite futile, but so many splendid actions are, aren't they? Shall I wait down here, or what?'

'Do you think it would be better if you came too?'

'Oh no. Worse. No, I didn't mean that. I meant, shall I go upstairs?'

'Upstairs?'

'Yes.'

'To – to bed?'

'Well, you were kind enough to say something about putting me up.'

'But if your step-father comes along?'

'Knowing him, I don't think it's worth while sitting up for.'

'Oh, all right, all right,' cried the overwrought Augustus in sudden desperation. 'Go to bed then. Go where you like. I'll jolly well have it out with this Prussian sire of yours. Where is he? Where do you live? That is to say, when you are not run out?'

'The only other house down the road. You can't miss it. Where is the bedroom I am to go to, please?'

'You can't miss that either,' said Augustus. 'Upstairs.'

He crossed the hall and flooded Rookery Nook with illumination wildly. Rhoda halted beside him and stretched out her hand. She spoke in a subdued tone of honest gratitude.

'You are being a dear to me,' she said. 'Don't think that I don't realise what I'm asking of you and that I don't appreciate your great, great kindness.'

'Oh-h!' breathed Augustus, gazing at her. Then, in words almost passionate, wrung from the depths of his tender heart. 'Forgive me if I sounded impetuous. There's nothing in the whole wide world I wouldn't do to help you. You trot along and make yourself at home. I'll see you through this, and I don't care a bean.'

'I have been lucky,' she said, 'to find you, of all people.'

She released her hand from his grasp and mounted the stairs, her dainty bare feet peeping from beneath a train of dressing-gown and encumbered by overlapping folds of sky-blue silk trousering. At the bend of the stairs she turned, divinely smiled and then disappeared from view.

He remained gazing upwards, until he heard the bedroom door gently closed.

Then, swinging round on his heel, he stared about him at the rich hall of Mrs Mantle Ham.

Stately, scrupulous hall, now in the throes of disorder unnatural and grotesque. On the hall table fugitive shirts; a case of pipes, burst open and with pipes scattered from their velvet sockets; vagrant ties, collars, a loofah, socks unpaired, two novels, one boot. On the hall floor a portmanteau, like a dreadful relic of some Roman orgy of tigers, torn asunder and raped of its vitals. Around it the vitals; horribly involved mass of intestines, tangled conglomeration of holiday packing.

And in his own not unscrupulous mind, a tangled conglomeration of conflicting emotions analogous with the condition of the stately hall. Suspicion – but this only to be compared with the little sock lying alone and banished upon the mat – misgiving, compassion, desperation, defiance, reluctance; above all, blinding, compelling enchantment.

For a moment he stared thus, like one awakening from a trance of fever. Then, buttoning his coat about him, he blundered across the hall and struck forth into the night.

CHAPTER VI

Augustus is Run Out

At the gate of Pixiecot he halted, having progressed to that spot subconsciously and piloted solely by instinct. His mind had been occupied by thoughts which took no heed of Lighthouse Road. But eventually realising where he was, encompassed about by gloom, in haunts unfamiliar, bent upon a mission weird and wild, at the gate of Pixiecot he halted and groaning dallied.

His groan was evidently audible; for, from within the portal of Pixiecot, which stood not far from the road, came the responsive challenge of a long-drawn and rattling growl.

Awed by this, Augustus decided not to open the gate, which would probably click. Instead, he scaled the gate, not without difficulty. This manoeuvre failed in its object, for the growl waxed crescendo; while, on the side of the house nearest the elm trees, a window was flung impetuously open.

Stumbling over an untended flower-bed, Augustus edged cautiously round the house in the direction from which the latter sound had emanated. Looking upwards as he went, he soon discerned, in the aperture of the window, the outline of a bullet head resting upon an adumbrant mass of shoulder scarcely outlined in the darkness.

His first sensation on beholding Mr Putz was one of surprise. Even by the unreliable light of the moon, it was evident that the step-father was not the man he had pictured. True, the bullet-head was in keeping with anticipation, but the militant moustachios were lacking.

Instead of the elderly but virile Viking of Augustus's conception, Mr Putz, so far as could be ascertained, bore the appearance of a rather bloated and time-worn student. The curious, intangible disparity which make any Continental un-English was perceptible even in the darkness.

Mr Putz looked down at Augustus with a queer, peering carriage of the head for some moments without speaking. He then suddenly disappeared; only to return, adjusting horn spectacles upon his broad, stubbed nose. He then said, quietly, but with deep menace:

'Who?'

'Look here, I say; are you Mr Putz?' began Augustus.

'Who?' repeated Mr Putz. 'Speak it out.'

'I'm the man that's got your step-daughter,' said Augustus, admirably concise.

'I do not care for you,' said Mr Putz.

'All the more reason to come and take your step-daughter back,' said Augustus.

'I have run her out already,' said Mr Putz.

'Yes, I know you have. And she's next door at my house in her pyjamas. And I tell you, I simply—'

'Soho. She wish to come back to my house. No?'

'No,' said Augustus. 'You're quite right, she does not. Well, naturally she doesn't while you treat her in this way.'

'Aller right,' said Mr Putz. 'What you make?'

'What?'

'Speak.'

'Damn it, I am speaking as fast as I can. Look here, you can't do this sort of thing. Turning ladies out late at night in their pyjamas – it isn't done.'

'It is done already also.'

'But dash it, I tell you I am alone in my house, and your step-daughter has come there in her pyjamas. It's impossible. I can't keep her there.'

'If she expresses sorrow she shall come back to my house immediately. If she doesn't express no sorrow, aller right. It is oder now oder never.'

'It's you who ought to express sorrow. What's she done to be – run out like this? Simply because she ate some wurts—'

Mr Putz's voice became more animated.

'It is not only that she eat die woits. It is that she disobey my order also to eat die woits.'

'And you mean to tell me that, just because she has eaten a few wurts when you told her you'd rather she didn't, you're prepared to lose her altogether and to hand her over to the first stray man that happens to be about?'

'Absolutely,' said Mr Putz. 'Order. To obey. She will not stop away long, I tink.'

'I think she jolly well will,' said Augustus boldly. 'If you're not careful I'll keep her.'

Mr Putz's face appeared to be wagging from side to side. He was evidently labouring under growing excitement.

'If she choose to flee from me without sorrow it is for her,' he cried. 'If with sorrow, then she may return immediately also already.'

'She didn't flee. And she's not with sorrow in the least. Now then. What about it?'

Mr Putz's voice deepened into a hoarse rumble which was echoed from the ground floor of Pixiecot.

'Too much. Immediately go.'

'I've a good mind to send for the police and have you run in,' said Augustus.

'And I,' cried Mr Putz triumphantly, 'have a good mind to come to my dog and have you run out.'

'All right,' said Augustus with finality, sheering off a few paces, 'if you want me to keep your step-daughter—'

'Go.'

'In my house—'

'Too much. Go.'

'In my bedroom—'

'Go, go. I loose my dog.'

'All night—'

'My dog shall run you out, biting strongly.'

'Half in her own pyjamas and half in mine—'

'Finish. I come to run you out.'

At this Mr Putz vanished.

Lights shot up within the house. Into the barking of the

dog crept the note of high-pitched delight characteristic of wild animals at meal-time. The voice of Mr Putz could be heard issuing a manifesto in response to an inquiry from an adjacent room. 'Aller right. A man come. I shall run him out.' There appeared to be every indication that the rupture of the brief negotiations was about to be consummated in no uncertain manner. Augustus, again tripping over the flower-bed, returned to the gate.

There he paused for a few seconds and listened. Between the expectant yelps of the dog came the sound of a rattling of door-chains. Augustus turned and walked away with what he flattered himself was an air of dignity. Not for many yards, however, did he walk. He heard behind him the gate flung open with a creak and a thud. He quickened his pace. Next a medley of pattering footsteps sounded in the rear, like the ghostly march of dead drummers; the big drum in muted quick-step, the kettle-drum in flickering variation. The dog had ceased to bark; instead a most dreadful hunting sound of nasal whistling fell upon the ear. Augustus, with a bravery which surprised himelf, halted and swung round.

'Look here!'

Mr Putz, a monkish, moonlight figure in a dressing-gown with a cowl, merely jerked the dog by the leader and stooped to release it, muttering, at the same time, some sinister foreign incitement, understood only by the dog:

'Phorr – putta-putta – phorr – putta-putta – phorr!'

Augustus hesitated no longer. He dashed forward into the drive of Rookery Nook, slammed the gate behind him in his stride, and, a few seconds later, flung himself, panting and perspiring, into the depths of the Chesterfield.

After a few minutes he raised his head and listened intently. He thought he heard the sound of that fiendish canine whistle on the other side of the closed front door. But even at this he could not summon sufficient energy to rise and bolt the door. The combination of physical exertion and panic seemed to have left him but a mere thread of himself, with all his energies liquefying from him.

For quite a long while he lay in this extreme; and as his abnormal fatigue wore off, the normal fatigue of eleven-forty-five weariness descended upon him. Presently, with a supreme effort, he bestirred himself and again listened. All was silence, save for the pedantic beat of the grandfather clock. Once more he surveyed, with a sigh of impotent misery, the chaotic condition of the hall. Then, struggling to his feet, he dragged himself upstairs to the bedroom door.

He knocked twice before being rewarded by a distant and sleepy invitation to enter. The electric lights were still burning in the room; but Rhoda had taken the precaution of drawing the blinds; though the sumptuous brocade curtains designed to shroud the bow of the centre windows remained hooked back at either side, like a couple of gorgeous Victorian sisters with pronounced bustles.

Rhoda, beautifully flushed in half-slumber, peered with a contented smile from the whelming trough of Mrs Mantle Ham's bed. On the bedrail hung, in grotesque company, a pair of dainty pink silk trousers, still sodden at the ends, and a heavy masculine dressing-gown. A comb lay in ridiculous isolation on the waste of dressing-table.

'Hallo!' said Rhoda. 'What happened?'

'I think you might have told me about the dog,' said Augustus.

'Oh, I'm sorry. Did he actually come down and loose the dog?'

'Yes.'

'I *am* sorry. And what did you decide to do?'

'Well, good heavens, what do you suppose I decided to do?'

'I mean about me?'

'You? The only thing I've decided about you is that you're not going back to that house even if you want to.'

'That is kind of you. I tell you what I thought you might possibly be able to do, though if you can't of course I shall quite understand, and we must think of something else. In the morning, I thought, you might be able to wrap me up in a motor coat or something and run me up to a friend's house in London in your car. I know it's a long way, but if we made an early start, that might perhaps solve the problem for both of us.'

Augustus shook his head slowly.

'I'd love to do it,' he said, 'but it's that sister-in-law of mine that is the snag. She'd nose it out somehow, if I buzzed off for a whole day directly I arrived here. She'd never rest until she'd found out what I was up to; and then every telegraph wire in the country would sparkle and crackle with slanderous rumours. It can't be done.'

'Couldn't you take her husband into your confidence?'

'Her husband? Have you ever seen an earwig get up on its tail in the middle of the road and knock a steam roller out of the light?'

'Oh dear,' said Rhoda. 'What can we do? Is there nobody that can help us?'

'Oh-h!' cried Augustus suddenly. 'Yes. Hold on, now. I believe I have an idea.'

She made no reply and he pondered, blinking sleepily but methodically for some moments.

'Yes,' he continued. 'It may mean your lying low here for the best part of tomorrow.'

'I don't mind that.'

'You might even have to hide.'

'Right.'

'Very well then. You go back to your beauty sleep. I believe I can get you up to town by tomorrow evening if you'll leave yourself in my hands.'

'I'd rather they were your hands than anybody's,' said Rhoda. 'I think you're priceless. You haven't by any chance got a new and unused toothbrush, have you?'

'I'm afraid not.'

'Never mind. I cleaned my teeth with my finger but it isn't very satisfactory. I suppose I'd better stay in bed tomorrow morning until I hear from you?'

'Yes, I think you had. Goodnight. Shall I switch out the light?'

'Thanks.'

As he quitted the bed-chamber he heard following him the soft whisper of a blown kiss.

CHAPTER VII

Harold Twine on the Blind Side

Dinner time found Mrs Twine unsettled and in unsettlement somewhat irritable. The fussiness that was characteristic of Clara existed not in the bosom of the elder sister. There was no call for it. Gertrude lived twenty-four hours in advance of Time. She specialised in a self-ordained forecast of events, known as 'the programme for the day'.

'Harold,' she would say immediately after breakfast – this always happened – 'Harold.'

Mr Twine would then raise his eyes from the paper, would put the paper on his chair and would sit on the paper. He would then fold his hands as though in watchful worship. Mrs Twine would then say, 'Fold your serviette'; and Mr Twine would unfold his hands, roll his napkin into an unsuccessful sausage, refold his hands and come again to sitting attention. Mrs Twine would then cross the room to her writing-table, produce a pencil and release one piece of paper from an exactly-sized collection of pieces of paper impaled upon a bill-hook. Mrs Twine would then return to the breakfast table, sit, and swell visibly about the bosom at Mr Twine. All this always happened.

Mr Twine was a short man with twin forelocks, a habit of licking his lips, and knickerbockers too voluminous for his legs which were woefully rectilineal. He had the consistently self-conscious manner of one who feels himself to be the subject of derisive conversation among his fellow-men.

'You first,' would say Mrs Twine. 'Golf at all?'

'Yes, dear.'

'At what time?'

'Ten – er – I think, forty. The caddy-master—'

'Ten-forty. Against?'

'Erm – Higgs.'

'v. Mr Higgs. Which Mr Higgs?'

'O. Higgs, dear.'

'v. Mr O. Higgs.' She would write it down. Then:

'Luncheon. At home? One–

'Ye – yes. I marght possibly be rather kept. If I lost the ball much, or—'

'One-fifteen. Be careful *not* to lose the ball. Remember what Admiral Juddy told you about lifting your right elbow.'

'Yes, I have tried.'

'You should practise driving alone, by yourself.'

'Yes, I will.'

'When?'

'Well – tomorrow.'

'Yes. I will make a note of it. After luncheon today, what?'

Thus him. Then her own programme for the day was rehearsed unchallenged. Then, in the kitchen, the cook's programme for the day. The housemaid's programme for the day. The gardener's. The chauffeur's. The cat's. There were no children.

Mrs Twine was a well-built woman, larger than Clara, bigger. Her eyebrows joined in the middle. Her nose, while not notable for size, was pronounced and pinched at the extremity. It seemed to shoot from her face, like a sort of advance agent of information on the scent. The line joining the pinched extremity and the crown of the upper lip was always very red. She had a mole on the left of her chin.

Mrs Twine had established herself in a position of great influence and authority in Swallow Road. Her tongue would cut into a dispute and settle the issue, like the flashing sword of a D'Artagnan. She was without fear of any mortal of either sex or any status. An admirable woman in the abstract; for, even in Swallow Road, to hold a position founded on jam with a pride which expresses itself in silent contempt for the sneer of superior inferiority calls for admiration. But Mrs Twine was not a pleasant woman. She was, indeed, that most diabolical specimen of all the daughters of Eve, the spiteful woman with a slow temper.

Of all strictly human mysteries the most universal is the most mysterious – the matrimonial mystery. Why he married her – why she married him. The mystery applies to almost every couple in almost every road, Swallow or otherwise. The parties to the marriages even ask themselves the question sometimes.

Mrs Twine would, occasionally, in a mood of cold banter, ask herself the question aloud in her husband's hearing. It is unlikely, on the other hand, that Mr Twine asked himself the same question even mentally. At his boldest he perhaps dreamt the question, and awoke with a startled eye for the pillow alongside.

But a very brief analysis of the Twine's courtship will solve the mystery of how they came to marry each other.

In a modest provincial town the elder Posset girl, masterful even at twenty-two, had elected to wed. A modest provincial town is deficient in County Nimrods or dashing Guardees; and Gertrude's choice of the very junior partner of a firm of local accountants had, at the time, appeared comparatively exalted. The nose, red even then at the baseline, had protruded into the baffled expression of Mr Twine in a sitting-out corner of the Town Hall. Fingers had stolen up and played little flipping exercises on his shrinking biceps. He had emerged into the Lancers, amazedly gripped, smilingly sweating, betrothed he scarce knew how. Clara, still only half out of a pig-tail, had reviewed the affair in the light of a wild orgy of romance; and she still preserved a copy of the wedding invitation (let down in a cream scroll by a bevy of gymnastic cupids) in a random collection of childhood's souvenirs. The real boom in Posset's Jams dated, incidently, from 1914.

The Programme for the day which was to welcome the Longhamptons to Chumpton had been vexed by complications. In the morning a telegraph boy had arrived at Frascati. Mr Twine, who was attending to the adjustment of a lawn-sprinkler with indifferent success, was summoned from the French window.

'Now kindly attend,' said Mrs Twine. 'This important telegram has arrived.'

She read it aloud.

Twine Frascati Chumpton Somerset

Mother poorly don't worry not fit but unfit travel am going there will bring her down later augustus coming alone so will want looking after till I come Clara

'Oh yes. Oh dear,' said Mr Twine.

'I wonder whether I ought to go to Mother.'

'Yes.'

'I don't think so. Clara says don't worry.'

'No. I only meant I wondered too.'

'I shall wait until I hear how Clara finds Mother. You had better go and send a telegram to Clara at Sutton, asking.'

'Yes.'

'You had better come with me into the dining-room and I'll get another slip of paper and we'll will go through the programme for the day again.'

'Yes.'

'You had better call and tell Noon to come and put the sprinkler right. As you have left it, it is simply flooding one portion of the grass and leaving the rest absolutely unwatered.'

'Yes.'

'You had better not wear your white shoes next time you experiment with the sprinkler.'

'No.'

Mrs Twine overcame, by degrees, her annoyance with the

perversity of Fate in cancelling her prearranged programme. She plunged into reorganisation, re-advised Mrs Leverett, sent and received telegraphic messages between herself and Clara, and by lunch-time was once more in a normal condition of settled prospicience. She even agreed to go out and play Bridge at Mrs Wintle's at eight-thirty. Augustus would have arrived in the course of the afternoon or early evening. He could be left to do his unpacking, while Harold could go to the Country Club. Thus, at lunch, she said,

'So, at last again, that is all right, isn't it?'

'Yes,' said Mr Twine. 'Most satisfactory.'

'Except that I don't think you can really mean that Mother being ill is satisfactory?'

'Oh no. I didn't—'

'Do you wish for any more stewed rhubarb?'

'No, thank you.'

'Let me see. What time is your game this afternoon?'

'Oh, I'm not playing a match this afternoon. This afternoon, if you remember, you wanted me to be back in good time for tea, so as to be ready to meet Clara and Longhampton.'

'But Clara is not coming.'

'Not now. But, if you remember, we arranged that I was only to do my approaching and putting practise this afternoon, so that when they arrived I should be here. My game with Admiral Juddy is tomorrow morning.'

Mrs Twine sorted pieces of paper frowning.

'I do so dislike being thrown out. It upsets all my programme. I do wish poor Mother wouldn't have these attacks. Oh yes. Today you are doing your approaching.'

'Yes. At two-thirty. Only I expect I may have to walk out a good way, because ordinary match couples will be starting and I might get in their way.'

'You can do your approaching and putting on the last green, near the club house!'

'Yes, but it's rather public. I don't – I didn't want the other men to watch me doing it very much.'

'If other men are watching you and criticising, it will make you do it more carefully.'

'Oh.'

'And you will be back by what time?'

'Four, I think you said.'

'Four, yes. Augustus will have arrived by that time I should think. Don't be later than four.'

But Augustus did not arrive. Dinner-time drew near and he had not put in an appearance.

'It is most vexing,' said Mrs Twine. 'I particularly wished to see that he was settled in before I went out to Bridge.'

'The worst of it is,' said Harold Twine, 'that I met Admiral Juddy on the links and promised to make up a four at the Club tonight. Otherwise I could stay and look out for Longhampton. Bother!'

'Well, we must have dinner. And you had better call in at Rookery Nook on your way down to the Club and see that Mrs Leverett is there, and tell her to wait there until Augustus arrives. And see that word is sent over here directly he does so.'

'Yes,' said Harold. 'But, dear, if you have to go out to Bridge and I am at the Club, will it be very much good our hearing?'

'What do you mean?'

'I mean, will it be very good their sending over?'

'I don't understand you,' said Mrs Twine. 'Express yourself.'

'I mean, if – suppose, for instance – he arrives at – well, say – ten; and sends word to us here—'

'We shan't be here at ten.'

'Exactly.'

'What do you mean "exactly"? Don't crumble your bread, dear, please.'

'I mean—'

'Hush! What was that?'

'Cook, I think.'

'Does cook hoot?'

'Oh. I thought you meant somebody sneezing. I think I heard—'

'Hush! I heard a hoot.'

'Oh.'

'Didn't you?'

'No. I don't think what I heard was a hoot.'

'Well, what I heard was.'

'But—'

'But what?'

'A hoot, dear?'

'Yes, a hoot, a hoot.'

'Er – what sort of a – er – hoot?'

'A hoot. A noise like a hoot.'

'I don't hear anything.'

'Well, of course you don't, if you keep talking. I thought it might be Augustus.'

'Oh, but—'

'But what?'

'Do you think he would come outside and hoot?'

'Wouldn't he hoot with his horn?'

'What, dear?'

'Hoot with his motor, with his horn. Hoot. Hoot with his horn, with his motor.'

'Oh. You mean you think he may have passed in the road hooting in his car?'

'Well, do you think I meant he was standing outside the front door playing a trumpet?'

'No. But it *marght* have been somebody else's car.'

'On the other hand it may have been his.'

'But surely he wouldn't hoot and pass? He would stop and come in, don't you think, most probably?'

'Not if he didn't know we lived here.'

'Oh, but he does, doesn't he?'

'Does what?'

'Know.'

'Why?'

'What, dear?'

'Express yourself.'

'Well, what I thought was—'

'Instead of thinking balderdash, you'd better go over to Rookery Nook and come back and let me know, before I go to Bridge.'

'Yes.'

'At once.'

'Yes.'

'You'll have to come back quickly.'

'Yes.'

'Do up your serviette. Tell Mrs Leverett to wait. That is to say, if he's not there. If he is there, see that he has all he wants for the night. Don't let him patronise you. You simply fawned on him at the wedding. You are as good as he is. Better, I hope.'

'Oh, my dear, remember, Clara told you he had improved a great deal.'

'These so-called men of the world. I know. Don't you allow him to try and lead you astray.'

'My dear Gertrude!'

'Oh, I know what men are when they get together. They tell each other coarse stories and things. I know he's that kind of man.'

'Oh, but you don't really think—'

'Oh, go, go, go, to Rookery Nook,' said Mrs Twine, as though chanting the refrain of a popular song.

Harold Twine went and returned. Augustus had not arrived. Mrs Leverett was still there. She was getting a little impatient. It must have been somebody else's hoot.

Mrs Twine, stiffening with suppressed indignation, went to Mrs Wintle's. Harold, breathing deeply in temporary respite, to the Club.

At eleven o'clock, Admiral Juddy, who was an old gentleman with a sunken chest, sky-blue eyes and enormous white eyebrows, leant forward and smote the table with his clenched fist.

'Hell's pit!' he cried. 'Why the blazes couldn't you give me back my lead?'

'Oh,' said Harold, 'But—'

'I had two solid tricks sitting, waiting in my hand. The queen of sparklers and the jack of shovels. What d'you think I led sparklers for? You only got the lead in your blasted hand once and then you go and shove out a miserable-looking dooce of bloodthumpers.'

'But I hadn't another diamond,' said Harold.

'Then you ought to have kept one.'

'Oh, but I never had one at all.'

'Then you ought to have got one somehow – curse and confound this!' said the Admiral. 'I'm not going to sit down under this. I'm going to have another rubber.'

'Isn't it rather late?' suggested Harold.

'I don't care if it's the crack of blasted doom,' said the Admiral. 'Cut.'

'I suppose we had better reckon up. It's after eleven,' said Miss Olive Creepe. 'Poor Mrs Twine. You have had a melancholy evening.'

'I have not had bad hands personally,' said Mrs Twine, bitingly. 'But they do not seem to have suited my partners!'

'Haven't we time for one more rubber?' asked Mrs Wintle.

'Ample, so far as I am concerned,' said Mrs Twine. 'I didn't suggest reckoning up.'

'Well, only one more,' said Mrs Creepe.

'I haven't heard any definite proposal to play six,' said Mrs Twine.

The final rubbers were in both cases speedily over. Admiral Juddy and Mrs Twine were respectively victorious. The parties thereupon broke up. Mrs Twine and her husband arrived in the hall of Frascati almost simultaneously, the latter in a state of informative excitement.

'Gertrude dear,' he cried, 'Clara has come after all.'

'What!'

'Yes, really.'

'How do you know?'

'Why, just now, as I was passing Rookery Nook on my way home from the club, I noticed that the lights were on in the big room on the first floor, overlooking Swallow Road. The blinds were down, but on them – on the blinds – I saw the shadow of Clara, standing and doing something to her hair. I saw it as plain as a pikestaff.'

'You saw what?'

'Her. It. The shadow.'

'Are you sure it was Clara? How could it be Clara?'

'Well, dear; how could it be any other woman? It was a woman. Honestly. I'm sure of that. I mean you could tell from her figure.'

'What!'

'Her attitude, that is. There she was, standing and combing long strands of hair from her head.'

'How long did you look?'

'Not long, of course. But long enough to make certain it was a woman.'

'What!'

'That is to say, I just looked up and saw this going on—'

'What going on?'

'This combing, dear. And then I thought to myself "Aha".'

'Why did you think "Aha"? What had you to "aha" about?'

'Nothing, dear, except I thought to myself "Hallo, Clara has come down after all".'

'This is very odd,' said Mrs Twine. 'She certainly said in her telegram that Mother was already practically well again; but she would hardly have started off and got down tonight. She couldn't have.'

'No,' said Harold. 'But there she was, in the bedroom there; as plain as the nose on your face.'

'What!'

'I say, there she was, as plain as the nose on my face.'

'How long ago was this?'

'Only about two minutes, dear. I was passing, on my way home—'

'Then they won't have gone to bed yet. You had better run and make inquiries. Don't hang about there. Come back and let me know at once. I will wait up until you come back and let me know.'

'Yes.'

'You had better go and look at the blind again first and see whether the light is still up in the room.'

'Yes.'

'If the light is out, you had better call up to the window from Swallow Road and make inquiries.'

'Yes.'

'Well, don't hang about then. Go and do it.'

'Yes.'

Harold Twine pattered back to the corner of Lighthouse Road. Quickly securing a convenient observation post, he scanned the first floor window. The light was still burning in the room.

Just as he was about to turn away he again saw a shadow thrown against the blind. Harold paused and peered, smiling in satisfied confirmation of his own perspicacity. For this time the shadow was unquestionably that of Augustus. He was standing in profile and obviously addressing some remark to the now unseen Clara. He was, so far as Harold could determine, still fully clad.

Harold trotted down Lighthouse Road and through the gateway of Rookery Nook, at the jaunty double of the unexpected but infallibly welcome visitor. As he approached the front door he noticed that Augustus had not yet extinguished the lights in the hall. Harold gaily popped up the steps and sought the bell. Mrs Mantle Ham's bell was not very easy to find in the dark, being almost entirely obscured by the very high-class creeper which ornamented her porch.

But why ring? It might inconvenience Longhampton, who was upstairs in the bedroom, and possibly alarm Clara. Harold tried the door. It was unbolted. Should he not walk heartily in and call to them up the stairs?

He thrust the door open and bounced in, fell with a sickening thud over an open portmanteau and bit the dust of a valuable Turkey mat.

When he regained a sitting posture on the floor, it was to see the figure of Augustus Longhampton crouching to spring, like some ponderous beast, at the bend of the staircase.

CHAPTER VIII

A Cat-Call from Harold Twine

'Hallo! It's you,' said Augustus.

'Yes,' said Harold. 'How are you? Welcome to Chumpton.'

'What the devil do you think you're up to?'

'Oh. I happened to trip over a portmanteau.'

'But what are you doing here?'

'I was just coming to call upstairs.'

'What! Have you any idea of the time? Do you generally make a point of calling on people at midnight?'

'Oh. I didn't mean calling in that sense. I meant coming to the foot of the stairs and shouting.'

'But, dash it, man; you can't come strolling into people's houses at the dead of night and shouting.'

'Oh. But all your lights were on.'

'I don't see what difference that makes. Because I happen to have my lights on, is that any reason for you to come turning cartwheels in my front hall and shouting like a sort of comic Curfew official?'

'Oh. But, you see, knowing that you hadn't gone to bed, and seeing that Clara had come down after all—'

'What!'

'I say, seeing that—'

'What do you mean about Clara?'

'I found out she was here after all.'

'Here?' echoed Augustus, instinctively lowering his voice.

'Yes. I saw her shadow upstairs as I was passing the house, on the blind.'

Augustus's jaw dropped, but Harold who was examining his left knee-cap, failed to notice, and by the time he again looked up, Augustus had decided upon a policy of peremptory confutation.

'I'm not surprised to hear you were on the blind,' he said. 'Speaking from my own experience, I think you were very lucky not to see anything worse than a shadow.'

'Oh, I say,' said Harold. 'But really, I saw her figure. And yours too. Only that was later on, after I'd come back, after I'd told Gertrude. Just now in fact. I'm sure it wasn't the same shadow both times, because she was doing her hair, and that could hardly be you, could it? At least, I mean – not combing it out in long waves, like that.'

'Get up off the floor and pull yourself together,' said Augustus severely. 'You're talking absolute drivel.'

'Oh, but surely she is up there, isn't she?'

'Who?'

'Clara.'

'Up where?'

'In that room? On the first floor.'

'Clara is at Sutton, you blithering idiot.'

'Oh, but surely there is some lady up there, isn't there? With hair.'

'Up there – in my bedroom? A woman, with hair? Twine, what the devil do you mean?'

'Oh. I beg your pardon. Only I could have taken an oath—'

'You'll take one or two from me in a minute. A woman with hair in my bedroom?'

'Oh. I beg your pardon. Of course, if there isn't that disposes of it.'

'So I should hope,' said Augustus. 'Unless you're going to accuse me of splitting a bedroom with a bald woman?'

'No.'

'Oh. Then that's that. I know what it is, of course; you're a little bit on.'

'Oh, no.'

'Yes, you are. It's all right. I've been like that myself before now.'

'Oh, but—'

'My dear fellow, it stands to reason. You see shadows of female beavers on the blinds and come dashing in here, looping the loop all over the hall floor. You're a little bit drunk. It takes different people different ways.'

'Longhampton! No, but seriously. This is a very queer hallucination.'

Augustus nodded agreeably.

'That's it,' he said in the tone of a doctor checking symptoms. 'Hallucination. Only, you'll find, as you get drunk a bit more often, that you won't see things until a later stage.'

'Oh, I say, quit funning,' said Harold coyly.

'I'm not funning at all. This is very serious. Did I understand you to say that – you'd been home and hiccoughed your tidings to Gertrude?'

'Yes. I told her I'd seen Clara. That's really why I came round here.'

'My God!' muttered Augustus.

'Why, what is the matter?'

'What? Oh, nothing. Only I'm afraid Gertrude may be rather annoyed when she hears she's been false alarmed at like this. She, I suppose, has gone to bed?'

'Not yet. In fact, she said she would come round here too if Clara was really here.'

'Well, I think you'd better run home and tell her to go to bed. You must make out the best case for yourself that you can, Twine. I'll leave that to you. You can think it over, as you run.'

Harold rose from the floor and performed nervous massaging movements with his fingers on various portions of his anatomy.

'But are you really *quahte* sure that there is no one in the house besides yourself?'

'There's a cat,' said Augustus.

'Mrs Leverett—'

'No, I meant an ordinary cat. Besides, even if Mrs Leverett hadn't gone, I should hardly invite her to my bedroom.

Apart from other considerations her appearance is enough to sicken a Mormon elder on a desert island.'

'Oh. Well, I had better get back at once to Gertrude.'

'Yes, by Jove, you'd better.'

'Yes.'

'And tell her you – well, you simply saw what wasn't there, that's all.'

'Yes.'

'And – oh, I say, tell her not to trouble to come over too early in the morning, because I shall probably sleep pretty late.'

'Yes.'

'Yes, and I expect you will too. One does. Good night, Twine.'

'Good night. But I can't make it out yet, you know.'

'That's all right. Don't let it haunt you. Push off, there's a good fellow.'

'Oh. Well – I'll see you in the morning.'

'Yes,' said Augustus. 'If you take care of yourself.'

This time he bolted the front door. He returned to the foot of the stairs and pondered. He felt a misgiving that his show of bravado had been insufficiently genuine to convince even Harold Twine. Dangerous, this. Gertrude might—

He remounted the stairs; again tapped on the bedroom door. Further precaution was essential.

'Come in,' chirruped Rhoda, and, as he entered. 'Was that my step-father?'

'No,' said Augustus. 'A complication from my side this time. I think it's quite on the cards that my sister-in-law will pay us a visit in about ten minutes.'

'Oh dear! Are you going to tell her?'

'No, I'm not.'

'Then what do you think I'd better do?'

'Hide,' said Augustus. 'Don't switch on the light.'

'I think it may be rather difficult to hide properly in the dark.'

'Well, hold on. Wait till I draw these darn great curtains. They saw your shadow on the blind, you see.'

'Oh, how careless of me,' said Rhoda calmly.

'Never mind. They haven't discovered anything yet. I'll draw the curtains and then we can switch on the light, and then we can choose a good place for you to hide in, close at hand; and then if you hear the front door bell, you can just nip out of bed and hide in it.'

'I see,' said Rhoda. 'But will your sister-in-law come up to the bedroom, do you think?'

'If she comes at all, she will come with that object,' replied Augustus.

'Oh, right you are then,' said Rhoda willingly. 'Under the bed?'

'No – o,' said Augustus, 'I don't think it had better be anywhere in this room.'

'Just as you think best,' said Rhoda, who was by this time sitting up in bed. 'Only I shall have to look rather nippy when I hear the bell, shan't I?'

Augustus blew out his cheeks.

'Dash it all,' he deliberated, 'the woman can't make a sort of grand tour of the house at this time of night. What do you think of coming downstairs again just for about half-an-hour, until we make sure whether she's coming or not? We could easily find somewhere for you to hide there.'

'By all means, if you like. Besides, it would be obvious that this bed had been got into, unless I made it again, which I suppose I'd better do. You can't very well have gone to bed in your clothes and got out again, can you?'

'By Jove, I should never have thought of that,' said Augustus. 'Would you get up and make it? I'm awfully sorry to disturb you in this way; and it may be just nervousness on my part.'

'Oh no, I think you're most wise to be prepared,' said Rhoda. 'And I think, as a matter of fact, I do know your sister-in-law by sight. If she's the woman I think she is, then you're certainly justified in taking every precaution. If you don't mind waiting outside, I'll get out and put on my dressing-gown.'

At the corner of Lighthouse Road, Harold Twine pulled up and sought counsel of the starry firmament. He had become accustomed to defeat, hardened to humiliation. It was not the rather disappointing reception which he had encountered that depressed his willing spirit. It was the unaccountable, violent, almost maddening disproof of a vision which, with his own eyes, he had beheld; nay, even studied. He was a very material person. He was no somnambulant and imaginative Bottom, to be waylaid by sportive fairies in the Swallow Road and made the victim of their midsummer pranks. After all, he had seen the shadow of Augustus quite clearly and identified it, and there, sure enough, inside Rookery Nook had been the man himself in confirmatory substance. No less certainly had Harold seen the female figure shadowed on the blind. Ah, there was something very queer going on, very queer and fishy and unpleasant. Suddenly with a gulp of apprehension, Harold realised what this might mean. Could it be possible that Augustus, so soon after his marriage, was being unfaithful? Harold had read often enough of cases where husbands had forsaken their wives in favour of another woman. Perhaps he had wondered, subconsciously over the newspaper, how the husbands ever came to be allowed to forsake, or why, having successfully forsaken, they should commit the suicidal act of subjugating themselves to another of the same species as the forsaken. But was it credible that Longhampton, even if guilty of so reprehensible and short-sighted a policy, should bring an inamorata along with him in his car and smuggle her into Rookery Nook? But there it was. He had seen that shadow on the blind. That, amid all his doubts and speculations, remained a definite, irrefutable fact.

Oh, but did this mean some dreadful matrimonial discord in which he would be involved, perhaps chiefly involved?

Did this portend his shivering in a witness-box and being torn asunder by some relentless K.C.? To one of his temperament no earthly ordeal more horrid could possibly be imagined. Harold stepped round the corner and glanced once more at the first floor window. Ah. The curtains had been drawn now. Fishy. Fishier and fishier. There was almost certainly something up. He must not, could not be involved. He would say no more to anyone; not even to Gertrude. After all, Augustus Longhampton has told him there was no one else there, so let it remain at that. Would that he had never flown to Gertrude with his first gushing presumption.

Fancy, though, Longhampton – disgusting; wicked! Gertrude had always said he was a loose man. But the bravado of it! At Chumpton. In Rookery Nook. It simply must mean that Longhampton had seized the first opportunity that circumstance offered, no matter how scandalously risky. Oh, how fast!

Luck was not with Harold. As he turned from the window he found the nose of Gertrude protruding into his face. Impatient and suspicious, she had arrived to make her own stealthy investigations.

'You are a very long time coming home.'

'Yes, I was just having another look at the window.'

'Why?'

'I was wondering whether the curtains had been drawn all the time.'

'How could you have seen shadows on the blind if the curtains were drawn?'

'Yes, that's just it.'

'Just what?'

'I don't see how I could have, but I didn't think they were.'

'You could have done what? What weren't they?'

'What, dear?'

'Express yourself.'

'I think the curtains have only just been drawn.'

'I don't care about the curtains. Have you been to the house?'

'Yes. Longhampton was there. But I must have made a mistake, because he said there was no woman.'

'What!'

'I mean, that Clara wasn't there.'

'What woman do you suppose there could be there besides Clara?'

'None.'

'Then what do you mean?'

'I said I'd seen, as I thought, the shadow of a woman doing her hair on the blind. And he said I couldn't have, because Clara wasn't there.'

Mrs Twine shot a sudden and keen glance upwards in the direction of the window. Her pinched nostrils contracted.

'But you told me you undoubtedly saw the shadow of Clara?'

'Well, of a – yes. Of Clara, yes; I thought—'

'A female figure, you said.'

'Yes, but perhaps it was Longhampton looking like a woman.'

'Combing his strands of hair from his head?'

'Oh. It may only have looked like that. He may really have been pulling off his shirt.'

'Had he his shirt on when you saw him?'

'Yes. But it may not have been the same shirt.'

'Why should he change his shirt?'

'I don't know.'

'You had better come with me.'

'Yes. Where?'

'There, of course.'

'Oh, but—'

'But what?'

'Is it necessary? I've satisfied myself.'

'About what?'

'About Clara not being there.'

'I mean to be satisfied about more than that. Did you go up to the bedroom?'

'Bedroom? No. Why, dear?'

'Because that was where you saw this female shadow.'

'Yes. But there is really nobody there.'

'No woman, you mean?'

'Yes. No.'

'How do you know there is no woman there if you haven't been up to the bedroom?'

'But he *said*. I said, "Is Clara here?" And he said—'

'What was his manner towards you when you went in? Did he seem pleased to see you?'

'Oh, I think so. I think perhaps he was a little tired.'

'How did he receive your news about you having seen this female figure?'

'He passed it off as a joke.'

'Oh, did he!' said Mrs Twine. 'Come.'

'That is to say, he rather laughed at me for seeing things that couldn't possibly be there.'

'Did you tell him that I was thinking of coming over?'

'Yes.'

'What did he say to that?'

'He asked you not to tonight. Really, I think the man was very anxious to go up to bed. In fact, he asked you not to come too early in the morning.'

'Indeed! Come along. Keep up.'

'Oh. But—'

'But what?'

'I forget what I was going to say now.'

'Well, when you remember it, don't say it. I don't wish to be heard talking outside the house.'

'Yes.'

'Don't make a noise with the gate and don't scrunch on the gravel with your feet.'

'No.'

'The lights are still up in the hall. He cannot be in such a desperate hurry to go to bed after all.'

'No. He hadn't quite finished unpacking. Some of his things were still in the hall.'

' 'Sh. Don't make a noise. What things?'

'Oh, various things. He was unpacking in the hall.'

' 'Sh. Why?'

'I don't know.'

' 'Sh. Didn't you ask him?'

'No.

'If you ask me, the whole thing seems to point very strongly to some sort of jiggery pokery.'

'Oh. But—'

'Hush! What is the use of my telling you not to talk?'

They approached the front door; she, in the moonlight, seeming to float up the gravel drive like a ghost bent upon vindictive domestic haunting; he, in her wake, reluctant but abject, mounting even to obsequious tip-toe at one half-turn of her head; but so hating the business as to indulge, at a more opportune moment, the undisciplined sustainment of a grimace.

The feeling of distressed and shrinking subservience to discipline was no novelty to Harold Twine. How familiar to him was the dire experience of meeting some erring female neighbour condemned to excommunication by Gertrude, of passing furtively by on the other side and of raising his cap one half-hearted moment too late, vainly feigning shortsight—a would-be Samaritan, forced to play Levite on the Swallow Road to Jericho! But seldom in his experience had he been possessed by an aversion so keen as that which he felt now. He knew there was some woman in Rookery Nook. He knew the potentialities of Gertrude. The woman would be discovered. A violent and exhaustive domestic (if not public) upheaval would inevitably ensue, in which he would inevitably be the mutual target of domestic (if not public) recriminations.

He was not inspired by sympathy with Longhampton. But he had been trained to a settled, if regulated existence, and the very thought of some appalling family embroilment affected him with an almost physical irritation. Never before had the awe-inspiring instinct of revolt stirred more dangerously within his bosom.

Meanwhile Gertrude had found, and rung, the bell.

The door was opened immediately by a laboriously artificial Augustus, self-primed to be hearty without over-acting the cordiality, to be sleepy without over-doing the inhospitality. The portmanteau had been removed and all its contents now lay upon the hall table, looking like the relics of a bazaar at closing-time. 'So here you are,' said Gertrude. 'So here I am,' said Augustus cheerfully. She sniffed and entered. The base-line of her nose was very red. Twine followed.

'I am annoyed that you should have been so late in arriving here,' said Gertrude. 'I wished to be here to install you. What time did you come?'

'To tell you the truth, I didn't notice,' said Augustus. 'Well, and how are you, Gertrude?'

'I left word most particularly that I was to be informed when you arrived.'

'Yes. It's my fault. I forgot that I'd told the daily woman I'd go and tell you. You're looking very well, Gertrude.'

'It seems very strange that you should have forgotten. I suppose you had the food I sent in for you.'

'Yes, rather. Ham and eggs. Splendid. Thank you for—'

'I should have thought that the fact that you were eating the food that I had sent would have reminded you that I was waiting to hear you had arrived.'

'Yes. It ought to have. But I had a lot to do in a hurry. Unpacking and so on.'

'Your hurry to unpack doesn't seem to have been very effective,' said Gertrude with a nose-contraction at the hall table.

'Ha! I couldn't get my portmanteau upstairs. It was too heavy. So I turned the things out here.'

'And you are now engaged in carrying your clothes upstairs in relays?'

'Yes. That's the idea.'

'To your bedroom?'

'Yes, of course. Why, isn't that the right place to put

them? If so, let me know, because, as a matter of fact, I haven't taken any of them up there yet.'

'In spite of your feverish hurry to unpack?'

'I've been taking them out of the portmanteau.'

'H'm. Then you have discovered where you are to sleep?'

'Oh, yes. Rather. Capital bedroom. Would you care to see it?'

This was a mistake. Over-acting. Gertrude shot a glance at him.

'Why should I wish to see your bedroom?'

'Well, my dear Gertrude, you have taken the trouble to come over here at midnight to see that I'm all settled in. I thought perhaps you wouldn't feel you'd done it properly until you'd seen that my room was all – you know – nice and ready.'

'Yes, I will see your room,' said Gertrude. 'Harold, you had better remain here.'

'Yes.'

'Do you know this house well?' continued Augustus pleasantly.

'Only the ground floor,' said Gertrude.

'Ah. The bedroom's up these stairs.'

'So I suppose,' said Gertrude.

'It's a very large room, overlooking your road apparently.'

'Why?'

'Well, because it was put that side of the house, I suppose.'

'But why should you remark on its overlooking our road?'

'Because Twine says he saw shadows on the blind. He seems to have mistaken my shadow for Clara's. I don't know why he should have thought I looked like Clara, but I'm sure it's very complimentary of him.'

Harold said nothing, licked his lips, feebly smiled.

'Never mind about that now,' said Gertrude. 'Show me the room.'

Augustus escorted her upstairs. Harold sat on the Chesterfield and breathed again. He was still firmly convinced that some woman had been in that bedroom. But Augustus had got rid of her. Where, goodness knew. But she had gone. He, Harold, could eat his words and all would be well. He knew the taste of ill-considered words well enough. In a negative sort of way he might be deceiving Gertrude, but it was for her own peace of mind in the long run. There were times when a man must take a definite and authoritative line of action with his wife. Besides, even if Gertrude found out, it wasn't as though he had rendered any practical aid to Augustus. He would never have dared to do that – elected to, rather.

Waa-ee-ow!

Harold sat bolt upright and gripped the arm of the Chesterfield.

All this time, from the moment when Augustus had set foot in Rookery Nook, the cat had remained in outraged contemplation, behind the china cupboard of the pantry. But it was not accustomed to being asked to spend the night behind the china cupboard and was damned if it did so without protest. Besides, it was hungry.

The pantry door stood open. The door giving access to the hall from the servants' quarters was, however, closed. Against this door the cat vainly rubbed its person and gave tongue.

Harold recovered himself. A cat only. He looked around him with wide inviting eyes. He chirruped softly with his lips and verbally replied to the call for supplication, 'Puss! Pussy – puss. Pretty pussy-puss-puss!'

The sound of a friendly voice, issuing from a quarter inaccessible, goaded the cat to the verge of frenzy. Laying its head well back, it closed its eyes and produced its top-note. Harold Twine now locating the voice of the cat, popped up benevolently from the Chesterfield.

Immediately he opened the door to the kitchen quarters, the cat gave a repetition of its lightning-streak method of progression across the hall into the dining-room, Harold, peering into the darkness of the kitchen quarters, chirruped in vain. No cat was there after all. He could have sworn he had heard a cat. Queer.

'Come along, come along, come along,' he whispered encouragingly. He even advanced a few paces, stepping cautiously through the kitchen and craning his neck inquiringly through the open door into the scullery beyond.

'Come along, it's all right. It's all right, come along,' he murmured gently.

Not Balaam himself was more astounded than was Harold by the hair-raising response of the cat.

'Thank goodness!' said the latter in cheerful human tones. 'I was getting cramp in my—'

Harold fell back into the lighted doorway, his scalp tingling with a cold thrill of shock and horror. On this, the cat added, in an altered tone, 'Oh Gosh!' and upset an enormous tripod of saucepans in assorted sizes.

Harold slammed the door behind him, reeled against the Chesterfield. Another woman! The same woman? Was this house stiff with women? If Augustus Longhampton thought he could conduct a private Agapemone at Rookery Nook without Gertrude finding out about it, he little knew, he little knew.

The rather husky voice of the suave Don Juan broke in upon his fevered meditations at this juncture from the staircase.

'What are you up to, Twine?'

'Oh. N – nothing – I heard a cat.'

'The sound we heard,' said Augustus, descending the stairs with Gertrude, 'was not the sound of one hearing a cat. It was the sound of one throwing coal-scuttles at a greenhouse.'

'What were you doing?' added Gertrude.

'Oh. I heard the cat mew—'

'What?'

'Mew.'

'You mean – mi-ow?'

'Yes. Mi-ow or mew. I have always called it a – a mew.'

'A mew,' said Augustus, 'in the singular, is a variety of sea-fowl, resembling a gull. In the plural, stables.'

'I heard the cat making its noise.'

'It didn't sound at all like a cat's noise to me,' said Augustus.

'No, I – I'm afraid I did that,' said Harold, lying valiantly from motives he made no effort to define.

'You did what?' asked Gertrude.

'Er – that noise.'

'What do you mean, you did the noise?' said Gertrude.

'I – I made it,' said Harold.

'Good God!' cried Augustus. 'You ought to go on the halls.'

'I went into the kitchen,' said Harold.

'So I should hope,' said Augustus. 'Next time you want to make noises like that you'd better go in the garden.'

'I went into the kitchen, because I heard the cat making the noise I spoke of.'

Gertrude handled Augustus to one side and took charge.

'I thought you said you made the noise yourself?' she said.

'Oh that noise, yes. I meant the cat was mewing – miowing – making its—'

'What – was – that – noise?'

'Oh. I'm afraid something in the kitchen was upset.'

'I should think it *was* upset,' said Augustus. 'It sounded peeved beyond measure.'

Gertrude swept round upon him.

'Turn up the lights in the kitchen,' she commanded.

'No, no; that's all right, Gertrude. I'll see to whatever it is. I'm afraid Harold isn't quite himself.'

'What?'

'Oh, I don't mean anything serious. Only he keeps on seeing visions and hearing cats. I expect the truth of the matter is he's half asleep. And I think, if you don't mind, the very best thing for all of us will be to go to bed.'

Gertrude leant forward and stared intently into her husband's face.

'Is anything the matter with you?' she inquired.

'I do feel a little dizzy.' said Harold.

'Dizzy?'

'Tired, dear.'

'H'm!' said Gertrude. 'Come home.'

'Yes.'

Augustus politely opened the front door and awaited them on the step. Gertrude, with a movement as though of gathering herself together for as dignified a departure as possible under the circumstances, followed him across the hall. Harold, still harassed by a mental conflict of doubt, misgiving and guilt, trailed behind her.

As he passed, he happened to glance at the door of the dining-room. There, in the doorway, stood the cat. He pointed towards it and, almost involuntarily, gave vent to a little cry of self-justification.

'There! Look! There's the cat!'

The cat instantaneously disappeared into the dining-room. Gertrude turned and cast an inquiring glance at the vacant aperture. Augustus, too, put his head round the front door and stared at the dining-room.

'Oh, it's gone now,' said Harold feebly.

'Come!' coldly responded Gertrude. 'Dizzy indeed!'

'Gertrude,' he ventured to begin, as they neared the front gate.

She halted and again peered at him in the moonlight.

'Are you drunken?' she asked curtly.

'Oh, Gertrude, dear!'

'Then why have you been behaving in this extraordinary manner ever since you came back from the club?'

'Oh.'

'Seeing things on blinds, and not being able to sit still on a sofa for two minutes without rushing and dashing things over in the kitchen—'

'Oh.'

'Looking for a cat that wasn't there—'

'Oh, but there was one really. In the dining-room.'

'Then why did you go and look for it in the kitchen?'

'Oh, but I think it was in the kitchen when I started looking, only I'm quite sure it was in the dining-room when I saw it.'

'You can't express yourself,' said Gertrude.

'I'm awfully sorry,' said Rhoda. 'That man came into the scullery and I thought it was you and came out.'

'That's all right,' said Augustus. 'He thinks it was a cat.'

'Oh, but I talked to him.'

'What?'

'I spoke.'

'The devil you did! Much?'

'A few words.'

Augustus held his head.

'And then what happened?'

'He ran back into the hall.'

'That woman will have it out of him. Thank goodness he didn't blurt it out while she was here. I'm going to double-lock that front door, and all the relatives in the world can come and ring at it and beat on it till they're blue in the face; and step-fathers can come and shoot through it, and dogs can come and whistle through it – I don't care. Go on. Trot off to bed. I'm going to sleep on this sofa. And first thing, I'm going to get up and arrange for you to push off to town. That sister-in-law will be round, breathing through her nose, at a pretty early hour, but we've outwitted her so far and with any luck we'll get through. After all, she's only got her husband's word for it, and she suspects him of being lit up, and, take it all round, I think we're doing very well. Good night.'

'Then it's really good night this time?' said Rhoda on the staircase.

She stretched down her hand to him and with fervent lips he kissed it.

'I must confess I'm rather loving this,' she said. 'I'm afraid you're not.'

'I think I enjoy these little lucid intervals best,' he replied.

He rolled up a towel and three shirts and made himself a pillow. He removed his boots and his coat. He squashed himself on to the Chesterfield. He heaved a long-drawn sigh and pessimistically closed his eyes.

Tick – tick – tick – the Grandfather clock. Augustus rose with an oath; the pillow of towel and shirts unravelled itself and slid gracefully to the floor. He seized the door of the clock and pulled it open. He tied one of the weights round the pendulum. He rolled up his pillow again. Again wedged himself to rest.

Why was it so light? Oh damn! He had forgotten to switch out the light. Never mind. Leave it, leave it. Oh-h!

Would slumber come? If it did, he would wake with cramp in every limb. Still, he might perhaps doze. Doze.

Waa-ee-ow!

Augustus opened his eyes, raised himself on an elbow and gently slid one hand down the side of the Chesterfield.

The excellence of his shot with the boot compensated almost fully for all the night's afflictions. It caught the already retiring cat full on the backside. It streaked under the dining-room sideboard, where it spent the remainder of a haunted but silent night. The boot spent the night in the middle of Mrs Mantle Ham's dining-room carpet.

Augustus, jumping up from the Chesterfield, closed the dining-room door, switched off the light and, gathering up again the disintegrated components of his pillow, rolled them together as best he could in the darkness.

Above his head, the bosom of Rhoda was already gently rising and falling in the blissful rhythm of repose. The hand which Augustus had kissed lay outstretched on the coverlet, as though waiting to be kissed again. In the hollow of Mrs Mantle Ham's yielding pillow was buried the smile of one lulled to sleep by celestial voices.

Harold was not at peace. Long before his troubled mind

received the first hint of sleep he was thrice prodded by an elbow and requested not to snore.

'Oh. But—'

'But what?'

'I didn't think I was snoring.'

'How can you possibly tell whether you are snoring?'

'Oh. But I didn't think I was asleep.'

'You don't even know whether you are asleep or not.'

'Oh.'

'Hush! How can I get off? Your conduct, from first to last tonight, has been most unaccountable and off-putting. I shall speak to Admiral Juddy.'

'Oh, but—'

'Hush, will you?'

At six-thirty Augustus was in the grip of a body of mediaeval torturers, who were testing for his benefit a new type of rack, which not only elongated his limbs but twisted them vertically in the process. Presently he sat up; a severe shooting pain still affecting his neck. He was in a completely miserable state of sleep-sodden dishevelment. He blinked himself slowly back into his surroundings. He glanced at the clock, cursed it for having stopped, and fumbled for his watch. He carried his head stiffly round, at the curious and awkward angle demanded by the shooting pain, and surveyed the staircase. The recollection of Rhoda spurred him to action and, kicking aside the relics of his pillow, he discovered one of his boots. After five minutes vain search for the other he gave it up, sought the wash-house and plunged his face into cold water. He then felt better, remembered the whereabouts of the other boot, assumed it and, throwing open the front door, was rewarded by the gladdening vision of a roseate morning and the greetings of birds.

And at the same hour Mrs Leverett, awakening from force of excellent habit, placed her right hand upon her husband's chest and levered herself from her bed.

Rhoda, in Mrs Mantle Ham's bed, was still asleep. Mrs Gertrude Twine, in her own bed, was still asleep. Harold Twine, in his wife's bed, was still awake. The cat, under the sideboard, was awake but comatose.

Augustus closed the door of Rookery Nook behind him and proceeded round the gravel sweep to the garage.

CHAPTER IX

A Cat-Call from Mrs Leverett

'Where,' asked Augustus, 'is the post office?'

'Ay?' replied the milkman.

'Ay. The post office.'

'Oo, the poost-arfs?'

'Ay.'

'Oo.'

The milkman, who was seated on a narrow plank running round the side of a wooden chariot of the type affected by milkmen, was a very venerable milkman with spectacles, white whiskers and an expansive Panama hat which gaily flaunted the colours of the Old Carthusians. He lowered his head and took a long scrutiny of Augustus in the car alongside over his spectacles. He then rose from his seat and said 'Wooee!' to his pony who made no reply.

'Wull now,' said the milkman, 'the poost-arfs. Wull now. If so be you warrnt to goo to the poost arfs, you warrnt to goo – ahh – do ye knoo the church?'

'I dare say I could recognise a church,' said Augustus.

'Ay. Wull now. The poost-arfs, he be the one, two three – the thurrd – noo, the fourth – ay – noo, the one, two, three – the thurrd maybe, or maybe the fourth turrn – noo, dash my buttons, he be the second – noo, nooo, noooo, the thurrd he be – wull, the poost-arfs, he bide round one o' they turrns be the church, ther' 'e bide, as sure as Christmas day.'

'Yes,' said Augustus. 'I rather wanted to get there before Christmas day if I could. Much obliged. Good morning.'

'Ah,' said the milkman. 'But it ain't no use your gooing to that ther' poost-arfs, mister.'

'Why not?'

'He don't open.'

'Don't open?'

'Noo. It be too early for 'un yet awhoile.'

'Good lord! What time does it open?'

'Oo,' replied the milkman speculatively. 'Wull now. Just about around the toime I do be getting around aback ther' from taking this here milk around about to all these here houses around, then it so generally happens that that ther' poost-arfs, he do be about open.'

'What time is that?'

'Ooo – about eight, I reckon.'

'Then the post-office doesn't open till eight?'

'About eight,' said the milkman cautiously.

'Oh, but the place must be open before that. Don't the postmen go in and out there, getting letters and delivering them in the early morning?'

'Ay,' said the milkman, 'the lazy diddlers!'

'Well, what time do they do that?'

'About around the time I do be getting around aback—'

'Oh, confound this!' said Augustus. 'I want to send off a most important telegram.'

'Oo,' said the milkman with interest.

'Are you quite sure I can't send it off till eight?'

'Ay,' said the milkman. 'Noo. About eight.'

'But I don't want to be out at eight. What am I to do?'

'Oo,' said the milkman. 'Wull now. How would it be if you was to give this here telegram to me, and when I do get around aback ther', I could go in ther' for yer and dispatch he?'

'That's very kind of you,' said Augustus. 'But are you sure you'd do it all right?'

'It don't call fer much doing, mister,' said the milkman. 'I can sook a stamp with any man.'

'But I haven't got it written,' said Augustus.

'Write 'un in this here milk-book,' said the milkman. 'I'll copy 'un careful.'

Augustus left his car and joined the milkman. The latter threw down his reins and said 'Hoi-ee-oo! to the pony, who remained stationary. The milkman then produced a time-worn notebook and a pencil which appeared to have been sharpened with the teeth.

Augustus deliberated. He dared not commit himself to elaborate detail in the publicity of a milk-book. Nor must he tax the copying capabilities of his elderly agent. The message he finally inscribed was as brief and cryptic as he could contrive, while yet likely to produce the desired effect. He then handsomely bribed the milkman and returned to Rookery Nook.

Before entering the drive, he clambered from his car and cautiously investigated the scene of his nocturnal interview with Mr Putz. Pixiecot lay ominously tranquil. The window through which Mr Putz had conducted negotiations was tightly shut. A thin veil of mist hung tenaciously over the neglected garden; not a romantic mist like the sleepiness in the eyes of awakening dawn, but a cheerless, cold mist obstinately forbidding Pixiecot to respond to the rapturous call of the morning. Even the birds upon the eaves squatted chilled and songless.

Augustus, invigorated by his early outing, stowed his car in the garage and hurried indoors. It was but seven o'clock. At eight the daily woman was due. 'Earlier,' she had said, 'I cannot be.' Good. There was yet an hour in which to rehearse the first of the several obstructive and evasive measures with which he was unquestionably destined that day to be employed. He did not anticipate much trouble over the daily woman. He could have a bath, rouse Rhoda, assume her place in the bed and stow her in a cupboard while the daily woman brought the tea. He could then bid the daily woman prepare the breakfast, and Rhoda could come forth from the cupboard and split the tea. Rhoda could then go back to the cupboard while the daily woman made the bed. The daily woman could then be discharged, as Augustus would be having lunch at the golf club and dinner at the Twines'. So much for the daily woman – all quite plausible and perfectly agreeable to everybody all round. A preliminary skirmish merely. The real battle would commence with the early arrival of Gertrude. Gertrude, having wormed the yarn of the lady in the scullery out of Twine, would be punctual and at her nosiest. Meanwhile, what of Pixiecot? What overtures were to be expected from that quarter? Would it not be possible, by threat or subterfuge, to secure at least a reasonable selection of Rhoda's wardrobe? Perhaps Rhoda herself could be persuaded to essay a temporary return under false colours, now that the affair was reviewed in the dispassionate light of morning. Failing this, surely not even Putz would refuse to clothe her. Or Nutts must succumb to the lure of bribery.

Active measures from next door were improbable. Putz's one idea had appeared to be to get rid of Rhoda. Having run her out, he didn't seem to care a blow what happened to her. The news that she was about to leave him for good would probably appease him to such an extent that he would readily clothe her for departure. On the other hand, the mentality of Mr Putz appeared to be beyond the scope of normal calculation. For the moment there remained the daily woman and Gertrude. Augustus tapped at the bedroom door, and, receiving no answer, entered the room on tiptoe.

Oh, how beautiful! Lovely as she had appeared in her animated waking hour of banishment and supplication, she was more lovely yet in the untroubled Paradise of sleep. How closely Morpheus clings to us in that last hour of a long, deep slumber, as though unwilling to let us slip from his arms back into the baneful turmoil of consciousness! Perhaps the wise old god knows better than we in which state we are the more progressive.

Clasped tightly thus in the embrace of sleep lay Rhoda, restful as some sleeping sea-nymph, buoyed up by the billows and lulled by the gentle swell of ocean. Augustus stood at the bedside and watched her, quite elevated. To disturb her yet seemed almost a crime. It was only just seven o'clock.

He left her and, from the jumble sale on the hall table, he

salved his shaving materials. These, with his towel, he bore to the bathroom. The water was, of course, stone cold. Curse! He had omitted that from his calculations. He must shave as best he could in cold water. He must also, for the first time in years, have a cold bath. A cold bath was, to Augustus, paradoxically, Hellish.

Mrs Leverett, lathering her ruddy forearms at the basin, responded to a deep Somerset imprecation from the bed in these terms:

'Be making an earlier start than that I had thought to make, I shall be able to get to work there sooner than what I had thought to get.'

'Ye-gurr neburr wurr thurr thurr yegurr wurr,' was the response issuing from the bowels of the bed.

'Up you get! said Mrs Leverett, gasping and hissing in ablution. 'Be five minutes I shall have started, and you must see the children up and fed before you go to your work. Nor don't you get putting Florrie's shirt on Cyril as on the last occasion.'

By ten minutes past seven the commendable woman was at the side door of Rookery Nook, fumbling in the depths of a string bag for her key. She found it and entered the house quietly. Excellent! By stealing this march on time she would no doubt be enabled to snatch an hour off after breakfast, waylay a friendly cart on the Swallow Road and get down to Chumpton to see the children off to school. She laid her string bag on the scullery table and glared with a slow misgiving at the shattered saucepan-tripod.

She opened the door leading into the hall and stood aghast. She opened the door leading into the dining-room and her opinion of Augustus was confirmed by the importunate outburst of the rescued and rubbing cat. Over the kettle for the bedroom tea she rehearsed, with strange contortions of countenance, a remonstrance almost amounting to notice.

Augustus gingerly lowered one foot into the bath grimacing horribly. Oh, but this was absurd. This was not ordinary cold water, which was never as cold as this. This was iced water. Oh, what a damn fool game! And yet all the laws of sportsmanship demanded that he must plunge. Presently. He would plunge presently. Or at any rate sit. He removed his foot and rubbed it, substituting the other foot to be gripped and congealed in its turn. After a while he had both feet in and was lowering his body from which his breath was already escaping in fluttering spasms. Oh, poisonous ordeal! He plunged, and was not alive again for several seconds.

Was not alive again before Mrs Leverett, wild-eyed, bosom-clutching, early-morning-tea-tray-shaking, breathless almost as Augustus himself, was hurtling back down the staircase, gulping forth to herself words inarticulate and astonished: 'Her from next door, my God, and in his bed! Her, in his very bed, my God, from next door!'

Rhoda slowly stirred, opened her eyes, closed them again, opened them again, closed one, with the other dully surveyed the window curtains, opened the other, turned her head calmly upon the pillow, smiled. The bedroom door was open. There was borne to her ears from an indefinite distance the sound of one fighting for life in cold water. She resumed her former attitude upon the pillow and again closed both eyes.

Back in her scullery Mrs Leverett stood, supporting herself on the table edge, her face looking more than ever purple in effort to remain above the Tartan, in her mind self-control and counsel battling with vindictive and scandalised wrath. At length a contorted and very sinister wink indicated that the former forces had prevailed. She emptied the tea-pot and replaced it on its shelf; she deliberately and silently replaced the saucepans and their tripod in the undignified position in which she had discovered them; she even crossed the hall and replaced the despairing cat in the dining-room. Having thus covered her tracks she re-locked the side door, replaced the key in her string bag, and glided, a curiously rotund harbinger of doom, into Swallow Road.

Presently Augustus, finally clothed but drying his ears, came to the open door and called through,

'Hallo! So you're up.'

'Good morning,' said Rhoda. 'No, I'm not. I've nothing to get up into. Except the dressing-gown.'

'I noticed your door was open.'

'I didn't open it.'

'Oh,' said Augustus. 'Perhaps I left it open. I looked in before, but you were asleep and I hated to disturb you.'

'Was that just now?'

'Some time ago.'

'How deceptive sleep is! I thought, for some reason, that you were in here just now.'

'Well, would you mind preparing to receive a council of war? It's getting on for half past seven and the daily woman will be here at eight.'

'The who? Your sister?'

'No. A general. Suspected of sympathies with the enemy. Up, Deborah!'

'A general? Oh, a servant? Gee! Where am I to hide when she comes?'

'Probably a cupboard. Anyhow, if you'll give me a call when you're ready, I'll come along and we'll go into it together.'

'And how long shall I have to remain in it?'

'That depends on how successfully I can wangle the daily woman. But, for the moment, if you would get a move on, and a dressing-gown—'

At the back door of the house known to herself as 'Thrushcato', Mrs Leverett summoned the heavy-eyed-housemaid of Mrs Twine with a rousing tattoo. After a lengthy and inquisitive greeting she was admitted and installed in the kitchen, where she underwent a species of third degree at the hands of the maid, who tested her with wild surmise, and the cook whose forte was sarcasm. Mrs Leverett, however, remained unshaken. Her tidings concerned only Mrs Twine. She demanded and waited the ear of that lady. Meanwhile budge she would not; either physically from her kitchen chair or informatively from her ominous reserve.

In retaliation the maid absolutely refused to call Mrs Twine before the appointed hour of eight-fifteen. To do so would involve disorganisation of the programme of the day at its first item. She was strongly supported by cook.

'We 'ad yesterday's programme upset,' stated the latter. 'With anything further of the same sort I cannot cope.'

Mrs Leverett therefore waited, bribed with tea, but inexorable.

'I don't think the daily woman can be coming,' said Augustus. 'She probably disliked the look of me last night and has thrown her hand in. So much the better.'

'Yes, the less time I spend in cupboards the better I shall be pleased,' said Rhoda. 'Though, of course, I'll go just where you think best and just as often as you like.'

'Talking of that, there's a very serviceable cupboard under the stairs,' said Augustus. 'I discovered it just now. There's a key in it; so you could lock yourself inside and I can say that it's been left closed. I think it'll be the very place for you while Gertrude's here. Will you come and have a look at it?'

It was now a quarter past eight. Augustus took a quick reconnaissance of the kitchen quarters. No daily woman nor any sign of a daily woman. He showed Rhoda the cupboard, which had been built in, under the hollow of the staircase and contained such articles as a collection of pictures too massive for the drawing-room, a croquet outfit, two disused bicycle pumps, a remnant of linoleum and an immense pile of the back numbers of *Country Life*. Rhoda peered into its gloom wistfully. 'I don't suppose your sister-in-law will stay very long,' she reflected manfully.

'Well, she won't be here yet, anyhow,' replied Augustus.

'Let's try and find some food. I expect there's some tea, and I know there's some bread and butter left over, because I left it and it's still on the dining-room table, unless that miserable cat has been at it.'

'There's a gas stove in the scullery. I noticed it last night,' said Rhoda.

'Fine! Half a tick while I just bolt or wedge all the doors, and then we will skirmish for victuals.'

'Excuse me, madam,' said the maid, 'but Mrs Leverett is here, wanting to see you.'

'H'm.'

'Excuse me, madam, but Mrs Leverett is waiting downstairs to speak to you.'

'H'm.'

'Mrs Leverett, madam, is—'

'H'm. H'm?'

'Mrs Leverett, madam, from Rookery Nook—'

'What? Oh, what?' This from the haunted Harold, suddenly leaping into a sitting position.

'H'mm – what are you doing? Lie down.'

'Oh. But Hannah said something—'

'Lie down, will you! What, Hannah?'

'Mrs Leverett, ma'am. She's downstairs.'

'Why?'

'She's come over from Rookery Nook—'

'Oh – h – what for?' cried Harold.

'Keep silent and lie down. You're only half awake. What does the woman want, Hannah?'

'She wants to speak to you private and particular about something, madam.'

'Oh – h!' moaned Twine.

'Stop that! To me?'

'Yes, madam.'

'What about?'

'She won't say, madam.'

Here Gertrude sat up.

'What is all this, Hannah? Come!'

'Mrs Leverett says she must see you in private as soon as possible, madam.'

'What about?'

'She won't say, madam. I think it must be something about the house.'

'About what house?'

'Rookery Nook.'

'Oh – hh!' from Harold.

'Stop that. Where is she?'

'Downstairs, madam.'

Mrs Twine, now very erect in bed, stretched and blinked herself into action. She brought one wrist slowly to the opposite shoulder as though practising an elaborate back-hand stroke at tennis, then, shooting the elbow forth, caught Harold nicely in an unrevealed but obviously sensitive portion of the anatomy.

'Ow! My dear!'

'Get up.'

'Oh. But–'

'Get up.'

'Very well, but–'

'Get up.'

'Hannah is still here, and–'

'Go away, Hannah. Tell Mrs Leverett to wait. Get up, you.'

'But, my dear, what–'

'What *what*?'

'What?'

'Oh, get up.'

'I am nearly up.'

'Then get quite up.'

'May I have my tea?'

'No. Have your bath.'

'Yes.'

'Don't you understand something is afoot?'

'Oh – h. What?'

'How do I know till I've seen Mrs Leverett?'

'Oh.'

'Go and shave.'

'Yes.'

'And have your bath.'

'Yes.'

'And call over the banisters and tell Hannah to send Mrs Leverett to me here.'

'Yes.'

And if you want tea you can come back here when Mrs Leverett has gone.'

'Yes.'

'*Do* you want your tea this morning?'

'Yes, dear.'

'I thought you would,' said Mrs Twine.

He went. She donned a dressing-jacket and a boudoir cap. Scarce was she comfortably settled in bed again before Hannah, reopening the bedroom door and standing on the threshold, was swept aside, and a rushing, flooding incarnation of hatred and dismay, panic and vengeance, burst through the portal and rolled to the bedside; a Gorgon, startling and unnerving, in a Tartan outfit. Even Mrs Twine pulled up the bed-clothes.

'Oh, ma'am—'

'Mrs Leverett, what on earth—?'

'Oh, ma'am; excuse me and believe me or believe me not; I 'ave strange words to tell. Oh, ma'am; bid Hannah shut the door and not listen at the keyhole—'

'Madam, as if I should think of—'

'Shut the door and go downstairs, Hannah. Mrs Leverett, control yourself. What has happened?'

'Oh, ma'am; believe me or not, I got up early and went to the 'ouse – is Hannah gone?'

'Yes. Well?'

'Oh, ma'am – whether you may believe this or believe it not – I was at the 'ouse 'o Rookery Nook be seven or seven-fifteen. And, oh, ma'am; I made tea and up I took it to the bedroom.'

'Yes, yes?'

'And oh, ma'am, the gentleman was not in the bedroom.'

'Well, I dare say he'd got up. Is that all that—?'

'No, ma'am; it is far from all. Though the gentleman was not 'imself in the bedroom, there, in the bedroom, in the bed – believe me or—'

'What? Quick! What?'

'Was a lady.'

'A lady?'

'Oh, ma'am – and what a lady!'

'Who? Quick!'

'She who lives next door.'

'What! Next door where?'

'Next door to Rookery Nook – the German lady. There she was in his bed asleep.'

'What!'

'Believe me or believe me not.'

'That woman who lives in the house down Lighthouse Road past Mrs Mantle Ham's?'

'Yes, ma'am. The young one.'

'You mean to say that you found that woman in Mr Longhampton's bed, asleep?'

'By the book,' said Mrs Leverett.

The scornful contradiction died on Mrs Twine's lips. Suddenly she recalled – startling corroboration – Harold's female shadow on the blind. Did Augustus then know these outlandish people? Had he consented to rent Rookery Nook in malice aforethought for the furtherance of his low reunion with this obviously fallen woman? Had he even inspired the idea of renting the Nook? Now that Gertrude came to think of it, the first suggestion that the Longhamptons should come to Chumpton at all had emanated from Clara's end. But Augustus had been extremely favoured by fortune, if this hypothesis was true. In the first place it was a coincidence that the house Gertrude had bespoken was next door that of his paramour. In the second place, how opportune for him the sudden breakdown of Mrs Posset and consequent detention of Clara. Possibly, finding that fate was lending him so helping a hand, he had seized his chance. Oh, but so deep-laid and hazardous a scheme of misconduct was surely out of the question. On the other hand there was the woman, in his bed.

'By the book,' repeated Mrs Leverett. 'Believe me or—'

'Stop talking a minute please, while I think,' said Mrs Twine.

Of course, this might have happened. He might have strolled out of Rookery Nook last evening and met the woman casually. They may have known each other before. Augustus was, no doubt, on familiar terms with half the loose women in London. He may have made an assignation on the spot and – well, carried it out. Poor Clara! After three months. Still, Gertrude had known it from the first. You could read it in his face. How lucky though that she had been the person to whom this information had been brought. She would deal with the matter herself and in her own way. She rallied Mrs Leverett with a steadying forefinger. 'Tell me exactly all you know, saw and suspect,' she said. Mrs Leverett took a chair and a deep breath.

'Nearly nine,' said Augustus. 'Well, it's quite certain the daily woman isn't coming now.'

CHAPTER X

Harold Twine is Run In

Clive FitzWatters, cousin to Augustus, had an obscure flat at Knightsbridge and a still more obscure job in the motor industry. The latter did not bind him to prescribed routine in an office or showroom. He was, as he asserted, 'an outside agent'. In pursuit of this calling he was wont to mingle with the world at large, in any locality which appeared to him propitious, and to sell it cars. On the morning with which we deal he intended to set forth and sell it cars at the Bath races.

With this in view his servant, Prosper, called him at the hour of nine.

'Your breakfast is on the table, sir. And there's a telegram just come, sir. Shall I bring it to you?'

'No, that's all right, Prosper,' said Clive. 'I'll attend to it when I'm up. It's only from Mr Pringle with a few certainties for Bath. I'm fed up with Pringle. His presentiments for Wolverhampton last week failed to encourage.'

'Yes, sir,' said Prosper. 'Myself, I favour Spotted Dog for the County Plate.'

Ten minutes later the young gentleman entered his sitting-room in very leisurely manner and a green shot dressing-gown. He picked up the yellow envelope, cut it neatly open and cast a dispassionate eye over the contents.

Clive, despite an admittedly woeful mode of existence, was rather an agreeable youth. He seemed to inherit, both in appearance and demeanour, a suggestion of those bygone days when elegance was the chief aim of the budding patrician. His nose was high and long and straight, his eyes the eyes of a Mephisto who has grown too lazy to do much harm. He was prone to grin, a characteristic seldom associated with elegance, but in this instance a saving grace, for on his sensitive mouth a smile would have been merely furtive, especially under those eyes. If, at first glance, he appeared a dandy and a cynic in days when no man can afford to be either, his grin could not fail to be reassuring.

It banished good looks and seemed to grin on in satisfaction at this achievement. It was a humorous conspiracy with the world at large. It did not challenge evil but it cheeked it. It had been a passport for policemen on boat-race night. It was still the whole difference between a bad man and a naughty boy.

Over this telegram the grin grew very pronounced.

FitzWatters 189A Knightsbridge London
Help Augustus

Clive over-poured his coffee into the saucer, inspected and discarded an egg, sat back in his chair and grinning meditated.

Help. Augustus.

The cousins were accustomed to exchanging railing for railing to a degree which might have scandalised Saint Paul, but would in greater probability have reminded that man of the world that such conduct is the hall-mark of genuine affection. Bosom friends were these two. A S.O.S. from Augustus was a matter of paramount importance to Clive.

Help? Now, wait a moment. Augustus had motored down on the previous day with Clara to a place called Chumpton in Somerset. At Chumpton lived the Twines. Mrs Twine. Help. Yes. This was something to do with Mrs Twine.

Mrs Twine it had been who had ferreted out the history of that bachelor escapade of Augustus's with Dolly Berkeley and had duly reported it. This was no doubt some similar line of trouble. Old Gussy at Chumpton had probably motored slick into some other superannuated Dolly, had got wind up and had been caught in that condition by Mrs Twine. This would explain the extremely perfunctory application for assistance. The mishap was evidently one of which no details could safely be committed to the telegraph office. Well, Clive, as it happened, was going that way and could, if necessary, push on to Chumpton for a few hours. But what form of help, in Heaven's name, did the fool expect him to render?

There was time to wire Augustus and receive a reply; but this might prove embarrassing at the other end. Clara might ask questions; might even open the telegram. Oh, but he could address it pointedly to Augustus, and Augustus had been married three months, and if he hadn't learnt by this time how to repress an inquisitive wife, he jolly well ought to have. Besides, if it was as important as all this, why couldn't he give at least an inkling of what he wanted Clive to do? 'Help!' Only Augustus could have sent such a footling telegram.

'Prosper!'

'Sir?'

'You noted down Mr Longhampton's holiday address for me.'

'Yes, sir. In your blotter.'

'Good! I want you to go and send off a wire at once.'

'Certainly, sir.'

'Where's the address? Oh, here. What's this – "Cookery Book?" '

'Rookery Nook, sir.'

'Oh. Righto. Well, hold yourself in readiness, hat in hand, while I compose something.'

'Certainly, sir.'

Mrs Twine came down to breakfast in icy mood, more silent than usual, grimly calculating. She had formed her plans.

Mrs Leverett had returned to her home in Chumpton, dragooned by a subtle blend of flattery and intimidation into an oath of unshakable silence. The next person to be considered was Harold. Mrs Twine directed a trenchant glare towards him over the breakfast table.

There had been something curiously evasive about Harold's manner on the previous night. Was she to believe that he was cognisant of what was going on at Rookery Nook and that he was deliberately withholding information? She had never had cause to suspect Harold of deceit before. Was the baneful Longhampton influence already at work upon him? She knew, too, that there existed among men a preposterous code, falsely attributed to honour, prompting them to hush up the sins of their fellows. And the more lewd and outrageous the sin, the deeper the hush. Could it be possible that Harold actually knew that Augustus Longhampton had spent the night in carnal vice and had not come and told her about it?

There was something very suspicious about Harold anyhow. He seemed restive in his seat and he was shirking her eye, while displaying marked inability to manage his fish balls, one of which he had already flicked twice from his plate and rescued from the cloth with his fingers, under the pretence of taking toast.

Better for the moment to leave Harold out of her calculations. When she had investigated and made discoveries she could confront him with them. He might then be able to supply any links in her chain which were lacking; he would also be taught a lesson in the duties of a husband which Gertrude could promise herself he would be unlikely to forget. Her decision to act independently for the time being was strengthened by Harold's transparent attempts, towards the end of breakfast, to obtain his bearings.

'You – er – you saw Mrs Leverett, dear?'

'Yes. Why?'

'Oh. Nothing. Only I suppose she – said what she – wanted to say?'

'Do you suppose she sat opposite to me in my bedroom and wirelessed to me?'

'No. But—'

'But what?'

'Is there anything wrong at Rookery Nook?'

'Why should there be?'

'Oh. Nothing. Only I thought perhaps Mrs Leverett coming here like that might mean that there was.'

'She came for instructions. Be careful. Some of your marmalade is going to drop off the edge of your toast on to the cloth.'

'Oh.'

He was very ill at ease, his conscience plaguing him sadly. One glimpse of encouragement from Gertrude and he would have plunged into confession. But Gertrude gave no cue for confession. She preferred disillusionment. She said no more until she rose and tweaked a piece of paper from the bill-hook.

'Your golf is at what time? Fold your serviette.'

'Ee – m, ten. v. Admiral Juddy.'

'What are you staring out of the window for?'

'I see a telegraph boy.'

'Well, are you afraid of a telegraph boy?'

'No, dear – but he's coming to the front door.'

'If he was coming to the back door, you wouldn't see him.'

Mrs Twine, nevertheless, displayed considerable interest in the telegram and snatched it from Hannah. Her eyes lighted up as she silently perused the message.

Twine Frascati Chumpton Somerset

Mother completely recovered shall bring her today by train leaving paddington one oclock please tell Augustus Clara

'The boy needn't wait,' said Gertrude.

Without comment she returned to her programme for the day. 'v. Admiral Juddy,' she quoted, inscribing.

'Good news, dear?' ventured Harold.

'Mother is much better. If you're starting at ten, you had better be getting ready.'

'Yes.'

'You'll have to walk to the links as I shall want the use of the car.'

'Yes.'

'Luncheon here at one.'

'Yes.'

'This afternoon, what?'

'I might perhaps show Longhampton the golf course.'

'H'm. I'll put that down tentatively. You'd better be off now.'

'Yes.'

Contrary to her custom, Mrs Twine did not immediately proceed to the kitchen. She went to her drawing-room and sat for a few minutes in deep meditation. Then, having revised her plan of campaign, she arose with decision, seated herself at a writing bureau and snatched a telegraph form from a pigeon-hole.

Longhampton Fairglebe Sutton Surrey

So pleased but come by eleven fifteen train most important you do so shall meet you at Bristol in car don't be alarmed but urgently necessary you do this

Gertrude

She rang for Hannah.

'Has the master left for the golf links?'

'Just this moment, madam. Shall I catch him?'

'Certainly not. Tell Coombes to bring the car round at once.'

'Drive to the post office,' she told the chauffeur. 'Then, on the way back, drop me at the corner of Lighthouse Road and return here with the car. Then be ready to take me out again soon after eleven.'

'Yes'm. Where shall we be going?'

'I'll tell you that when the time comes. Kindly do not mention my movements at all to any of the servants or anybody. Drive me to the post office. Be careful of the church corner. Last time you nearly drove me into a dray. Hoot when you are nearing it.'

Harold Twine walked a few yards from his front gate in the direction of the golf links. He then halted and moaned aloud. How could he go and play golf in this miserable predicament? How could he endure to labour round that exhausting course, divoting the soil with his half-hearted brassie, battling in sand-troughs with his impotent niblick, flustered rather than aided by the raucous snatches of education from the foul lips of Admiral Juddy? How could he face this, feeling that the time thus devoted to enjoyment might be employed in preventing, by diplomatic intervention, the convulsive family rumpus which he knew instinctively to be brewing? Was it not his duty at least to see Longhampton, to warn him that he had actually seen the woman not only on his blind but in his scullery, to plead with him to abandon this risky and inconvenient passion for the sake of domestic quietude if for no better motive? Yes, yes; he simply couldn't go and putt with this on his mind. He would miss all the putts and Juddy would be sarcastic and oh, all golf and all life would be wretched. He must, he must make an effort. What was the time? Five and twenty to ten. By running he could get to Rookery Nook, advise Longhampton in a few well-chosen words to desist from this mad amour, and be on the first tee, incapacitated for driving but, at any rate, relieved in mind, by the time appointed. He must, he must. He did. He ran. He ran to Rookery Nook.

The ministrations of Rhoda had restored the home of Mrs Mantle Ham to a condition resembling its normal decorum. The hall had been cleared and the belongings of Augustus stowed neatly in the angular dressing-room. An impromptu but adequate breakfast had been served and enjoyed, and its traces removed. There was nothing to be done now but sit in the hall and await developments. Augustus varied this employment by reconnaissance work from convenient windows respectively facing the quarters from which interruption might be expected. Rhoda remained on the Chesterfield, still in pyjamas and dressing-gown, calmly submissive, like some blonde Circassian belle awaiting the disposals of her pasha.

So far no sign from Pixiecot, no sign from Frascati, no sign of the daily woman.

Then, at about twenty minutes past nine, Augustus called down from the head of the stairs.

'Your step-father has opened his front door and is standing there, sniffing the breeze. The dog is also there and also sniffing.'

'Let me see; I don't get in the cupboard for Father, do I?' responded Rhoda.

'No, I suppose not. I don't think he's coming here in any case. He simply seems to have opened the door to have a sniff.'

'That's very unusual,' said Rhoda.

'I'll have another peep at him,' said Augustus. 'He's probably having a good look-see over here while pretending merely to sniff the air.'

'I don't think he'll come here,' said Rhoda. 'And I'm not going back with him if he does.'

'Quite so,' said Augustus. 'Still, it would be rather nice for you to get some clothes if that could be managed.'

'No, he's gone in again,' he added a minute later. 'But he was on the prowl all right, because I think he saw me and pretended to be showing the dog something in this direction.'

'You can't see into this house from there. I've tried,' said Rhoda.

'Oh, good. That gives us rather a pull over him. I'll just have one more look. Hallo, yes, here he is coming out again complete with dog and hat.'

'Well, if he comes here, don't say anything about my going to London.'

'Righto. Stay there a moment. I'll just make sure of his movements and then come to you.'

From a bedroom window Augustus saw through a gap in the elm trees the figure of Mr Putz passing through the garden gate of Pixiecot. He was wearing a black alpaca jacket of the type favoured by dentists and board-ship stewards, roomy grey trousers and a bowler hat. From the distance, his cheeks, which were not full but very pendulous and which hung over his collar on either side of his face, gave him an appearance rather resembling that of his dog. He strolled, as though without purpose beyond that of gentle exercise, past the gate of Rookery Nook and on to the corner of Lighthouse Road. Here he turned and commenced to stroll back again. Augustus, dodging from one point of vantage to another, witnessed his progress eagerly.

'Does he generally do this after breakfast?' he called down.

'Never,' Rhoda replied.

'He doesn't seem to be taking any interest in this house,' said Augustus. 'I suppose it's just his way of sort of baiting me.'

'Or me,' said Rhoda.

Mr Putz regained his own gate, wheeled round and again commenced his perambulation. The dog, obviously delighting in his unaccustomed outing, described happy circles of nosing investigation around his more sedate master. Suddenly, however, the dog sprang to attention, his ears pricked and his body stiff but quivering; while from his nose issued that peculiar and excited whistling sound associated, in his case, with the hunt. At the same moment the figure of a short man in baggy breeches, running, not swiftly but methodically and with pains, hove into sight round the corner of Lighthouse Road.

'Golly!' cried Augustus from the landing window, 'here's Twine!'

'Who?'

'My brother-in-law.'

'Oh dear! I suppose this is where I start going into the cupboard?'

'Yes, I'm afraid so. He's the man you interviewed last night in the scullery. He's such a perfect fool that if you stood behind the hall door and said you were an umbrella-stand he'd probably believe you. Still, I think it would be wiser to go to the cupboard while I hear what he's got to say.'

Harold had advanced several yards down Lighthouse Road before he saw the bull terrier. The latter had begun to move towards him, still very stiffly but with accentuated quivering of the body. Harold, seeing this, made the fatal mistake of pulling up and pretending to walk. Mr Putz, after taking very deliberate stock of Harold, issued a sharp word of caution to the dog in the language understood only by themselves.

'Hoo! Na-na-na-na! Putta-putta no.'

The dog, cowed by this, contented himself with meeting Harold and escorting him to the gate of Rookery Nook smelling his breeches. It is not easy to open a gate gracefully with a bull terrier smelling one's breeches; and Harold, after an inquiring glance at Mr Putz, who utterly disregarded him, pushed the dog gently with his foot as he fumbled with the latch. A moment later he was dashing full tilt up the drive of Rookery Nook with the dog whistling and gnashing behind him.

As Augustus threw open the front door the dog made a final spring and caught Harold by the baggy portion of the breeches overlapping the knee. The impetus of Harold and the tenacity of the dog resulted in both being hurtled together into the hall. Down the drive, at the gate, Mr Putz had halted and was vainly repeating his quaint formula. 'Ho – ho, Na-na-na-na! Na-na-putta. Ho ho, lu-lu-lu-lu!'

'Oh, quick! Oh, help! Oh, help! Oh, blow!' cried Harold. 'This dog has got me by my breeches.'

'I say, I wish you wouldn't bring dogs in here; especially that dog,' said Augustus.

'It belongs to that man at the gate. Oh, but quick! Do something please. It's worrying me dreadfully.'

'Yes, it's worrying me too,' said Augustus. 'The best thing you can do is to go back to the gate, dragging it by your breeches. Then you can give it back to the man.'

'Oh. Can't you pull it off?'

'No,' said Augustus, 'I don't think so. It seems to have a very firm grip.'

Harold clutched the arm of the Chesterfield and attempted to kick the dog off with the foot of which he retained the full use. The result was that he fell over. The dog released his hold and with an ugly snarl went for Harold in full earnest. Augustus caught it by the hind quarters only just in time. The dog, swooping round, transferred its attentions to Augustus. The latter,with surprising agility, leaped on to the hall table and kept the now infuriated dog at bay by well-timed kicks. The dog decided that its former prey was the softer thing and, wheeling round unexpectedly, sprang once more at Harold. Harold jumped on to the Chesterfield and fell over the back. The dog followed.

At this critical moment the door of the cupboard flew open and the dog received a hearty jab in the ribs with the upper end of a croquet mallet. It leapt back with a howl of pain and rage; and Harold, rescued, so far as his disorganised senses could determine,by the hand of God, rolled out of the immediate danger zone and clutched a footstool for protection.

'Conrad! Get back, get out, go on, how dare you? Go on, go home! Naughty dog!'

The effect was miraculous. The dog lowered its head and slunk round the wall towards the doorway. There it halted, took a final baffled view of the hall, whistled plaintively through its nose and trotted out into the drive.

'I thought I'd better come out,' said Rhoda to Augustus, who was now seated on the table. 'Conrad does so hate those rather loose kinds of breeches.'

Harold Twine remained on the floor, hand to head, gazing upwards at the bewildering female who had delivered him from the jaws of death.

A very striking-looking woman. But what had she on? A dressing-gown too big for her. Beneath, apparently men's pyjama trousers and socks uncouth. Her upper portions were fortunately completely hidden by the enveloping Jaeger.

So this was the woman that Longhampton was – with. But how came she to possess this divine power over savage beasts? Oh. But she knew the dog. Conrad. The man, then, at the gate was a party to this amazing concern. The man at the gate – why, that was surely the man who lived at that little house down the road – that German man. Ah! Then this must be the daughter that Harold had heard mention of. A very much nicer-looking woman than he had anticipated from all accounts. But why here and in this extraordinary attire? A very good thing for Harold that she *was* here. She had unquestionably saved his life from the dog.

'Thank you so much,' he heard himself murmur as he struggled up from the floor. 'You saved my life from the dog.'

'Yes,' said Augustus. 'He was just going to get you by the throat, Twine. By the way, I don't think you know each other, though you met for a moment in the scullery last night. Mr Twine, Miss Rho – er – the lady from next door.'

'How do you do?' said Harold.

'You owe her a great debt of gratitude, Twine,' said Augustus.

'Yes, I do indeed,' said Harold.

'All right then. Just sit up and take notice while I tell you what's going on here, because I think it's quite on the cards that we shall want your help.'

'Oh. My – my help?'

'Yes. I shall have to stick to the house this morning; but there will be two or three little odd jobs to do, and you will be just the man to do them.'

'Oh. But I only just looked in to see you about – something and I've got to go and play golf.'

'You can't do that. We shall want you here. Dash it, when a lady has just sprung in with a croquet mallet and saved your throat from a man-eating dog, the only thing you can possibly do is to render any small service in return. You can't turn round and say you're going to play golf.'

'Oh. But I can't stay here. Gertrude is coming and—'

'If Gertrude is coming that's all the more reason for me to rope in any help I can find. I suppose Gertrude knows that this lady is staying with me?'

'I don't know. That's just what I wanted to talk to you about.'

'Then you didn't tell Gertrude that you'd met this lady in the scullery?'

'No. I – not yet.'

'Oh, stout fellow!' cried Augustus. 'Then no one besides you and Mr Putz and Conrad knows that she is here.'

'What? I think Gertrude has an inkling.'

'What do you mean? Either she knows the lady is here or she doesn't. You can't have an inkling about a thing like that.'

'Oh. But her manner is strange and – I thought rather – what shall I say?'

'Now look here, Twine. This lady walked in here last night from next door without any clothes—'

'What!'

'She had been caught eating wurts and got run out. Now, I put it to you, that is the sort of thing that would cause Gertrude's manner, if she knew about it, to be a great deal more than merely what shall I say. Therefore, we may take it for granted that Gertrude does not know. Well, I think it's very important that Gertrude *should* not know, because, between ourselves, women are always apt to misjudge any rather singular occurrence of this sort.'

'Oh. But, I – I don't quite understand myself what it's all about.'

'Try and be intelligent. The whole thing simply is that this poor girl got turfed out of the house next door and came here for protection. So naturally she stayed here.'

'Oh. All night?'

'Yes, you damned fool. You don't suppose she waited a couple of hours and then went home for the dog watch. She was definitely and conclusively run out by Putz, who is her step-father. So she came here, and is staying here until this afternoon when I have arranged for her to leave for London. Nobody except her step-father is to know that she's here, and her step-father is not to know that she's going anywhere else. So you see we can do with a little intelligent help. You, having had your life saved by her from the dog, will naturally be only too pleased to stay and render it.'

'Oh, but Gertrude doesn't know I'm here, and she is coming and will be cross if she finds me here. Also she'll want to know what I'm doing here instead of playing golf.'

'That's easy,' said Augustus. 'There's a very good cupboard here. This lady is going into it when Gertrude turns up, and you can go with her.'

'Oh. But what should I do if I stayed here? What is there for me to do?'

'We'll go into that when things are a little less hectic. At the moment you say Gertrude is on her way here, and Putz and Conrad are still prowling about outside. Conrad will probably attack Gertrude and one thing and another. So I think we'll just wait and see how we stand after Gertrude's been. You'd better leave me the croquet mallet when you go into the cupboard.'

'Oh, but Longhampton,' burst forth Harold in distracted supplication, 'do please let me just say what I want to say and go. Really I don't think I can do any good by staying here. And, oh, I do really think that Gertrude has some knowledge of this, because, I meant to tell you, Mrs Leverett came over to our house this morning and saw Gertrude, and it was after that that Gertrude's manner became so particularly – what shall I say? And oh, think – it might mean a most terrible scandal and trouble in the family, and really I think it would be much better if Miss – the lady – went home or something before anything really awful happens.'

'But she's not going home, you breathless idiot. I've told

you already. Do you suggest that the lady who has just gallantly torn you from the jaws of the dog should be sent back to be brutally ill-used and very likely run out again? She's *got* to stay here. And so have you.'

'Oh. But why?'

Augustus vaulted off the table and stepped quickly to the front door.

'Well, for one reason,' he said, 'because Gertrude is at this very moment coming up the drive followed by Conrad.'

'Quick!' said Rhoda. 'This is the cupboard. There's plenty of room for both of us.'

'Oh. But this is horrid. Hiding from my wife—'

'Well, if you don't want her to see you—'

'No. I don't. But – oh, very well.'

As the cupboard door closed upon Harold and Rhoda, the voice of Mrs Twine could already be heard from the drive.

'Will you kindly call your dog off? I will not be – Augustus! Come and tell this person – Will you kindly call off your most offensive dog?'

'Hoi! Lu-lu-lu-na-na. Putta no!' came from the direction of the gate.

'Augustus!'

'Hallo, Gertrude. Good morning.'

'Come at once and—'

The sound of the side door bell ringing loudly in the ears of Augustus drowned the remainder of her command.

'Gosh! Who's this?' he muttered agitatedly. 'The other door! This is getting rather thick. Half a moment, Gertrude.'

'This dog is biting my skirt.'

'Na putta. Na. Lu-lu-lu!'

'I must just go and see who's at the side door and then I'll come and lend you a hand, Gertrude. Go away, sir. Bad dog! Put down the lady's skirt.'

'Look at that man standing there and gibbering like a monkey. Am I to be torn in pieces. Augustus! *Will* you come to my assistance?'

'It's all right,' replied Augustus, who was veering round the sweep of the drive which led to the side door. 'That man is coming up from the gate to rebuke the dog.'

'I don't wish to have anything to do with that man,' said Gertrude who was describing very small circles with Conrad. '*Will* you let go my skirt, you loathsome dog! What are this man and this dog doing at this house?'

'Nothing,' said Augustus. 'At least, the dog came in with you, and the man is coming in after the dog.'

He ran round to the side gate, at which a telegraph boy was by this time beating with his fists.

'Here, quick! Give it to me,' he hissed.

The boy handed the telegram over, extracting at the same time from his wallet a piece of naked toffee which he commenced eating.

Augustus tore open the envelope.

Augustus Longhampton Rookery Nook Chumpton Somerset

What do you mean by help am just off bath and could come on but please define requirements more lucidly you priceless ass Clive

'Wait,' said Augustus to the boy. 'I'll reply to this.'

The boy sat automatically upon the step and ate.

'That is to say, follow me,' said Augustus.

He returned hastily to the front door, the boy crackling at his heels.

Gertrude was now in the hall but still gyrating. Conrad was still gyrating with her. Mr Putz was leaning half in the hall and half out, clapping his hands and reprimanding Conrad in violent dog-language. Augustus rushed past him into the hall, clasped his brow, glanced at the cupboard door, discreetly kicked the derelict cap of Harold Twine into the dining-room, passed swiftly into Mr Mantle Ham's study and fell upon a batch of telegraph forms pigeon-holed on the writing-table.

'*Make* it let go. Come and seize it! You are only inciting the dog. Augustus! This man is only inciting the dog. *Will* you come?'

'Yes, in one half tick. If he can't make it let go, I don't suppose I can. But I'll try in a moment. Only I must just—'

'Ar'ch! This cannot go on. Don't keep talking that rubbish; come and *seize* the dog.'

'If seized,' said Mr Putz, 'the dog will angrily bite. Now he plays only already.'

'It has torn my skirt to ribbons. I shall charge you. Augustus!'

' 'Ere,' said the telegraph boy, speaking with difficulty but nobly advancing. 'Oi'll bash 'un.'

He picked up the footstool and aimed it at the dog. The footstool caught Mrs Twine full on the left ankle, but had the desired effect. The dog released the skirt and darted at the telegraph boy.

'Ho!' cried Mr Putz in dismay, coming forward into the hall. 'It is now done. Now there will be great biting. Lu! No! *Na*-putta!'

The telegraph boy bolted through the door into the kitchen followed by Conrad. Mrs Twine, maimed by the footstool, tottered unwillingly into the arms of Mr Putz. In the cupboard, Harold, his gills throbbing almost audibly, found himself clasping convulsively the unseen but calming hand of Rhoda. From the kitchen came a sudden and appalling crashing sound, accompanied by a fearsome medley of animal noises.

The telegraph boy emerged with the air of an admiral returning from successful naval action.

'It be orl roight now,' he announced. ' 'E's got going with the cat.'

In the study Augustus scrawled the final anguished words of his fevered appeal.

FitzWatters 189A Knightsbridge London

Mean what I say help aid assistance support succour

ministration deliverance Manna in wilderness Balm in gilead Smooth ruffled brow Temper wind shorn lamb Lay flattering unction soul. Come over macedonia and help help help help help Augustus

CHAPTER XI

Mrs Twine Forms an Unholy Alliance

Of help Augustus certainly appeared to be in dire need at that moment. Three very ill-assorted couples demanded his careful attention. In the centre of the hall, Gertrude and Putz; in the cupboard, Twine and Rhoda; in the kitchen, Conrad and the cat. The telegraph boy, Chorus to this interlude, had returned to his position in the front doorway, against the post of which he leant, chewing his toffee contentedly.

'Kindly leave go of me,' said Gertrude. 'I have now partially recovered. Thank you.'

'Don't mention with much pleasure absolutely,' said Putz.

'Now then,' said Augustus. 'Please go and remove that dog from the kitchen. Listen to it. It is doing the cat to death.'

'I have spoke to him already without it make any good,' replied Putz. 'The cat has caused him to furify and angrily disobey.'

'Rubbish!' said Gertrude. 'My skirt was being torn to ribbons and all you did was to stand and babble some very offensive-sounding bunkum. No one made any effort to assist me, except that boy; and all he did was to hurl a stool at my foot.'

'Well, anyhow,' said Augustus, 'I don't think we ought to allow the dog to sit in the kitchen, eating a valuable cat, without making some sort of effort to choke it off. Here, take this, boy. Send it off at once and keep the change.'

' 'kew,' said the boy, opening his wallet and removing his toffee from his mouth.

Augustus opened the kitchen door tentatively. Out shot the cat, hotly pursued by Conrad. Augustus, stepping hurriedly back, trod on Gertrude's other foot. Mr Putz clapped his hands and cried, 'Lu! Na-na-na!' and the cat shinned up the grandfather clock.

Here once more the croquet mallet came into play. Augustus took it up quickly from the chair against which it had been left and handed it to Putz. The latter swung it gingerly several times and finally dealt Conrad a smart crack over the skull, at the same time crying very loudly, 'Boomfa, boomfa!' This temporarily decided Conrad, who staggered to the wall, sat back on his haunches and watched the cat with his tongue out.

'And now,' said Gertrude, who was leaning up against the cupboard on one foot, 'take it away before it goes mad again.'

Mr Putz politely returned the croquet mallet to Augustus and proceeded to the doorway where he stooped and smote his knees very often and rapidly with the palms of his hands. Conrad, with a reluctant glare at the cat, thereupon rose, stretched himself and slowly followed. Augustus, in whose heart arose a great throb of thankfulness, closed the door sharply behind them and turned with a pleasant smile to Gertrude.

'There we are!' he exclaimed.

Gertrude tottered to the Chesterfield. Her eyes were fixed upon the door and she seemed on the point of referring to the late visitors, but for some motive of her own she desisted from doing so, though Augustus, standing over her, made profuse apologies for a visitation which, he assured her, was no design of his.

'Never mind about that,' Gertrude interrupted at length. 'The brutal dog has torn my skirt and I've a good mind to institute proceedings for damages. However, I had better tell you what I came over to tell you.'

'Yes?' said Augustus, eyeing her furtively.

'In the first place,' said Gertrude, her manner changing to one of considerable affability, 'I have heard from Clara who asked me to give you the message that Mother is much better. In fact, Clara thinks that with proper care she may be able to come here after two or three more nights.'

On the last word Gertrude glanced keenly sideways at Augustus, who, without noticing her, mumbled his pleasure at her tidings.

'Unfortunately,' continued Gertrude, 'I have got to be out all today – away, that is.'

'Oh dear,' said Augustus.

'And the trouble is,' said Gertrude, 'that Mrs Leverett came to see me this morning and told me that she is afraid she cannot after all accept the daily work here. So, as I have got no one else to turn to on the spur of the moment, I am afraid you will have to look after yourself entirely today. I shall not be back until quite late this evening, and so I shan't see you again till tomorrow morning, by which time I hope to have fixed up another daily person for you. If you like I could send a maid over to make the bed for you etcetera.'

'Oh, don't bother,' said Augustus heartily. 'I can manage. I don't mind making a bed etcetera.'

'And as for your meals,' added Gertrude, 'I would suggest your lunching at the golf club or at an hotel, and dining also at an hotel. There are one or two here that will, I think, do.'

'Oh rather. I'll look out for myself,' said Augustus.

'Well, now I must go,' said Gertrude, 'as I have to leave almost at once. I promised to motor over to see some friends at Maiden Blotten. I was going to take Clara. What a pity – never mind. I must take her later. Harold is at the golf club. You can look him up if you feel inclined.'

Gertrude ceased and wetted her lips with her lying tongue. She was not a woman who practised untruth. But in that after-breakfast deliberation, she had come to the conclusion that, after all, the guile employed to defeat guile was so closely connected with truth and righteousness as to become, ipso facto, honourable and indeed laudable. She had devised a scheme whereby she could march into the house at about two-thirty with Clara and her mother. Augustus, his misgivings allayed by her brilliant diplomacy, would still undoubtedly be sporting with his shameless Amaryllis in the shade. R-r-r-red handed! Gertrude had lingered upon the glorious word to herself in her drawing-room. On the last occasion that Gertrude had thought it her duty to warn Clara concerning the patently bad man she had married, Gertrude had been snubbed for her pains. She would receive no snub this time. Clara would see for herself and – well, must decide for herself. It was just as well that the mistaken marriage should be annulled before Clara became a mother. There were other far more eligible men than this, to whom she could turn for consolation. Getrude had particularly in mind one – a Knight of the Order of the British Empire and a Member of Parliament.

Indeed that day might witness a tremendous, a sweeping change for the better in the prospects of her younger sister. To accomplish so gratifying a feat lay in Gertrude's power. In order to do it she must wholeheartedly lie to this man Augustus. And now it was done. She saw in his normally fatuous countenance the gleam of gratified surprise and voluptuous relief. The only tiny qualm felt by Gertrude was due to the practised ease with which she found she could lie.

Subconsciously, though, she was aware of two other little obstacles which had occurred to her since her arrival at Rookery Nook. She turned from Augustus and cleared her throat, trying to concentrate her mind while she pretended to examine further her ruptured skirt. Oh, yes.

The telegram. Who was that from? And why the avid intentness of Augustus with regard to it? What was the other thing?

Ah! That man – Gutz, or whatever his undesirable name was – that man. Why should he be lurking there outside the gate? His presence certainly confirmed Mrs Leverett's remarkable assertions, but was he there as friend or foe? Was he party to this infamous wenchery? Evidently. For he had entered the house and strolled out again without making any attempt to regain his borrowed mistress. Was it then possible that the woman might have left Rookery Nook by the time planned by Gertrude for her swooping exposure? Had she gone already?

Gertrude bit her lip. On this point it would be fatal to make investigations however innocently framed. The truth about the telegram was easier to ascertain.

'Yes,' she said with a little click of the tongue 'That horrid dog did tear my skirt and now I must change it before I go to Maiden Blotten. What a bother! I do think, Augustus, that you might have done something to the dog instead of worrying about some wretched telegram. Was the telegram so terribly important?'

'I'm so sorry,' said Augustus. 'Yes. It was from my stockbroker about some shares that are behaving like rockets; and he told me I must let him know what I wanted to do without wasting a minute. Besides, as I said before. I don't think I could have prevailed on the dog if Putz couldn't.'

'If who couldn't.'

'Er – that gentleman with the dog – the Hun gentleman. His name is Putz.'

'Oh. Was that who it was? How on earth did you know his name?' asked Gertrude with casual good-humour.

Curious, that of the two liars the more experienced should be the one to trip.

'Er – m – er, Mrs Leverett told me. I was asking about my neighbours last night.'

He lied so awkwardly that Gertrude accepted his ready and preconceived lie about the telegram as a statement of fact. In any case, she was too eager to take adva age of the opening he had given her to bother any further about the telegram.

'Putz,' she said. 'Yes. I believe that is his name. But that is the first time I have ever spoken to him. He is rather a mystery in Chumpton.'

'I should think he'd be a trifle out of the common in most places,' said Augustus.

'Well, I hope you won't encourage him to walk up and down outside your gate with that horrible dog. I know he keeps people out of his own house – the Rector had a most disagreeable experience with him – but he can hardly be allowed to behave like a kind of sentry in front of this one. I wonder why he should suddenly take to walking outside here. I'm sure he never used to when the Mantle Hams were here.'

'I'm sure *I* don't know, Gertrude,' said Augustus innocently. 'Unless, not having had any visitors himself lately he's afraid the dog may get a bit out of training.'

Gertrude hesitated, and decided to abandon the dangerous subject. If she had only known a little more about lying – that is to say, about combating black guardism with guile – she might have ventured further. As it was, she rose and inspected the drive.

'He seems to have moved on now,' she remarked, 'and I must get back home and change my skirt. I shall come and see you tomorrow morning, with, I hope, a new domestic. Meanwhile, I am sure, you can manage just for one day.'

'Thanks, Gertrude. Easily. I'll investigate the local hostelries. Good-bye.'

He watched her as far as the gate, where she stood and looked anxiously to left and right. Then, as she went her way, he returned to the hall, closed the front door and threw up his arms, like one of the prophets in the study, to Heaven, in demonstrative thankfulness. After a tentative scratching on the panels, the cupboard door was opened and Harold emerged with cramp and Rhoda with caution.

At the corner of Swallow Road Gertrude halted with a start. There was Mr Putz. He held Conrad by means of an enormous Bandanna handkerchief which had, unseen, been enfolding his own ample middle. Seeing Mrs Twine he bowed elaborately and indicated the repressed state of Conrad with a gesture.

'Do not fear,' he said. 'He shall not again bite. I hold him by my belly handkerchief.'

Mrs Twine retraced her steps for a few yards nervously. She could not be seen in company and conversation with Mr

Putz; and it was just at this hour that Mrs Wintle and the Creepes and people went down to the town to do their shopping. Her first instinct was to ignore Mr Putz and hurry past him. Then an idea crossed her mind. She edged a few yards further back into the shades of Lighthouse Road. Mr Putz, mistaking her movement for a lack of confidence in the resisting power of his handkerchief, followed her, demonstrating his complete mastery over Conrad by jerking the latter severely in different directions.

The high and exclusive fence of the Mantle Hams swept down Lighthouse Road in a curve which afforded cover from Swallow Road at no great distance from the corner. Mrs Twine found herself performing an action of which yesterday no power on earth could have persuaded her she was capable. She shrunk against the protective fence and summoned Mr Putz with a series of backward jerks of the head accompanied by an expressive and conducive exercise of the eyes.

Mr Putz, halting at a short distance from her, witnessed these allurements with a slow surprise. He even took his horn spectacles from a pocket in order to confirm his impressions. He then took a few paces forward, raised his hat again, and said. 'I beg your pardon, what you make?'

'I wish to speak with you in private,' said Mrs Twine. 'Kindly take your dog in your arms and hold him securely by the collar.'

Mr Putz shrugged but complied. Holding the struggling Conrad in both hands, he came quite close to Mrs Twine and offered her his polite, if somewhat divided, attention.

Gertrude assumed the rather forced manner of one introducing herself on the strength of a mutual acquaintanceship.

'I find you are a friend of the gentleman who has just arrived at this house?'

Putz shook his head glumly.

'Friend? No. I do not care for him.'

'Oh. But I happen to know that your – the young lady

from your house is a great friend of his. So I thought you must be too?'

'I do not care for her either also,' said Mr Putz.

'Oh, come,' said Gertrude. 'I know as well as you do that she has been in this house all night. Whether you care for her or not, you must either favour her being there all night or dislike her being there all night. That is to say, you must surely either wish her to continue there or wish her to leave there. I happen to know a good deal about the young man in there, and I may be in a position to help you over what is bound to be rather an awkward situation.'

'For me?' asked Mr Putz.

'Well, is it not? The girl comes from your house. Are you going to allow her to go to and fro between your house and this house as she pleases?'

Mr Putz became more animated.

'She is gone from my house now also, absolutely finish,' he stated with a gesticulation which almost released Conrad.

'Oh!' exclaimed Gertrude with great interest. 'Then she acted against your will in going there last night?'

'No,' said Mr Putz simply. 'I ran her out.'

'I beg your pardon?'

'Where she go I do not care for it. What she do I do not care for it. Last night she leave my house already, absolutely finish. I run her out.'

'Oh!' repeated Gertrude with the facial expression of a lost Continental explorer at grips with a local patois. 'Then you expelled her from your house?'

'Absolutely,' cried Mr Putz firmly.

'And she went to this house and stayed there?'

'Where she go I do not care for it.'

'She is still there,' said Gertrude casually, 'isn't she?'

Mr Putz employed Conrad for purposes of a sweeping gesticulation.

'So, yes,' he said. 'She cannot flee.'

'Why cannot she – er – flee?'

'Wit'out die clothes, wit'out die money—'

'Without the clothes?' echoed Gertrude.

'In her night-clothes only she go to it.'

'You turned her out of the house in her night-gown?'

'Absolutely,' replied Mr Putz, with a satisfied smack of the lips. 'Run out.'

Any amazement which Gertrude might have felt over the procedure adopted by Mr Putz was overshadowed by satisfaction. Augustus certainly possessed no means of clothing the abandoned lady from his present resources; and in any case her night-gown was probably the form of attire which would find the greatest favour in his sight. It was equally out of the question for him to take and dump her in a night-gown anywhere locally, even if he wished to do so. She was not only undoubtedly still at Rookery Nook, but undoubtedly bound to remain there, unless Augustus could obtain very confidential assistance. He could certainly obtain no such assistance in Chumpton. Ah, the telegram again—

If he had been lying about his stockbroker and was attempting to seek assistance by wire from some one at a distance, it was improbable that the some one could arrive on the scene before Clara. If the some one arrived simultaneously with Clara, the result would probably be to involve Augustus even more deeply. To be caught smuggling a woman off the premises was surely worse than to be caught complacently keeping a woman on them. In the latter instance he might possibly devise some plausible excuse; in the former his action would be in itself a confession of guilt. As a matter of fact, Mr Putz's revelation as to how the girl had got to Rookery Nook rather exploded Gertrude's theory of a premeditated programme of debauchery on the part of Augustus. But there was evidence enough of his guilt. He had refrained from informing her of his arrival. The woman had been found in his bed. His whole attitude towards Gertrude, on the occasion of both her visits, had been that of a criminal sneak.

By meeting Clara at Bristol with the car, she could get her to Rookery Nook by two o'clock. She could of course send the car for Clara, and herself remain on guard over Rookery Nook; but it would be far more advantageous to land Clara there with a mind already nurtured, in view of the horrid disclosures awaiting her. Gertrude realised that she must go and meet Clara and get this nurturing done. Clara might be difficult enough as it was. She was inclined to be obstinate and self-satisfied about Augustus. Still, Gertrude would have a car-drive for an hour to do the nurturing in, and her mother would be there, which was an asset.

As for the possibility of the woman escaping from Rookery Nook in the meantime, this was negligible. Gertrude had cleverly lulled any fears that Augustus might have felt. He thought he was going to be left alone for the day. There he was, a very dissipated man, left for a day in a house alone with a young woman in a night-gown. Was it likely that they wouldn't still both be there at two o'clock?

But she must not get any clothes. That was the one last link in the cable which was to bind Augustus. As had already occurred to Gertrude, the woman would most likely leave the clothes off if she got them, but she must not get them. Gertrude again attracted the attention of Mr Putz who, during her deliberations, had been shuffling awkwardly from side to side and apparently attempting to adjust a portion of his costume, a matter rendered difficult by the fact that to hold Conrad in one hand for more than two seconds was beyond human power.

'I suppose,' said Gertrude, 'That before long the – the lady will try and get you to give her some of her clothes?'

'A moment please,' said Putz. 'I am in some trouble already. I wish I had not taken for my dog this handkerchief from my belly.'

'Please don't trouble about that for one moment. I just wish to ask you whether you intend to hand over any of her—'

'I must trouble,' broke in Mr Putz. 'My trousers descend.'

Mrs Twine fell back against the fence with a little cry of fear. Mr Putz, vainly attempting to spare a hand for his attire, politely turned his back upon her. Beneath the alpaca jacket the seat of his trousers certainly appeared to have become dangerously elongated. The struggles of Conrad became intensified. Mr Putz, addressing Mrs Twine over his shoulder, issued his ghastly ultimatum.

'Oblige kindly by holding up the trousers while I again obtain the handkerchief from my dog. If not, the trousers will absolutely descend.'

'I – how dare – I – you – oh, I cannot hold up your trousers for you,' said Mrs Twine.

'Then I will lose my dog!'

'Hold that dog. I will not be attacked again.'

'If I do not lose my dog, my trousers will rapidly descend. Already my shirt flops forth.'

'Do not let that dog go. Oh dear! Some one is certain to see me. Look out! The dog snapped at me then. Hold him tightly.'

'I cannot both hold my dog and both hold my trousers. Kindly oblige for the trousers, and I will re-obtain my handkerchief.'

'You should wear braces,' cried Gertrude passionately, as she clutched nervously at the seat of the trousers.

'Alas!' replied Mr Putz. 'I yesterday boist my brace.'

'Well, I cannot go on holding up—'

'A moment also. I untie my belly handkerchief.'

'And kindly do no go on talking to me about your belly. It is most unrefined. In England gentlemen do not accost ladies who are practically strangers with information about their bellies.'

'So. No?' asked Mr Putz inquiringly. 'Die handkerchief for the middle belly-band, is it not so spoken of?'

'I think you mean a coomerboond,' replied Gertrude, still retaining an agonised grasp on the seat of Mr Putz's trousers.

'Ach so!' said Putz. 'Please to pardon. Wait. The handkerchief is confused and the dog struggle. Hoi. Na-na-na. Hold firmly up my trousers please.'

'How can I, while you keep moving. Besides, it makes the

trousers – inclined – to slip. Oh, goodness me, if any one should happen to—'

'Wait,' said Putz. 'I can thus untie. I will place the dog between the knees, thus to use both of the hands. Fear not. I will place his tail also in your direction. Continue kindly to hold. My shirt already is absolutely out.'

'Now!' cried Augustus heartily in the hall. 'That ordeal's over. Gertrude's going away for the day, Twine – to Maiden Something in a car. So we've got the place to ourselves.'

'Oh, but Longhampton, I must go. I don't *larke* this business.'

'Don't like it, you ungrateful devil! When you've been rescued from a dog and hidden from Gertrude. Pull yourself together, Twine. Your first job is to go to the gate and reconnoitre for Putz. If he's still in the lane, come back and I'll show you a way through the elm trees to his house.'

'To his house?'

'Yes. You must go there and try and get some clothes.'

'Oh, but—'

'I'll give you full instructions later. The first thing to do is to find out where Putz is. I think you'll find it will be much easier to get some clothes from the house next door if Putz and Conrad are still out.'

Harold took a good deal of persuading. Might he not be allowed to run round to the golf club first and make his excuses to Admiral Juddy? No. Might he not go and make certain about this sudden resolve of Gertrude's to spend the day at Maiden Blotten. It was the first he had heard of it, and Gertrude always told him at breakfast where she was going to be during the day. No? Oh, but – well, frankly, *marght* he not then make a final appeal to Longhampton. He had never before had any little secret from his wife; the sensation of having one was odious. Besides she would learn the truth sooner or later. Longhampton knew how discerning she was. Oh, please? No.

Oh – h.

Rhoda remained silent throughout. She avoided Harold's occasional and piteous glances. She was in the hands of Augustus and his word was law. Before very long Harold was at the gate.

Almost immediately, however, he was back at the side of Augustus, who had followed him into the drive. Augustus heard what he had to say, eyeing him doubtfully. Then, motioning Harold to follow, he noiselessly crept along the border skirting the tall fence, pausing every now and then to listen or to frown silence upon Harold whose scouting potentialities were limited.

'So,' said Mr Putz. 'It is better. Kindly tuck in for me my shirt, binding my trousers up with my handkerchief.'

'I cannot,' said Mrs Twine. 'You must do that yourself.'

'I also cannot. If I hold the dog with one hand on the ground already, I cannot in this manner tuck shirt and tie trousers. If I raise the dog from the ground he demands both of my hands. I cannot therefore in this manner tuck and tie. Kindly oblige.'

'I simply cannot do it in any case while you stoop in that manner. If you will stand upright holding the dog, I will see what can be done. Please make haste. This is terrible.'

'The handkerchief,' announced Putz, flipping that object round his back at Gertrude as he clutched Conrad between his knees.

'Well, if I render you this service I shall expect you to help me in return,' said Gertrude.

'Certainly,' replied Putz. 'But surely you too are not also requiring to be fastened?'

'No, certainly not. But I want you to promise me something about this young woman of yours.'

Augustus pressed his ear to the fence. His mouth was wide open. He signalled briefly but severely to Harold not to be so audibly out of breath.

Putz's reply was relentless.

'She get no help from me. I do not care for her. She may go to the deffel.'

'I'm not asking you to help her,' said Gertrude gently. 'That's right; stand upright, holding the dog in your arms. Then I can tie you up. Raise your coat for a moment with one hand. Oh dear, yes, your shirt is out. But I'm not *asking* you to help her.'

'What you make then please? Quickly tie. The dog struggle.'

'I want you to see that she doesn't obtain any of her clothes from your house.'

'I shall give her no clothes you bet your word for it,' said Mr Putz. 'But why you should so wish it?'

'I'll tell you why,' said Gertrude, a note of sly amusement creeping into her tone. 'Try to keep still, please. I cannot think how you ever got this coomerboond to meet. I'll tell you why.'

'Tuck the shirt first also already,' said Putz.

'Never mind. I think I can manage if you will keep still. I will tell you now. That young man in there is my sister's husband.'

'So? But my shirt is very uncomfortable.'

'He is not a good husband to her and I wish to teach him a lesson. My sister is coming down here today, though he doesn't know it. If she arrives and finds that young woman of yours there with him, he will get a fright which will do him a great deal of good. Of course, no *harm* will come of it – nothing, I mean, which is likely to involve you. Just a sort of practical joke, if you understand. Only, to make sure she is there when my sister arrives, she must not be allowed to get any of her clothes. Undo the lower button of your jacket. It is caught in the coomerboond.'

'Soho,' said Mr Putz. 'I tink there will be a battle then in this house. My step-daughter will also find herself in some riot already.'

'Oh,' said Mrs Twine reassuringly. 'Nothing serious.'

'What!' cried Mr Putz excitedly. 'When the weib come and see her wid the yung man—'

'If you don't wish her to get into trouble, I will make my sister—'

'I wish it,' said Putz.

'Oh! Well, of course, I expect it could be made rather unpleasant for her.'

'It is good,' said Putz.

'Though, of course, you yourself would not be involved in any way.'

'For me, if they would get me into some trouble also let them come to my house and try for it. I will run them out with my dog.'

'Please do not jump about so excitedly. I cannot possibly do up your trousers. Very well then, that's quite satisfactory. There! That will allow you to get home at any rate, and you can tie yourself up more comfortably when you arrive indoors. Good morning, Mr Putz.'

'Wid pleasure. By and by we meet again already I hope so,' said Mr Putz, again placing Conrad between his knees in order to raise his hat.

Augustus led Harold back on to the lawn of Rookery Nook and regarded him with a slow and stolid shake of the head.

'Twine,' he said. 'I am afraid your wife is behaving in a very deceitful and spiteful manner.'

'Well,' murmured Harold, 'I told you she had an inkling.'

'She is trying, by a very low-down, female bit of trickery, to get Clara down here today, while this poor girl is still in the house and to raise Cain between Clara and myself.'

'Yes, but—'

'There can be no "but," Twine. She has even descended to allying herself with that Hun brute in order to work her mischief to her own satisfaction. Well, now, I consider it's up to you. If this is the kind of game that Gertrude is capable of, it shows you up in a pretty foul light.'

'Me?'

'Yes, you. Isn't it the duty of a married man to exercise an influence over his wife?'

'Oh—'

'This either means that you have neglected your duty as a husband, or that your influence over Gertrude has been a stinking influence. Well, Twine; it's up to you to make amends. Gertrude is trying to make a hideous row and smash up my very great happiness with Clara. With your help I can stop her, but only with your help. Come, Twine, as man to man.'

'It's all very puzzling. I don't—'

'As man to man, Twine. Are you going to stand by and see my happiness with Clara ruined, just in a bit of female spite?'

'Oh, dear me – I—'

'Come along. Quick! You see what your wife's up to. It's your duty, not only in the cause of honour, but as her husband and – and master to do all you can to prevent her from doing this criminal thing.'

'Yes, I know, but—'

'Yes. There you are then. Good man, Twine! Of course any man would do the same thing. Now then, the first thing for you to do is to cut through those elm trees and sneak over to that house without being seen from the road. Get there before Putz and see Nutts.'

'Oh. What? Who? Oh, but—'

'Nutts. A woman named Nutts. Tell Nutts that Miss Rhoda is in Rookery Nook and must have some clothes by hook or by crook. You can easily remember that because it's in rhyme.'

'Oh but the man is going back there with the dog.'

'All the more reason for you to hurry.'

'Oh, but, Longhampton, this is all a very unpleasant business. I don't think—'

'What do you mean – "I don't think." I *do* think. It's what comes, Twine, of letting wives get the upper hand. Let it be a lesson to you. Learn this very day to reassert your authority, and when you have reasserted it, don't you go and lose it again. Come on. There's a ditch the other side of the elm trees. I'll show you a place where you can jump across.'

'Oh, no, no, no. I still don't think—'

'Come on; get a move on, do. Putz will be back there if you don't buck up.'

He grasped Harold by the lapel and led him at a stealthy double across the lawn towards the elms.

'But there's a great deal I don't understand,' protested Harold.

Augustus, without slacking speed, turned his head back towards the fence.

'There's only one thing I don't understand,' he said. 'And I expect we shall require an explanation of that before we're through.'

'What?' asked Harold. 'What don't you understand?'

'I don't understand,' replied Augustus, 'what Gertrude was up to, taking Putz to a quiet corner of Lighthouse Road and making him take down his bags.'

CHAPTER XII

Pleasure at the Helm

The Great-Western engine bore the eleven-fifteen express into Bristol Station, punctual to the minute, and took a deep breather of steam. Clive, comfortably installed in a corner nearest the platform, looked out of the window and yawned. The station at which he changed for the train to Chumpton lay further down the line, and the express condescendingly halted there.

Clive watched with languid amusement the turmoil of the platform, which at this season of the year was considerably augmented by the proximity of Weston-super-Mare. Fathers with bowler hats and bow ties, their ginger moustaches sticky with the perspiratory cares of excessive parenthood, were stampeding officials for the information which the latter were repeating the whole time as loudly as their excellent lungs could permit. Mothers, craning to check the information received by Father, so as to be quite certain he got it right, were at the same time addressing instructions to the family in tones which almost drowned those of the officials. Porters propelling enormous trucks stacked high with luggage were charging down whole platoons of maidens shrilly occupied in meeting and greeting, and pointedly advising them to mind their backs, these being indeed, in most cases, totally unprotected from assault of any description. Boys, with a strange assortment of merchandise carried on trays, were besieging the train and advertising their wares by the curious expedient of singing very loudly in Russian. Ladies who had been disappointed by the non-appearance of expected friends were flitting from one carriage to another, peering within, and treating the peaceful occupants to wild soliloquies of disquietude.

The methods of one of these ladies differed, however, from those employed by her frustrated sisters. Her research was limited to the first-class coaches. The thirds she avoided with a rather emphasized air of superior detachment. She thus failed to notice the third-class Clive, but he saw her as she passed him by and sat up stiffly and with keen interest. He even rose and watched her progress through the open centre window of his carriage. The grin was in evidence.

'Hallo!' he said to himself. 'Dirty work at the railway junction!'

Surely to goodness, Gertrude had not been sent to meet *him?* What possible freak of circumstances could have ranged her with Augustus and thus excited her active sympathies with his undefined agony? Oh, but if the trouble had been anything to which Gertrude could be a party, the fathead Augustus would have been more explicit in his telegrams. Besides, why should Gertrude be searching only the first-class carriages? She surely would know that he would be in a third. The journey was an expensive one, and the state of the car-market putrid.

Some one else then, besides himself, had been expected by this train; some important arrival in the opposite camp. It must be some one calculated to contribute in no small measure to the enigmatical anguish of Rookery Nook if Gertrude had taken the trouble to come all the way out to Bristol.

She returned in Clive's direction, and he removed his head from the window and buried it in *The Sportsman.* He still, however, furtively watched. He saw her being asked whether she had any luggage by an accommodating porter and replying in terms which caused even his hardened spirit to blench. She then took an exhaustive survey of the clamorous platform, straining her head upwards and swaying it, as a school-teacher, at an irksome children's outing, strains to catch the eye of a consultative curate. The Babel of arrival had now begun to give place to the equally animated Babel preliminary to departure. Gertrude's agitation became more marked. She returned to a final heated inspection of the carriages, upsetting a bunch of bananas from the tray of one of the Russian choristers. She even included a few of the more respectable-looking third-class carriages in her search. In vain. She was roughly ordered to stand back please by a guard whose manners she would certainly have spoken about at any other time. An upraised copy of *The Sportsman* swam, as part of a fruitless and fleeting panorama, before her still searching eyes, as the train passed smoothly on its way.

Clive lowered *The Sportsman*, closed his eyes and indulged in a mental riot of fantastic speculation. The possibilities were boundless. On two points only could he feel any certainty; firstly that Augustus was in a desperate strait; secondly, that Augustus wanted to get him to Chumpton before the person that Gertrude wanted to get to Chumpton got to Chumpton.

At Ditchlow Junction Clive rose from his seat with characteristic languor, took his hat and stick from the rack and strolled out of the train. On the platform he found Augustus in a state closely resembling the state of Gertrude at Bristol. Augustus, on perceiving Clive, immediately bolted out of the station into the yard, started up his car, and sat in it with his cheeks blown out. Clive gave up his ticket and jauntily followed,swinging his stick.

'Hallo, old bean!' he said grinning. 'Cherchez la femme?'

'Get in,' said Augustus.

The distance from Ditchlow Station to Rookery Nook was roughly six miles. Augustus negotiated the awkward turning out of the station yard and settled himself more comfortably in his seat.

'Now listen,' he said. 'The salient points are these.'

He told Clive the salient points.

The indisposition of Mrs Posset. The arrival, solo, of himself at Rookery Nook. The arrival, in pyjamas, of the pathetic, perfectly pure and indescribably beautiful Rhoda. The bedding of Rhoda. The seeing, by that miserable little worm-eaten, hag-ridden, slobbering little chump, Twine, of the shadow and subsequently of the substance of the lovely girl at Rookery Nook. The mysterious getting to know, by Gertrude, of the presence of the lovely girl at Rookery Nook (probably due to Twine though he swore it wasn't). Putz. The callous brutality of Putz. The dour, unremitting antagonism of Putz. The formidable running-out methods of Putz. Conrad.

The lying, sneaking, double-faced, treacherous procedure of Gertrude. The mean and sinister conspiracy of Gertrude with Putz (carried already to lengths which even he, Augustus, who had overheard them, could scarcely credit).

The attempt (unsuccessful) of Twine, prompted from the elm trees, to get clothes from Nutts. The sending of Twine to procure some food for lunch. The subsequent waiting in patience (what more could be done?) for the hour of Clive's arrival. The leaving of the unreliable, incompetent little blighter, Twine, to guard the garrison while Augustus fetched Clive from Ditchlow. The glory to God that Clara had not stepped out of the same train as Clive at Ditchlow, heralded by Gertrude.

Clive, who had been listening cheerfully alongside, tapping the buttons of his spats with the ferrule of his stick, reassured his cousin with regard to the movements of Gertrude and Clara, thereby causing Augustus to swerve with joy across the road, pinking a wayside pig with his near wing.

'Well, anyhow, that's the poisonous position I'm in, and the only thing to do is for you to get me out of it,' resumed Augustus. 'You can manage to clothe her and get her up to town this afternoon somehow or other. You'll like the job. She's not only one of the most lovely girls I've ever seen but a very attractive and pleasing girl too. You don't often get the two together.'

'M'yes,' replied Clive, in the rather nasal and drawling voice which seemed eminently suited to his personality. 'Yes, of course I anticipated a lady of some description. Only I thought the boot was probably on the other leg, and that

I had been sent for to tackle the average and habitual type of body-snatcher.'

'Nothing of the sort,' said Augustus.

'All right. I am quite willing to put up my sword. Only I've been spending the whole morning at visionary grips with entirely the wrong type of female. I've been side-tracking our old friend a daughter of a colonel in the army. I've been recovering the letters from the woman with the puce eyelids, and putting a dictaphone on the member of the Snow-ball Club. I see I must wash all that out. This appears to be something much less fierce and more dangerous.'

'Why more dangerous?'

'Oh, I'd much rather help a beautiful girl than fight her,' said Clive. 'But it's always a game that is fraught with far greater peril.'

'There's no peril about Rhoda,' said Augustus. 'She's perfectly straight and nice.'

'Yes, yes, I know all about that. I can picture the sort of girl she is exactly. The sort of girl who can tell the age of a horse and plays the piano with her tongue out. But, as far as I can see, I shall land, pretty late at night, in London along with this girl who will still, presumably, be in pyjamas.'

'Well, she can't stay at Rookery Nook in them. And she says she's got friends in town.'

'Yes, but they'll want finding. And even then one can't be sure what view they'll take of this particular form of rescue work.'

'When you see her,' said Augustus, 'you'll want the job.'

'It would be easier if she could get some clothes. What happened when this poor soul Twine approached the housekeeper?'

'The fool rang the bell, and Nutts opened the door, and when she heard what he wanted she simply shut it again. I happened to be waiting, and naturally I made him go back and have another shot; but this time she was waiting too. Apparently she gave him a severe biff in the stomach with the butt end of a broom. Putz and the dog turned up at the gate just at the same moment, and I only managed to get Twine back into Rookery Nook just in time. Another second and Conrad would have had him by the pants again.'

'Makes it rather difficult,' commented Clive. 'Summer fashions are becoming fairly unbridled, but dash it – a pair of pyjamas. I don't see how I'm going to get her from Chumpton to London, unless I can kid the police that I'm taking her to a fancy-dress ball.'

'You can go by car.'

'This car?'

'No, you can't take this car; because when Clara comes I'm going to sit tight and lie in my teeth, at any rate till Gertrude sheers off. No, you'll have to hire a car.'

'My dear boy, you can't stroll about the Somerset countryside in silk pyjamas, hiring cars.'

'We can send Twine to hire a car.'

'Ah, true. You seem to have won Twine over very successfully. Is he revolting or something?'

'Yes,' said Augustus. 'He's one of the most revolting specimens I've ever struck. Still, I had to get help where I could.'

'I mean revolting against Gertrude, you ass.'

'Oh. Well, he ought to be. I got him behind a fence, listening to Gertrude and Putz engaging in the most remarkable exchanges. I believe it shook Twine. A firm hand, and I think he is ours.'

'Well!' cried Clive. 'In that case, of course, the whole thing's a cinch.'

'What do you mean? What are you going to do with Twine?'

'Send him along to get some of Gertrude's clothes, you poor mutt,' said Clive conclusively.

Augustus swerved again.

'Oh, glorious thought!' he said. 'If Clara missed that train of yours she can't get here till about half-past four, even if Gertrude motors her from Bristol. The day is, I think, won. This is Swallow Road. Round this corner on the right is –

whoop! – Lighthouse Road. That, on the right, is Rookery Nook. That, on the horizon in front, is Putz.'

'I warm to this,' said Clive.

Stump – *stump* – STUMP. Down Swallow Road in the direction of Frascati from the golf links marched an irate old gentleman, not with the watchful agility of the stalker but with the ponderous, haunting, inevitable tread of the avenger. The grim finality of Rachmaninoff's Prelude was in the sound of his foot-beat. Stump – *stump* – STUMP.

Admiral Juddy consoled and encouraged himself as he went by muttering aloud weird profanities of the Chinese. His great grey eyebrows were all twisted and intermingled in a lingering scowl of wrath. He was a sight very unnerving. Any of his acquaintance who chanced to meet him took but one glance and, cowering upon the opposite pathway, slid past him discreetly. One, a somewhat fanatical lodging-house keeper, widow of a warrant-officer of the China Fleet, caught a random observation from the Admiral's lips, fled into the sanctuary of a friendly gateway and crossed herself.

To the front gate of Frascati – undeviating, inexorable stump – *stump* – STUMP. Up the gravel path to the front door of Frascati,calamitous visitation upon Frascati sudden and desolating as an Old Testament visitation of Heaven upon a refractory tribe – stump – *stump* – STUMP. Upon the door-bell of Frascati – a pull-bell on a chain, pulled down to the very limit of resistance and held down for a few moments before release almost as strenuous as the downward pull – a clang devastating, wire-straining and charged with a cruel shriek like the laughter of elated devils.

'Another telegram,' said Cook to Hannah. ''Ow many more? It's that red-'aired boy you'll find. Tell 'im if he rings like that again, I'll speak to 'is father for 'im.'

Hannah opened the door. The Admiral gripped his walking stick and gave vent to a very long and extraordinary preliminary noise at the back of his nose.

'Where's yer master?' he asked with laudable restraint. 'Come on. Where is he?'

'He – he hasn't been back to lunch, sir.'

'I haven't come to lunch with him. I want to know where in – I want to know where he is.'

'I hardly know, sir. Of course this morning he went to golf.'

'Oh – h – h,' muttered the Admiral, turning and fortifying himself with a brief but fervid monologue. ('Tzai-poo-la! M'sai kwah! P'twee!') 'I tell you he did nothing of the sort. That's just what I want him about. Bla – h'm!'

'Reely, sir?' said Hannah. 'Then I'm very sorry, sir, but I've no idea where he can be.'

'Where's Mrs Twine?'

'Gone out for the day in the car, sir.'

'He gone with her? What? Eh?'

'No, sir.'

'Sure? Hah?'

'Yes, sir.'

'Well then, where the – where *is* he?'

'Reely I don't know, sir.'

'Yer don't suppose an evil beast has devoured him, do yer?'

'I hope not, sir,' said Hannah.

'Do yer?' said Admiral Juddy. 'I don't.'

Stump – *stump* – STUMP. ('Poon-chee-la! Boochong!')

At the gate he turned.

'I'm going round to my house for a little while. When he comes, you tell him I'll be back soon. Tell him that I spent the whole – that I spent the whole morning mucking a – messing about and couldn't get a game. I'll be back. Tell him. I'll have him. You tell him I'll have him.'

'What?' cried Cook, when Hannah told her. 'Never went to 'is golloff?'

'No.'

'What? Didn't keep to 'is programme?'

'No.'

Cook made an abortive attempt to whistle.

'Queer things is up,' she said. 'First of all that Mrs Leverett; then off she goes all day in the car; then telegrams come; then 'e don't keep to 'is programme. You mark my words, queer things is up.'

Augustus drove the car right into the garage of Rookery Nook and led Clive back, round the gravel sweep, to the front door. This was closed. The only sign of activity within was the impression of an ape-like figure performing darting sentry-work at the mullioned windows. As they entered Rhoda was standing over by the cupboard with a hand to the latch, alert and watchful. Twine, licking his lips, remained self-consciously in the foreground.

Clive murmured, 'By Jove!' and without further ceremony crossed the hall to Rhoda and offered her his hand.

'How d'you do?' he said. 'I understand I am to have the great pleasure of seeing you to London.'

She glanced at Augustus and then took the hand of Clive. There was no levity in her manner. She said, 'You are all being very, very kind.'

Over her pyjama jacket she now wore a striking blazer. The dressing-gown was employed chiefly as a skirt. The golf stockings and voluminous shoes of Augustus covered her feet. She was not a girl, it struck Clive, with whom a flirtation was possible. Her presence seemed to banish any suggestion of the half-hearted sentimentalism of an 'affair.' Her character, like her beauty, seemed elemental and consummate. This was a girl of extremes; the only girl in the world for some one, but for some one only. To others a friend; an eminently desirable friend, no doubt, but no more.

Even Clive, you see, was quite inspired by the unaffected grace of this target for the stones of Swallow Road.

'If you can really get me to London I shall be ever so grateful,' she went on. 'I'm only so sorry to make it difficult for you by not having any clothes.'

'Oh, we'll soon fix that,' replied Clive cheerfully. 'Hallo,

Twine. I hope this finds you as it leaves me at present. Oh, we'll soon fix that, Miss – er—'

'Marley.'

'Miss Marley. Come and sit down on this sofa and let's just decide exactly what we hope to do. Have a cigarette. These are Turkish and these are Chinese. Said to contain opium. I smoked sixteen of them yesterday and dreamt I was playing water-polo in Jermyn Street, seated upon an ostrich. Don't go, Twine. You're in this.'

'Oh. I think I've done enough.'

'Enough!' echoed Augustus.

'Enough, Twine!' said Clive. 'We haven't started yet, my dear fellow. I haven't told you the first of my plans, you poor fool. You know what they're trying to do to old Augustus, don't you, old boy? It's up to us, in the name of all that is cousinly and brotherly, to get him out of the cart, you blithering idiot.'

'Oh, but – you chaps. You must see that this puts me in a very awkward position with Gertrude.'

'Gertrude,' said Clive, 'is trying to work up a very discreditable piece of hate on Augustus. You, as her husband, should feel it your duty to prevent Gertrude doing what you know to be a most unworthy action. Her motives may be honourable, but you know as well as I do that they're utterly mistaken. Quite apart from the consequences to Augustus and Clara, it's positively your job, as her husband, to do all you can to stop her behaving in a way which is obviously rotten and discreditable. In other words, it's up to you to help us put a spoke in her wheel, and with any luck, a wheedle in her spoke.'

'Oh dear!' said Harold. 'Well, what do you want me to do now?'

'Well, as a matter of fact, your part of the stunt *does* come first. I want you to trot along to Romano's—'

'To where?'

'To your own – house—'

'Frascati?'

'Oh. All right. Don't interrupt. You can call it the Regent Palace Hotel if you like. But, anyhow, I want you to go along there and go upstairs to Gertrude's room and get some bags—'

'What!'

'Bags. Or a bag if you've got a good big one. A good big bag or bags, either your own or Gertrude's – it's immaterial whose bags you get. In the bag put – now listen – Miss Marley, perhaps you'll just check me over this, because it will be more or less guess-work on my part – in the bag put one pair of thin com – er – lady's summer underwear—'

'What! But what do you mean?'

'Oh, don't make it difficult for me, Twine, with Miss Marley listening and everything. A pair, or suit, of lady's—'

'Combies,' said Rhoda. 'That's all right. But in the summer you know, we don't—'

'I do *not* know,' said Clive. 'How should I know? Wait, Twine. In summer they don't.'

'Oh, but I say, FitzWatters, in any case, you are surely funning? I simply couldn't—'

'Look here. We've only got two hours in which to organise and carry out the whole of this flight. Do you suppose that I should sit here and fun? Especially in rather doubtful taste in the presence of a lady. Miss Marley will explain to you herself exactly what comes first in summer. Then she'll want a pair of silk stockings, a pair of walking shoes, a petticoat of suitable texture and some sort of a dress. Oh, and something to put over the dress.'

'Oh, and something to put under it, please,' said Rhoda.

'I thought I'd done all that was necessary there. A corsage, Twine.'

'A thing with no sleeves and little buttons and a tape,' said Augustus. 'Isn't that right?'

'Well,' said Rhoda, 'if he could just manage a pair of cami-knickers and a Princess petticoat—'

'You got that, Twine?' said Augustus. 'Manage as stated. And some sort of head-dress.'

'True,' said Clive. 'Not a dashed great thing with feathers though, Twine. You won't be able to manage that with already two bags. But bring some appropriate type of hat, bonnet, tile or coif. You can take it off in the car,' he added to Rhoda.

'Oh, if we're going to drive all the way, the most important thing will be a really serviceable overcoat,' said Rhoda.

'Yes, but we can't be quite sure what lies ahead of us, and you may as well be more or less rational all through. Still, Twine, you hear that? Concentrate particularly upon a likely great-coat, spencer, mackintosh, burnoose or poncho.'

Harold, who had been making vain attempts to impede the progress of the conference, now advanced to the Chesterfield with arms outspread and fingers quivering, after the manner of a ballerina performing 'The Dying Swan'.

'Oh, but I say. Oh, but I say, you chaps. Oh, but I say, no, this is too much.'

He had better have yielded at the first. Precious minutes were wasted, valuable energies expended. Harold knew himself to be in the grip of opposing forces against which his small powers of resistance were futile. It had been bad enough before this blandly dictatorial, airily inconsiderate worldling, FitzWatters, had arrived. Now he was done for. He attempted to put forward a stammering argument showing that their efforts to preserve the domestic peace of Augustus and Clara were bound to result in the shattering of his own happiness with Gertrude, and that if he was obliged to spend the afternoon in the prevention of a family embroilment, charity surely began at home. But they either didn't understand him or wouldn't; and as they kept talking back at him the whole time, he found it impossible to express himself.

The person who clinched the business, however, was Rhoda.

'May I just say something?' she asked.

'Certainly,' said Clive. 'Don't go on talking, Twine. Miss Marley is going to say something.'

'You know,' she said, addressing herself to Harold, 'when we were alone here together just now, I told you, didn't I, that my one object was to try and stop any possible trouble arising from my having come here and being treated so kindly. If I thought there wasn't a good chance of my being able to get away now, before I start causing anybody to kick up a row, I'd walk out as I am and get taken to the nearest lunatic asylum. I think your wife has got hold of entirely a wrong impression about me. If she, or any other kind-hearted person, knew the truth about me and about the way I've been treated at home and all that sort of thing, instead of trying to land me in difficulties they'd do anything they could to help me out. After all, you've seen me and talked to me and you know that I'm not the kind of girl your wife thinks I am; and if she'd had the same opportunity I hope she'd alter her opinion too. You know that your wife's doing me a great injustice. Won't you do what you can to stop it?'

'Oh – h!' sighed Harold.

'There's a garden gate leading straight on to Swallow Road, Twine,' said Augustus. 'I should come and go that way if I were you. I'll be on the look out and lend you a hand with the bags.'

CHAPTER XIII

Footling Behaviour of Harold Twine

Gertrude relapsed on to a platform seat, dished; stung; her programme for this momentous day sadly adrift. The young of a tripper came and sat beside her and had whooping cough.

Gertrude again took up a standing position in the midst of the platform and remained, tapping at her extremities, her toe tapping the ground, her tongue tapping her teeth, concentrating her thoughts.

Clara then had either failed to get her wire or had been prevented from carrying out her instructions. Here the hat of Gertrude was pushed violently to one side by a child preposterously young to be allowed a shrimping net.

In that case Clara had probably wired to Frascati in reply to Gertrude. How could this be ascertained? Frascati was not on the telephone. Should she ring up some reliable neighbour and get her to go in to Frascati and get and read the reply wire? Who reliable was on the telephone at Chumpton? And this would mean Gertrude having to wait and ring up again in order to find out what Clara said, after the neighbour had got the telegram and returned home from Frascati. No. At this point a parrot in a cage, toppling from the heights of an overladen truck that was passing, fell with considerable commotion at Gertrude's feet and said, 'Have this with me'.

There was, however, no reason to suppose that Clara would fail to arrive by the next train. The next train was due at Bristol at three. The time now was one-thirty. By returning in the car at top speed Gertrude could perhaps reach Chumpton just in time to meet the train again at Bristol by returning from Chumpton to Bristol immediately and again at top speed. Oh, how irritating! A young man with one of those lemonade bottles, which are so seldom successfully opened by hitting down a compressed glass ball with the butt end of a pocket knife, brought it off, greatly to his surprise and pleasure, over Gertrude's skirt. She then left the platform and returned to her car.

'I must come back here again to meet the train at three,' she told the chauffeur. 'Drive me to Fortt's. Be very careful of the trams.'

Hannah, running into the hall of Frascati, welcomed her prodigal master with two fatted telegrams and an expurgated version of the message from Admiral Juddy. She saw him, physically and mentally overwrought, weak-kneed, lip-licking, handle the missives with nervous misgiving. His demeanour was an open confession of a guilt and fear far exceeding the guilt of his treatment of Admiral Juddy, and the fear of the maledictory consequences. Indeed, as regards Admiral Juddy, he replied with comparative complacency, 'Oh, tell Admiral Juddy, I'm so sorry. I tried to let him know but couldn't. Tell him I'll come and play tomorrow morning.'

'Oh sir,' said the good-hearted girl, silent witness of how many a scene of oppression, 'is anything amiss? Can I do anything to help you, sir?'

'Oh. No, Hannah, thank you. I must open these telegrams and then I must go up and – oh. What time did the – er – missus leave?'

'Before twelve, sir. In the car.'

'Yes. I had better open these telegrams, I suppose.'

He sneaked with them into his dining-room, and she back to her kitchen door and the vigilant spectacles of Cook, flashing interrogation.

Harold opened the telegrams by prising up the flaps, so that he might close and stick them up again if he found he ought not to have interfered. They ran as follows:

Twine Frascati Chumpton Somerset

Got to paddington in time for eleven fifteen but couldnt catch owing mother slight relapse and sick in cab have taken her great western hotel will take one oclock train if she better which think will be do wire here what up is anything serious matter Clara

Twine Flushuti Chumpton Somerset

Just off to catch one train no wire from you mother better but still unsettled so dont meet in car bristol think would jog mother and bring on trouble again hope all well Clara

Suddenly and with great abandon Harold, after a brief reverie, flung the telegrams on to the dining-room table and cried aloud:

'Oh, blitheration take the whole of this bothered business!'

'Swearing!' said Cook to Hannah. 'What did I say? Remarkable things is up.'

Harold, recovering himself, drove ill-considered desperation from his mind and, for the first time that afternoon, strove calmly to face the situation. His one prevailing instinct at the moment above all the jumble of conscientious motive and Quixotic obligation was a fear that had now become almost greater than fear, a lingering anticipatory horror of his day's work as it would appear in the eyes of Gertrude. Was there no way in which he might possibly reconcile what he had done with the functions of Gertrude's frequently-defined ideal of a husband? Calmly let him just take stock of affairs as they stood, before dashing into this wild work with bags.

Gertrude, thinking that the girl at Rookery Nook had been frail with Augustus Longhampton (how Gertrude ever discovered she was there at all goodness only knew, but Gertrude always got to know things), had wired for Clara and was going to meet her at Bristol. But he had found out, in the meantime, that the girl was not really a frail girl, but had been driven to Rookery Nook by the brutality of her step-father. Harold had himself tested the step-father to see whether he was as brutal as all this and had found that he was.

Being unable to communicate with Gertrude and assure her that she was misjudging the girl (except by stepping out of a cupboard where he was hidden with the girl, a move which had not recommended itself at the time), Harold had been driven to act independently. He was convinced that Gertrude, had she met the girl, would have been impressed with the girl's innocence. Why then, she would naturally ask, had Harold contrived her escape before Gertrude's return? Snag.

How had Harold come to find out about the girl at all if he had spent the morning at golf? Oh, but he hadn't. Why not? Had he known, then, of something fishy going on at Rookery Nook at the time of his leaving Frascati for golf? If so, why had he not mentioned it to Gertrude? Snag.

Where had he been at the time of Gertrude's visit that morning to Rookery Nook? In the hall cupboard with the girl? Oh never. Utter snag.

If he refused to play any further part in this escapade what would happen? Gertrude and Clara would arrive, find the girl, make a dreadful scene. Into the midst of the dreadful scene would be lugged by the protesting, contentious Longhampton, he. He would be called upon to testify. He could deny and retaliate, but to what purpose? What chance had he in argument against Longhampton and that shattering other fellow, FitzWatters, in the presence of Gertrude, who would be overwhelmingly prejudiced by the first minor revelation that he had gone to Rookery Nook instead of to the golf club? Longhampton and FitzWatters would be vexed with him for not having fulfilled his promise and brought the clothes and would not spare him. Gertrude would hear all. The meeting in the scullery. The concealment in the cupboard. Oh, and whatever happened; if

Fortune, in some unforeseen and miraculous hazard, caught him by the hand and led him out of this labyrinth of adversity back into the sunshine of his ordinary, everyday, humdrum, bullied but contented existence, even then Admiral Juddy was certain to meet Gertrude, would stop her, would blow his great nose and clear his great throat and out it would all come – bit by bit – the full story – the entire confession. He could see himself making it. He could see Gertrude hearing it – opposite him – her bosom swelling at him – holding herself in check – waiting till she had heard every detail. And then—

It was a choice of evils. He might as well continue in sombeody's good graces. He might as well carry out his appalling promise to the inmates of Rookery Nook. To break it now would only mean fresh and immediate tribulation. So, after hesitating for a moment as to whether he should commit suicide or get bags, Harold Twine crept upstairs to the box-room to get bags.

'Hi! You!' cried Augustus from the garden gate of Rookery Nook. 'Boy!'

The telegraph boy brought his bicycle to the halt by banking steeply and using one foot as a brake.

'Hallo! You're the boy that came to my house this morning, aren't you?'

'Yup,' said the boy.

'Ah. I expect you've pretty well used up your toffee by this time. Here's a shilling to get some more. And as you go past Mr Twine's house down there, just slip in and leave this note. See? Good boy.'

'It's 'is 'ouse Oi be a-going to,' said the boy.

'The devil it is! With a telegram?'

'Yup.'

'Oh. Well, hurry up then. Go and leave your telegram and deliver your note and buy your toffee. Good afternoon, boy.'

Hannah peered through a window commanding the front door and returned to the side of Cook.

'Hannah!' called an anxious voice from upstairs, 'if that's Admiral Juddy—'

'No, sir, it's a telegram.'

'Oh.'

'Another!' said Hannah to Cook.

'It's what I said,' replied Cook. 'Something extraordinary is on the tapes.'

'Goodness!' cried Hannah from the door. 'It's for me.'

' 'Ere. And a note fer the gent,' said the telegraph boy.

'This for me, and a note for him,' exclaimed Hannah, bursting back at Cook.

'It's what I said,' repeated the latter, drying her hands busily on her apron. 'Something quite out of the common is on foot.'

'It's from the missus,' said Hannah. 'Listen.'

> Smeddon Frascati Chumpton Som.
>
> See that mrs Leverett is at Frascati at four fifteen certain to remain there till I come   Mrs Twins

'I'll take the message meself,' said Cook. 'I happens to want to go into the town. Something—'

The note Hannah carried upstairs to her master whom she strangely found in Mrs Twine's bedchamber holding a large canvas-covered suitcase in one hand and toying self-consciously with the door of a wardrobe with the other. He moaned to see the note, as a superannuated and decrepit pirate would moan to receive the black spot, while still doing his best under onerous conditions.

He took it to the window and read it, Hannah waiting.

> DEAR MR TWINE,
>
> *And* some hair-pins, please. I forgot.   R.M.
>
> P.S. Buck up.   A.L.

P.S. If you meet anybody who asks you what you've got in the bags, be bright and ready. Assuage any curiosity that might find its way to the ear of Gertrude. Your best plan will be not to meet anybody. Also select articles that Gert. will not be likely to miss for a day or two. I should have mentioned this. I expect she has two of everything. Thanking you for past favours,

C.F.

P.S. Some move on also immediately get already please.

PUTZ.

P.S. Grrrrrrrrr—

CONRAD.

'Oh,' said Harold wretchedly. 'Hannah.'

'Yes, sir?'

'Oh! No, never mind, never mind.'

The good girl unreservedly pressed her services upon him, told him of her wire from Mrs Twine, urgently desired his confidence. He, wiping his brow and with a great effort of self-restraint, declined her good offices. 'I might get you into trouble,' he said. 'I'd see you didn't, sir,' said she with decision. 'Oh, Hannah; but if I ask you for something, I – I don't want you to let the missus know.' 'Oh, sir,' replied the girl more faintly, 'what?' With great yearning, so she thought, he gazed at her, licking his lips. 'Well, sir?' she cried. 'If you'll let me know what it is you're after—?'

'Some hair-pins,' he gasped.

Hannah gaped at him, but dutifully departed to her own chamber. Not hers to reason why. Cook's though. Cook was in the next apartment, putting on her hat. She inquired what Hannah was in search of. Hannah told her briefly and hurried from an atmosphere which rung with querulous homilies on strange happenings and the marking of words.

She found the master with one foot in the open suitcase and his head apparently wedged in an open chest of drawers.

He liberated it, however, and received the hair-pins with a murmur of gratitude. She attempted to make a further puzzled overture but he nodded her from the room and again plunged at the chest of drawers. Hannah pensively returned to the kitchen. Cook, hoisting and buttoning herself for the town, was already at the back door.

It was the hour at which Swallow Road, awakening from siesta, contemplated a variety of cretonnes and ducks and the ardent prospect of afternoon pastime. Mrs Fludyear was about to set forth upon a maladroit but vindictive battle (with half-an-hour off for tea) at the Ladies' Croquet Club with Mrs Preen. The already snarling components of a mixed foursome were converging from various points in Swallow Road upon the Ladies' Golf Club. Miss W. Creepe was on her way to catch her skirt with her racquet and say, 'Yours, partner,' at the Whigham-Pitts's. Mrs Wintle was leaving her house to play Bridge at the Firmstone's. Mr Twine was leaving his house to play what and where? Carrying a green suitcase? Mrs Wintle held him up. It was nothing short of a duty.

'My dear Mr Twine! You look as if you are eloping. And I saw Mrs Twine going off somewhere in the car this morning. Really, this won't do.'

'Ha!' said Harold mirthlessly. 'Yes, I'm just – ha – going to – haha! Yes. I'm just taking some things to Rookery Nook. My wife's sister is there you know.'

'Oh. Then she has arrived? I heard she couldn't come after all owing to your wife's mother being dangerously ill; but I suppose it was only Chumpton gossip as usual. The way people gossip here is terrible. But why has Mrs Twine gone away for the day if her sister has just come?'

'Ah. But – yes. No. My sister-in-law hasn't come yet. Only her husband.'

'Oh, I see. Then has some of his luggage gone astray or something?'

'Er – yes. That is, he hasn't got quite all he wants in the house, so I'm lending him some things.'

'I see,' said Mrs Wintle. 'Hot, isn't it?'

'Oh, very,' said Harold.

He had indeed placed the suitcase on the path beside him during the brief conversation. Mrs Wintle now passed on and he resumed it. Mrs Wintle turned to glance at him as she went, then, halting abruptly, stared at him. Harold, prospecting up Swallow Road in the direction of Lighthouse Road, saw Mrs Fludyear and Colonel Bagley bearing down on him in company. With what he was pleased to consider a wonderfully expressive gesture implying that he had suddenly recollected some important obligation in Frascati, he turned and hurried back through his own gate. Mrs Wintle met Miss W. Creepe and stopped her. The two ladies conversed animatedly.

'—with a pair of lady's shoes, one in each pocket of his coat,' concluded Mrs Wintle. 'I saw them distinctly sticking out. The heels. Rather queer, surely; if only the husband is there.'

'Most,' said Miss Creepe. 'But I suppose there's some reason.'

'Of course. But you know what people are. Somebody else might notice and gossip about it and all sorts of extravagant stories might get about which would be a great pity. I'd have asked him about them myself, only I didn't notice them until I'd passed on.'

'There isn't any other girl staying at Rookery Nook, is there?'

'Oh no. I'm sure I should have heard. Besides, hardly another girl alone there with the husband, before the wife comes down. I really must try and find out what he's up to.'

'He ran back into his own house in rather a guilty sort of way I thought,' said Miss Creepe.

'Yes,' said Mrs Wintle. 'I thought so too. Hot, isn't it?'

Stump – *stump* – STUMP. Admiral Juddy, mollified somewhat by whisky, but still eyebrow-entangled and lapsing occasionally into Chinese, came Rachmaninoffing down his garden path into Swallow Road, bent once more upon his vengeful pursuit. He paused to reprimand his gardener. 'Clear all this junk off the quarter-deck, God split my soul!' Stump – *stump* – STUMP.

Brooding and muttering, with lowered head, Admiral Juddy failed to notice Miss W. Creepe. Miss W. Creepe, scanning eagerly the windows of Rookery Nook from Swallow Road, failed to notice Admiral Juddy. Just outside the garden gate of Rookery Nook they collided. ('Oh! Admiral Juddy, I *beg* your—' – 'Can't you look where you're – oh, all right, all right. Pongchoo! Twee-p'tswai-pee!')

'Going to play tennis, heh?'

'Yes. I'm going to the Pitts's. I suppose you're off to golf. Or do you find a round in the morning enough, this weather?'

This was asking for it; got it. Miss W. Creepe heard things about Mr Twine. Sturdily retaliated. Told Admiral Juddy things about Mr Twine. He was at this moment at home, preparing to take a rather queer assortment of things over to Rookery Nook in and out of a green suitcase. Who exactly was at Rookery Nook? Did the Admiral know?

No, and didn't care. N'ze-ho-la. But was grateful to Miss W. Creepe for her information. Would get to it at once. Rachmaninoff.

'Is that Twine outside the gate?' asked Augustus.

'I think not,' replied Clive.

'Who is it then?'

'I should be rather sorry to say. You seem to have chosen rather an extraordinary place for your holiday. It's either somebody making a film or an open-air meeting of a sub-committee of the League of Nations.'

'Is Twine at it?'

'I think not.'

'He's the devil of a time,' said Augustus anxiously.

So busily occupied had been the Admiral and Miss W. that they had missed something. They had missed seeing Harold appear round the bend of Swallow Road, groping nervously along the wall with his green suitcase, and pull up all standing within only a few yards of them. They had missed seeing him glare wildly at them, almost dropping the suitcase, and spurred to strategical inspiration, dive down Lighthouse Road and round the covering sweep of Rookery Nook fence as the Admiral stumped past the corner.

Saved! Harold almost forgot his woes in the little glow of triumph with which he watched the avenging greybeard tack across Swallow Road and pound onwards to Frascati.

Harold had had enough of Swallow Road. He would go in by the front gate of Rookery Nook. He placed the suitcase on the ground and fingered his collar which had collapsed under the strain of the day's doings and was not very comfortable. That was better. This lamentable business of the borrowed clothes was, for weal or woe, nearly completed now. They would be pleased with him and would perhaps let him go now. In that case he could overtake Juddy, appease him somehow and even, possibly, concoct an alibi for Gertrude. He seized up the bag and scuttled ahead down Lighthouse Road, round the final little bend to the front gate of Rookery Nook and into the arms of Putz.

'Here, milk!' shouted Cook, stepping into the road and waving an ex-parasol. 'Are you a-going to the town?'

'Ay, that Oi be,' said the milkman.

'Then you can take me with you,' said Cook. 'These 'ot pavements catch me feet something crool.'

'Oo,' said the milkman. 'Ay, to be sure. Wo-ee! Can 'ee hoist yerself?'

'Yes, if the pony don't move on,' said Cook.

'If you lingers on that back step 'e be more loike to move oopwards,' said the milkman. 'Where may it so be that you was thinking o' gooin', missus?'

'Mrs Leverett's,' she told him. 'It's something concerning that there house Rookery Nook. Something very mysterious is current.'

'Oo?'

'Do you 'appen to know anything of the folks that is in that house?'

As it so happened the milkman did. Knew summat of the gent. Had fulfilled a commission for him that very morning and had found him a very nice-spoken and open-handed gent. Cook shook her head. From casual references to Augustus, overheard in Frascati, she had formed a very different opinion. The note of argument crept into the conversation in the milk-cart. When the note of argument creeps into a conversation in a milk-cart prudence and indeed pertinence fly to the four winds. The milkman heard all about Mrs Leverett; Mrs Twine's departure; the telegrams (two for 'Twine' and one for 'Smeddon', the latter again summoning Mrs Leverett); the callous non-observance of the programme for the day by the master; the long, unexplained absence of the master; his fleeting reappearances and strange behaviour in bedrooms; his staggering request for hair-pins. All of these events were undoubtedly connected with the mystery of Rookery Nook.

The milkman retaliated by repeating his good opinion of Augustus in greater detail; presently by producing, and turning the well-thumbed pages of, the milk-book. Was sorry he had done so when he saw the enormous interest and fresh, but now secretive, satisfaction afforded Cook by his revelation. It was entirely the gent's own affair, he said, and should not be bandied about by such as whose affair it was not. Cook's retort took the form of a further breathless recital of the known facts on arrival at Mrs Leverett's door, of snatching the milk-book from the milkman's hand and showing Mrs Leverett the milk-book; of enjoining Mrs Leverett to tell all she knew in return. Mrs Leverett, frowning in occult misgiving over the tidings of the master, the packing and the hair-pins, replied that she would be at Thrushcato at the time appointed. Until then, and for aught she knew after then as well, 'her mouth was silenced'. The milkman, sorely conscience-smitten, reclaimed his milk-book and drove away, leaving the two ladies still wrangling upon the doorstep.

Sorely conscience-smitten. The gent had treated him very liberally and, now that he came to think of it, *had* mumbled something about keeping the matter dark. These females were up to getting the gent into some sort of trouble. That Mrs Twine was at the head of it. That Mrs Twine had recently complained to him of the quality of milk which he had himself with his own hands drawn the very same morn from the finest dun in the medder. He disliked that Mrs Twine. And now, it seemed he had gone and played into the hands of that Mrs Twine at the expense of the friendly and liberal gent. At four-fifteen, so these women had mentioned, the net was to close upon the gent at Rookery Nook. He would darned well be around about Rookery Nook at that hour. Maybe he could do summat to retrieve any damage his indiscretion had wrought.

'Halt!' said Putz.

He held Conrad by a leader. Harold eyed the front gate, edged a yard or two out from the fence.

'Move further also,' said Putz, 'and I lose my dog.'

'What do you want with me?' pleaded Harold.

'Wid this trunk also what you make?'

'I beg your pardon?'

'Speak.'

'I'm afraid I don't quite—'

'Immediately speak. You have it here a trunk. Inside is what?'

He advanced upon Harold, Conrad straining at the leader and whistling.

'Aller right,' said Putz consolingly to the latter. 'Not yet. Na-putta. Presently you shall bite.'

Harold turned in the direction of Rookery Nook and opened his mouth to shout for help. He felt the suitcase torn from his hands. He clutched wildly at it and managed to retain a hold. He was dragged into the road. Blindly clutching he desperately fought. Conrad, entangled by the leader somewhere in the midst of the fray, was whistling and gnashing violently. Weird grunts of effort and foreign snatches of self-encouragement came from Putz. With a decisive tug he wrenched the suitcase from Harold and it burst open.

The wrench momentarily disconcerted Putz, who, overbalancing beneath its impetus, sat in the road, and still further involved Conrad, who had got the leader round three of his legs and his head under the lid of the suitcase at the moment of the bursting open. Harold seized his opportunity. He made one swoop at the suitcase, gathered in both arms whatever garments came to hand, made a dash for the gate, slammed it behind him with his foot and fled, impeded by flapping and slipping articles of attire, up the drive.

Though none pursued he never ceased to run till he gained the porch. Here his energies failed him. Utterly spent, his heart thudding at his throat, robbed of speech, the perspiration bursting from every pore, an effervescent wave of white linen sprouting in frills from his chest, he sank against the door-post of Rookery Nook like a Marathon herald yielding up his spirit at the goal.

Clive, standing at the angle of the house, called coolly over his shoulder in the direction of the garden gate.

'It's all right. He's here.'

'Here?' came the reply. 'How the devil did he get here? Has he got the things with him?'

'He's got some things.'

'Hasn't he got the bags?'

'I can't quite see what he's got yet. You'd better come and see for yourself.'

'All right, I'll come. But what's the matter with the fool? Can't he talk?'

'Apparently he can only wag his head from side to side.'

'Well, but you're there. You can see. What's happened to him? What does he look like?'

'You'd much better come and decide for yourself,' said Clive. 'To me he looks more like a very hot cauliflower au gratin than anything else I can think of on the spur of the moment.'

Augustus made his appearance and the inquisitors descended on Harold.

'Is that all you've got? What's the matter with you? What's up? What's happened? Where are your bags? What have you done with the other things? What have you got here? You weren't told to bring a pair of these things in any case.'

He could only gulp and helplessly gesticulate. Clive turned with some anxiety to Augustus.

'My God!' he said. 'I believe that Chinese gentleman we heard outside the garden gate has got hold of him and put him through some dreadful form of Chinese torture.'

They bore him into the hall and dumped him on the Chesterfield. Presently he managed to gulp out the essentials of his narrative. How, leaving Frascati, he had encountered Mrs Wintle. How he had been bright and ready, as per instructions in the note. But had seen Mrs Wintle talking to Miss Creepe and Miss Creepe to Admiral Juddy. How Admiral Juddy was stalking him for cutting golf. How, by strategy, he had outwitted Admiral Juddy only to fall a prey to Putz. Of his struggle and partial victory against odds. He finished, breathless again and with hands protestingly outspread.

'What more could I have done?' he asked.

'What less, you pipsqueak?' rejoined Augustus. 'Clive, if that blighter's still outside the gate with the bag I think it calls for action.'

'Come on then,' said Clive. 'You too, Twine. Your job will be to draw Conrad while we tackle Putz.'

'No,' said Harold. 'No more.'

'Look here,' said Clive quite kindly, persuasively. 'You have already endangered the success of this enterprise by your behaviour. You can at least come and draw Conrad. That's a thing you've already proved yourself quite good at.'

By the time they got to the gate, however, Putz was just

entering his own, carrying the green suitcase. Conrad turned his head and whistled at them.

'Too late!' cried Augustus desperately.

'But he's got my wife's bag and my wife's clothes in it,' whined Harold.

'Well, of course he has, if you gave them to him, you bloody fool,' said Clive.

CHAPTER XIV

Admiral Juddy in Wonderland

Down the high-road of Life, nearing the corner, stumps many an Admiral Juddy, his shoulders bent with the cares of well-nigh seventy years that are past and with the crowning, heavier-than-ever cares of the year that is present – everything wrong; his digestion, the Government, the behaviour of the rising generation, the state of India, the state of Ireland, the state of the whole Empire if it comes to that. The state of England – these blasted swabs of Labour people – how the devil the authorities permit such a set of – oh, well; it's too late for him to take a hand now, but if he were a young man—

Life. The prospect of the limited number of years remaining to him – what? Pottering about in this God-forsaken place – Why didn't he move? What the devil was the good? Any other place would be just as bad. That fool of a doctor had advised him to winter abroad. Winter abroad indeed! Did the doctor think he was going to undertake all the labour and expense of carting himself and his wife off to some beastly foreign hotel to be waited upon by a set of howling Dagos, while his house at home was left to the mercy of whatever Goths chose to come and take it and smash all his valuable Chinese curios and dispute the inventory? No fear. This place was good enough for him.

But the trouble was that even in those recreations with which he sought to beguile the monotony of well-earned retirement, things always went wrong. Wrong. Always wrong. At golf. What the deuce was the pleasure of golf when things always went wrong? Times without number had he stood out there in the rough at the tenth, far, far, from home, and had cried aloud to Heaven a vow that he would never, never again come out playing this God-damned and fiend-begotten and utterly blasted and withered and pestilent and putrid game. Wrong. It wasn't as though he didn't know the game. He did know the game – a long sight better than a great many better players. He could teach people the game; did. But once he got in that blasted rough—

Again, just as he was in position for a fine long raking iron shot to the very pin – feeling like it – something would go wrong – something. Perhaps he would catch a glimpse out of the tail of his eye of some supercilious young blood stamping with impatience on the tee behind; and into the bunker would go the infernal ball and into the turf would go the iron and off would fly the head of the rotten, accursed iron, and into the bunker would be flung the head and over the bunker would be flung the shaft – wrong; wrong. Oh – hell! And this was pleasure! Totally and to the uttermost limit, damn!

Or, again, take Bridge. It wasn't any use anybody telling the Admiral he didn't know all there was to know about Bridge. He'd played Bridge long before it ever came to England. He'd played it in the eighties at Foo-Chow as the guest of the Mandarin Yat Hoo. As a matter of fact he'd half invented the filthy game.

But somehow or other whenever he sat down to a rubber at the club at Chumpton things seemed to go wrong. Half the time, of course, his poor, miserable, benighted partner didn't understand his play which was naturally advanced. What was the good of telling a man like Twine for instance what was the conventional response expected of him following an original call of a couple of bludgeons? The fool would go and say what he'd been told to say right enough, but there he'd been found to be sitting with a fist-full of bloodthumpers, and, my God! if the Admiral had only known that d'you think he'd ever have called bludgeons? He could have swept the board. Wrong! Things had gone wrong as usual, just for lack of a little common savvy. And this again was pleasure was it? Even when the Admiral got his own way and played the hands himself things generally went wrong.

Stump – *stump* – STUMP. Back bent; beard sunken on chest, eyes bright blue, glittering upwards in defiance of the menace of wrong-goings and increasing infirmity. And he had been a great man in his time, they said – a fine sailor. Well, he must have been. His career spoke for itself. Had he been ten years younger he might have niched his name on the monument of undying renown. As it was, all he had been allowed to do in the war was to potter about at the Admiralty, carefully superintended by mistrustful experts whom he could remember beating in the gun-room.

He knew that he was regarded as a standing joke. He knew that his ill-temper and abuse were tolerated by his neighbours half in amusement,half in pity. But there were times when they might have observed a glint in his eye which would have warned them that he was still a man to be reckoned with at a pinch. On these occasions, however, he was generally alone. They were the occasions when he would stump down to the so-called Promenade and would stand gazing out towards the alleged sea. Then, perchance, there would be borne to his ears the desultory cry of the gull and to his great nostrils the tang of the salted breeze; and he would grip his stick and turn to face the wrong-goings and vexations of the day a trifle fortified, a trifle more erect; as though the kindly hand of memory had removed a care or two from his burdened shoulders.

Admiral Juddy stumped to Frascati and again interrogated Hannah. The harassed girl asserted something or other, but the Admiral didn't wait to hear what it was. If Twine wasn't at home, he knew where to find him now. He had gone to Rookery Nook with a green bag, and ladies' footwear sticking out of his pockets. What he thought he was up to the Admiral didn't know, but, by thunder, he would find out.

He was on his way back to Lighthouse Road when Mrs

Belcher called him from the gate of 'Dunwiddy', Swallow Road, and asked him to come and give an opinion on her roses. Admiral Juddy was an acknowledged expert on roses. True, his own roses had gone wrong that year. His blazing nincompoop of a gardener had blazed too thoroughly. Still, Mrs Belcher always seemed to think she could grow roses better than anyone else and he was glad of an opportunity to correct that impression.

When Rhoda Marley, from an upper window of Rookery Nook, saw her step-father carrying the green suitcase into Pixiecot her expression would have disabused the most sceptical witness. Some men, unlike Augustus and Clive, might have hesitated long before crediting her story, so deep in its very simplicity, in its very artlessness so ensnaring. A naturally cheerful girl she was, with enough depth of character to be able to find a reflective amusement in life even though she viewed the world from behind prison bars. Caged as she had been, in as strange a home as could well be imagined, for the past eighteen months, her first instinct in almost any eventuality was still to laugh. Perhaps it was this trait which had incurred the deliberate and indeed unwilling hostility of Putz.

There was little mirth in her face as she watched him now; but there was no indignation nor regret. Her lips were set with determination and in her fine eyes was a gleam of challenge.

The flagrantly illegal and unscrupulous methods adopted by Putz in this campaign on Rookery Nook rather appealed to her. They were characteristic of his ruthless and in some respects admirable nature. 'He is more what a man is intended to be than other men are,' had declared her spellbound mother. Perhaps in his arbitrary, unswerving tenacity of purpose he was. But the despotic stepfather of Rhoda was far removed from the indulgent consort of her late, foolish and favoured mother. The breach, long-anticipated, inevitable, had come to pass.

Rhoda descended into the hall just as the others returned from the drive. Even Harold found some consolation in her charming reception of his failure and in her reiterated gratitude for services so ill rendered. She even mildly rebuked Augustus who was becoming dispirited and rather blunt in his observations to Harold.

'I know what my step-father's like to tackle,' she said. 'He was interned most of the war, otherwise we shouldn't have won it.'

'If they hadn't let him out for the peace,' grumbled Augustus, 'we might have had one. Now he's gone and leagued with Gertrude and he jolly well means to keep you here until they come and catch you—'

'Bare-footed,' suggested Clive.

'Don't you make any mistake,' cried Rhoda. 'That's not his game at all. He may look as if he's trying to keep me here. As a matter of fact he's doing all he can to make me go back. He expected me to come weeping on the doorstep half an hour after he'd run me out last night. Now that he sees I'm not going back of my own accord he's trying to force me to do it. That's what's up.'

Augustus protested, 'But he tells every one he doesn't give a penny hoot where you go or what happens to you.'

'That's bluff,' said Rhoda. 'It's very important to him that I shouldn't leave him altogether and go off to London. If you want to see him go really off the deep end you watch what he does when I drive out of here in the car.'

Augustus waved wild arms.

'But *are* you going to drive out of here in a car? What are you going to do it in?'

'Don't lose your nerve, Augustus,' said Clive. 'We can hire a car. There's a car-hiring place in the town, isn't there, Twine?'

'I don't mean what make of car, or in the car of or belonging to whom, or anything else about the car, you hearty ass,' said Augustus. 'What I mean is that Twine, having fallen among Putz, has turned up with a selection of odd clothing which makes it quite impossible for Miss Marley to go dashing about the country in cars.'

'Why impossible?' asked Clive. 'Do you mean it would be cold or illegal?'

'Both,' said Augustus. 'Probably the best you will be able to raise in this benighted town is an open Ford. And you'll have to get a chauffeur to drive you.'

'Why?'

'Well, they won't hire out a car without one.'

'Even so. Are you suggesting that the chauffeur will be so overcome by the appearance of Miss Marley that he won't be able to drive his car?'

'No, but don't you see, you fool, that if you were driving the car yourself, you might be able to smuggle her along as she is – or will be.'

'Well, if you won't lend us your own car—'

'How can I? I want the car here when Clara comes, as a sort of alibi.'

'I see – all right. There's no necessity to be febrile. I know we've wasted precious hours in attempting to get some clothes for Miss Marley and have failed. This makes it all the more important that the same thing doesn't happen when we try to get her a car. To this end you should endeavour to refrain from behaving like a jazz drummer and be calm and calculating. Now, listen. I shall go to this local car place and say, "I wish to hire a car to drive myself to town in."—'

'They won't do it.'

'They will do it. I shall have with me a local celebrity who will act as my guarantor in the matter: a gentleman of unsullied, if not of unbullied, reputation; of ample means, a prominent churchman, an eminent member of the local council of the Girls' Friendly Society—'

'Oh! Twine?'

'Twine. I shall have Twine with me in the car place. They will probably offer to *give* me a car. We will drive it back here to the garden gate. By that time Miss Marley will have seen what she can do with the material provided for her by Twine and will come downstairs, looking like an illustrated interview with a film star at her Hollywood home, and off we shall go.'

'But can you manage with these things?' asked Augustus of Rhoda pessimistically.

'Let's have a look,' said Rhoda. 'Well, here's a pair of stockings for a start—'

'When sitting in a car,' remarked Clive, 'a pair of stockings come really at the wrong end to be aptly described as a start.'

'Oh,' cried Harold with flushed recollection. 'I forgot. I have some shoes in my pocket.'

'Still the wrong end, Twine,' said Clive.

'And some hair-pins,' murmured Harold.

'Good!' exclaimed Rhoda gratefully.

'Good,' commented Clive. 'But I wish you wouldn't go to such extremes. How are we off amidships, Miss Marley?'

'Not very well off, I'm afraid,' said Rhoda. 'You see, this thing is a bust bodice, but—'

'You fool,' cried Augustus severely to Harold. 'You've only brought about three articles. You might at least have brought them in decent condition.'

'And this—' continued Rhoda, 'is – m'yes. There's not very much, is there? I dare say that by borrowing a pretty large quantity of string, or possibly by sticking safety-pins through my flesh I may be able to carry it off.'

'I'll tell them to put a rug in the car,' said Clive. 'After all, with a rug and a greatcoat and a windscreen – but we shall have to drive the whole way of course. I can't bear to think of you trying to hold your pieces of string together through your greatcoat and fighting for a seat in the Bristol express.'

'Well, I'll go up and see what I can do,' said Rhoda.

'That's right,' said Augustus. 'Clive, you push off with Twine and get the car. It's getting late, you know.'

'Come, Twine,' said Clive.

'Oh. But must I?'

'Haven't you been listening?'

'Yes, but – if you are seen – I mean, if people see you

walking with me – I mean they will look at you and wonder who you are.'

'I'm used to that,' said Clive.

'No, but the people here are so curious.'

'Yes, I've noticed that.'

'No, but I mean, someone is certain to see you with me and then they'll ask Gertrude who it was.'

'What do you mean – it?'

'It. You.'

'What *is* your trouble. Take a deep breath and be grammatical.'

'Oh-h. All right, I'll come,' said Harold desperately. After all, the walk would be in a good cause. He was going to get rid of this baffling FitzWatters as a result of it. Having taken the plunge he walked so resolutely that even Clive was hard put to it to keep pace with him. His abandon was rewarded. Down the length of Swallow Road they scarcely met a soul except an aged man jogging along in a milk-cart and too concerned with his own speculative mumblings to turn his watery eye in their direction.

Rhoda, gathering together her meagre borrowings from the hall table, turned suddenly to Augustus and spoke with great candour.

'With all said and done, if your wife walked in here and saw me as you saw me; if I told her about myself as I told you; if she saw my step-father and Conrad and used her common sense, would she suspect?'

'Yes,' said Augustus. 'Because she will have been primed by this Gertrude. If I could get her to myself I'd soon put her right. I mean to tell her all about it in any case. But it is essential to flabbergaster Gertrude. When Gertrude and she arrive you will not be here; you will never have been here; Gertrude has been making some howling and outrageous mistake. My wife, who is really a dear little girl, will arise in defence of her falsely accused and innocent boy, and Gertrude will retire baffled to Frascati. Then, gently, I can put my wife wise to what has happened.'

'Don't you think your sister-in-law will go to my step-father and try to get him to come along and testify?'

'If your step-father is likely to be as annoyed as you seem to think at your having got away with it, he will probably only run Gertrude out, which will be a sight for the Gods.'

Rhoda deliberated.

'I think he'll try and make things as awkward for you as he can out of pique,' she said.

'Oh, that'll be a nice change, won't it?' replied Augustus not without sarcasm.

With a quick movement Rhoda threw the things back on the table and came to him impetuously and with hands out-stretched.

'I'll chuck it,' she said. 'I'll go back to him. I wanted to cut myself adrift from him once and for all, and I know you wanted me to want it. You've done all you can for me, and I've no right to involve you like this. It's not too late and I can stick it if I try. Give me a greatcoat and I'll go back to him and ask to be taken in.'

Augustus seized her hands and clasped them tightly.

'No, by Allah!' he cried.

He saw the light of thankfulness and hope renewed in her eyes, and his resolution tightened with his grasp.

'That wouldn't help anyhow, good heavens!' he went on. 'There you'd be in the next house; and Gertrude and Putz both know you stayed last night here. It would only make things look suspicious, where they're really as innocent as day. To go back now would be to do yourself a great injustice, quite apart from what you'd be going back to. Besides—'

'Yes?'

He drew her a little closer. The good, fat fellow was deeply, impulsively in earnest, but Rhoda seemed to find only inspiration in a spectacle which was, truth to tell, a trifle ludicrous.

'I don't care for all the rights and wrongs and suspicions and innocencies and Gertrudes and Putzes in the world,' he told her. 'You're beautiful and in trouble and I'm going to get you out of it. As for your going back to be unhappy – no, by God! You're going away from here, and I only hope you'll let me go on helping you, and we'll find happiness for you somewhere.'

His grasp on her hand relaxed and his hand stole up her arm to the shoulder. The gentle pressure of her outstretched palm upon his chest recalled him to his senses, a pressure not reproachful, scarcely protesting. Nor, dash it, was he open to reproach. Here, in this house with him, for the best part of a day, had been this lovely creature, at his mercy, in his hall, in his bed, half in his pyjamas – he was a good fellow, but it was all very well – it was very tantalising, mark you.

But that tender hand on his chest reminded him that the more tantalising it became, the better must be his fellowship. That and her words, half laughed in her happiness – 'You're a brick.'

A brick. A brick is a hard thing to be. No darling can ever be a brick, no brick a darling. He released her, but not disconcerted with her. The tiniest bit disconcerted with himself; with her stimulated. So many girls he had known would have kissed him and taken all his pains as a matter of course.

'Well then, I'd better go and string myself and pin myself,' she said. 'Have you any string? Where are pins?'

'There's a ball of string in the study and some pins in my dressing-room,' said Augustus. 'Don't go and commit suttee, or anything.'

She gathered up the packet of hairpins and the clothes. 'You've forgotten the shoes,' Augustus said. 'Never mind. I'll try them on when I get down,' she replied over her shoulder.

Scarcely had she gone when an inspiration seized Augustus. He called after her and she answered from the study. Thither he hurried. Conveniently found her at the writing-table. The inspiration was of an epistolary nature.

For the final and utter rout of Gertrude one precaution had yet to be taken. As Rhoda had suggested, Putz might contribute and elaborate accusations, if appealed to.

Remove Putz from the scene of action during the all-important hour of the visitation, and the triumph was complete.

Was Rhoda certain that Putz would use every endeavour to prevent her from leaving Chumpton? Yes, she was quite sure. She had reasons for being quite sure. He knew where she would go if she got to London, and he particularly desired her not to go there. Never mind about London; could she count on his pursuing if she went in the opposite direction to London – to Taunton for instance? He probably would so pursue. Why?

'Listen,' said Augustus.

Rhoda must write Putz a note. 'Who's to deliver it?' asked the practical girl immediately. 'Oh, *I'll* have a dart for it. Don't interrupt please,' said Augustus, and continued. She must tell Putz in the note that, since he had driven her from home, she had been forced to obtain what shelter she could. The kind friends who had hitherto watched over her were transferring her by car to an hotel at Taunton, where she was to stay that night. In the morning she was to be seen to London. She was writing the note at the moment of departure for Taunton. Should he relent, he could probably find her at Taunton.

'I needn't say that last bit,' remarked Rhoda. 'He won't relent, but he'll make a bee-line for Taunton in any case.'

'Don't you think it's a remarkable bit of strategy?' said Augustus.

'Yes, I think it's worth trying,' said Rhoda. 'He'll certainly believe it, because he knows I never tell lies.'

'It's magnificent,' said Augustus. 'He'll dash off to Taunton and spend the evening slitting the throats of hotel proprietors. By the time he gets back I shall be ready for him. Try it on.'

'It may make him more watchful to see that I don't escape.'

'If he comes and watches here I shall tell him you've gone. And you can always sneak round at the back and get out through the garden gate. Besides, you probably *will* have gone by the time he gets the note.'

'Just as you think,' said Rhoda. 'Righto, I'll write it.'

Five minutes later Augustus emerged cautiously from the front door of Rookery Nook. His head was turned in the direction of the elm trees. Stooping at the hedge of the drive, he craned with his tongue out to catch a glimpse of Pixiecot. When he straightened himself he bumped, with a little cry of surprise, against a figure of a dejected and very obsequious milkman.

'Hallo!' said Augustus. 'It's you. What's up.'

'Sur,' said the milkman. 'Oi toold. This morrn, when you give me that ther' telegram, you toold me I warn't to goo tellin' 'un; and Oi toold. And no sooner hadn't Oi not gone and toold like as here Oi be telling you Oi toold, than Oi thinks to meself – "Thurr! Oi bin and toold". And Oi thinks Oi better be comin' and tellin' you, sur, o' this here tellin,' and to be tellin' you that if thur be ought Oi can do fer having done this here tellin', then if you will be tellin' me what ter do, you jest tell me and, dash my buttons, Oi'll do he.'

'Stop,' said Augustus. 'Enough. You remind me of a gramophone record of a chorus sung by a Honolulu orchestra. I understand that you've gone and split to someone about sending off that telegram for me, and that you've decided to come and confess this to me and, if possible to expiate your indiscretion. Is that it?'

'Ay,' said the milkman. 'I reckon that'll be around about it.'

'Oh,' said Augustus. 'Very well then. I won't recriminate but I'll tell you what you can do. You can jolly well go and deliver this note at that house next door.'

'Ay,' said the milkman. 'Oi will that.'

'Optimist,' muttered Augustus. 'But wait a moment. Into whose ear did you hiss this disclosure of yours about the telegram?'

'Oi toold,' said the milkman, 'a wumman.'

'Flirt,' said Augustus. 'What woman?'

'Ay, an oold wumman,' said the milkman.

'Broadcaster,' said Augustus. 'What old woman? *Your* old woman?'

'Never, pray God,' said the milkman. 'Missers Twine's cook I toold.'

'Oh, the devil you did,' said Augustus. 'Then you can not only take the note next door but wait for an answer as well.'

'Not a bad show,' admitted Admiral Juddy grudgingly at the gate of 'Dunwiddy'. 'But you won't have a thing to show next year – not a bloom, not a blud – bloom – bud. Blight, my good madam, blight. Syringe your blight, good G – great Scot. Send for me if I'm alive. I'll come and syringe the blight off yer. I know what it is. Had it myself. Killed me this year – stone dead – not a bl – nothing to show at all. My beastly gardener – (n'ze-g'hoo-la, p'tchee-wot) – thought the best way to kill the blight was to cut the – was to cut the tree down. You mind what I say. If you don't syringe that blight off yourself, this time next year you won't have a d – you won't have a daisy. Good day to yer.'

Presently Augustus, waiting anxiously in the hall for sounds of readiness above and of activity from either flank, more philosophical now, calmer, but highly strung and inclined to blow his cheeks out at his watch, caught the sound of Rachmaninoff on the gravel drive, and with a new apprehension slid to the front door. Admiral Juddy stood before him, wiping sweat from his conglomerate eyebrows.

'Day to yer,' said Admiral Juddy. 'You're the tenant here for the holidays, heh? Mrs Twine's brother-in-law, I believe, ha?'

'Yes,' admitted Augustus anxiously. 'What about her?'

'T'isn't her,' said the Admiral. 'It's him.'

'Him? Whom?'

'Twine,' roared the Admiral, boiling suddenly over. 'Twine, by the holy dog. I know he's here. Want him. I'll have him. Juddy's my name. Admiral Juddy. You've heard of me, I dare swear.'

'I'm sorry,' said Augustus. 'My education's been rather neglected and—'

'Well, I don't care a fish's teat whether you have or not. I want Twine. He's here and I want him. I'm sorry to be curt, but to tell the truth I'm a bit annoyed.'

'Really, sir?' said Augustus. 'I'll keep your secret. But Twine, as a matter of fact, is out.'

The Admiral flourished his beard.

'Won't wash,' he said decisively. 'Don't want to be curt and rude but—' his bony knuckles whitened as he strove to hold himself in check – 'stick my liver, that won't wash.'

'Your liver would certainly appear to require some sort of attention,' said Augustus. 'But Twine is not here.'

'He was here just now. You can't deny that. He was traced here, carrying a b – carrying a bag. Where is he? I'll have him. I've been after him all day.'

Augustus hesitated. This irate old gentleman's attentions during the critical hour might be somewhat obstructive. Here, it might seem, was another likely candidate for Taunton. He temporised.

'You appear, if I may say so, to bear some slight grudge against our friend Twine,' he said. 'Would you mind giving me an idea of what you want him for?'

'Well, God's truth, do you think I want to kiss him?' shouted the Admiral.

'No,' replied Augustus, 'I think probably not. But even if you do I'm afraid I can't help you, because I really haven't an idea where he is.'

The Admiral gave vent to his famous and terrific nose noise and scowled past Augustus into the hall. Then, emitting an ear-splitting yell of triumph, he pointed a quivering finger at the table.

'Those shoes! They were in Twine's pocket. I know. Now then!'

'I daresay they were, sir. But really I must expostulate.

The sight of a pair of shoes which Twine very kindly brought here for my domestic use should not I think cause you, if I may say so with great respect, to carry on like the Chief Red Rattlesnake at the sight of fire-water. If you—'

He broke off. Both he and the Admiral swung round in the direction of the elm trees.

'Hell's tongs and trivets!' cried the Admiral. 'What's this?'

'Hi, mister,' cried the agonised voice of the milkman. 'Help! Oi be corrt be the barrb. The dog be after me. Help, sur. The dog be after me and Oi be corrt be me bags on the barrb.'

From the porch the milkman appeared to be suspended by some hidden agency, like a marionette, and his spasmodic but ineffectual movements of the limbs were in keeping with this impression. Occasional glimpses of Conrad could be obtained, as he leapt in and out of the picture from some unseen level.

'Who's that man?' demanded the Admiral.

'That is the milkman,' said Augustus.

'What the devil's he doing here?' asked the Admiral.

'At the moment,' said Augustus, 'he appears to be sitting on some barbed wire.'

Outbursts from the milkman confirmed this statement.

'Hi, sur – the barrb – corrt hi, mister – the dog—'

'Hold on,' cried Augustus. 'I'll come.'

'Ay, Oi'm not a-holdin'; Oi be held,' corrected the milkman.

Admiral Juddy glared after the retreating Augustus, then again turned inquiringly towards the hall. To what amazing environment of impudent young men, impaled milkmen, savage dogs from neighbouring houses, ladies' shoes, had the quarry Twine allowed himself to be lured from duty? To whom, in the name of the seven demons of Ping-hai, had Ham gone and let his house?

The Admiral mounted to the top step and sniffed the atmosphere of the hall searchingly. He was tempted to enter and investigate, but hesitated. Next moment he [illegible] to hesitate. He was borne, venting some horrid imprecation of surprise and annoyance, into the interior by a combined and panic-stricken onrush on the part of Augustus and the milkman. The former made a desperate attempt to slam the front door, but this was frustrated by the foot of Admiral Juddy, causing that gentleman to call down a most undesirable plague, in Chinese, upon his host's sister. The Admiral remained, one-legged, against the hall table. Augustus took to the dining-room; the milkman to the drawing-room. Conrad followed the milkman.

The milkman, cornered, gave a yell of fear and fell heavily against a china cupboard. Almost before the moment of impact two china shepherdesses within shivered into eternity. The extreme panic of the milkman proved, however, to be premature. A more succulent victim was at hand.

On a peaceful and highly ornamental window-seat the cat had been enjoying the long overdue bliss of a sunny nap. Now, awakening to a horror almost incredible, she sprang into a bristling arch of hostility. Conrad, ignoring the milkman, approached the window-seat stealthily, his flanks wagging like those of some uncivilised dancer working up for an unbridled whirl of abandon.

The cat leapt to the curtains, clung swinging an inch from Conrad's first snap; thence to a picture which crashed with her on to Conrad's head; thence to the china cupboard, whither Conrad pursued, immolating shepherdesses as though with a field gun. Her next move was to the mantelpiece, sending a whole line of delicate ornaments tinkling like hail into the grate. Conrad, thoroughly infuriated, sprang indiscriminately upon sofas and chairs, ripping cretonnes, rending and flinging aside inoffending and expensive cushions. The top half of the milkman which still remained in the room from the open window made very half-hearted attempts to restrain him with noises associated with the hunting field and the clipping of fingers. Augustus, boldly returning and standing in the open doorway, merely held his head and cried aloud to a discreet selection of saints.

Gathering courage from these, he seized a stick from the hall and sprang into the fray. The cat, gauging an opportunity to the second, bounded from the mantelpiece through the doorway and across the hall. Conrad had scarcely gained the doorway by the time she was through the curtained aperture of the gents' hat department and he lost her. Nothing dismayed, however, he immediately flew for Admiral Juddy.

For an old man the Admiral made the staircase in capital time. Further, he showed a marked ability for dealing with his assailant during the ascent. Perhaps he had, in his time, warded off the attacks of wild dogs in the deserts of Kwung-Tung. In any case, by mounting backwards and discriminately butting rather than kicking Conrad with the sole of his foot he succeeded in gaining the first floor. During this episode words very regrettable fell in a constant stream from his lips.

The landing gained, Admiral Juddy paused only to give a final foot-stab to Conrad; then bolted into the first room to hand. As he closed the door behind him he heard Conrad fling himself against the woodwork. With a great gulp of exhaustion the Admiral sank into a providential chair and drew forth his handkerchief to mop his head.

For once the ready expletive died upon his lips. Amazement drove the fury from his face as the sunlight swims through the storm-clouds. The girl, peering at him with a startled expression over her left shoulder, shrank from him towards that wing of the bedroom which had been designed as a boudoir. She held her white arms close to her sides and clasped herself very tightly.

Automatically, stammering he knew not what, the Admiral staggered to his feet and to the door. The girl, profiting by this, gained the cover of an armchair, from which only her face, wildly beautiful in affright, remained visible.

With his hands upon the door knob the Admiral again paused. Against the outer panels, Conrad, desperately foiled, hurtled and whistled in seething rage.

The Admiral turned again into the room, incoherently spluttering, vaguely hand-wagging. Again confronted the startled face of the fugitive nymph, cowering in her chair. For one stupendous moment could only stare; then, clutching his beard, fell back once more against the door.

Gods! He knew this girl's face. The face of that girl from down the road. Miss 'No Thank you'. Gods, and here! In this house – this room – at mid-afternoon. And, save for a pair of silk stockings – Gods! Gods!

CHAPTER XV

Abandoned State of a Lady

The spacious approach to Temple Meads Station, Bristol, is situated on the 'Up' side; and, leaving your conveyance here, it is necessary to walk the breadth of the station over a bridge if your business is on the 'Down' platform. Gertrude, however, was in no hurry.

By the time the one o'clock train from London steamed in, she was again in good position for observation. And indeed she spotted Clara in her first-class carriage almost at once. The hands of the sisters met on the door handle.

'So you're here,' said Clara. 'Tell me what the matter is quickly. I must go back to Mother. She has been ill again.'

'I cannot possibly tell you in a breath,' said Gertrude. 'I will tell you as we go along in the car.'

'But we're not going in the car. I told you in my telegram. It would jolt Mother and upset her.'

'What telegram?'

'Never mind about that. Do for goodness sake tell me what is up at Chumpton.'

'I tell you I cannot in a sentence and upon a platform. Do be sensible. Bring Mother out and I will help her into the car.'

'Be sensible yourself, Gertrude,' replied Clara sharply, turning as she spoke to catch a glimpse of Mother. 'Mother is not fit to—'

'No, I should just say she wasn't,' said an acrimonious female voice from within the carriage in that feminine speciality the unintentionally audible tone.

'Who is that?' demanded Gertrude.

'Don't take any notice. A rather unpleasant woman and

her husband. She has been making remarks all the way, ever since poor Mother began to feel ill again.'

'Some people,' said Gertrude in a ringing voice, 'have the manners of Lenin.'

'Tell me quickly. What is all this that you've been wiring about and coming to meet me about?'

'It is absurd about Mother and the car,' replied Gertrude. 'My chauffeur drives very carefully. Where is Mother? I will ask her myself.'

'Excuse me,' said a lady with feathers in her hat, bursting suddenly from the interior of the carriage, 'I heard what you said just now.'

'No, no, no. No, I say – no, Clarice,' protested the voice behind her of, presumably, the male Lenin.

'I'm very glad you did,' said Clara. 'Most people would do all they could to help an old lady who is ill in a railway carriage.'

'People who are going to be ill have no right to come into railway carriages. It is very undesirable.'

'No, I say – I say, no, one moment, Clarice, I say—'

'She wasn't actually ill in the carriage,' said Clara. 'If she had been it would have been owing to your refusing to give up the seat nearest the corridor.'

'I paid for my seat just as much as you did, and what's more I got there first, and there I intend to stay until I get to Weston-super-Mare,' said Mrs Lenin.

'No, Clarice, please, I say—'

'Stop that,' said Mrs Lenin. 'I won't be bundled in and out of carriages by people.'

'Now, now. Look here, shall we—?'

'No. We won't. Don't you keep "no-noing" at me—'

The feathers were again wafted into controversy within the carriage, completely obliterating a semi-prone and apparently unconscious figure in the far corner.

'Mother!' cried Gertrude, wedging herself into the corridor entrance.

'Is that you Gerty?'

'Yes, Mother. How are you, dear?'

'Awful,' said Mrs Posset.

'I've got a car, dear, to take you on from here. That will be much nicer.'

'Much,' agreed Mrs Lenin.

'I'm better here,' said Mrs Posset. 'You let me be, there's a good girl. If I tried moving from where I am I think I should give way again. As for driving in a car—'

'I told you so,' said Clara.

'T'ck, t'ck,' said Mrs Lenin.

'Now, now, Clarice,' said Lenin.

Gertrude swung her head from side to side, stamped with annoyance; then turning, vented her rage upon the feathers.

'I didn't know that people with third-class behaviour travelled in first-class carriages,' she spat.

'If you're going to start telling us all the things you don't know I'd better take a season,' was the unhesitating retort.

'Clara,' said Gertrude, 'come out on the platform.'

'All right,' said Clara. 'I've been there once. Why can't you say what you want to and have done with it?'

'Don't leave me for long, dears,' said Mrs Posset. 'I've got rather a queer feeling coming over me again.'

'Then the best thing you can do is to go out on the platform too,' said Mrs Lenin.

'Now then, quick,' said Clara, as they gained the platform. 'What's up?'

'How much longer do we wait here?' shouted Gertrude to a passing official.

'Due away three-fifteen,' called back the official.

'I didn't ask what time we were due away. I asked what – I asked how long more—'

'Oh, come along,' said Clara. 'What – is – up?'

'You don't deserve to hear if you won't make an effort to get Mother out into the car. The only thing I can possibly do now is to go on to Weston in the car. You have a long wait there and I can see you again. Perhaps, by that time, Mother will have been ill again and be feeling better and be able to come in the car. At any rate she'll have to be driven to the house from Ditchlow station, unless she expects to be carried there in a litter or something.'

'But will you tell me—'

'Don't interrupt me. I wish to collect my thoughts. I have never known such an off-putting and unreasonable—'

'Will you kindly come back to the carriage,' said Mrs Lenin. 'The lady shows signs of giving way again.

'Well, if she can't control herself that's not my look-out,' returned Gertrude. 'Wait, Clara, while I think. Will you kindly go away please, you? I am speaking privately to my sister about something.'

'Much more of this,' said Mrs Lenin, 'and I shall ring for the guard.'

'Now, listen,' said Gertrude. 'I shall go over and get into the car and drive to Weston. You will be there before me; but wait in the ladies' – no, wait! I have a better idea.'

'Look here, Gertrude,' said Clara. 'I don't want your ideas and instructions, thank you. What I want is to be told—'

'I am trying to scheme out the very best way I can of telling you and you won't—'

'Taye, lady?' asked a small but enterprising Russian of Gertrude, butting in hopefully with his tray.

'No. Go away this instant.'

'Choc'layee? Cig̓'raeedes? Megzee? Lemnaheede? Bot-lemnaheede, lady?'

'No, you pernicious little brat,' cried Gertrude. 'Go away immediately or I will report you to the station-master.'

With a strange swallowing sound of wrath she swung round again upon Clara.

'Go in to Mother,' she cried. 'I will go and get a ticket and come with you. The car shall meet us at Ditchlow. When I come back I will help you with Mother into a carriage away from these vulgar profiteers of people. Then I can tell you what I have to tell you.'

'I don't care what you do,' said Clara. 'Only if there's any bad news I think you might do what I ask and tell me here and now. Is it anything to do with Gussy?'

'What?'

'It *is* something to do with Gussy. Is he ill?'

'No,' said Gertrude. 'Wait. I will tell you all.'

'Gerty! He's not – dead?'

'Dead! Ha! Dead! No, he's very much alive. Oh, very much. Ha. Dead! No, he is certainly not dead.'

'Well, I think your mother is,' said Mrs Lenin from the carriage door.

'Stay there,' said Gertrude with much self-control, 'I will join you immediately.'

She moved swiftly away up the steps and over the bridge to the far platform. Dodging through an archway she hurried towards the spot where she had left the car, rounded a corner leading to the station approach and was rammed by a commercial traveller.

'Damnation!' said the commercial traveller.

'Why can't you look where you're going?' said Gertrude.

'Because I'm deaf and dumb,' replied the commercial traveller, a noted wag in Clifton commercial circles.

'Kindly get out of the way,' said Gertrude. 'You haven't bought the station, have you?'

'No,' said the commercial traveller, 'but I don't mind making you an offer for it. How much is it?'

Coombes, a stolid West-countryman, affected by the shafts from his mistress's tongue about as severely as Gulliver was affected by the arrows of Lilliput, received his instructions unmoved, and goaded Gertrude not a little by his careful observation of her face, which she knew to be overheated. He was to drive the car to Ditchlow Station. Owing to the long wait at Weston he would be there before the train. Mrs Twine, Mrs Posset and Mrs Longhampton would all be getting out of the train at Ditchlow. Did he understand? Perfectly, and fore-fingered his peak. Gertrude flounced to the booking-office.

At the booking-office, for some preposterous reason, was a queue. Gertrude, desperately rotating her face for a clock, managed to steal two places in the queue by taking advantage of an old lady with an open purse and a schoolgirl with a loose stocking. At the window of the booking-office was a man who had asked for a ticket for some place which necessitated the booking-office clerk going to some inner shrine where tickets for obscure places were hoarded, taking whole minutes to find the required ticket and having to write something on the ticket when he had found it. From the middle distance echoed a minatory blowing of whistles. Gertrude edged her way out of the queue and pattered up the steps to the bridge.

Half-way across the bridge she pulled up, grasping the rail. Too late. It was going. Thc train was going. Moving. Shunting forward merely perhaps. No, definitely, inexorably going – gathering speed. There it went – the last of it – the guard's van – rounding the corner – out of sight. Gone. Lost.

Lost. The train lost. The car gone and lost. Oh, sudden, swamping, black desperation of muddle and quandary upon her, like a blow, descending. Oh, knock-out of circumstance.

A woman hostile to the world caught suddenly by the hand of fate and made to face the world's hostility. On all sides, at every turn, in this which was to have been her cruel, ascendant hour, hostility. Not one giant hostility standing in her path, but a host of little teasing hostilities impeding her progress like mischievous brownies, contributing in turn to this crowning, flattening hostility of the lost train, the gone car.

The hostility of Mrs Posset to be sick. The hostility of that insolent time-wasting, gorge-raising, nose-poking woman in the carriage. The hostility of the commercial traveller, the guard, the magazine boy, the booking-office – of all Bristol Station, of all Bristol, of all England, of all the world. The hostility, only at this moment realised, of the sun and the heat and of the responsive diaphoretic tendencies of the human frame, causing the face to flush and perspire and the underclothing to irritate. Above all, the unexpected, the cool, the infuriating hostility of Clara.

Clara.

We desperately struggle and are beaten. We fight and cling and strain beyond our strength and fail. It is in that bitter moment that the cry of conscience most clearly sounds, most pointedly. As the sweeping melody of the strings breaks in upon the blaring tumult of the brass it comes. Even Gertrude, in the anger almost of tears, heard it as she stood there in her defeat.

What, at heart, had been the motive pricking her, goading her in this day's work? Why had she, in her modest country existence, in her futile, petty environment of the paltry jealousies and halfpenny snobbery of Swallow Road, heard of Clara's engagement with resentment? Why had she, with her shrinking little unpresentable husband, grudged the gay, race-going, club-frequenting young man about town of Clara's choice? Why had she listened to the bride's elated prospect of a dear, happy little busy town with plenty of amusements going on all round when she had the time and inclination for them, of light-hearted trips abroad perhaps, of plenty of jolly friends of course – ah, why had Gertrude listened to all this with no better grace than a sniff? Why, when that train had arrived just now, had she caught sight of Clara looking young and keen and very becoming in her smart hat only to compress her lips and to hurry forward to the carriage door, impelled by a quickening thrill of vengeful spite? Thus conscience upon the strings. Not a very alluring refrain perhaps; just the simple tune of honesty.

In again blared the brass, clangorous, deafening. Motive? Why, the husband had been caught in the act. Out with him! Out with Clara's placid superior pride! Tear it down. Motive indeed! What motive was here but a plain duty?

The sun struck through a pane of coloured glass in the roof of the station. The shaft of light fell upon Gertrude as she stood there upon the station bridge, illuminating her as the limelight from the wings plays down upon a performer on the stage.

A green light. A green light.

CHAPTER XVI

Uttermost Farthing of a Milkman

Immediately outside the bedroom was a frenzied and lashing dog. To leave the bedroom was to court assault of a very painful and undignified nature. There had only recently been a hydrophobia scare. To leave the bedroom might be, literally, madness.

Inside the bedroom was the young woman from down the road practically stark naked. Admiral Juddy had been up against some pretty formidable situations in his time; but this, as he mentally decided, was a toughish thing. He remained, however, inside the bedroom.

'Did you get chased up here by the dog?' asked Rhoda round the chair.

'Of course I did,' replied the Admiral. 'Can't you hear the – can't you hear the dog outside?'

'Yes,' said Rhoda.

'Yes. Well, what the – what d'you expect me to do? I'm not going out of here to be torn by a dog. It's a very fierce dog if a man's got nothing to defend himself with. If I had my service revolver with me, by God, I'd put its light out. But as it is, what d'you expect me to do, heh? I'm not going out of here to be torn by a dog.'

'How did the dog come here?' asked Rhoda.

'How did it come? Why, good night, it came in after the milkman. Chased him into the house – him and the tenant.'

'Who?'

'The tenant. That young feller who's taken the house.'

'Oh.'

'It came from next door. You live there, don't yer? Whose dog is it? Is it your dog?'

'Yes, I expect it came from there. No, I don't live there

any longer. No, it isn't my dog. It's my stepfather's dog.'

'Well, have you got any control over the dog?'

'Yes,' said Rhoda. 'It always obeys me.'

'Then in the name of Heaven go to the door and shoo the dog,' said the Admiral.

'I'm sorry,' said Rhoda. 'But I'm afraid I'm not in a condition to run about the place shooing dogs in front of you and the milkman and the tenant, even in the name of Heaven.'

'Oh lord, that's all right,' said the Admiral more persuasively. 'You need only just run to the door and shoo a bit. You needn't mind me.'

'To tell you the truth, I wasn't bothering very much about your feelings in the matter,' said Rhoda.

'Well, dash my wig, if the dog stays there and you won't go and shoo it, it means I've got to stay here and – well, dash my wig, there we are,' said the Admiral. 'And what the deuce are you doing here anyway?'

'I'm staying here for the moment,' said Rhoda. 'You live in this place, don't you? I know you by sight. I'd explain to you exactly what has happened and how I come to be here and – like I am – I mean undressed, and everything else; only I don't feel like doing it round the back of a chair like this, because it's rather a long story.'

'Oh, that's all right, my girl,' said the Admiral. 'Don't you worry about a little thing like that. You just pop out and put your clothes on. I'll wait for yer.'

'Certainly not,' said Rhoda. 'Besides I can't do that in any case.'

'Why not? Come along now. I've been in places where the women never wear a stitch o' clothing from one year's end to another unless they strike a typhoon. It's nothing to me.'

'Even if I'd do such a thing I haven't any clothes to put on, so I can't,' said Rhoda.

'God Almighty! I seem to have walked into a bagnio,' said the Admiral.

'If you're rude,' said Rhoda. 'I shall come out and let the dog in.'

'All right, all right. Only, here you are in this house, strolling about the place in the middle of the afternoon– er'm er'm – stripped to the wide and without any clothes to put on even if you wanted to. Dash my wig, this is toughish.'

'I came in pyjamas,' said Rhoda.

'Whaat?'

'I came from the other house in pyjamas. Oh! I know. Get my pyjamas from the bed there and throw them over the top of this chair, and then go and sit down and put your face in your hands until I tell you to look; and then I'll come and explain things to you.'

'H'm. I'll get your pyjamas for yer,' said the Admiral. 'As for hiding my face and all that bunkum, poon-chu to that. I'm an old hand at this stuff.'

'Well, sit over there. I think I can manage in this chair. Throw the pyjamas from a long distance, and mind you throw them far enough.'

'They're odd,' cried the Admiral from Mrs Mantle Ham's bed. 'Half blue and half pink, God dash my head.'

'That's all right,' said Rhoda. 'The blue half is the tenant's.'

'What?'

'They're that gentleman's downstairs.'

'Yes, I can see they're somebody's downstairs. But do you mean to say you came along here without your own downstairs?'

'I had to borrow his trousers,' said Rhoda. 'Come along, please. You'll have to hear all about it now, whether you want to or not. That's quite close enough. Now throw.'

In the midst of the battered drawing-room stood Augustus and blew out his cheeks. And he had been placing great reliance in the severely ornate and orderly appearance of this room. Hither it was that he had decided to lead Clara on her arrival; in this calming environment, following the confutation of Gertrude, were the true facts of the curious case to have been disclosed. His unvarnished tale could scarcely fail to ring true in the atmosphere of this elaborate confessional.

And now. Was he to attempt to convince his rather sensitive bride that he had provided a strictly decorous night's shelter to a fugitive damsel, in a room which bore every evidence of prolonged and unlicensed debauchery? On the contrary. It would be advisable to keep Clara clear of the drawing-room. And she would probably ask to be shown it first thing. While Gertrude was still there. Blast this! 'Milkman!'

'Sur?'

'Come in here. All of you.'

'Ay, sur.'

'Help me to clear up this room. Pick up that cushion and try and wangle the cover somehow so that the hole doesn't show. Help me to collect all these darned little things from the grate. You'd better try and open that cupboard and clear out all those smashed women. Where is the dog now?'

'Oi 'ear 'un, sur, somewheres. Oi reckon the cat must 'a run outside.'

'I should think it's more likely inside by this time,' said Augustus. 'The fool's simply been asking to be eaten all day. What happened to the old gentleman? I suppose it's too much to hope that he's been eaten too?'

'Oi reockon 'e be fled likewoise,' said the milkman.

'Well, let 'un boide for the moment,' said Augustus. 'Shut the door. Now, my aunt, look at this sofa-cover thing.'

'Oi thinks as 'ow Oi 'ears the dog oopstair', sur,' said the milkman from the doorway.

'Oh the devil! Never mind. It can't do much harm upstairs. Leave it till we've done what we can with this room. Then you can go out into the drive and entice it down by making noises like the cat.'

For five minutes they worked assiduously. Then Augustus,

standing with his back to the fireplace, surveyed the results of their efforts with a diffident shake of the head.

'I know you've been doing your best,' he told the milkman. 'It's really my fault for not having noticed the condition of your boots before you started. Besides, as I've kept on telling you, you've been too impetuous. I mean, you could surely have hung that picture up without putting your foot through the gilt cane of that chair? However – the best thing you can do now is to leave me to try and polish things up a bit, and you go and discover the whereabouts of the dog, and, if necessary, alter them. Good man.'

The milkman stealthily regained the hall. Yes, the dog was unquestionably on the first floor landing. The milkman deliberated, pulling the lobe of his ear. He had surely by this time done enough to redeem his indiscretion over the matter of the telegram. At this moment, however, Augustus put his head out of the drawing-room.

'Milkman!'

'Sur'

'Here. I forgot. Here's another five bob for you. Thanks very much for all your help. Yes, you're quite right. The dog is upstairs. Get it down, will you, and see that it doesn't come back, and then that will be all.'

The drawing-room door closed again. The milkman pocketed his bribe and stole up to the bend of the staircase. There, placing the first two fingers of his right hand to his mouth and taking a deep breath, he emitted a strange sound not unlike the note of an owl. It sufficed. Within five seconds he was in the drive. So was Conrad.

'You tell me,' said Clive, 'that in this car place there is no car?'

'I do,' said the proprietor. 'That's just why I do. If I didn't I wouldn't. There's two of our cars out on the road, and won't be back till nightfall; and there's that car there, which you might have, only it's got no radiator and at the moment about half its right quantity of piston rods. So there you are.'

'I most decidedly am not, thank you,' said Clive. 'Only it's an astonishing thing to me that when a respected and desirable resident of this place like Mr Twine comes along here and asks for a car you can't think of some means of supplying him.'

'Mr Twine's got a car of his own,' remarked the car proprietor.

'That's just the very reason why you ought to jump at the opportunity of getting him to sit in one of yours,' said Clive.

'Well, I 'aven't got one, and that's that,' said the proprietor. 'How many more times—?'

'Twine,' said Clive, as they withdrew from the garage, 'this is serious.'

'Yes.'

'Unless we are very careful, this is going to defeat all our precautions. It's getting rather critical. We can't allow a little thing like this to go and put the bird-seed in the raspberry and currant.'

'No.'

'Now, think, Twine. Is there any other place within hail where it might be possible for us to hire a car?'

'Er – no.'

'You seem doubtful. Are you doubtful?'

'No. Of course—'

'Of course what?'

'It *marght* be just possible that you could hire a cab.'

Clive halted.

'Now don't go and rouse the old Adam in me, Twine,' he said. 'Do you seriously consider my starting off to drive from here to London, a matter of some two hundred miles, in a local cab with a very nearly naked young girl?'

'No.'

'All right then. Only try and think before you burst into speech, because it only clouds the issues so to speak and makes things more difficult. We must now go back to Rookery Nook. We shall probably have to use Augustus's car after all and leave him to explain as best he can. Come along now. Briskly, Twine. You went like the wind when we were on our way down.'

'I think the dog has gone now,' said Rhoda.

'Never mind about that – go on, go on, my dear,' said Admiral Juddy.

For the second time within twenty-four hours Rhoda found herself confronting a strange gentleman and rehearsing the curious details of her domestic unhappiness, while clad only in pyjamas. On the first occasion it had been in her own interests. Now it was necessary for her to allay any misgivings that might arise concerning the character of her splendid protector and ally Augustus. Modesty became a secondary consideration. The Admiral must learn the truth, ere he dashed hot-headed back to Swallow Road with some staggering perversion of last night's events at Rookery Nook.

The Admiral reclined upon the bed. His hands were tightly clenched and his bright blue eyes gazed piercingly at the beautiful vision before him. Rhoda was seated in a chair in the centre of the room. The rays of the sun beating through the windows warmed and irradiated the limbs faintly outlined in their embrace. It is improbable that the Admiral took in all she said, but he heard enough. Enough to convince him of the unaffected sincerity of this adorable creature. Enough to stir within his weather-beaten bosom a stinging, rejuvenating impulse of active vengeance upon this unspeakable Boche, swaggering in unopposed brutality in their very midst. What the hell the authorities thought they were doing – oh, well, never mind about that now. Go on, child, go on. By all the sacred grandfathers of the Ming dynasty the Admiral was going to take a hand in this.

The child went on. Piercingly he watched her, at times his thoughts straying into a little rhapsody of inattentive admiration and delight. Nothing like this had happened to the Admiral since he had accepted the hospitality of a night's lodging in the inner courts of the Mandarin Tan Wat Hi at Ning-po in 1879.

Getting straight; getting straight. Augustus, having armed himself with a dust-pan and brush from the pantry, again, after many minutes, paused to take stock of his handiwork. Getting straighter. Not that the room would do for Clara as it was; not to kick off with at any rate. Better though. He had managed to clean up most of the shepherdesses, and all the beastly little ornaments were back on the mantelpiece. Of course the confounded clock couldn't be made to start again; but he could say that had happened bef—

He swung round sharply towards the open window. The milkman was half-way into the room again.

'Get out of that,' roared Augustus. 'What the devil are you doing? Bringing half the flower beds into the room just as I've managed to—'

'It be after Oi, sur,' cried the milkman. 'It be snopping at Oi where Oi stand. Can't ye hear 'un?'

'Yes, I can,' replied Augustus. 'Don't you come in here though. Work yourself up on to the outer ledge and let it go on snopping till I come. I wish to heaven I'd got a gun.'

Placing the dustpan on the hall table, he ran out through the porch and round the house in the direction of the drawing-room window. The aged milkman was now standing upon the outer sill performing a confined and hazardous one-step, with Conrad in unremitting attendance from the pathway below. Augustus, who had snatched up a stick from the hall, flung this at Conrad. The latter, swerving in the midst of a spring, accordingly pursued Augustus down a garden path. The milkman seized this opportunity to descend from the window-sill and bolt towards the back gate. The observant Conrad abandoned the chase of Augustus and returned to the pursuit of the milkman.

The milkman gained the gate and jumped into his waiting cart with a jerk which rudely disturbed his slumbering pony.

Conrad darted after the milkman through the open gate into Swallow Road. The pony took fright and bolted. Conrad, not to be denied, bounded alongside the milk-cart, alternatively attacking the wheels of the cart and the legs of the pony. This only served to increase the agitation and speed of the pony; while Augustus, arriving in Swallow Road, was delighted to see that the milkman evidently thought he could discourage Conrad by flogging at him with his whip. Augustus knew Conrad better than that.

Here, at least, was an admirable solution to one difficulty. The pony seemed a sturdy one and there was no reason to suppose that either he or Conrad would surrender until the chase had lasted for quite a number of miles. So much, temporarily at any rate, for Conrad.

Augustus watched the milk-cart out of sight. It seemed to be gaining rather than slackening speed. He turned and looked in the opposite direction. No sign of a car, of Clive, of Twine. He returned to the garden of Rookery Nook, closed the gate and wiped his brow. For some moments he remained leaning against the gate, seeking the breath worthily expended in the extradition of Conrad.

Out of sight, round the gravel sweep, Putz halted in the front porch and inquiringly peered into the hall. He entered and again paused, glancing stealthily at the several doors which gave access to the hall. Save for a cat, eyeing him distrustfully round a curtain, the place seemed deserted. Then, from aloft, the sound of distant voices caught his ear. Very deliberately he stole up the first flight of stairs and craned his bullet head to listen. Again he advanced; to a bedroom doorway; again listened; opened the door; entered.

The Admiral, who was by this time prone upon the bed, gave vent to a rather inconsequential Chinese desire to see the mother of whomever the visitor might be smitten with leprosy and struggled into a sitting position. Rhoda sprang up from her chair. Putz took small notice of either. He merely nodded, with an expression of some interest on his face, to the Admiral and said 'So?' To Rhoda he half-turned and said 'You leaf here, no? I do not tink you leaf here.'

With these words he swept the oddments of Gertrude Twine's wardrobe into his arms from an ottoman and again very calmly left the room.

About two hundred yards short of Swallow Post Office there was in the middle of the road a large heap of stones. Down in this part of the world the employees of Urban District Councils display unwonted sagacity. The stones were to be used for patching a side of the road. To dump them on the side of the road destined for excavation would be of course preposterous. To dump them on the opposite side of the road would involve the labour of transferring them from one side of the road to the other. Obviously the one place in which to dump the stones was the middle of the road.

Sitting with his back against the heap of stones and smoking a pipe, was a representative of the Urban District Council. He was safeguarded against intrusion by a red flag which projected from a bank a short distance away, together with a notice board bearing a partially obliterated warning:

CAUTIO

R AD-MEN ERS AT WORK

The afternoon was sultry and the ruminations of the road-mendeı pacific. For a long time he nodded dreamily over his pipe before, with a very gradual manifestation of misgiving, he removed this article from his face and raised his head in the manner of one who thinks he has heard a distant threat of thunder.

He had scarcely gained his feet before the inevitable collision occurred. He saw the runaway milk-cart bearing down upon him and discreetly gave way. He heard the frenzied injunction of the straining charioteer, 'Hi! Stop he, stop he!' but failed to comply. The red flag proved the last straw to the already panic-stricken pony. It shied and swerved. The milk-cart crashed into the heap of stones. The milkman half fell, half leapt into the arms of the road-mender. Conrad, dodging the overturning milk-cart, received a crushing blow from an enormous can discharged from its deck.

This knocked a good deal of the spirit out of Conrad, who withdrew, yelping with pain to a neighbouring meadow. Here for some time he remained, nursing his aching limbs. At length, reviving somewhat, he took the opportunity of destroying and partially devouring a duck.

From no great distance there was still borne to his ears a confused clamour of broad Somersetshire argument and lamentation. Conrad grinned and turned contentedly homewards.

CHAPTER XVII

Passover Work

Augustus, rounding the porch and entering the hall, ran full into Putz. 'Stop him,' he heard the voice of the Admiral shout from the staircase, and he dived for Putz's knees and brought him down. Putz, striking out, caught Augustus a heavy blow on the chest, and was on his feet again and behind the table before Augustus had picked himself up from the doormat. By this time, however, the Admiral was below.

Still resting against an angle of the wall was the croquet mallet. The Admiral snatched it up as automatically as the buccaneer of fiction whips up a handspike. Putz paused only to throw a dust-pan containing shattered china shepherdesses at Augustus and backed heavily into the study. The cat departed quietly inwards from the gentlemen's curtain, absolutely sickened with existence.

Before Putz was through the study door the Admiral had discharged the croquet mallet at him. It missed Putz but splintered a pane of the door. The Admiral, rending the air with Chinese war-cries, shot forward to regain his weapon. Augustus also advanced.

Putz, at bay at the writing-table, clapped his hand to an inkpot and hurled it at the doorway. He caught his sleeve in a curtain and the inkpot flew upwards and hit the bust of the pensive Dan Leno-like gentleman on the top of the bookcase. Leno tottered but retained his equilibrium, though sadly disfigured by ink about the features. The Admiral shortened his grip on the croquet mallet, accidentally rapping Augustus severely over the knuckles, and charged forward from the doorway, triumphantly brandishing. 'Now then! Hands up; you son of a cock-eyed coolie.'

Putz leant back against the writing-table, supporting himself with both hands, straightened his back and shot out a foot. The Admiral dropped his croquet mallet, clutched his stomach and fell back with a gurgle of anguish against the wall. 'Buddha! He's got me in the guts. The dirty – oh-h-h! Go on; tackle the b— oh-h-h! Plumb in the guts, by Buddha!'

Incapacitated thus, the Admiral could only writhe against the wall, from which Saul, in somewhat similar circumstances upon Mount Gilboa, vividly reflected the cut of his stricken jib.

Augustus recovered the mallet, but by this time Putz had availed himself of a cylindrical oaken ruler which he twirled as a sergeant-drummer twirls his baton. 'Look here! Cut all this out,' said Augustus. 'You're smashing the house up.' 'I hope,' responded Putz, and flicked a pen-tray neatly to the floor with the ruler.

Augustus backed watchfully to the doorway. From the wall the Admiral rallied him with broken-winded snatches of reprimand and incitement. Putz continued to twirl his ruler in his right hand, while with his left he prudently relaxed the pressure of his front collar-stud upon his windpipe.

'Come now,' said Augustus, after a few moments, 'this can't go on.'

'Can't go on!' cried the Admiral. 'Hasn't – ough – started yet. You wait till I'm – a'ach—'

'Aller right,' agreed Putz twirling. 'I wait for it. Wait so long as you like it. Recover your belly. I battle with both.'

'How did all this start?' demanded Augustus of the Admiral.

'Oh, Hell's forks, don't stop to ask – ouff – questions now,' replied the Admiral. 'Is this a – owee – debating society, split my eyesight? Go and hit that son of a knock-kneed water-carrier with your – m'mf – croquet mallet, and then I'll tell yer.'

'What the devil are you in my house for?' asked Augustus sternly to Putz.

'Battle,' replied the latter simply.

'By the dog, you shall have it in a minute,' said the Admiral.

'Aller right,' said Putz. 'Do not hasten. I wait for it. Recover absolutely if you please.'

He ceased to twirl the ruler and replaced it on the writing-table. Instantly Augustus decided. It were better to settle with Putz now. This invasion only proved what his line of conduct was likely to be in an hour's time. Augustus raised his mallet and lunged suddenly. Putz side-stepped, caught the mallet with his right hand, tore it from the hands of Augustus and threw it at the Admiral; seized Augustus round the waist, swung him from his feet, threw him after the mallet and left the room.

In the hall he pulled up sharply. Clive, running in from the drive, felt himself caught by the shoulders and spun against the door of the cupboard. Putz, on the doormat, stooped to regain the clothing which still remained scattered in that region; while in this unbalanced attitude was collided into violently by the incoming Harold, fell, intermingled with a devastated conglomeration of Harold, over backwards, and dealt his head a stunning blow against the substantial carved leg of the hall table.

Next moment Augustus was upon his chest. A moment later the bewildered but willing Clive. Their precautions were unnecessary. By the time the Admiral, alternately flourishing the mallet and whetting his fingers, had arrived from the study the three allies were on their feet again, Putz in a sitting attitude holding his head.

'It's all right,' said Augustus. 'He's pretty nearly out. My cousin put him out in the hall here.'

'Not I,' said Clive. 'Twine put him out.'

The Admiral gripped the still utterly dumbfounded hero by the hand.

'Proud to be associated with you in this, Twine,' he said.

'Now then. What about this swine? Is his light out?'

'No,' said Augustus. 'He's only knocked a bit silly.'

'It is over,' murmured Putz. 'I am defeated already. Peace.'

'Peace my elbow!' said the Admiral. 'I've got you now, you dog. You try and move from where you are and I'll—'

'Ah, but he's got to move,' said Augustus politely. 'I want to get rid of him. He can't stay here. As a matter of fact his step-daughter's here too. She can't stay either. There are one or two things you don't quite understand.'

'Stop that,' said the Admiral. 'I understand everything. I've seen the girl.'

'These fellows have just called to take the girl away from here in a car,' said Augustus.

'No, they haven't,' said Clive.

'No, they haven't,' echoed the Admiral. 'Yer needn't worry about that girl. That girl's coming along with me. I'm going to look after that girl. What I want to get at is what the devil are we going to do with this swine on the floor.'

He indicated Putz with his foot, causing the latter to remind him of the rules governing civilised warfare.

It was Clive who finally took charge of the situation.

'Look here, we're wasting precious time,' he said, 'This is all tommy-rot. There must be a certain amount of information which each of us lacks about one another. Now, you—' he pointed to the Admiral – 'I don't think you know about Clara, do you?'

'You mean the girl upstairs?'

'I do *not* mean the girl upstairs. There you are, you see, you don't know about Clara. I, on the other hand, have yet to have the pleasure of knowing who you are or how you happened to breeze in on this affair. The best thing we can do is to go up to the room where the girl is and reorganise ourselves.'

'But Putz?' broke in Augustus waving his arms.

'That's easy,' said Clive. 'Would you oblige me, sir, by handing your croquet mallet to Twine. Twine, you will remain on guard here. If the gentleman who is sitting on the floor attempts to take the smallest liberty, slosh him over the head with the croquet mallet and shout loudly.'

'Oh, but—'

'That'll do, Twine. There's no time to stop and argue. You've already knocked the man out once and that was before you had a croquet mallet.' He turned to the Admiral. 'Shall we go upstairs?'

'Certainly,' said the Admiral. 'Only yer needn't worry your head about who's going to look after that girl up there, because I am.'

The two cousins led the way to the staircase. Admiral Juddy lingered for a moment and with an air of considerable ceremony handed the croquet mallet to Harold.

'Take it,' he said. 'And don't you hesitate to use it. Don't wait till he asks for it. Personally, I should hand him one every few minutes just to keep him quiet.'

'It is aller right,' said Putz. 'I am surrender. On parole. I do not t'row away my honour. We are now no longer in China.'

The Admiral marched towards the stairs; then again turned with a flourish of the eyebrows to Harold.

'And I've got a bone to pick with you, Twine,' he said.

'I know,' replied Harold with a sigh. 'That golf this morning. I'm so s—'

'Golf be damned,' said the Admiral. 'But here you've been all day, knowing what was going on in this house and never sent for me to lend a hand.'

Restored to his normal dignity he withdrew to his conference stump – *stump* – STUMP. Harold, holding the croquet mallet at an apologetically menacing angle, sighed, licked his lips and unenthusiastically mounted guard.

Greatly to his relief Putz ignored him utterly. The prisoner, after rubbing his head slowly for some time, turned over on his side and with a prolonged moan lay at full length on the floor. He made no attempt to move from this attitude even when, after what seemed a very long time, the federation from the bedroom again made its appearance in the hall. Clive led the way.

'Do you know, Twine,' he said, 'what we have decided to do next?'

'Oh, my gracious, no, I do not,' said Harold. 'Anyhow, I think I've done enough, surely? I—'

'You must now,' said Clive, 'get into the front seat of Augustus's car.'

'Oh, but—'

'The seat beside the driver. Augustus will drive. In the rear seat of the car will be Mr Putz. You will continue to carry the croquet mallet and while Augustus drives the car you will kneel up on the front seat and threaten Mr Putz with the croquet mallet. When you have reached a thoroughly outlandish spot about five miles or so away, you will drop Putz, lower the mallet and return with Augustus in the car.'

'Oh, but I say, FitzWatters, this cannot be.'

'It's going to be,' said Augustus. 'And very soon be too.'

'But we shall go down Swallow Road,' cried Harold.

'I don't know what road you'll go down,' said Clive. 'You know the roads about here better than I do. That's another very good reason for your joining the party.'

'That's it,' said the Admiral coming alongside and rubbing his hands gleefully. He stooped and prodded Putz with his toe. 'Come on. Get up, you. You're going to be marooned.'

Harold button-holed his aged neighbour with the specious irresolution of a curate raising a point at a Sunday School meeting.

'But, Admiral Juddy; if I go like that down Swallow Road, I mean, everyone will see and talk and oh, really I think—'

Very suddenly the Admiral's whole countenance became one vast flame of fire.

'Obey orders,' he roared.

'Oh, I beg your pardon,' said Harold and obeyed orders.

The Admiral again hoofed Putz.

'Get up you. None o' that skulking or I'll have your intestines for garters.'

'What you make?' asked Putz dismally. 'Enough already. My head ache very strongly. Peace please.'

The Admiral raised his head and in blank amazement apostrophised the assembly.

'Peace, again! God burst my belt, this beats the band.' He flung a horny forefinger at the drive. 'Take him away and maroon him. Here, you, Twine, take his feet. Don't throw your croquet mallet away, yer poor fool. You, what's yer name – Augustus? – take his head. Get him into the car and get him out away somewhere. Put him in a bog or something. Now, you – the other feller—'

'Admiral,' interrupted Augustus, as he bent to take the resigned and surprisingly tractable Putz by the shoulders, 'you'll remember that this is all a dead secret, won't you? You won't go and repeat anything that's happened?'

'Repeat it?' shouted the Admiral. 'Course I shan't repeat it. P'chu-tai. What d'yer take me for? You won't hear me breathe a word of it.' His voice rose to a hoarse bellow. 'Not a word. Not a whisper—'

'That's all right,' said Augustus. 'Now – hup, Twine.'

Very suddenly and violently Putz began to struggle. 'Ahh! I thought as much,' cried the Admiral. 'Hand me that mallet.' But Putz, who had gained the use of his feet at one kick, stood erect and raised a protesting hand.

'Enough!' he said. 'Now absolutely finish. I now altogether surrender. I take back my daughter.'

For a moment the Admiral could only choke. Fortunately by the time he found tongue he noticed Rhoda upon the staircase and lapsed into Chinese.

Rhoda came down very imposingly in her pyjamas and faced her step-sire.

'I am never coming back to live with you any more,' she said, a trifle pale for the moment in indignation but retaining her composure. 'You can make up your mind to that. I forgive you for your treatment of me. But I don't think you had better remain in this country. When I get to London I shall see the lawyers and claim my property. I shall make you an allowance on condition that you live abroad. Now, will you please go over to Pixiecot and tell Nutts to bring me my clothes?'

Putz watched her dully. His eyes contracted slightly. His head was lowered like a bull's. For a few seconds he worked his mouth without making reply. Then he said,

'Deine mutter—'

'Oh, fight fair,' cried Rhoda passionately, suddenly transformed into a magnificent Amazonian figure of righteous wrath. Then she relapsed into her wonted calm. On every side of her, open-mouthed male witnesses gazed motionless with enraptured awe.

'Well?' said Rhoda. 'Will you go and send Nutts?'

He shook his head. In German he informed her that though he was prepared to admit defeat, this did not indicate the abandonment of his principles.

'I like you for that,' said Rhoda. 'That's the best side of you. But I'm afraid it means you must go for your drive.'

'That's right,' said the Admiral.

'Twine,' said Clive, 'you had better hand me the mallet and let me do this escort job. I know your spirit is willing, but I don't think your flesh is very strong. And they will fool you yet, these Junkers. Now, are we ready?'

'Yes, all ready,' said the Admiral. 'Go on. March him off. Put him in the car. Put him in a bog. Put him in a bunker. Here, Twine – I want you. You've got to stay and guard this house see? And don't you budge from the house for anyone, heh? And if anyone comes before the others come back, put 'em off the scent, hah? That's your job. Pretty soft one too. I'm going to see this other woman, Nutts or whatever they call her. I'll give her nuts.'

Putz's eyes gleamed. For a moment it seemed as though he contemplated a final fling for freedom. Then he swayed, placed his hand to his brow, and suffered himself to be conducted without further protest to the garage. Rhoda watched him go with steady eyes. When he had passed through the porch and out of sight she nodded to her thoughts and quietly went upstairs again.

'Have you known that girl before?' asked the Admiral.

'No,' said Harold.

'Were you by any chance the feller that gave her the name of "Miss No Thank You"?'

'No,' said Harold.'

'Oh, you weren't, heh?' said the Admiral. 'Well, that's a damned lucky thing for you.'

The car drew up outside the front door. Clive, kneeling on the front seat, armed with the mallet, shouted back into the hall.

'Which way, Admiral? Where are the most desolated spots in this part of the map?'

'Well, if yer can't take him out to sea, you'd better turn to the right,' replied the Admiral. 'Then bear to the left. There's a road turning off Swallow Road which runs alongside the golf links on yer starboard. You'll find some pretty good tiger country along there. Take him a bit off the line at the tenth and leave him there. That ought to settle him.'

'Righto, that'll do; we'll fix him,' said Augustus. 'Twine, don't stand there all the day idle. Go and clear up the study.'

Five minutes later Admiral Juddy stumped to the front door of Pixiecot and beat upon it. After a prolonged interval suggestive of furtive espionage the door was opened two inches and an eye appeared. 'Go on; open up!' commanded the Admiral. 'Call that opening a door? What's the matter with yer? Are you a nun or a leper or something?'

The aperture widened a little, and the features of the guardian of Pixiecot, in physiognomy not unlike Dante, were revealed.

'Are you this Nutts?' asked the Admiral.

'What do you want?' returned Nutts in the voice of a bronchial parrot.

'I'll soon tell yer what I want,' said Admiral Juddy. 'Up you go to your young lady's room and pack all she's likely to want in a bag and bring it down to me and look almighty quick about it or, by my living soul, I'll give you to the crows.'

The door-space lessened, but by this time the Admiral had nobly inserted some gout in the opening.

'It's against my orders,' said Nutts.

'Orders, my stars and foo-pwit-la to them,' said the Admiral. 'Up yer go! I'll dashed well come along with you and see you do it.'

The streets of Bristol, heated, hostile, on an afternoon in mid-August sweltering, throbbing. The pavements of the city of Bristol like sheets of candent metal in the flame of the sun. The trams and cars and ruthless, head-splitting, heart-stopping traffic of Bristol, rounding unanticipated corners at speed unlicensed and angle perilous. The racking, unceasing whirr and hubbub of the business of Bristol swelling to the fermenting penultimate hour of the day's work. Hostility here; the most terrible hostility.

The most terrible hostility in the world here. The hostility of the battling, arrogant Mammon of the great community to the unwanted pilgrim irrationally straggling, virulently despairing, despisedly petitioning in its furious midst.

'Taxi! Here! You! Man! I must have a taxi,' said Gertrude.

'Where to?' asked the taxi-driver, doubtfully slackening speed.

'To Chumpton.'

'Where?'

'I tell you to Chumpton.'

'Where's that?'

'About thirty miles I think. Through Weston. As quickly as you can without danger.'

' 'Ere, leave go 'o my door. I 'aven't got the petrol,' said the taxi-driver.

'Well, there is a quicker way if you go over the marshes.'

'Gawd, what d'you take me for? A tank?' asked the taxi-driver and drove on.

'Taxi!' said Gertrude. 'Stop will you!'

'No,' said the second taxi-driver. 'Can't you see I've a fare?'

'Taxi!' said Gertrude.

'Yes'm,' said the third taxi-driver more propitiously.

'I want you to drive me to Chumpton, please.'

'Chumpton!' said the third taxi-driver.

'Chumpton, yes.'

'What, right down there by Bridgwater?

'It isn't nearly as far as Bridgwater.'

'Ho. Well, it's a darn sight too far for me, missus, wherever it is.'

'Nonsense. You *must* take me. You are on hire.'

'Yus, but that's *all* I am,' said the third taxi-driver. 'Your quickest way to get to a place like that will be to buy some-one.'

Gertrude flung herself towards a policeman in the middle of the road. A newsboy on a push-bicycle sang past her ear. Devastating dray-horses plunged about her bosom. She re-turned to the pavements. The taxi-driver had departed. Hos-tility here.

At length she dragged her weary feet more by fortune than design into a public garage. The chauffeur on duty was a thickset man in shirt-sleeves who stood with his hands in his breeches pockets and moodily regarded the streets while addressing her. He was expecting a car back before long – about a quarter of an hour or so most likely – might be twenty minutes – not more than half-an-hour anyhow. Without turning his head he invited Gertrude to sit upon an upturned box if she liked. Gertrude sat on the box. The chauffeur on duty, remaining perfectly stationary, whistled 'Ain't we got fun?' 'The Sheik of Araby', 'Don't scrap the British Navy', and 'Hot Lips'.

'Come on you boys!' cried Admiral Juddy to the returning car, as he stood upon the top step of Rookery Nook and performed excitable semaphore. 'We've done this on them all right. She'll be down in a minute. Here, you! Don't you go and stow that car. We'll take her over to my house in it. Plenty o' time. What have you done with that great stiff?'

'He's somewhere in the marshes half-way to Hong Kong,' replied Clive with satisfaction. 'He gave but little trouble. I had to prod him in the stern to get him out of the car, but apart from that he was comparatively quiescent. Where's Twine?'

'Up on the study bookcase, washing down that figurehead,' said the Admiral.

'Well, collect him,' said Augustus to Clive. 'He'll be better out of the way now. He's about shot his bolt.'

At this Harold, now very materially polluted in appearance by the day's doings and carrying a bucket, was summoned from the study. His appearance in the hall coincided with that of Rhoda, who descended the stairs, radiantly transformed, in normal summer attire.

Little time was wasted. Clive, relieving Rhoda of her bag, hastened with it out into the car. Harold, following, stated his intention of walking and was spoken to very rudely.

'I'll have the car back here for you in plenty of time, old man,' called Clive to Augustus. 'Come along please. All aboard.'

The Admiral barked some retort to this injunction over his shoulder and remained in an attitude of expectant gallantry in the porch. Rhoda came to Augustus and held out her hand.

She found no words, but the yearning gratitude in her eyes was very expressive. Augustus rapturously gazed upon her; then stooping raised her fingers to his lips.

'Oh, poon-chai to that,' growled the Admiral restively. 'This isn't a blinking dancing class.'

A minute later the car swung round the corner of Lighthouse Road; almost immediately afterwards pulled up all standing at a hoarse injunction from the Admiral on the rear seat. Up the front path and into the hall of Swallow Lodge stumped the Admiral and roared like a lion for attendance. A startled housemaid came edging from her retreat.

'Where's yer mistress?'

'Sir, she's out. Playing golf, sir.'

'Oh, so she is. Good job too. I hope she's bunkered. Take this bag. This young lady's coming in here for a bit. Twine, you get home. You, young feller, you take that car back and then go and join Twine. In you come, my dear.'

In she went. Off went Harold. Back went the car to Rookery Nook. Up Swallow Road, scarce two hundred yards behind it, came another car – a closed car. Outside it, the cautiously hooting Coombes. On the top of it, boxes, boxes. Inside it, the eagerly peering Clara, the chin-sunken and eau-de-Cologne-bespattered Mrs Posset.

Glancing behind him at the corner of Lighthouse Road, Clive saw the car. Instinctively was wise to the car. Again at the front gate of Rookery Nook he turned his head. Yes. The other car was rounding the corner.

Up the drive of Rookery Nook he, like an arrow, shot; jerked over his shoulder an admonitory thumb for the benefit of Augustus dumbly agape in the porch, and came to rest with a rip of studded tyres in the garage.

Augustus, foolishly babbling inquiries, came trotting round the angle of the house after him.

'Up socks, old bean!' said Clive, vaulting from the car. 'They're here. Me for the back gate. A near thing but a gay one. The stiff lip with Gert., remember. Tact with Clara. Return your jar and you're twopence in, and tan choo pong to *you.*'

CHAPTER XVIII

A Lady Member Leaves her Seat in the House

In a lovers' meeting the journey ended. Augustus dutifully clasping his young wife held her suddenly to him more closely, with genuine ardour pressed his lips to hers, dwelt on the embrace. Her eyelids, closed in the blissful moment, nestled into his cheek. How sweet she seemed after twenty-four hours absence! His honest heart quite leapt. Dear little Clara, how truly dear to him he had not realised. He hugged her, that she uttered a little squeezed sound of loving surprise. His little wife. How could he have feared that challenge and contention would find a place in the Paradise of this passionate reunion?

'My darling, darling Gussie!' cried she. 'And here you are! And how are you? And is anything the matter? Gertrude has been sending me wild telegrams, and met us at Bristol, looking half distraught, and didn't seem to know whether she was coming back by train or car and finally appears to have missed both. Darling Gussie! Is all well with you?'

'Yes,' said Augustus. 'You sweet little girl! Of course it is, now.'

Clara turned from his embrace to the car; showed signs of buzzing.

'Help Mother out of the car, will you, darling? I think she had better go straight upstairs to bed.'

'Oh,' said Augustus. 'Yes, certainly I'll help her. Hallo, Mother? What's the matter? A bit tired with the journey, I expect.'

'I have been sick,' said Mrs Posset, getting out of the car, 'almost from the moment I left home, and I haven't finished yet.'

'Oh dear, how trying!' said Augustus. 'Fancy! All that time! But why start?'

'How could I help starting?' returned Mrs Posset a trifle testily.

'I mean starting the journey,' explained Augustus gently. 'Let me give you an arm up the steps.'

'Where's the servant?' asked Clara from the hall.

'What? Oh, there isn't one. I mean, she's thrown her hand in. I'll tell you all about that in a minute. We'd better just get Mother—'

'No servant! But is there a room ready for Mother?'

'What? Oh. I don't know. Yes, I suppose so, isn't there?'

'Well, my dear boy, I don't know, till I've had a look round. Anyhow, the room you had last night is all ready, I suppose. We'd better take Mother there to begin with.'

'Oh. Shall I just run up and see that it's all right for her?'

'So long as it's got a bed, that's all I'm particular about just now,' said Mrs Posset.

'You'd better leave it to me,' said Clara. 'I'll manage. But if there is anything seriously wrong, please tell me straight away.'

'There's nothing wrong at all,' replied Augustus. 'I think Gertrude has gone off at half cock about something or other. But we'll go into that directly. Do let me just see whether everything is straight for Mother.'

'No,' said Clara. 'Leave all to me, darling. I'm glad nothing serious is up. What's the matter with Gertrude, I wonder?'

Augustus gave an elaborate shrug and mentally determined that, following this act of Divine intervention at Bristol, he would try and be a little more observant in his religious exercises.

'It looks quite a nice house,' said Clara, pausing half-way to the staircase with Mrs Posset on her arm. 'But it's in rather a funny state, isn't it? What on earth are those things doing lying about in the hall? And that bucket?'

'Ah,' said Augustus, nodding like a china ornament with a

spring neck and beaming a good deal. 'Yes. You see, I was just trying to get the place a bit straight. Owing to having no servant.'

'But those things, lying over there in the corner. What are they. They look to me like underclothes of some sort.'

'Ah. Yes. The woman we took the house from left some of her linen lying about.'

'Did she? But surely not on the hall floor?'

'No, but – they got there. Darling, just see Mother upstairs and then come back, and I'll tell you all that I've had to cope with.'

The first hint of a cloud appeared on Clara's brow.

'I know there's some sort of mystery going on,' she asserted. 'Gertrude wired that I *must* come today. There she was at Bristol Station, all sort of darting about and mysterious and unsettled. You, all bowing about and smiling, as though you were trying to get in front of something and keep me from seeing it – If there's anything wrong, for goodness' sake tell me, and tell me now.'

'Nothing at all is wrong, darling, nothing. I'll—'

'Oh, do please take me to the bedroom,' said Mrs Posset.

'Yes, let *me*,' said Augustus.

'Come upstairs with us and show us which is the room,' said Clara.

'Er – yes, this way,' said Augustus, moving towards the staircase; but Mrs Posset had already gained it, leading, rather than supported by, Clara.

'Is this the room, facing us?' asked Clara, at the head of the stairs.

'Yes. Shall I—?'

'No, darling. I must look after Mother alone. I may have to help her take off some of her things. You wait downstairs and I'll join you.'

She conveyed Mrs Posset into the bedroom. Closed the door of the bedroom with a rather peremptory snap. Augustus descended to the foot of the stairs and blew out his cheeks. If only he could take her into his arms again and in the bountiful influence of that mutual, Elysian reliance recount the irreproachable but distressing details of the day's work! Ah, but already that hard note of perplexity and inquisition had crept into her voice; already that pucker of resentment into her little face – her pretty but just the tiniest bit usual little face so quick to express the emotions of a nature of genuine gold, no doubt, but of gold unpolished.

Appropriate the Posset connection with fruit. Gertrude was all stone; Clara nearly all plum. But bite down too hard into her and you would get a jar all the more severe for its latency. Soft, succulent little golden plum; hard, imperforate little core. Strangely it seemed to Augustus that this might after all have been easier had Gertrude arrived blatant and ridiculous in accusation. As it was, Gertrude, apparently, had gone wildly adrift. It was left to him to tell Clara that he had housed a fugitive young woman and packed her off. That sounded quite innocent in all conscience. But he knew Clara. A cheerful, light-hearted recital of the facts would incur her resentment; worse, her incredulity. And this portion of his task he had discounted as easy and not to be bothered about. In that embrace on the doorstep it had melted into a positive cinch, already as good as performed. Now – that hard note in her voice – that pucker – she was going to be difficult. He felt it – he knew it. She was going to be difficult.

Stroking his hair he went to the front door. From the door-mat he scraped with his foot the clinging relics of broadcast shepherdesses. From behind the scraper he rescued the dust-pan and, running out into the garden, flung it far into a flower-bed.

Wait! Now he knew what he would do. Of course. Now he knew. He would get Clive and Twine over. In a body they would confront Clara with the whole absurd story. On his right hand Clive, lubricating the discursive machinery with the merry quip; on his life Twine, ready, when called upon, to put in his guileless and unimpeachable spoke. Good! Yes. He would temporise prettily with Clara for a while. Then in would burst her two relatives, and they would sit her down on the Chesterfield and surround her and in chorus rehearse the lively score of this comic opera of a day's doings; turning the lowering darkness into the sunshine of happy day, into a lasting smile of contented amusement the hovering frown. Of course. Augustus went down the garden path and opened the back gate.

'Ah!' he cried. 'You! Where are you going?'

'To Mrs Twine's. Mind your own business,' said Mrs Leverett.

Now here was one of the enemy. Why? Let him think. In what way had this woman proved herself to be one of the enemy? He stretched out a hand and detained Mrs Leverett; busily, tapping his brow with his other hand, Pelmanised upon Mrs Leverett. Ah, yes.

'Mr Twine told me that instead of coming here this morning you went to his house and saw Mrs Twine. What did you want to go and do that for?'

The peculiar make of Mrs Leverett forbade her to perform the action of drawing herself up, but she managed to strain her head an inch higher above the Tartan and wagged it from side to side.

'If you must know,' she said, 'I did come to your house this morning. Whom, 'owever, had I but foreknown—'

'Ah!' cried Augustus. 'You came into my house and saw something – or someone – and so you sneaked out again and went and told Mrs Twine? I see.'

'I know my dooty,' said Mrs Leverett. 'Kindly let mer be.'

'Mrs Middlemiss—'

'Me name is Leverett.'

'Mrs Leverett, you do not know your duty. I will let you be, but not kindly. This is asking too much. You came in and no doubt saw a young lady in my house. Instantly you surmised the worst. Not only that, you went and spread it to the public.'

'I did not,' said Mrs Leverett. 'I jest went and told Mrs Twine. I know where my path lies.'

'To tell Mrs Twine is much worse than spreading it to the public. It is like inoculating the public with it unawares. And the whole affair was really the most harmless and simple incident which can be explained as easy as winking.'

'Explain it then,' said Mrs Leverett practically.

'Don't be absurd,' replied Augustus. 'I haven't got the time to stand here and start explaining the whole thing to you now. But the construction you've chosen to put on it will quite possibly land you in an action for defamation of character.'

'Eh?' said Mrs Leverett with a sudden little jelly-like shiver of the Tartan.

'Still,' said Augustus, 'if I can convince you of the error of your ways by any other means, I'll do so. Do you know Admiral Juddy?'

'I do that,' said Mrs Leverett.

'That young lady is at the present moment in Admiral Juddy's house, just as earlier in the day she was in mine.'

'Ah,' said Mrs Leverett. 'But is she in his bed?'

'Do you think that Admiral Juddy is the kind of gentleman who would take into his house a young lady who is capable of any unworthy line of behaviour?'

Mrs Leverett seemed to harbour doubt on this point and made no reply.

'Now, Mrs – for some reason your name always seems to escape me—'

'Me name is Leverett.'

'Mrs Leverett. Now, Mrs Leverett, you are, as you told me yourself last night, a busily employed wife and mother. I remember you gave me an inventory of your encumbrances. I don't want to be hard on you. I daresay you acted as your conscience told you, but it told you wrong. I should like to make friends again. I should like to offer you a pound note just to prove I mean it, but I suppose if I did that, you'd think I was trying to bribe you.'

'Oh,' said Mrs Leverett. 'I'm ready to admit meself in the wrong if in the wrong I was.'

'Good enough,' said Augustus, producing his note case. 'Even great people make mistakes, Mrs Leveller. The greatest are those who find them out and admit them in time to cover their tracks. Now, I'll tell you what I want you to do. I want you, when you get to Mrs Twine's, to see if Mr Twine is at home. If he is there, or another gentleman, a young gentleman who is wearing spats and grins, ask them to come over here to Rookery Nook together and as soon as possible.'

Mrs Leverett duly made her destination. Immediately on her arrival Cook dashed at her with a telegram addressed to her at Frascati. Mrs Leverett opened it with an air of bored aloofness and perused the contents with a now almost contemptuous expression which irritated the absorbed Cook to the borders of assault. Eventually Mrs Leverett threw the telegram on to the kitchen table, stated her intention of taking no further part in these matters and bade Hannah conduct her to Mr Twine. Cook reclaimed the telegram and devoured it.

Leverett Frascati Chumpton Smst

Detained Bristol wait till I return not a word but if the person we have in mind leaves rookery nook try and find out where for Mrs Twine

'Ah!' said Cook. 'I knew I was right. Things *are* blowing up for something.'

When Augustus returned to the hall of Rookery Nook he met, with some apprehension, Clara emerging from the drawing-room with her eyebrows somewhere in her fringe. She said,

'This seems to be an extraordinary sort of house. That bedroom seemed very well-appointed and all that sort of thing, but things seemed all out of place and messed about. The same with this drawing-room.'

'Oh, my dear, that drawing-room!' said Augustus. 'I tell you, it looks a great deal better now than it did a little while ago. I spent part of the afternoon, as a matter of fact, trying to put the place a bit straight. At one time it looked about as tidy as a Russian railway station.'

'But how very strange of these people, the something Hams,' said Clara. 'What is there over here? A study? Look at the door. That blemish looks quite new.'

'Yes, I believe that was done recently by a friend of the Hams, rather a violent old gentleman, an Admiral. Let's go and sit in the garden, shall we, darling?'

'I haven't had any tea yet, have you?'

'No,' said Augustus. 'I could certainly do with some tea. I'll show you the kitchen quarters. I expect you can soon fix up some tea.'

Clara paused again in the hall.

'I really do *not* understand about those pieces of underwear lying about the place,' she said. 'That's a thing I do *not* understand about.'

'I know,' agreed Augustus. 'It is queer, isn't it? Sounds like an account of a murder – "Portions of under-clothing were found lying about the place".'

'Pick them up and let me look at them,' said Clara.

'Clara!' This from Mrs Posset aloft. Clara obediently returned to the foot of the stairs.

'Yes, Mother?'

'Come up, dearie, please. I want you.'

Clara jerked her chin, annoyed. 'Very well, I'll come,' she called out and advanced to Augustus, taking him by the lapels of his coat, looking into his eyes very earnestly. He made as though to embrace her again but she restrained him, and her manner, in any case, forbade a repetition of that first blissful moment of their meeting. You cannot buzz and be Elysian.

'I know something's the matter,' she said. 'I know it instinctively. I should have known it even if Gertrude had never telegraphed and dashed about. Directly I started talking to you I could see that you were standing first on one leg and then on the other and trying to make up your mind whether you'd tell me something. I shall get quite worried if I don't find out what it is. Tell me, now. Quickly. Because I've got to go up to Mother.'

This was, of course, beyond the bounds of possibility. One of the first essentials to a successful statement of the facts was unlimited time. They were facts which required to be stated very gently, in fairness to her no less than in fairness to himself. Clara was so awfully touchy about this kind of thing. No. He decided and replied without hesitation.

'Look here, my darling; there's absolutely nothing that you need worry your head about in the least.'

She released his lapels and turned; then looked at him again quickly. She was twitching her left shoulder as though something were irritating it. He remarked at that moment her likeness to Gertrude.

'Nothing,' she asked, 'that it would make any difference or matter my not knowing?'

'That's it,' said Augustus. 'Nothing at all.'

'In fact, you've nothing at all to tell me?'

'Clara!' from upstairs.

'Nothing,' said Augustus. 'Oh, except Clive's here.'

'Clive? Why?'

'I asked him down for the day.'

'Why?'

'He was going to Bath races. I wired and asked him to come on here instead.'

'Oh? Because you were left here all alone or something?'

'Clara!'

'Yes. Quite so,' said Augustus quickly.

'But where is he now?'

'Clive? Gone out.'

'Where?'

'With Twine.'

'With Harold?'

'Yes, with Harold.'

'How is Harold?'

'Clara!'

'Oh, in the pink. I say, darling, do run and see Mother. Come down again as soon as you can.'

'Then there really is nothing?'

'Nothing in the least,' said Augustus.

She went upstairs. He to the porch. Worse – this was getting worse. Buck up, Clive. Twine, run.

Why hadn't he told her just now, when she gave him the opening? But how could he? He would just have started – 'A girl from next door stayed here last night. She turned up in pyjamas just as I was turning in. So I put her in my bed and—' Then 'Clara!' from upstairs or something, and it would be ten minutes before he could finish his sentence and meanwhile Clara would have been getting all sorts of notions into her head. No, for this job, time was required. Also Clive. And Twine. If Clara hadn't been so *touchy*—

Then he heard Clara's voice calling him from the bedroom. He went upstairs with the sudden gait of one not far from the end of his tether. If he were going to be called upon to spend the evening of this hectic day in helping to minister to Mrs Posset, he was through. A little of his mother-in-law went a long way even when she was in normal health.

On entering the bedroom he found, however, that Mrs Posset was apparently much better. She had removed her hat, coat and shoes and was sitting on the bed, buoyed up by pillows. Her expression was fixed but all-seeing like the expression of a hawk. Her nose was the mother of Gertrude's nose.

'I'm just trying to get things straight,' said Clara. 'You saw where Coombes put all the boxes in the hall. You might bring up Mother's two, will you?'

'I'll try,' said Augustus willingly.

'And Gussy?'

'Yes, dear?'

'I see you've put all your belongings in that little dressing-room next door. That's quite right. But you'd better put these with them.'

She produced from behind her the blue silk pyjama

trousers of Augustus, who accepted them with creditable unconcern.

'Mother found them under the quilt,' continued Clara. 'But there seems to be no sign of the coat that goes with them.'

'Oh, it's probably in the dressing-room,' said Augustus.

'Rather funny that the two portions of your pyjamas should have strayed apart like that! Unless you went to your dressing-room this morning with only the coat on?'

'Really I can't remember,' said Augustus. 'What does it matter, anyhow?'

'I suppose they *were* the pyjama trousers you wore?' put in Mrs Posset from the bed.

'Certainly,' replied Augustus with dignity. 'Why?'

A challenging finger shot from the bed to the towel-horse.

'Then who wore those?' cried Mrs Posset.

Augustus turned his head sharply. 'A woman's,' he heard Clara affirm in measured accents. On the towel-horse dangled in deplorable abandon, with one dissolute and dishevelled end flung over the other, a pair of silk pyjama trousers of a fetching shade of pink.

All the self-control burst from Augustus as the torrent bursts from a broken dam.

'Oh, how grossly careless!' he cried.

CHAPTER XIX

Here's Luck

On his right hand Clive, hands in pockets, lolling in a chair, thinking, apparently, that the drivel he was talking was calculated to appease Clara; whereas anyone but a self-opinionated ass could see that it was positively cementing Clara; grinning – why couldn't the fool stop grinning? Precious little to grin about.

On his left hand Twine, eating a straw hat, and, even when called upon to attest, attesting in a lip-licking, eye-rolling way that did more harm than good.

In the centre he, hand-spreading, gently, kindly explanatory but distressfully finding that every good point he brought forward was countered by a question arising out of that point and incidentally knocking all the stuffing out of that point. On the Chesterfield Clara, tight-lipped, cementing.

Why, when the girl came, hadn't he gone straight over to Gertrude? Why had he taken the directly opposite course of keeping the presence of the girl in the house a secret from Gertrude.

'Well, but Clara dear, you know what Gertrude is. I mean, poor Gertrude, she doesn't always look at things in their most – how shall I put it – blameless light. I mean, she – Twine, you can attest to that. Without saying anything derogatory to Gertrude, you'll admit she is a bit nosey in these sorts of affairs. Isn't she? Come, now.'

Lips. Eyes. 'Oh. I don't think you can *quahte* say that.'

'I should hope not,' said Clara.

Why keep the girl at all? Why admit her? Was there something so very pitiable about her? Well, even if she had fallen out with her step-father and been driven from home, that surely was a reason against, rather than for, this extraordinary procedure? Presumably there was a great attraction in this girl? Oh, no, no. Oh no. Just an ordinary girl. Oh, yes. Quite ordinary.

Then why not continue to let her remain here until Clara arrived? Why all this desperate dispatch for Clive; this fearful anxiety to smuggle her out of the house? What was Clive going to do with her? Take her to London, was he? H'm. Rather hard on Clive, if the girl were so ordinary as all that.

The step-father. What of the step-father? If Augustus had decided to interest himself in the case to all this extent, why hadn't he propitiated the step-father? Why hadn't he got the step-father here to explain his conduct in turning this poor girl away from home? Where was the step-father now? Not available? Why not? Was there, to come to the point, a step-father at all? Well, where was he? Why not go and get him? H'm.

Above all, why, when Clara had first arrived, had Augustus lied and said nothing unusual was up? Why had she been left to discover for herself that there had been a woman in the house, in that room, that bedroom? Oh, he was going to tell her about it later, was he? And when was he going to tell the marines about it?

'Well, if you won't trust me—' said Augustus.

'Why didn't you trust *me*?'

'You haven't heard the details. You've only just heard the bare facts.'

'I discovered the bare facts,' said Clara. 'If you'd been clever enough to have told me the facts I might have been more likely to believe the details.'

Here Harold Twine sighed and, consulting his watch, asked to be allowed to leave. Nobody gainsaid him.

'As far as I can make out,' he said, 'Gertrude ought to be home soon.'

'Please send her over here directly she arrives,' said Clara.

Things were not progressing. Augustus glanced despairingly at Clive, who was, however, occupied in making faces at the departing Harold.

Than the departing Harold no one was in lower spirits. All his energies had been expended in vain. The family row, which he had incurred Heaven knew what to avert, was impending if it hadn't actually started. Moreover the moment was now approaching when he render an account to his wife.

Gertrude had missed her train and had evidently had rather a trying day all round. Had his conduct throughout the day been exemplary he would have had to face a certain amount of sardonic complaint. What would be her estimation of him after a series of enormities so flagrant and extravagant that he found his own memory of them scarcely credible? And what had he to show for them? What, except a family row far more widespread and volcanic than it would ever have been had he never interfered?

Then, at the corner of Lighthouse Road, he pulled up, seized with a sudden, a great inspiration. Yes, at last Lighthouse Road justified its name.

What, in the fact of all perplexities, had impressed him with the absolute innocence of Augustus in this affair? Was Augustus himself so unimpeachable by nature? Alas, no. But who could meet and associate with that girl for two minutes and doubt her incorruption, her incorruptibility? Not even Gertrude herself. Clara certainly not. Should he, on his own responsibility, make this last, desperate fling? It couldn't make matters worse than they were. It couldn't make everybody more furious with him than they respectively had been all day or were going to be all night. At the corner of Lighthouse Road Harold licked his lips very quickly and often for the space of twenty seconds; then turned to the left and hurried to the house of Admiral Juddy.

Clara at length consented to hear the details, but they seemed to satisfy her very little. Furthermore, in the enumeration of the details, Augustus and Clive showed a tendency to fall over each other like dogs over a meal and to snap at each other accordingly. The tale became rapidly more involved, incoherent and anachronistic. The trump-card of Augustus, namely Gertrude's malevolent intrigue with Putz, carried to the point of doing up his trousers for him in the public highway, lost a good deal of its sting owing to the fool Clive chipping in with an inopportune account of the rape of Gertrude's green suitcase. Ultimately Clara rose very stiffly from the Chesterfield, saying that she must prepare for her mother's transfer to Frascati for the night, whither she would, in all probability, herself accompany the matron.

'Dear boy,' said Clive, a minute or two later, 'you are doing no good by kicking Gertrude's lingerie about the floor and vilifying me. There's no need to give way. We've still some perfectly good witnesses to produce. Personally, I should be inclined to rope in the Admiral and let him lie in wait for Gertrude. I bet he'd teach her the error of her ways. At the same time we might be able to collect Putz and Conrad. We could shut Putz up with Clara and Conrad with Mother. That ought to bring the Posset faction to reason.'

'If Clara sees Rhoda,' said Augustus, 'that'll put the last nail in the coffin.'

'That must, of course, be avoided at all costs,' agreed Clive. 'If Rhoda had a permanent squint and one leg shorter than the other we might risk it.'

'Besides,' said Augustus, 'I'm not going to have the poor girl lugged over here again to be bullied and charged with all sorts of shocking improprieties. It would be scandalous treatment. Why, I don't suppose that girl *knows* things. She probably still goes about looking at raspberry bushes with a half-incredulous interest.'

'And in any case,' added Clive, 'however much she got charged it would be you who'd have to do the settling, old thing.'

At this moment Clara, supporting Mrs Posset, reappeared at the bend of the stairs.

'I've been telling Mother some of the extraordinary things that you say have been going on here,' she said, having conducted Mrs Posset to the Chesterfield. 'She says that if it is all as innocent as you make out, why don't you let us see the person, instead of dashing her off to someone else's house just the very moment we arrive. Mother says you'd better go and bring her back here, and then we can see what sort of a person she is.'

'I'm afraid I'm not prepared to accept Mother as the arbitrator in this affair,' replied Augustus softly.

Then burst the tempest – tears in full flood, thunder of wrath, lightning flashes of aspersion. Not a healthy storm, as are some storms, clearing the oppressive air, but a storm of devastation, havoc-spreading. The row, Harold, which you with horror had glimpsed, was on.

For ten minutes it raged; then Clara ran upstairs to the bedroom where she had left her hat. She would get Mother's hat at the same time. They would both go over to Gertrude's at once.

Mrs Posset remained, flickering with lightning on the Chesterfield; spasmodically thinking of fresh things to say and saying them. Augustus, with a great final heave of resignation, went to the study. Clive followed him.

'Go up to her,' he said. 'This is getting serious. Go up to her.'

'What's the good?'

'Go on. If you don't, I will. All this over nothing at all! She can't really think that you've been careless with a girl from next door.'

'The old woman does.'

'The old woman is the mother of all Possets. Go up to Clara.'

'What's the good?' repeated Augustus, but went.

In the bedroom he discovered Clara kneeling against the bed and crying on to it. He went and put his hands on her shoulders which she shook without looking up. He leant over and spoke to her very gently.

'Clara, do you think I could have kissed you like that when you came if I'd done anything wrong?'

She raised a countenance which looked more than usually plebeian in the disfigurement of grief.

'Oh, I daresay you didn't do what you call wrong. But it's all this secrecy and evasion and plotting. Why can't you trust me? That's what hurts me so.'

'Do you think you are proving yourself very trustworthy?' asked Augustus.

She said nothing to that, but began to cry again. He held her more closely in his arms

'Let Mother go over to Gertrude,' he said, 'and you stay here alone with me. We'll soon put this to rights, old lady.'

She sobbed those long, heavy sobs which are the last stage of tears. She made no effort to relax his hold upon her. But after a while she said,

'I should still like to see the girl.'

'Would you?' replied Augustus cheerfully. 'I wouldn't. That's all finished with. Come on, bring Mother's hat downstairs and I'll get Clive to take her over in the car. Only, first of all, give me another kiss, like you gave me when you came in.'

He drew her to her feet, to his bosom. For a moment she seemed to struggle, then slowly yielded. A capricious, April girl. But only very few months married, remember. And a Posset; though easily the best of them.

'No,' she said presently, 'you couldn't love me like that and be false to me. I ought to have known. I've made a fool of myself I suppose. I went and said dreadful things to you.'

'No, you didn't, darling. It doesn't matter if you did.'

'But Clive heard me; and Harold. I feel so ashamed.'

'That's all right,' said Augustus. 'I'll soon see that Clive doesn't get the wrong impression. And Harold is used to it.'

She took Mrs Posset's hat and ran downstairs ahead of him. At the foot of the stairs she abruptly halted.

Mrs Posset was still seated on the Chesterfield. She seemed only half conscious of the fact that Harold, who was bobbing in front of her, with his straw hat clasped to his chest, in a manner suggestive of oriental salutation, was attempting to explain something. Clive stood near the study door with one thumb in his mouth. At the table was Admiral Juddy, grasping a gnarled and ponderous stick and glaring at Mrs Posset, as though he were on the point of inflicting corporal punishment upon her. Framed in the doorway, standing in an unaffected attitude of modest subservience, was the beautiful subject of controversy.

Clive was watching Clara's face. He saw the happy little smile which she was wearing fade into a stare of perplexity and he bit on to his thumb. For many seconds Clara stood thus, staring. Then a great light of amazed joy shone forth from all her features. She leapt forward from the bottom stair. Mrs Posset's hat skimmed from her hand into the beard of the Admiral.

'Rhoda!' she cried. 'Rhoda! Is it you?'

'Clara Posset!'

'Rhoda!'

'Clara!'

'Rhoda'

'Clara!'

'Good gracious!' said Harold Twine. 'I believe they know each other.'

'Know her!' said Clara. 'The dearest schoolfriend I ever had.'

She turned from embracing Rhoda and surveyed the round and utterly bewildered expression of her husband on the staircase.

'So *this* was the girl?' she exclaimed.

'Is that man your husband, you lucky thing?' chimed in Rhoda.

'And you told me she was ordinary,' said Clara.

'That was the only lie we told you, Clara,' said Augustus.

CHAPTER XX

Roost in the Rookery

It was nearly seven o'clock when the inferior hired open car containing Gertrude, chilled to the marrow by the long drive after the heated atmosphere of Bristol, drew up at the gate of Frascati. The extortionate fee demanded by the driver was settled without prolonged argument. In the hall Cook received her belated mistress.

'Where is Mrs Leverett?' were the first words of the determined woman.

'Upstairs in bed, 'm,' said Cook.

'What! Mrs Leverett?'

'Oh, her? I thought you meant Mrs Posset. So much has been afoot that I got a bit mixed,' said Cook. 'Oh, Mrs Leverett, she's gorn 'm. Hours ago.'

'Gone? And Mrs Posset is here? Where is your master?'

'He's at Rookery Nook, I think,' said Cook. 'He come back here with Mrs Long'ampton and Mrs Posset. And they leaves Mrs Posset and they takes some champagne out of the cellar and off they goes again.'

'What! Oh, well, I will see Mrs Posset. I have had no tea. Hannah had better make me a cup of tea.'

'I'll do that, 'm,' said Cook. 'Hannah's gorn to Rookery Nook too.'

'Hannah has?'

'Yes, 'm. Mrs Long'ampton she says as how she wants her services for a little while over there, you not having been able to secure anyone as you 'ad 'oped.'

'Oh indeed?'

'Yes, 'm. From what I could judge I think as how they 'ave some company there unexpected.'

'Company? What are you talking about?'

'Well, p'raps Mrs Posset may know. Meself, apart from knowing that something unusual is in the atmosphere, 'ardly can say what it is that is occurring.'

Ten minutes later Gertrude again set forth from Frascati. They had not done with her yet. Did Clara blindly accept the odd coincidence of this girl having been a schoolfriend of hers as proof of her innocence? Naturally the girl had been to some school or other. The fact that she happened to have been to Clara's school and had, at that time, been above suspicion, surely did not render her so indefinitely and for all time? According to that theory no educated female could be suspected of incontinence, which, in the present state of society, was as about as ridiculous a notion as could possibly be devised. Perhaps when Clara got to know that this dear friend of her girlhood had actually spent the night in her husband's bed, she might begin to sit up and take notice.

There were no signs of the alleged 'company' at Rookery Nook. The car was evidently out, for the front gate stood open. The front door, on the other hand, was closed. No sounds of conviviality were heard from within. Gertrude rang sharply and waited on the top step.

Much to her distaste the door was immediately opened by Augustus.

'No bottles thank you,' he said. 'Oh, it's you, Gertrude. I beg pardon. Back from Damside Parva? Please come in.'

'Where is Clara?' asked Gertrude icily.

'Clara is upstairs unpacking. Rhoda is with her, the girl from next door, a friend of hers – such a nice girl. Clive, who is here you know, has gone out in the car to buy provisions. So has Harold. Let me see, who else is there? Mrs Latherer has retired from the diplomatic service and has gone home to lather her young. Putz has gone to Weston to buy a pair of braces, and Conrad has been run over by a milk-cart which was shattered in the process and has just cost me an enormous sum in compensation, but which I cheerfully stumped up as I understand that it has left Conrad with a chronic pain beneath the coomerboond. I say, do come in, Gertrude.'

'I will go away until I can see Clara alone. I did not come over here to be insulted.'

'Come in,' said Augustus sternly. 'You've been the cause of all this trouble. Come in here. You and I are going to have it out.'

'I tell you I wish to see Clara.'

'You shall see Clara when I've finished. But believe me, if you don't come in and sit down and be told what I've got to tell you, I shan't allow you to see Clara at all. If, on the other hand, you go away now, you'll stay away. So you can choose for yourself.'

Gertrude, very erect, entered the hall with an air intended to convey that she was doing so entirely on her own initiative.

'In here, please,' said Augustus, opening the door of the drawing-room.

Gertrude raised her voice and called shrilly up the staircase, 'Clara!'

'Clara will do exactly what I tell her,' said Augustus. 'In here, please.'

He entered the drawing-room behind her and closed the door.

'Now,' he said, 'listen to this, Gertrude.'

Gertrude raised her shoulders and turned to the window.

'When this girl was driven from home,' continued Augustus, 'and was forced to come and stay here last night – in my bed, which I naturally offered her, though it meant my having to sleep in all my clothes in the hall – my one idea was to prevent your getting to know. The way you've carried on today has proved my wisdom. You happen to find out and your first thought was to make mischief. If I could have trusted you I should simply have handed her over to you to look after, and before you'd talked to her for two minutes you'd have found out the kind of girl she was. Instead of that you lied to me and actually plotted with that German brute to try and get me involved. You nearly succeeded, because I lost my nerve and sent for Clive and did my best to compromise myself by getting rid of the girl before Clara came, knowing as I did that you had gone to meet Clara and tell her the tale. Fortunately someone who is a great deal wiser than either of us intervened and guided my steps to the path of wisdom.'

'You can at least abstain from profanity,' cried Gertrude.

'I didn't mean God,' said Augustus. 'I meant Harold.'

'Harold!'

'Yes, Gertrude, Harold. I daresay you know that Harold played golf with Admiral Juddy this morning. Well, after he'd – er – finished with that he came round to see me. He brought Admiral Juddy with him, or rather, the Admiral came soon after. I confided in Harold what had happened. He met the girl and saw, as any decent-minded man would, that she was a perfectly straight and nice girl. I was trying to get her away all this time, and Clive too; but Harold, with great diplomacy, put difficulties in the way of our doing so. Then this blighter Putz had the nerve to walk in here and create a disturbance. We tried to put him out, but he's a strong devil and he showed fight. He struck poor old Juddy and put him out; he picked me up and flung me across a room and he threw Clive the whole length of the hall. Well, of course, this was too much for Harold to stand and look on at, so he went for Putz and knocked him clean head over heels. That settled Putz. I don't think he expected to run up against a man like Harold. Then, just to let Clara and your mother arrive here without a lot of fuss and misunderstanding, we had the girl taken over to the Admiral's house, and when they were settled in here and we could explain, Harold and the Admiral brought her back. Clara immediately recognised the greatest friend she had had at school and all was well. Only just consider, Gertrude. Consider the trouble you might have caused by misjudging me and thinking me a bad man; when I am, with perhaps one exception, as good a husband as you'll find anywhere from here to John o' Groats. There you went, plotting and sending wires and dashing off to Bristol, and inciting Putz to come and perpetrate his hate in this house – yes, you did; I heard you doing it. You have proved yourself a very spiteful and disloyal sister-in-law, and, in my opinion, a very unworthy wife to a man whom I shall always remember for what he has done in a day of great tribulation. Thank goodness he was ignorant of the fact that he was working in opposition to you, or I daresay his extreme sense of duty would have made him quit. Possibly long association and his own modesty have blinded you to the qualities of Harold. Or perhaps you may be looking for the same qualities in your sister's husband as you find in your own. If so, it's no good looking for them because I haven't got them. But I can assure you that Clara's happiness is quite safe with me without any outside management. That will be all for the present. Now you can go and see Clara.'

Gertrude had not endured this homily without restlessness. Indeed she had been making an extensive tour of the drawing-room, pursued by Augustus, during its delivery. The conclusion found her in an advantageous position near the door. Of this she made haste to avail herself.

A few minutes later Clara rejoined her rather exhausted husband in the hall.

'It's all right,' she said. 'Gertrude won't give any more trouble. In fact she'll apologise to you, if you'll let her.'

'No, that's all right,' said Augustus. 'Only, Clara, I do hope she won't take it out of that – out of Harold.'

'Harold! Why, Gertrude's been trying to get me to promise that Harold shall never be told what she's been up to.'

'Oh, what a chance in a lifetime for Harold!' said Augustus. 'But I don't suppose he'll take it. Where's Gertrude now?'

'Upstairs in the bedroom, talking to Rhoda,' said Clara.

Later in the evening Mrs Posset, who was now able to take a little nourishment, took it in company with her elder daughter. Her son-in-law was dining out.

Her son-in-law had, as a matter of fact, finished dining out by this time and was seated in the hall of Rookery Nook, a trifle more flushed and excited than usual, listening, with Clive, to some of the more fantastic reminiscences of the career of Admiral Juddy in the China Seas. Augustus and Clara had disappeared into the garden with Rhoda. Harold, presently emerging from the hall, discovered the young couple alone in a summer house.

'Oh, I say,' he stated, 'Admiral Juddy wants to play Bridge.'

'Righto,' replied Augustus. 'There are cards in the study.'

'Yes, but he wants a fourth.'

'He'll have to want,' said Augustus. 'I'm talking to Clara.'

'Oh. But where's Miss Marley?'

'Never you mind,' said Clara. 'Run along, Harold.'

The Admiral had therefore recourse to three-handed Bridge, a game which, as he pointed out, was poor fun, as a player of any distinction could simply sweep the other two off the face of the blasted map. He had swept, with remarkably indifferent success, for three hands when the host and hostess, once more in company with Rhoda, put in a reappearance.

'Listen to me a moment, please,' said Rhoda. 'I've something to tell you.'

'Hah?' ejaculated the Admiral suspiciously.

'Yes, I've just seen my step-father.'

'On purpose?' asked Clive.

'He's in rather a chastened frame of mind.'

'So I should – so I should hope,' said the Admiral.

'I'm going back to him,' said Rhoda.

'Whaat!'

'Yes. On my own terms. You see, if he gives me any further trouble I can simply walk in here to these dear people. I shall be over here most of the time in any case.'

'So shall I,' said the Admiral.

'I'm thinking of staying myself,' said Clive.

'I'm rather fond of my step-father really, you know,' said Rhoda. 'especially now, that I needn't put up with him if I don't want to. Anyhow, he's on a month's probation. And he's coming round here in a minute or two to apologise.'

Even as she spoke the figure of Putz appeared in the doorway. He carried the green suitcase of Gertrude. Placing this article on the floor, he bowed to the company, produced his horn spectacles which he carefully raised into position on his nose, and cleared his throat doubtfully.

'All right,' cried Admiral Juddy. 'Yer needn't say anything. Look here! Do you play Bridge?'

'Absolutely,' replied Putz.

'Then come and cut,' said the Admiral. 'Come on you, young feller, cut. Twine! Now you! Now me! My God, I'm his partner.'

The game had not long been in progress before Augustus, after a brief whispered consultation with Clara, stole quietly out and hurrying down the garden path, made his way across Swallow Road. In twenty minutes time he returned. But not alone. Gertrude was with him.

Harold, seated with his back to the door, turned at the sound of the familiar footfall and instinctively rose from his chair.

'Don't move, dear,' said his wife. 'I will look after myself.'

'Come and sit with me on the sofa,' said Rhoda.

'With pleasure,' replied Gertrude. 'I hope you are winning, Harold.'

'He's not,' said the Admiral. 'At last I've discovered a partner who knows the difference between a bludgeon and a shovel. My call? Three blood-thumpers!'

A tranquil scene. In an armchair Augustus and his Clara, jointly reclining, their hands clasped in a lingering embrace; on the Chesterfield, at Rhoda's side, Gertrude, watching the face of her preoccupied but slightly self-conscious husband with a new interest, almost a new curiosity. A scene tranquil as the night outside, where the August moon now reigned serene over her cloudless kingdom.

So tranquil a scene that from the curtain at the far end of the hall the cat plucked up heart of grace to emerge and to curl in purring conciliation on the knees of Augustus. So tranquil that, when from the darkened doorway came the sound of a tentative pattering, it needed only the reassuring voice of Putz from his Bridge table – 'Aller right! No fear. *Na*-putta. No further biting!' – to set at rest the momentary, dovecot flutter of uneasiness within the hall and to bring Conrad, stretching the cares of the busy day from his shoulders, to sink with his head between his front paws at the feet of Rhoda. Gertrude restored her own feet to the floor, and continued to gaze at Harold. The cat lowered her head and purred herself back into slumber.

From Chumpton Town the church clock once more boomed forth the hour of eleven. Augustus's eyes widened a trifle. To Rhoda too the sound seemed to have its associations. Exactly twenty-four hours before – She turned her head and glanced at Augustus. Smiled her divine smile.

Momentarily, in keeping with his thoughts, his grasp on Clara's hand must have relaxed; for she pressed his fingers and murmured, 'Darling?' So he leant back in his armchair and drew her closer to him, resting her head against his shoulder.

Mrs Posset had been asleep before Gertrude had left her. Hannah, who had long since returned to Frascati, was asleep. Even Cook was nearly asleep. The milkman was asleep. Nutts was asleep. The road-mender was still asleep. Mrs Leverett was asleep.

From the floor in front of Rhoda echoed a long-drawn and blissful sigh of abnegation and composure. Conrad was asleep.

The head which rested on the shoulder of Augustus had become very still. Even Augustus himself had closed his eyes and was breathing rather deeply and steadily.

Dear night! As woman bears to us the gift of love, so you bear in your arms the gift of sleep. True love, untroubled sleep – and what matter the tangled unrealities of our day?

THE END

A CUCKOO IN THE NEST

'The Cuckoo is a bird that lays
other birds' eggs in its own
nest and viva voce.'

Schoolboy's Essay

PART ONE
'Come He Will'

CHAPTER I

Westward Ho!

Peter, after the manner of man at his breakfast table, had allowed half his kedgeree to get cold and was sniggering over a letter. Sophia looked at him sharply. The only letter she had received was from her mother. Sophia's mother was not a humorist.

'I've got a letter from some people I have often heard of but never met,' he explained, noticing her expression. 'Some people called Bunter.'

'Bunter? Do you mean the titled people who sent us an ornamental vase for a wedding present?'

'They are titled. He is Sir Stirling Bunter. They inherited it. As for the ornamental vase, I should say it's extremely likely. It seems to go, doesn't it – Sir Stirling and Lady Bunter, Ornamental Vase? I daresay they inherited that too. I've never set eyes on them, but they were old friends of my people and they've always kept up with me in a sort of way, if you know what I mean.'

'I'm afraid I don't quite,' said Sophia.

'Oh, yes, you do, dear. For instance they always, every year, send me Christmas cards; generally the awfully hearty sort of Christmas cards that people do send to other people that they don't know at all well. You know. The kind that have mottoes like

Here's rattling good luck and roaring good cheer,
With lashings of food and great hogsheads of beer.

And then, when you see the Bunters, you probably find that they are the most melancholy old folk with malignant diseases. I've always noticed that about Christmas cards.'

'But why do they write to you now? It isn't Christmas yet.'

'They don't both write. Fanny Bunter writes.'

'That's Lady Bunter,' commented Sophia for her own satisfaction.

He read the letter aloud. Sophia listened with the studied air of one for whom, even in these days, a title possesses some surreptitious allurement. During the three months of her married life she had often secretly admired and attempted, herself, to assume the genuine nonchalance of Peter in dealing with Bunters.

'My dear Peter,

'It is ridiculous to think that we should not even know each other by sight. My husband and myself had intended to come to your wedding, but then found we couldn't. Still, the occasion served to remind us that the last time we set eyes on you was at your Christening. It makes me quite ashamed to think of, especially when I think that your dear parents would have counted on us to keep in touch with you. But we never come to London from year's end to year's end. It does not suit Stirling, and the last time he ventured there he had what might have been a most serious accident in a handsome cab.

'Handsome – *sic*,' commented Peter.

'Sick?'

'She thinks it was called a hansom-cab because it was good-looking, poor old dear. Never mind. Where are we – "handsome cab", yes':

'At the time of your wedding we resolved to ask you to come and pay us a visit. I remember we did ask you once or twice before, but you have never been able to come. We are asking one or two friends to the house for the shooting and we shall be so pleased if you and your bride will join the party. Can you come on Thursday, the 18th of this month, for a few days? I suppose you shoot. Your dear father was such a good shot I know.

'With kindest regards,

'Yours very sincerely,

'FANNY BUNTER.'

'A very friendly letter,' said Sophia with suppressed gratification. 'Where do these – Bunter people live?'

'At the Knoll, Rushcombe Fitz-Chartres, Somerset. One moment':

'P.S. All our friends tell us that much the best train down is the one that leaves Paddington just about one o'clock. By this you only have to change at Bristol and then at Glastonbury and then you get on to our little local line. By the other train – the one in the morning – the journey is supposed to be rather long and muddling.'

'Well,' said Sophia after a brief pause, 'why laugh?'

'I'm not laughing.'

'You were laughing to yourself over it.'

'Oh, was I? Perhaps I was a little tickled by the near thing in the handsome. I wonder what the dear old soul would think of our little turnout. By the way, dash it, Sophie, we can't drive down there. These blighters say the car won't be in running condition for a month.'

'Who said we wanted to drive down there?'

'If we don't want to,' said Peter, 'so much the better, because we can't. Unless of course we hire a car.'

Sophia stared. Such a suggestion seemed almost unprincipled to one who had been accustomed to hover on kerbstones and fight for standing-room in the Chelsea bus.

'Hire a car to go all that way?' she asked incredulously.

'I don't know. Why not?' replied Peter, watching her with inquiring humility.

Sophia raised her eyebrows and pushed her chair back with a quick impulsive movement of the body.

'Are we going there at all is the first question,' she said.

'Yes,' said Peter.

'You seem very certain that I want to, I must say.'

'I don't at all. I simply meant "yes" about that being the first question.'

'I don't quite understand you. Are you going to eat that kedgeree? We haven't any other engagements that I know of, but should I like it there? Are they smart sort of people? Who will be there, do you suppose? I didn't know you shot. Do you shoot?'

Peter sat up to the table with the rather vacant smile of a man who appreciates the value of a secret grievance.

'I don't want my kedgeree. You would like it, I feel sure,' he began.

'I don't want it.'

'No, I mean the Bunters. I haven't a notion what sort of people are likely to be there. They are not smart at all, but County, don't you know? I shoot.'

Sophia hesitated. Peter's acquaintances were a very mixed assortment. Certain male specimens had put in an appearance at her wedding. Her mother had smelt them out like a witch doctor and had stigmatised them generally in two damning words, 'Fast fishes.' The female of this species of Peter's friends was understood to be more deadly even than the male and quite uninviteable, especially to his wedding. On the other hand, Sophia had discovered that Peter was on intimate terms with a large number of respectable, married personages, some of whom stood so high in the social scale that she found their patronage almost humiliatingly grateful.

With these people Peter enjoyed a magnificent assurance and ease of manner, which was the secret envy of his less confident bride. The vision of this country house party both enticed and embarrassed her. She carefully suppressed these feelings from Peter. And, when she came to think it over, what had she to fear from any country house party? She had a beautiful trousseau. And intelligence. Sir Stirling and Lady Bunter – her mother would be pleased.

'All right,' she said.

'Oh, we are to go then?'

'Certainly. You seem keen and I'm quite willing to go. Next Thursday week. We will go by the afternoon train as Lady Bunter suggests.'

'Changing at Bristol and at Glastonbury to get on to the little local line,' remarked Peter. 'The inferior morning train must be first cousin to a Polar expedition.'

He rose from the breakfast table, submitted to a brief catechism as to his programme for the morning, and went his way.

Two months earlier he had returned to that specially consecrated flat from his honeymoon. He was the picture of happiness, his bright young face was wreathed in smiles, his fair hair waved from his forehead, he was plump and content as any bridegroom of twenty-four with an independence – pecuniary – should be. To nobody but himself did he confess that he had erred in his conception of what marriage to Sophia held for him.

To himself he owned that before his marriage he had regarded Sophia as a sort of superior goddess, whom he could enshrine in the consecrated flat and burn incense to whenever he felt so disposed. Instead he found himself settling down, fairly happily, to be ruled. Peter had never been ruled before. Even during the war he had been in the Air Force.

But, after all, a goddess ought to rule, and Sophia proved herself deserving of incense. True, she demanded all the incense he had at his command. She had taken a very early opportunity of showing him this quite clearly.

He had met a friend, a male friend, one of the male friends who had been at the wedding. They still preyed upon him in the window-seats of clubs and behind the swing-doors of lounges, luring him back to intermittent confidences and hurried, extemporaneous refreshment. Of this friend he had inquired casually who was feeding Bobbie Kensington at the Piccadilly Grill nowadays. The friend had replied by insisting on Peter trotting down to Hammersmith Broadway to pay his respects to that queen of the front row chorus. A harmless episode; but at the consecrated flat tea and tenderness grew cold in company.

Peter returned, shamefaced at his dallying but quite frank as to his movements.

'You are never punctual,' said Sophia.

'I always am as a rule,' said Peter. 'Very punctual. As a matter of fact I am generally ahead of time. I am like the 6.30 edition of the evening papers. I am super-punctual.'

'Where have you been?'

He informed her cheerfully.

'Bobby Kensington? He sounds fast,' said Sophia with disapproval.

'It isn't Bobby, it's Bobbie,' said Peter. 'There's a wealth of difference. Bobbie, in the feminine, you know. As in – well, Tommie and Billie. I even seem to have heard of a Freddie somewhere.'

'You needn't think you are going to do that sort of thing now,' said Sophia.

'My dearest Sophie—'

'I daresay you used to mix with those sort of women before, but now—'

'I never mixed,' remonstrated Peter.

Bobbie, however, was ruled out firmly and finally. Peter bowed to the decision. His worship of Sophia grew but stronger for being enforced. Her unforeseen authority served merely to reinforce the spell of wonder and admiration which had constrained him ever since his first vision of her.

She was like a Beardsley *Salome*, he had said. And indeed she had the narrow eyes and the high cheekbone of that creation, and as nearly the sinuosity as is compatible with human symmetry. His wooing had been brief but incisive. He had carried off his prize in the teeth of unremitting opposition from Sophia's mother.

What this good lady's ambitions for her only child had been she never clearly defined. After receiving Peter Wykeham cordially in the first instance, as any fond mother should receive the suitor who pays his respects in a seven-hundred guinea runabout, Sophia's mother gradually cooled and finally froze completely. Unfortunately, however, for the determined lady, Sophia, who had inherited the determination, continued to favour Peter, and Sophia's father proved himself, as usual, pig-headed and unwilling to assert his authority, such as it was. Finally, after much vexed domestic wrangling, the frozen mother was thawed into an awe-inspiring maternal-bridal costume of dark lilac, and the parties were married early in June at St Peter's, Cranley Gardens.

'First stop Bristol. Take your seats, please,' said the guard, with an air of long-suffering authority, like that of the headmistress of a large kindergarten.

'Take your seat, Peter,' echoed Sophia. 'I wonder why it is that men must always stand on the platform and look, just when their train is going.'

She spoke through the open door of their first-class carriage.

'I stand,' replied Peter, 'because one can't very well sit down in the middle of the platform; and I look to see why the bookstall girl hasn't given me all the papers I paid for.'

'Never mind that now. The train will go without you if you don't take care.'

'I'll take jolly good care it doesn't do that,' said Peter, fumbling with a disordered accumulation of journals. 'But where's my *Life*? Half a moment, Sophia. Just hang on to these, will you? I'm going back for my *Life*.'

'Nonsense. They're shutting the doors. Come into the carriage.'

'But my dear, I paid the girl. If she didn't mean me to see

Life she wouldn't have let me give her my ninepence. She didn't look that sort of girl at all.'

He bundled his collection of literature through the carriage doorway, and, turning, retraced his steps in the direction of the bookstall. Sophia sat back in her corner, with an impatient tilt of the chin.

Without the least indication of hurry or ostentation, but with that smooth, gliding motion which characterises the departure of a Great Western express, the mighty train moved almost imperceptibly forward. Even Sophia, who was on the qui vive, remained for the moment incredulous. Then she struggled to her feet with a cry of dismay, upsetting the literature in a morass on the floor of the carriage. The door was slammed upon her by a porter who might have been recruited from an institute for deaf mutes.

Sophia leant gesticulating wildly through the window. A stout Hebrew on the platform raised his hat and waved encouragingly back. In the distance Sophia caught a fleeting glimpse of Peter. He had turned from the bookstall and, standing with his back to the train, was engrossed in conversation with a lady, or woman; a lady, or woman, who left in Sophia's mind an impressionist vision of ample proportions, blonde hair and expensive furs.

The train gathered speed—

'By Jove, Margaret! Haven't seen you for years and years.'

'I hope it doesn't look years and years, Peter. What are you doing here?'

'Just come back to have a look at *Life*,' said Peter, displaying the periodical.

'Still? I should have thought you would have given up doing that now. You're a married man now.'

'All right. You're a married woman now, too.'

'Yes, I am.'

'And where's your husband, Margaret?'

'Oh, he's busy. He's in the House of Commons, you know, and he is very conscientious. Where's your wife?'

'My wife,' said Peter, turning, 'is in that—' He broke off and stared open-mouthed at a disappearing guard's van. 'Oh God!' he murmured faintly. 'My wife,' he explained, turning again to his companion, 'is somewhere between here and Bristol.'

'Bristol? That wasn't the Bristol express, was it?'

'It was.'

'What a bother! I thought – what time was it supposed to start?'

'I'm not quite sure,' replied Peter. 'But it certainly did it.'

'Bother!' repeated the lady. 'I was to have caught that train.'

'I did catch it,' said Peter. 'But I seem to have let it go again.'

CHAPTER II

A Stream and a Tributary

Revolution, whether of the red species advocated on the backstairs of Labour, or of the more refined but scarcely less violent kind noticeable in the drawing-rooms of the West End, is well named. It is not, as most imagine, a pulsatory movement. It is a revolutionary movement, like the movement of a wheel. It *is* the movement of a wheel. It is the movement of the wheel of Time.

For the last thirty years Mr Middling, of the Suburbs, has been sitting in the same railway carriage of his suburban line. His children will not sit in it. The railway carriage will still, no doubt, be in use, but it will be occupied by the children of the present engine-driver. Mr Middling's children will be driving the engine.

And the engine-driver's children will say, 'What a menace these fellows are.' And the guard's nephew will reply from across the carriage, 'They won't be satisfied till they've had a revolution.'

Sophia's father was a dealer in wholesale ironmongery. What with the war and what with his wife and what with one thing and another, the good, plain man found himself in more genteel circumstances at this period than had ever fallen to the lot of any of his ancestors. Then came Peter; and, briefly, the cause of Peter's variance with the wholesale ironmonger's wife was, like all such differences, attributable to the rotating wheel of Circumstance.

With centre Burlington Arcade and radius Burlington Arcade – National Sporting Club, describe a circle. The circle thus described was roughly the social circle of Peter Wykeham before his marriage. His bride's mother had no hesitation in describing it as a very vicious circle indeed;

but that was only when she discovered that Peter was diffident in inviting her inside it.

It is a circle which will be found to include all the best and several of the worst restaurants, the headquarters of all the most reliable bookmakers and every serviceable stage-door.

It also includes Berkeley Square, the Savoy and Piccadilly Hotels, Shipwright's, Thurston's and the Royal Automobile Club.

In order to marry Sophia, Peter had voluntarily enlarged his social circle; but he seems to have conveyed by suggestion to the slowly freezing mother that Sophia was the only member of the family whom he regarded in the matter. Mother very rightly resented the slightest hint of condescension. She considered that the exclusiveness of Peter's circle was due not to its distinction, but to the fact that it was an inner Babylon of prodigality and whoredom, from which every honest Kensingtonian held aloof, except on the conventional tip-and-run excursions in pursuit of shopping, tea and theatres.

If she ever found herself borne on the revolving wheel of Circumstance and landed in Berkeley Square, she was quite prepared to modify her views.

Meanwhile she certainly could not be said to pave the way for Peter's happiness. He disregarded her and she said he was a snob. For Sophia's sake he twisted his countenance into an amiable grin and tried to be hearty. Sophia's mother said he was trying to patronise her. All this time Sophia's father sat stolidly on the fence. On one occasion he accepted an invitation to lunch at Peter's club, whence he returned in so noticeable a state of exhilaration that he would have served his prospective son-in-law's interests far better had he remained and eaten his lunch upon the fence as usual.

At the marriage feast of Peter and Sophia the usual water and wine were in evidence. The water took the form of a narrow stream of semi-proscribed relations and specimens of recently arrived neighbours. Peter's friends were undeniably the wine of the party; and the best wine arrived last in the form of a small company of glorious young patricians who walked from the church and presented themselves at the tail end of the reception queue. The wine was too well-bred to display its opinion of the water, but the mixture was naturally a trifle insipid, though the water strove to augment the shortage of wine by bubbling with imitative effervescence and the conversation of novels.

But the friends of Peter, departing in a body, exchanged horrified confidences as they went their way.

'Poor old Peter!'

'What has he gone and done?'

'What a bunch!'

'Did you remark the old sort of head-squaw with beads? A great aunt of the bride, I understood.'

'Did I not. Where can she possibly have bought her hat?'

'I can only suggest Christie's. And who was Old Bill in the grey summer suiting?'

'Idiot! That was the host. The bride's father.'

'Oh, God!'

'No, not God. That was the bride's mother. I can't conceive a happier description of her.'

'What in all the Ministry of Munitions are these people?'

'Father is something in the hardware line, I am told.'

'Oh, hardware? Well, I should think he must be pretty good at his job if he produced that daughter.'

'Poor old Peter!'

It is necessary to return to the wedding in order to place on record a circumstance which was regarded as nothing more serious than a regrettable inconvenience by anybody, and by some even as a boon. Of the clergy, relatives of the bride, who had been invited to perform the marriage ceremony, one failed to arrive. They waited for him until the arrival of the bride at the church, when the service proceeded without him. It was very annoying because the announcements for the 'Marriage' columns of the morning papers had already been carefully compiled, thus:

On 2nd June, at St. Peter's, Cranley Gardens, by the Rev. Willmott Staines, uncle of the bride, assisted by the Rev. Andrew Cathcart Sloley Sloley-Jones, cousin of the bride, Peter Withington Wykeham, son of the late Hugo Wykeham, to Sophia Clarice Willmott, only child of Mr and Mrs Ferdinand Cox Bone, of Oakley St, Chelsea.

Besides, it was very unbecoming that a girl in Sophia's position should be married by only one clergyman at a time. Her mother was exceedingly vexed about it. But even she had to confess that Uncle Willmott made the most of his opportunity. He addressed the young couple at great length, informing Peter severely that he was the fortunate recipient of a priceless gift. Peter, when he understood that this referred to Sophia, resented the allusion. He had discovered that Sophia was priceless and was surely entitled to be considered the best judge in the matter. However, he got a little of his own back an hour later, when he pressed Uncle's hand and said, 'Good-bye. And many thanks for your priceless gift. We wanted ladles.'

But where was the Rev. Andrew Cathcart Sloley Sloley-Jones?

He had duly descended that morning in his provincial Vicarage, clad in his wedding garment, his spectacles sparkling joyously in the morning sun. Nature could afford a gleam of partiality for the spectacles of this enthusiastic, inquisitive, genial, annoying parson. He sounded well-connected, but he was in happier circumstances than that. He was well to do.

His housekeeper, Mrs Pugsley, unlike Nature, did not reflect his cheerful humour. If no man is a hero to his valet, Heaven defend the bachelor parson from his housekeeper.

'The cab has been ordered to call for you at ten,' said Mrs Pugsley.

'The cab? Good. I had thought of cycling to the station, but—'

'Not in those trousers,' said Mrs Pugsley.

'Beg pardon?'

'Bicycling in your best trousers before the wedding?'

'No. P'raps you're right. A cab. Right. Have we any sugar, Mrs Pugsley?'

Mrs Pugsley took about as much notice of this inquiry as the blonde behind the marble counter takes of the inferior waitress when the latter says 'Tea for one.' When she returned to the room five minutes later she brought the sugar with her, but only incidentally and along with other matters. This was Mrs Pugsley's way with sugar.

'Butt has called to see you.'

'Butt? The sanitary inspector? Queer. The man's a heathen. A hard case, Mrs Pugsley. What can he want. Delighted to see him of course, still—'

'He's come about the drains, I think.'

'The drains? Oh, but surely our drains are simply A1?'

'Any 'ow, he's standing looking at the man-hole in the front,' said Mrs Pugsley. ' 'Ere's your sugar.'

'Oh, I say, thanks. The man-hole? Righto. I'll join him in two two's.'

At the conclusion of his meal the vicar duly discovered the nether portions of his visitor protruding on to the garden path. One shoulder supported the tilted lid of the man-hole. Sloley-Jones stooped and cleared his throat. Mr Butt thereupon withdrew his head from the man-hole.

'Morning, Mr Butt. My housekeeper told me I should find you looking at the man-hole. Shall we go inside?'

'I've seen as much as I want,' replied Mr Butt, crawling to his feet. 'I didn't come 'ere to inspect you. That' – he indicated the man-hole – 'was jest by way of 'aving a busman's 'oliday, as they say. You're what they call the church clergyman of this place, aren't you?'

'Certainly. I'm the vicar of the parish church. Rather.'

'Well, if that ain't the same thing it's near enough for me,' said Mr Butt. 'And speaking for myself, and man to man and face to face' – he leant his own face slightly forward as he spoke – 'I don't 'old for religion.'

'I know. I've heard about it. Rotten state to be in, you know, Butt. Disastrous! But perhaps you've been thinking it over and want advice.'

'No,' replied Mr Butt firmly, 'I haven't and don't. But my old mother, Mrs Butt, who lives in my house in Redlands Road, was once given to it.'

'To what?'

'To religious belief.'

'Oh, good! Well?'

'And she's been sick.'

'Been sick? How rotten. What upset her do you think?'

'Been sick for years, she has.'

'Been sick for years? How awfully trying for you all.'

'It don't appear,' said Mr Butt contemplatively, 'that she can go on being sick much longer.'

'No, I should think not, poor soul,' said the vicar.

'And having been once a woman with religious thoughts, and having been sick over a number o' years, her thoughts 'ave returned to religion. Mind you, I think, meself, she's a bit weak in the head, owing to the constant sickness.'

'Well, well. Well?'

'Last night,' continued Mr Butt, dropping his voice mysteriously, 'she called me to her bedside, and I went and bent over her and she said something very low.'

'Really?' said the vicar with greater interest. 'I'm sure she didn't mean it. A trifle delirious perhaps. What did she say?'

'She spoke in a low tone.'

'Oh, I see. Yes?'

'She said she thought she was soon to go home; and she would like to see a church clergyman about the state of her condition.'

'Oh, good! I see what you mean. You want me to come and see her, poor old lady. You bet. Delighted to do anything I can.'

'Yes, now,' said Mr Butt.

'Er – yes,' said Sloley-Jones. 'I'm awfully sorry I can't come this morning, but—'

'Why not?'

'Oh, as a matter of fact I'm just off to London.'

'Ho,' said Mr Butt grimly. 'And where do you suppose my pore old mother is jest off to?'

'I'm sorry. I've got to go to a wedding. A family affair.'

'I thought your church clergyman's job in the parish was to visit the sick and needy?'

'So it is, but—'

'But instead o' coming and 'elping a pore old lady out with it, off you goes, gallivanting off to a wedding.'

'No, no. Come, I say, Butt. That's not fair. Below the belt.'

'When pore old ladies in the town and parish,' said Mr Butt, raising his voice after the manner of sanitary inspectors in argument, 'are sick and dying and suffering from pangs—'

'Below the belt, Butt,' protested Sloley-Jones.

'From pangs of conscience, or what they imagine are such, where's the church clergyman?'

'Come now, reason, reason!' said the vicar.

'Reason, a wedding,' said Mr Butt with great scorn.

His voice was now rising to a shout in a hopeful effort to swamp that of his antagonist.

'I'm sorry,' repeated Sloley-Jones. 'Can't come this morning. Imposs! Any other day.'

'Not that I care. I don't hold with religion. But what I want to know is this.'

Mr Butt's face was crimson and he shook a very dirty finger in the direction of the man-hole.

'When did you last have your drains inspected?' he cried.

'I don't know,' replied the vicar with dignity. 'They don't want inspecting, thank you. They are absolutely tip-top drains.'

'Ho! And are you aware that the local municipal authorities require every householder to be liable to fine or imprisonment if his drains are found out of order and he takes no steps to have them inspected with view to rectification?'

'I tell you—'

'And 'ave you had it done?'

Mr Butt glared at his victim with bloodshot eyes. Then, producing a worn notebook from his pocket, he turned the leaves, licking his thumb at intervals, with accompanying glances of menace at the vicar.

'I fail to see what my drains have to do with the case,' said the latter boldly. 'I know they are perfectly sweet. I should have detected the smallest flaw in my drains. Besides, you say you came here to see me about your mother. If you had been so offensively cautious about your own drains perhaps the poor old lady would not have been so dreadfully sick.'

'I know my dooty,' remarked Mr Butt, making an entry in the notebook.

The vicar shifted uneasily.

'But, Butt. Mrs Butt – your mother – will not – is not expected to pass away today, is she?'

'The longer she's sick the nearer the end,' said Mr Butt proverbially.

'It's awfully inconvenient,' murmured Sloley-Jones. 'My curate is away.'

'She asked for you,' said Mr Butt, looking up from his notebook with the air of one offering his victim a last chance.

'For me in person?'

'Yes,' said Mr Butt. 'She asked for you in person. Her mind has been wandering lately. Fer the last day and a 'alf she has been in a state bordering on absolute como.'

'But she doesn't know me personally?'

'She 'eard you speak once.'

'Oh, come. That's gratifying. When?'

'She 'eard you speak in your church. I think she went inside by reason of being caught in a thunderstorm.'

The vicar did not appear to credit this explanation. He adjusted his spectacles and glanced at his watch.

'R-redlands R-road,' he cogitated. 'I have my motor-bike.'

'Number thirteen,' said Mr Butt. 'And I don't mind reckoning this an inspection, though intended as a busman's 'oliday. I'll send a 'and to overhaul that man-hole o' yours.'

The cab waited outside the vicar's dwelling until such time as the London train was due to leave the local station, when the driver enjoyed a brief altercation with Mrs Pugsley and departed. Ten minutes later the vicar, pushing his motor-cycle and covered with dust, reappeared at his gate.

'I sent the cab away,' said Mrs Pugsley.

'Judicious,' he replied. 'But how rotten! I've missed the wedding.'

'That's the second London wedding you've missed in three weeks owing to bi-cycling about at the critical moment,' remarked Mrs Pugsley severely.

'I know. Though this was far the most important. I was going to do part of the service in this one. The other didn't matter so much. I wasn't invited even. Still, I should have liked to have gone. The bride was a Social Worker. Splendid woman! She married an M.P. too, by Jove. I should have enjoyed meeting him, Liberal as he is. But this is a much worse case, Mrs Pugsley.'

'Then you should not go bi-cycl—'

'Couldn't help it absolutely. I was ministering to the sick. I suppose I'd better go and wire to the people in London. I'd try and get there on my bicycle, but it isn't running well. In fact it isn't running at all. I think I must have got some dirt in my carburettor.'

Thus it was that towards the end of her wedding festivities, Sophia received the following belated telegram, as transcribed in the cryptography of the post office:

To Mr and Mrs Wkkeham oakley st Chelsea

Most awfully sorry cannot participate detained Duty a Thousand regrets apologies business before pleasure but terribly disappointed sorry congratulations and All good wishes future happiness cathcart sloley-Jones.

CHAPTER III

Margaret

'Why are you going to Bristol?' asked Margaret.

'I'm not,' replied Peter. He spoke ruefully. Already during his brief married career he had experienced more than one sharp correction. Not that he resented this. To hear Sophia speak sharply was merely one of the less gratifying of the many varied surprises which marriage to Sophia held for him. But he had never been guilty of a lapse so serious as this confounded affair of the missed train. The situation was pregnant with misunderstanding and reproach.

'My wife is, and I ought to be, on the way to visit some people at a place called Something Fitz-Whatnot in Somerset,' he went on to explain.

'Rushcombe Fitz-Chartres?'

'Good heavens, are you Mrs Bradshaw?' cried Peter in admiration.

'The Bunters?'

'The Bunters.'

'Funny. I'm going there too.'

'How extraordinary and delightful,' said Peter. 'So we're both going to the same place – though we're not exactly plunging there at the present moment, are we? Are you friends of the Bunters then?'

'I used to stay there when I was a girl. They've asked me to bring my husband down there for the shooting.'

'Oh, yes, and to bring yourself for the ratting I gather. I notice you've got your ferret with you in your muff.'

'That is Pansy, my Schipperke pup. I couldn't leave her. Well, what are you going to do now, Peter?'

'Where's your husband?'

'Busy with his politics. I decided to go down ahead of him

because he is always so very uncertain in his movements.'

'Sounds a likely sort of a man to go shooting with,' commented Peter.

'So now I suppose I must travel down tomorrow instead. You will be doing the same thing, I take it?'

Peter did not reply for a few seconds. He was deliberating.

'It's a nuisance,' he said at length. 'You see, my wife doesn't know the Bunters from Adam and Eve – well, I don't myself if it comes to that; but I have a sort of feeling that she will be rather put out at having to spend the first night there alone without me. She never said so to me, but I think it would be a great relief to her if I could get down there this evening. I don't know why exactly, but I have a notion that she rather counts on me. I suppose it is because I have had more experience at this sort of stunt. I've got so used to meeting ladies who might quite easily be Eve that—'

'But you can't get down tonight.'

'I can if I put my mind to it,' said Peter. 'Hold on a moment now. I've got an idea. It's now one o'clock. How far is it to this place by road? I suppose two hundred miles covers it anyhow. My car's laid up, worse luck, but I know where I can hire one. Thirty into two hundred – you haven't got a piece of paper? – all right, *Life* will do. Six isn't it? Roughly six hours. Two – three— Good heavens, Margaret, I can get down there by eight o'clock, and so can you.'

'I'm game,' said Margaret with perfect calm.

'We return forthwith to my flat,' continued Peter exultantly, 'you, I, your luggage and Pansy. We eat. I telephone. The car arrives. We buzz off and get to Fitz-Thing as soon as, if not before the train. Can do?'

'Can do,' said Margaret.

'Good!' said Peter. 'As a matter of fact I was keen on doing the journey by road all along.'

A taxi was speedily summoned and Margaret's extensive luggage placed upon it.

'What will your wife do?' she asked, as Peter took his seat beside her and Pansy inside the vehicle.

'Don't ask me,' he replied. 'I'll tell you after she's done it if I survive.'

'I mean – will she go straight on to the Bunters'?'

'One cannot go straight to the Bunters' apparently, but she will find her way there of course. At least, I hope so. She's got all my gear.'

'She knows that you will follow her down immediately, which will be some consolation to her.'

'Yes, and when she sees me tonight she'll be so bucked that she'll probably let me down quite lightly after all. Oh, she's such a wonderful girl, Margaret.'

'She has to be, I expect,' said Margaret.

A few minutes later they were at Peter's flat, where refreshment was improvised by Sophia's housemaid while Peter succeeded in engaging a car by telephone. The housemaid had seen previous service in the household of Sophia's mother and was consequently influenced by strong anti-Peterite views, which were by no means mollified by his sudden return in company with a strange lady of an appearance which the housemaid decided without hesitation was worldly.

This was not the first occasion upon which Margaret's appearance had been the subject of adverse comment. Such is always the lot of a good-looking woman with expensive furs. It is quite possible that she may be blameless in character. It is a tiny fraction more possible that she is not.

And if a really striking looking woman is blameless she may ignore, but she cannot hope to remain unmolested by, the aspersions of Jealousy. And Jealousy swallows surmises as an Anglo-Indian swallows appetisers.

Margaret should never have been a Londoner. She was one of those large-limbed, healthy, cheerful women who seem more at home following a pack of hounds on a windy moorland than monopolising more than their fair share of the inadequate pavements of Bond Street. She provided a strong contrast to the other maidens there; hence perhaps the fascination which she seemed to exercise over men; hence Jealousy; hence, in due course, a scandal.

It was not a very serious scandal. Something connected with a married artist and a notorious studio-flat. But it sufficed. Margaret, dignified still, but maligned and deeply mortified, shook herself free and plunged into good works at charitable institutions. Margaret should never have been a Londoner. In the country you can be kind to any poor, disreputable Lothario and get away with it.

The men redoubled their attentions. Some of them loved her despite it all. Some of them loved her all the more because of it all. Some of the younger ones had mothers and allowances, but were prepared to go to Australia with her.

Margaret, however, shrouded herself in a veil of reserve and retirement. She seldom obstructed Bond Street now. She was usually to be found at an orphanage at Walthamstow or a crèche at Islington. She saw few of her old friends. And few of her old friends saw her. Jealousy triumphant retired.

Then came the announcement that Margaret was to marry Mr Claude Hackett, M.P. The tidings surprised everybody. An undistinguished Wee Free member for a secluded Eastern County constituency – why, a provincial mayor's daughter might have thought twice about him! Who was he anyway? A young man of the highest ambition and a modest fortune acquired rapidly in the Far East.

'My hat!' said Peter, when he heard. 'Poor old Margaret, who might have chosen the reddest rosebud in the garden, has been driven to settle down on what sounds like a good-looking cauliflower. See what comes of turning into a chrysalis just because somebody calls you a butterfly and you don't like it, my boy.'

The boy addressed murmured some conventionality. He didn't seem as interested in the subject as Peter was.

'Oh, it's all very well for you to say she has made her bed and must lie on it,' proceeded Peter. 'Why should she lie alongside a husband like that? I haven't met him but he sounds extraordinarily dour and I bet you he's as good a Methodist as was ever Prussian to a fallen housemaid.'

'Why doesn't Peter marry the girl himself, if he makes such a song about her?' Thus club gossip backbites. 'Instead of striking out that line of his own in artistic ironmongery?'

Enough. Both Peter and Margaret were duly married in accordance with their own tastes in the matter. Both appeared entirely satisfied and both received at the time telegrams of congratulation from each other, from Lady Bunter and from the Rev. Cathcart Sloley Sloley-Jones.

Margaret's mother, who was a mere incarnated scent-bottle at Bath, had long since ceased to count. That dear old, inconspicuous, reliable friend of a former generation, Lady Bunter of Rushcombe Fitz-Chartres, was of more practical value. She had never for one moment credited the horrid stories that had been circulated. Margaret careless with a married artist? Unthinkable! Lady Bunter had had Margaret down to stay with her at the time when the trouble originated. And, now that she was happily married, she must bring her nice M.P. husband down for the shooting.

The well-appointed limousine from Gamble's garage drew up outside the block of flats. The driver, who was a large man with a red moustache, carefully selected and pressed Peter's bell. This brought the house-parlourmaid, who asked the red man sharply what he wanted.

'Car ordered here for a long trip – name o' Wykeham. That's right, ain't it?' he explained according to his wont.

The housemaid took a frowning survey of the car and stiffened visibly.

'When were you sent for?' she asked.

'Ordered by phone from Gamble's garridge not a matter of a quarter of a hour back. A long trip I was told. Right away somewhere. Will that luggage be for me, miss?'

He indicated the extensive pile of heterogeneous baggage

affected by Margaret, which had been deposited in the hall of the building.

'I don't doubt,' said the maid trenchantly, following his glance.

The driver entered the hall and took stock.

'Would this be a 'oneymoon outfit?' he inquired slyly.

'Certainly not,' said the maid.

'Ah,' proceeded the driver with interest, commencing his operations by placing one box on the top of another, removing it again and selecting the nethermost. 'I generally knows by the look of the outfit. For such as is interested in such studies luggage is full of interest. 'Oneymoon, I thought, 'ere. Not long married, miss, you grant me?'

The housemaid stiffened again and shook her head.

'Though none of your business,' she replied, 'the couple is not a married couple.'

The driver paused in his action of raising the first box, turned his head and whistled.

'Not living in sin?' he suggested faintly.

'How dare you say such things to me?' said the housemaid.

'Don't take it amiss. They aren't the only ones.'

'That'll do from you,' said the housemaid.

She shook indignant shoulders. The driver resumed operations with the box. He jerked it into the required position and remarked:

'I throw no stones.'

'I don't wish to hear from you again,' was the reply. 'You get about your business.'

The driver complied with a final and somewhat vague statement of his willingness to take the rough with the smooth, which he seemed to consider disposed of the matter amicably. Peter, Margaret and Pansy then put in an appearance.

'I don't seem to know you,' said Peter, as the process of loading was completed. 'I thought I knew all the men from Gamble's. What's your name?'

'Dann,' said the driver.

'Dann. And can you shift pretty rapidly if put to it, Dann?'

'Infringement risks yours, sir?'

'Of course.'

Dann stole a furtive glance at Peter and scratched his red moustache.

'And I take it I don't altogether fade from the mem'ry when I've got you there?' he asked.

'I wish Gamble's had sent one of the men who know me,' was Peter's comment.

'Right, sir; that's all right,' said Dann hastily. 'I can take any o' them on any time. I was a Air Force motor-cyclist at one time, I was.'

'Were you though! Well, look here. Hounslow – Bath – stop when you get to Glastonbury, and I'll ask the rest of the way.'

Dann made no verbal assent. He merely expectorated and grasped the gear lever. His red moustache bristled with zeal. Peter smiled faintly and climbed in.

'I shouldn't be surprised if we get down to the Bunters' for tea,' he said.

CHAPTER IV

The Nest

The village of Maiden Blotton was as miniature and as isolated as any to be found on the Somerset countryside, and remains so today. There are a few desultory houses in the neighbourhood, and it was, no doubt, on behalf of the occupants of these houses that the quaint little church with the high pews was originally erected away there in the fields, for even country folks require continual admonition of the soul and ultimately a hallowed acre for the body. But there was not a Vicarage at Maiden Blotton, the admonition referred to being the secondary Sabbath consideration of a hard-riding parson from Downblotton, five miles away. Yet Maiden Blotton ranked as a place, being openly advertised as such to the high road traveller, though, so far as can be ascertained, that inscription on the cracked signpost along the Glastonbury road – 'Maiden Bloton 2¼m.' – constitutes the only written record of her existence in the whole of geography.

Maiden Blotton or Bloton (the phonetics of the sign-writer are unreliable) possessed one redeeming feature. The church, standing in damp estrangement, with the churchyard walls worn and crumbled into gaps through which moody cows were wont to stray in order to scratch their backs on the grateful Bathstone of the monuments; the three or four cottages across the road, painted black for economy and inhabited by rustics connected with the maintenance of the cattle aforesaid, or, less vivaciously, of turnips – these alone would barely have justified the signpost. But fifty yards down the road, linked to the cottages by a prosperous plantation of crab-apple trees, stood an inn – and Maiden Blotton was a place.

It was an inn with a double frontage of bar and parlour respectively, easily distinguishable from without by the degrees of refinement in window inscriptions; the parlour being labelled 'ales', and the bar 'beers'. Of the fact that stabling could also be provided no advertisement was necessary.

At about 7.30 on the evening of the eighteenth of September, the landlady of this inn came through the open doorway into the road to perform the regular evening ritual known to her as 'taking a last look round'. This consisted of stepping into the middle of the road, literally looking round her in all directions and returning again to the inn, the door of which was then closed and further custom neither invited nor esteemed. This practice had originated in the days when the landlady's late husband conducted the affairs of the inn; though his last look round had usually taken the form of a final and opportune breath of fresh air before he went, or was put, to bed. Since his wife's accession the last look merely served to inform any of the gentlemen interested in turnips further up the road that if they intended to patronise the bar that evening they would have to run; and was in this respect a totally futile measure; all the gentlemen in question having invariably found their way to the inn a good half-hour before.

This evening the landlady took her last look round somewhat hurriedly, for there was the chill of approaching autumn in the air and on each side of the road the mists were settling upon an almost unbroken horizon of turnips. There were already lights in the windows of the inn, and the signboard which stretched between those of the first floor, setting forth the announcement 'The Stag and Hunt by A. Spoker. Beers. Beers', was scarcely legible in the waning light.

Mrs Spoker glanced with satisfaction at the lights in the windows as she retraced her steps into the inn. Her bedroom accommodation usually more than sufficed her; claims to that extent upon the hospitality of the *Stag and Hunt* were few. At the moment, for a change, both the bedrooms available for visitors were occupied. The room above the bar was assigned to an old lady who, it seemed, having suddenly become bedridden, had had the misfortune to be at Maiden Blotton when this calamity had occurred and, lacking friends and relatives, promised to remain ridden above the bar till further notice. The room over the parlour was being patronised by Mr and Mrs Love, owners of one of those desultory houses in the neighbourhood, at which house repairs, which apparently amounted practically to demolition, had driven them temporarily to the inn.

Mrs Spoker, who was a long, bony woman with high shoulders and a moustache, indulged a severe self complacency at these unwonted circumstances. This took the form of a voluntary statement, to everyone with whom she came in contact, in these terms – 'I am completely occupied.' This Mrs Spoker regarded as a polite interpretation of the more vulgar 'I am full up,' a phrase which she could not in her mind disconnect with certain deplorable episodes in the curtailed career of that A. Spoker commemorated by the signboard. And, since Mrs Spoker found no occasion to employ this satisfactory report of her condition as a pretext or apology, its frequent reiteration must have been a modest boast which was undoubtedly justified by the exceptional nature of her occupation.

Even so, it was strange to hear Mrs Spoker boast; for she was a woman of the most rigid and inexorable principles. Irreligious thought and worldly motive were to her as the defilement which she shook from her duster, as with averted head and disgusted expression she stood for a few vigorous morning moments in the open window of her parlour. By some paradoxical evolution rancour and intolerance have been established in the vanguard of primitive Christianity. Mrs Spoker, in common with many of the stricter disciples of righteousness, was as inclement in demeanour as she was cadaverous in aspect.

Mrs Spoker closed the inn door and retired into an

artificial room, which had been constructed by partitioning off a corner of the hall. This served as the reception office and possessed the regulation glass shutter through which intending patrons could be inspected, an album for purposes of registration, a keyrack, the landlady's account books and cashbox, a Christmas calendar for the year before last and various other of the recognised conventions of such a chamber. It spoke highly for the cleanliness which was next to godliness in Mrs Spoker that the dust of disuse had never been allowed to settle upon any of these articles; but even her watchfulness had been unable to prevent the frame of the glass shutter from warping in such a manner that it was now impossible to raise it; with the result that, on the rare occasions when an intending visitor appeared, the latter was first treated to a display of dumbshow by Mrs Spoker from within and afterwards forced to enter the office in order to sign the register, which remained heavily chained to its counter.

The shutter, being thus permanently closed, excluded sound from outside. Mrs Spoker remained unaware of footsteps and a conversation in the road before the inn door, and sat surveying her accounts by the light of a candle with that concentration of her thick eyebrows which is characteristic of moral rectitude intent on getting its money's worth.

'Ha!' cried Peter, releasing one of the smaller but by no means the lightest of Margaret's valises and gazing intently upwards to discern the legend between the windows. 'I told you there was bound to be a pub at Maiden Bloton. Here you are – "The Stag and Hunt by A. Spoker. Beers. Beers." Doesn't that warm your heart?'

'It's more than two and a quarter miles,' said Margaret with some ingratitude.

'Never mind, we're here,' said Peter. He indicated the bar window as he spoke. 'Beers, again. This is really most encouraging. Beers! There's something peculiarly alluring in the use of that plural. I feel sure we have found our haven at last, Margaret.'

'Well, what about going into it?' said Margaret.

She opened the door, and Peter, who still carried one bag, again raised the other and followed her into the inn. The hall was illumined only by the light of Mrs Spoker's candle shining through the glass shutter.

'At last!' repeated Peter, dropping Margaret's luggage in the hall with a sigh of relief. 'What a fatigue! Are you dead, Margaret?'

'I am tired rather, I'm afraid.'

'Hungry?'

'Yes. Are you?'

'Am I? If I hadn't felt so confident that there must be a pub at a place with a name like Maiden Bloton I should have devoured Pansy on the way here. Anyhow, all is well now. We'll get some dinner of sorts here and a couple of bedrooms of sorts and some breakfast of sorts, by which time Dann will arrive, and then Bunter ho!'

There was little of Peter's usual exhilaration in this optimism. Even his spirits had dropped beneath the ordeal of carrying two heavy bags for miles along an otherwise deserted road in the twilight of an unreasonably dark September evening. Margaret's gentle complacency had suffered still more perceptibly. To engage voluntarily in a cross-country walk is a very different proposition to being suddenly evicted from a car which develops a violent leak in the radiator in a locality which appears to be first cousin to a prairie, and being forced to tramp dejectedly in search of shelter for the approaching night. Conversation on the road, at first speculatively merry, had gradually hardened in tone. Margaret had more than once expressed her desire to return to the car; Peter had insisted on his visionary inn at Maiden Bloton. And even now beneath the promising sign of the *Stag and Hunt*, with the smell of cooking mingling curiously with the permanent evidence of the stabling, Margaret felt that it required an effort beyond her present capabilities to accord Peter his due. She contented herself with sitting uncomfortably on one of the bags, as the only alternative to standing for a moment longer, and with saying with as much equanimity as she could muster:

'Well, do please let us get the rooms and order the dinner, shall we?'

'Rather,' said Peter. He moved forward and looked through the glass shutter. 'That's right. This is evidently the bureau,' he reported.

'Is there anyone there?'

'Yes, a rather curious looking man in a blouse.'

'Knock him up,' said Margaret, suppressing a yawn.

The surprise in Mrs Spoker's face gave way to a hard smile of pleasure as she scented the possibilities of this stranger. If to be completely occupied was gratifying, the opportunity of turning a solicitous wanderer from her door was an almost undreamt-of luxury. For some moments she and Peter engaged in mutual gesticulation through the glass.

'Pull that shutter thing up and talk to him,' urged Margaret.

'The damn thing's stuck,' said Peter, 'and I can't talk to him for two reasons. In the first place it's not him at all, it's a woman; and in the second place she's deaf and dumb.'

'Then go in and write things,' said Margaret.

Peter was about to comply when Mrs Spoker appeared from the door of the office bearing her candle, by the light of which she inspected her visitors with a hopeful scowl.

'Good evening. We want two—' Margaret began.

'I am completely occupied,' said Mrs Spoker.

'Oh, I'm so sorry; I thought you looked busy,' said Peter. 'But, you see we had to let you know we'd got here, didn't we? We've had a misfortune with our car and we shall have to dine and sleep here tonight.'

'Where are you going to sleep?' asked Mrs Spoker.

'Well, I suppose you know where your bedrooms are better than I do,' said Peter.

'I tell you,' repeated Mrs Spoker. 'I'm completely occupied.'

'Oh, you mean you're full up?' cried Peter, his jaw dropping.

'Completely occupied,' said Mrs Spoker.

Peter met Margaret's eye and winced.

'But can't we get put up anywhere here?' he asked desperately.

Mrs Spoker shook her head and gave vent to a long whistling negative.

'Oh, hell!' whispered Peter to himself, but not too softly to evade the ears of Mrs Spoker, who frowned deeply. 'We can get some dinner here anyhow, I suppose?' he continued.

'Not if you blarspheme,' said Mrs Spoker.

'I'm sorry,' said Peter. 'I didn't mean you to hear it.'

'The Almighty heard it,' said Mrs Spoker.

'How do you know?' said Peter with growing irritation.

Mrs Spoker turned severely to Margaret.

'You should know better than to allow him to blarspheme in my 'otel,' she observed.

'I do,' answered Margaret, who noted the necessity for conciliation. 'I didn't hear him or I would have stopped him.'

Mrs Spoker shook her head.

'The vile word is spoke by that time and soon forgot most like. But the entry is made against him in the book from which there is no rubbing out,' was her pessimistic comment.

'Can we have some dinner?' asked Margaret.

Mrs Spoker drew herself up and gave vent to a prolonged hiss like a doubtful serpent.

'I am not at all sure that you can have any dinner neither,' she temporised. 'We're very strict 'ere. This is my 'otel, and into it I admit only such as meets with my own approval.'

'I'm surprised to hear you're full up,' said Peter.

Both ladies treated him to frowns.

'We're very tired and hungry,' said Margaret in imploring tones, 'and we've still to find a night's shelter.'

'By the way, is there a telephone here?' asked Peter.

'No,' snapped Mrs Spoker.

'Where's the nearest town?'

'Downblotton, five miles on,' said Mrs Spoker.

'Five miles, good Lord!'

'What was that?'

'I said "five miles with a good load." It's a long way. Have you a cab or a cart or anything of the sort?'

'No.'

'Well, is there one to be got in the place?'

'What place?'

'Why, this conf – confraternity – this village.'

'No.'

'My God – h'm – my godmother lives not far away,' said Peter. 'If I could only find some means of communicating with her.'

Mrs Spoker, who saw through this, contented herself with a cold shiver of the shoulders. For some moments nothing further was said. Finally Margaret tried again.

'When can we have some dinner?' she asked.

Mrs Spoker turned and watched her for a few seconds, as though deliberating whether the appearance of the lady visitor compensated for the evident godlessness of her companion to the extent of justifying a meal at the exacting *Stag and Hunt*. At length, raising her rasping voice, Mrs Spoker called:

'Gladys.'

'It's as well for you, madam,' she went on, 'that you take no part in your 'usband's ways: and as well for him also. He would get no dinner from me else. Blarsphemy, I ab'or.'

'Look here, this lady is not—' Peter stopped short, as he noticed Margaret shaking her head with an animated frown in his direction.

'Is not what?' asked Mrs Spoker.

'Is not able to do any more walking tonight. Are you sure you can't put her up?'

Before Mrs Spoker replied the parlour door opened and a miniature domestic appeared. The landlady turned upon her as though she had surprised her in the action of robbing the till.

'Gladys, why 'ave you not lit the 'all lamp? Bring it immediate.'

The foolish virgin thus admonished was about to comply, when she was again accosted.

'And there will be another two dinners when Mr and Mrs Love 'as finished.'

Gladys's only comment was a sigh – a form of expression to which she was justifiably prone, and which, in co-operation with chronic adenoids, was not easily distinguishable from an habitual grunt. As she proceeded to the rear of the hall to obtain the lamp, Mrs Spoker returned to the subject of her rooms with some avidity.

'Both my bedrooms are completely occupied,' she repeated. 'If it were not so, seeing the circumstances, I might offer you one of them.'

'And there is not another pub – lic hotel, or even a cottage, where we could—'

'Cottage?' cried Mrs Spoker. 'In the cottages here they sleeps so unhealthy already that I wouldn't ask a dog to share 'em – not a dog, no, nor yet a cat. Seven and eight in a room – immoral in my way of thinking.'

'You're quite right,' said Peter pacifically. 'It ought to be stopped. I never heard of such an orgy. I shouldn't dream of trying to get a bed there under those circumstances.'

'Nor you wouldn't if you wanted,' said Mrs Spoker.

At this point Gladys reappeared with a large oil lamp, which, by stretching to the very limit of her reach, she managed to balance precariously on a wall bracket in the hall. The effort called for such a rapid and strident succession of grunts that even Pansy, who had hitherto remained asleep in Margaret's muff, commenced to display symptoms of uneasiness. No sooner, however, had Gladys performed her dangerous task and retired again into the parlour, than another individual appeared with a sudden, rather tentative movement from the road.

This was a swarthy young man of local farming type with a red face, a shifty eye, and ex-army breeches. As soon as he noticed Mrs Spoker he made as though to retire into the road, but the landlady was on him in a flash.

'Out with you,' she cried. 'I'll have none of you here, as you should know by this time.'

The young man hesitated in the doorway and turned his shifty eyes inquisitively towards Margaret.

'Aa – aa oonly called in fur to see 'Arry 'Ook who's inside o' thet bar o' yours, Missus Spooker,' he murmured.

'Out with you,' repeated the landlady, making waving motions in his face with her fingers. 'I'll have none of you corrupting of my 'otel nor of Harry 'Ook neither, which is a respectable married man. Out you go.'

The abashed farmer allowed himself a last, lingering glance at Margaret and retreated into the road with a submission which was astonishing in one so robust. Mrs Spoker closed the door after him with a bang and turned in triumph to her visitors.

'There you see,' she cried. 'If I chooses not to 'ave any undesirable person in my 'otel, out they goes.'

'What's the matter with him?' asked Margaret wearily.

'Matter? 'E's a sinner, that's what the matter is with him,' said Mrs Spoker comprehensively. ' 'E goes about with young women.'

The idea that the undesirable patron might have been able to render assistance spurred Peter to ill-advised protest.

'But surely it is not a crime for a man to go about with young women?' he said with the smile of a curate in controversy.

'It is here,' was the brief reply.

'His intentions may be honourable.'

'His aren't,' said Mrs Spoker.

Peter sighed.

'I don't see how they are ever going to get to know each other,' he remarked.

Margaret was frowning again.

Mrs Spoker drew herself up for a crushing rejoinder.

'That man,' she declared emphatically, indicating the inn door with a quivering forefinger, 'the first time as 'e ever came to this 'otel, 'e asks for accommodation, which I, not knowing him, and not being at the time completely occupied, gives 'im. 'E was travelling with a young woman, 'is wife 'e gives it out, just as to all intense and purposes you and your wife has arrived here this evening. But was she 'is wife? No, she was not 'is. She was the wife of another, and there 'e was taking 'er about the country as though they was united into 'oly wedlock according to the sight of God.'

'Perhaps they didn't occupy the same room,' suggested Peter, with a fugitive glance at Margaret.

Mrs Spoker laughed such a suggestion away bitterly.

'It is not a nice subject,' she said. 'Nor was it till a week later that I discovered the truth. And whatever rooms they occupied, do you think I should 'ave took 'em in here, and they travelling the country together, and she with her husband, a commercial up in the Midlands and in ignorance of they so doing?'

'I see,' said Peter. 'So that the fact that they were travelling together—'

'Is enough for me,' said Mrs Spoker. 'Do you think I don't know what such is up to? It is not a nice subject, especially before your wife. But I'm just a-showing you what happens to persons who comes here when I don't consider them desirable.'

Peter turned slowly to Margaret with a thoughtful tilt of his eyebrows. Mrs Spoker followed his movement with a gleam of dawning suspicion on her stern face. From Peter her glance travelled with deadly swiftness to Margaret. The latter was regarding her with a complacent smile of patient innocence.

'Do you think that Mr and Mrs Love will have finished their dinner soon?' she asked.

CHAPTER V

'Sing Cuccu Nu'

Having completed the first course, which was soup, Margaret looked up almost shamefacedly from her plate. All the brightness had returned to her expression. She laid her hand gently on Peter's sleeve.

'Forgive me if I was irritable, Peter. I did want my food.'

'My dear Margaret – irritable nothing, as they say in Congress. In the first place you weren't irritable; and, in the second, if you were so fiendishly hungry as to want this soup you must have put up a truly wonderful show of patience. No, it was I who nearly put the hat on it.'

'Never so nearly as when you were on the point of saying that I wasn't really your wife. If she knew the truth we shouldn't have been allowed in the stables.'

'And now I wonder what the dickens we had better do about sleeping,' said Peter. 'You see, even if we go on, Dann won't find us in the morning.'

'Yes, but on the other hand, if we could get on to the next town, we might be able to telephone to the Bunters.'

'Five miles! My dear Margaret, you are certainly a wonderful advertisement for this soup and a very weak whisky and soda.'

This was true. From the weary traveller, sinking in the last stages of fatigue on to her baggage in the hall, Margaret was already transformed to a strong and vigorous young woman with a high colour and a gay enthusiasm for their minor adventure. She was very human. Had she not found cause to drill herself to studied reticence of recent years she might perhaps have been an emotional woman. She gave this impression now, as, alone with Peter, she allowed full play to that careless animation which follows hunger appeased. The most rapid and the most seductive transition in all human nature is that which attends the palliation of a ravenous appetite. There is something humiliating about it. Can you, who lay down your fork or your tankard with a purr of urbane satisfaction, be he who, but a few moments ago, was cursing a willing waiter for refusing to alter all the laws of Thermology in the cooking of your steak? Can those harmless but refined fellow-diners be the selfish cads whose gluttony and personal appearance so raised your contemptuous wrath on your arrival? Were you not childishly hasty in projecting an assault upon one of the younger of them for smiling when you shouted at the waiter? Ah, it is not the least cause for condemnation in Judas Iscariot that the greatest crime in history was committed at the conclusion and not in the dire necessity of a meal.

Having done full justice to the soup, they discussed the prospect cheerfully. Already the clouds were rapidly dispersing. There remained an interval of three long hours between them and normal bedtime. Tomorrow, at all events, they would make Rushcombe Fitz-Chartres. If they had to remain awake until then, they had often done the same thing at a dance. And this was just as much fun as a good many of the dances they had known. After all, they were in England. Why had they allowed their spirits to behave as though the leak in the radiator had suddenly been sprung upon them in the heart of the Caucasus? And so on.

Then Margaret turned to Peter quickly, as though struck by a thought.

'Peter, how selfish I've been. I've nothing to worry about. You have.'

'What?'

'Your wife.'

Peter laughed.

'That sounds like a good old back-hander for Sophia,' he said.

'Don't be foolish. You know what I mean. You were so keen on getting down so as not to disappoint her. And now—'

Peter raised his eyes thoughtfully to hers. There was a faint suggestion of restrained humour in his expression.

'It's a very dangerous subject here, Margaret. If the old lady heard us discussing my wife she would countermand the next course, which I judge from sounds of labour in the passage to be imminent.'

He was right. Gladys entered at that moment with hash, which she placed before them with clumsy haste and abandoned with a snort of relief.

'Anyhow,' said Margaret, 'I shall be able to assure your wife that noble sentiments inspired you to take Dann.'

'Careful,' said Peter. 'I think Gladys has only gone for veg.'

'She gives due notice of her coming,' said Margaret.

Peter was silent. The reference to Sophia seemed to have dispirited him. Margaret smiled at him gently with her kind eyes.

'Tell me, Peter,' she said quietly, 'just between you and me and Andrew Usher, how does married life strike you?'

Peter stroked his hair, deliberating.

'I think it's awfully purifying,' he said slowly. 'It makes you realise that half the ideas and aims in life which you considered great are really frightfully punk when analysed. Marriage analyses. Within three months I've discovered that a great many of the instincts and things which I thought gold are in reality the other muck – alloy or whatever it's called. Aren't I poetical?'

'Very,' said Margaret.

'I think Sophia has a stronger will than I have. If I'd known that I was going to have to do some of the things I have to do now, I wouldn't have got married; and yet I find I do the things now not because I have to do them but because I want to do them. Do you get me?'

'No married person could help getting you, Peter.'

'I thought when I got married that I was going to do what I liked. Instead of that, I find it's exactly the other way round. I like what I do.'

'And does she like it?'

'She ought to. She thinks of it. I don't suppose that Sophia is the sort of girl who shows her feelings much. Now you are, Margaret. Anyone can see that you're happy. It's simply written in your face these days.'

'Thank you, you dear,' said Margaret with genuine pleasure.

'I hope Sophia's happy,' he went on more pensively.

Margaret gave him a little intimate smile of approval.

'Go on really hoping that, Peter, and you needn't worry one little scrap about all the doing of all the things in the world.'

'Beware,' said Peter. 'Hunting noises without. Enter Gladys with veg.'

They entered upon the second course with undiminished relish, Pansy participating.

Presently, however, Margaret paused and sat upright with her chin raised, listening. Simultaneously Peter performed an exactly similar action. Their eyes met.

'Horse!' said Margaret.

'And cart!' said Peter.

They were on their feet in an instant. Margaret stepped to the window.

'Quick, Peter! Run and stop it.'

'I will, if it doesn't stop of its own accord.'

'Don't risk it. It's coming nearer. It doesn't seem to be pulling up. Peter, you must stop it, by hook or by crook.'

'Righto,' said Peter, eyeing the doorway reluctantly, 'but I hope it will save me the trouble. I wonder whether the driver knows about the beers – beers. I must say I rather hate the idea of running and trying to stop a horse by hook.'

'Now!' cried Margaret from the window. 'Quickly! Oh, all right; it's stopping.'

'Thank heaven!' said Peter.

'It's a waggonette – going our way,' reported Margaret, shading her eyes. 'Peter, I think we're saved.'

She returned briskly to Peter's side.

'All that remains,' she said, 'is for you to go and be awfully tactful. You will be better without me. I expect it is a job which will best be done in the bar.'

The driver of the waggonette had already entered the hall. He was a thin, pink man of the type indubitably connected with stables. He seemed familiar with the formalities of the *Stag and Hunt*, for he merely rapped on the glass shutter with his knuckles and summoned Mrs Spoker with a jerk of his head. They conversed in an awe-struck undertone at the office door.

'I'll tell them,' said the landlady at length, moving rapidly towards the staircase. 'You bide here. None o' that bar now. You may be required hurried.'

She mounted the stairs and a moment later could be heard knocking at the door of the bedroom above the parlour.

Peter stepped from the shadows of the parlour threshold into the hall. Within a minute he returned, nodded encouragingly to Margaret, and mixed a whisky and water. His next stay in the hall was of longer duration.

Margaret was more than once on the point of following him, but refrained, wisely conceiving that the rescuer might prove less amenable if confronted by his supernumaries *en masse*. The sight of Peter's face when he again entered the parlour was ample reward for her patience.

'Well done, Peter,' she exclaimed, without waiting for his report.

'My dear, it's better than that,' he answered. 'The most wonderful stroke of fortune!' He replaced the glass on the table and seated himself in a leisurely manner. 'There's no panic. I'll ring for the pudding,' he added.

'The stage thunder' – Peter pointed upwards to the ceiling, whence, indeed, proceeded a series of rumbling noises, punctuated by an occasional bang – 'is caused by the Loves packing.'

'Packing?'

'Packing in hot haste. Our friend the cart has come to fetch 'em away, fetch 'em away, fetch 'em away—'

'Where to?'

'Home. They are local people. Their home is being "done up", as they say. They must be rather foolhardy to leave their house and all that it contains to be crashed by navvies, but they did. One of the things they left was a genuine antique woman, Mrs Love's mother.'

'Well? Surely she hasn't been crashed by navvies?'

'That is precisely what has occurred,' said Peter dramatically. 'It doesn't take much to make a navvy put anything down, and our guardian angel had no difficulty in persuading one of the navvies to put down his bucket. His reason, it seems, was that he had to put down his bucket because he was going to think about a ladder. Anyhow, at that moment Mrs Love's mother comes round the corner, avoids the ladder for luck, and takes a prize toss over the bucket. Oh, isn't it perfectly splendid?'

'But why?'

'Why? My dear Margaret, the old lady is eighty odd. You can't go cartwheeling about over buckets at that age. Even in the profession you'll generally find that anything over sixty simply holds the handkerchief and rests on her laurels. The Loves are not a troupe, though they sound like one, and the old lady rested with great force upon her hip. She is now in bed with the doctor— I'm not talking scandal; the driver is my authority. They seem to be people of queer habits altogether. The driver eventually had to leave me because Mr Love put his head over the staircase and told him with some heat to go upstairs and help him lash his wife's trunk. Rather waste of time, I thought, even if a relief to the feelings.'

'But I really don't see how all this affects us, Peter.'

'Why, what more do you want? In about three minutes the room upstairs will be completely unoccupied.'

'Oh, I see. But that's only one room, Peter.'

'I don't want a room. I'll encamp in this parlour or anywhere. The point is we can get fixed up without having to slog along to the next village.'

'But won't it be very uncomfortable for you?'

'Not a bit. It's a magnificent solution. Directly the tumult and the shouting dies we will interview the landlady and—'

He paused. They interchanged a significant glance.

'Yes, we shall have to go rather warily with that landlady,' said Margaret with a short laugh.

Peter rose and peered into the passage.

'There seems to be no response to that pudding bell,' he remarked. 'I think we'll leave it, shall we?'

'Yes, I've had quite enough. But look here, Peter. About this business. If we tell that woman that we're not married—'

'She'll out us without a moment's hesitation. Fancy if all hotels were so strict. Brighton front would be one large dormitory.'

'It makes it a little bit awkward,' said Margaret dubiously.

'We might pretend to be brother and sister.'

'Oh, nonsense! We've already given her to understand that we're married.'

'Well, that's all right, Margaret,' said Peter, a little self-consciously.

'It's not all right. If we take the bedroom why should you sleep in the parlour?'

'My dear Margaret, of course we know that it would be all right, but while people continue to cherish such nasty minds I think it would be better for me to sleep in the parlour.'

'Oh, don't be silly, Peter. What I am asking you is – what will the landlady think of the husband who sleeps in the parlour?'

'Ah, I follow your meaning with reluctance,' said Peter. 'Well, I don't see why the landlady should know anything about it. We can book the room and climb up to it together with candles, like any old, fed-up married couple. When the house is quiet I'll sneak back here. You needn't start to undress till I go.'

'I should hope not,' said Margaret.

'I don't see why you should hope not in that strain,' protested Peter. 'I thought it was rather a brilliant idea.'

'What about the morning?'

'In the morning I sneak out again and moon about till you come down. The whole thing is perfectly simple.'

Margaret hesitated, her fingers playing restlessly with a locket at her breast. In her placid eyes was the reflection of painful memories. She seemed to drive them away with sudden resolution.

'Yes,' she said. 'It's the only thing to be done. We simply daren't risk a confession to the landlady after what she said. She may be difficult enough to manage as it is. And, after all, we needn't tell anyone that we even pretended to be married. Anyone outside the inn, I mean.'

'No, I won't lie awake composing a song about it for Sophia,' said Peter.

Margaret was about to deprecate this attitude and to prepare a list of possible participants of the secret, commencing with Claude and Lady Bunter, when the conversation was interrupted by a medley descriptive of domestic traffic from outside the parlour. The boots of heavily laden men began to beat an uncertain tattoo on the stairs. Dislocated stair-rods twanged ominously. The sharp tenor of Mr Love and the pessimistic bass of the driver engaged in what appeared to be a laborious anthem, swelling during the descent into a crescendo of 'Go on, go on. – Steady, oh, steady, sir. – Go on, I say. – Oh, steady a moment. – Go on, I say, go on.' Female voices, raised in lamentation and instruction from the landing above, blended effectively; while the fact that Gladys had been commissioned to partake in one of the more strenuous of the tasks connected with the move was suggested by an intermittent sound not unlike that produced by the low notes of a flute.

From the parlour door Margaret and Peter watched the procession with thoughtful interest. Mr Love and the driver carried between them their former perquisite, the trunk of Mrs Love. Behind them a smaller but substantial piece of luggage was borne by Gladys and an aged male retainer, seconded from duties in the bar. That both Mrs Spoker and

Mrs Love, in the rear, were heavily laden with minor impedimenta gave the watchers reason to hope that the evacuation was to be complete and final.

The departure was not unduly prolonged. In the road Mr Love and the driver favoured the company with a brief chanty running 'Got it? – No, I ain't, 'old on. – Got it? Got it? – No, 'old on, sir.' Within the door Mrs Spoker hastily imparted to Mrs Love a few final sentiments on the subject of Divine Intention in the disposition of buckets; farewells and last commiserations; a deep, guttural instigation to the horse; and the wheels of the waggonette crunched heavily away into obscurity.

'I think you'd better tackle her,' said Peter.

Margaret, refreshed, certainly had a persuasive charm about her. Mrs Spoker was duly lured into the parlour on her way back from speeding the Loves, was spoken fair and thanked for the excellence of her dinner, Peter remaining diplomatically in the background. Margaret exercised the most admirable discretion. She listened with an impressed air to a home-made parable concerning the elder Mrs Love and the bucket. Beneath her softening influence Mrs Spoker became quite human. She agreed almost cordially to allow Margaret the use of the bedroom. Having done so, however, she seemed momentarily to regret the decision, as her darkening frown rested on Peter. She turned again to Margaret and inquired in a transparently false tone of conversation how long she had been married. Three months, Margaret told her with innocent promptitude. Mrs Spoker nodded grimly.

'Very well,' she said. 'I will see to the girl making the bed up.'

In the doorway she halted and directed another somewhat inimical glance at Peter.

'You will have to sign the book,' she told him, as though pronouncing an ultimatum.

'Certainly,' said Peter, with creditable coolness.

'And – what is the name?'

'May I come in?' said a voice – a high-pitched effusive, male voice.

Mrs Spoker turned sharply and threw open the door.

'Oh, thank you. I – I hope I don't intrude,' said the owner of the voice, entering the parlour.

He was a clerical gentleman of about thirty-eight. There was something exasperatingly dry about his appearance. His clothes were very dusty and he had a habit of working his mouth open and shut as though his throat were dusty too. Round the ends of his trousers were khaki leggings of the type affected by marines. His hands and the cuffs of his shirt were sadly dirty. In one hand he held a spanner, not aggressively but as one would hold a pencil. In contrast, however, to his deplorable condition his manner seemed philosophically hearty; and his eyes, magnified by large gold-rimmed spectacles, seemed positively to flash forth sparkling beams of good cheer.

'Good evening, good evening,' said this parson blandly. 'I looked in to see whether I could borrow a little oil.'

'I am complee—' Mrs Spoker began from force of habit; but she broke off, amazed at the procedure of the reverend gentleman.

'Good gracious!' exclaimed the latter, bounding forward with both hands outstretched to Margaret. 'Mrs – Mrs – er – Hackett, yes, Hackett, as I live. I almost forgot your married name for a moment. First time we have met since before the happy event. Sorry I couldn't be there – sickening! Still so glad to see you now.'

'O – h,' responded Margaret, skilfully disguising vexation as surprise, 'fancy meeting you here, Mr Sloley-Jones.'

'You're staying here?' pursued the other keenly.

'Er – yes. Just for the one night. Are you?'

'No,' said Mrs Spoker.

'No,' agreed Sloley-Jones. 'I just looked in to see whether I could borrow a little oil.'

'No,' said Mrs Spoker.

Sloley-Jones paid no heed to her. He had turned with a

fresh burst of enthusiasm to Peter, radiating flashes of pleasure from his spectacles.

'First time we've met,' he cried, as he seized Peter's hand and commenced to wring it. 'Delighted! How-do-you-do? Splendid. How are you? Well done! I'm first rate, thanks – A1. Hope you're the same? Good!'

CHAPTER VI

Tally-ho!

Sophia did not lose her head. True, she glanced at the communication cord above the window of the railway carriage, but only for a moment. There is a wealth of sinister inference about that warning against improper use. It is not so much the five pounds; it is the probability of tedious and perplexing argument with autocratic officials, of police court proceedings, of snapshots in the daily press.

Moreover, to Sophia, who was an eminently reasonable young woman, it appeared extremely improbable that the guard, if summoned, would consent to back the train into Paddington from Ealing in order to regain Peter. Again, it was unlikely that Peter would wait expectantly for this solution; especially now that he had picked up this blonde woman. Ah! That was the thought which rankled in the mind of Sophia, far outweighing the grievance of Peter having missed the train and having kept the tickets in his waistcoat pocket.

Sophia sat watching the uninspiring scenery of the Thames Valley with dull eyes. She gradually mastered her impetuosity with an effort of which only a wholesale ironmonger's daughter was capable. Had she been in the retail trade she would have sounded the alarm signal long ago, or perhaps have thrown herself bodily from the carriage as the train started. As it was, she kept such vulgarly headstrong impulses in check. She sat back in the corner seat of her first class carriage and froze the desire to do anything excitable or undignified with a cold douche of wholesale self-control.

The long suffering nature of the British Public is never more strongly emphasised than when the British Public travels. One has only to undertake a short journey on one of the underground railways of London to observe a great flock of human sheep submissively yielding to the insolent tyranny of one barking whelp at the gate. Great, potent men, on their way to devastate a whole meeting of querulous shareholders; fierce, opinionated women, bound for Westminter on acrimonious political deputations, are cowed into obedience by the lashing tongue of that one, sharp-nosed slave-driver and meekly pass right down the car.

This affords an amazing commentary on the British public character; and it is a noteworthy feature that, when protest is raised, the protestant, for whose sentiments the whole flock of sheep has a sneaking sympathy, is unquestioningly regarded as a goat of the worst type. For this reason the better class sheep prefer to show their utter contempt for the hound in charge by appearing not to heed him at all, and by merely obeying his orders as though they happen, by some coincidence, at that very moment to be desirous of passing right down the car in their own interests.

Sophia belonged decidedly to the better class of travelling sheep. She stifled the inclination to make a scene with the guard, even though she was the sole occupant of her particular compartment. She also determined that when the official should appear to inspect the tickets, rather than endure a single sentence of expostulation she would pay her fare over again.

Meanwhile she stared casually at wet fields and thought of the blonde woman.

Sophia possessed none of the haphazard bonhomie of the class into which she had married. There were many girls of Peter's acquaintance (some of them had learnt the news of his engagement with unwonted wistfulness) who would, in Sophia's position, have felt deep vexation at his carelessness, especially in regard to the tickets, and who might have expressed indignation against his blonde friend for having been instrumental in making him miss the train. But they, knowing Peter, would not have brooded through the windows all the way to Swindon with dark suspicions of a prearranged *coup*, visions of secretive and unlawful pastimes, premonitions of every detail of a brief, unhappy marriage being bared to the public eye on flaming posters.

Sophia came of a stock which rejoices in the due advertisement of its successes, but counts public investigation of its failures as only less desirable than a Presbyterian conception of the Day of Judgment. While Peter, without courting notoriety of any description, would have accepted it quite impassively and would, no doubt, have thrived on it, his wife shrank back into her corner from the thought that her private affairs might be subjected to the investigation of those apparently half-informed but sedulous gentry who fill two pages weekly with a list of the Things which, as they bluntly confess, they Want to Know.

But Sophia was a spirited girl. It was not her intention to see Peter decoyed on the very morrow of his marriage back into the excesses of his unrevealed bachelorhood. She was temporarily in awe of his social standing, but the ironmongery had not entered into her soul to the extent of compelling blind subjection.

At Bristol she would wire to announce that she was returning immediately. This would warn Peter that he must get rid of the blonde without delay and thus avoid the unpleasantness of an unforeseen passage of arms. Besides, Sophia felt more confident of her ability to deal with Peter in the absence of the blonde. She would take the first train back to London and she would hear, quite calmly, what Peter had to say. Of course she might have to threaten to wire to her mother. Sophia sat more upright in her corner seat as she began to realise the strength of her position.

She would, beyond all question, bring Peter to his knees. He would plead forgiveness, which would be granted in the full love of a woman's nature. Sophia was a connoisseur of matinées.

So Sophia paid her first-class single fare to a rather puzzled official and withered his attempts at conciliation. At Bristol she imperiously superintended the collection of her luggage and Peter's into a large but neat pile on the London platform, sent her wire and had tea.

The up-train was due to leave at five o'clock, arriving at Paddington at 7.30. Sophia was in some doubt as to whether she ought to send a wire to Lady Bunter, but was stayed from this course by the thought that Peter had possibly done so. The arrival at Rushcombe Fitz-Chartres of two conflicting telegrams was not calculated to improve the outlook for the Wykehams' domestic resettlement.

Eventually Sophia regained Paddington. After a wait of several minutes she secured a taxi. On reaching home she found the flat forsaken, the door locked, the maid absent, Peter—

Sophia had to assist the driver of the taxi to remove the luggage. The driver then cursed her roundly and drove away. Sophia sat on the stairs till eleven o'clock. She did not go to her mother; her sense of justice was very keen; she would hear Peter before taking any step which she knew to be irredeemable. She was very hungry. She was very tired. She was unloved, deserted three months after her marriage. And, as the hunger and the weariness increased, there came to her, together with a lump in the throat, the knowledge that this was all a foolish gloomy surmise; that Peter loved no woman but her, that he was as honourable as she herself, that she was impetuous and unjust and that what she wanted more than all the world was to hear Peter's step on the stairs and to throw her arms round his neck.

But no Peter came up the stairs. The lump in her throat hardened, and her heart slowly hardened too, as though determined to assert its mastery over the remorseless husband. And the shadows of the coming darkness preyed upon that dreary staircase and closed down on her in her self-inflicted misery; while, through the narrow landing window above her, peered the last streaks of mocking daylight, like the suggestive glances of that dreaded Society Peeping Tom, intent on the examination of one of those many, curious Things he Wanted to Know.

At eleven the maid returned and found her mistress crouched on the stairs in a dire stage of fatigue and distress. Through Sophia's poor aching brain the fragments of the conversation which followed echoed like the foolish inconsequences of a French Primer.

'Has the master gone? – Yes, he left at 2.30. – Was he alone? – No, he was not alone. – Was the lady blonde? – Yes, and the small dog should not have been allowed in the drawing-room. – Had the lady luggage? – Yes, and the couple left in a car. – Open the door if you please. – My telegram is in the letter-box. – Give me some meat, some bread, and some wine.'

The wine, which was thin claret, proved to have a woeful influence on Sophia in her exhausted condition. It not merely refreshed her, it fired her to fresh indignation and action. In her regained animosity, headstrong and reckless of the consequences, seeing that the mask was now thrown aside and that her husband had definitely schemed to trick her and to desert her, Sophia took action forthwith. She rang up her mother.

Sophia's mother was one of those ladies who when once roused from sleep go off like a released spring into garrulous conversation. From the moment of awakening she invariably talked at the wholesale ironmonger until he sprang out of bed and ran into his dressing-room in sheer self-defence. Occasionally she awoke in the middle of the night and talked.

On this occasion she had already been in bed for nearly an hour, and her conversation was relapsing into a drowsy monotone. Her husband had given up replying and was hoping sleepily. He had almost lost consciousness when he was prodded in the pit of the stomach by an elbow and told to go and answer the telephone. It is doubtful whether any treatment more trying to the temper than this could possibly be devised. But Sophia's mother was not the woman to brook defiance. After a few moments' vain remonstrance her husband complied. His manner and appearance were suggestive of a satiated sea-lion.

A minute or two later he returned in triumph. It was she who was wanted. Sophia wanted her. Sophia? Sophia had gone to Somerset. Well, perhaps she was speaking from Somerset. Did she say so? No, he hadn't asked her.

'Well, go and ask her while I put something on.'

'Oh, it's you she wants. You go and ask her.'

'I am going as fast as I can. Don't you get back into bed now.'

'Why not?'

'You may be wanted.'

'Wanted?'

'Yes, wanted – required.'

'What for?'

'How can I tell till I've spoken to Sophia? If you haven't got the sense to ask her yourself—'

'I say, for goodness' sake button up that thing in the front. The servants may see you.'

'The servants are in bed.'

'I wish to Heaven I was.'

'Wait now till I return.'

'Yes, I will; but I may as well get into bed.'

'No you may not. You are to wait up. You may be wanted by Sophia.'

'In Somerset?'

'Don't waste time talking. Wait till I return. You may sit *on* your bed if you like.'

'I knew it,' said Sophia's mother, returning after a great while.

'I had to get in. I felt cold.'

'I don't mean that. I knew it all along. Go and put on your clothes this very instant. Don't put on too many, and don't take too long in putting them on. I knew this would come. I sensed it from the first.'

'What would come? Why dress? Sensed what? What is all this – that's what I want to know – what?'

Sophia's mother seized a stocking from the chair where her discarded garments had been placed, and, shooting a slipper the whole length of the room from her foot, balanced herself on one leg and prepared to clothe the other. In this attitude she cried out dramatically:

'Sophia's husband has left her. I knew it. Another woman. Don't waste time dressing. He gave her the slip at Paddington. Go and dress at once. I foresaw this. They left in a car with luggage. Don't waste time. Just put on your shirt and breeches and things. I knew it all along. You will keep me waiting, you know. I shall be so angry if you do. I am not going to put on my corsets or anything. A blonde woman with furs.'

'But when did this happen?'

'Today of course. When do you suppose it happened? Will you go and put on your breeches?'

'But where?'

'Where? I've told you, Paddington. I shan't be two minutes, you know. When you've got something on, go and get a taxi.'

'But is Sophia in Somerset?'

'Are you trying to be funny?' asked Sophia's mother, doing things with shoulder straps.

Towards midnight the parents discovered their daughter in the midst of the formerly consecrated, now desecrated, flat. She had surrounded herself with all the conventional properties of the deserted wife – the *déshabillé*, the tears, the smelling salts. The very break in her voice as she recounted her story was in due keeping with the traditions. Her mother stood with her lips compressed into a hard, narrow line, and listened with a series of quick nods, which seemed to indicate that events had transpired exactly in the manner she had always anticipated. From time to time she inserted a comment to the same effect.

'Tessie says that he seemed in excellent spirits,' said

Sophia, as she reached the conclusion of her narrative. 'The car was hired from Gamble's garage by telephone. The driver, even, seemed suspicious.'

'And well he might be. I knew this,' said Sophia's mother.

'When he told the driver where to go, the driver appeared unwilling. Finally, though, they all got into the car; he, the woman and the little dog—'

'I sensed that.'

'And drove away – away.' Sophia broke down here. Even at this moment she was subconsciously comparing her rendering of the part of the forlorn bride with Miss Marie Lohr's.

'Poor child!' said her mother. Then, turning to her husband, who was standing apart, fingering the sparse hairs of his crown, she continued in a voice subdued into menacing intensity:

'What are you going to do?'

'What?' said her husband.

'Yes, what – what?'

'I – I don't know. What?'

'Oh don't keep repeating. Have you been listening? Have you heard what Sophia has been telling you? Do you understand what is afoot?'

'What is a foot?' repeated her husband with sleepy stupidity.

'Act, act!' hissed Sophia's mother. 'Do something.'

'Yes, but what? That's what I'm trying to get at – what?'

'Your daughter,' said his wife, with a sweeping gesture, 'is being lugged into the divorce court. Lugged! And you stand there and say "what, what?" '

'Well, what suggestions can you make?'

The hard mouth was contracted again during rapid deliberation.

'Get detectives,' said Sophia's mother.

'Oh, detectives – nonsense! Especially at this time of night! You might as well say, "Go and hire a pack of bloodhounds." '

'This man must be found and brought to book.'

'Brought to where?'

'Book, book! Don't yawn. Act!'

The wholesale ironmonger was fingering his hairs again.

'It's all very well,' he remarked very slowly and stupidly, 'but I don't see that we've any definite proof—'

Both women were on to him in a flash.

'No definite proof! Oh, no definite proof!' they cried in varying inflections of irony.

'After all,' he pleaded, 'he saw Sophie go off in the train to Somerset, and he comes home and takes a car. What does that look like? Looks to me like he's meaning to go after her.'

Sophia merely tilted her chin in silent and forbearing derision. Sophia's mother leant forward into her husband's face and said 'Poof!'

'The other – the lady – may have been – well, may have been going the same way or something like that.'

'Huh!' exclaimed Sophia bitterly.

'Oh, poof!' cried her mother.

'I bet you' – the nettled husband and father raised his voice – 'I bet you he's down with those people in Somerset by this time, at the baronet's place, and wondering where the dickens she's got to.' He jerked his thumb at Sophia. 'I'll wire there in the morning.'

'That's right,' said his wife. 'Lug it into the public eye.'

'Anyhow it's no good our standing here all night. I've only got my pyjamas on underneath and one thing and another. We can't do anything until the morning, and I'll bet you that everything will be explained perfectly openly.'

'I shall stay with Sophia.'

'Do by all means—'

'No, don't, mother. I'm all right now.'

'I prefer to.'

'I would rather you didn't.'

'Oh, toss up for it and let's get to bed,' said the other parent with growing asperity.

He was a kind man and relented a moment later, bidding Sophia a tender good night and assuring her that his theory was sound. She remained silent.

'After all,' said the good man, 'he can't always be expected to carry on in the same way as us. We must remember that. His ideas are a bit different from ours; he's been brought up in a different – what's that word – environment. He—'

'I thought you said you wanted to go home,' said his wife.

'I'll wire that place in the morning. Sir – what? Sir Stirling Bunter; Rushcombe Fitz-Chartres. I'll wire him first thing, and I'll bet you – yes, all right – coming, coming. Good night Sophie. And don't you worry now.'

Sophia, who awoke languid and irritable, remained in bed; but her mother, who returned to the flat at breakfast time, plunged enthusiastically into investigation. Her first move was to ring up Gamble's garage. No, the car was not returned and they were without news of it. No, they didn't know where it had been bound for; a long journey – that was all they had understood, and, knowing Mr Wykeham so well, they had left it at that. Eh? Oh, the driver was a newish man but quite reliable. Name of Dann. Yes, they'd see he was sent along to see Mrs Wykeham when he returned.

On reaching his office Sophia's father called for telegraph forms and settled himself for composition. He could rattle off a business letter with any man, but delicate social interrogation of this sort was another matter. He rapidly destroyed a preliminary half-dozen forms and then began to ponder the matter really deeply.

In the first place it was necessary to discover whether Peter was at these Bunters; secondly to explain why Sophia was not; and to do so in a style which was at once succinct and apologetic – these Bunters being obviously howling swells – with an underlying suggestion that there was an entire absence of panic but that Sophia was a trifle anxious. The composer scratched his depleted crown with a pencil, and rehearsed hypothetical telegrams aloud to himself with strange facial contortions:

Can you kindly send news wykeham think some mistake wife caught train he missed so returned—

Is wykeham with you wife missed him started to come but missed him so returned home but miss—

Outside the private office a departmental manager, two ledger-keepers, a lady clerk and three travellers awaited decisions on a miscellany of ironmongering matters and chafed audibly like wild animals at feeding-time. Their director tore the batch of half-written messages from his desk and flung them savagely into the waste-paper basket.

'I'll ring up the flat at lunch-time,' he decided, 'and if there's still no news then I'll – I'll send a wire. Come in, Hopkins.'

CHAPTER VII

The Roosting

Sloley-Jones?

Peter could not avoid a certain abstraction of manner as he returned the hearty greeting bestowed upon him by the parson in the parlour of the *Stag and Hunt*.

Sloley-Jones? Peter had heard Margaret address the stranger by this name, and to him, too, it seemed faintly familiar. In his mind he connected it vaguely with Sophia. Why he could not tell.

'Yes, it was a blow being prevented from coming to your wedding,' continued Sloley-Jones garrulously. 'You got my wire, I expect.'

Yes, this seemed in keeping with Peter's veiled conception of what the name ought to signify to his mind.

'Thank you, we did, yes,' said Margaret quickly.

'Oh, yes, we did, thank you,' said Peter.

'Of course,' resumed Sloley-Jones to Peter, 'I've heard of you often enough.'

'From my wife?' ventured Peter.

'Well, yes, from your wife of course, and from other sources too,' said Sloley-Jones. 'A man like you can't hope to remain in obscurity, you know. Ha.'

This sounded rather more formidable. Peter shifted uneasily and sought Margaret's eye.

'I met your wife last just before you were married – at a poor children's guild.'

'A poor children's guild?' repeated Peter feebly.

'Why yes, and you were to have been there too. You were detained in the House I expect,' said the reverend gentleman unctuously.

In the nick of time Peter remembered that to this genial

muddler, as to Mrs Spoker, he was Claude Hackett. He was no longer Sophia's husband; for the time being he was married to Margaret. He felt a return of the subconscious feeling of pleasurable novelty which the contemplation of the small deception had given him. All right! He was not over-pleased to be Claude Hackett, M.P., but the idea of being Margaret's husband was queer and, alas, enticing. But he must do the thing thoroughly. Peter shook off his abstraction and became quite buoyant.

Mr Sloley-Jones's stay in the parlour of the *Stag and Hunt* lasted barely ten minutes, but during this time he succeeded in working havoc. The observant Mrs Spoker ascertained that the name of her guests was Hackett and – unexpected development – that Mr Hackett was a Member of Parliament. Mr Sloley-Jones appeared to cherish the long exploded theory that every member of the House of Commons possesses a secret fund of political intelligence; and despite the lateness of the hour and his shortage of oil he seemed disposed to make the most of this opportunity to remain and pump Margaret's husband upon the secret personality and policy of every member of the Cabinet in turn. Fortunately for Peter Mr Sloley-Jones had a habit of framing his questions in such a way as to leave little doubt of the answer he hoped to obtain. Perhaps a long classical association with the interrogative particles *num* and *nonne* was responsible for this helpful characteristic; perhaps, as a parson, he realised that the best-informed parishioners are invariably the least talkative and therefore require a strong lead.

At the same time he was little short of astonished to find this confirmed Radical agreeing with ready complacency to some of the most advanced principles of the Sloley-Jones die-hard Imperialism.

'Indeed?' he cried at one point. 'Is that really your true estimate of the Labour people?'

'Yes,' said Peter. 'Oh, yes, I think – I think what I said just now.'

'Ah, and that opinion is – beneath a veneer of bigotry – excuse me using such a term—'

'Not at all,' said Peter.

'That is the true conviction of most of the Free Liberals in the House. Is it not?'

'Oh, you bet it is,' said Peter.

'Really? Enlightening! But you wouldn't care to make the admission in the precincts of the House I am sure?'

'Oh, no, rather not.'

'Dear me. This is entertaining – an eye-opener. Humbug it all is though, isn't it?'

'It is, isn't it?' agreed Peter in a cheerful tone.

Mr Sloley-Jones lowered his voice into a rather sinister whisper:

'What is Lloyd-George's real view of the miners' report?'

'I – I don't know.'

'You don't know? Oh, come now. I suppose you won't say. Is that it?'

'Well, yes,' said Peter. 'I – I hardly care to say.'

'Ah. I ought not to ask I suppose?'

'No – er – I think it would really be better if you didn't.'

Sloley-Jones turned again to Margaret, flashing enthusiasm from his spectacles.

'It is splendid to meet your husband, Mrs Hackett – in such candid mood too – glorious! I never expected to find myself in sympathy with a "Wee Free" – encouraging! Hope you don't mind my calling you by that nickname?'

'Not a bit. I like it,' said Peter.

'Ah. Good egg! Well, I must be off – I really simply must. My good woman, are you sure you cannot allow me to borrow a little oil?'

'What sort of oil would that be – lamp oil?' asked Mrs Spoker.

'No no. Loobericating oil.'

'Well, what's the difference, except that I haven't got any of either of 'em?' was Mrs Spoker's reply.

The parson sighed.

'I felt I was in for trouble,' he informed Margaret in a melancholy tone. 'I shall seize up altogether if I don't get some looberication. I walked for about a mile here because I felt myself over-heating – nasty! Besides, my pistons keep making curious noises – tricky business! I don't like it. However—'

'Well, you can't stay here not if you burst a blood-vessel,' said Mrs Spoker discouragingly. 'I am completely occupied. I have just let my last room to Mr and Mrs 'Ackett.' She plumed herself on her mastery of the name.

Peter winced slightly.

'Where are you making for?' asked Margaret encouragingly.

'Ah. Only Downblotton. Downblotton is my headquarters. I am doing a little tour – so awfully nice! I'm looking up some of the architectural remains in this part of the country. Fine local specimens – I daresay you know them, Mr Hackett? You do? Bravo. Well, as I say, I really ought to be going. I simply must. I only wish I could borrow a little oil. I suppose, Mrs Hackett, that you and your husband came along here by road? There's no railway station for miles.'

'Yes, we did. But our car broke down some miles away. That is why we are stopping here for the night.'

'Oh, bad luck!' cried the clergyman. 'I only trust I shan't be compelled to return here under similar circumstances.'

'Indeed I hope not,' agreed Margaret cordially.

'I am completely occupied,' put in Mrs Spoker warningly.

'Yes. By Jove. I should have to sleep in this parlour or somewhere. Ha, ha!'

'Ha ha!' echoed Peter in repudiation of so ridiculous a notion.

Mrs Spoker treated the proposal to a grunt of contempt.

'After all, Downblotton's only five miles from here,' said Margaret.

'Your motor-bike ought to be good for five miles,' added Peter.

'Yes, it's only five miles,' admitted Sloley-Jones. 'Besides I've had a chance to cool down nicely. I think I can safely be going, don't you?'

'Yes, I really think you can,' said Peter.

'Yes. So we will say good night, shall we? Good night, Mrs Hackett – au revoir. Unexpected pleasure! It's made me feel quite cheerful again. I was getting down in the mouth I can tell you – thought I'd broken one of my inlet-valve springs at least. Still I think I only let myself get a little overheated. I'll try and regulate my mixture a bit better. I think I'm a trifle rich. Good night, my dear sir.' He extended a begrimed hand. 'Such a pleasure to meet you. We must have another little confidential chat one of these days – most exhilarating! Good night, my good woman.'

'Don't you come back now,' said Mrs Spoker. 'Because I couldn't allow this parlour to be slept in, not under any circumstances.'

'But if my looberication fails half a mile down the road—'

'Not if you has heart failure in the churchyard,' said Mrs Spoker firmly.

'Well, well, we must hope for the best, mustn't we? I'm a good deal cooler now and I dare say I shan't konk.'

Mr Sloley-Jones faced the door with an effort, then again turned.

'Good night again, Mrs Hackett. Good night, my dear sir. Ah, hallo little dog! Good night, little dog! Is this your little dog, Mrs Hackett?'

Margaret replied with a succession of quick nods.

'Ah!' Sloley-Jones bent and caressed Pansy, who regarded her mistress with questioning eyes and sneezed.

'Good night, little dog! Dear little dog – pretty little dog!' said the parson.

Mrs Spoker held the parlour door widely ajar and cleared her throat.

'Well, well, I ought to be nicely cool by this time,' said Sloley-Jones. 'Good night – er all!'

The landlady accompanied him from the room in a manner which she might well have acquired from dealing with undesirables in the bar. Peter sought Margaret's eyes with a rueful smile. Her expression was that of a hostess at the conclusion of her afternoon-at-home.

The front door was heard to slam loudly and Mrs Spoker was back in the parlour. Two hard lines of inquisitorial interest stood out between her eyes.

'So you are a member of the House of Parliament?' she asked.

Peter blew his nose conveniently, but Margaret came to his rescue with ready confidence.

'Oh, yes, my husband is in the House of Commons,' she said.

'I shouldn't 'a thought it,' commented Mrs Spoker. 'Now which side would you be, Mr 'Ackett?'

'Er – which are you?' asked Peter cautiously.

'Are you for or against the brewers?' pursued Mrs Spoker relentlessly.

'The brewers? Oh, I'm for them,' said Peter without hesitation.

'Oh, are you?' cried the landlady savagely.

Peter's face fell.

'I – I'm – I'm a supp – a strong supporter of – of beers,' he ventured.

'Oh, I don't suppose you're one of these Pussyfoots,' said Mrs Spoker, 'not by a deal. But what I want to know is, why don't you gentlemen up there study the question of the public houses?'

'Oh, but I do,' said Peter. 'It's a subject I – I'm awfully keen on.'

'Then why don't we hear of you doing something more for us?' said Mrs Spoker. 'What was that he called you – a wee flea?'

'Free,' explained Margaret. 'Free.'

'Oh, free? Free with promises I suppose, like the rest of 'em. 'Owever, I shall be obliged, if when you come to the office and sign the visitors' book, you'll please put in the letters and all after the name. It will be a object of interest in these parts.'

Peter glanced at Margaret and bowed. His attitude was intended to appear condescending but failed signally in this respect.

'What time will you be a-going to bed?' continued Mrs Spoker, turning her attention to Margaret. 'We keep early hours here.'

'Any time – now if you like,' said Margaret. She stooped as she spoke and raised Pansy in her arms.

'What are you a-going to do with that dog?' asked the landlady suspiciously.

'Take her to bed.'

'To your bed?'

'Yes, of course.'

'To bed with you?' Mrs Spoker's voice was undergoing rapid inflections of shrill astonishment.

'Yes.'

'You and Mr 'Ackett and that dog in one bed?'

'Certainly. Why? Have you any objection?'

''Ave I any objection?' Mrs Spoker turned swiftly on Peter. 'And are you in the habit o' sleeping with a dog?' she cried.

'I – oh yes – rather. This little dog always – always sleeps with – with us.'

Mrs Spoker shook her head decisively. She reproduced her strange doubtful, hissing noise.

'No dog sleeps in my bed,' she stated.

'I dare say not. I admit it's an acquired taste,' said Peter. 'But—'

'Such a thing I never heard of,' said Mrs Spoker. 'Why, it's worse than what goes on down at them cottages. It's unsanitary to my way o' thinking. And you a member o' the House of Parliament!'

'Why shouldn't a Member of Parliament sleep with a dog?' asked Peter rather irritably.

'I allow no beasts in my bedrooms,' declared Mrs Spoker in a tone of finality.

'Then all I can say is, this must be a very remarkable country inn,' said Peter warmly.

Margaret interposed with her customary discretion.

'Very well, Mrs Spoker. Just as you like. But where can the poor little girl sleep?'

'Little girl?'

'Little dog.'

'In the stables,' said Mrs Spoker, regarding the poor little girl with a ferocity which seemed to widen the already considerable extent of apprehensive white eyeball in the latter.

'Oh!' sighed Margaret tenderly.

'There's nothing else worth speaking of in the stables,' went on Mrs Spoker briskly. 'She'll have a deal more room there than what she would have in the bed with you and Mr 'Ackett.'

'She'll be so lonely,' objected Margaret, stroking Pansy affectionately. 'She may howl.'

'It don't matter if she do 'owl. No one will hear her from the stables,' said Mrs Spoker triumphantly.

'Can't she sleep on the floor of the room?' asked Margaret persuasively.

'No, madam,' was the firm reply. 'No beasts in my bedrooms.'

Pansy was surrendered and commenced to tune up for the stables with a series of crescendo squeaks. Before leaving to deposit her, Mrs Spoker repeated her request that the visitors' book should receive Mr Hackett's attention. She relit the candle in the office and, inviting her guests to enter, bore away Pansy who was now in full rehearsal.

'Look here, Margaret; this is the very devil,' said Peter. 'I must draw the line at forging your husband's name. There are limits. Besides, I'm not quite certain how to spell it.'

'Well, I'll do the writing,' said Margaret readily. 'After all, my name's Mrs Hackett, isn't it? One can't be convicted for half a forgery, can one?'

'Good idea!' said Peter. 'The only alternative is for me to write it so badly that nobody could read it. Of course I could do that; especially in hotel ink. Still, I think on the whole you had better do the deed.'

'Date – 18th of September,' quoted Margaret as she bent over the massive album and commenced to inscribe. 'Visitors' name – C. Hackett, M.P., and Mrs Hackett. There, Peter. The deed is done. Oh – Room number?'

'Oh, give that a miss and hope for the best,' said Peter.

But it was not to be. Mrs Spoker returned with startling suddenness just as Margaret had restored the pen to its tray. The landlady inspected the inscription keenly.

'Room number two,' she said, presenting Peter with the pen.

'Oh yes,' he murmured in a tone of obligatory surprise, as he proceeded to make the kind of 2 which he attributed to Margaret's style of chirography. Then he turned and met her eye with a rather sheepish smile.

'And so to bed,' he said.

Mrs Spoker had already lighted two candles which she handed to them in candlesticks of discoloured metal.

'What time are you to be called, please?' she asked.

'Oh, I – I'll call myself,' replied Peter.

'H'm. That's as you please of course,' said Mrs Spoker.

'Seems to be about the only thing that is,' muttered Peter to himself as he followed the landlady and Margaret upstairs.

Room number two of the *Stag and Hunt* provided an immediate and striking problem to any mind occupied with the interesting subject of upholstery. The door of the room was so small as to necessitate the parties entering in single file. The carefully closed windows seemed ill-proportionately smaller than the door. Yet by some uncanny means so large a quantity of massive furniture had been conjured into the room that the floor space resolved itself into narrow alley ways between bed and wardrobe, washing-stand and chests of drawers. Of the latter there were two, a yellow and a mottled. Nor did it appear possible that these articles had been imported limb by limb and, when once inside, built up into a substantial whole, for every one of them had the solid appearance of having been hewn out of one huge trunk. The double bed in itself monopolised a vast proportion of the available space, a tall, ponderous structure covered with a counterpane of a rather livery yellow shade. In several places this appeared to be vainly endeavouring to conceal forbidding-looking hummocks of mattress which protruded aloft like the humps of camels. The carpet, evidently an afterthought, had been cut round the various appointments and was in consequence sagging sadly at the edges. The usual rush mat, so familiarly distressing to cold bare feet, lay before the washing-stand. The walls of the room were decorated with superannuated Christmas cards of a religious nature affixed with drawing-pins, a large framed picture of a soul with a pitiable squint being conducted by discreetly clad angels through a thunderstorm, and copious texts. Peter was examining one of the latter which hung immediately over the centre of the bed, as Mrs Spoker with a curt 'Good night to you,' retired and closed the door.

Peter and Margaret looked at each other for a moment in silence. Then simultaneously they laughed aloud.

'Under the circumstances, dear Margaret,' said Peter, 'I feel it was hardly tactful of them to put "Suffer little children to come unto me" just over your head tonight.'

'Listen!' said Margaret. 'And when we hear her go to bed you can creep down to the room where we had dinner. I hope you won't be most dreadfully uncomfortable.'

'I hope we neither of us will,' said Peter disconsolately. 'You seem to take all this extraordinarily calmly, Margaret, but I must say it looks to me as if we might be working up for considerable trouble.'

Margaret laughed again.

'Nonsense, Peter,' she said. 'Nobody we know will ever find their way to this place, and if they do they won't be any the wiser. Why shouldn't I have stayed a night here with Claude?'

'And what will Claude say?' argued Peter.

'Claude? Why, he'll be amused.'

'Will he?'

'At any rate he'll understand,' said Margaret, inclining her head to one side thoughtfully. 'So, I suppose will Sophia?'

'Oh, yes – Sophia. Oh, Lord, yes – if – when she hears about it,' said Peter carelessly.

'Well then, there you are. Who's going to cause any trouble?'

Peter hovered restlessly.

'What about that turbulent priest – Something Up-Jenkins, or whatever you say his remarkable name is?'

'Oh, I don't count him,' said Margaret. 'I'll explain to him next time I see him. He'll think it a joke too. I'm sure he's a sportsman.'

'H'm. He strikes me as being the sort of keen idiot who crops up at the very worst moment and drops bricks. Besides, I sort of feel that he knows Sophia and her people. It seemed to come back to me.'

'Oh, Sophia's people?' said Margaret with a slightly mischievous smile. 'Still I don't think you need be worried, Peter. I'll manage Mr Sloley-Jones.'

'It's only you I'm at all worried about,' said Peter.

'Then stop worrying, my dear,' she replied. 'Go and listen quietly at the door and see whether you can obtain any indications of Mrs Spoker, because I rather want to go to bed and sleep.'

Peter and Margaret were not the only persons in the *Stag and Hunt* who were considering the possible activities of the Reverend Mr Sloley-Jones. As Mrs Spoker locked the house door she paused for a moment in thought. Unlocking the door again she opened it and peered out into the night. For a few seconds she listened intently. The only sound that was borne to her ears was a long-drawn, stifled squall, pitched in a high key and succeeded by a rapid peroration of breathless yappings. Mrs Spoker again closed the door, again locked it, and removed the key. Then, as though to make assurance double sure, she turned and locked the door of the parlour, and, gathering up her candlestick from the floor, carried both keys, together with those of the bar and the office, upstairs with her to bed.

CHAPTER VIII

Pilgrims of the Night

Creaking movements resounded from staircase and landing. Peter turned from his keyhole reconnaissance at the bedroom doorway.

'All clear, I think,' he announced with a wistful smile.

Margaret had been investigating the contents of the two bags which by the joint agency of Peter and Gladys had been conveyed from the derelict car to the bedroom of the *Stag and Hunt*. She was now awaiting the retirement of Mrs Spoker with an air of apologetic impatience and modified unbuttoning preliminaries of a highly tantalising nature.

Three minutes later these had developed in privacy to an extent which entirely precluded the propriety of Peter's return. Margaret heard the sound of a faint scratching at the bedroom door with a quick turn of the head, and, shrouding herself with instinctive modesty, made her way thither between the projections of furniture.

'Is that you, Peter?'

'Y – es. Can I come in?'

'N – o. Why?'

'I must.'

'You can't yet.'

'May I presently?'

'Why do you want to?'

'Because, Margaret dear, I can't sleep in the what's-its-name-parlour.'

'Nonsense,' said Margaret, raising her voice slightly in protest, 'you can't have tried yet. You've only been there about three minutes.'

'But I can't even try, dash it! The old woman has locked the parlour door and sleeps with the key under her pillow.'

'Oh dear. How very unfortunate,' said Margaret. 'So where are you going to sleep?'

'That's precisely what I'm wondering,' said Peter.

'I'm very sorry for you,' announced Margaret through the keyhole, 'but you can't come and wonder here now, Peter.'

'May I open the door a crack?'

'No.'

'It would be easier to talk.'

'Are we going to talk very much?'

'I'll shut my eyes if you like.'

'Kindly keep the door firmly closed until I tell you you may open it,' said Margaret. 'I am in the middle of undressing.'

'Oh, what torture!' came in a muffled groan from the passage.

'Go and sit on the stairs for five minutes and then come back and ask again,' commanded Margaret.

'I think my watch has stopped,' whispered Peter fatuously.

'Then count five thousand sitting on the stairs,' said Margaret.

'Great heavens, am I Pelman?'

'Now, behave, Peter.'

'Behave! I am capable of behaving myself perfectly decently without having to sit on some infernally draughty stairs counting.'

'Well, as far as I can see, you'll probably have to sit there all night. But you may come in and talk it over with me when I am in bed.'

'And what if Mrs Spoker comes down and finds me crouched on the staircase muttering numerals?'

'Oh, don't meet troubles half-way,' said Margaret.

'That's just what I'm trying to avoid doing,' said Peter, retiring with very ill grace to the staircase.

So on the staircase he sat and heaved a little sigh of discomfiture. And if that sigh had been caught upon the night breeze and borne eastward, it might have encountered another little sigh, emanating from another staircase, the staircase of his flat in London. O melancholy circumstance! Here is a charming young couple, but three months married, sitting dejectedly at ten of a September night and sighing in helpless misunderstanding on two widely separated staircases.

Peter waited until he had cramp in the left leg, when he arose rather testily and returned to the bedroom door. Even a woman, dash it, ought to have had time to get into bed since his last call. He scratched again on the woodwork and opened the door a few inches.

'Wait! Not yet! Go away!'

'I will wait here,' said Peter. 'I will *not* go away. When it's "yet", let me know.'

'What on earth is all that commotion?' he added a moment later. 'Is the room on fire or something?'

'I am just getting into bed,' replied Margaret.

Peter sighed.

'Now I hear a noise like a band tuning up. I suppose that is the bed being got into?'

'Yes,' said Margaret. 'You may come in.'

She was sitting up. Her arms were spread over the yellow counterpane. Her bright hair had been brushed back and was held in a plait by a white ribbon. She eyed Peter from beneath her long lashes with a benevolent smile. He returned the smile with critical interest, as he advanced and seated himself uninvited on the foot of the bed.

'So that's what you look like, is it?' he remarked.

'It is,' said Margaret. 'Though you didn't come back here to tell me that.'

'All right, all right,' said Peter. 'I simply remark, in passing, that you look extraordinarily becoming in bed, that's all. Your taste in night-wear is simple, but effective.'

'I didn't invite you in here to exercise your alleged humour on the rather delicate position in which we find ourselves,' said Margaret firmly.

'No, but it interests me,' rejoined Peter. 'I rather like a

plain sensible nightgown myself. Sophia, now, wears a nightgown that looks like an enlarged spider's web which has caught some blue butterflies. And a boudoir-cap. You simply wouldn't believe the time she took to decide which boudoir-cap I was to see her in at the Bunters'.'

Margaret inclined her head speculatively.

'Doesn't it occur to you,' she said, 'that your wife takes thought on such matters simply with the idea of pleasing *you*? It's precious poor fun for a girl to take all that trouble and be laughed about for her pains.'

Peter stirred restlessly on the bed and his smile vanished.

'Well,' he said. 'I suppose I shall have to go down to the stable and sleep with Pansy.'

'Yes,' agreed Margaret cheerfully. 'Good idea!'

Peter sat pulling the lobe of his ear and watched her for a few moments in thoughtful silence.

'I suppose,' he said at length, 'that having gone so far, you wouldn't allow me to try and get an hour or two's rest on the floor of this room?'

'For once in a way,' replied Margaret, 'what you suppose happens to be absolutely correct.'

Peter sighed again.

'You are lucky,' he murmured. 'I wish I had a bed like that.'

'Then you can't be hard to please,' remarked Margaret testing a hummock. 'You will take to the stables like a duck to water.'

Peter arose from the bed and, thrusting his hands into his trousers pockets, commenced a somewhat restricted promenade of the bedroom, swinging his toes in front of him, as though he were kicking odious convention from his narrow path.

'It's all such rot,' he said. 'As far as I can see, Propriety is decided and limited not by the niceness of people's minds but by the nastiness. I may give you a lift in my car and nobody turns a hair. I may dine with you. I may sit on the foot of your bed – that's perfectly permissible. One might as well say a man might not go and see a girl in a nursing home. But if I lie down on the floor with my feet under the bed instead of on it, then immediately all the nasty-minded people in London come swarming and buzzing on to you like bees on a queen or a drone, or whatever it is bees do. One might just as well say, when you come to think of it, that it is immoral for a man to sit next to a woman in a bus. I shan't be anything like as near you as I should be in a bus, and we shall both have just as much on – you probably rather more. If you weren't allowed to travel on a bus with anyone you weren't married to, then there really might begin to be some chance of getting about London on the cheap.'

'On the other hand,' said Margaret gently, 'it would be rather uncomfortable if every man who met you in a bus could claim to sleep in your bedroom. It sounds like a newspaper report of early conditions in Russia under Bolshevism.'

'But with old friends, Margaret – I ask you.'

'Yes, you asked me before,' said Margaret.

Peter halted and stood over her. She looked up at him with a masterful smile of confidence. The plaited tail of golden hair had fallen over her left shoulder. Her strong, beautifully moulded arms, bare to the elbow, were still spread out before her. In the dim light of the candle her face looked pale, but her eyes were bright with what looked like rather heartless amusement. Margaret certainly looked very pretty in bed.

Peter placed his right hand gently upon hers and leant towards her slightly.

'Good night,' he said.

'Poor Peter. I'm really awfully sorry you haven't got a bed.'

'You look it,' said Peter.

'We must be common-sense,' said Margaret.

He leapt at what seemed a possible cue for further argument. Margaret withdrew her arms and placed them between the sheets.

'If we are going to be common-sense,' said Peter, 'I really fail to see why I shouldn't sleep on the floor.'

'No, Peter. I've suffered before now for being indiscreet.'

Peter turned from the bed.

'Of course,' he said. 'I forgot. I understand what you've got in mind now; I dare say you're quite right. Yes. Damn! Good night.'

But he halted near the doorway and examined his thumbnail critically.

'Though, of course,' he added. 'It's different now. I don't see that it's anybody's business but ours and your husband's.'

'And your wife's.'

'Er – yes. Hers too, I suppose.'

'It doesn't do to be too logical in these affairs,' said Margaret. 'You might as well say that if I elected to walk down Bond Street in my underclothes it wouldn't be anybody else's business but mine. Anybody else would see to that.'

'I don't suppose,' said Peter, 'that anybody else would notice anything unusual.'

'I'm really very, very sorry you haven't a bed, but I don't think the floor would be any more comfortable than the stables.'

'Well,' said Peter, glancing dejectedly round the room, 'I could get to sleep here anyhow. I could borrow a rug or a pillow or something—'

'Oh, I'll give you a pillow to take to the stables.'

'Oh, that's awfully good of you. And what, may I ask, is going to happen when Mrs Spoker hears more noises and comes down to investigate and finds me fooling about in the stables with Pansy and a pillow?'

'All right. I meant it kindly,' said Margaret.

'You mustn't forget this,' said Peter. 'In the eyes of the *Stag and Hunt* we are married. If we go and give Mrs Spoker or Gladys or the old man in the bar a hint that we are not really married, we shall probably be bunged out into the night. Our names are in the visitors' book as man and wife. That blighter – you know – O. Henry—'

'Cathcart Sloley-Jones?'

'Yes – has met us here as man and wife. We shall certainly have to explain to your husband in any case—'

'Well, of course I shall do that,' said Margaret. 'And to your wife too.'

Peter sighed.

'Well, if your husband and my wife, who are the only people that matter, hear about what we have done so far and don't mind, surely in Pity's name, they won't grudge me the small additional licence of lying down in the draught with my head under the dressing-table and my feet sticking so far under the bed that I shall bark my shins if I have a dream.'

Margaret laughed softly.

'Oh, I don't suppose Claude would mind,' she said.

'Well, there you are. My own wife is my own affair.'

'Claude,' continued Margaret, 'is not one of the husbands who say rather silly and unkind things about their wives.'

'Nor am I. Nobody could be fonder of his wife than I am of Sophia. I am passionately devoted to Sophia. Now, do let me have that spare pillow and take a chance for a few hours 'neath the shade of the washing-stand.'

'Peter!'

'Um – h – m.'

'Are you asleep?'

'Why?' asked Peter suspiciously from the darkness of the floor.

'I'm so sorry; I forgot to open the window. That is to say, I tried to, but it stuck. Would you do it?'

'Open the window? Do you want me to die?'

'We must have air,' said Margaret in a tone of sleepy virtue. 'Fresh air is essential or I shall have a headache in the morning.'

'I find I've got quite enough air as it is, without asking for any fresh, and I've got a neck-ache now. All right. I'll do it.

Have patience. I will disentangle my extremities from the towel-horse.'

Two minutes later he resumed his recumbent attitude on the floor, dusting his hands together with faint ejaculations of disgust. From the bed there echoed faint cooing sounds suggestive of gratitude.

With a prolonged effort Peter settled himself and drew his overcoat round such portions of his person as the furniture allowed. Again silence reigned, save for soft, regular sounds of breathing. Suddenly from the night without came the muffled but indomitable voice of Pansy. It was repeated – a long-drawn yell, followed by a series of quick, high-pitched squeaks. With a great whirl of bedclothes Margaret sat upright in bed.

'Peter!'

' 'Ullo.'

'Listen. Can't you hear my darling?'

'Are you addressing me?' said Peter rather grumpily.

'Pansy! Poor little dear. Can you hear her, Peter?'

'No,' said Peter.

'You can't be listening. There she goes again.'

'I think I can hear an owl,' said Peter.

'Nonsense. It's Pansy. Oh, I can't bear to hear her.'

'Oh Lord – all right – I'll shut the window again.'

'No, no. Oh, Peter! We can't let the poor little dear go on doing that all night.'

Peter sat up with a groan.

'Well, how on earth do you suggest stopping the damn little – dear little – poor little brute?' he asked.

'If you were only Claude, you would go and bring her in,' said Margaret.'

'If I were only Claude I shouldn't have cramp in my spine.'

'Peter, can't you?'

'Oh, my dear Margaret,' wailed Peter. 'I – I – I would like a shot if I really thought there was the slightest chance of my being able to get to the stables.'

'Why?' said Margaret. 'Only just now you were thinking of going down to sleep there.'

'I wasn't,' said Peter. 'It may be laid down as about as good a cinch as anything that has never been actually proved that that back door leading to the stables is warranted to baffle Houdini.'

'It's probably only bolted,' argued Margaret with drowsy insistence.

'My dear Margaret,' said Peter with a little groan, 'if a woman takes the trouble to double-lock her parlour and keep the key under her pillow, it stands to reason that the door to the yard is hung all over with burglar alarms. It probably has Yale locks and a portcullis.'

'Listen to that poor broken-hearted little darling,' cried Margaret in tremulous tones. 'Oh, how can you be so stony-hearted, Peter? If you had any love for dumb animals—'

'Dumb! God wot!' remarked Peter.

'You wouldn't lie there talking rubbish. I don't suppose you have any idea what a portcullis is.'

'I haven't,' said Peter. 'But you needn't get so animated about it. I don't think it's anything indecent, and even if it is the fact of sleeping in the same room as a lady would seem to justify a certain amount of licence in one's conversation.'

'You're taking rather a mean advantage of me if you're going to force me to get up and go down myself,' said Margaret.

Peter with a moan stirred himself into activity, lit a candle, and sought his discarded boots and jacket.

'One thing about Sophia,' he said. 'She confines herself to moulting lovebirds.'

CHAPTER IX

The Sleep of the Just

Peter halted before the small door at the end of the passage through which Mrs Spoker had borne Pansy to the stables. After examining it by the light of a match until he burnt his fingers, he cautiously tested the bolts which guarded it. Though there was nothing unusual in their appearance, they were curious bolts. The bolt at the foot of the door was loose in its socket and could be withdrawn with one finger. It was, in fact, if anything too loose for Peter's liking; it gave forth loud rattling sounds during the operation, at the conclusion of which the head of the bolt fell with a noisy thud against the woodwork of the door.

The topmost fitting offered a direct contrast. It appeared to have been welded into its socket. Still burning matches in reckless profusion Peter exerted himself upon it in vain. He shifted his position and attempted to work the head of the bolt up and down as a vague but hopeful preliminary to shooting it back. The head of the bolt yielded half an inch with a squeak which seemed to resound through the whole house.

Peter set his teeth and made a further effort. The bolt flew back with a sudden staggering surrender and a loud crash. Peter, partially overbalanced for a moment, recovered himself with a gasp.

The door was still held by a turned key. Why Mrs Spoker, who had so carefully guarded the keys of all the other doors on the ground floor, had allowed this one to remain turned in its lock is one of the mysteries which only arise – but always arise – when a woman gets an idea into her head.

After listening anxiously for any evidences of disturbance on the floor above, Peter turned his attention to this key. It was very stiff. Peter found a very good pencil in his pocket and attempted to employ its aid in the difficulty, inserting it through the eye of the key and thus gaining a purchase. He was handicapped by having to hold lighted matches in his left hand throughout the operation, and when he placed a burning match on the floor and used both hands to the key the match went out and he broke the pencil at almost the identical moment.

'That woman,' he said to himself, 'must have the wrists of Tarzan.'

Perhaps the beastly thing wasn't locked after all. He turned the door handle and pulled. No, it was locked. He fingered the key again deliberately. Yielding to an almost unintentional movement it turned quite easily from left to right, in the direction usually employed for locking a door. Peter sighed, lit one of his few remaining matches and groped on the floor for his two pieces of pencil.

He pulled the door open. Oh, he was not yet in the yard. Here were sculleries or something. He was in a dim atmosphere of tea-leaves, crockery and wet floor-cloths. He struck another match and peered his way down a further narrow passage to the real back door.

Here the bolts were more normal. He opened the back door stealthily. Outside the night was dark, but the way to the stables was not difficult to ascertain. Pansy was still unsettled.

Peter stepped out; then suddenly drew back with a shudder. Rain, fine drizzling rain of the most thoroughly wetting variety, was falling with silent persistence.

He stood for a moment in the doorway and turned up his coat collar. His mind dwelt upon the woman upstairs – in bed. What an extraordinary woman she was. A little earlier that night, as he had sat on the end of her bed watching her, he had been swept by a sudden wave of admiration of the homely, settled, unambitious comfort of her nature. Sophia, the artistic, the emotional, the uncertain, had been mentally subjected to unfavourable comparison with Margaret, lying there so cosy and unartificial in her old-fashioned nighty. But Peter could remember Margaret gay and excitable – too excitable. Since she had retired to do penance she had apparently made the discovery that penance was the best form of existence.

As Peter had seen her tonight, Margaret had suggested a breathing definition of home comfort and of intransitory fondness possessing none of the rather erotic emotions of Sophia's *ménage*. Yes, he must confess, he had looked upon her in her homeliness and for the moment yearned. Now he was gaining early and first-hand experience of the lot which awaited the husband of a Margaret.

He must be willing, nay, was expected cheerfully to volunteer to go forth into the cold, wet night after a little blasted barking dog. What would married life mean to such a man? The episode was suggestive of an ordered routine of kind smiles and dull sweetness. No, the impassioned flexible Sophia was Peter's woman – exacting, querulous, at times bitter; but how much more exciting; and really, when one came to the point, no less reasonable. Sophia would never have demanded this dog-fetching business.

Interesting, though, and instructive to spend a night with old Margaret. Poor old Margaret! She had been awfully badly maligned and had been driven perhaps to overdo the domesticated, strictly ordinary part she had assumed. Peter regarded her still with great affection and a sort of indeterminate sympathy.

And now for her confounded dog!

No wonder they had heard the little wretch. The top half of the stable door had swung open. As Peter looked within there was a desperate scramble in the straw and the sharp yelps of Pansy seemed to change in tone from complaint to welcome.

Peter entered the stable. He struck yet another match and stooping over Pansy caressed her kindly. She licked the proffered hand. From head to foot she was trembling in a manner which resembled one continual shiver. The hairs of her ruff bristled. Her tailless hind-quarters seemed to be subject to a separate and more excessive vibration than that which affected the rest of her small black person. Her pathetic eyes with their usual expression of intense fear glanced shiftily to and fro. She ceased to howl only to give vent to a series of long plaintive whistling sounds through her thin sharp nose.

'Shut up,' said Peter.

Pansy glanced nervously from left to right and whistled again.

'Shut up,' repeated Peter.

He raised his right hand very slowly and softly patted the quivering flank.

Pansy raised a sudden shriek of agony. Peter had no idea how sensitive his little friend was on matters of this sort.

'Look here, stop that, or I really will hit you,' he said.

He slowly raised his hand again. Pansy did not wait. She shrieked and springing suddenly aside sped out of the stable into the night.

'Damn!' cried Peter following.

He stood for a moment on the threshold of the stable. He looked around him, making little chirruping noises with his lips and clipping noises with his fingers. He failed, however, to catch sight of Pansy. He stepped out from the stable. The rain had increased in volume.

'Come here!' said Peter in a hoarse whisper, groping among what appeared in the darkness to be pig-buckets. 'Look here, do come here. Dear little Pansy, come on. I won't hurt you, you infernal little brute. My God, if I catch you – Pansy! Little Pansy! Here, dearie!'

Far, far away, amid the wet undergrowth of the crab-apple plantation, Pansy fell foul of a tree-trunk and gave tongue.

Peter turned with blasphemous comment in the direction from which the note of fear reached him. He blundered blindly into a hand-pump which stood at an angle of the inn wall. He careered into the largest of the pig-buckets and dislodged a salmon-tin. He found himself lost in a dripping morass of weed and stones, where, at the extreme confines of the *Stag and Hunt*, what had formerly been a portion of the inn yard was now the property of vegetating Nature. He butted against another small out-building, unseen in the darkness, from which issued the throaty anticipations of a doubtful hen. He tripped over a derelict broom. He paused and listened only to receive a large globule of accumulated rain on the bridge of his nose from the branch of a tree.

'Oh, damn this!' said Peter. 'And when I get the little brute I know what it will be. She'll be too wet to get into the bed and I shall have to nurse her on the floor. I'll nurse her, by Gad. Here, little Pansy! Pansy-Pansy! Co-ome along then, dear little dog!'

A wire fence separated the *Stag and Hunt* from the crab-apple plantation. Peter found it somewhat unexpectedly. Having found it he leant against it and again listened intently. All was silent save for the dull hiss of soaking rain.

Lingering in a semi-reclining attitude, Peter suddenly realised that he was intensely weary. Almost any situation was preferable to that in which he found himself. Better to return to his hard and draughty bed on the floor – to the stable even. Yet he seemed unable to summon the effort. And as he waited hopelessly, uselessly, leaning against the wire fence he longed for the comfort and cleanliness of the refined spare bedroom at the Bunters' where Sophia lay asleep.

A feeling of blank despair, a sort of shock at the realisation that this was really he and these circumstances were really his, combined with the almost mocking summons of sleep, overcame him. He must make an effort – he couldn't. But what was there to be miserable about? All he had to do was to go back. It didn't matter whether he slept or not. Besides he was so sleepy now that he hardly knew what he was doing.

No, but there was something really the matter at the back of his mind. What was it? He hadn't done anything wrong – nothing that he would be ashamed about to Sophia, or that she wouldn't understand – after a bit. And yet this feeling of intense depression had some connection with Sophia.

'Good heavens!' said Peter to himself aloud. 'I know what's the matter with me. I'm blowed if it isn't that I'm home-sick.'

It was. For the first night since their marriage he found himself parted from his wife – from the wife whom he went about criticising to his female friends. And now when he was really left to his own resources, and his own resources resulted in his getting wet through and extremely exhausted in trying to find another woman's stray dog at the dead of night in a dirty little pub at some Godforsaken village in Somerset, he began to realise what drivel he had talked to Margaret about Sophia.

Sophia was hard sometimes. He had learnt to love her hardness. If she was hard ever it was because she was made like that, and he loved her. Perhaps as she learnt how dearly he really loved and treasured her and how home-sick he was when he spent a night away from her she might grow a little softer.

Margaret now was too soft. Damn her shivering little fool dogs.

Rousing himself with a great effort the happy husband returned to the *Stag and Hunt.*

He manipulated the various bolts and locks with as little noise as possible; to which end he ignored the topmost bolt of the inner door entirely. The stairs creaked ominously as he commenced his wary ascent. He sat down upon the staircase and removed his boots. They were very wet.

As he hovered outside the bedroom door he again seemed to hear sounds of restlessness on the floor above. He turned the door-handle silently and crept into the room.

Margaret ignored his entry. Peter lit a candle and carried it inquisitively to the bed.

Margaret lay back on her pillow with closed eyes and a little smile of blissful contentment playing about her lips. Her head was poised slightly on one side, and her cheek and neck had that soft, pink fullness which is irresistible. Peter shaded the candle with his hand and bent over her, holding his breath.

She stirred slightly and her left hand which lay across her breast moved a few inches. The wedding ring on her finger caught the gleam of the candle light. Peter withdrew his head and straightened himself with thoughtful eyes.

He was thinking of Sophia again. Sophia was lying asleep too in her solitary spare bedroom at the Bunters'. Or perhaps she was lying awake, thinking of him and feeling herself that unsettled sensation of discomfort at being parted from him for the first night since her marriage.

Peter shivered in his wet coat and glanced helplessly around him. He would go. After all, though he and Margaret and Margaret's husband and – after reasonable explanation – no doubt Sophia, too, would fully understand and approve this necessity for his sleeping in Margaret's room, perhaps it would be as well for him to take a chance on the staircase or even to try and snatch a few hours' sleep on the bed vacated by Pansy in the stable. For some reason which his overtired brain refused to analyse he did not want to sleep in Margaret's room now. He somehow felt that it was impossible to sleep in spirit with Sophia with his feet under Margaret's bed.

He looked down again upon Margaret asleep. That soft round of cheek and neck was only comparable to a vision of chocolate *éclairs* to the eyes of a schoolboy. Yet this seemed only an additional reason for departing silently and courting Sophia in spirit in the stable.

Peter sighed deeply.

'This is a fiendish outfit,' he said. 'Wandering about wet through and frantically overtired, with my mind having a sort of irresponsible beano on its own. Oh, what the devil shall I do?'

'What dear?' asked Margaret, opening startled eyes.

'I said "What the devil shall I do." '

'Oh!' Margaret blinked at him several times.

'Where's Pansy?' she said at length.

'Well, Pansy, as a matter of fact, is looking out for herself. She didn't want to come in with me, so I let her run off and enjoy herself. She's so happy.'

'Oh, Peter! Wouldn't it be kinder to go and bring her in?'

'No, I don't think so,' said Peter hastily. 'And in any case I don't suppose I could find her now if I wanted to.'

'Why not?'

'Because the night outside is about as black as the spot-boy's white gloves on the Saturday evening of a billiard match.'

'Where is she?'

'Last time I heard of her she was enjoying herself awfully among some trees.'

'But, Peter – you're wet!'

Margaret raised herself in bed and stretched out a white hand to the arm of his coat.

'Oh, my dear, you're wet through.'

'That's all right,' said Peter carelessly. 'Not through. Only rather.'

'You're soaking; absolutely soaking. How did you get so wet? Is it raining?'

'Oh no, my dear Mrs. Watson; I've been standing under a hosepipe.'

'You must get some of those things off immediately. You'll get pneumonia or something. Now, how are we going to manage about this?'

She was sitting up in bed by this time, sweeping the hair from her forehead with busy fingers. She ceased to do so in order to use the hand for gesticulating at Peter.

'I know,' she said. 'Put out the light and remove your outer garments and hang them over a chair to dry. Then wrap yourself in this blanket and keep warm on the floor. After an hour or two the things ought to be dry enough to put on again.'

'God of battles!' said Peter. 'Are we spending the night, or doing "Saved from the Sea" for the cinematograph?'

'Do what I tell you. Remove your outer garments at once; only kindly blow out the candle first.'

Peter cast one appealing look towards the bed and obeyed. The room was plunged in darkness. He removed his wet coat and boots. As he stumbled to his feet he realised that his socks, too, were damp. He balanced himself on one leg to make closer investigation, tottered, overbalanced, and clutching at the nearest object to hand, sent a china basin from the washing-stand crashing to the floor. Margaret raised her head with a muffled cry of alarm.

'What on earth are you doing, Peter?'

'Nothing, nothing. I knocked over a jug or something. Nothing, nothing.'

'It made an awful row,' said Margaret.

'I think it only *sounded* loud,' murmured Peter.

'Is it broken?'

'I can't see. I shouldn't think so. A bit of it may be.'

'Don't be footling,' said Margaret. 'Hurry up and put your blanket round you. It's hanging over the bed-post. And then go to bed quickly on the floor.'

'Hush!' said Peter quickly in a whisper. 'Listen!'

They listened. Yes. Footsteps were descending the stairs. They drew nearer and halted outside the bedroom door.

Peter paused open-mouthed. The flickering light of a candle shone through the abnormally large crack between the door and the mat. He drew a deep breath. To be subjected to a verbal inquisition from Mrs Spoker at that hour and in those circumstances was more than even he could face. He groped his way stealthily round the bed. Mrs Spoker knocked and he hesitated no longer. He clambered into bed beside Margaret and drew the bedclothes round his neck. Margaret appeared to give her silent consent to such a course. She uttered no remonstrance; nor did she reply to the sound of knocking which was now repeated from the landing.

'Pretend to be asleep,' whispered Peter.

Margaret made no reply. Mrs Spoker pushed the door a

foot open and peered in. The silence was broken only by the sounds of heavy breathing.

Holding her candle aloft, Mrs Spoker advanced a pace into the room and scrutinised the bed and its occupants severely. She could descry the two heads of her visitors lying close together on the pillow. Mrs Hackett's face was slightly raised and wore a smile of seraphic innocence. Mr Hackett's face was downturned, half-buried in the bedclothes.

Behind the landlady, the face of Gladys, wearing an expression of mingled alarm and stupor, appeared, surmounted by curl papers, round the door. She, too, surveyed the sleeping Hacketts. In accordance with her unfortunate habit, she snorted loudly.

'Don't you go making that noise here; you'll wake 'em up,' whispered the landlady, propelling Gladys by pushing movments of her own hind-quarters back on to the landing. 'You get back to bed. It ain't them. If I hear any more of it I'll have Alfred up and make him look downstairs.'

'It's cats,' volunteered Gladys, as Mrs Spoker followed her out and closed the bedroom door silently behind her.

'Cats, rubbish!' said Mrs Spoker. 'You get to bed.'

She stood for a moment with candle raised, frowning down over the banisters, a gaunt figure in her dressing-gown and nightcap. Then, turning with a shrug, she held a brief auditory examination of the state of the bed-ridden old lady above the bar. From this room the sounds of unbroken sleep could be heard even on the landing; and finally Mrs Spoker bore her candle slowly back up the second flight of stairs.

'Peter! Get up and get out at once.'

'Oh, Lord! All right, all right. I was nearly asleep.'

'Come on now. Get up at once. This won't do.'

'All right. Don't prod me, merciful heavens.'

'You may wrap your blanket round you and sleep on the floor.'

'Oh, yes. Thanks very much.'

'Only please do so at once.'

'All right. Don't make a row. You'll have that accursed

old woman down here again. Don't push. I'm trying to find the floor with my foot.'

'If you're sleepy, that's all the better,' said Margaret. 'You'll be able to get off on the floor.'

'What I want to know is – what's going to happen if I'm still asleep when that bleating girl brings in the tea in the morning and finds me on the floor. What am I going to say?'

'Use your sense. Say you are looking for one of your socks.'

'I've got my socks on.'

'Then take one of them off and lose it, and then you can really be looking for it.'

'Oh, confound this, Margaret, really—'

'Hush! Don't make a noise. And mind you get as warm and dry as you can. Good night. Oh – and, Peter—'

'Yes? What? Damn! Half a second. What?'

'Do be careful not to lie down on the broken bit of jug.'

PART TWO
'He Sings all Day'

CHAPTER X

The Vicar's Egg

The rain had ceased, but the morning was gloomy and threatening. If Nature forbore, for a while, to weep for the follies and foibles of mankind, she continued to frown heavily upon them. Ponderous clouds hung over the face of the sky. The prospect of one passing smile of sunshine seemed remote.

Yet Nature, even in this embittered mood, found a devotee. He leant through the front parlour window of a small lodging-house in the town of Downblotton and exclaimed,

'By Jove. Rain overnight! Good! The roads wanted it badly. No sun either. Capital conditions for biking. I'm off to Glastonbury for the day, Mrs Wigger. Breakfast ready, you say? Well done. Bacon? Excellent. Thank you, Mrs Wigger. Egg? Bravo. Fried? Good!'

Mrs Wigger, holiday landlady to Sloley-Jones, was a little woman of rosy contentment. Hers was an eminently smoothing nature. Her dimpled hands were generally busy smoothing a table-cloth or a pillow-case; and, failing these objectives, Mrs Wigger would employ them temporarily in making smoothing movements over her own ample bosom. Her manner was invariably sweet and cordial, but studiously noncommittal, as becomes a smoother.

She stood and smoothed herself now, as she watched her boarder stride enthusiastically to the breakfast table and seat himself, bringing the large palms of his hands together with great smacks of delight.

'Would you per'aps care to take your dinner with you – your lunch, that is?' she suggested. 'It will in all probability only make a small parcel and will save you spending whatever it is on whatever it is you get to eat at Glastonbury or wherever it is you get it, that is, if you don't take it as I suggest.'

'Ah – happy thought!' said the reverend gentleman, smiling up at her while yet in eating difficulties with his fried egg. 'Yes. Good idea indeed, Mrs Wigger. What can you give me now?'

'Well, there's always egg,' said Mrs Wigger tentatively.

'Egg! Never too often for me. I love egg. This egg, by the way, is simply tip-top.'

'Very well then, sir. Egg. Hard-boiled, that will be, of course.'

'Hard boiled? No? How too splendid!'

'And what time will you be starting?'

'Let's see now. I'm going to the garage for a bit first. Before I start out today I mean to get thoroughly oiled. I expect they'll want me to clean out my carburettor. I may have to change my plugs. Say shortly after ten, Mrs Wigger.'

'Very well, sir. I'll try and see whether I can't let you have your egg and that ready for you at about shortly after ten or thereabouts. Have you pretty nearly all you require now, sir?'

'Rather,' said Sloley-Jones. 'Rath-err. Except my boots.'

Shortly after ten the parson sallied forth. He wore a pepper and salt Norfolk jacket, which bulged with what Mrs Wigger described reticently as 'the egg and cetera', and which she herself stuffed in a neat parcel into the clergyman's pocket with the air of a benevolent aunt three days before Christmas.

Sloley-Jones had again assumed his marine's leggings against the mud. The sky remained menacing, but he somehow managed to extract a glint of sunshine to catch his spectacles as he waved farewell to his landlady, who stood smoothing herself and watched him out of sight. That the garage had oiled him thoroughly was obvious to more senses than one long after he had turned the bend of the road towards Maiden Blotton.

He slowed down in almost unconscious compliance to his

train of thought as he neared the *Stag and Hunt*. The front door and nearly all the windows were open to the morning. Through the window of the bedroom above the parlour Mrs Spoker shook a duster at him with the facial expression of one who is cleansing her premises of an evil smell. Sloley-Jones saw no sign of the Hacketts. They had evidently continued their journey.

His mind was still busy with that charming openhearted woman and her rather surprisingly nice husband as he swung round a corner of the road a mile beyond the inn. Then, quick as thought, came a sudden distraction. Sloley-Jones gripped his brake, skidded madly, and saved himself and his bicycle from destruction by plunging an intuitive leg into the hedge. The small boy remained in the middle of the road and witnessed the brilliant manoeuvre with a broad grin.

Sloley-Jones drew his foot from the hedge. He groaned, wiped his brow and adjusted his spectacles. Then he faced the small boy and shook his head sadly.

He was a very dirty little boy and his grin was malicious rather than humorous. His general appearance seemed to savour of the industrial rather than of the rural. He had the obdurate demeanour of a Trade Unionist in the bud.

'I say, boy,' began Sloley-Jones, 'you simply mustn't walk in the middle of the road. It's dangerous – awfully. I was very nearly into you.'

The boy merely grinned offensively.

'Don't grin now. You must take more care. You – Good gracious!'

For the boy, unwilling to remain and debate the subject, was preparing to move on. He twitched a string which he held in his right hand. The twitch resulted in a sharp yelp and from behind the legs of the boy was hauled the figure of a small, expostulating, black dog.

Sloley-Jones opened his mouth wide and, stooping over his cycle, subjected the dog to a closer examination. At the same moment the boy moved forward and the dog, stubbornly refusing to follow voluntarily, was dragged for several yards on four stiffened legs through the slush of the road.

'Wait a moment,' commanded Sloley-Jones. 'I know this dog. This is not your dog. Where did you get this dog? I know this dog.'

'No, yer don't,' said the boy.

'Yes, I do,' said Sloley-Jones. 'Don't contradict. I know this dog. Did you find this dog?'

The boy hesitated and glanced shiftily from Sloley-Jones to Pansy who avoided his eye with an almost human expression of apprehension.

'I was talking to this dog only last night,' continued Sloley-Jones. 'I was also talking to the lady the dog belongs to. Where did you find this dog?'

'It ain't a dog,' said the boy.

'Oh yes it is,' said Sloley-Jones. 'I suppose you think it isn't a dog because it hasn't got a tail. It is a dog. It is a Dutch dog, known as a Schipperke, from the Dutch word which means a skipper or sea-captain. The dogs are called that because out there in Holland the barges on the canals are all guarded by dogs of this sort. Of course it is a dog – absurd! Did you suppose it was a cat? Now then, where did you find this dog?'

'It ain't a dog,' said the boy.

'You seem to be a very silly boy, besides being very rude and contradictory to those who know better than yourself. I tell you this is a Schipperke dog belonging to a lady I know.'

'If yer think this is a dog,' said the boy, 'yer don't know much.'

'You're the most offensive boy I think I have ever struck,' said Sloley-Jones severely. 'If it isn't a dog, what is it?'

'It's a bitch,' said the boy.

Sloley-Jones turned aside with a sharp, irritated clicking of the tongue. He returned to the charge with a greater assertion of his authority.

'Did you find the d— her?' he asked positively.

'I did that,' said the boy.

'And what do you intend doing with er – her?'

'Train 'er,' replied the boy twitching the string sharply.

'She does not require any training, thank you.'

'Yes, she do,' said the boy. 'She can't even walk proper.'

'Now look here,' said Sloley-Jones severely. 'You must give me that dog at once. I'll see that—'

'It ain't a dog,' cried the boy enthusiastically.

'You must give me that – well, why not? – that beech immediately, and I'll take her to her proper owner,' said the parson.

The boy shook his head slowly.

'Mebbe, there'll be a reward for 'er,' he suggested.

'Nonsense, a reward! Ridiculous! Much more likely you'll get into trouble for stealing her.'

'Any'ow,' said the boy, 'I'll wait a bit and see whether there ain't going to be no reward.'

'But it's ridiculous! I never—'

The parson's hand had strayed to his pocket. An immediate inspiration dawned upon him.

'Now, look here,' he said. 'I do not intend to offer you any money for the do— any money. But if you hand over that do— the little creature without any more fuss I tell you what I'll do, though I don't really consider you deserve it. I'll give you something very nice to eat.'

'What?' asked the boy promptly.

'Well, I'm not quite sure,' proceeded Sloley-Jones, withdrawing the paper parcel with some difficulty from his pocket. 'Egg, for one thing. Are you fond of egg?'

'Let's 'ave a look at it,' said the boy doubtfully.

'There you are,' said Sloley-Jones, opening the parcel. 'Lovely things to eat – scrumptious! More than you deserve.'

Having regained Pansy he administered a severe chiding to a boy who had evidently been brought up to speak in the most rude and argumentative way to his elders and betters, and who showed in addition a strong tendency to interest himself in the study of sex-problems which were almost bound to produce evil influences in one of such tender years. The boy, who had meanwhile withdrawn to the farther side of the road, busied himself in consuming hard-boiled eggs and sandwiches in a manner which only the digestive organs of a boy can permit. Finally Sloley-Jones buttoned Pansy, greatly against the latter's will, into the chest of his Norfolk jacket, and turning his bicycle set off at full speed for the *Stag and Hunt.*

Mrs Spoker had completed her cleansing operations on the first floor and was standing at the entrance of the inn as the parson drew up. She peered at him, as he placed his cycle on its stand, with the expression of a short-sighted pessimist.

'Good morning,' said Sloley-Jones.

'I thought I saw you going the other way,' said Mrs Spoker.

'Yes, you did; but I came back.'

'It's no good your doing that,' said Mrs Spoker. 'I am not yet open to the public.'

'I want to see Mrs Hackett,' said Sloley-Jones, placing a hand inside his Norfolk jacket.

'She's gorn,' was the reply. 'Both she and Mr 'Ackett. And a good job too.'

'Oh, I say. Come! That's not very complimentary. I think they're most awfully nice people myself – topping!'

'That may be,' grumbled Mrs Spoker, 'but the noises there was going on last night in this 'otel was 'ardly creditable.'

'Noises in the night? Why?'

'That's what I wants to know, why. Mr 'Ackett, 'e started of it, goin' out for to let the dog loose. I got that out of 'im this morning when I found one of the bolts o' the door unclosed. But what caused some o' the other noises that took place after, I don't know. It was not them, for I went down to their room to look and there they were in bed and asleep. It wasn't you come back after all, I suppose?'

'I? No fear. No, if I had come back I should have woken you up.'

'Well, whatever it was did wake me up,' cried Mrs Spoker

angrily. 'So much so that I never got a wink o' sleep all night. I made sure at first it must be you outside there with more complaints in your bicycle and wantin' to come in.'

The parson shook his head with a soft smile.

'Sorry to hear you had such an awfully disturbed night,' he said. 'But it was nothing to do with me. I got home all right. Lucky! I was red hot and hissing like anything. Why did Mr Hackett let the dog loose? I expect the noise you heard afterwards was caused by the dog.'

He displayed the shivering form of Pansy as he spoke.

'Talking of the dog,' he said, 'here she is. That's why I came back. I suppose Mrs Hackett was rather upset about her?'

Mrs Spoker looked with great severity at Pansy for a few moments before nodding curtly.

'In that case,' continued the parson, 'I wonder that Mr Hackett went and let her out like that.'

'So do I,' said Mrs Spoker bitterly. 'Out in the pourin' rain, gettin' all his clothes wet, which had to be dried this morning before 'e got out of 'is room. And all that disgraceful noise and that at night, and all for a dog.'

Pansy turned a guilty eye from the speaker.

'Well, I suppose Mr Hackett knew what he was doing.'

'I doubt it,' said Mrs Spoker. 'And the noises I 'eard after couldn't a' been made by the dog, for the noise was inside the 'ouse and the dog was somewhere outside, 'aving run away.'

'What kind of a noise was it?'

'Crashing,' said Mrs Spoker. 'And there was a basin broke in the room Mr and Mrs 'Ackett had this morning. But it couldn't 'ave bin that either, because I was in their room 'ardly a minute after the crashing noise come, and there they were, as I tell you, in bed and asleep together.'

'H'm, mysterious – very! Quite queer!'

'So I made sure,' continued Mrs Spoker, with renewed suspicion, 'that you and that bicycle o' yours was at the bottom of it.'

'No indeed,' said Sloley-Jones. 'Anyhow the point is, what are we to do with the dog?'

'Mrs 'Ackett, she spent 'alf a 'our lookin' fer that thing this morning,' said Mrs Spoker contemptuously. 'After their motor-car 'ad come and all, when they was all ready to start; and when she gave it up she left me the address she was goin' to for me to send the dog, if found.'

'Oh, well done – that's prime,' cried Sloley-Jones. 'I'll go after them with the dog – that is if they haven't gone a tremendous distance. How delighted Mrs Hackett will be. What's the address?'

Mrs Spoker retired to the office, whence after a few moments she returned bearing a half-sheet of note-paper.

'Care of Sir Stirling Bunter, Baronet', murmured Sloley-Jones aloud as he read the inscription. 'Oh, Rushcombe Fitz-Chartres. That's only about fifteen miles from here, isn't it? Yes, rather, I know. You can get there across the common – Baynton, or whatever the place is called. Or of course you could go straight on through Downblotton and Turnholme, but that's a long way round.'

'It doesn't concern me,' said Mrs Spoker with a shrug. 'I'm not goin' either way.'

'Which way did the Hacketts take, do you know?'

'No, I do not.'

'Oh, Baynton I expect, though I dare say the road's pretty dud. Anyhow I'll chance it, shall I?'

'Yes, do,' said Mrs Spoker quite encouragingly.

'Right. The only thing is, have you got a basket or anything I can put the poor little thing in? I've been carrying her inside me, here, and I don't think either of us find it very comfortable.'

'That dog's bin more trouble to me than I 'ardly dare trust myself to say,' said Mrs Spoker. 'I 'ave no basket. You must take her inside your clothes as heretofore.'

Ten minutes later the Reverend Cathcart Sloley-Jones sailed through the town of Downblotton at a speed which made the country policeman on duty heave up a nodding head and survey the scene around him with a slow gaze of stupefied horror.

And outside the post office of Downblotton stood, unoccupied, a large and well-appointed limousine. And inside the post office stood Margaret, wrestling with a local telephone directory.

And still more deeply submerged in the post office, in the small telephone box itself, stood Mr Dann, crushing his red moustache against the mouthpiece in an uproarious recital of his movements for the benefit of Gamble's garage, London.

And three doors off Peter reclined, sleepy yet, in the chair of the Downblotton barber.

And at this very moment Sophia's father, in his office at Holborn Viaduct, was flinging his discarded attempts at social telegraphy into his waste-paper basket.

And Claude Hackett, M.P., was asking the hall porter of the Reform Club for details of the trains to Bristol.

And Sloley-Jones, knowing none of these things, but glistening with heat and zeal, joyous in well-doing, was speeding onwards to the Bunters', rehearsing in his mind the full details of the account he should render; with Pansy, reduced to a mere cowering embodiment of dumb panic, in his bosom.

CHAPTER XI

Going and Coming

Running an unkempt forefinger over the western portion of a large automobile map, while he held the telephone receiver in the other hand the manager of Gamble's garage gradually succeeded in piecing together the fragmentary remarks of Dann into the semblance of a definite report. He gathered that Dann was conversing with him from a place called Hold On, which, after an interval for consultation with the postmaster, developed into Downblotton. The leak in the radiator had first occurred on the road, miles from anywhere. Mr Wykeham and the lady had stopped in a pub at a place called Half a Tick.

'You don't seem to get the hang of the neighbourhood very satisfactory,' commented the manager.

'No more wouldn't you down in these parts,' replied Dann. 'They still calls their places by the names they was given by Julius Caesar when 'e first came along.'

A further brief interval followed while Dann inquired of the postmaster the name of the little place down the road.

The Downblotton postmaster, who had grown old and grey at his post of duty, considered that efficiency was only to be defined in terms of deliberate and punctilious caution. These quick people with motor-cars who rushed his post office and subjected him to questions in rapid fire he regarded as a serious menace to the peace and rectitude of his native town. He had already experienced quite enough trouble for one morning from the lady of the party, who, having at length arrived at the conclusion that the Bunters were not on the telephone, had left the post office.

The postmaster left his counter and came slowly forward to the door of the telephone box.

'The name o' the place down the road?' he repeated.

'Ah,' said Dann with a sharp nod.

'Down which road?'

'Why, down that road. The place I just come from.'

The postmaster, who by reason of a drooping eyelid could only use one eye for staring, used it at Dann.

'There's a lot o' places down that road,' he said. 'A 'eap of 'em, there is. 'Ow do I know the name o' the place down that road you jest come from? If you don't know the name o' the place you jest come from, 'ow can I tell you the name o' the place you jest come from down that road? There's a 'eap more places than one down that road by a great deal. There's a lot more of 'em than one by a whole 'eap.'

' 'Old 'ard,' said Dann on the telephone. 'I'm just asking Julius Caesar. I find 'e's still 'ere.'

'If folks comes in and says "What's the name o' the place I jest come from?" 'Ow do I know? They ought to know. They come from 'em, not me. What kind of a place was this you jest come from that you wants to know what place it was?'

Eventually the manager of Gamble's elicited the news that the party had stayed overnight at an inn designated the Stunted Hag in a village named Maid's Blotter. No such definite information could be given concerning the destination for which the car was now bound. Rushcombe Fitz-Chartres was beyond Dann's power of memory.

'You'll find it on the map easy enough,' said Dann to his manager. 'O'Brien something it is, I think; or MacPherson – something or other. You'll find it on yer map. It ain't far from 'ere, that's all I know. And if I'd a' known all the rar which would ensue I wouldn't a' rung you up at all, I wouldn't.'

'You needn't 'ave for all the good you've done,' returned the manager.

'No, and I won't do it no more, what's more I won't,' retorted Dann, who between manager and postmaster was becoming somewhat heated.

'That'll do,' said the voice of the manager. 'I don't wish to 'ave no more backchat from you.'

'No more don't I from you ruddy well neither,' said Dann.

This concluded the conversation.

In one respect it sufficed. Within five minutes the manager had endowed Sophia's mother with a full share of the information at his disposal.

No sooner therefore had the wholesale ironmonger plunged into the morning flood of his ironmongering matters than a knowledgable lady clerk interrupted him with a confidential whisper. He was wanted on the telephone by Mrs Bone.

'Oh, Lord!' murmured the harassed man. 'All right. Tell her to – that is, ask her to hold the line one moment. Say I'm just in the middle of something important. Hand me those telegraph forms, will you, please?'

He tore now at the sparse hairs of his crown. Seizing a pencil he began feverishly to compose afresh:

> Sir Stirling Bunter. Rushcombe Fitz-Chartres. Somerset. Have you any news wykeham he started yesterday for you with wife but got left behind wife started but returned think he started too in car wife has lost track wants to know what to do is he with you—
>
> Wykenam missed wife he—
>
> Is wykeham with you mrs wykeham will come if he is wit—
>
> Wykeham missed train wife caught but—
>
> Yesterday mrs wykeham missed mr wykeham—

'Mrs Bone is through to your private line, sir,' said the lady clerk.

She was. The overwrought husband on lifting the receiver found that his wife was already delivering the peroration of a lengthy harangue.

'Are you listening?' she asked, pausing in the midst of a peculiarly puzzling passage.

'Yes, dear.'

'You are? Then why not say so? Have you telegraphed to the people in Somerset?'

'Yes, indeed I have.'

'Then you have been exceedingly foolish. The last thing I said to you was "don't".'

'Well, I think I still might be able to stop the telegram going.'

'H'm. You can't have sent it off very promptly. Why half-do a thing?'

'Do you want it to go or not?'

'What?'

'Do you not want it to go?'

'What?'

'The telegram, dear.'

'No, of course not. Hasn't it gone?'

'I say – I – I think I can stop it.'

'H'm. When did you send it? How can you stop it?'

'I'll try anyhow. But why do you want it stopped?'

'Why? Because as I tell you I know he is not there. I have found out where he is. Why can't you listen?'

'Where is he?'

'I have told you. He is living with that woman in an inn.'

'Oh, nonsense, my dear. Living! He can't be living like that. He only left home yesterday.'

'He lived with her there last night. I'm not surprised. I knew something of the sort was up.'

'Oh, nonsense, Constance.'

'What?'

'I say nonsense.'

'I can't hear. Do you understand? He went to this inn. They are living—'

'Yes, I say nonsense, Constance.'

'What is monstrous nonsense?'

'All this, about his living at an inn, is nonstrance – nonsous – is non—'

'What? Speak more distinctly. Put your mouth closer to the telephone.'

'What I say, Constance, is that this is nonst – I tell you this is all absolute nonsense.'

'Don't mumble. We must act. Come home here, to the flat.'

'I can't. I don't believe all this non – all this story about the flat – inn.'

'Have you got anything in your mouth?'

'No. Listen—'

'Listen indeed! This line is awful. I think it's mostly your fault. Enunciate.'

'What?'

'Come back here to the flat.'

'I can't. I'm busy. There's nothing really the matter. Where is this inn?'

'Somewhere in Somerset. We must go there at once.'

'Somerset? Well, there you are. What did I say? He went after Sophie.'

'After Sophia? Ridiculous! He went away from Sophia.'

'But not on purpose.'

'Oh, poof! Do you mean to tell me he didn't live with this woman on purpose?'

'He didn't live with her, whoever she was. You can't call it that.'

'I prefer to call it that. It's the most refined way of expressing it.'

'But what evidence have you?'

'Oh, evidence! I have evidence that he and the woman stayed together at the inn last night. That's good enough for me. I know what men are. It's no good your telling me they didn't live.'

'But I tell you this is preposterous, Constance.'

'What? Speak up.'

'He went after Sophie in the car. He must have been going after her. She had all his things.'

'Things?'

'Yes.'

'What things?'

'Clothes and things.'

'What?'

'Things. Clothes and things. His things. Don't you see?'

'What things?'

'Oh, Lord, all his things. He was on his way to the Bunters' no doubt. Is this inn near the Bunters'?'

'I don't understand you. What I am telling you is the clear fact that he lived with this woman—'

'Nonsense, Constance – prepon – you're mistaken. He went after Sophie. He thinks she's at the Bunters' with his things.'

'In that case, pray, why didn't he go to the Bunters' instead of to this inn?'

'Well, perhaps he—'

'With a woman?'

'Well, I—'

'Oh, come home,' said Mrs Bone.

The barber's shop at Downblotton, whither Margaret repaired on leaving the post office, appeared on her entrance to be combining its tonsorial functions with those of the headquarters of the local debating society. Peter had caused the barber to suspend operations and to engage in voluble argument by asking him the best way to Rushcombe Fitz-Chartres. The barber, the barber's apprentice, a completely bald farmer who was having his hair cut by the barber's apprentice, a man with a sheep-dog and the assistant from the bootshop next door were telling him.

Margaret did not wait in the shop. She had made up her mind that there should be no delay in acquainting Sloley-

Jones with the facts concerning the pilgrimage to the *Stag and Hunt*. Here was her chance.

She experienced little difficulty in ascertaining the house where he was staying. Every small boy in Downblotton knew the cycling clergyman.

Margaret went her way down the main street of the little town, a tall, conspicuous figure in her London costume and furs amid the rustic surroundings. There was something in her attitude, a slight unusual stoop, which suggested that she realised this and shrank from it. She, who was the godmother of a dozen homes for the destitute young, seemed almost to resent, this morning, the attention of small open-mouthed natives. Truth to tell, Margaret's peace of mind was excessively disturbed.

She was afraid of public opinion. She had felt its sting. It was unlikely enough that public opinion would ever glean the interesting details of last night's escapade; but if by any ill chance she found herself confronted with the accusation that she had passed off Peter as her husband and had shared a double room at the *Stag and Hunt* with him, then her own clear conscience in the matter would only serve to accentuate an injustice. At such times conscience must be regarded as an incubus rather than a saving grace.

Fortunately she could count with absolute confidence upon the complacent good sense of her husband, Claude – the dear, charitable, sensible, unemotional man. But there again she must remember that he was a public character. His seat was insecure. An alleged lapse on his wife's part would rob him of the support of every self-respecting Liberal lady in the constituency and would further provide considerable political capital for the threatened female Labour candidate who was the mistress of a Trade Union leader.

With what ecstasy of relief had she first set eyes upon that ill-fated inn. She was beginning now to wish she had never done so. Would that she had spent the night restless and chilly in the foundered car; with Dann, a ponderous chaperon, fumbling at the radiator.

Margaret's spirits rose as she approached Mrs Wigger's. The thought of staying the enthusiastic and communicative parson was in itself a relief. And it was really most unlikely that a committee of Claude's female constituents would find its way to the *Stag and Hunt* or that it would obtain much change from Mrs Spoker if it did.

For that was the chief cause of Margaret's apprehension throughout; love and admiration of that quiet, desperately serious man whom she had married; fear of prejudicing the career which was his pride and ambition.

She knocked at Mrs Wigger's door confidently. She would merely recount their weary discomposure on discovering the scruples of Mrs Spoker and, in merry mood, would thank the parson for having supplied a much-needed touch of reality to their half-formed plot. There would be no necessity to enlarge upon the details of the plot's development.

Mrs Wigger, more than usually non-committal and smoothing herself like an early morning bather, ventured to think that Mr Sloley-Jones was not at home. He had in fact practically left the house well nigh what must be by this time pretty near an hour almost ago.

Margaret's eyes narrowed.

'What time will he be back?' she inquired.

'And that I should really almost hesitate to venture on guessing,' said Mrs Wigger.

Margaret returned slowly to the main street where the car stood. She took her seat in it and waited for Peter. She was thoughtful and strangely depressed. Unpleasant associations crowded to her mind. Last night, before bedtime, she had made light of the friendly parson's blunder. Now it seemed to possess dangerous qualities. She knew what a cheerful gossip that man was.

Other fears possessed her; fears that recalled the misery of being a welcome topic to every cathouse in Kensington.

Margaret was a modest woman. That was, of course, the root of all the trouble. Because she was modest and had preferred philanthropic seclusion to the society of her traducers, the latter had inferred that she had assumed the veil of the guilty penitent. This was an entirely mistaken view. Any one of them would have welcomed her return. Society would as soon think of burning a fortune-teller as of excommunicating a young woman whose romanticism had outstripped her prudence. Margaret knew this, but she refused to go back to the sunshine of some of the gloomiest drawing-rooms in London, if only because it would mean her pleading guilty by inference to a lapse of which she was innocent. She preferred her own quiet backwater in any case. But the injustice scorched her still.

Peter's flippant mood on this horrid morning served only to increase Margaret's distress. This had alienated them ever so slightly. Her insistence on inaugurating a search-party for Pansy before breakfast had widened the breach.

Peter, for his part, as he sat only half listening to the farrago of local geography which was still being poured forth for his benefit in the barber's shop, took mental stock of the complex character of his companion in adventure with a growing frown. Her bright good nature of the previous evening had forsaken her. Surprising woman! How disillusioned might one become on closer acquaintance with the most reliable of the sex. He could rely on Sophia anyhow. He had only to clasp her in his arms and assure her that no unforeseen mishap could ever cause his loyalty and devotion to swerve by a hair's breadth. He felt sure of this – or, at all events hopeful. In an hour's time he would be with her again and could put it to the test. He rehearsed his opening remarks in involved convulsions beneath the barber's towel.

CHAPTER XII

As Good as a Mile

At the top of a steep hill, sheltered by deep overhanging trees, Sloley-Jones dismounted and wiped his brow, gazing around him indecisively. He must be nearing the end of his journey. These woods on either side of the road might be part of Sir Stirling Bunter's estate. He would make inquiries. Pansy, realising that the moment of her long-delayed but inevitable extermination was now at hand, made one sudden and desperate effort to free herself from the confines of the Norfolk jacket, but without avail.

A few yards further up the road sat a very aged native. Sloley-Jones advanced towards him. The native was one of those old gentlemen who enjoy promiscuous employment connected with hedges and ditches from a somewhat casual Urban District Council and regard themselves with some justification as licensed, if not subsidised, beggars.

The old man failed at first to notice the approach of an almost infallible victim. He was a very old man and his eyesight was growing dim. He sat nodding on the bank, mumbling a quaint West-country jargon to himself and fumbling with a shredded remnant of tobacco in the crown of a hat which must have seen well nigh as many years as its owner.

As the parson halted beside him he glanced upwards, not quickly but stealthily. He scratched with a quivering and horny forefinger at the spot formerly covered by a forelock. His sunken and watery eyes brightened perceptibly.

'Good morning,' said Sloley-Jones. 'I say, could you tell me—'

'Good morn' to you, zur, tho' 'taint a ver' good morn' to be sure.'

'No, not very,' said the parson. 'Still, it might be worse. I want to find out—'

'It do look to me as though it be blooin' oop – blooin' oop, ye see,' said the old man.

'Yes, it does. Squally! I must hurry. Tell me, where—'

'If 'twarn't so early in the year fer snoo, Aa should a' said it might be it were gooin' ter snoo,' remarked the old man.

'Oh come, it isn't cold. I'm hot personally – perspiring in fact. I wish you would tell me—'

'Mebbe it be a gooin' ter thunder.'

'Maybe. But I think it's more likely to pour with rain. That's why I want to be getting along. Where is Rush—?'

'Aa aint seed no lightenin' in these parts fer many a day,' reflected the old man.

'Where is Rushcombe Fitz-Chartres?' cried the parson.

The old man frowned deeply as though the name was borne to his mind from the dim memories of the past.

'Rooshc'm?' he repeated slowly. 'Ay.'

'Yes?' said Sloley-Jones encouragingly.

'Be you a-goin' ter Rooshc'm then?'

'Well, I hope so. I want to. Must. Why? Is it far?'

'Ay,' said the old man bluntly.

'It is far?'

'Ay. Rooshc'm. Ay, Rooshc'm be a tidy step to be sure.'

'But I'm not stepping. I'm riding.'

The old man admitted this consideration with a nod.

'Ay, it won't be so far then,' he observed.

'Which direction is it?'

'Seein' that you be ridin', mister,' said the old man scratching his head, 'you'd be, you'd be about 'alf-way ther'.'

'Half-way from where?' murmured the parson helplessly.

' 'Alf-way from Rooshc'm,' replied the old man patiently.

'Yes, yes; but half-way from Rushcombe to where?'

This baffled the old man for some moments. He turned his watery eyes up and down the road as though engaged upon a search for a missing landmark.

'Well, wher' else did yer think o' gooin'?' he asked eventually.

Sloley-Jones removed his right hand from the breast of his Norfolk jacket for purposes of gesticulation.

'All I want to know is how do I get from this spot to Rushcombe.'

'What might you have ther'?' asked the old man with sudden interest.

'A dog, but that has nothing to do with it. At least I suppose I ought not strictly to say that because it has, but—'

'A dug? It doan' look like a dug to me.'

'I daresay it doesn't. It's not a very common type of dog. At least it is fairly, but I don't suppose you see a great number of them in these parts. It's a Schipperke.'

'A whatawhat?' cried the old man.

'A Schipperke. But never mind about that. I must get on. Imperative! Where is Rushcombe Fitz-Chartres?'

'Oo, it ain't a dug then?' said the old man, struggling to his feet and examining Pansy with great curiosity.

'Come now, leave her alone, please,' said Sloley-Jones, resisting this attention. The old man's face was now protruding into the hollow of his coat, his head being on a level with the parson's aquiline and somewhat discriminating nose.

The old man poked at Pansy with his bent finger. He was rewarded by the weary groan of one hardened to torture to the point of tedium.

Several of the more irritating of our national proverbs deal with the latent potentialities of the seemingly trivial. If the benevolent Sloley-Jones had only known the immense value of the seven minutes he wasted at the hill-top for the benefit of that aged man, who seemed to find an almost abnormal satisfaction in gouging every available portion of Pansy's anatomy with his horny finger, the parson would have crushed the rural entomologist beneath the wheels of his bicycle rather than yield one precious moment.

As it was, he allowed himself to be led once more into a dissertation upon the nature, habits and nomenclature of the

Schipperke. The old man displayed a keen appetite for information but singularly deficient powers of digestion. Seven minutes passed before Sloley-Jones again buttoned Pansy into his chest with an air of long-suffering finality and said:

'Now I simply really must be getting along. Absolutely. Now do please tell me quite briefly firstly, where is Maiden – dash – Rush – yes – Rushcombe Fitz-Chartres, and—'

'Ay, Rooshc'm—'

'Yes. And secondly—'

' 'Old on, 'old on,' said the old man. 'Aa ain't told ye yer firstly not yet Aa ain't.'

'Which is the way and where is it?' asked the parson firmly, hitting Pansy's head by mistake with a demonstrative forefinger.

'Ay, be all o' that secondly?'

'No, no. Never mind about first and secondly. Simply which is the way and how far is it?'

'Ay, ye said "Where is it" just now.'

'Well, tell me, where is it?'

'Where is it, or how far is it?'

'Oh dear, both.'

'Ay, booth. Ye didn't say that, mister. Ay, booth to be sure. Booth where is it and how far be it.'

'Yes,' said Sloley-Jones.

'Wull,' said the old man. 'Wull now. Rooshc'm. She be over ther'; over ther', ye see.'

'Yes, yes.'

'Ye see. Ye go on, ye see, the way ye do be gooin'.'

'Yes, yes, yes.'

'Ay. Ye go on the way ye be gooin' to be sure. Ye see. And ye go on a matter o' – oo – oo – oo – oo – oo – oo—'

'Yes, yes, yes, yes?'

'A matter o' – oo – oo, mebbe a 'alf-moile, ye see.'

'Yes, yes, yes.'

'An' when ye get on a matter o' a 'alf-moile, why – ye'll be a bit more'n 'alf way ther', ye see.'

'Yes, yes, yes, I see. Yes,' said Sloley-Jones, mounting his cycle quickly. 'Thanks. I quite see. Yes, yes. Thanks. Many thanks.'

'Ay,' cried the old man warningly. 'Ye go on, ye see, the way ye do be gooin'—'

'Yes, yes, yes, yes, yes,' cried Sloley-Jones, working his long legs in great strides on either side of the cycle.

'Ay,' said the old man.

And by the time the latter had moved from in front of the cycle, which was not before the parson had had to pause and dive his hand into his trouser pocket, Lady Bunter had left the Knoll in company with her depleted shooting-party. Seven minutes earlier Sloley-Jones would have stayed her with tidings of one of the two missing couples whose failure to arrive on the day appointed had caused the aristocratic old lady no small measure of bewilderment.

It must of course be her fault. She had muddled. There could be no possible doubt on that score. In the first place they would have wired had it been a question of a missed train. Besides two entirely separate lots of young married people couldn't go astray like that in one day without a word of explanation.

'No, I'm afraid I must have muddled dates,' she said. 'I wrote to both couples at the same time I think, so I probably made the same muddle in each case; repeated my muddle, as it were. They can never have started. But now they may suddenly arrive at almost any moment when we least expect them, not realising, of course, that I muddled and thinking that we shall be expecting them then; so I have made a sort of double muddle.'

Lady Bunter laughed her little cooing laugh at her own expense.

'But haven't you got their letters back, confirming the date?' suggested the old pink man like a design for a Toby-jug, to whom the above confession had been brought on the evening before.

The Bunters were people who had a Napoleonic way with trouble. They never retreated from trouble. They advanced and sought it out. They were generally at grips with trouble of some sort. They challenged other people's troubles besides their own. They always won.

They were both very old-fashioned and pink in the face and countrified. On Sunday they went to a miniature village church and sang hymns about heaven and hell in a manner that suggested that, poor, unscientific, old people, they still believed in these places; which they did. Their lungs were full of clean air and their minds of sweet thoughts and charity. Neither of them had the slightest fear of anything in the whole wide world from Death to earwigs.

'Haven't ye got the letters confirming the date, dearie?' said Sir Stirling.

'No. How careless! I remember I made them into squills.'

'Into what, my love?'

'Into squills. The things you light your pipe with.'

'Spills?'

'Spills if you like. One can say squills, I believe. I always say squills. My mother always used to call them squills.'

'Oh, really?'

'Of course I may be displaying my ignorance. I thought it was squills.'

'Ignorance? Not at all. You're quite right. One can say squills. In fact I believe that squills is really the more correct.'

'Oh no, Sam dear, I'm afraid it isn't. It's my ignorance.'

'Oh, please don't argue, my dearie. It is such waste of time. I happen to know, in this case, that the word is perfectly correct. The point is, what are we going to do about it. Tell ye what. Shall I run down to the study and start unrolling all the spills – squills I mean – the word should be squills, you are quite right, it comes back to me – unrolling all the squills that are there? We might find these people's answers.'

'No, my dear; you mustn't think of taking all that trouble.

It won't bring the people here even if we do find their letters among the spills. All the same I am worried to think in what way I could possibly have muddled. I got the date right in my letters to the others – the people who have turned up; Joe Mock and Mr Goodie.'

'Besides, you don't as a rule make blunders like that. Now if it had been I who had written and asked them—'

'Oh no, Sam, on the contrary, you're very accurate about those sorts of things. I always muddle.'

'Fanny, that's not true and I really won't have you saying such things. You know as well as I do that if anything has got to be done properly and decently in this house you're the only person who can do it. Talk about muddling! I've never known you muddle.'

His manner was quite incensed. A casual observer would have understood muddling to be a domestic virtue of which he sorely felt the lack. After many years the only severe words which ever passed between the Bunters were invariably occasioned in defence of their respective standards of unselfishness.

'Whenever I don't muddle,' said Lady Bunter, 'it's because you see in time what I am doing and stop me.'

'Nonsense. Nothing to do with me at all. This is not very fair of you, Fan. I never interfere. If I did, there would be some muddling if you like.'

'What makes me feel that I really do not think that I made any mistake in my letters to these people was that I believe I showed you what I had written,' said Lady Bunter. 'If I had stuck down something silly, you would have seen it and pointed it out.'

'I should have done nothing of the sort,' replied Sir Stirling sternly. 'Not that there would have been the smallest likelihood of there being anything silly for me to see.'

'Still it must be my fault,' said Lady Bunter shaking her head with a kind and reflective smile. 'Otherwise Margaret would have wired. I don't know about the Wykeham boy, but I should think he would have wired too – Helen Wykeham had very strong views about being careful not to upset people in those ways. But Margaret certainly would have wired.'

CHAPTER XIII

'Sing Cuccu, Sing'

Sir Stirling had white chop-whiskers and a vast red waistcoat, which bulged mountainously like the hindquarters of old ladies of the crinoline period. He lived exclusively in the country, almost entirely within the limits of his own modest estate. Never, since that day when he had experienced the narrow shave with the hansom-cab, had he been to London. For on that occasion he had known a loss which was unique in the whole three and sixty years of his history, a loss which had grieved and sickened him once and for all with the angry tumult of the town. He had lost his temper.

Now and again there would dawn upon Sir Stirling Bunter an awful, haunting suspicion. He suspected his wife. Fanny, too, hated town. At least so she always pretended. But he remembered still the flush of pleasurable excitement which had warmed her still girlish cheek amid all the amusement and gaiety which had preceded that finishing fracas with the traffic. There were times when he still conjectured that her rooted dislike for London life was all a part of her accursed unselfishness.

For in many other matters, great and small, Fanny had proved herself similarly untrustworthy. Butter beans provided a case in point. Sir Stirling loathed butter beans. He had only himself to blame for Fanny getting to know it, but he had let it leak out during the days of their engagement. Fanny had, in consequence, eschewed butter beans and had kept up a rigorous pretence that her soul revolted from them. They had been married ten years before, returning one day unexpectedly to lunch, he had discovered her in the midst of what was nothing short of a secret and gluttonous orgy of butter beans in his absence.

Since that day he had never been able to feel any real confidence in Fanny. If a woman would go to those lengths over a trifle like butter beans, how was he to know her many other impenetrable cravings? What was the honest conviction of her mind in regard to theatres and the gay life? In every one of her dislikes he read a skilfully disguised passion. When she said she would never allow any motor-car to supplant her love of old Dobbie and the rather weather-beaten old waggonette, the distrustful husband's reply had been to allow himself to be welshed into providing her with the noisiest and most unreliable automobile of its year. There had been tears then; tears of love and wistful gratitude mingled with tears of disappointment. How could she explain that this outburst of generosity was the most ungenerous thing he had ever persuaded himself to do? For the only time – the first and the last – their sunshine had known the passing menace of a tiny cloud.

Since then the Bunters had continued to question and combat each other's accursed unselfishness in the abstract.

Never throughout the thirty-eight years of their married life had one unkind word or thought threatened the peaceful harmony of this unyielding war of abnegation. When an agreement on any subject was vital – as, for instance, on the question of procedure in succouring a friend or neighbour in misfortune – it was only to prevent the affair developing into an absolute deadlock that Sam gave way finally to Fanny. This was generally the solution. But the trouble she had to persuade him that he would be doing her a kindness by allowing her to yield to his opinion proved what a stubborn, anti-self-opinionated old husband he was to manage.

They did not entertain frequently. Lady Bunter was fond of welcoming her own intimate friends to the Knoll, but she had a shrewd suspicion that they got on Sam's nerves. Rather than make such a confession, Sam would, she knew, have demolished every nerve in his system. He, for his part, did not encourage shooting parties because he had an idea that, at heart, Fanny possessed conscientious objections to the slaughter of wild game. She had never said so of course. She had never said so because he knew that she had a foolish notion that he enjoyed shooting. He had told her ten million times that he didn't care one rap about shooting. Every time he said it he said it more loudly. It was no good. Fan still refused to believe him. What hell it was for a decent man to be asked to prove worthy of so impossibly sweet-natured and self-sacrificing a woman.

The question whether Sam loved Fanny more than Fanny loved Sam fortunately never arose. It could only have culminated in an explosion.

The shoot which had been arranged for this morning had been deprived of three guns, owing to the absence, unexplained, of Peter Wykeham and Mr Hackett and that, explained, of Mr Mock. Mr Mock had spent many years in the Far East and was subject to sudden attacks of gout and liver. This morning he said he had the former, and had the latter.

Undismayed, Sir Stirling roped in two neighbours at the eleventh hour, but set forth rather pessimistically with his remaining guest, Mr Goodie, a Scots gentleman of middle age and rather Winkle-like sporting propensities.

Lady Bunter accompanied them armed with lunch and other mysteries. Her secret intention was to spend most of the period of slaughter in ministering to the confined wife of a gamekeeper.

It did not occur to her to remain at home in the hope of being able to greet any of her four stray guests. She had muddled and, in all probability, had muddled thoroughly. They might arrive in a month. She certainly did not expect to see them for at least a week. Lady Bunter was always getting into trouble with her almanac. She would have kept one of a less complicated sort had she not known that Sam favoured the kind showing saints' days and pictures of the moon. The Knoll was full of articles that neither of the Bunters cared for as much as each thought the other did.

Sir Stirling and Mr Goodie stood by the trap in the front drive, awaiting her ladyship, who was fussing over the final provisions for the comfort of Mr Mock. The latter, a yellow old skeleton with whiskers which sprouted out of his face diagonally like a cat's, accompanied her to the door on a stick. Sir Stirling, who had been attempting to inspirit himself and Mr Goodie with predictions of a glorious day's sport, rather puzzled the Scotsman at this point by telling him loudly how much, on the whole, he hated shooting.

'You will have the place all to yourself,' said Lady Bunter to her afflicted guest. 'Mind you have a good lunch.'

'Tiffin!' cried Mr Mock. 'Good night! I can't eat.'

'Oh, try. I've ordered curry specially for you. I'm sure you'll like it. You'll be hungry by that time. You had no breakfast.'

'I'm hungry now,' said Mr Mock. 'But I can't eat. I simply can't face the thought of *makan* in any shape or form. If I'd realised how sick I was today I wouldn't have had any *chota haziri*.'

'Never mind. You can take it easy here and get well again. You won't be disturbed.'

'Much obliged to you, Fanny. Hope I shan't, I'm sure. But what about that crew who failed to turn up yesterday? They will probably come bursting in and—'

'Oh, no. I don't think there's the least fear of that,' said Lady Bunter. 'I feel confident I muddled by more than one day.'

'Ready, my dearie?' cried Sir Stirling. 'If we're going to start on this dreadful business, we may as well be getting along.'

Lady Bunter, encumbered with baskets, pattered busily down the steps towards the trap.

'Yes, I am quite ready. Joseph is afraid that some of the other people may come, but I'm sure they won't. It's just possible,' she called out, as she took her seat, 'that one of them may send a telegraph. If so, please open it and answer it if necessary, will you, Joseph?'

'I suppose you mean a telegram?' replied Mr Mock with a slightly injured air.

'Yes, if you like,' said Lady Bunter, settling herself with elaborate dispositions of rug. 'One can say telegraph, can't one?'

'Of course you can,' agreed her husband, hiding his impatience to start and directing a sharp glance of reproach at Mr Mock. 'Telegraph is really the correct expression. Telegram is a what's-its-name. Ye don't sign letters with your autogram, do you, Joe?'

'Oh, *mana boli!*' argued Mr Mock. 'Telegraph is an adjective. Of or belonging to a telegram. Telegraph pole. A pole of or belonging to a – a pole for sending a telegram.'

'I don't care. You can send a telegraph. I know you can. Can't you, Goodie?'

'I should say,' replied the judicious Mr Goodie, who was experiencing some difficulty in getting into the trap, 'that the wudd was oreeginally a correption which—'

'Put your other foot up first, Mr Goodie,' said Lady Bunter. 'It's the way this trap is built. I ought to have told you.'

'Anyhow,' shouted Mr Mock, 'anybody with any sense calls it a cable. So if a cable comes I'm to open it, am I? And how the deuce am I to know what to reply?'

'Never mind then,' said Lady Bunter soothingly. 'Are you two all right there? I am so excited and looking forward to your starting to shoot.'

'Hi! *Nanti sikit*! Wait a moment! Here!' cried Mr Mock.

'What?' asked Lady Bunter, checking the somnambulant Dobbie.

'Which of those two men who ought to have come here yesterday and didn't is the one who has been out in the Straits?'

'Oh, Joseph, I've told you. Mr Hackett, the M.P. Don't start talking Malay to the wrong one. Not that it matters because neither of them will be here for some days.'

'Hackett. All right, I only wanted to know just in case. Well, so long, Sam. Hope you have a good day.'

'Oh, I don't much care either way. I'm not really keen on this sort of thing,' murmured the host in reply as the cavalcade departed.

Seven minutes later, when Mr Mock had already conquered his gout and was initiating a campaign against his liver with a strong whisky and soda, he was startled by what seemed to be a machine-gun practice in the front drive.

He arose with an Oriental expletive and sought the library window.

A few minutes later old Francis, the butler, discovered him in an attitude of timorous hostility, like that of a man who anticipates the attentions of the black hand.

'Excuse me troubling you, sir,' said Francis, 'but would you mind having a word with a gentleman who has just called. He come with a dog.'

'Oh, God! Why?' said Mr Mock.

'He happened to find it, sir.'

'Yes, but why do you want me to see him?'

'Seemingly,' said Francis, 'he expected to find Mrs 'Ackett here.'

'Mrs who? Oh, Hackett. Mrs Hackett, yes, I know. Well?'

'He seemed surprised to hear that Mrs 'Ackett was not here, and, when I tells him that her ladyship is also out, he asks whether any of the guests was in the house and I took the liberty to mention you, sir.'

Mr Mock sighed and blew his nose with terrific force.

'Is this the padre with that stinking bicycle?' he asked.

'It is, sir,' said Francis.

'All right. Damn! I'll see him, Francis. Tell him I can spare him a few moments. A dog? What the deuce—?'

Sloley-Jones, who still carried Pansy but who would in any case have been in a soiled condition, was shown, delighted, into the library. He adjusted his spectacles and radiated.

'Mr Muck?' he inquired.

'Mock.'

'Oh, Mock? Sorry. I misunderstood the butler. May I introduce myself? My name is Sloley-Jones.'

'Oh,' said Mr Mock. 'Well, sit down. What have you got there – a Schipperke bitch?'

'By Jove!' cried Sloley-Jones. 'You know the breed?'

'Good Lord, yes. Man I knew in Java had one.'

'Oh, Java? Yes of course that would follow. They're Dutch dogs and Java of course is Dutch.'

'Well, good heavens, d'you think I don't know that?' retorted Mr Mock irritably. 'You'll start telling me William I – 1066 next. Sorry. I've got a liver, or rather gout. Apologise. But don't say things like that. Java Dutch! Have you ever been to Java?'

'N – o, I haven't as a matter of fact,' replied Sloley-Jones cautiously. 'I should love to go. Adore it. It must be a ripping country – priceless! Poor climate though.'

'It's a magnificent climate,' said Mr Mock. 'Finest climate in the world. Call this a climate? What do you know of the *mata hari?*'

'Er – I beg your pardon?'

'I say what do you know of the *mata hari?*'

'You mean the matter of the climate? Sloley-Jones, my name is.'

'*Mata hari.* Means sun. Malay.'

'Oh, I beg – I see.'

'Literally "eye of the day." *Mata* – eye. *Hari* – day. *Mata hari*, eye of the day – sun.'

'Oh, I see. I thought you said, "what do you know of the matter, Harry?" Eye of the day. Yes, awfully picturesque. Poetical quite.'

'So what I say to you is – what do you know of the sun in this beastly country?'

'Ah. Yes, yes. Quite. Ha ha! Still, it's been pretty warm at times lately.'

'Warm! You ought to be in Singapore.'

'Yes, I wish I was,' said Sloley-Jones.

'Well, well. What can I do for you? Have a *stingah?*'

'A – er?'

'A drink. *Stingah* we call 'em. This,' said Mr Mock indicating his mixture, 'is a *stingah.*'

'Yes, it looks it,' said the parson blandly. 'No, thanks.'

'We get the habit out East you know,' proceeded Mr Mock, imbibing apologetically. 'Can't get along without it after a bit.'

'Quite so,' said Sloley-Jones. 'Oh, I should love to go there. It must be glorious. However, I brought this dog along here because I chanced to find it in the road.'

'Well, I don't want it,' said Mr Mock.

'No, no. Quite. But as a matter of fact I know this dog. Rather queer. I'll tell you what happened.'

He did so in full detail. Mr Mock failed to display any marked interest in the nocturnal peregrinations of the Hacketts, but grew very apprehensive on being informed of their imminent approach.

'Good Lord!' he exclaimed, as the parson terminated his exhaustive account. 'Then these people may be here at any moment?'

'Oh, rather,' said Sloley-Jones. 'Absolutely. I expected to see them either here or on the road.'

'But I can't deal with them,' cried Mr Mock. 'I don't know what room they go into or anything else. What a bl – blithering nuisance.'

He rose from his chair and executed a series of half-circuits of the hearthrug in a state of indeterminate vexation.

'Oh, I shouldn't worry,' said Sloley-Jones. 'I expect the butler knows. Sure to. Shall I ask him?'

'Yes, yes, do something for Heaven's sake,' said Mr Mock. 'Ring the bell. I suppose you can't jump on your bicycle and go and tell Lady Bunter?'

'I shouldn't worry, you know. From what I know of the Hacketts, they'll make themselves quite at home. Very likely they'll go out and join the shooting party.'

'M'yes. Glad it's the Hacketts anyhow, if it's got to be anyone. I've something in common with Hackett. He's been East.'

'Has he indeed?'

'Course he has. Didn't you know? That's how he made his money so quickly. Rubber. I thought you said you knew him?'

'No, I really only knew Mrs Hackett. I never actually met him till last night, and he didn't say anything then about having been – er – East. Funny!'

'Well, did you ask him?'

'N – o, I didn't really have any occasion to.'

'Well, then, you can't be surprised at his not saying so. A man doesn't as a rule dash up and say "I've been East," unless he's asked, does he?'

'You did,' replied the parson gently.

'Oh, fiddle!' said Mr Mock, breaking off impetuously. 'Do, for goodness' sake, ring that bell.'

'I have,' said Sloley-Jones.

At this point Francis appeared.

'Oh, I say, butler,' said the parson keenly, 'do you know which is Mr and Mrs Hackett's room and all that sort of thing?'

Francis surveyed the dirty clergyman with dignified surprise.

'I do, sir,' he replied.

Francis possessed a fund of restraint which was seldom tested in that house. But his 'I do, sir' was quite patently Franciscan for 'Who the devil are you, coming in to my Knoll and raising domestic queries?'

'Oh, that's all right. Splendid!' said Sloley-Jones, shifting rather restively and clearing his throat at Mr Mock. 'So you can fix them up – er – etcetera, can't you?'

'I beg your pardon, sir?' said Francis.

'Not at all. Only, you see – they are on their way here now. I spent last night with them – or part of it at least – so I happen to know – oh yes, I told you of course, didn't I, when

I was explaining to you about the dog? Only Mr M – this gentleman—'

'Oh, do shut up,' said Mr Mock. 'You'll confuse the man. It's all right, Francis. These Hackett people will be here for tiffin, that's all. It's nothing to get excited about,' he added, frowning severely at Sloley-Jones.

'Very good, sir. Everything will be quite prepared for them,' said Francis, unable to resist raising disdainful eyebrows at the object of Mr Mock's scowl.

Sloley-Jones turned from one to the other with a manful effort to screen his discomfiture. He sniggered with palpable exertion. He tested Francis with one heliographic flash from his spectacles but looked in vain for any confirmatory glow.

'Well, well, well, then, that's splendid,' he said. 'I'm so glad. That's simply top-hole. Now I – you know, I really ought to be thinking of – er pushing off. I've got to cycle to Glastonbury. It looks like rain too. Rotten! However. Well, I'm so glad I called and put – er – everything all right. Yes, well – good-bye, Mr – good-bye. Oh, where shall I leave the dog? Good-bye, butler. Will you take the dog? Yes, thanks. Well, good-bye. Good morning.'

He pushed the paroxysmal Pansy into the arms of Francis and fled into the hall. Before the sedate butler had taken two paces in pursuit the machine-gun practice recommenced in the drive.

'Francis,' said Mr Mock. 'I believe that man is *gila*.'

'I shouldn't be surprised, sir,' said Francis.

'Anyhow he's *booso*,' said Mr Mock.

'I'm afraid he is a trifle, sir,' said Francis.

'Quite upset me,' said Mr Mock. 'I think I must have another *stingah*. Do it for me, will you, Francis? Steady with the soda.'

CHAPTER XIV

Nemesis en Route

For the second time in two days Sophia found herself westward bound by express train from Paddington. On this occasion she was accompanied by her mother, who sat upright in a corner seat, working her rather pendulous jaw in strange chewing motions of private verbal rehearsal. Sophia's father was there too. At least, he was in the corridor.

Mrs Bone had brought one bag, a loose-leather antique, into which had been flung the nightwear and toilet accessories of all three and two teagowns. It was uncertain where the party was likely to spend the night but in any case they would manage with two teagowns. Mr Bone apparently was expected to manage without a teagown. There had only just been room in the bag for his clean collar and he had to carry one of his hairbrushes in the pocket of his overcoat.

In justice to Mr Bone it must be stated that he had not wished to bring any portion of his property or indeed of himself on this journey. He had not even yet consented to do so. But there he was in the corridor. Seen from the carriage there was a motionless misery about the appearance of his back, like that of an ass standing and doing nothing in a field.

Sophia was pale and very handsome this morning. Her eyes were piercing and defiant. She was in a shocking temper, angry with the whole world. She was angry in chief with herself for having caused all this shameful disturbance, angry with that masterful matron opposite, who seemed to find a certain vindictive satisfaction in her misery.

Yes, Sophia was more angry – more definitely out of temper and methodically cross – to-day than at any period of the evening before. It was a different state of temper and it was directed against a different objective. Peter had ceased to be the leading villain of her inglorious domestic tragedy. Her first outburst of fury against him had slowly died away and another resentment more subtle and even more bitter had gripped her.

Sophia had been herself only subconsciously aware of the change. She had not troubled to analyse the medley of undefined grief and wrath which possessed her heart that morning. The truth was borne in upon her as she sat watching the beady eyes blinking rapidly and unseeing through the window opposite; the heavy lips busy with hypothetical recitation. And, as she watched, Sophia's shoulders shivered suddenly with irresistible aversion.

Peter? Yes, Peter had wrought her a lasting injury no doubt, though Sophia knew that at heart she was still willing, anxious to remain incredulous. But it was the gloating self-satisfaction of her mother, triumphantly assured of his guilt and elaborating its visitation, that had slowly beguiled Sophia's sympathies back to the side of her husband. Why had she been such a fool? Why had she, in the first tempest of remorse, cast all her cards upon the table to be played by that massive, domineering, unsparing hand? There was probably as much jealousy as mercy in poor Sophia's revulsion of feeling.

Why should her mother assume complete command of this wretched punitive expedition? She, Sophia, alone was entitled to dictate terms. Terms? The recreant would get blunt enough terms from his mother-in-law. Then, with a quick yearning, Sophia knew that she wanted to offer generous terms – any terms – any. She wanted Peter back. She loved him.

'Mother!'

Her voice was so sharp that Mrs Bone dislocated a hat feather. Even Mr Bone turned an inquiring head from the corridor. Mr Bone was wearing a grey bowler which became him but poorly.

'What?' said Mrs Bone. 'Don't be so sudden, Sophia. What?'

Sophia leant across the carriage at her mother searchingly. There was an emotion deeper than anger in her dark eyes. She caught her lip between her teeth in a half-hearted attempt at self-control.

'You seem to be glad,' she said.

'I don't know what you mean,' said Mrs Bone. 'You've interrupted my train of thought. What do you mean?'

'You seem to be glad that Peter has done this. You seem to enjoy the idea of this miserable – chase.'

Mrs Bone glanced questioningly through the window and expanded her nostrils.

'I don't think you are in a fit state to talk about it,' she said. 'If you think that I am glad to discover that your husband is a bad hat, then all I can say is that the shock must have been too much for you. I am very excessively distressed to discover it. Not surprised, mind you, in the very least, but genuinely shocked. And the sooner it is thoroughly understood that he shall not and will not be allowed to make your life an absolute hell—'

'What?' asked Mr Bone, peering in with a patient smile from the corridor.

'Go away,' said Sophia's mother. 'I am not talking to you.'

'But, mother, it's no good your pretending you weren't pleased when I got engaged to – to Peter. You were simply delighted about it.'

Mrs Bone shook her head with a wry smile.

'You say you always knew this would happen,' continued Sophia heatedly. 'You were remarkably secretive about it, I must say.'

'Well, if you want to know the truth, Sophia, I never from the very outset cared for that man or trusted him the smallest bit.'

'I don't believe you,' cried Sophia, ablaze. 'You turn round on him now and pretend to have been immensely knowing, but when we first got engaged and you found out that he had money and smart connections you were off your chump with pleasure.'

'Control yourself,' said her mother severely. 'Be refined. My chump! Chump!'

'Yes?' said Mr Bone, appearing wearily in the doorway.

He was waved out again with violent fanning movements of a convenient *Daily Telegraph*.

'You never had the slightest inkling that Peter was anything but very kind and very good,' said Sophia, now thoroughly wound up. 'And I still don't believe he is anything else.'

'Then all I can say is, Sophia, that I am horrified to discover that you are the sort of docile, downtrodden wife who encourages a man to be loose.'

'I'm not,' said Sophia. 'And Peter is no more loose than Father is.'

'Nearly every man,' said Mrs Bone, with an introspective blink towards the corridor, 'is loose by nature. Much rests with the wife.'

'Peter may not have meant—'

'Now, don't start that to me,' interrupted her mother. 'You're as bad as your father. I don't want to rub it in about this man, but here he is, living—'

'I don't believe that,' cried Sophia vehemently. 'At least – he may have been led astray.'

'Led astray by appointment at Paddington?' suggested Mrs Bone sweetly.

'There's no reason for you to gloat over it anyhow,' said Sophia with tears of anger.

'Sophia! You don't know what you are saying.'

'Ever since you first heard about it you have been revelling in it. One would think that to discover your daughter was in trouble with her husband was the most glorious thing that could possibly happen.'

'Poof!'

'There's no poof about it,' said Sophia choking back her tears. 'I suppose you think it's smart and fashionable, just because every other couple is being divorced and scandalised about in this filthy world.'

'That is exactly the reason why I—'

'Oh, why must you be so theatrical, Mother?'

'Theatrical! If anyone is being theatrical, you are.'

'I was last night,' confessed Sophia boldly. 'Now I'm trying to keep natural. Why do you want to go dashing down to the country with Father and all the rest of this unnecessary rubbish?'

'Do you suggest that I should sit at home and knit?'

'Yes,' said Sophia. 'I wish I'd come alone. I want to see Peter alone.'

'Ah!' cried Mrs Bone, pouncing on this admission. 'Yes, you would like to go and see him alone and would swallow the first fairy-tale he chose to invent. That would be the beginning. You would forfeit your influence over him once and for all. In six months' – Mrs Bone gesticulated dramatically with five suede-gloved fingers and a thumb – 'you would lose him altogether. Then there would be a nice public scandal right enough.'

'Why mayn't I deal with my own husband in my own way?'

'I'm telling you. Because your own way is simply to encourage him to be a loose fish and a fast man and to make a terrific public mess of your marriage.'

'I never asked you or wanted you to do all this. You've taken the whole affair into your own hands, and—'

'My only reason for taking the affair into my own hands' – the express steamed beneath an archway with a sudden roaring rattle. Mrs Bone raised her voice to a shrill scream – 'is to hush it up,' she shouted.

'What's the matter?' said Mr Bone. 'The train was going through that little tunnel so I didn't catch what you said.'

'Will you stay in the passage?' said his wife.

'My dear, I am doing so.'

'Then do it.'

'I am doing it.'

'Then continue to do it.'

Mr Bone turned a sympathetic eye to his daughter. He caught a fleeting glance from her in return. It was the glance of a scolded, impenitent child seeking a friend in need. Mr Bone surveyed his family with bewildered concern.

'What's all this hick-boo?' he ventured to ask.

'Will you go into the corridor and shut the door between it and us?' demanded his wife.

'Aren't I going to be allowed to sit down at all on this blessed journey?'

'You have sat. You did a lot of sitting at the beginning. Why don't you smoke? Go along the corridor to a smoking carriage and sit.'

'Why am I brought?' cried the outcast, apostrophising the whole carriage with outspread hands.

'Why shouldn't Father come and sit down?' asked Sophia bluntly.

'Because I should be very sorry for him to overhear your extraordinary sentiments.'

'You know he'd take my side and back me up,' said Sophia.

'Take your side?' echoed her father. 'Ah, I thought there was a rumpus on. What is all this?'

'At home,' put in Mrs Bone monitively, 'you do nothing but want to smoke like a factory. You have your chance. Smoke.'

'I have been telling Mother that I desire to be allowed to put things right with Peter in my own way,' cried Sophia in clear, challenging tones.

'Well, so I should hope,' muttered her father.

Mrs Bone drew in a long acrimonious breath between her teeth.

'She says,' proceeded Sophia, with a flash of her dark eyes, 'that if it's left to me I shall forgive him. Well, if he's sorry I probably shall. That, surely, is my concern.'

'You've got to find out whether there's anything to forgive him for first,' said Mr Bone.

'Oh!' exclaimed his wife.

She arose with as much dignity as is possible in a train travelling at sixty miles an hour.

'Then, no doubt, you would like me to go and stand in the corridor while you and Sophia plan to lug each other into continual misery and public shame.'

When the party alighted at Bristol Mrs Bone's star was still obviously in the ascendant. She was the first to gain the platform ponderously brisk and alert. She took the platform at a little bound, which set her cheeks and other less evident portions of her anatomy quivering like jelly. She snapped at a solicitous porter as a dog snaps at a fly.

Sophia's fury had given place to the languid dudgeon of fatigue. Mr Bone wore the flushed and constrained air of a defaulter who has just endured an hour's solid cursing from his colonel.

'We will drive from here,' said Mrs Bone. 'Have you got the bag? We cannot rely on being able to hire a motor anywhere else. We will have some lunch in the station buffet. Go and find out where we can hire a motor. Meet us in the buffet. Put your hat on straight.'

'What?' replied Mr Bone, who landed on the platform just as she completed these orders.

She repeated the gist of them.

'I say, don't shout, dear,' said her husband. 'People are looking at us.'

'They are looking at you. Look at your hat. What do you look like?'

'Don't, don't. You confuse me. What a horrible station this is. Which buffy? How can I know where to get a car? We don't even know the name of the place we are supposed to be going to. How can I tell the man?'

'What man?'

'The man. The car man.'

'Get the car. I will tell the man where to go.'

'But, my dear Constance, one cannot go and get men like that. The man will want to know where he is to go.'

'I say, I will tell him.'

'But you will be in the buffy. Am I to bring the man to the buffy? The man will probably refuse to come to the buffy.'

'Of course,' said Mrs Bone loftily, 'if you are afraid of men—'

'I'm not. But what I want to know is – why engage a car till I have had my lunch. I want lunch. It is half-past one. I have an absolute craving for food. Why can't I come to the buffy with you and then go and get the car?'

'Because you will waste half the afternoon getting it.'

'Oh, I see. So I am not going to be allowed to have my lunch until I get the car. A sort of bribe.'

'Ferdinand! Don't make a scene. People are looking. Cannot you understand that if you go and get the car while Sophia and I get some food we shall kill two birds with one stone?'

'Do you want to kill me? Am I to eat?'

'You can take something with you in your hand and eat it while you go and get the car.'

'Oh, God!' said Mr Bone.

'Sophia and I will be in that buffet. You can come and buy whatever you want to take in your hand first.'

'Oh, very well, very well,' said the husband after a moment's reflection.

They proceeded to the buffet. Sophia followed them at a distance, having decided to appear entirely disconnected.

Mr Bone's purchase was remarkably moderate for a hungry man. The garage seemed, on the whole, unlikely to be his first port of call in the streets of Bristol.

'Now,' he said, turning again to his wife. 'What is the name of this place we're going to? The man is sure to want to know.'

'If you are so afraid of the man as all that, you can tell him that it is a village called, I think, Blotto. It is—'

'Oh, ridiculous, Constance! Blotto! It can't be. This isn't Scotland.'

'If it is not Blotto, it is very nearly Blotto. Unless the man is a fool he will know what you mean. Besides, if you will kindly listen to what I have to tell you, you will be able to make it quite clear. It is near a town called something else Blotto.'

'Well then it's probably something Blotto too.'

'Why?'

'What?'

'Why?'

'Oh, Lord, I don't know. Let me go. Here is the bag. How far is this place?'

'I don't know. It cannot be far.'

'Why shouldn't it be? It may be miles and miles.'

'It cannot be far because those two motored from London there in a few hours. Have you no nous?'

'No what?'

'Oh, go; go.'

He went. By the time he returned Mrs Bone and Sophia had grown completely disgusted at the somewhat insipid atmosphere of the buffet; and the former had threatened to report a waitress, who had informed her that it was not a waiting-room, to the general manager of the Great Western Railway Company. Mr Bone, on the other hand, appeared to have been revived and invigorated by his sojourn.

'Come on,' he cried. 'I've got a car.'

'So I should hope,' said his wife. 'By the time you've taken, one would have thought you had got an omnibus.'

'It's the deuce of a way,' continued Mr Bone with malicious relish. 'It will take hours and cost a fortune. Come on.'

'It won't cost so much as divorce lawyers' fees,' said Mrs Bone.

'Mother!' protested Sophia.

'Now don't you start that again,' said Mrs Bone, raising a warning finger. 'Where is the motor, Ferdinand?'

'Outside. Did you expect it to drive into the buffy?'

He marched forth. Mrs Bone overtook him and peered down into his face suspiciously as they walked.

'Ferdinand. I am almost tempted to believe that you have been to a public house.'

'I have,' said Mr Bone. 'I had to. Do you think I am a camel?'

'Why could you not take what you wanted in the buffet instead of keeping us waiting while you went and glutted yourself like a workman? It is most thoughtless and horribly undignified.'

'I can't help that. I wanted it.'

'What have you had to drink?'

'Beer. It's done me a lot of good.'

'You seem to have taken quite enough.'

'I took as much as I could. I had a quart of beer.'

'H'm,' said Mrs Bone. 'So, while we were waiting in that stuffy disgusting buffet of a place, you were standing in a public house saturating yourself with quarts of beer?'

'Yes,' said Mr Bone boldly. 'I'll go home if you like.'

'You can sit on the outside seat of the motor next to the driver,' said his wife. 'You want wafting.'

'I want what?'

'Do what I say. It is nauseating.'

'I'll go home if you like,' said Mr Bone.

CHAPTER XV

Coming and Going

Mr Mock paraded the library, his hands at his back, his knees bent and his face contorted by curious twitchings of his feline whiskers. He appeared to be rehearsing; as was, indeed, the case. He was rehearsing the reception of the Hacketts. If, confound it, he was doomed to the task, he would do it with as good grace, as pleasantly and as briefly as lay in his power.

He paused occasionally and directed a sharp glance, from beneath his bushy eyebrows, down the drive. Before very long the unmistakable sound of a car changing gears as it rounded the topmost slope reached his ears. Mr Mock stood at the window, eagerly muttering the opening pleasantries on which he had decided.

Another, less decisive, rehearsal of what should be said and what should be left unsaid in the first few moments of arrival was taking place inside the car. If Margaret had failed to conquer her forebodings she disguised them. She leant forward scanning the house as they approached it with a frank smile of confidence.

Peter did not lean forward. He had lighted a cigarette and was attempting to assume the necessary posture of careless ingenuousness. Both occupants of the car were experiencing the feelings of amateur artistes pluming themselves in the wings for a big scene which might, or might not, be received favourably in the sight of an unreliable audience.

'I shall leave you to get rid of most of the preliminary and explanatory matter, Margaret,' said Peter. 'Get it off your chest in the sort of hearty, "what rotten luck" style. Can you see the front entrance yet?'

'Yes.'

'Is anybody standing there?'

'No. The front door is closed.'

'Good. It would have been just my luck if Sophia had been waiting on the mat. I rather feel that I shall want my second wind for Sophia. I bet you she's the first person we see.'

'That's all right,' said Margaret. 'I'll get out first and ring the bell. You can stay inside the car until we discover exactly who is in the offing.'

'Thanks, yes,' said Peter. 'You might even be able to make your opening speech and then sort of turn and haul me out of the car at the dramatic moment. "And so here is Mr Wykeham" style of thing. It all depends on where Sophia is. I bet you she's placed.'

The car drew up. Dann stretched himself and clambered laboriously from his seat.

There was no need to ring the bell. The front door was opened before Margaret had moved from her seat.

Francis stood at the entrance. He turned his head and called to somebody behind him in a voice which could be heard clearly from the car.

'Hann! 'ere, Hann. Mr and Mrs 'Ackett!'

But it was not Francis and his embarrassing warning which struck unpremeditated and paralysing misgiving into the hearts of the car's inmates. No sooner had the front door been opened than a small black object had appeared, quivering with one last forlorn hope, in the portal and, after standing for a moment with ears erect, had darted forward with an outburst of frenzied gratitude and flung itself with exultation against the wing of the car.

'Pansy!' cried Margaret.

'How the devil—?' exclaimed Peter craning forward cautiously to gain a view of the hall.

'Some one has managed to get your little dog here, mum,' said Dann informatively.

'Yes, thank you; so I see,' replied Margaret. 'Take all the luggage down and put it into the house, please.'

She turned to Peter with a little gesture of dismay.

'Somebody has been here before us,' she said.

'Yes. With a yarn,' added Peter significantly.

'But who?'

Peter pushed back his hat and stroked his brow. 'Ask the butler,' he suggested.

Margaret nodded.

'Wait here,' she said.

She descended from the car and confronted Francis with a pretty smile. The butler, who was assisting Dann, politely released his end of a trunk on to the driver's foot and bowed his attentions.

'Lady Bunter and party, 'ardly expecting somehow that you would arrive so soon, though, no doubt, delighted to find themselves incorrect in the matter, madam, 'ave proceeded shooting,' he explained.

'Oh yes,' said Margaret readily. 'I'm so glad they didn't stay in for me – for us.'

'They doubtless would 'ave, 'ad they known, madam,' said Francis, inclining his head deferentially.

'I'm glad they didn't know,' said Margaret. 'I couldn't come yesterday. I missed my train. But, tell me, how did my little dog get here? I lost her last night.'

Francis beamed blandly at the reclaimed Pansy who was worrying her mistress's skirts with every sign of rampant hydrophobia.

'Oh yes, madam; I heard all about the trouble you had experienced with the little – er – the dear – little animal. It was brought here not half a hour ago by a friend of yours. He told us of your movements and that was really what enabled me to expect you and Mr 'Ackett to arrive.'

'Oh. But what friend?'

'A clergyman, madam; a Mr – let me see – Only – no.'

'Sloley-Jones?'

'Ah, yes, madam.'

Margaret nodded thoughtfully.

'I see,' she said. 'Would you like the chauffeur to give you a hand carrying my boxes upstairs?'

'Thank you very much, madam; but we can manage. Will your chauffeur be staying here, madam?'

'No. Oh, no. Thank you. All right. I just want to have a word with Mr – h'm – Hackett. Oh, by the way—'

'Yes, madam?'

'Has Mrs Wykeham gone out with the shooting party?'

'Mrs Wykeham, madam?'

'Yes, Mrs Wykeham. She is staying here, isn't she?'

Francis raised his eyebrows and assumed an air of confidential ambiguity.

'No, madam. We were expecting both Mr and Mrs Wykeham yesterday but – er – they did not arrive, and we are – er – without information regarding their – er – intentions in the matter.'

Margaret turned slowly towards the car. She made a scarcely perceptible movement with the fingers of her left hand, and a round, inquiring face within the car disappeared from view.

'Oh, and one other thing,' she said, again addressing Francis, 'Lady Bunter and the others had left of course before Mr Sloley-Jones called here; so they don't know what happened to – to us?'

'Exactly, madam. Otherwise, I am sure, her ladyship would 'ave remained in. Only me and Mr Mock is aware.'

'Mr Mock?'

'Yes, madam. Another of her ladyship's guests. A gentleman who 'as – er – been East, madam.'

'Oh, indeed? And Mr Mock saw Mr Sloley-Jones.'

'Oh, certainly, madam. For some considerable period.'

'Thank you. I only – I'm so sorry that I – that we should arrive when you don't expect us.'

'Not at all, madam; thank you very much. I quite expected you, having seen Mr – the – the reverend gentleman.'

'Ah,' said Margaret with an effort. 'That's all right then. If you'll kindly see after my luggage—'

Francis bowed and retired into the hall.

Margaret returned to the window of the car. Peter peered expectantly from the back cushions.

'Peter, don't, whatever you do, let the butler see you.'

'What?' cried Peter. 'In Heaven's name what is up now? How can I possibly avoid the butler seeing me? Am I Aladdin or somebody?'

'The butler knows all about the *Stag and Hunt.*'

'All, Margaret?'

'I don't know how much he knows. Sloley-Jones brought Pansy here.'

Peter groaned.

'I thought as much,' he said. 'Confound these priests. And he's about the most dangerous of the whole crowd. Wolsey was a stop-gap curate to that man. May he too be forsaken in his grey hairs and dwindle into a mere advertisement for pants. Where is Sophia?'

'She's not here.'

'Oh, that's better. Come, that's much better. Where is she?'

'She never came here.'

'Never came here?' echoed Peter with amazed distortions of countenance. 'Well, what on earth happened to her?'

'I don't know. The butler says you were both expected but never arrived.'

'Well, I could have told him that I never arrived. But Sophia – Sophia?'

Peter rose to his feet in the car with every sign of extreme perturbation.

'What on earth can have happened to the poor dear girl?'

'Perhaps she put up at an hotel with a young man,' suggested Margaret dryly.

'Oh, shut up, Margaret. This is awful. Do you suppose she went back home? I'd better go back.'

'Well, that was what I was going to suggest,' said Margaret. 'I told you not to let the butler see you for that reason. If they've heard what went on at the *Stag and Hunt* it will be just as well for you not to disembark here at all. I can say that my husband had to go back suddenly to town and—'

'And then he'll probably arrive by the next train,' said Peter wildly.

'I don't think he's likely to come till tomorrow,' said Margaret.

'But we were going to tell these people that we got hung up and stayed the night at the *Stag and Hunt*. Why all this evasion? Anybody who thinks that two people can't stay at a pub without spending the night in the same room must have a mind like a sink.'

'But don't you see,' explained Margaret gently, 'that, in order to find out where to bring Pansy, Sloley-Jones must have gone to the *Stag* and cross-examined Mrs Spoker. What did Mrs Spoker tell him – that's the point.'

'Did you ask the butler that?'

'Certainly not.'

'Do you think it likely that, even if Mrs Spoker told Sloley-Jones that Mr and Mrs Hackett performed the extraordinarily usual custom of splitting a bedroom with each other, the ass would have taken the trouble to repeat it to the butler?'

'It might have leaked out over the story of Pansy's escape and that sort of thing. Besides, why should we tell anybody that it wasn't really Mr and Mrs Hackett who put up there. If you go back to town now, before anyone sees you, and find your wife, I will say that I and my husband put up at the *Stag and Hunt* last night and came on here this morning, and that he had to go back at once and is expected again tomorrow. Then, when Claude arrives tomorrow I will tee him up about it, and you will arrive in a day or two with your wife and nobody will be a halfpenny the wiser.'

'Of course,' said Peter, 'if you're such an accomplished liar as all that—'

Margaret smiled dismally.

'I'm only thinking of what will be best and wisest for everybody,' she said. 'After all, there are lies and lies.'

'Yes,' said Peter. 'And this is one of the lies.'

'You want to go back to town in any case to see your wife; and one thing and another.'

'Yes,' said Peter. 'But one of the other things is that that poop Jones will come crashing down upon us all here one morning and completely upset the entire apple-cart.'

'Well, you can't sit hiding your face in the car all the morning, and the butler is beginning to nose about again,' whispered Margaret briskly. 'We must decide one way or the other. What am I to say?'

'I shall go back now with Dann. I leave you to your own horrible devices. But if and when I return here with Sophia how the dickens am I to know what you've said?'

'It all depends on how much I find the butler and the other man know.'

'What other man? Jones, you mean. These priests are a bane. I forswear religion. Talk about Rasputin the rascal monk. Jones has him beaten to a frazzle.'

'I didn't mean Sloley-Jones. I meant—'

Whom she meant was revealed dramatically enough. Mr Mock, having perfected his plans for a hearty and original welcome, threw open the library window.

'*Mana itu orang, tuan Hackett?*' he shouted in the direction of the car, his yellow face wreathed in a smile of jocular amiability. '*Panggil dia sini. Sia mahow chuckup summa dia. – Tabi la lu. Tabi tuan, tabi s'kali. Tabi, mem.*'

'Gosh!' exclaimed Peter. 'What in the name of all that is zoological is that?'

Margaret had turned with a quick intake of breath. She managed to summon a nervous smile in response to Mr Mock's welcome; then she again sought Peter's agitated countenance.

'I think it's Malay,' she said.

'Your what?'

'Malay. I've heard Claude use language like it. It's a guest here, a Mr Mock. He's been there. He thinks you're Claude, you see.'

'Yes, this settles it,' said Peter. 'I am off, dear Margaret, with all convenient speed. Where's Dann?'

'Here, sir,' said Dann returning at that moment.

'Dann, I'm going back in the car with you to London. Shift.'

'*Mari sini, mari sini,*' bawled Mr Mock.

'Maraschino to you,' murmured Peter. 'Shift, Dann. Tell 'em what you like, Margaret, and put it down to my account.'

'All right. Leave it to me,' said Margaret.

'Shift, Dann,' said Peter.

'*Hi. Nanti sikit. Mana piggi?*' came from the library window.

Dann, the unquestioning, cranked his car, leapt into his seat. With a rasping of studded tyres on the gravel drive the car swung round and straightened into an immediate twenty-five miles an hour down the hill.

Margaret watched it disappear. She mounted the steps into the house and encountered Francis with a ready smile.

'Mr Hackett has gone back again,' she said. 'He heard news from – he heard news which made him think he ought to go back to London at once.'

'Indeed, madam?' said Francis gravely.

'I expect he will be back soon,' said Margaret.

Accents changing from heartiness to bewildered annoyance could still be heard ringing plaintively from the library.

'*Apa matcham? Mana tuan Hackett suda piggi? Apa matcham skarang; mana boli, mana boli?*'

CHAPTER XVI

Nests in the Storm

It was not long before the baffled Mr Mock came forth to investigate. Margaret returned his greeting warmly and repeated her fiction of the recalled husband. The Anglo-Oriental displayed considerable disappointment and inquired whether she, too, spoke Malay. He was on the point of returning to the library to reinforce himself against the task of entertaining a lady in nothing but English for the course of an entire tiffin, when Margaret called him back.

'I am so sorry that you were bothered with having to receive my friend Mr Sloley-Jones this morning.'

'Not at all. Glad you got your dog back, my dear lady.'

'Yes,' said Margaret. 'We – I was awfully worried about losing her. I suppose you heard the whole story about how it happened?'

Mr Mock chuckled slyly and rubbed his hands.

'Oh yes. O-o-oh yes, I heard all about it,' he said.

Margaret hesitated and encouraged further comment with an inquiring nod.

'What a night!' added Mr Mock.

'You seem to find it amusing,' said Margaret pleasantly.

'I dare swear I find it more amusing than your husband did,' said Mr Mock.

'Why?'

'Well, my dear lady! Not much catch to be slung out of bed in the middle of the night and sent out in the rain to let the dog loose; eh? Ha ha!'

'Ha ha!' responded Margaret. 'Still, my husband got out – got up of his own accord. We couldn't sleep. The dog was howling.'

'Oh, was that it? No wonder the poor feller got slung out of bed. I've had much the same experience with tigers before now. Only they were even worse.'

'Yes,' said Margaret. 'I think I would rather deal with Pansy than a tiger.'

'Sometimes in the jungle,' Mr Mock went on reminiscently, 'the blighters used to keep me awake all night. All night. Not a wink of sleep. Glad to hear you didn't suffer to that extent.'

'I beg your pardon,' said Margaret curiously.

'Ha ha!' said Mr Mock with a mischievous twinkle in his somewhat rheumy eye. 'You weren't long in getting to sleep after the dog business, believe me. Ha ha ha! I seem to know more about what happened last night than you do yourself; eh?'

'You seem to know quite enough,' said Margaret in a manner of demure reproof.

Mr Mock returned to the library in high spirits. Delightful woman! He was no longer assailed with doubts as to his ability to pilot her felicitously through the *tête-à-tête* tiffin. He was quite stimulated by the prospect of tiffin. He anticipated tiffin. He drank her health.

Presently he saw Margaret leave the house and seek a wicker chair on the terrace overlooking the broad sweep of venerable velvet turf at the front of the house. She had already changed her travelling costume for a coat and skirt of rough tweed. Stockings of a striking plum-colour were displayed. On her feet were brogues of the type which flaunt those rather unnecessary tasselled tongues.

Mr Mock, at the library window, watched her progress, rubbing his nose critically with his forefinger. There was still that little stoop, unnatural and slightly furtive, in Margaret's walk, as though she knew she was being scrutinised but desired to appear unconscious of the fact.

The sky was cheerless and overcast. The wind was stirring the elms to an extent which caused incessant perturbation to a protesting colony of rooks; but Margaret paid small heed to the weather. She took her seat in the wicker chair and surveyed with troubled eyes the fair prospect of lawn and shrubbery and the foul prospect of domestic intrigue and equivocation to which her folly had committed her. She deliberated with a deepening frown. She looked rather like Violet Hopson at that stage of the film when she realises that unless she can get the hero to pull the favourite the squire will prove who her mother was by blackmailing the bishop.

Margaret's thoughts were undoubtedly gloomy, but the atmosphere of the Knoll awakened a half-forgotten suggestion of peace and rest in the midst of trouble. She had known the grateful influence of that mellow garden before, its sweet immutable repose, quelling all the vicious, emotional flagrancy of London, as its owners were wont to quell the strife of neighbours, by sheer impassiveness.

She sat on in silence save for the breeze and the rooks. Away down in the shrubbery a bent old gardener was performing vague, childish manoeuvres with flower-pots. A shaggy cocker spaniel appeared from somewhere and, having investigated Pansy with unemotional civility, rubbed his back ingratiatingly against Margaret's chair and licked her hand. In the midst of her dark reflections Margaret closed her eyes and surrendered herself to the blissful influence of the old country garden.

Who could willingly engage in deceptions here, however pressing the need? The fact that a mislaid dog had been found and restored by a friendly parson was surely not a circumstance which called for a full investigation of her movements for the last twenty-four hours. Why worry? She would not be cross-examined on the subject. She would tell Lady Bunter, perhaps, in confidence what had occurred. There would be no necessity to elaborate a fiction for the benefit of the rest of the party.

Claude she could rely upon. She could picture his thin, keen face knitted in perplexity and slowly melting into one of his brief smiles of conciliatory amusement. Mrs Spoker was unlikely to be heard of again. Sloley-Jones?

Yes, it would be as well to circumvent Sloley-Jones before

he and his overheated bicycle went sailing more dangerously afield. She would take Claude over to Downblotton one morning and they would explain matters.

But stay! Sloley-Jones knew the secret which that disastrous mountainous double bed at the *Stag* had to tell. Caution was required here. Save for the actual witnesses of that fatal simulation of sleep Sloley-Jones was the most formidable figure in the field. The butler and Mr Mock had not set eyes on the alleged husband. Sloley-Jones had held him in exuberant conversation for ten minutes. Mrs Spoker had subsequently told Sloley-Jones about the bed. Perhaps, after the manner of the landlady with a tale to unfold, she had conducted him upstairs and shown him the bed. At all events he knew all there was to know about the bed and possibly surmised supplementary details for himself. Yes, caution was required here.

Peter too. She had allowed the hare-brained, irresponsible creature to dash away without pausing to formulate any definite line of defence, should the unfortunate occasion arise. There was no knowing what incongruities of explanation might not be promulgated at the very outset for the benefit of the inquisitorial Sophia.

An ugly belt of cloud came bowling over the elm trees. The rooks, blacker and more distrait beneath its shadow, increased their hoarse lamentation like the stricken survivors of a devastated village. The old gardener raised his head, dropped a flower-pot, and shuffled away into shelter. The spaniel ambled off with a suggestion of *sauve qui peut* about his apologetic hindquarters. Down came the rain. Once more Nature was weeping for the follies of Humanity.

For the innocent follies in chief, no doubt. It is the innocent folly which causes most of the tears. Margaret went indoors, unsettled still.

Ere long Francis performed a brief selection upon a muffled and deferential gong in the hall, summoning Mrs Hackett to her lunch and Mr Mock to his tiffin.

The progress of the meal proved to be less fluent than the

latter had anticipated. Mrs Hackett responded to his several ventures in conversational urbanity much in the spirit of one ingratiating a talkative child. It seemed as though the curtain of some lurking care was shaking her sensibility from the sunshafts of his gallant humour. Mr Mock languished beneath the strain and after relapsing into a distressing silence sought relief in abusing his food.

'Curry!' he snorted. 'Call this curry? They can't make curry in this benighted country. This is not curry – not even hot. No Bombay Duck! Just as well perhaps. Insult to any decent Bombay Duck to be asked to be eaten with hash. I'd show 'em how to make a curry. I wish I had my boy here. Have you and your husband got a boy, Mrs Hackett?'

'A boy? No,' replied Margaret modestly. 'We've only been married for three months.'

'Oh, good night! I didn't mean – all right – never mind,' said Mr Mock with some confusion. 'Anyhow it's quite evident now that you can't possibly have one.'

Margaret laid her knife and fork (Mr Mock was using a spoon) on her plate in slow astonishment and blushed.

'I'm afraid I don't understand your observation at all,' she said.

'I know,' said Mr Mock readily, waving a conciliatory hand. 'You don't understand. That's the trouble. Never mind. I thought you'd know what I meant. You must get your husband to explain to you. It's a sort of custom. Anybody who has been East will tell you. I thought everybody over here knew all about it.'

Margaret sat back in her chair and looked round anxiously for the absent Francis.

'I see you still don't savvy what I'm driving at,' pursued Mr Mock. 'I'll explain.'

'No, no; please don't,' said Margaret anxiously.

'But my dear lady, don't you know that a large number of the men who have been East bring a boy back with them to this country?'

'Oh, you mean a servant?' said Margaret with sudden relief.

'Of course I do. Good night, you don't – yes, a servant, a boy.'

'Oh, yes, yes,' said Margaret. 'No, Claude didn't.'

'Ah. Then I don't suppose you've ever tasted decent curry,' said Mr Mock.

'I like this curry, I must admit.'

'Exactly,' grunted Mr Mock. 'Oh, what you miss! No decent curry. No real turtle. No Manila cigars under Heaven knows what price. No *goola Malacca.* Sometimes, by Jingo, I'm tempted to go back East.'

'I should yield to the temptation if I were you,' said Margaret.

That passing glimpse of solace which she had seen and lost awhile in the first brief moments of retreat on the terrace appeared not again. Just as her customary peace of mind seemed to be haunted by some shadowy apprehension which she could not shake off, so the soothing atmosphere of this dear old house was addled by the domination of this outrageous Mr Mock, disporting gloomily in its sacred shade, like a great ape violating a forsaken temple of prayer.

Mr Mock concluded his tiffin, stalked to the latticed window of the dining-room and surveyed the weather. It had improved. The rain storm had passed. A fitful glimmer of sunshine appeared and disappeared in the face of the sky line like a cynical grin. Mr Mock, too, had improved. He said so. He said he had improved to such an extent that he now intended to take the air, to ascertain the whereabouts of the shooting party, and, unless the distance was too great, possibly to join it. He invited Margaret to accompany him. She declined courteously.

So Mr Mock trudged forth alone. The sun began to shine more steadily upon the peaceful terrace. The gardener came forth and resumed his finicking occupation. Pansy frolicked coquettishly around the prone and forbearing spaniel. A whistling boy with a bicycle came up the drive and delivered a telegram.

Margaret took it from him. It was addressed to Lady Bunter. She weighed it for a moment between her finger and thumb, speculating upon the yellow envelope with distant eyes. Then, taking it indoors, she handed it to Francis, who thanked her and propped it up with a clothesbrush on the hall table.

People are almost as optimistic about missing a rainstorm as they are about missing death. Though the heavy shower which had passed had been threatening to begin at any moment during the morning, quite a large number of people were caught in it and got wet. Sir Stirling Bunter was one of this number. Lady Bunter, who had left the cottage of the wife of the gamekeeper just as the storm broke, but who did not turn back because she was not quite certain what time Sam wanted his guests to have their lunch, and was quite used to rain, so it didn't really matter, was another. The two neighbours of Sir Stirling who had joined the shoot were likewise very wet. Mr Goodie, who had been in a particularly exposed position, was practically liquid. A little circle of pools gathered around them as they assembled for lunch in the inadequate shelter of a coppice.

'This is rotten,' said Sir Stirling. 'Fanny, my dearie, you're frightfully wet. I vote we quit this.'

'I'm not a bit wet,' responded Lady Bunter. 'I had my Asquithcutum.'

'Ay!' cried Mr Goodie with a burst of unusual enthusiasm. 'That is a grand wudd for it, Lady Bunt'r. It's a jooke I should 'a liked to have oreeginated. The Asquithcutum – proof against all political storrms. Ay, that's grand.'

'Haven't I used the right word?' asked Lady Bunter timidly.

'Course you have,' said her husband. 'That'll do, Goodie.

To return to the subject, I say that you are wet, my dear, and must go back home.'

'No, I'm not; but I think we will go back home because you and the others will all get colds, and—'

'I shan't,' cried Sir Stirling. 'I'm as dry as a bone.'

'Oh, Sam dear! I can see the water running off you.'

'Only off my mackintosh. Look here, Fan. Do go home yourself.'

Lady Bunter deliberated for a moment.

'It's a pity to spoil your sport,' she began.

'Rotten day,' put in Sir Stirling. 'I'm sick of it already.'

'Then let's all go home,' said Lady Bunter triumphantly.

And other wayfarers were caught and drenched in the unsparing progress of that storm. It caught an aged rustic idling at the roadside and drove him over the bank into the plantation, grumbling in high-pitched expostulations as though of pain.

It did not wet Dann very severely. He was overtaken by the first downpour as he stood, his cap pushed back and his coat slung over the wing of his car, investigating the second collapse of his lamentable radiator. He quickly got inside the car and pulled up the windows; after which he sat patiently watching the rain, chewing a rather greasy thumb, and wondering aloud with much frankness of expression why such visitations invariably overtook him on the most isolated and unfrequented roads in the country.

It wetted Peter. Peter was almost too preoccupied to care. He was walking at full speed into Downblotton, mentally commandeering special trains, composing telegrams, rehearsing telephone messages.

The storm passed Bristol and swept eastwards before the Bones had gained that objective. Mr Bone had called attention to it. Mrs Bone had said that it was small wonder he wanted to change the subject under discussion, if it were only to talk about the weather.

In the same train, three carriages away, in that very smoking carriage which Mrs Bone had recommended to her husband for sitting, Claude Hackett heard the sudden lash of rain upon the windows, and glanced up from his monthly review with a quick frown.

One of the most likely people in the world to be caught and wetted by a rainstorm which he had thoroughly anticipated was Sloley-Jones. He happened, however, to have made Glastonbury before it broke; and passing quickly into the precincts of the inn, where he intended to redeem the loss of his egg, got only slightly wet.

One of the least likely people in the world to fall a victim to caprice, even the caprice of the weather, was Mrs Spoker. But, despite the employment of an umbrella of dimensions which suggested that it had been bred by golf out of perambulator, Mrs Spoker got a little damp. It was but seldom that she allowed herself the worldly relaxation of a few hours away from the *Stag and Hunt*. Today, as it chanced, she had handed the care of the bedridden lady, the keys of the office and the respectable reputation of her inn to the joint agency of Gladys and Alfred, the old man of the bar; and, accepting the offer of a lift in the waggonette of a passing farmer of proved reliability, had set forth to enjoy a midday meal with her old acquaintance, Mrs Wigger, of Downblotton; together with what that punctilious lady was wont to describe for purposes of invitation as 'a few verbal words.'

CHAPTER XVII

'Well Singes Thu, Cuccu'

Mr Claude Hackett, having lunched in the train, took the first opportunity of proceeding by rail to Glastonbury. It was here that the hiatus, which made the morning journey from London to Rushcombe Fitz-Chartres so troublesome, occurred; and, as he had previously been led to expect, he had an hour and a half to put in before he could obtain the necessary connection.

Having checked these details and deposited his luggage at the station, he went forth into the town. He did not saunter. It was not the nature of Claude Hackett to saunter. In order to put in the time, he was going to look at ruins which, truth to tell, interested him very little indeed. But, since force of circumstances demanded, or practically demanded, that he should go and look at ruins, he went to look at the ruins by the most direct route and at a brisk pace.

On arriving at the ruins he looked at them for the space of at least three minutes. He then looked at his watch.

Time itself seemed to be infected by the immobile grandeur of those patriarchal pillars and walls, standing yet indifferent to the speed and clamour of a modern environment. Claude Hackett wrinkled his brow whimsically at the thought and, attempting to bestir his very inert sense of duty towards the ruins, decided to walk round them once and to view them casually from every aspect.

He turned a corner and halted. He found himself confronted by a strange group of objects.

Immediately in his path stood a motor-cycle, propped up on its stand. A few yards in front of the cycle, projecting from behind a buttress of the ruined wall, were black human hindquarters. Watching these hindquarters furtively, while with one foot he was attempting to kick back the stand of the cycle, was a small boy.

Claude Hackett realised without a moment's hesitation that this meant mischief; that the small boy was intent upon amusing himself at the expense of the hindquarters to the probable detriment of the motor-cycle. He therefore cried aloud in a stern voice:

'Now then! What are you up to there?'

The effect of this was that the small boy, profiting by a long course of study in the topographical possibilities, disappeared completely and instantaneously; while conversely, by a remarkably laboured procedure, the whole of Sloley-Jones disengaged itself from the buttress.

'What's the matter?' asked Sloley-Jones. 'I'm only investigating something. I'm sorry, but it's quite all right surely? Are you a curator?'

'No,' said Hackett. 'I—'

'I'm only investigating something,' said Sloley-Jones. 'Besides, if you're not a curator, was it really necessary to shout like that? I bumped my head. Rotten.'

'I wasn't shouting at you,' said Hackett. 'Is this your motor-cycle?'

'It is, but really I must say I don't see why you should ask. I don't wish to appear ratty about it, but was it necessary to shout like that? It isn't in your way, is it? There seems to be plenty of room to get past. I'm awfully sorry, but I really fail to see why I shouldn't leave my motor-bicycle there; especially as you say you are not a curator or anything.'

'Look here, sir,' said Hackett, 'if you will allow me to explain, perhaps I may succeed in mollifying your apparently somewhat ruffled feelings.'

'Oh, I beg your pardon. I don't wish to appear ratty in the least. Only you gave me an awful jump and I bumped my head.'

'If you want to know, there was a little urchin trying to kick your bicycle over, and I shouted at him.'

'Oh, I say, I'm most intensely sorry for what I said,' cried Sloley-Jones. 'You must forgive me. I had no idea of course. To be startled and to bump one's head like that makes one a little impetuous. Thanks most awfully for looking after my bicycle.'

He advanced into the sunshine and tested the equilibrium of the cycle on its stand with a hand begrimed with his investigations.

He sought Claude Hackett's face and gave vent to a brief apologetic laugh on a single note. Hackett merely nodded. His long white face displayed no indication of amusement.

'I seem to have saved your cycle a bump at the expense of your head,' he observed.

'Oh, it's quite all right now – absolutely. Where did the boy go? Was it a boy?'

Hackett nodded.

'You said an urchin,' said Sloley-Jones, smiling. 'If the word urchin cannot be used in the feminine it ought to be able to be. Ha!'

'This was a boy,' said Hackett. 'He ran away when I shouted.'

'Very wise of him,' said Sloley-Jones loudly, as though to warn the boy against further activities should he have been listening, which he was. 'They ought not to allow these wretched children to come playing about here. They are a perpetual nuisance – unspeakable. They deface the beauties of the walls and molest people who take an intelligent interest. I should like to take it up with the curators. In my opinion it is nothing short of desecration. Don't you think so?'

The question was rhetorical. The bump which the parson's head had received was not so great a shock as was the brisk manner in which the stranger took up the unintentional challenge.

'No,' said Hackett. 'Since you ask, I can't say that I agree with you.'

The discomfited Sloley-Jones gazed in great surprise at

the well-dressed, gentle-mannered stranger who thus unhesitatingly proclaimed himself a champion of the Goths.

'No? Really? You – you surprise me, I must say. Surely you agree that it is a pity that a magnificent old – pile – edifice like this should become a – a playground for people with no veneration? Oh, it's awful. Do you know that a woman named Bertha Harris has actually had the indecency to carve her name with a penknife on that buttress? If people are Vandals and Yahoos they might surely stay away. Why should anybody be allowed here who has no respect for remains, which are without parallel, remember? You can't replace them when Bertha Harris and other slubberdegullions have done their work. I would have no one near the place who was not prepared to do it honour.'

The parson spoke not without heat, but with due intent to exercise gentle persuasion upon his puzzling interlocutor.

Claude Hackett raised his head deliberately and gazed at the outraged buttress with the eyes of a cynic.

'I am not prepared to honour it, I am afraid,' he said in his well-modulated, rather nasal voice.

He seemed about to say more but forbore. Sloley-Jones could only scratch the bridge of his nose and feel at singular loss for words.

Hackett's eyes returned slowly to the round, inquisitive spectacles. A smile, which was more like the promise of a smile unfulfilled, flickered over his keen countenance.

'No,' he said, as though continuing an argument. 'There are some temples which can never be defaced, far less destroyed; but they are temples not built with hands. Temples of Science, temples of Literature, where the worshippers may gain knowledge and refreshment in the pursuit of knowledge. Those are the temples which I would have held sacred. As for an old church' – he waved his hand expressively towards the ruin – 'what's the good of it? Bertha Harris is of far greater importance to me than the stone she cut her name on.'

Sloley-Jones had opened his mouth half an inch but made

no reply. He looked with increasing interest at the tall, commanding man who stood before him. The face was so long and thin as to suggest that in his infancy it had been caught and squeezed like a lemon, but the prevailing expression emphasised by the clean-cut, pointed chin seemed to imply tenacity rather than resolve. The eyes, deeply set, were kind and forbearing, in direct contrast to the austerity of mouth and chin. For the rest Sloley-Jones noticed shamefacedly that the stranger was undoubtedly a man of unusually cleanly habits. His hands and linen were spotless. He was clothed quietly but with a finish. He was certainly the last man whom one could expect to find engaged upon an occupation which he confessed was objectionable, and defying harmless tourists whose only desire was to investigate piously and in peace.

This thought seemed to occur to the stranger too. There was an apologetic note in his voice as he continued:

'I don't wish to inflict my views upon you. Every one is entitled to his own.'

'Oh, that's all right – quite. I like it,' said Sloley-Jones.

'I am afraid I took you up rather briskly,' said Hackett. 'I should like to make my meaning clear if I can.'

'Oh, do. I say. This is quite interesting. Well?'

'I see you are a clergyman. Those who profess to have any respect for the clergy are usually apt to proceed to the other extreme and allow their precepts to pass unchallenged.'

Sloley-Jones repeated his one-note laugh.

'On the good old principle of casting the first stone, perhaps,' he remarked. 'Don't mind me. Go on. I like this.'

'I should have thought,' said Hackett gently, 'that the worship which you appear to devote to a mere pile of stones was hard to reconcile with your spiritual principles. It is the work of men's hands; and whether it is a piece of antique masonry or a golden calf appears to me to be immaterial. That, however, is beside the point.'

'One half tick,' cried Sloley-Jones. 'By Jove, this is splendid. I can see I'm going to have a perfectly topping argument with you. But first of all, aren't your own spiritual principles the same as my own, may I ask?'

'I should think it is very unlikely,' said Hackett.

'You are a Christian?'

'Certainly.'

'Church of England?'

'Yes.'

'Well then. If I may say so, you are hardly the sort of person whom one usually finds oneself up against; the sort of person who seems to find a wretched form of amusement in going about cheeking the Church. You have already associated yourself with Bertha Harris. You now seem to be on the point of joining forces with the bicycle urchin.'

Sloley-Jones grinned broadly with the joy of controversy and rubbed his hands.

'Yes,' replied Hackett. 'If I had known that you, a clergyman of the Church of England, were really prodding about behind that wall from a sense of duty, I think I should have felt rather inclined to kick your bicycle over myself, as a mild form of active protest.'

'Isn't this too priceless?' was Sloley-Jones's comment. 'Now, what's your point?'

'Well, very briefly, this. All around you' – Hackett waved a white, comprehensive hand – 'while you employ your energetic piety upon this buttress, there is raging a continual battle. The battle against poverty and' – he twisted his mouth sardonically – 'other forms of sin.'

'I know,' cried the parson. 'You needn't tell me that. I don't shirk the battle, believe me. This is my relaxation.'

'But the forces opposed to you in the battle are without exception the first-fruits of this archaism which you pause to admire; doctrines and heresies and prejudices as obsolete as these walls. The only difference between them is that this is a helpless ruin; they are the opposite extreme. They are a prison.'

'Antiquity' – he raised his voice as Sloley-Jones showed signs of interrupting – 'is no blessing to us. It is a curse which should be rooted out of every present-day calculation. The only relics we should venerate are those I spoke of – the records of Science and Literature. In other respects custom and dogma are as great a curse as the diseases which still survive from previous generations to poison our own.'

'By Jove,' said Sloley-Jones, 'I believe you are a Socialist.'

'Oh yes,' agreed the other readily. 'Though that is a term which is abused as a political label.'

'Abused? I should have thought that the most violent section of the Labour Party would have been too tame for you.'

Hackett shook his head with one of his brief, fluttering smiles.

'I deprecate violence,' he said.

'Anyhow,' said Sloley-Jones, 'I should put you down as an advanced Liberal.'

'Not advanced,' was the reply. 'Some of the old party who thought more of their prize than their creed have advanced. Some have retired. True Liberals have done neither. I have done neither.'

'Ah,' said Sloley-Jones. 'You know I'm awfully glad we met – uncommon glad. Of course I can't take an active part in politics; but I'm frightfully keen on the subject – keen as mustard. Personally I'm an old-fashioned, full-out, die-hard Imperialist Tory of the most bigoted and relentless type; so we could have a simply topping debate. But I dare say you haven't time.'

'Oh, my dear padre,' said Hackett in a tone which appeared almost light-hearted in comparison with his former zeal, 'I really don't wish to inflict my views upon you. You mustn't think that I attack every stranger I meet in this manner. Circumstances seem to have thrown us into contention.'

'Not at all,' said Sloley-Jones. 'I really am awfully glad we struck each other. I don't suppose it's any use our trying to convert each other. But one doesn't often get the chance of a discussion with a really genuine Liberal nowadays.'

'Ah, I think the wish is father to that thought,' said Hackett. 'The race is by no means extinct, I assure you.'

Sloley-Jones adjusted his spectacles and beamed past the face of his disputant, gleefully preparing his master-stroke.

'I suppose,' he said, 'that you wouldn't believe me if I were to tell you that the Free Liberal party in the House of Commons is simply sitting on the fence waiting to see which way the cat is going to jump?'

'No,' said Hackett cordially. 'I shouldn't.'

'I'm really sorry for you fellows,' went on Sloley-Jones. 'There must be quite a large number of you who are genuinely consistent to your creed; but you can have no idea how you are being hoodwinked by your members and leaders.'

'Really?' observed the other darkly. 'This is very interesting. I can't say that I was aware of this spiritual wickedness in high places.'

'No,' said Sloley-Jones, pursing up his lips and assuming a very matter-of-fact tone, 'I don't suppose you are. I only happen to know what I am talking about because I had it straight from the horse's mouth only last night. I was talking to a friend of mine, who is himself a Free Liberal member, and he told me quite openly and without any compunction that the whole bunch of them are simply waiting to sell themselves to the highest bidder.'

'Indeed?' said Hackett with honest surprise. 'I happen to know one or two of the party members. Who, may I ask, was this rather outspoken friend of yours?'

'Oh, I don't want to give him away,' said Sloley-Jones quickly. 'I might damage his reputation in the party. For all I know you may be a member of the House yourself.'

'Yes, I am,' said Hackett.

'Oh dear,' exclaimed the parson. 'Then I – I don't think I ought to say more.'

'Are you sure you ought to have said as much?'

'What?'

'Please don't be offended; but doesn't it strike you that

this anonymous reactionary of yours is rather the sort of figure that one connects with underhand election methods?'

'Oh, come! You must take my word for it that I really did have the conversation.'

'I don't doubt it for a moment, if you say so. But the gentleman in question must have been a greater friend of yours than he is of his party.'

'No, as a matter of fact,' burst out Sloley-Jones, 'I expect you honestly take your politics a sight more seriously than the majority. This was really the first time I had ever met this man, though I have known his wife for years. He was stopping with his wife last night at an inn not far from here, and I happened to call in and find them there and the wife introduced me to him. He was perfectly frank and open about his politics from the first. Of course he said he shouldn't care to repeat all he told me from his seat in the House; but I gained the impression that he was heartily sick of the entire outfit.'

'Oh well,' said Hackett, the light of solution appearing to dawn upon his perplexed features, 'I needn't encroach further on your confidences. I know the man you mean. He's going to resign almost directly.'

'He didn't tell me that,' said Sloley-Jones, sinking his voice unconsciously in intimate curiosity. 'That's queer – extraordinary. His wife would have told me anyhow I should have thought.'

'You are speaking of Bruce Gladwin, are you not?'

'No. Well, don't let it go any further, but I am speaking of a man called Hackett.'

Claude Hackett was carrying a straight walking-stick of handsome snake-wood. He leant forward, with both hands upon the heavy gold knob which surmounted it and executed a little pirouetting half-turn with his weight on the stick. When he raised his head his tongue was stuck in his cheek, which gave a singular expression of masterful irony to his long grave face.

'I'm very much afraid, padre,' he said, 'that you have been imposed upon in this matter. I have my own reasons for saying that the man you conversed with last night could not possibly have been Hackett.'

'Oh, but you're wrong, excuse me. You're absolutely out. I saw both—'

'Why he should have represented himself as Hackett I have no idea but I do happen to know that Hackett was in London last night.'

'Oh no, look here, you can't pass it off like that,' said Sloley-Jones, smiling still but showing some evidence of resentment in his voice. 'I tell you the man was there with his wife. I have known his wife for years. She was Margaret Bliss – you know, the Margaret Bliss Home for Children – and—'

'Yes, that's right,' assented the other sharply. 'She married Hackett. Well?'

'I say, she was there with her husband. She introduced me to him. They were motoring and had got stranded. I found them at this inn at a place called Maiden Blotton, a village about three miles from here. They stayed there last night and went on this morning to the Bunters' place at Rushcombe. So you see I know my facts.'

He paused with a long and triumphant intake of the breath. That he had gained his point was obvious from the baffled expression of his disputant. He saw the keen eyes narrowed as though the possessor were making a mental calculation.

Sloley-Jones was not the man to miss driving his advantage home. The point under discussion seemed to his energetic mind to be of intrinsic value to the political argument. He held a Liberal M.P. flabbergasted in debate. It was delicious. He sailed hotly in to complete the rout.

'You say you know Mrs Hackett,' he said. 'If you know her as well as I do, you will realise that she is not the sort of woman to pretend that a man is her husband when he is not, just for a joke.'

'No, no. I quite agree with you there,' acknowledged Hackett. 'Mrs Hackett is a very honourable and a very irreproachable woman in every way.'

'I'm glad to hear you say so,' said Sloley-Jones. 'I have always said so too. There was some mischievous scandal about her at one time. Jealousy, I expect. Disgusting! That was really why she started all her philanthropic work. They say she would never have married Hackett if she hadn't meant to chuck her own society crowd. However, I was very agreeably surprised with Hackett. I had always been given to understand the man was rather an ass.'

The other tapped his toe impatiently with his stick and glanced around him quickly. He seemed to be in two minds. Sloley-Jones was delighted with his success. He had this rooted Liberal by the hip, he felt, on any subject.

'If you still feel any doubt in your mind about what I have told you,' he said casually, 'I can soon disprove it quite finally. The Hacketts remained at the inn for the night. In the middle of the night Hackett got out of bed and went down to let out their dog which was howling, and lost it. As a matter of fact I found the dog this morning and returned it to them. The landlady of the inn was disturbed by queer noises in the night – probably caused by the dog – and went down to their room and found them both asleep together in bed. So there you are. We both know Mrs Hackett well enough to let it stand at that; though I fancy one of us must know the husband rather better than the other does.'

Chortling over which sarcasm Sloley-Jones turned rapturously to his bicycle.

Hackett's eyes were wide open now, but they had lost all their forbearance. His brows were knitted. The drawn austere face displayed no sign of anger. For a moment there passed over it that shadow of a smile, as though in answer to one merry little thought struggling in the complexity of his mind. He made a sudden movement with his hand as though to regain the parson's attention; then thought better of it and brought the hand slowly back to the knob of his stick.

He stood watching Sloley-Jones's fidgety attentions to his bicycle with an abstracted stare, as the idler of a harbour town watches a ship at sea.

He drew himself up and threw back his shoulders.

'I think it's time that I was making a move,' he said.

'A – h!' responded Sloley-Jones, glancing up from the bicycle. 'Well, we haven't had much of a debate after all – pity!'

Hackett nodded pleasantly and turned, swinging his stick.

'And, I say,' added Sloley-Jones mischievously, 'don't split on me to Hackett. And, I say, don't take your politics too seriously. Nobody else does. Cheero.'

Round the corner whence he had come first upon the bicycle, the urchin, the hindquarters, Hackett paused and apostrophised the ruined walls in a sinister whisper.

'Do I dream?' he said.

Then he walked at top speed to the nearest garage. He did not pause to ask his way. He seemed instinctively to discern the shortest route.

Ten minutes later Sloley-Jones was just in time to see him depart with his luggage from the station. He had chartered a local car. Sloley-Jones knew that car.

The parson dismounted and watched the car curiously as it sped out of the town. He turned to the porter who had been assisting at its loading and who was now standing and indolently whistling as he fingered his largess.

'I say,' said Sloley-Jones. 'Do you happen to know who that gentleman is?'

The porter, who apparently valued his music above his manners, shook his head without ceasing to whistle.

'Didn't you notice his name on the labels of his luggage or anything?'

The porter shook his head in a manner which only served to emphasise the high note which he had achieved at this moment.

'Do you happen to know where he is off to?' insisted Sloley-Jones.

The porter frowned, ejaculated 'Main Blon, I believe,' and continued whistling.

'Maid-en B-lotton?' repeated Sloley-Jones suspiciously.

The porter nodded almost imperceptibly, dug his hands into his trouser pockets, turned towards the station doorway and took a flying kick at a piece of waste paper in his path, all without the loss of a note.

'How awfully rum,' murmured Sloley-Jones aloud. 'What's his game? Dash! This is awfully rum.'

He mounted his cycle deliberately. There was a back-fire like a revolver shot and the porter, turning his head quickly, was gassed out of tune by superfluous lubrication, as Sloley-Jones commenced his pursuit of the mysteriously inquisitive Liberal M.P. in the car.

CHAPTER XVIII

'Pass, Friend'

Peter, his light overcoat buttoned haphazard over his shoulders and distorting his whole appearance, entered the Downblotton post office in a manner so violent that the postmaster thought he was being held up by a bandit. When he recognised the young man who had been in the company of the interrogative lady with furs and the red-moustached chauffeur that morning, his hostility became, if anything, intensified.

'I've got to get through to London quickly,' cried Peter. 'How long does it take?'

The postmaster removed a worn portfolio containing stamps from the counter and placed it in a drawer. He tried to close the drawer which was ill-fitting and stuck. He pulled the drawer open again and repeated the experiment. Again it stuck. He pulled the drawer completely out of its seating, which he examined minutely, stooping with his aged head on a level with the counter. He then blew into the seating and attempted to replace the drawer. After two or three efforts he succeeded in wedging the drawer into its aperture. Exerting considerable energy he pushed it home. He then pulled it out again to see whether he had jammed it. He had jammed it. Finally he managed to pull it out again and to push it in again two or three times without a jam. He then removed the stamp portfolio from the drawer and replaced it on the counter. He turned a very inhospitable scowl in Peter's direction and said:

'How?'

'Yes, how long?' repeated Peter, who was lathering his perspiring brow with a coloured silk handkerchief.

'How long how?' said the postmaster.

'By telephoning of course. How do you imagine I want to get through to London? Do you think I want to bore a tunnel there or something? Come on; shake a leg for Heaven's sake. I'm in a hurry.'

The postmaster rearranged the position of the portfolio upon the counter.

'How long do it take to get through to London by telephone?' he declaimed.

'Yes,' said Peter. 'How long to London by telephone. There can have been nothing like you since the days of Moore and Burgess.'

'Well, 'ow can I tell 'ow long it may take?' said the postmaster. 'Sometimes it takes a great deal longer to get through to London from 'ere than at other times by a lot. Other times it don't take so long not to get through than you might expect by quite a time.'

'Where do I speak from?' said Peter quickly.

'If folks comes in 'ere and says " 'ow long does it take to get through to London?" 'ow can I say 'ow long it may take?' grumbled the postmaster. 'There's more—'

Peter was already in the telephone box, having at length discovered its whereabouts by his own observation.

He was intensely worried; but, to do him justice, it was the fear that Sophia had undergone an ordeal of weariness and depression by reason of his own neglect which distressed him far more than the prospect of retribution. The knowledge that he would never be able to make Sophia believe this did not detract from his agitation.

He decided that he would remain in that telephone box until he succeeded in communicating with the flat. It was not a pleasing prospect, for the box was very close and rancid with the long imprisoned fumes of cheap tobacco. But Peter could not face a long vigil in the company of the postmaster. In his present state of mind he might be driven to kill the postmaster, which would only add to the already sufficient complications in which he was involved.

Resolutely curbing his impatience, he engaged in negotiations with a succession of female voices which sounded like the efforts of aspirants for the part of the canary in a Maeterlinck fantasy. The drums of his ears were assaulted with frequent but unexpected detonations of the most rending and horrisonous description. He overheard fevered conversations, now rising to a bellow, now fading to a distant screech of endeavour, as though the principals were straining every nerve to allow him to eavesdrop. Another bombardment would follow; then the chirrup of one of the canaries, blissfully greeting the lull after a thunderstorm. He breathed back fervent directions and imprecations into a receiver around which the stale tobacco fumes seemed to have concentrated in an almost visible integument of glutinous substance.

For how long he remained in that telephone box, Peter never knew. For how long he implored, resisted, argued, he lost all reckoning. His most trying altercation was with a voice which claimed to belong to 'trunk supervisor', which sinister title seemed appropriate to a vulture rather than a canary, though the voice yielded to none in its qualities of chirrup. Fortunately, just as Peter was losing his temper with the trunk supervisor, a motor-bus with a missing engine apparently took up its position between them; and by the time this moved on the supervisor had departed and had been succeeded by a breezy gentleman who asked Peter confidently whether he was Mrs Rowbottom.

At the end of twenty-three minutes there quavered in Peter's ears, out of the chaos of earthquake, fire and thunder, the shrill but distant echoes of a still, small voice. He recognised with amazement, unable to avoid the impression that they reached him only by some superhuman coincidence, the accents of the bitter housemaid, Tessie, of his London flat. Even then he was assailed by an over-exacting canary, who interrupted the first outpourings of his inquiries to ask him whether he was speaking.

The charity that thinketh no evil cannot be cited as one of Tessie's most luminous characteristics. She had views as to the most probable course of Peter's procedure during the last few hours beside which Mrs Bone's assumptions were sunny optimism. Tessie had certainly never anticipated this glorious opportunity of contributing her quota to the miscreant's discomfiture. She made the most of it.

Without venturing to state her own feelings in the matter, she gave Peter a vivid impression of the reckoning awaiting him. She described the return of the forlorn and weary Sophia, the advent of Mrs Bone, the investigations and discoveries of that matron, the final vigorous swoop of the entire family, refreshed by enlightenment and unremitting in vengeance, upon his inadequate refuge in the by-ways of Somerset. Ten thousand miles of telephone line could not have modulated the ring of virulent triumph in Tessie's voice, as she greeted Peter with these galling facts.

How had Mrs Bone discovered where he was? Ah. *She* found out, never fear. Tessie lingered over the point with an underlying hint of reproach that Peter should ever have issued such a challenge to that master intelligence. At length she disclosed the means whereby Mrs Bone had achieved this *coup*.

Peter rang off. He burst from the telephone box, threw a florin at the postmaster and ran out into the street, deaf to the flood of squeaky protestation which followed him. He passed rapidly up and down the street in anxious search for any evidences of a garage. He escaped collision with a butcher's cart by a hair's breadth. He participated, under protest, in the struggles of some small boys who were inaugurating the football season. Presently, more by luck than good management, he discovered the local policeman.

No, there was no garage in Downblotton and a good job too. Was there a cycle-shop? Yes, there was a cycle-shop. Where? There. Peter dashed on.

He was in no mind for haggling. He was as clay in the hands of the cycle dealer, who invented record terms for the loan of a bicycle with a saddle which might have been invented as a mild mediaeval torture. The dealer could have sold Peter the bicycle had he known.

Peter paid in advance and sped away. The bicycle emitted a strange protesting groan at every circuit of the chain. He paid small heed. He was as hungry and nearly as weary as on the last occasion when he sought the *Stag and Hunt*. But every other consideration gave place to the frenzied hope of short-circuiting the retributive Mrs Bone ere she held him, forsworn and abject, in the meshes of her net.

If only he could see Sophia first, could explain; failing explanation, could plead. It would be obvious to her that his love was genuine and immutable. Peter pushed on, indifferent to the galling saddle, indifferent to the faintness of hunger; seeing only the relentless vision of Mrs Bone mounting the staircase of the *Stag and Hunt* to view the bedroom, having completed her grim investigations of the office register.

He plied the pedals to the limit of exertion, freewheeling occasionally only as a means to gather strength for a further onslaught. Fortunately the road was clear. It was a narrow road and muddy, but there was no traffic to impede his progress. The female figure hastening towards him was the first he had encountered since leaving Downblotton.

The female in question, who had been hurrying, halted on seeing the bicycle and remained in a huddled attitude at the extreme edge of the road, apparently under the impression that this was the only means whereby she could avoid being knocked down by any passing vehicle. Peter, straining ahead, glanced at the female as he passed. He recognised her face. More, her face bore some subtle connection to all the tumult of fear and misfortune which possessed his thoughts.

He slackened his pace and turned in his saddle before he actually identified the face. The female was standing gazing after him. Peter stopped.

'Hallo!' he cried. 'It's – what's-your-name.'

The female, who was out of breath, responded with an ingurgitation of assent.

'Yes, that's right,' said Peter, returning towards her. 'The *Stag* girl.'

The female's appearance was hardly in keeping with this rather pastoral description. She nodded and snorted her assent in a manner which suggested that the 'Girl-stag' would have been more appropriate.

'Gladys, isn't it?' continued Peter.

Gladys snorted and nodded.

'Where are you off to?'

'Downbl—' replied Gladys, catching her breath at the second syllable and completing her information with a demonstrative thumb.

'Downblotton? Why? Tell me, what has happened at the pub – the inn – Stag – Hunt?'

'Goin' – ter get – Mrs Spo – ker, I am,' said Gladys.

'Mrs Spoker? Why, is she in Downblotton?'

Gladys nodded and snorted.

'Good,' murmured Peter. 'But why get her? What's up?'

The old lady, Gladys explained with much difficulty, had told her to go into Downblotton as quick as she could and bring Mrs Spoker back at once.

'The old lady?' Peter turned and scanned the road before him with haunted eyes.

Gladys nodded several times.

'Damn!' whispered Peter.

'What is this old lady doing? Where is she now?'

'In the bedroom,' said Gladys.

'Oh, my God!' said Peter. 'Why does she want Mrs Spoker? Look here, Gladys. It's no good your going and getting Mrs Spoker. I'm on my way to the *Stag* now and I'll see the old lady and tell her all she wants to know.'

There was little room in Gladys's face for any signs but those of heat and bronchial distress. Peter's offer brought only a glimmer of mild surprise to her expression. She shook her head.

'I 'ave to get Mrs Spoker,' she affirmed. 'The old – lady

was in a terrible – state when she 'eared as 'ow – Mrs Spoker wasn – ther. She's very sick I reckon.'

'I reckon she is,' agreed Peter. 'But, look here, Gladys, I know what I'm talking about. If that old lady saw Mrs Spoker she'd only go and get Mrs Spoker into great trouble. I know what she's after. You simply must not go and get Mrs Spoker. It's a most extraordinarily lucky thing that Mrs Spoker isn't there.'

'I 'ave to,' insisted Gladys. 'The old – lady may be goin' ter die for all what – I know. She looks – 'orrible.'

'Die, nonsense! Why should she die? I wish – well, anyhow, she always looks like that.'

'She don't, I don't think,' said Gladys. 'She's mutterin' awful and 'er eyes is all rollin'.'

'Good Lord, she must have worked herself into a state,' reflected Peter disconsolately. 'Did she ask you many questions?'

'Not many,' said Gladys. 'She jest says, "Wher's the lan'lady? What do she mean by bein' out when I – most wants 'er?" she says. "Go and get 'er – back this minute," she says.'

Peter nodded gloomily.

'I know,' he said. 'You give quite a vivid impression of her, Gladys. I can imagine exactly.'

'Yes,' said Gladys with smouldering resentment. 'She was like that from the moment she first come.'

'Yes, and a good while before that if you only knew,' said Peter. 'But you needn't think she's ill. She's always like that.'

'No, she is ill, I'm sure o' that,' said Gladys. 'From the look of 'er she may easy be goin' ter die.'

'Oh, don't go on talking in that ridiculous way,' said Peter irritably. 'Why on earth should she die?'

'She'll 'ave ter die sometime,' replied Gladys with a shrug.

'Yes, I suppose so, with luck,' said Peter. 'But you needn't think she's going to lie down and die on this particular afternoon, because flukes like that only happen in books for very small boys.'

'I 'ave ter get a doctor to 'er anyway,' said Gladys pertinently.

'A doctor? Who says so?'

'She did.'

'She said she wanted to have a doctor? Then she really has been taken worse. This is more interesting. What's the matter with her? What are her symptoms like?'

'She didn't show 'em to me,' said Gladys.

'But was she ill when she arrived? By the way, I suppose the others were with her? A gentleman with a moustache and a lady?'

'No, she come by herself and she 'as bin by herself all the time. Gave it out she 'ad no friends,' said Gladys.

'I should think she might be quite right about that,' said Peter. 'But are you sure her husband wasn't with her?'

'No,' said Gladys emphatically. 'Nobody.'

'And her daughter; her daughter's my – h'm, yes. Well, when did she come; at what time?'

'At what time o' day?' said Gladys opening her mouth and assuming a reminiscential air.

'Yes.'

'About six-thirty, I think it would be.'

'Oh, look here, don't be ridiculous, Gladys. I'm only trying to help you with this old lady. What time did she arrive at the pub? Now think.'

'I can't rightly remember,' said Gladys. 'It wer' three weeks ago or more.'

'Three wee—' Peter wheeled upon her with a suddenness which frightened Gladys not a little. 'What old lady are you talking about?' he cried.

'The old lady above the bar,' gasped Gladys.

'Oh, thank Heaven!' said Peter. 'So all that has happened is that the old lady above the bar has been suddenly taken ill? Is that it?'

'Yes,' said Gladys.

'Oh, thank Heaven,' repeated Peter fervently. 'That's splendid. Then nobody else has turned up at the *Stag*?'

The startled Gladys could only display her tongue and shake her head again.

'Good!' exclaimed Peter springing on to his bicycle. 'Now, don't you go and frighten Mrs Spoker. She needn't hurry back. The old lady probably grudges her an afternoon off. Tell Mrs Spoker that. Say it will be all right if Mrs Spoker strolls home in the cool of the evening.'

The instructions were rather lost on Gladys, who had already been walking for an hour and was prepared to continue her journey without respite. She was fully convinced in her own mind that the spirit of the old lady would inevitably pass that evening, unless Mrs Spoker could be summoned in time to forbid it to pass; in which case, as Gladys knew from experience, it would have to be a very bold spirit indeed if it still insisted on passing. Unless, however, she used her best endeavour to secure Mrs Spoker, the spirit might pass before that lady had obtained a chance of checking it; in which case Gladys would be a murderess and have her photograph in the *News of the World*. Gladys therefore watched Peter out of sight curiously; then, summoning her energies, hastened forward to Downblotton.

'It might be worse,' thought Peter, as he pedalled on in the opposite direction. 'Nobody's shown up so far. Mrs Spoker isn't there. Gladys isn't there. I may be able to get there first and see how the land lies. As long as I can keep it dark about that damned bed, I ought to be able to pull off the reconciliation stunt. If only I can clear them out before Mrs Spoker gets back. Just my luck if that blinking incumbent had run into them and worked up some more of his priestcraft. Still, at the moment, it does look as if it might be worse.'

His feet kept pace with his busy mind. He ploughed onward along the heavy road for five and twenty minutes; at the end of which he was rewarded by a distant prospect of the *Stag and Hunt*, standing, deserted and at peace, in the afternoon sunshine.

CHAPTER XIX

Alfred and the Shining Hour

Peter opened the inn door cautiously and peered inside. There was no sign of life. He waited in the hall for a moment irresolutely, then ascended the stairs. From the bedroom above the bar echoed a distant wheezing sound. Otherwise all was still.

Peter returned to the hall, pushed open the door which led to the bar and entered. Old Alfred was reclining in a semi-comatose state in a cottage chair. His head was resting against the fireplace. He struggled with a grunt of surprise into a sitting posture.

He recognised Peter with a sleepy nod. The latter had recruited the services of Alfred that morning in the search for Pansy, and, fortunately, had rewarded him extremely handsomely for doing nothing and doing it very slowly.

'I've come back, Alfred,' Peter announced. 'There are some people coming to see me here this afternoon, but you needn't disturb yourself in any way. If they want anything I'll tell you. I've seen Gladys and know all about everything. I haven't had any lunch. I should like a sandwich and some beers.'

'Ah, ye can't get nothing to eat out o' me, sir,' said Alfred. 'It's too late. As fer beer, it's too late for that too be rights.'

'Rights, Alfred? What are rights?'

'Wrongs mostly,' replied Alfred philosophically. 'Well, if ye don't say nothing I'll give ye some beer, sir.'

'That's the spirit,' said Peter. 'You may as well be thoroughly independent while you are about it and give me quite a lot of beer. Join me, Alfred, join me. Let us drown rights.'

Alfred effected the preparations for this programme with

furtive zest. He also found some antique biscuits. Within two minutes Peter was feeling in better fettle for the reception of Mrs Bone.

'Now, look here, Alfred,' he proceeded, as he refreshed himself, 'let me give you a word of warning against these people who are coming here this afternoon. They are up to no good. They are trying to make mischief about me and about the *Stag*. We don't want Mrs Spoker to lose her licence. By the way, here's another five shillings for you, Alfred. Now, if these people ask you any questions, you just pretend not to know anything at all.'

'Anything about what?' asked Alfred, rubbing the tip of his nose with his pewter pot in a mystified manner.

'Anything about anything,' said Peter.

'Well, I don't,' said Alfred.

'Good,' said Peter. 'The best thing you can really do is to have another beer and go to sleep quietly in here.'

'Oh, I got to look arter the place, sir,' said Alfred, 'or ye never know what might not 'appen. Still, ther' might be something in what you say about 'aving another. Funny about me, I allus gets thirsty arter rain.'

'Right,' said Peter. 'You carry on, Alfred. You'll be all right. The weather hasn't settled yet.'

He placed his pewter upon the bar counter as he spoke and, raising his head, listened intently. From without came the unmistakable sounds of a car approaching and slackening speed. The moment had arrived.

'These will be the people,' he said quickly. 'Remember what I say, Alfred. Don't even see them if you can help it, and, if you can't, pretend to know absolutely damn all.'

'About what?' asked Alfred insistently.

'Pretend to be a perfect silly fool,' said Peter.

'Oh, I can't do that,' said Alfred. 'It ain't natural.'

'Oh well, I dare say it will be quite all right if you can be natural,' said Peter.

He closed the bar door behind him quietly. The hall door had not yet been opened from outside. Peter crossed the hall and entered the parlour. Creeping eagerly to the window he held the curtain a little on one side and peeped out.

A tall, spare man turned from issuing directions to his chauffeur, who touched his cap, operated his side break and stretched himself. The tall man swept the exterior of the *Stag* with a cursory glance and stepped rapidly towards the door.

Peter released the curtain.

'The doctor,' he reflected. 'Dash it, I never thought he would turn up so soon. This may complicate things.'

He assumed a careless attitude upon the hearthrug of the parlour and waited. He heard the inn door opened and closed; a firm step in the passage. It passed the parlour and proceeded towards the office. After a moment it returned. The parlour door was pushed open rather roughly.

'Oh,' said Hackett.

His manner had the troubled preoccupation of a slow man in a hurry.

'Oh, good afternoon,' said Peter.

'Can you tell me where I can find the landlord?'

'Yes, there isn't one,' said Peter pleasantly. 'There's only a landlady and she's out. You're the doctor, aren't you? The old lady you've come to see is upstairs in bed. You can't mistake the way, because there are only two bedrooms. Hers is the one above the bar.'

Despite his hurry Claude Hackett allowed him to complete these unnecessary instructions. It was a habit of his to hear all that another had to say to him. Peter met the kindly eyes with a discomforting sensation that he was being searched.

'I am sorry,' said Hackett, 'to disappoint the old lady in question. I am not the doctor.'

'Oh, I beg your pardon,' murmured Peter hastily.

'You are a guest here no doubt? I—'

'No,' said Peter. 'Oh no, I – I merely just happen to be – to be here, as it were, at the moment; don't you know?'

'I wonder,' continued Hackett, waiting again for this explanation in full, 'whether you could be so kind as to inform me where I can find somebody who represents the management of this establishment. I fail to see any signs of activity outside.'

Peter chortled agreeably. 'If you wait for another quarter of an hour, my boy,' he was thinking, 'you'll see all the activity you want.'

'The landlady,' he explained aloud, 'has gone off into Downblotton apparently for an afternoon on the buzz. I told you about the old lady above the bar. Well, she's been laid up here for weeks and has of course been taken ill at the most inconvenient moment; so the inn maid, Gladys, has also pushed off to Downblotton after the landlady and a doctor. That's why I thought you were the doctor.'

Hackett nodded gravely.

'And are the landlady and Gladys the sole custodians of the premises?'

'Yes,' replied Peter. 'At least, there is an additional old man to be found somewhere in the depths of the bar, but I'm afraid he is *non* pretty well *compos mentis*, as they say.'

'I dare say he will serve my purpose. Thank you,' said Claude Hackett, turning towards the door.

'I'm afraid he won't, you know,' said Peter, restlessly preparing to follow. 'If you will allow me—'

Hackett paused. His face had grown slightly sterner.

'I know pretty well all there is to know about this pub,' continued Peter. 'If there's anything I can do for you—'

'No thank you,' said Hackett politely. 'I called in to make some private inquiries. Which is the bar, please?'

Peter indicated the opposite door with a somewhat grudging finger.

'There you are,' he said. 'You mustn't mind my saying so, but really making private inquiries of Alfred is one of the most piffling occupations one could possibly choose. However, you'll discover that for yourself. If I can assist you in any way, I shall be in the parlour.'

Mr Hackett's face showed no resentment at this gratuitous

comment. He entered the bar. Peter returned to the parlour with a shadow of unwelcome suspicion on his brow.

'Private inquiries?' A sinister mission for this sinister man to undertake. What private inquiries could he have to make at the *Stag*, and who had sent him to make them? A solicitor, was he? No, Peter told himself, he would be a very unusual solicitor. Solicitors were men with moustaches, which got wet when they drank tea, and curious trousers. His father-in-law might easily have been a solicitor. This man looked more like a barrister. Or a detective. A detective! Peter tiptoed back to the door and listened.

He heard nothing. The door was a heavy, old-fashioned door which excluded conversation. Peter passed on to the front door, and, opening it, looked out. The chauffeur, who was reading a time-worn sporting newspaper, glanced up and then continued reading. Peter eyed the luggage piled upon the back seat of the car, and advanced casually.

'Are you Alfred?' demanded Hackett with nasal severity.

Alfred started up with a guilty look and brought his tankard into immediate and prominent notice by hiding it beneath the cottage chair.

'Ay, ay,' he said.

The strange gentleman tapped his stick on the floor before him, leant forward upon it with both hands, and assumed an attitude of withering mastery over Alfred.

'The landlady is out, I understand? Are you the only representative of the hotel who is at home?'

Alfred directed a watery gaze past the stranger towards the door. He slowly gained his feet and stood scratching his neck.

'I don't know,' he replied.

'This is the only inn in the place, is it not?'

'I don't know,' said Alfred.

'How many guests were there stopping in the hotel last night?'

'I don't know,' said Alfred.

'How many rooms are there for the accommodation of guests?'

'I don't know,' said Alfred.

'Your knowledge,' remarked Claude Hackett, 'appears to be limited. Perhaps you could tell me how many shillings make five.'

'I don't – oh, I might,' said Alfred.

The long, white fingers of Mr Hackett sought his waist-coat pocket.

'Who is the gentleman out there? What is his name?'

'I don't know,' said Alfred.

The fingers were withdrawn from the pocket.

'I don't, honest,' said Alfred.

'Was he staying here last night?'

'I don't – 'e might 'a bin,' said Alfred.

'But it wasn't *he* who—' Hackett broke off with startled eyes. An inspiration of the most objectionable kind appeared suddenly to have possessed him. He advanced towards Alfred a step and gesticulated vigorously with his stick in the direction of the door.

'Was it he who had a lady with him?'

Alfred hesitated, scratched his neck again, blew out his cheeks and avoided Mr Hackett's face.

'Why don't ye ask him hisself?' he finally compromised by suggesting.

'Where is this lady now?'

'I don't know.'

'Is she in the hotel?'

'I don't – no, sir.'

'She is not? Where has she gone?'

'I don't know,' said Alfred.

'What was this lady like in appearance?'

'Oo, she were a good, big woman,' said Alfred fast-idiously.

'A – lady of ample proportions?'

'Ay, she were a good, big woman,' repeated Alfred. 'A good bust on 'er, she 'ad.'

'Indeed,' commented Mr Hackett without enthusiasm. 'A lady of what age?'

'Oo, a young 'un, as women go,' said Alfred.

'She was a lady, was she not?'

'Oo, yes; a lady she were, such as ladies is,' agreed Alfred.

'Then say so. Stay. Had this lady a little dog with her?'

'To be s—' Alfred restrained himself and cocked a thoughtful eye upon the fingers which still lingered in the region of the waistcoat pocket. 'I ain't sure,' he stated.

The fingers left the waistcoat pocket and ascended to their owner's chin. The chin looked longer and thinner than ever, as though the teeth above it were set. But there was more anxiety than anger in Hackett's eyes.

Alfred watched the movement of the fingers critically.

'I ain't at *all* sure,' he said.

Hackett did not ask any more questions. He stood in deep thought for the space of a minute. Then with an effort, as though hardening his heart against his will, he roused himself. He handed Alfred five shillings without a word, and walked to the door.

He returned to the bar almost immediately.

'That room down there seems to be an office.'

'Ay, sir, that it is.'

'Bring me the key of it,' said Hackett.

With a groan which might have represented laziness or embarrassment Alfred retired to the secret lair of the keys in Mrs Spoker's absence, and after considerable fumbling selected the desired specimen. By the time he gained the hall Peter, also, had reappeared upon the scene. The latter walked up to Hackett, who was waiting darkly by the office door, and addressed him with a slightly extravagant air of jauntiness.

'I say, look here, you know, I wish you would let me help you if there's anything I can possibly do for you.'

'Thank you,' replied Hackett with a foreshortened bow of acknowledgment. 'If you will have the kindness to wait for me inside that little room, I think I shall be able to take advantage of your offer.'

'Oh – er – all right,' said Peter, losing a trifle of his bravado. 'But I really meant inside the office here. I mean, I know my way about and all that sort of thing, if you – if I – you know.'

Hackett made no further reply. His eyes rested critically on Peter for a moment. Then he took the key from Alfred's shaky hand and inserted it in the lock.

Peter remained in the passage, rubbing the calf of his left leg gingerly with his right toe. The dilemma in which he found himself was now so awful that he felt he would have welcomed the appearance of Mrs Bone in the front porch almost with relief. For during the few minutes which he had spent in small-talk with the chauffeur outside, Peter, unlike the Glastonbury porter, had taken advantage of Claude Hackett's labels.

Mr Claude Hackett, M.P.
Rushcombe Fitz-Chartres.
Via Bristol and Glastonbury.

For the first fraction of a second the label had conveyed to Peter's mind a distant and not unpleasant impression of past amusement. The truth dawned upon him with a cold shiver which seemed to creep lingeringly down his back. He emitted a little gasp and turned open-mouthed to the inn. He wavered, uncertain whether to hasten, whether to linger, whether to hide.

'Private inquiries!' he repeated below his breath. 'Yes. This is nice. Claude Hackett. Followed hotly by Bones. And I actually hurried here and hurt myself behind with my bicycle saddle.'

Gathering his wits, Peter realised that this Claude Hackett could, after all, have no idea that it had been he who had been the participant in last night's fiasco. His real name had never been mentioned. At the worst Hackett would only have ascertained from some obscure and diabolical agent of rumour that Mrs Hackett had been traced to this retreat in company with a stranger unknown. The thought restored a little of Peter's shattered confidence. Indeed, by cultivating an air of indifferent readiness to assist the investigator, he might be enabled to divert any inexpedient suspicion. It was in this spirit that he accosted Claude Hackett outside the office. The latter's request and the manner in which it was made dampened the spirit not a little.

He knew all. Peter saw that at a glance. But how did he know?

There was something masterful, inexorable in the psychology of Claude Hackett which had a very disturbing effect on Peter; something which made him feel like a little, guilty boy in the presence of a master bent upon ruthless discovery. In fact Peter had an uncomfortable sensation that he was years and years younger and several feet shorter than his antagonist. As he shuffled restlessly in the passage he stole a glance through the glass of the warped shutter. Hackett had the visitors' book open and was examining the entries methodically.

Even then, when he saw his worst suspicions confirmed in the handwriting most familiar to him, Claude Hackett's face revealed to Peter no trace of what was passing in his mind. It remained a long, grim, expressionless mask. He closed the massive book with a snap, and turned away.

Peter retired towards the appointed parlour and lingered in the doorway. Alfred was the first to emerge from the office. To the old man the whole course of proceedings was as baffling as the ritual of a Chinese funeral. Peter eyed him with a sudden suspicion. Perhaps, after all his precautions, this unjust steward had let him down. There certainly was a hang-dog air about Alfred as he returned the glance. Peter summoned him closer with a jerk of the head.

'You haven't told him I was here last night with the lady, have you?'

'No,' replied Alfred in an imitative whisper. 'No, I ain't told 'im. Leastways; no – 'e asked me, ye see.'

'When he asked – did you tell him or did you not?' said Peter with growing misgiving and irritation.

'No, I didn't tell 'im,' croaked Alfred in his somewhat unsuccessful undertone. 'Leastways, 'e asks, yer see, and—'

Both glanced nervously towards the shadows of the office. The tall, portentous figure was emerging. Peter dismissed Alfred with a quick gesture and receded into the parlour.

'You blithering old idiot!' he articulated. 'Give me back my five bob.'

PART THREE
'Go He Must'

CHAPTER XX

The Quick Way with Mr Mock

Margaret descended the stairs quickly. In the hall were Lady Bunter, Sir Stirling Bunter, Mr Mock, Mr Goodie and Francis, together with a vast and conglomerate disorder of mackintoshes, wetness and steam.

'Where is Mrs Hackett, Francis?' Lady Bunter was saying. 'Sam dear, I should really leave that mackintosh in the porch. Oh, here is a telegraph. Now mind you men have baths.'

'I'm dashed if I have a bath for anybody,' said Mr Mock.

'Not you. The wet ones.'

'I'm not wet,' said Sir Stirling. 'If anyone ought to have a bath it's you, Fanny.'

'Well, I insist upon Mr Goodie having one,' said Lady Bunter.

'I'm quate agree'ble,' said Mr Goodie.

'Ah, here is Margaret! My dear, my dear! give me a kiss. My dear, what a joy to see you! You go and get in, Mr Goodie.'

The fond old lady drew Margaret into her arms, forgetful that her mackintosh had been only partially removed, and embraced her with great affection and at considerable length.

'This *is* a pleasure,' she continued. 'We were so surprised and delighted when Mr Mock told us you had arrived. I thought I had muddled.'

'Told her she hadn't,' said Sir Stirling advancing. 'She never does. How are you, Margaret?'

'I think I must have nearly muddled,' said his wife, releasing Margaret, 'because the Wykehams haven't come. Margaret, you know Mr Mock, of course. This is Mr Goodie – Mrs Hackett. Now do go and pop in, Mr Goodie.'

'Well, there's a telegram,' cried Sir Stirling. 'I expect that's from the Wykehams.'

'Yes, I'll see to it in one minute. My dear Margaret. I am so sorry about your husband having to rush off in that disappointing manner. Mr Mock told us of all your adventures. How funny about the little dog. Kind of the clergyman. Will your husband be able to come back soon?'

'Oh, yes,' said Margaret. 'Almost directly. He had to dash off on some business or other. Some Parliamentary business very likely. I expect he will be here again tomorrow.'

'Oh. But how restless and expensive. How dreadfully one seems to have to dash in order to keep pace with these times. Sam, dear, I do think you might change even if you won't bath.'

'I'm going to change. I should like to have a bath too. But I am not going to have a bath unless you do. You're the person who really wants a bath.'

'Well, we'll see. I may. Let's all go to the library just while you finish your pipe. Not you, Mr Goodie.'

'I haven't finished my pape,' said Mr Goodie.

'Then finish it in your bath. I've never seen such obduracy. You know, Margaret, if we women didn't look after men, they would all die of pneumonia in a week.'

'Yes, I know,' said Margaret softly.

Lady Bunter led the way trippingly to the library. The sun was shining again through the windows, lending additional brightness to the already cheerful comfort of oak and leather. The walls were peopled with the happy old-fashioned creations of Dendy Sadler. From ample shelves smiled the warm bindings of complete editions of Punch, Scott, Dickens, Thackeray, George Eliot and the Hackney Stud Book.

Mr Mock edged, crabwise, to one corner of the room, where on a small table stood the components of another much-needed *stingah.*

'But Margaret.'

Lady Bunter, standing with her short straight back to the

fireplace was studying her telegram with a very puzzled expression.

'This telegraph's from your husband, dear. In London.'

'Oh,' said Margaret coolly. 'He's been very quick.'

'It was sent from London this morning.'

'Well, he can't have sent it then, can he?' said Margaret.

'It's signed Claude Hackett. It says "Please expect me today arriving four thirty Claude Hackett." '

'Perhaps he sent it yesterday,' suggested Margaret, rising casually.

She walked to Lady Bunter's side and stood overlooking her hostess with one arm on the latter's shoulder. Sir Stirling was watching her with critical appreciation. 'Marriage suits Margaret. Fine looking woman,' he thought.

'Well perhaps he did send it yesterday, and I'm muddling,' said Lady Bunter hopefully. 'It says the date of the telegraph here – the 19th. Yes, that was yesterday, wasn't it?'

'Yes,' said Sir Stirling.

'*Mana boleh*?' interrupted Mr Mock. 'Today's the 19th.'

'Oh yes, so it is,' said Lady Bunter. 'Annie Hopwood's birthday.'

'Well, perhaps it was her birthday yesterday,' said Sir Stirling.

'No, darling, the 19th is her birthday.'

'I know it is; but yesterday may have been the 19th.'

'No, it wasn't really. I thought it was for the moment, but I was muddling up. Well, Margaret dear, this telegraph must have been sent today. Oh, my dear, how you squeezed my arm.'

'I'm so sorry,' said Margaret. 'It was only a little squeeze of affection.'

'You darling,' responded Lady Bunter with a ready smile, 'it is lovely to have you back here with us. But this telegraph. I can't account for it. Your husband was with you this morning down here and yet here is a telegraph which he sent off from London at – at eleven. Surely it is very strange and queer and complicated and altogether funny.'

'Well, he couldn't have sent it off himself and that I'll swear,' said Mr Mock, advancing, *stingah* in hand. 'I saw the man myself, didn't I, Mrs Hackett?'

'I didn't know,' said Margaret calmly.

'Well, I saw you drive up in the car. He was in the car, wasn't he?'

'Perhaps,' suggested Margaret abruptly to her hostess, 'he told one of the servants to send it off this morning.'

'My dear,' said Lady Bunter with interest, 'have you servants? How lucky and clever. I am told that in London they are as rare as castles in Spain. I have a friend, Gertrude Box. You know the Boxes, people who had the Gubbins' place for the shooting one year – when was it? She—'

'But, look here, Mrs Hackett.' Mr Mock had stepped to the ladies' side, his yellow face wearing the satisfied grin of the amateur logician. 'How can your husband have told the servant to send the cable saying he was going to arrive today, when, if it hadn't been for your breakdown on the road, you would have been here yesterday?'

'I'm afraid that's too involved for me,' replied Margaret with a rather inaffable smile.

'I'm sure it is for me,' said Lady Bunter. 'It sounds like a riddle of the sphinx. Or do I mean the riddle of the sands?'

Mr Mock directed a shaking finger towards the telegram.

'Now, look here,' he said. 'You and your husband started off yesterday in a car intending to get here. But you had a smash or something and had to put up at a rest-house. Your servants didn't know that. They can't have sent the cable. If your husband was with you down here, *he* can't have sent it. Besides, he says he's going to arrive by the train getting here at 4.30. He's not. He's been here once. It's one of the queerest things I've ever come across.'

'Well, never mind,' said Lady Bunter. 'It will all be explained sooner or later. Who's going to have the bath next?'

Mr Mock turned aside with ill-concealed asperity.

'I'm cursed if I have a bath,' he said. 'I've said so twice.'

'Sam, dear, have you finished your pipe?'

'Yes, all right, all right. Look here, Fanny dear, don't go standing about in those wet things all the afternoon.'

'No, my dear, I am just going up now. Margaret, I suppose we are to take it that your husband is not arriving at 4.30? It's all so complicated that it looks as if we are almost bound to make a muddle.'

'How can the man be going to arrive at 4.30 when he left here for London only two hours back in a motor?' interposed Mr Mock, pointedly.

'I hardly know,' said Margaret, eyeing the obstructionist with some disfavour. 'Does it matter much either way?'

'Not the slightest, except that we shall like to see him as soon as he can possibly come,' said Lady Bunter. 'Come upstairs with me, Margaret. I am going to change. Sam, I do trust you will do the same.'

Mr Mock watched the two women pass in company from the room with a scowl of mortification. He turned almost fiercely to Sir Stirling.

'Women! 'Pon my soul! Here's a damned mystery and nobody seems to take the smallest earthly interest in it. No heads!'

Sir Stirling, in the act of following his wife, glanced at Mr Mock on the way, with a look of fatuous toleration.

'Don't you worry, Mock,' he said. 'Leave it to Fanny. You never need worry over anything on earth if you'll only just leave it to Fanny.'

Margaret overheard this advice, as she followed her hostess across the hall to the staircase. She paid special heed to it, as she happened to be worrying considerably over something on earth at the moment. Within two hours Claude would arrive. Unless she could contrive some means of instructing him, he would inevitably give her away. Even then, all would be well, were it not for the evil presence of Mr Mock. The rather suggestive details of her unhappy experience would make the strongest appeal to him. He would carry the story back and chortle over it with other old yellow, half-civilised, toping men at his club. The story would soon be all over London, for such as cared to hear it. It would proceed without delay to the House and to the constituency.

Margaret quickened her step and overtook Lady Bunter as the latter reached her bedroom door. The younger woman had decided. She would leave it to Fanny.

Fanny seated herself on the bed, removed her shoes and stockings, and began to dry her feet with a face-towel. She had launched forth upon an abstruse reminiscence of bathing in company with Margaret's mother when they were girls of twelve, but Margaret cut her short.

'Dear,' she said, 'listen. I want to explain to you about that telegram.'

'The telegraph – gram – from your husband, or rather, not from him but from the servant or somebody, do you mean? My dear Margaret, you really do not know how fortunate you are to have servants in London.'

'It *was* from my husband.'

'Oh, but how and when? Don't explain if it's very difficult to understand.'

'Claude travelled from London today. The man I was with last night was somebody else.'

'Margaret! Who?'

'Peter Wykeham.'

'Margaret!'

The toe-drying movement continued automatically. Lady Bunter sat upright on the bed with her eyes and mouth opened to their fullest capacity.

'I will tell you exactly what happened. Then you must help me.'

'Margaret!' Lady Bunter paused for two or three seconds, then nodded several times with much intensity. 'Go on,' she said. 'Don't keep me on the horns of – whatever the expression is.'

Margaret told her. Lady Bunter was too horrified to interrupt. From time to time she uttered a little painful squeak, as though instead of drying her foot she was lacerating it, as indeed by this time she unconsciously was. Margaret concealed nothing. She sat in a basket chair in the window and coolly revealed every incident of her progress from Paddington to Rushcombe Fitz-Chartres. The conclusion of the recital found Lady Bunter, barefoot still, circumambulating the bedroom at a disquieted trot. She tore the hat from her head and cast it from her to lighten the already excessive pressure upon her brain.

'So now you understand,' said Margaret. She spoke in a definite and final tone which seemed to disarm expostulation. 'What am I to do about it?'

Lady Bunter's eyes and hair were wild. She made nervous intertwining movements with her fingers. The entire responsibility for Margaret's indiscretion seemed already to have been transferred to the shoulders of Fanny.

'Margaret! Margaret! Margaret! Oh, my dear, Margaret! Oh, Margaret dear!'

'There's nothing to worry about if we can keep it dark,' said Margaret. 'We must keep it dark from Mr Mock.'

'Nothing to worry about! But, my dear, there is. What will your husband say?'

'My husband is as calm and reasonable a man as yours is.'

'Oh, well, he's all right, then. But just think what you have done. What do you suppose the other girl, the Wykeham girl, will think? You don't seem to grasp the true awfulness. You actually slept in the same room as this young man. Even if you hadn't and they thought you had it would be bad enough. You seem to be remarkably calm about it I must say. Although I know there was no actual – harm, I can't help feeling it was really just a tiny bit disgraceful. And so appallingly dangerous. I'm astonished at that Wykeham boy. I should have thought he was the last person to have horrid habits. I dare say he did nothing actually wrong, but he might have had more consideration for you; and, oh, dear Margaret, after all that has happened previously, why didn't you have more consideration for yourself?'

'Well, if you'll only help me to hush it up, no one will be any the wiser or any the worse.'

'But, my dear! Suppose the Wykeham girl takes umb— that word. I dare say you know a great deal better than I do that the very fact of your having been seen in the same inn for the night as this boy, not to say bedroom, is enough to get you divorced.'

'No, darling,' said Margaret gently, 'I shouldn't get divorced because there would be nobody trying to divorce me. I should simply be the co-respondent.'

'Simply!' repeated Lady Bunter with a gasp. 'The calm way in which you take this! Anyhow, I may be muddling about which would be the one to be divorced; but I know, from reading the reports of some of these horrid cases, that it only has to be proved that people stayed together at the same hotel for a night, and then *houp la*! that settles it.'

'Why *houp la*?' asked Margaret patiently.

'What I mean to say is the thing's done – like a conjuring trick.'

'Oh, I think you mean "hey presto",' said Margaret.

'*Houp la* is good enough for me. And it may be *houp la* with you, Margaret, unless something is done.'

'Well, put your shoes on for a start. You'll get cold.'

'I am bursting with heat,' said Lady Bunter.

'I must be the first to see Claude when he comes,' continued Margaret, turning to the window with watchful eyes. 'I will meet him at the station and tell him. Then we can invent some reason for his coming back here so soon and—'

'Oh, Margaret! Margaret! You won't lie, dear?'

'Won't I?' said Margaret.

'No, no, no. We must explain the matter more or less truthfully and yet in a way which will camel – what's that word they used to use in the war?'

'Camouflage. And how do you propose to camouflage it?'

'I don't know. Must we try? We're all old friends here.'

'Mr Mock?'

'Oh, Joe Mock is an old friend of mine. I think he will

hold his tongue if I tell him to. It isn't as if he was a woman.'

Margaret shook her head.

'He strikes me as being rather a mischievous old person. I suppose you can't get rid of him for the afternoon somehow.'

'My dear Margaret, I can't very well drive him out of the house, just because you choose to take young men into your bedroom.'

'No, but you can shut him up. He's so very inquisitive.'

Lady Bunter sighed deeply.

'I'll try,' she said. 'But quite apart from Joe Mock we have the Wykehams to deal with.'

Margaret sighed back.

'I know,' she said. 'I have been haunted all day by a feeling that some one will go and let the whole thing out.'

Lady Bunter had ceased her exercise and stood regarding Margaret with an expression which she considered severe.

'When one thinks, my dear child,' she said, 'of all you have had to put up with before now through being indiscreet, I am simply amazed and bewildered at your having run this risk. It shocks even me. If anyone but you had told me that you had done it I should have refused to believe them. This time, at any rate, they have something to go on. It is dreadful.'

'I don't care two straws,' said Margaret quickly, as she turned from the window and smiled into the piteous wrinkled face, 'so long as nothing is done which can harm Claude. Public men are very exposed to all these sorts of calumnies. If they used his wife's reputation in the constituency to try and ruin his career, I should never forgive myself.'

The words brought a look of the greatest tenderness to Lady Bunter's sensitive countenance.

'You do love your husband very dearly, Margaret?' she asked softly.

'I love him above the earth and all that therein is, the heavens and all the powers therein,' said Margaret earnestly.

'Oh, my dear, hush! isn't that a little profane?'

'My love for him isn't profane anyhow,' said Margaret. 'It is a sacred love.'

'M'yes,' said Lady Bunter. 'I feel I ought to be able to say something rather clever now about your observation of the thing you hold so sacred, but I haven't got the brain, so never mind. But now, quickly, what are we going to do and what are we going to say? Goodness knows what may happen next at almost any moment. Unless we put our heads together we are bound to make a muddle.'

'You suggest,' said Margaret, 'and I'll do whatever you think best unless I can see any glaring miscalculations.'

'Very well, my darling,' responded Lady Bunter, pausing to embrace her protégé. 'But I don't see quite how anyone can suggest anything until we know for certain that your husband and the boy's wife are prepared to condone what you have done. Then, of course, worst of all, there is that parson with the silly name. He has already repeated the whole story to Mr Mock. He is probably at this moment at the other end of the county, telling somebody else.'

Here Lady Bunter was absolutely correct.

'But never mind,' she went on. 'I'll tell Sam of course and see what he suggests. With your help and his I may be able to pull the thing out of the fire somehow.'

Fanny was at grips with trouble again and her spirits rose.

She entered upon the first of her duties immediately. She told Sam. It proved to be a slow task. Sam seemed incapable of understanding Margaret's story; and, when at length he understood it, he refused to believe it. When reassured by Fanny that the story was true, he wasted a good deal of time in blaming young Wykeham. Fanny said she did not think, on the whole, that young Wykeham was more culpable in the matter than Margaret. Sam, upon this, readily agreed with Fanny that Margaret was chiefly to blame. Fanny, on the other hand, inclined to Sam's opinion and exonerated Margaret at the expense of Peter. At the conclusion of half an hour, the interview had resulted in an absolute deadlock: each side refused to yield an inch from support of the view originally expressed by the other.

The discussion then took more practical lines. Fanny's next duty arose, that of devising some means of curbing the curiosity of Mr Mock. In this, too, she consulted Sam. Sam's opinion was that the only practical way of curbing the curiosity of Joe Mock was to clear Joe Mock out of the house and keep him out until all this tyranny were overpassed. From which observation developed suddenly a brilliant inspiration.

It was Fanny's idea. That was agreed upon. As a matter of fact Sam first hit on it, but he attributed it to Fanny; and, since the perpetration of a minor untruth was involved, Fanny preferred that it should not be laid at Sam's door. Wisely she refrained from saying so. Otherwise Sam would have claimed sole author's rights and there would have been another deadlock.

Sam, preening himself in his false feathers, descended the stairs to the library door, paused for a brief facial rehearsal on the mat, and entered. Mr Mock was seated on a settee grumbling indeterminately. Mr Goodie was standing at the fireplace drying his ears.

'My dear fellows,' said Sir Stirling, 'something rather unfortunate has happened.'

'Oh. *Apa matcham*?' growled Mr Mock.

'Just at a most inconvenient time, when you, my dear Joe, are practically an invalid and—'

'What has occurrerred?' asked Mr Goodie.

'It's all my fault. Entirely mine. I don't know how to apologise sufficiently—'

'Oh, what the devil is wrong?' cried Mr Mock.

'Why, this. I've just made a most disagreeable discovery.'

'What is it?' asked Mr Goodie. 'There has note been an eccident I hoope?'

'No, but – what d'ye think I've just discovered?'

Only Mr Mock answered the question and his voice was

muffled. It was in his direction that Sir Stirling turned in making his dire revelation.

'I have run completely out of whisky,' he said.

Mr Mock gripped the arm of his settee. He half-rose. His weak eyes were wide and horrified.

'Impossible!' he gasped.

'That,' said Sir Stirling, indicating the dregs of the decanter on the table, 'is all there is left.'

'*Hoi – ya*!' said Mr Mock, following the direction of his host's finger. 'Barely enough for one *stingah*. Not enough. Barely enough for a *sookoo*. But what the devil are we going to do about it? You might have broken it gently, Sam. Thought you said it wasn't anything bad.'

'Of course,' said Sir Stirling, 'if I had only the means of sending to the people who supply me at Taunton, I could get some more straight away.'

'Well, send in Heaven's name!' said Mr Mock.

'I can't go myself. I've something else on. Francis, who generally does it, has another job on hand this afternoon too. All the other servants are busy; besides, I shouldn't let them drive the trap. The car has got to take Fanny out and Wemblow, the chauffeur, is the only man who can drive the trap as well.'

'But almighty Providence! I can drive a trap, can't I? How far is Taunton?'

'Oh, my dear Joe, you're not fit. It's very kind of you, but—'

'Not fit! Good Lord, I've driven a buggy through ten miles of semi-jungle before now with a temperature of 104 with denghi fever. Something must be done. The house can't go dry like this.'

'I shouldn't like you to go alone,' said Sir Stirling, shaking his head sagely. 'Perhaps if Goodie would be so awfully good as to keep you company—'

'I'm quate – I'm agree'ble,' said Mr Goodie, without enthusiasm.

'That will be immensely good of you,' said Sir Stirling.

'The old mare is rather sensitive and she knows you, Goodie. But if you'll go, Joe, in the capacity of buyer, and select a good brand—'

'Right!' said Mr Mock. 'Though it's none of it drinkable these days. All I can do to get some of the stuff down.'

'You're sure you're all right to go, Joe? It won't make your gout worse?'

'Gout? Good night! I haven't got gout. Had a touch of liver, but I've shaken that off. When will the buggy be round?'

'I'll order it. It really is most obliging of you both. I think you had better wait and have tea in Taunton.'

Mr Mock's eyes were shining. He rubbed his bony knuckles.

'Give me a chit to these people,' he said, 'I shan't want tea.'

CHAPTER XXI

Seconds in the Ring

That feeling of defenceless juvenility returned to Peter with redoubled force as Claude Hackett followed him, with slow strides, into the parlour of the *Stag*. The very manner in which the door was closed was vividly reminiscent of bygone interviews in which one party had been considerably more pained than the other.

Claude Hackett remained composed and deliberate. He found time to remove a small accumulation of dust from his trousers with his handkerchief. When at last he looked into the shifty eyes of Peter it was with interest, almost, it seemed, with respect.

'Would you oblige me by telling me your name?'

Peter fidgeted and made a rather lame effort to summon fortitude.

'Why?' he returned.

'I have reason to believe that you are a friend of my wife's. I am sure that is sufficient excuse for my curiosity.'

Peter thrust his hands into his pockets and attempted to bore a hole in the carpet with the toe of his boot.

'My name's Wykeham as a matter of fact,' he said.

'Oh? Mr Peter Wykeham?'

'M'm.'

'Oh, yes. You have known my wife for a long time?'

'Oh, rather.'

To Peter's great surprise Mr Hackett stepped forward and extended his hand.

'How do you do?' he said.

'Oh – er – how are you?' responded Peter with growing embarrassment as he limply held the white and supple fingers.

'There is apparently no need for me to tell you who I am,' proceeded Hackett returning to his former position.

'No,' replied Peter glancing at the calm eyes with some enmity. 'I saw your name on your luggage.'

Mr Hackett permitted himself that scarcely perceptible tilt of the eyebrows which his friends had learnt to associate with irony.

'It is my luggage then?'

'Isn't it?' said Peter quickly.

'It seems almost reasonable to harbour a misgiving that *you* might claim it,' said Hackett.

Peter's only reply was a little sniff not far removed from open hostility.

'I must confess,' went on the master of the situation, 'that I am at a loss to understand all that has taken place during the last twenty-four hours. I look to you for a great deal of enlightenment. It appears that my wife failed to reach her destination last night and took refuge here. You were with her.'

'Well, why not?' said Peter.

'You were not with her?'

'Yes, I was.'

'You were. Why?'

'Why not?'

The eybrows were tilted again.

'We seem to be in danger of becoming involved in a vicious circle of conversation,' said Hackett. 'I only desire to learn the circumstances which threw you into company with my wife.'

'Well, if you want to know, we both missed the same train at Paddington.'

'Thank you. And then?'

Peter changed feet and continued his boring operations.

'We both missed the train. My wife caught it.'

'*Your* wife?'

'Yes, my wife. I have a wife.'

'Indeed.'

'Yes indeed,' said Peter chafing beneath the cool sardonic manner of his catechist. 'A very good one too. I suppose I can have a wife if I like?'

'Of your own, certainly,' conceded Hackett. 'But please continue. Your own wife caught the train. My wife missed the train. You missed the train.'

'That's right,' said Peter. 'We were all bound for the same spot, the Bunters'. I, having missed the train, gave your wife a lift down in a car. The car went phut two miles from here. So we came here and stayed here. What more do you want?'

'Only a few details of additional information,' said Hackett, examining the grain of his stick and polishing a portion of it with a wash-leather glove.

Peter fidgeted again. This man galled him more than all the Bones in Christendom. How the devil Margaret could ever have—

'Being a married man with a wife of your own – a very good one—' pursued the even, nasal voice, 'you will sympathise with my desire to ascertain that my wife suffered no evil consequences from this unforeseen mishap. The accommodation here, for instance, seems decidedly limited. She procured some food and a bedroom?'

'Oh, we looked after ourselves all right,' muttered Peter.

'I'm very glad to hear it,' said Hackett. 'So you both procured some food and – bedrooms?'

'Oh, yes,' replied Peter stretching his shoulders in a nonchalant manner and turning towards the window.

'In that case,' proceeded Hackett without the least variation in his dispassionate method, 'I am afraid that you yourself cannot have enjoyed a very tranquil night's rest in the company of the old lady above the bar.'

Peter wheeled round. He could restrain the words which burst from his lips no more easily than he could govern the strange tingling of his skin.

'Stop that, Hackett,' he cried. 'This is a true bill. If you think your wife is capable of doing anything that isn't absolutely decent and honourable, then all I can say is you're damn well unworthy of her.'

The kind eyes, now close to his, brightened immediately in a keen appreciation. For once Claude Hackett became animated to the borders of excitement. He clapped his hand upon Peter's shoulder and gripped him.

'Don't waste your breath,' he said.

'There was nothing wrong, nothing,' said Peter.

'Wrong!' cried Hackett. 'Who dares suggest that there was anything wrong? Do you imagine that for a single moment I ever allowed the thought to cross my mind. Thank you, Mr Wykeham, you needn't trouble to defend my wife's honour to me.'

Peter fell back with his mouth open.

'Well, what the dickens is all this buzz about?' he asked in plaintive amazement.

'Come,' said Hackett, 'we're on level ground now, I think. Let us be honest with each other.'

'I *am* honest,' said Peter. 'Damn it, I only looked after your wife and tried to fix her up comfortably. We got into a bit of a hole, I agree. And when you come along snuffling about and making sarcastic investigations, naturally I don't stand up with my hands behind me and work off the whole unlikely yarn at you like a Sunday School child. I shouldn't have been doing my duty to Margaret if I had.'

Hackett bowed his head. The ghostly smile flickered over his countenance and was gone.

'You are right,' he said. 'My discoveries here led me to the belief that you had become rather entangled between you in your efforts to secure a night's lodging. Perhaps I allowed myself to be a little sarcastic at your expense. I will be quite frank with you. And you, please, will be quite frank with me. What happened?'

Peter breathed heavily, scratched his nose and sat down on a horse-hair sofa.

'I don't suppose you'll believe me when I tell you,' he began.

'In which case,' remarked Hackett, relapsing into his former manner, 'I shall be obliged to possess myself in patience until I hear the true facts from my wife.'

'Well,' said Peter with an effort at concentration, 'what happened was this.'

He paused and scratched his nose again.

'It sounds an awfully thin story,' he groaned.

Hackett adjusted the knees of his trousers carefully and seated himself astride the arm of a chair.

'So much the easier,' he said. 'It hasn't got to penetrate a very narrow mind.'

Peter cocked an ultra-cautious eye upon him.

'Before I begin; I only want to – Look here, you meant – you were absolutely in earnest about what you said about Margaret, when I said about her, how she was absolutely – above suspicion? Because—'

He did not complete the sentence. Hackett held up a protesting hand.

'Come, come,' he said, 'we shall probably find that there is plenty for us to disagree about. I shall very likely say that your precautions for Margaret's comfort last night were extremely ill-considered. Don't let us waste time in harping upon the one subject on which there cannot be the smallest dispute. If you doubt whether I am being honest with you on that subject I shall be in danger of losing my temper. I shook hands with you. I am not Judas, I hope.'

'Well, when you hear this yarn, don't be Pilate. If you're influenced by what ordinary convention thinks an enormity you'll probably get pretty warped over this show.'

'Oh, please come to the point,' said Hackett briefly.

Peter found it far from easy to come to the point. The task had, however, been rendered less complicated by the astonishing revelation that Claude Hackett was an ally. As he proceeded along the treacherous path of his story he stumbled more than once. His companion made no effort either to assist or to implicate him, but sat watching the fireplace steadily, as though his thoughts were far away. Peter gradually warmed to his subject. From the outset he made no attempt at further concealment. On the contrary he reviewed every incident of the previous night with an attention to detail which threatened at times to become laborious. Whether Claude Hackett found it laborious or not was impossible to determine. As the narrative approached its most poignant point Peter glanced more than once with supplicatory eyes at his auditor. But the latter made no sign.

The car journey, the leak in the radiator, the long footslog to the *Stag*, the reception accorded them by Mrs Spoker, the complete occupation of Mrs Spoker, the incident of the undesirable friend of 'Arry 'Ook, the departure of the Loves, the furtive plans for utilising the parlour as a sleeping apartment, the arrival of the inevitable and undesirable Sloley-Jones, the banishment of Pansy, the wangling of the visitors' book, every episode was recorded with explicit, if occasionally rather grandiose veracity. Then came the test.

Peter faltered, pulled himself together with a little shake of the chin and plunged boldly on. The impassive figure opposite never stirred a hair.

The locked doors, the ensuing arguments (complete with reiteration of the comparative indelicacy of riding upon buses and sleeping upon floors); the bed on the floor, the window, the voice of Pansy *in extremis*, the descent and wetting, the return. The broken basin. The visitation of Mrs Spoker. The bed. A nervous glance here. Peter gulped and hastened on.

The rest was easier going. Peter deposited Margaret at the Bunters', heard of the fatal activities of Sloley-Jones, returned with Dann, left Dann on the high road and telephoned from Downblotton; received warning of the Bones, bicycled back to the *Stag* upon a rack and—

'Well, there you are,' said Peter. 'And I suppose you'll say I've made a howling mess of things.'

Hackett opened his eyes a trifle, but did not raise them from the fireplace.

'Yes,' he answered. 'But only because I cannot hit upon a more expressive word than "howling" at the moment.'

'Well, I'm awfully sorry,' said Peter.

'My wife – Margaret' – Hackett leant back very slowly and looked at Peter – 'is a woman quite without any rival in sympathy and understanding. I am very loath to think that any advantage should have been taken of that sympathy.'

'None was,' said Peter anxiously.

'There I entirely disagree with you,' said Hackett. 'However, if we are going to proceed together to the Bunters', please don't tell Margaret that I think so. I shouldn't like her to think that I did not approve of one of her kind actions.'

'By Jove,' Peter exclaimed almost involuntarily, 'you are an extraordinarily good sort of fellow, Hackett.'

The manner in which his confession had been received had banished his bashful timidity in one instant.

'I am a reasonable man, that's all,' replied Hackett. 'And, being a reasonable man, I expect you to comply with a favour which I have to ask you.'

'Of course I will,' said Peter. 'What is it?'

'You will consent to come with me to the Bunters'. You will forgive me if I consider your story so unique as to require confirmation before I definitely accept it.'

'Yes,' said Peter with a slightly mournful laugh. 'I suppose that's reasonable enough. All right. I'll come along with you if you want me.'

'You see, Wykeham,' said Hackett more pointedly, 'if, when I have heard the really official version, I find that it does not tally with yours; if, that is to say, I discover that some definite advantage has been taken of my wife, I shall appreciate having the man who took that advantage close at hand.'

'I shan't run away,' said Peter. 'You'll find the facts are exactly as I've told you.'

'Thank you,' said Hackett politely. 'Then that is agreed.'

'Of course,' said Peter, 'I shall have to wait until I've seen my wife and her crowd. I hope I shall be able to bring her along too, if you can tackle both of us. She may cut up rough and refuse to come. I expect she's been pretty well primed by her mother.'

Hackett's gaze returned to the fireplace. He tilted his eyebrows as he deliberated.

'Does your wife's mother know the facts of the case?' he asked.

'No, but she'll jolly soon find 'em out,' said Peter pessimistically.

'Don't you think it might be advisable to keep your wife partially in ignorance of all that occurred until you have the opportunity of explaining to her alone?'

'Yes, but it can't be done,' replied Peter.

'Why? I may tell you I should never have come to this place, had I not, by a strange coincidence, chanced upon an informant whom I now have no difficulty in identifying as your friend, Sloley-Jones.'

'That scheming, meddling mendicant!' cried Peter.

'It is hardly likely that he will waylay your wife's family as well,' said Hackett suggestively. 'They must be relying entirely upon conjecture as to your – behaviour. If we can mollify their suspicions, surely that will have the desired effect?'

'Oh, well,' said Peter, 'personally, of course I'm prepared to lie like a trooper if only I can put Mrs Bone off the scent. She wouldn't take it like you have. But, naturally, I'm not asking you to chime in and lie too.'

Hackett rose quite suddenly. The quick movement was unusual in him. It was as though he had recalled to mind an appointment which he had failed to keep. His expression, too, was changed. The kindness had left his eyes.

'Look here, Wykeham,' he cried. In his voice rang a new note of stern challenge. 'I was driven to this inn by a haunting fear; a fear that the thing I hold more precious because it has been foully wounded once was in danger. I mean my wife's reputation. I've little enough to thank you for. You've taken very pretty measures to guard her name from some of her dear friends. Be that as it may, the danger's present, and by any means in my power, fair or foul, I'm going to squelch it.'

'Good man!' cried Peter rapturously. 'I'm damned sorry for what I've done and you can trust me to back you up in the squelching for all I'm worth.'

'Very well,' said Hackett more collectedly. 'Your best plan will be to persuade your wife to accompany us to the Bunters'. Who else is to be expected?'

'Her mother and father. The father's all right. He won't give any trouble. He's a poop. The mother is like one of those females of the classics with snakes instead of hair.'

'I think, perhaps, you had better allow me to deal with the mother,' suggested Hackett.

'My dear fellow, do,' consented Peter in the most generous tone.

'What time do you expect these people?'

'Judging from what I heard on the telephone I thought they'd be here now. What about fortifying ourselves? You help to make the laws; help me to break one for a change.'

Claude Hackett, now completely restored to his former almost lethargic ease, consulted his watch and nodded.

'Yes,' he said. 'I think I may as well have a whisky and soda.'

'I think you're wise,' said Peter presciently.

CHAPTER XXII

Thin Ice

'This is the place,' shouted Mrs Bone, rapping the window of the car with the butt end of an umbrella. 'Stop! Will you stop! Driver! Tell him to stop; this is the place. Stop, driver! Ferdinand, will you wake up and tell him! Stop, I say. This, thank goodness, is the miserable place.'

Mr Bone aroused himself with a jerk which dislocated his grey bowler.

'Sorry, my dear,' he said. 'I was asleep. Dropped off. Where are we?'

'Blotto,' replied Mrs Bone with asperity. 'Get out.'

Mr Bone turned incredulously to the driver.

'Is this Blotto?' he asked.

The driver, who seemed far from certain on this point, was craning his neck to look backwards towards the inn they had just passed.

'Looks like it,' he admitted.

'Oh. Well, it's been a long way,' said Mr Bone.

'Yessir. A good bit longer than I estimated.'

'I suppose you've come by the shortest route?'

'Of course I have,' said the driver. 'Why shouldn't I have?'

'We seem to have been half over Somerset,' said Mr Bone meekly.

'So we have bin,' said the driver. 'This *is* 'alf over Somerset.'

'Oh,' said Mr Bone.

'Will you get out?' said Mrs Bone.

'Half a moment, Constance. The man is going to back I think. You will back the car to the inn, please. All right, my dear; one moment. I knew a man who broke his leg getting out of a car when it was being backed.'

'I'm not surprised,' said Mrs Bone. 'Just the sort of fool you do know.'

'Look out,' said Mr Bone. 'There's another car there. Don't run into it.'

The driver gave vent to a brief appreciation of this advice beneath his breath and brought his car to rest, after sundry manoeuvres, in the rear of Claude Hackett's. Mrs Bone dismounted and sniffed the air of Blotto menacingly. Sophia followed her. Mr Bone, who had been issuing instructions to the driver, turned a little nervously to his better half.

'What?' exclaimed the latter. 'Says he can't wait here long? Let me speak to him. Get the bag from inside the car. I will speak to the man. Will you try and keep out of the way for one moment of time?'

Mrs Bone thereupon turned her back to the inn and challenged the driver. Mr Bone read the inscriptions on the bar and parlour windows and pretended not to. Sophia, after regarding the whole of the exterior with an expression of puzzled disdain upon her handsome face, moved towards the inn door and tested the handle. Next moment, with a stifled cry, she found herself clasped in the arms of Peter.

Found herself; for, in the first shock of this unexpected greeting, she certainly lost herself. Then, after a momentary struggle, she saw who it was, realised with a sudden rush of emotion that the husband upon whom all her affections had been centred in growing expectation and renewed hope throughout that day's long, weary journey, held her as a lost child clings to the mother restored. The floodgates of Sophia's better nature were loosened.

'Peter! Peter, my darling!' she cried, and fell upon his neck.

He drew her into the parlour, his arms around her still, reluctant to release her. In the hall doorway the face of Mr Bone peered stupidly like that of some surprised beast.

'Sit down here, my dear one,' said Peter. 'How tired you

must be. Don't let's start explanations and things for a minute. You will want a breather after all this.'

'I only want you,' said Sophia. 'Stay here with me.'

'You bet,' said Peter.

Sophia turned her attention to the tall figure standing with his back towards them by the window.

'Who?' she whispered a little apprehensively.

'Oh, Mr Hackett!'

The figure turned.

'Mr Hackett is a friend of ours,' explained Peter. 'He is all part of the – mess up. He is the husband of the lady I was talking to when the train left Paddington. And oh, Sophia, I am frightfully sorry about that effort.'

Sophia seemed to pay small heed to the apology. She was smiling quite amiably and shaking hands with Mr Hackett. After all, if the husband knew all and remained on the best of terms, there could be little for her to worry about.

'Oh, so you are still here?'

Mrs Bone had appeared in the doorway and was taking stock of the situation with a pose which seemed incomplete without a lorgnette. She relinquished this in order to turn her head with a sudden movement of annoyance which suggested that she was being prodded from the rear.

'Yes,' said Peter. 'At least, I came back here when I heard you were coming. How awfully jolly to see you all down here. May I introduce Mrs Bone – Mr Hackett?'

Mrs Bone appeared rather uncertain as to whether he might. She advanced two short paces and bowed coldly.

'And Mr Bone,' proceeded Peter cheerfully. 'Where is he?'

'Come into the room,' commanded Mrs Bone.

'I couldn't before,' expostulated the husband.

'And close the door.'

'All right. Give us a chance,' said Mr Bone.

'S'sh,' said Mrs Bone. 'This is my husband,' she added bluntly to Hackett.

'So I – How do you do?' replied the latter.

Peter was on his feet at Sophia's side. He still held her hand.

'I should like to tell you all for a kick-off – for a start,' he said, 'that Mr Hackett is the husband of the lady I was talking to at Paddington when I missed the train.'

This announcement rather took the wind out of the sails of Mrs Bone, who, ever since setting eyes upon Peter, had been silently contemplating a dramatic opening and had decided upon 'And is your mistress still with you?'

'Yes, I am very sorry that Mrs Wykeham should have been so inconvenienced.'

It was Hackett who spoke, and he made a formal little bow of apology to Sophia as he did so.

'From the purely selfish point of view, the oversight suited my wife and myself admirably,' he continued. 'It enabled Wykeham to offer her a lift in his car. He, of course was anxious to follow Mrs Wykeham without delay. I followed her in *my* car.'

Peter looked up amazed at the coolness and calculation with which this refined liar was taking charge of the situation. Sophia's expression was wistful but satisfied. Mr Bone was murmuring involved sentences of trite gratification. Mrs Bone silenced him with a flourish of the hat and breathed heavily through her nose.

'Oh,' she said. 'But may one ask why your wife didn't wait and come with you?'

'One is naturally prompted to do so,' replied Hackett amiably but with complete gravity. 'I expected to be detained indefinitely by a deputation of constituents, which, however, failed to materialise.'

Mr Bone uttered a little coo of reverential interest.

'Are you an M.P.?' he asked.

'I have that peculiarity,' said Hackett. 'It has ceased, I am afraid, to be "that honour".'

'Oh, I don't know. H'm. By Jove. Fancy!' said Mr Bone, pulling down his waistcoat and smiling very affably.

Mrs Bone was making restless movements of the shoulders and lips. She returned, undefeated yet, to the attack.

'So you heard that this – son-in-law of mine had brought this – wife of – your wife to this – inn; and followed them here?'

Hackett bowed acquiescence.

'Exactly,' he said. 'I happened, fortunately, to hear that they had met with a mishap and had taken refuge here. So I came here too.'

Mrs Bone contented herself with murmuring 'Very fortunately indeed, I should think' beneath her breath, and with directing a glance at Peter which only had the effect of tightening the clasp of Sophia's fingers.

'Seems a funny sort of pub,' remarked Mr Bone, who rather flattered himself that he was rescuing his wife from an embarrassing predicament with considerable conversational skill. 'They seem to leave you to your own devices. Where's the landlord?'

'The landlady's out,' said Peter. 'There's nobody about.'

'Oh? I thought I saw an old man looking out of the window.'

'Oh, he's the barman.'

'The barman, is he? Well, I may as well go and have a word with him,' said Mr Bone carelessly.

'Why?' demanded Mrs Bone in a subdued but threatening tone.

'Oh. Just to – tell him we – don't want anything.'

'Stay here, please. I may as well tell you,' said Mrs Bone with severity to Hackett, 'that we accompanied my daughter here, because we heard that my son-in-law was at this place with—'

She hesitated and pursed up her lips. A china ornament on the mantelpiece apparently distracted her.

'With us?' suggested Hackett gently.

Mrs Bone still made no reply. Every moment seemed to make it increasingly difficult to explain to this cool, unexpected husband exactly why she *had* accompanied her daughter there.

'Didn't you think it was quite nice for me to be here with Mr and Mrs Hackett?' asked Peter, carrying the war into the enemy's camp with some foolhardiness.

Mrs Bone seemed to relish this interruption. She wheeled on Peter. The very hairs of the bearskin coat she wore seemed to bristle.

'All we knew was that you had abandoned Sophia in the train and that you were last seen in company with another lady. I, for one, was not surprised. When we heard that you had brought the lady to this inn for the night, I, for one, pricked up my ears. Perhaps if Mr – hum – here knew some of your lady friends, he would not be so ready to allow Mrs – hum – his wife to go motoring in your company.'

'Oh!' replied Peter, grasping Sophia's hand tighter than ever. 'Have you any evidence that I have neglected Sophia in any way, since we married?'

'Your reputation before your marriage, I think, justifies a certain amount of precaution in the matter,' returned Mrs Bone, in sweeping and grandiloquent sarcasm.

'Gosh!' was Peter's sole and rather obscure comment to this.

'May I interrupt by suggesting that what has been an evident misconception, however plausible, has been cleared up?' said Hackett. 'I'm anxious to be getting under way for the Bunters'. If Mrs Wykeham is ready to make another motor journey, I shall be very glad to give her and her husband a lift.'

'Oh, but I can't go there tonight,' said Sophia. 'Nor can Peter. We – I, that is, left all our clothes at home.'

'It's no good going all the way up to London and down again just for our clothes,' said Peter. 'It'll be all right if we don't have any clothes at the Bunters' just for the first night. The Bunters are awfully simple sort of people. We can telephone for our clothes from Downblotton or send a wire. They'll be down tomorrow.'

Sophia looked inquiringly up into her husband's face. She knew that the prospect of making the return journey to London in company with her parents and the reclaimed Peter was even more odious than that of casting herself upon the mercy of Lady Bunter with a teagown and a toothbrush. Then again came the vision of a smart country house party; of herself, shorn of all her saving appurtenances, being subjected to the critical gaze of the guests. As she hesitated an inspired solution occurred to her.

'What did you sleep in last night, Peter?' she asked.

'Oh, a bed,' replied Peter in an off-hand manner.

'Yes, but what did you wear?'

'Wear? Oh, I borrowed some – some wear.'

'Oh. How did you manage that?'

'Well, as a matter of fact, I managed to borrow some stuff from the hotel. It was pretty rough, but it served.'

'I told you,' said Hackett kindly, 'that before you decided to spend the night as you did you should have consulted me.' He turned to Sophia with his fleeting smile. 'I could have supplied him with more suitable arrangements,' he added.

Sophia smiled back.

'Because I was thinking,' she went on to Peter, 'that we might stay here tonight. Mother could have our things sent down tomorrow.'

Mrs Bone, who had been reinforcing herself by opening the door and making a further brief reconnaissance of the dingy hall and staircase, returned in time to notice the grimace of sharp apprehension on Peter's face and wondered what she had missed.

'It surprises me,' she said, addressing Hackett, 'that you should all have found room to sleep in this place.'

'The accommodation is not very extensive,' acknowledged Hackett.

'How many bedrooms are there?' asked Sophia of Peter keenly. She could see no reason why the proposal to spend the coming night at the *Stag* should not solve the whole difficulty.

'Two,' said Peter. He shifted his position uncomfortably and glanced at his mother-in-law, who was watching.

'Oh, there *are* two bedrooms then,' said that lady with a movement of the shoulders which seemed to imply that she was suffering from an irritation between the blades.

'Where are they?' asked Sophia.

Mrs Bone did not fail to detect the little frown of discouragement with which Peter greeted this cross-examination.

'One is over this room.' It was Hackett who spoke. He addressed the remark to the whole company. 'The other is opposite. Above the bar.'

'Oh, is *that* where the bar is?' soliloquised Mr Bone.

'Well, we should only want one, shouldn't we?' said Sophia. 'Which did you have last night, Peter?'

'The one above here; but – it's awfully uncomfortable. I simply couldn't allow you to—'

He dropped his voice to a whisper and, seating himself on the arm of the horse-hair sofa, engaged his wife in earnest confidence. She warmed to his ardent consultations for her comfort. All her bitterness had long since vanished. She was smiling and winsome as any maiden in playful argument with her sweetheart.

Mrs Bone did not intend to be left out of this. She advanced a step or two and listened unblushingly. Suddenly a thought struck her and she turned again to Hackett.

'Did you and Mrs – hum – find the other room very uncomfortable too?' she asked.

'My wife failed to get a wink of sleep in it all night,' he answered with dignified resentment.

'H'm.' Mrs Bone inclined her ear again to the whispered controversy, hovering menacingly like a cat preparing to spring upon the innocent discussions of two mice.

Peter was finding the very reasonable proposal of Sophia exceedingly difficult to contravene. He was becoming more involved, his arguments were growing more specious every moment. Sophia made no secret of her antipathy to the proposed arrival at the Bunters' with her toothbrush and her teagown. Peter, too, had no clothes, dress or undress. Here they were at the *Stag* with a room awaiting them. What could be more reasonable than to avail themselves of the inn for the one more night? As Peter fidgeted and stumbled and glanced nervously towards the window, Mrs Bone sprang.

'Yes,' she said. 'Most practicable and proper. I cannot have Sophia appearing at strange country-houses like a savage. Moreover, your father-in-law will leave you his pyjamas. Ferdinand, do not chew your hat. Open the bag.'

Mr Bone sighed, laid down his hat and commenced operations as dictated. His wife superintended the unpacking of Sophia's belongings and of his own striking Swan-stripe slumber suiting, which the poor man exhibited with the rather shamefaced manner of a schoolboy whose over-fond mother has decked him in ridiculous attire. Sophia leant back on the horse-hair sofa with a little chuckle of satisfaction. Peter seized the opportunity to steal one last, despairing glance of entreaty at Hackett.

The latter did not appear to notice it. He bestirred himself slowly and moved across the room towards the door.

'I must really be preparing to leave,' he said. 'I agreed to go to the Bunters' this afternoon, and my wife, no doubt, thinks that I am already on my way.'

In the doorway he turned and addressed himself pointedly to Peter. In the depths of his genial eyes there was the faintest possible glimmer of innuendo.

'You will decide whether you are coming with me, won't you?'

'Thank you so much. We are going to stay here,' said Sophia.

'Ah,' said Hackett. 'Well, I am going to see my wife.'

The door closed behind him, but his footfall could be heard a moment later on the stairs.

'Where is he off to now? Where is his wife then?'

Sophia had turned quickly to Peter. The latter was gazing upwards towards the corner of the ceiling. His face wore a smile of fatuous solicitude. Sophia noticed it with a shadowy frown of misgiving. Mrs Bone, too, was all attention.

Peter lowered his eyes and banished the fond smile. He saw, with complete satisfaction, that it had taken full effect.

'The idea is,' he explained, 'that the lady up there is not fit to go on today. You see, she had a very trying and tiring experience. However, she won't let Hackett stay with her. We haven't been able to communicate with the Bunters, and I suppose they will be expecting the Hacketts just as they are expecting us. She's expecting to go from here tomorrow. She said something about feeling as if she wanted to go home, but—'

'Oh, so that woman is still here?' cried Mrs Bone.

'Yes, rather. She's still here.'

'But her husband is leaving her here?'

'Yes. I say; she doesn't want Hackett to delay pushing on to the Bunters'.'

'She can't be feeling very ill,' said Sophia darkly.

'Oh, I don't think she's really at all ill,' said Peter. 'Just tired and so on.'

'Is she still in bed?' asked Mrs Bone severely.

'Yes, she's staying in bed today,' answered Peter. 'She's in bed in the room above the bar.'

'But who's looking after her, now that her husband's going?' asked Sophia.

'Oh, I don't think she wants anyone to look after her,' said Peter. 'But now that I am going to stay here – and you, of course—'

'Who is at the Bunters', do you know?' said Sophia, her dark eyes roaming in contemplation.

'No one practically but the Hacketts and ourselves,' said Peter.

'Because I think I'd rather change my mind and go on there with you and Mr Hackett now,' said Sophia.

CHAPTER XXIII

'Lhude Sing Cuccu'

Sophia's decision was obviously final. She arose quickly and gathered the garments which her father had managed with considerable disorganisation to transfer from the bag to the floor of the parlour.

'Tell Mr Hackett, please, that we will go with him after all. And get some paper from somewhere,' she said to Peter.

'Righto,' said Peter.

Disguising as best he could the elation which this development had wrought in him, he passed from the room into the bar. He was conscious that his movements were being followed with no little interest by his father-in-law, whose offer to lend a hand met, however, with a brief but unqualified veto from the parlour.

Pausing only to impress upon Alfred the necessity of remaining absolutely natural and devoid of the smallest semblance of intelligence, Peter secured some sheets of newspaper and returned. Even when confronted with the prospect of making her bow at the Bunters' with her worldly possessions enclosed in the advertisement sheets of a Sunday paper, with the song of the week, 'I went on eating my banana,' conspicuous to every eye, Sophia never wavered in her determination. At the worst she would go to bed on arrival at the Knoll and stay there until her clothes came from London. Anything was better than remaining at this wayside inn, with the rival who had lured Peter from his place of duty awaiting his ministrations in the bedroom above the bar.

Sophia was no longer jealous, no longer resentful. She knew that her influence over Peter was supreme, so long as she could remain at hand to exercise it. But she had seen that foolish, infatuated grin on his face as he gazed upwards towards the room where Mrs Hackett lay. She almost pitied the poor boy in his weakness. She could afford to now. The embrace with which he had greeted her on her arrival had been proof enough of his penitence and true devotion. But he was easily led astray; and Sophia's quick temper had flared up again for one harsh second, as her thoughts turned to that languid seductress in her stronghold above the bar. The husband, good, easy man, was only too obviously a tool in her hands. Why had she persuaded him to go away and leave her? No, no; the atmosphere of this inn was not calculated to prove very beneficial to poor Peter. She would remove him at all costs and by the quickest possible means.

Together at the Bunters' they would stroll in the woods and she would recall all the sweet early raptures of their happy marriage. She knew he would yield to her influence as he had yielded himself to her arms at their moment of meeting just now. And when Mrs Hackett arrived at the Bunters' – Sophia smiled at the thought. She would be ready for her.

So off they went, with Hackett. Little time was wasted. Neither Peter nor Mrs Bone made any overtures towards apology or reconciliation. Sophia merely instructed her mother to have all the clothes she would require dispatched by passenger train without fail on the following morning. Peter found time to bribe the Bones' driver and to suggest that the latter should refuse to remain at the *Stag* for more than, at the most, five minutes longer. This small negotiation was conducted in the highest possible spirit of concord.

Mrs Bone remained in the parlour. She heard the engine of the car, the changing of gears, the warning toot of the horn. She glanced through the window just in time to see a little cloud of dust on the road leading to the church and the small black cottages. She relapsed on to the horse-hair sofa. She was silent and ruminating. She had tasted defeat; and worse, she saw in her husband's solid expression of sagacious boredom the unkindest cut of all.

'Oh, don't grin,' she said suddenly.

'Not,' retorted Mr Bone concisely.

'Well, don't nibble your bowler hat. I've told you already.'

'All right, Constance. It's no good being sick about it. We ought to be very glad.'

'Who's being sick?' said Mrs Bone.

'Of course I knew all along that Wykeham was a perfectly straight and decent young chap. You would have it he was a blackguard. Now I've proved you wrong, let's go home.'

'You have proved me wrong! As if you would have come down here if it hadn't been for me.'

'Well, it was hopeless waste of time, I agree,' said Mr Bone. 'Anyhow, let's go home now.'

'I want some tea,' said his wife.

'Oh, I'll go to the bar and see if I can get you some if you like.'

'You want to go and drink again, I know,' said Mrs Bone.

'Yes, I do. I could do with another drink of beer quite easily.'

'Do you suck beer like this all day long when you are supposed to be at the office?'

'No, but I want a drink now. So do you; you've just said so. One man's drink is another man's – or rather – one man's beer is another—'

'Oh, stop talking rubbish,' said Mrs Bone.

'I don't expect you can get any tea here,' continued Mr Bone, stooping to repack the bag. 'But you can get some tea at Bristol. In the buffy. Or, perhaps, you may be able to buy some on the way and take it in your hand in the car.'

With this Parthian shaft the triumphant husband retired with the bag into the hall.

Mrs Bone chose to ignore it. She leant back upon her couch and closed her eyes, as though in prayer. She opened them again almost at once.

Machine-gun practice in the road.

'You!'

'You!'

The voice of her husband and Cathcart Sloley-Jones

blended in a crescendo of astonished cordiality from the front door.

'I've got Constance inside there,' she heard the former remark at the conclusion of these preliminaries. 'I've got!' Mrs Bone resented that way of making the announcement.

'What are you doing here? Come inside,' she commanded.

'Look 'ere. I can't stay messing around 'ere indefinitely any longer,' cried the voice of the Bristol hireling from the roadway.

'All right, all right. Just coming,' replied Mr Bone.

'That man has been engaged and must do what he is ordered,' said Mrs Bone sharply. 'Come in, Cathcart. Where have you come from?'

'Damned – going on – messing abart – damned – going back,' came in contemptuous snatches of protest from the road.

'How do you do, Constance? The last person I expected to see here, absolutely. Well, I'm jiggered. By Jove. Fancy this now. My hat!' said Sloley-Jones entering the parlour and greeting his cousin.

'S'sh. S'sh. All right. In one moment.' Mr Bone's voice could be overheard to promise in the hall.

'Why are you here, Cathcart?'

'As a matter of fact I ought to have been here long ago. I had some awfully hard luck with my bike. I've been suffering a lot of trouble of one sort or another lately. This time it was my sprockets, I think, chiefly. I think I got some oil on my magneto as well. You know if you get oil on your magneto, you're done. I cleaned my magneto of course; and then I found I was vibrating and popping.'

'Never mind about your bicycle. I wish to know what you are doing, coming to this inn?'

'Not ruddy well your property – engaged to drive – not to ruddy well pose—'

'All right. All right. Constance dear, when do you think?'

'Come inside this room and close the door. It is not very pleasant to have a husband who is afraid of a rude man.'

'But the man wants to know—'

'Come inside and shut the door,' said Mrs Bone.

'Just coming. Je-ust coming,' said Mr Bone to the roadway, as he unwillingly obeyed.

'I say, look here, don't let me keep you, you know – whatever happens,' said Sloley-Jones. 'I was really coming to this inn to – well, to see somebody else. Tremendous surprise to me this. Weird.'

'Whom were you coming to see?' asked Mrs Bone, leaning forward, dropping her voice and directing a very stealthy glance at her husband.

'Well, as a matter of absolute fact, I was following somebody. The whole business is rather strange. I happened to meet a man at Glastonbury, and to tell him about this inn and some people I knew who were stopping here last night; and he immediately leapt in a car and dashed off here. So I naturally followed. I mean to say. It struck me that perhaps I had told him too much. Shall I tell you all about the whole thing?'

'Yes,' said Mrs Bone with growing intensity. 'Ferdinand, do sit still. Why must you waggle your hands about?'

'The man's come round to the window,' said Mr Bone.

Mrs Bone rose snorting.

'Your whole life seems to be spent in fear and trembling of men,' she said.

She sailed from the room. Within two minutes she was back. The driver had returned, a mere crushed worm,to the seat of his car, where he remained formulating hopeless little designs for turning.

'Now,' said Mrs Bone.

In course of time the driver recovered. He stirred slowly in the seat. He was thawing into shame of his outraged importance. He had allowed his dignity to be openly disgraced. He had been ticked off by a ratty old woman. Again he scrambled from his seat, jerked his head in the manner which indicates decision in a gentleman of his nature, and again sought the parlour window.

Mrs Bone sat forward on the horse-hair sofa. Her eyes were staring wildly at the opposite wall, as though she saw a vision; but in the quick puckering of her lips there was an insinuation of relish. Her hat was awry. She was making little pinching movements of the thumb and first finger of either hand.

Seated at the little table where Peter and Margaret had partaken of dinner the night before, Mr Bone was, unmolested now, chewing the brim of his grey bowler with fervent relish. There was little change in his usual facial expression of obstinate stupidity.

Sloley-Jones stood at the fireplace. His great, dirty hands were outspread before him in gesticulation. His spectacles looked larger than usual. He was speaking impressively; arguing, it seemed. Whenever he ceased doing so his mouth remained open and he turned to Mrs Bone with a forlorn smile of protesting innocence.

Mrs Bone turned on him suddenly, delivering, to judge from her appearance, some devastating ultimatum. The parson wavered, nervously buttoning and unbuttoning the top button of his Norfolk jacket. Then, with a gesture of unwilling assent, he crossed the room and opening the door climbed rather laboriously up the staircase. Outside the door of the bedroom above the bar he halted and knocked timorously. As the response came from within he screwed his head round, rather in the manner of a blackbird investigating a doubtful worm. Then he entered the bedroom.

He had left the parlour door ajar. Greatly daring, the driver entered the hall and was about to renew his attentions to his clients when he overheard the altercation which was proceeding within and paused to listen.

'So now who's the fool?'

'I don't believe it even now. It's all rot. I'm going home.'

'Are you? I am going to Rushcombe Fitz-Chartres.'

'Nonsense, Constance. You can't do that.'

'I am going to.'

'Well, I'm not. The whole thing can be explained, I expect. We've made one hopeless hash and—'

'You are afraid of coming and saving Sophia from—'

'Yes, all right. I'm afraid. I bet you this fellow, Cathcart, is making some ridiculous mistake. I'm not going to burst into other people's houses and make a damned fool of myself for anybody.'

'Not for Sophia?'

'I tell you there's nothing to show that Soph—'

'Not for me?'

'No,' said Mr Bone courageously. 'I'm going back to Bristol in time to catch the 5.30.'

'You realise what this means? You are leaving me?'

'Oh, nonsense, Constance. I simply—'

'Very well. Go. Thank goodness I have got Cathcart to look after me.'

'All right. Only don't go and lug the poor devil into more trouble. You don't want to get our family a name for—'

'The next time anybody hears your family name,' said Mrs Bone leaning forward at her husband, 'will be in the divorce reports if I don't have my way and you have yours.'

'Oh, Lord,' moaned the wretched Mr Bone. 'What are you going to do now?'

'I am going to tell Sophia that her husband spent last night in the same bed as Mrs Hitchcock. I am going to see her husband and I am going to see Mr Hitchcock. If, as I suspect, that is not really Mrs Hitchcock in that room up there, I am also going to see Mrs Hitchcock. I am going to show all these people that, even if my daughter has married into a gang of vile and dissolute people, she is not going to be made a victim of their loathsome Society practices.'

'How are you going to get there?' asked Mr Bone, brightening suddenly.

'I shall take the car on to Rushcombe Fitz-Chartres immediately.'

'You won't,' said the driver dramatically in the doorway.

Mrs Bone drew herself up, quivering.

'Oh, so you are here, listening to our private conversation, are you?'

'I am that,' said the driver.

He turned to Mr Bone.

'Coming back to Bristol with me now?' he inquired. 'Say yes or for ever 'old your tongue.'

Mr Bone wilted.

'You know really, Constance,' he began, fingering the bag.

'Go then. Go,' cried his wife. 'Leave the bag and go.'

'No, but I don't want to go and—'

'You do. You have said so. Go and leave me.'

'Constance, I—'

'I'm just going to start the car up,' whispered the driver warningly.

'Oh, Lord. All right, I jolly well will go,' said Mr Bone.

He lingered in the doorway of the parlour. There was something pitiably appealing in the droop of his moustache.

'Good-bye,' he said softly.

'Good-bye,' said Mrs Bone frigidly.

In the hall Mr Bone collided with Sloley-Jones who had descended the stairs deep in thought. Mr Bone passed him without a word and crept wearily out into the car.

'It is as I feared,' was the parson's report. 'Rotten. I simply cannot for the life of me make out what can have been up. That's no more Mrs Hackett than you are – not so much. Well, perhaps just about as much, to be strictly accurate. There must be some extraordinary mistake somewhere – astounding!'

'Mistake? Poof!' said Mrs Bone.

'Hallo! Where's the car going? I say, it isn't pushing off, is it?' asked Sloley-Jones, striding to the window.

'Ferdinand is going back to London.'

'I say! But what are you going to do?'

'I am going to Rushcombe Fitz-Chartres. So are you.'

'Oh, but, Constance. I simply don't like to do that.'

'I,' said Mrs Bone, 'do not like to do it. It does not promise to be a very pleasant duty for either of us.'

'Oh, but, I say; do you mind if I don't come?'

'You must come,' said Mrs Bone in a monotone. 'You owe it to me and to Sophia. You are my informant. You must be there to witness my charges.'

'Oh, can't we write or something? You know—'

'Write! When the only question is how are we going to get there by the quickest means. Those two men have stood here and lied. I mean to get there while Sophia is still enduring the first shock of finding out that she has been tricked. Then will be the moment for your story.'

'Oh, how dreadful; how perfectly rotten! I protest, Constance. I cannot. This is too much.'

'Why on earth did you follow this man here if you didn't mean to interfere?'

'I didn't know who he was. I don't now. I cannot believe that Mrs Hackett – I think really the idea at the back of my mind was to protect Mrs Hackett.'

'Indeed? She seems to possess a great influence over young men. Well, here is your chance to protect her. You will be with me when I launch my accusation. You can protect her.'

Sloley-Jones groaned and stroked the Adam's apple of his long neck.

'All right,' he murmured at length.

'Now,' said Mrs Bone. 'How far is this town where you live?'

'Downblotton? About five miles.'

'You must take me there. When we get there we can hire a conveyance for the rest of the way.'

Sloley-Jones, who knew the shortcomings of Downblotton, nodded.

'But how are we going to get as far as that?' he asked. 'Can't walk you know. Frightfully tiring.'

'I would run,' said the determined mother, 'if it wasn't going to take too long. As it is—'

She cocked her head thoughtfully towards the road.

'Have you one of those little places behind?' she asked.

'I beg your pardon?'

'On your bicycle?'

'Oh, a carrier. Yes, of sorts. But, my dear Constance, that at any rate is absolutely out of the question. Quite – quite out.'

He surveyed his cousin's figure critically.

'In the first place my bicycle is only two and a half horse-power,' he remarked innocently.

'I will come behind you as far as Downblotton,' said Mrs Bone.

'But, my dear Constance—'

'We will leave my bag and umbrella. I will return here for the night. Come. There is no time to lose.'

'But look here. Honestly—'

'My mind is quite made up,' said Mrs Bone. 'Come out. Mount. Wait. Give me your coat to sit on.'

'There is a little seat there,' said Sloley-Jones nervously. 'But—'

'Mount,' said Mrs Bone.

CHAPTER XXIV

Precipitations of Moral Rectitude

England owes her status not to the characteristics of her sons, but to those of her daughters.

True, the sons have frequently been turned loose to perform most of the violent work. But they would never have been capable of performing it had they not been the sons of the daughters of England.

This, like most facts, is ungallant. England, as she is today, may well be regarded as the product of persons of the most disagreeable type.

Nor was Waterloo won on the playing fields of Eton. It was won at the childbed of a large number of big, haughty, rather contemptuous and absolutely indomitable women.

Had Mrs Bone possessed a son, he would have been a very different creature from his father. He would have been a vilely conceited, quite unconquerable young man with rows of war ribbons and no sense of humour.

Only a few women of each generation contribute to their country's weal. The brunettes of the green-room and the garage and the suburban tennis court are merely of recreative value. For creative value look to your big, stolid blonde. She remains laboriously in the background, as the strong, silent member of an acrobatic troupe receives, ignored by the audience, the skipping posturers on his shoulders. Yes, the history and the destiny of the country are centred in that speciality of ours, the big woman. And Mrs Bone had the hips of a stallion.

The motive which impelled Mrs Bone in reckless pursuit of Peter and his innocent dupe, her daughter, was not vindictive resentment of his lies and treachery. Her motive was rather a subtle satisfaction. From the first she had maintained – had sensed – that Sophia had been the victim of a wicked plot. The plotters should be hunted down, immediately, inexorably; should be shown, to their cost, the ability and the energy of that force which they had unwisely omitted from their calculations. The ponderous cheeks, bobbing and quivering with the vibrations of Sloley-Jones's motorcycle, were flushed with imperious excitement.

The discomforts, and indeed the danger, of her position as she clung, shaken like a cork on the ocean, to the parson on that precarious journey were nothing to Mrs Bone. Had she been swept to Rushcombe Fitz-Chartres on an aeroplane to be dropped at the Knoll by parachute, she would not have faltered. Her thoughts were elsewhere; triumphantly contemplating the discomforts, and indeed the danger, of the outrageous gang she was about to shatter.

That she had been momentarily outwitted at the inn was not unprofitable. Bump! For it incriminated the husband. The husband in fact was a party to this disgusting assignation. Bump, bump! How unthinkably vile! Hoot! One read of such things sometimes in the law reports – Bump! – in the awful sort of chaotic state in which the lower grades of Society found themselves – Ho-oo-oot! – following the war.

At this point Mrs Bone was carried suddenly in a ghastly vertical slither to the extreme side of the road, where, releasing Sloley-Jones, she was slung from the bicycle and alighted, in a sitting posture, on a low bush.

A market cart, which had swerved to the other side of the road in order to escape colliding with the cycle, halted a few yards further up the road. From inside it the heads of the driver, Mrs Spoker, Mrs Wigger, Gladys and the chemist's assistant from Downblotton were craned inquiringly back.

Sloley-Jones, who had retained his seat, relinquished it voluntarily and hastened to the bush.

'My hat! My goodness, Constance, I say I am most awfully sorry. That cart was to blame, you know. Entirely. By Jove, I am sorry. Are you hurt?'

'No,' said Mrs Bone.

'By Jove, I am sorry,' said Sloley-Jones. 'I couldn't absolutely do anything else. The cart—'

'Remove me,' said Mrs Bone.

'Anybody 'urt or hinjured?' asked the driver of the cart.

'Take my hand and give yourself a little sort of heave if you can,' said Sloley-Jones. 'I know it's rather difficult to sort of heave like that out of a bush. No grip, so to speak. I've tried it myself. Sure you're not hurt?'

'Not physically,' retaliated Mrs Bone, vainly heaving.

'I am so beastly sorry,' said Sloley-Jones. 'Now, again. Hup!'

'Any damage?' inquired the cart.

'Not physically, I believe,' called Sloley-Jones. 'Now. Hup! Hup!'

'How can I?' protested Mrs Bone. 'Stop doing that at once.'

'Oh, sorry,' said Sloley-Jones. 'I say, I am frightfully sorry. How awfully rotten for you! Do you think you could sort of worm up by yourself?'

'No,' said Mrs Bone.

'Well, what are we to do? Are you sure you're not hurt? Could you sort of use my shoulders as a lever and work yourself out.'

'No,' said Mrs Bone. 'Leave me alone.'

'I say. You are not too shaken to move, are you?'

'No. Fortunately I am not.'

'Well, I say, do see if you can't try and get out. You simply can't go on sitting in a bush. Do let me have one more try and see whether I can't hoik you out.'

'Wait,' said Mrs Bone. 'I think I am caught.'

'Oh, I see. Oh, well, half a tick. Don't let's tear your skirt. I wonder whether I could sort of oil round underneath you, so to speak, and disentan—'

'Stop!' cried Mrs Bone. 'Go away. I will do it myself. Go right away. Don't watch me.'

'Oh, all right,' said Sloley-Jones. 'By Jove, I am sorry about this. What sickening luck!'

He turned and faced the cart. The occupants had descended and were approaching.

'Hallo! It's Mrs Spoker. How queer. I say, Mrs Spoker, this won't do.'

'Tell those people to go away,' said the voice of Mrs Bone, laborious in gymnastics, from the bush.

'Mrs Wigger, too, as I live! Why, Mrs Wigger, what are you doing here?'

'Will you tell these men to go away?' came in strained accents from the bush.

'Be the lady demmidged?' asked the driver, who was an elderly man with baggy knees and no teeth.

'No, thanks,' replied Sloley-Jones. 'Not hurt. Just caught. She doesn't want—'

'Corrt?' exclaimed the driver advancing. 'Ay. Leave 'er to oi. Oi'll worry 'er free.'

'I don't really think she wants any help, thanks very much indeed all the same. She asked me not to help. I—'

'Go away from me,' cried Mrs Bone in the voice of one purple with effort.

The driver, a noted local Lothario, merely grinned and bared his wrists.

'Don't 'ee straggle now,' he exhorted. 'Oi'll settle 'un. Ye stand by, Robby, and leave 'er to oi. Oi'll worry 'er free.'

Robby, who was the chemist's assistant, stood by with interest. His feminine companions ranged themselves in the background; Mrs Spoker frowning upon the driver's chivalry, Mrs Wigger anxiously smoothing her bonnet strings.

'Cathcart! These men! Will you—? Don't touch me. How dare—'

Leaning forward the driver had seized Mrs Bone by the waist. Her struggles were sporadic but violent, like those of a hen frightened in a coop. Sloley-Jones hovered ambiguously at her side.

'Leave me go. Leave me go!' commanded Mrs Bone.

'I say, leave the lady go. I know it's kindly meant but she

doesn't want— There! By Jove, you nearly had her off. Once more!'

'Cathcart! Order him to stop. You encourage the man. I will not—'

'Oh, let him, Constance. Now, once again.'

'I am being assaulted and you stand by and—'

'No, no, really. It's for the best. You can't go on sitting in a bush. Now! Hup? No. Now again! Hoop!'

'Hup!' echoed Robby.

'Hup!' repeated the driver.

'Stop! Stop this instant! I am being—'

'Hup hup!' said Sloley-Jones encouragingly.

A final struggle. A long-drawn whistle of rent apparel. And Mrs Bone was free.

The driver deposited her on her feet in the road and wiped his brow.

'You great, clumsy rowdy!' cried Mrs Bone, her face disfigured with highly-coloured patches of heat and rage. 'You have torn my dress in halves.'

'Ah, oi 'ad to do that in order to worry 'ee free,' explained the driver.

'Go away, all of you,' repeated the poor lady, almost in tears. She turned rampant to Sloley-Jones. 'Idiot!' she added briefly.

'I say, I'm sorry, Constance, but—'

'Sorry you stood by and encouraged?'

'It was kindly meant you know. Frightfully. After all, you were absolutely hung up—'

'My skirt has been lacerated. Send those people about their business all of them.'

'I say, half a tick! Don't be ratty with these people. I know these people. They're awfully decent people. That one is Mrs Wigger, my landlady; and the other is Mrs Spoker, *your* landlady. I know these people.'

'What was that you said?' asked Mrs Spoker sharply.

'Oh, are you there, Mrs Spoker? Yes. This lady is coming back to put up at the *Stag and Hunt* tonight. She—'

'No,' said Mrs Spoker interrupting with decision. 'I am completely occupied.'

'Oh, but surely there is one room? Joking apart, I say.'

'I am not joking,' announced Mrs Spoker frowning heavily. 'I am completely occupied owing to Mrs Wigger, who is returning with me to 'elp nurse.'

'Oh,' said Sloley-Jones blankly. 'I say, Constance, this is rather a snag. Troublesome! I wonder what we'd better—'

Mrs Bone had retired several paces further down the road and was examining the damage to her skirt. The news that she would be unable to return to the *Stag* seemed, if anything, to soothe her slightly.

'You see, sir,' said Mrs Wigger, advancing a little and engaging the parson confidentially, 'Mrs Spoker, 'aving 'eard the old lady was said to be ill, asked me if I could possibly go and, perhaps, lend a 'and. So I 'ardly felt I could do other than do anything else but do so.'

'Yes, I see, Mrs Wigger. Rather. Of course. But how rotten—'

'Not,' interrupted the harsh voice of Mrs Spoker, 'that I am so sure that I should choose in any case to put up ladies who think fit to be seen in the public road riding bicycles bareback.'

Mrs Bone proceeded a few yards further down the road with the air of one avoiding an evil smell.

'Say good-bye to your friends and join me,' she said with great scorn to her cousin.

He returned to her side immediately, expostulating and apologising profusely. The cart party re-formed and continued their journey.

Mrs Bone snapped the chattering Sloley-Jones into silence.

'Now,' she said. 'Is your bicycle intact?'

'My bike? Yes, I saved it. Narrow squeak though. My brakes are rather dud and—'

'Then we will go on,' said Mrs Bone.

'Go on? But, Constance, are you fit?'

'Don't waste time. Remount.'

'Oh, but is this wise? Do you think we really—?'

'We will, at all events, go to the place where you are staying, Oldblotto, or whatever it is called. Take me to your rooms.'

Sloley-Jones adjusted his glasses and inspected the bicycle, which reclined in the hedgerow, very dubiously.

'Honestly, Constance,' he said, 'don't you think it looks – don't you think it looks rather – rather as if we are not *meant* to go on, in a sort of way?'

Mrs Bone really flared up then. She waved demonstrative gloves at Sloley-Jones and his bicycle, and arraigned them in a voice which quivered with fury.

'So,' she cried, 'when you are fool enough to catapult me into a thicket, you have the presumption to explain that it was an act of Divine Intervention. How dare you, Cathcart? I am losing all patience with you. Mount!'

'Oh, I don't go so far as to say—'

'Mount!'

She was full of grit, this matron.

They arrived at Downblotton without further mishap. Their appearance in the town was greeted with spasmodic bursts of enthusiasm by citizens of the lower order. Mrs Bone kept a stiff lip.

In Downblotton town Sloley-Jones was commanded to make inquiries for a vehicle in which to complete the journey. The result confirmed his anticipations. No such vehicle was available. Old Stacey, they were informed, had a goat-carriage which he had obtained from a cousin away down at the sea-side, who had gone broke; but, now their informant came to think of it, there had been some rumour that the goat was dead. Mrs Bone arrived at her cousin's lodgings with temper and spirits sadly impaired.

Here was a letter addressed to Sloley-Jones by Mrs Wigger. It set forth, by a tortuous process of epistolary smoothing, the reason of her absence; during which her lodger's needs were to receive the attentions of Ruby Kettle, of next door.

Mrs Bone soon made herself at home. She routed out Ruby Kettle, whose first duty was, appropriately enough, to serve the wayfarers with tea. Meanwhile a careful examination was made of the damage sustained by the skirt.

This proved to be extensive. At the moment of the accident Mrs Bone's bearskin coat had flown open. In the subsequent worrying free the skirt had been torn to ribbons. The effects of all she had endured at Sloley-Jones's hands, and the contemplation of all that she might be destined yet to endure had already caused the brave woman for the first time to waver. The skirt decided her.

'I will stay here,' she said. 'I will write to Sophia. You will take the letter, and you will bring back Sophia with you, unless these people, the Bunkums, have the decency to provide her with a car. Give me ink and a pen.'

Sloley-Jones provided her with these articles without comment. He placed his spectacles upon his forehead and blew his nose, cogitating as he watched her write. If he raised any objection to going it was a thousand to one that Mrs Bone would devise some devastating alternative. Besides, he rather wanted to go on his own account. He was curious to learn the truth of Mrs Hackett's adventure. Of course he did not for one moment suspect that Mrs Bone's suspicions were justified. But something of a decidedly piquant nature must have occurred.

He was ruefully conscious of a sentiment that even if Mrs Hackett were proved to have behaved in the most naughty fashion, this fact would make her only rather more attractive than otherwise. The charity that thinketh no evil is often difficult to distinguish from the curiosity that thinketh very little good.

Having completed the letter, Mrs Bone arose and handed it to him with a ceremony and finality which he found rather disconcerting.

'You promise me upon your word of honour as a gentleman – in holy orders – that you will hand this letter to Sophia and will not return to me without an answer unless Sophia herself accompanies you?'

'Righto,' agreed Sloley-Jones glancing at the letter nervously.

'You may read it if you like. It is a plain statement of fact.'

Sloley-Jones read it. His face became graver and graver during the process. Mrs Bone was watching him eagerly.

'Take it or leave it,' she exclaimed, the moment he looked up from the page.

'Righto,' sighed Sloley-Jones, folding the letter and placing the envelope in the pocket of his Norfolk jacket. 'But why take all this trouble to destroy Sophia's happiness with her husband? I mean to say – even supposing this is true—'

'*Destroy* Sophia's happiness? I am r-rescuing her happiness. The only thing to keep that man straight is a lesson.'

Sloley-Jones turned unwillingly towards the door. He seemed to be about to continue the argument, but contented himself with a sigh.

'I ought to change my clothes before I go,' he said.

'Poof,' said Mrs Bone. 'You'd be just as dirty again by the time you got there.'

'Righto,' said Sloley-Jones. 'Mind you,' he added, turning in the doorway, 'I may not get there. I've had a great deal of trouble today already. I may get oiled up. I dare say you heard, when you were sitting behind me, how I was popping and the queer sort of twanging noise that was going on in my valves.'

Mrs Bone 'shoo'd' him out, as the housewife 'shoo's' an errant hen.

She proceeded upstairs to the private apartment of Mrs Wigger, where she removed her skirt and inaugurated an extensive raid for thread and needles.

She went below again and sat in Mrs Wigger's parlour in her petticoat, stitching.

For hours she seemed to sit and stitch, stitch at her torn skirt. Her elderly limbs were stiff and weary from the unusual experiences which that day had appointed them to suffer. Ruby Kettle came and went. The head drooped over the stitching but still the dogged hands worked on as though mechanically. The impulsive, mettlesome mind began to wander, to dream.

Dreamt, perhaps, of the long-passed, undisclosed days of her own youth and of the penurious content of an unambitious suburb, long before the first seductive visions of wealth and of that chimera, a place in Society. Whatever her dreams, they seemed to bring the unfamiliar and half-bitter comfort of human tenderness even to Mrs Bone; for the heavy eyelids, lowered in frowning determination over the stitching, were wet.

The long afternoon dragged into evening. The sun gleamed weakly through the windows of the little parlour and departed. Shadows fell. But Sloley-Jones returned not again.

CHAPTER XXV

Bad Manners and Evil Communications

Peter did not succeed in presenting his wife with a full and clear statement of the case during their journey in the car. The car had not been built for confidences. Nor did Sophia, who was in an exhilarated frame of mind, invite or encourage any further details of his recent experiences. Peter, after one or two false starts, decided to postpone revelations until after their arrival at the Knoll.

Lady Bunter, who was by this time prepared for almost any eventuality, sustained the appearance of the two simultaneous and apparently cordial husbands, to say nothing of the odd wife, with admirable presence of mind. Sir Stirling, taking his cue from the only reliable prompter, mumbled some rather baffled greetings and retired into the library to hold his head. Margaret was not in evidence, and her husband, who appeared to enjoy some sort of tacit understanding with his hostess in the matter, immediately disappeared without explanation, in search of her.

The homely charm of the dear old lady set Sophia's last fears at rest. The smart country house party faded into the prospect of a complacent holiday in the company of some of the least awe-inspiring people imaginable. True, Mrs. Hackett might prove to be a lady of the challenging type. Already Sophia found it impossible to picture her as anything else. But however smart Mrs Hackett might prove, Sophia felt little misgiving in a house where the hostess treated the announcement that two of her guests had arrived without any luggage as though it were an incident of the most satisfactory, if not usual, nature.

But an hour later found Sophia in her bedroom. She was sitting forward, supporting her face between her hands. She had removed her hat, and her black locks hung over her eyes in a manner which lent a savage comeliness to her appearance. Opposite her, supported by the edge of a dressing-table and in the direct line of fire from those half-hidden, reproachful, searching eyes, stood Peter.

'I want to know why,' Sophia was saying. Her voice was deep and earnest. 'You went out of your way to say that Mrs Hackett was still at the inn. She wasn't. She was here the whole time. What's the point? Why was it necessary for you to lie to me?'

'I didn't mean to lie to you,' said Peter.

'You didn't mean to lie, when you distinctly—?'

'Not to you. I meant to lie, but I didn't mean to lie to you. I only meant to lie to your mother.'

'I want to trust you and to love you,' said Sophia. 'I thought I could. How can I now? I know Mother was suspicious and rather hostile. I dare say you resented that. I did myself. But why lie to Mother even?'

'Oh, dash it all; I had to do that,' said Peter.

'But why? Why?'

'What?'

Sophia rose with an impetuous toss of the hair and a sound like an isolated sob. She walked across the room to the window. From the hall below them Francis' gong cheerfully invited them to drown their sorrows in tea.

Peter remained at the dressing-table, stroking his chin and watching his wife moodily. If she cut up like this over the first paltry item of his confession, how the dickens was he going to tell her all?

'Is that the woman?' asked Sophia suddenly in a hard tone, without turning her head from the window.

Peter crossed the room and joined her. Along the terrace below the window Mr and Mrs Hackett were strolling towards the house door. She was talking quickly and gesticulating lightly with her left hand. Her right lay on his coat-sleeve. Hackett's attitude was that of a doctor, listening with courteous reserve to the patient's statement of the case.

'Yes, that's Margaret – Margaret Hackett,' said Peter. 'You'll like her, you know,' he added sedulously.

'She's older than I imagined,' commented the woman.

'Oh, yes. You'll like her all right,' affirmed Peter.

'He lied too,' said Sophia sharply, frowning beneath her tresses. 'Why? He seemed so nice, I thought. I want to understand why you both lied about her.'

She faced Peter and shook back the hair from her eyes. She stretched a pleading hand out to him.

'I was happy again,' she cried. 'I want to go on being happy, Peter. Is there any other little thing you've been keeping back from me?'

Peter raised his eyebrows speculatively.

'In a way I suppose there is,' he confessed.

'Ah!'

She nodded gladly into his face. He took her hand in his but dropped his eyes.

'Tell me everything.'

'I should love to do that,' he said. 'In fact I've been waiting to. But it's nothing in the least – wrong, and it will take a long time to explain fully and you've got to do your hair and put your hat on again and tea's ready. What about taking a little walk after tea?'

Sophia turned towards the dressing-table.

'Is it anything you're ashamed of telling me?' she asked.

'No, my dear, no.'

'If it is, Peter, tell me. You must trust me.'

'It isn't,' he answered.

'I'm glad of that,' said Sophia, 'though I hope you would keep nothing back in any case. Just tell me the salient points while I do my hair.'

Her nimble fingers were already busy. Peter cleared his throat unnecessarily and glanced at the sharp features in the looking-glass. She was in a restless, changeable mood, he thought, a dangerous mood.

'It's rather difficult to pick out the exactly salient points,' he said. 'I missed the train and met Margaret – Margaret

Hackett, and took her in the car – in pursuit of you, of course. You know all that.'

'Yes, yes. And you took Mrs Hackett to the inn. And you all stayed there last night. That was true, I suppose? When did Mrs Hackett come on here? That's what I want to know.'

'Today.'

'How?'

'In the car. Our car. The car we started in.'

'Then the car did not really break down?'

'Oh, yes it did. It broke down but then it broke up again. I mean Dann fixed it up.'

'Dan? Is that Mr Hackett?'

'No. A driver chap.'

'Who came here with Mrs Hackett then? Why didn't you?'

'I did.'

Sophia turned her head. A band of raven hair fell over her cheek and she swept and held it aside as she looked at Peter.

'Lies again,' she said. 'Why did you both tell me these lies?'

'I told you there were more, and we didn't tell 'em to *you.* We told them to Mother.'

'But why tell them to Mother?'

'Because she came down simply boiling over with accusations.'

'Lying to her wouldn't make it seem any less likely,' said Sophia petulantly. 'I'm surprised at Mr Hackett. Why should *he* lie?'

'Oh, thanks,' said Peter. 'I'm quite as honest a man as Hackett. I expect as a rule he lies a great deal more freely than I do. He's an M.P. But, in this case, he lied because he didn't want anybody to suspect his wife's honour.'

'He seems very nervy about it,' said Sophia with sarcasm. 'Besides, there was surely nothing very outrageous in being stranded at an inn for the night. You couldn't help yourselves. Why should Mother have been suspicious?'

Peter rose excitedly and kicked at a footstool.

'She had made up her mind to be suspicious,' he answered. 'She came down today in malice aforethought, full out and breathing through her nose, to try and get me into trouble. If she hadn't been so fiercely punitive I wouldn't have lied.'

'If you'd been a little more harmonious with Mother since we married she would trust you more,' said Sophia, snatching angrily at a falling hairpin.

'I've never known such a woman,' was his reply. 'She's like nobody on earth; for sheer enmity she beats the band. The only people who can hold a candle to her are those Mexican bandits in films, who blow into a township and shoot up the minister just for the joy of making trouble. I'm innocent – incapable, I mean, of anything disgraceful. You believe that. Why can't she? I lied to her simply because I can't trust her to believe the truth. That's probably what makes liars of most – liars.'

'Don't speak like that of Mother,' said Sophia with a quivering lip. 'She did everything for her love of me.'

'I thought she did it for her hate of me,' said Peter.

Sophia rose briskly and snatched her hat from the bed.

'And that, I suppose, in a nutshell, is all?' she asked.

'That's all before tea,' said Peter firmly.

She burst into a passion.

She stamped her foot. She flung her hat away from her. It performed a graceful half-circuit of the room and fell at her feet. She threw herself forward on the bed, her face buried in her hands.

'Sophia! Look here, my dear girl, really—'

Peter's hand was on her shoulder. She shook it off.

'Go away,' she sobbed. 'Go down and have tea with Margaret.'

He hesitated. She raised her face for a moment. It had lost all its attraction and was merely forbidding. Peter made a little appealing movement of the hands, as though offering to raise her.

A minute later he found himself in the drawing-room,

avoiding Margaret's eye and murmuring vaguely at Lady Bunter.

'She's tired, poor dear. She ought to have had tea directly she arrived. How thoughtless and muddling of me.'

Thoroughly in her element, the good lady presently ascended the stairs. In her hand she bore a cup of tea, with slices of bread and butter in the saucer. Lady Bunter had anticipated some such crisis. The hand which bore the tea trembled with anxiety. Indeed, by the time she reached Sophia's room the bread and butter had become positively uneatable except in a humid condition resembling pudding.

Sophia accepted the tea gratefully but declined comfort. She wished to be left quite alone and not to see anybody. No, she didn't want Peter to come up again yet. She was all right, she thought, but had a splitting headache. Lady Bunter was very kind. She understood, didn't she? Sophia was very sorry to collapse like this, but she'd be better soon if she was left to herself.

Lady Bunter did not quite understand, but she said she did. She could only regard the frenzy of this dark, emotional girl with the imaginative pity of the seeing for the blind. She allowed herself to be awed into submission to the younger generation. She told Peter that his wife must be left alone to rest. Peter hung about on the staircase indecisively for ten minutes; then plunged away into the grounds with his hands in his pockets.

It would be hard to determine which of the young couple felt the more injured.

Lady Bunter still hovered on the landing. Margaret joined her at one point, penitent and sympathetic. Should she see the girl? Lady Bunter shook her head decisively. Solitary reflection was the best palliation, she said. 'Palliative, dear,' suggested Margaret. 'Never mind what I mean. Please help me by doing what I say,' replied Fanny.

So Sophia was left to brood alone in her temper and shame. Nobody suspected for a moment that the worst had yet to be told her.

Peter stormed about in woods, hacking at ferns; hacking mentally at the chains which bound Sophia to her dogmatic, proprietary mother. He would fight the old woman this time and for all. He would then take Sophia away – to the Continent or something – and would lull her into a permanent and confident devotion.

He stalked on. The leaves were already falling fast and lay in damp masses at his feet. He kicked them as he walked. At length upon a grassy plateau beneath an oak tree he sank exhausted in mind and body, and tried to regulate the disordered, injured medley of his thoughts.

Yes, Sophia would want some lulling, though. At one moment she had clasped him to her with soft endearments, at the next had flung him from her with weeping and gnashing of teeth. Still, with concentration and opportunity he thought he would be able to lull her all right.

He lay on his back and gazed at the blue sky above him. There was rhyme and reason after all in the old standard music-hall jokes about mothers-in-law. He had married beneath him, that was the trouble. Not that he wanted to go back on Sophia. But her mother might have been discovered in a seaside boarding establishment. All the more reason to stick up to the old devil.

Peter pulled his hat over his eyes.

What a day he had had. Waking in that room in the *Stag* with poor old Margaret in an awful state of panic. Then looking for her little worm of a dog. The car ride here and back again with wind up, only to break down on the road. Fairly running all the way into Downblotton. Oh, that postmaster and his infernal telephone!

Fancy, now the life of that postmaster. Extraordinary how some people were content to go through this world in a groove, seeing nothing of life.

Good Lord, he had left that bicycle at the *Stag*. Couldn't be helped. He'd see about it some time – some time.

How funny Sophia was. There were two of her. He was like that picture of Garrick between the Muses. Only Sophia was both Muses at once, smiling comedy and rabid disfigured tragedy. Were they Muses? Whatever they were anyhow. Garrick it was, wasn't it?

He liked the comedy Muse – woman, whatever-you-call-her best. She had funny people round her. Old Bone and Alfred and a tall, grave man – yes, Hackett, all dressed up in the costumes of cross-talk comedians and exchanging side-splitting banter about kippers. Hackett didn't seem to see anything funny in it. Old Bone had on striped pyjama bags. He did look an ass, but he seemed to be pleased.

There was only one Muse creature now. There had only been one all the time really. Oh, they had left all the other people now and were – where was this? Why, it must be above the bar. Oh, dash it, he couldn't sleep on the floor again. It was so wet. It was wringing wet. She needn't be afraid. He wasn't that sort of person. He only wanted to lull her. Lull her. Lull. Lull.

Lady Bunter met Peter in the hall when he returned. His clothes were untidy, his eyes vacant. Lady Bunter immediately thought that he had been attempting suicide and her hand went to her heart. Fond of trouble as she was, she had had enough for one day.

'Sorry, Lady Bunter,' he said. 'I went out for a walk and sat down under a tree and went to sleep.'

'To sleep? What a one you are for sleeping. You always seem to have been doing something connected with sleeping every time I hear of you.'

'I've had rather a tiring day,' said Peter.

'Yes,' said Lady Bunter. 'So have I.'

'Is Sophie still upstairs? I think I will go to her now.'

'She's gone.'

'Gone?'

'Yes, she – she went.'

'Went? My dear Lady Bunter, where?'

'A parson came. I think he had been here before today. He–'

'That man again?' cried Peter. 'Is he a familiar, or something?'

'Yes, he was rather,' said Lady Bunter. 'But I think he meant to be nice. He is a cousin of yours, you know; by marriage.'

'But what had he got to do with it? Did he abduct Sophia?'

'My dear boy, be careful what you are saying.'

'There's nothing wrong in "abduct",' said Peter.

'Oh, then I'm muddling it with something rather dreadful. But what occurred was this. He brought her a note from her mother. When he saw me, when he first arrived, he asked me to take it to her as he said he had promised her mother that he would give her the note, though he said he thought the mother was wrong in her supposals – things – wrong end of the stick, you know.'

'Yes,' said Peter. 'But *he* needn't talk. Well?'

'I took the note up to her room. When she read it she got much calmer, I thought. But she said it confirmed her worst – things. Of course I told her–'

Lady Bunter gave a little helpless heave of the shoulders.

'I tried to tell her that you had really done nothing actually bad, and that Margaret Hackett was an old friend of mine and quite incapable of it. But it was no good. She said she wanted to go back to her mother. So I tried to find you of course. Fancy going to sleep out there on the grass. I expect you've caught your death of cold; the grass was dreadfully wet. I will get my husband to lend you some underclothes. You really ought to have a bath, if you can with all this on your mind.'

'When did she go?'

'Oh, a long time ago. She went in our car. I had to lend it to her. She asked for it.'

Peter jerked his head towards the drive.

'And the – parson fellow? Did he go with her in the car?'

'Oh, no. He went back on his motor-bicycle thing. I know because I heard him exploding as he went. By the way, he implored me to tell him all I knew about last night.'

'And you did?'

'Yes, you see, I thought if he knew that it was all perfectly innocent, he might be able to persuade your wife and her mother so. But I'm afraid he was rather shocked.'

'Not the last shock he'll get,' commented Peter.

'He said he hoped he wouldn't be lugged into it,' said Lady Bunter pleadingly.

'I like that. He's been lugging, himself, all day. But where did Sophia go to, Lady Bunter?'

'I don't know. The car ought to be back by now, so you can ask the chauffeur. Also, I noticed after she had gone, that she had left her mother's letter lying on the floor of her room. I didn't read it of course, but I picked it up. I don't know whether you ought to read it either, but, if you want to go after her and try and make it up, the letter may tell you where she is.'

'Please let me see it,' said Peter.

Lady Bunter fumbled at the pocket of her tweed skirt.

'And where were Mr and Mrs Hackett all this time?' asked Peter.

'They went out again. A friend of ours who is staying here came in from buying some whisky for my husband. He's rather a weak man – well, he's been living in the East, poor man, and of course that makes a lot of difference. But he started to ask Mr Hackett, and Mrs Hackett too, some rather awkward and offensive questions about their movements, so they went out. I only hope *they* haven't gone to sleep on the grass. Still, Mr Hackett has his own underclothes and things here. Here is the letter.'

'Thanks,' said Peter.

He glanced quickly over the closely written page.

'Look here, I'll read it to you,' he said. 'Then you'll be able to form some sort of idea of what I am up against.'

'Only if you think I ought to hear it. And don't forget that you acted in a rather provoc – what's that word? – way with poor Margaret.'

'To the pure all things are pure,' said Peter. 'You are pure. So is Sir Stirling. Absolutely pure, therefore best. So is Hackett. Why can't these people be pure?'

'I think I ought to be able to say something rather clever about you and Margaret to that,' remarked Lady Bunter. 'But I can't, so don't let's waste time. Read me the letter.'

'This is what Mother says,' observed Peter:

'MY DEAREST CHILD,

'You will have discovered by the time you get this that all your husband and the other man told us at the inn was a tissue of Lies.

'I am writing from your cousin, Cathcart Sloley-Jones's lodgings at Oldblotto. He brought me here on his motor-cycle throwing me on the way and tearing my skirt and shaking me or I would have come the whole way to fetch you.

'He happened to be at the inn last night and your husband was there with the woman alone. She introduced him to him as hers. Later your husband and the woman SLEPT in the SAME BED. He happens to know this.

'I am sorry to have to tell you this like this but it is no use blinking it.

'I got Cathcart to tell me much against his will what I suspected from the very first. This woman, Mrs Hackett, is NOTORIOUS. I seem to have heard something about her before now, he tells me.

'Come back to me at once. Ask Lady Bunthorne to lend you a car. She cannot refuse. If she does, get up behind Cathcart but make him ride very slowly and not SWERVE.

'We will consult quietly as to the best course. But what I say before I repeat. He must not be allowed to think he can treat you as a mere chattel of his among his other pleasures. When he has learnt that I shall be content to bide by your decision.

'My poor child. But I knew it from the first and we must strike while the iron is HOT.

'YOUR LOVING MOTHER.

'P.S. Your father, thank goodness, has gone back to town.'

'Now how am I going to get there?' asked Peter.

'My dear boy,' said Lady Bunter. 'Stay here quietly and have some dinner and change your underclothes and go off there afterwards, when everybody is less excited and muddled.'

'No. I must go now. I – I want her, you see.'

'You dear boy,' said the old lady affectionately. 'You are like your father. But I can't let you have the car yet, can I?'

'I'll walk and meet it,' said Peter. 'Good-bye.'

CHAPTER XXVI

His Own Nest

'Where is Sophia?' asked Mrs Bone. 'Why are you so late? You have kept me waiting in suspense all this time. I have had some food and sent the girl, Kettle, away. Why have you been such hours? And where is Sophia?'

'Isn't she here?' replied Sloley-Jones, wiping the dust from his glasses wearily.

Mrs Bone restrained herself as best she could.

'Oh, don't ask me where she is, you – She is not here.'

'Well, she ought to be. Very funny. She started for here ahead of me in a car. Altogether rather rum, this.'

'Ah, she *did* start to come here?'

'Ra – *ther.* In a car.'

'When she had read my letter?'

'Yes.'

'Did she look very upset?'

'I didn't see her. I understand she was resigned. By Jove, it *is* awful. Can't something—'

'You did not see her?'

'No, she was in her room. Lady Bunter negotiated.'

'Where was the husband?'

'Which husband?'

'Her husband of course. Are you trying to be stupid on purpose?'

'Whose husband, Lady Bunter's?'

'No, you fool. I beg your pardon, but it is your own fault. Sophia's husband.'

'Oh, Peter?'

'Sophia's husband.'

'I don't know.'

'He was not with her?'

'With whom?'

'Oh! With Sophia, of course. Did you think I meant with Lady Bunter?'

'Yes.'

'He was?'

'No, I say I thought you meant with Lady Bunter.'

'Arrch! Did you see the man?'

'What man?'

'Arrch! Sophia's husband.'

'No. I told you so.'

'You didn't. So Sophia read my letter and asked for a car and came away?'

'Yes. I told you that anyhow. I say, do let me get some grub, will you? I'm awfully done.'

'And her husband didn't get wind?'

'Wind?'

'Yes. Did not discover that she was leaving?'

'No. I say, I'll tell you everything in a mo. Do give me a chance to get a wash and find some prog.'

'I want to know first why Sophia isn't here.'

'She'll be here in a minute. Driver's lost his way perhaps. Does not know the way perhaps. Doesn't know exactly where this house is very likely. She'll be here in a minute.'

'Go out in the road and toot your bicycle as a signal,' said Mrs Bone.

'Oh, Constance, I can't. I'm awfully spent and frightfully upset over all this. That Mrs Hackett. I'd have staked my life on her honour. A welfare worker.'

'You would have lost your life then,' retorted Mrs Bone. 'I'm afraid you must be a very susceptible man, Cathcart. Anyhow I cannot sit here in this suspense. Go and toot.'

Sloley-Jones did as he was bidden with no very good grace. His signal was unanswered. He returned and commenced his meal. Three times during the course of it he was driven into the street to toot. Finally he was stopped and severely cautioned by the Downblotton policeman.

It was Mrs Spoker's hour for her last look round. She took it hastily and returned to the inn, closing the door. She glared suspiciously at a push bicycle which remained leaning against the outer window ledge of the bar. In the hall lay a Gladstone bag and a lady's umbrella. Mrs Spoker sniffed at them, as she had sniffed at them when she had first seen them lying in the parlour, and as she had sniffed at Alfred when he had been unable to throw any light upon them.

Presently Mrs Spoker, descending the stairs from one of her frequent visits of inquiry to Mrs Wigger concerning the life or death of the old lady above the bar, heard the sound of a car drawing up outside the inn. She stood before the door pluming herself. The door was opened by a chauffeur. Mrs Spoker backed a pace. It was not often the visitors to the *Stag and Hunt* had the door held open for them by a chauffeur.

'Are you the landlady?' asked Sophia.

'I am. But I am completely occupied,' said Mrs Spoker.

'I have been here before today. You were out then.'

'Oh,' said Mrs Spoker. 'Then are them things your things?'

Sophia glanced at the bag and umbrella indicated by the bony finger.

'Yes,' she said, after a moment's hesitation.

'Then I must ask you to take them elsewhere because I am completely occupied tonight. There was another lady said she was coming here, who I saw riding on the bicycle of a clergyman who has been a great deal about here these last two days, and I thought they was hers. Are they yours?'

'Hers and mine,' said Sophia. 'I am her daughter.'

'And at *her* age to go bareback,' commented Mrs Spoker. 'So you have called for them have you, Miss?'

'Yes and for something else,' said Sophia authoritatively.

'What else?'

'Information,' said Sophia.

Mrs Spoker's brow darkened.

'As to what?' she asked.

Of her own accord Sophia led the way into the parlour. Mrs Spoker, too startled by such an unusual display of independence in her *Stag* to protest, followed; and Sophia closed the door behind them.

'Very queer stories are being circulated about this inn,' said Sophia, drawing herself up and facing the landlady with a command which was the legacy of her mother. 'I am concerned in them. You must tell me what I wish to know.'

'Queer stories about my inn?' repeated Mrs Spoker, her high shoulders rising like a cat's in ominous hostility. 'What are they and who dares to tell 'em?'

'A gentleman who was here last night – a clergyman, a Mr Sloley-Jones, is my informant. He says—'

'Him!' cried Mrs Spoker with a snort of contempt. 'He'd say anything, the sawney.'

'He met a lady and gentleman here. They were staying here. Did they stay here alone?'

'Do you refer to Mr and Mrs 'Ackett, M.P.?' replied the landlady with hauteur.

'Yes. At least – Did they stay here alone?'

'Why should I answer such a question?' said Mrs Spoker. 'They *did* stay 'ere alone, if you must know; all but a dog, drat it, which was with them.'

'You must answer my questions,' said Sophia, 'or I shall be obliged to send lawyers to you.'

'Lawyers!' cried Mrs Spoker. 'What are you wishing to imply about the manner in which I conduct my inn. Lawyers! We are very strict here, allow me to tell you, young lady. Anythink that is not strictly above suspicion never sees the light o' day inside o' here.'

'Perhaps you have been imposed upon,' said Sophia.

'I – imposed on? Indeed? I should very much like to 'ear in what respect,' replied Mrs Spoker with set teeth.

'You are sure that the gentleman who was here with Mrs Hackett last night was really Mr Hackett?'

'Is that what that clergyman 'as bin sayin'?' snapped Mrs Spoker. 'And me takin' as usual all proper precautions in the matter. Is it likely that a M.P. would 'ave such audacity and wickedness?'

'The point is that it may have been some one masquerading as the M.P.,' explained Sophia.

'Masqueradin'! Nothin' of the sort. If you send your lawyers 'ere they'll get a job o' slander against your clergyman friend if 'e don't mend 'is ways.'

'But how can you prove that the gentleman here last night was really Mr Hackett?'

'How can I prove it? Didn't 'e sleep with Mrs 'Ackett, and me as it 'appened by chance, see them at it?'

'Does that prove it?' queried Sophia with a slight quiver of the lip.

'H'm. This is nice from a young lady, I must say.'

Mrs Spoker thrust her chin into the air and turned, scowling, towards the door. Then a thought struck her and she faced round.

'Prove it? You follow me, if you please. You will see whether this will prove it.'

Sophia's eyes brightened. Hope and fear fought within her as she followed Mrs Spoker down the narrow hall into the office.

Mrs Spoker laid her hand upon the large closed register of her guests.

'The names,' she announced, in the manner of a conjuror in his introductory stages, 'is entered in this book accordin' to the law. I saw Mr 'Ackett, M.P., enterin' the names with 'is own 'and with my own eyes. Would an M.P. forge? Per'aps you can recognise 'is writin'.'

'Let me see,' said Sophia quickly.

Mrs Spoker relinquished the ledger with a superior sniff. Sophia opened it and turned anxiously to the latest entries.

'You say you saw – Mr Hackett – write this?'

'He was completin' it just as I come in from shuttin' away the dog,' said Mrs Spoker.

Sophia looked up from the page at the little window pane before her as though she could perceive the figure of Peter, maligned and innocent, awaiting her beyond it. The bold handwriting in the album was certainly not disguised; nor, in any case, could Peter have been capable of so complete and subtle an improvement upon his customary scribble. Sophia closed the book with a jubilant snap.

'Thank God,' she said.

'Whatever you may 'ave discovered, there can be no excuse to be blarspemous,' said Mrs Spoker severely.

Sophia made no reply. She was already in the hall, stooping to take up the bag and umbrella. Mrs Spoker followed her, arms akimbo, working her moustache to and fro querulously.

'And *now*, 'ave you any complaint to make about the manner in which my 'otel is conducted?' she challenged.

'No,' said Sophia. 'No. It must all have been a mistake. Thank you. Good night.'

Her mind was still perplexed with little doubting questions which had still to be explained. 'Where did Peter sleep last night then?' whispered one. 'Why should he say he slept here?' asked another. 'Perhaps there was somebody else and the Hacketts are keeping it dark for him,' suggested a third. Sophia shook them from her head. The one, cardinal fact was proved. Peter had been falsely accused. He had tried, in his poor old blundering way, to tell her all, and she had lost her temper and driven him away unheard.

'Where now, 'm?' asked Wemblow, the chauffeur, with patient anxiety.

'Back, please.'

'Back to the 'ouse, 'm?'

'Yes.'

'Hi! Stop!' shouted Peter. 'Is that Lady Bunter's car?'

Wemblow's sigh was drowned in the deeper sigh of his studded tyres.

'Yessir,' he called back.

'Well look here. Lady Bunter said I might take the car back to Downblotton. I want you to take me to wherever you've just taken Mrs Wykeham. I'm sorry but it's awfully important.'

The door of the car was thrown open.

'Peter!'

'Sophie!'

'Oh, Peter.'

Peter sprang inside. The door closed again. Wemblow cocked his head up philosophically and awaited further orders.

'Sophie, my darling, I want to explain; I want to tell you everything.'

'Don't,' she answered. 'Don't tell me anything now. You can tell me everything some other time perhaps. I only want you again. Oh, Peter, what have I done? Forgive me.'

'Never mind, my dear one,' he said. 'That's all over now, isn't it?'

'Yes, yes. Go on kissing me.'

'Right. But you do really mean it to be quite all over now, don't you?'

'Oh, I promise. Let's forget it.'

'Yes, let's,' said Peter. 'Let's go right away from here by ourselves and forget there was ever anything the matter.'

'You darling! Can we do that?'

'We jolly well will,' said Peter. 'We'll go straight away into Downblotton. There's sure to be a night train. We can write to Lady Bunter and go and see her another time together.'

'Oh, yes,' whispered Sophia. 'Yes, I want to go right away with you alone now.'

'We'll do it,' said Peter. 'What's to stop us? But why were you coming back? Had you thought better of it, Sophie?'

The head against his cheek nodded gently.

Peter kissed her forehead. Then he raised his head and called through the window of the car.

'Can you drop us at Downblotton?' he said.

Wemblow was understood to assent.

'And I am not to tell you all I have to tell you now, am I?' said Peter with a shade of anxiety as they went their way.

'No, no,' said Sophia. 'Some other time. And only then if you want to.'

'Of course I want to.'

'It wasn't anything disgraceful, was it, Peter?'

'No my darling, I promise you that.'

'I almost wish it had been,' she confessed softly. 'Then I could have shown you how I forgive.'

Now there is in Downblotton a Cinema. As the car drew up doubtfully in the market square and Peter descended to make a few necessary inquiries before risking its departure, the first of the two evening performances at this Cinema had just concluded. The natives were wearily trooping from the doors, their minds restored to the sobering spectacle of the familiar streets, after dwelling for two blissful hours in the Nirvana of an American palace, kidnapping heiresses and devouring sandwiches served on wheels. Peter crossed the road and questioned one of the more elderly devotees of Norma Talmadge.

'Dann!' he cried.

' 'Ullo, sir?'

'What are you doing, Dann?'

'Spent all day what with blacksmiths and whatnot on that darned radiator,' replied Dann. 'This *is* a lamentable and one-'orse town, believe *me*.'

'Have you got her patched?'

'Yes,' said Dann. 'I settled 'er this time, sir; but too late to make a start 'ome tonight.'

'Where's the car?'

'In the blacksmith's yard. There ain't even a garridge at this so-called town.'

'Dann. I've got to get back to town straight away. You must take me. I'll make it worth your while.'

'Well, you was very considerate to me when we parted this morning,' reflected Dann. 'So, if you wants me and will continue considerate, I'll do what yer damn well please, sir.'

'This is better,' said Peter, returning to the side of his wife. 'Three quarters of an hour ago I was hoofing along the road and feeling very depressed about it. I have now two powerful cars at my disposal. We will make London tonight, Sophie. The Bunters' car can report our movements to the Knoll. First of all we will eat. We will go in the Bunters' car to a public house and eat and write, and then we will go in Dann's car home. I never hoped to do the thing in such style.'

Fifteen minutes later they sat at meat in the *George and Dragon* Hotel at Downblotton, having returned the conciliated Wemblow to Lady Bunter with a slightly involved covering letter.

'I think,' said Sophia, 'that before I go back with you, I ought just to let Mother know that she needn't worry over us any more.'

'Yes,' said Peter. 'We might let Jones know at the same time.'

'It might save a certain amount of trouble all round. Shall I call at his lodgings and see them?' suggested Sophia.

Peter hesitated.

'You know, I don't think you'd better go,' he ventured. 'If Mother saw you she would probably become very talkative again. If she only saw me it would probably have the very opposite effect. We want to make London by the morning. Shall I go alone and just put things right with them?'

Sophia watched his face with a loving but still somewhat puzzled gaze.

'Well, suppose I write a letter to Mother, saying that we have made it up?'

'Yes,' agreed Peter. 'And that there wasn't really anything to make up.'

'There wasn't, was there, Peter?' asked Sophia keenly.

'Of course not, my darling—'

'Still, there is one thing I do rather want to get at. Mr Hackett was at the *Stag* all the time with Mrs Hackett. I've found out that for myself,' said Sophia with rather pert satisfaction. 'But where really *were* you? Were you there too?'

'I thought we had decided not to have all this now,' remarked Peter softly.

'I just want to know that.'

'Well, I was there most of the time,' said Peter quickly. 'But you see there wasn't another room so I – I had to sleep where I could. I spent part of the night on the floor of one of the rooms, and part in the stables and part in the garden and – one place and another.'

'Oh, but how miserable!'

'Yes it was. I got awfully wet too.'

'Oh, but Peter! How dangerous!'

'Yes it was rather dangerous.'

'But even now I fail to see exactly why you and Mr Hackett shouldn't have told the whole truth about it before.'

'Before, dear?'

'Yes. All those – all that exaggeration about Mrs Hackett being still at the *Stag*, when she wasn't.'

Peter placed his hand gently on hers with a knowing smile.

'I thought I knew the quickest way of getting you to come with me, Sophie.'

'But why shouldn't we have stayed at the *Stag*?'

'Do you wish we had?'

'Not now,' said Sophia.

'Well, there you are, dearie, you've got what you want. I thought I was doing the best thing. Look here, sit down and write your mother a cheery little line and I will find out where Jones lives and will leave it complete with bag and umbrella.'

'This is very awkward,' said Sloley-Jones.

'Awkward!' said Mrs Bone. 'Is that all it is to you, with my child somewhere on the high road, lost in a car?'

'Well, I really don't think it would be any use my going and looking again. I've done it six times. She's sure to be all right in the Bunters' car. No, when I said awkward I meant about us.'

'Us?'

'Yes. If no one else comes we shall be – h'm – yes. I – Constance, do you think it is – what shall I say – all *right*?'

'What are you talking about?'

'I mean – we shall be alone in the house. Rather – I mean – I suppose it is all *right*, isn't it? I mean – ought we to be alone?'

Mrs Bone rose very stiffly and slowly.

'What are you suggesting?' she demanded.

'You can sleep in Mrs Wigger's bed of course—'

'I shall not sleep. I am too anxious. I shall rest upon the bed you speak of. What bed do I understand you to suggest that I shall r-rest upon?'

'Oh, Mrs Wigger's every time. Ra-ther. But, my dear Conny—'

'Conny?'

'Constance, then, if you're so particular—'

'I am very particular,' said Mrs Bone decidedly.

'What I mean is, do you think it is possible for you to stay here tonight without being just a tiny bit injudicious?'

'What is all this?' demanded Mrs Bone. 'Pull yourself together, Cathcart. I scarcely like to think what you are driving at.'

'Don't take offence. I should love you to stay with me, but it just occurred to me that if we were to be alone together here for a night something might come of it; and then I should feel so awfully uncomfortable about it. You too. Probably more uncomfortable than I should.'

'You are mad,' said Mrs Bone heatedly.

'Not a bit. I am only asking your opinion. You know much

better than I do what is considered improper. If we are left alone together here tonight, do you think we shall be proper? I don't.'

'Cathcart! You are not attempting to make suggestions to me?'

'Yes, I'm afraid I am. I did intend to hint—'

'What, what? What, pray, did you intend to hint to me?'

'That people might say just the same things about us as you – as they have been saying about your son-in-law.'

'How dare you draw such a comparison? How dare you suggest that anyone should whisper such scandal about me?'

'You know what people are,' said Sloley-Jones, wiping his nose humbly. 'You know how stories get about.'

'Poof!' said Mrs Bone.

'Just as you like, Conny – Constance. I only hope it will be all right for you in Mrs Wigger's room. You can sleep in my room if you like. I don't mind a bit. I'll sleep in yours – hers.'

'I have seen the room,' said Mrs Bone. 'It will do, under the circumstances.'

'Which room?'

'Your landlady's of course.'

'Oh, right. But – er – what will you wear? I suppose you'll want something to put on – I mean – you know, nightgown.'

'Your landlady has a spare nightgown, I take it?'

'Oh, you take it? Right. Yes, I suppose she has. I don't remember having – yes. No. Righto.'

'I will look and make quite sure that I have all I want,' said Mrs Bone. 'There will still be time to send the girl, Kettle, to borrow anything I require.'

'Oh, right you are,' said Sloley-Jones, accompanying her rather nervously as she again ascended the narrow staircase of the cottage.

Mrs Wigger's room was of modest dimensions and was but sparsely furnished. It scarcely seemed to hold out the promise of being able to satisfy the requirements of so large a lady as Mrs Bone. Sloley-Jones stood and massaged his chin disconsolately as he watched his guest operating chests of drawers and holding an inspection of Mrs Wigger's night-wear, of which the rare specimens were of a red and somewhat raw flannel.

'I say, would you like to borrow a pair of my pyjamas?' said Sloley-Jones.

'No,' said Mrs Bone.

'Because I thought – we wouldn't send out if we could help it. We don't really want to draw attention to our – to the fact that we are spending the night here alone—'

'Stop that!' cried Mrs Bone. 'I am sick of such rubbish. I shall have to send out to try and borrow some linen. Not that I shall sleep. Why can't you have the spirit to go and find Sophia for me instead of following me about the house, murmuring the most loathsome insinuations. Open the door.'

'I say, I'm sorry—'

'Will you open the door. I wish to go downstairs.'

'Certainly. I only – Hallo!'

The rebuked parson had turned to the door which he had allowed to swing to behind him when he had followed Mrs Bone so attentively into the bedroom. He grasped the handle and pushed. Then, with eyes wide and still magnified in width by his glasses, he turned ominously to his guest.

'The door has been locked,' he cried.

Mrs Bone, who seemed not altogether unprepared for some such occurrence, advanced upon him in the most peremptory manner.

'Open that door at once, and kindly desist from trying to be humorous at a time which is most inappropriate,' she commanded.

'Honestly, Const—'

'Open the door!'

'But I can't. It's been locked from outside. The key's outside. Somebody must have come upstairs quietly while we were talking in here and locked it.'

'Stuff and nonsense!' said Mrs Bone. 'Give the door a shake. Locked it! Who can have locked it? And why? It is jammed. Shake!'

The parson shook. He turned again with a piteous little smile of innocent endeavour, and shook his head. Beads of perspiration appeared upon his brow and trickled slowly down on to his spectacles.

'It's locked – some – joke or something. I – wonder—'

'Shake again,' said Mrs Bone. 'Shake. Have you no strength in your arms? Let me come.'

'Do, do. See if you can do it. I bet you don't do it, but come and can if you do. Do if you can. There you are. Isn't it absurd? I wonder who on earth can have—'

Mrs Bone, spent with a brief but violent wrestle with the door, wheeled upon him, quivering with wrath.

'You arranged this,' she cried.

'I – I swear. Conny, you mustn't say such things. I—'

'Who locked that door?'

'How can I tell? Somebody must have sneaked in from the road and done it for a joke. Most reprehensible. I can't think—'

'We must get out at once.'

'Well, I don't see how we're going to.'

'We must. You do not suggest that we are to be imprisoned here all night, or until Sophia comes?'

'No, I – I – I don't suggest it. That is, I don't desire it. Not the smallest bit. But I don't see how we're going to get out.'

'Make noises,' said Mrs Bone. 'Arouse the neighbours. Make noises.'

'No, no, I say, don't. I shall be made a laughing-stock. So will you. Worse. Gossip. You know what people are. Oh, what miserable luck! Don't let's lose our heads and do anything we might be sorry for.'

Mrs Bone retired to the bed and flounced upon it, shaking in every limb with fatigue and rage. Sloley-Jones, removing and wiping his spectacles, regarded her feebly.

'Well,' she cried at length. 'Do you intend to stay all night in this room with me?'

'Oh, don't,' he replied faintly.

'Unless you exert yourself at once I shall shriek for the neighbours.'

'Oh, I say, don't do that. They'd – they might think I was – taking ad – doing something – One half tick. I'll try and bust the door open, but it will probably make an awful row and attract attention.'

He turned unwillingly again to the door, hesitated, and again faced Mrs Bone, wetting his lips deliberately.

'I – I suppose it *is* the only thing to do? I mean, I suppose we couldn't possibly – No. Oh, dear! Yes.'

He took a very short run and jolted the door half-heartedly with his left shoulder. Beyond the slight noise of the concussion the attack was altogether without result.

'Push, push! Harder!' commanded Mrs Bone.

'Oof! Bah! Oof!' cried Sloley-Jones, trying again.

'Harder, harder!' exhorted Mrs Bone.

'Oof! Kahr! Erph! Oof! I say, don't make too much noise, Constance. We don't want people to hear, do we? I mean, you know what people are. Ooof! It's no good.'

CHAPTER XXVII

Other Birds' Nests

When Peter, having found the cottage of Mrs Wigger open to any member of the public who cared to investigate it, had strolled noiselessly into the front parlour, he had been surprised. The room was unoccupied, but there were signs that Sloley-Jones had been there. The parson's evening meal had evidently been consumed there not long before. A portion of it remained on the floor, another portion on the sideboard.

Peter placed the bag and umbrella on the floor of the parlour. He fingered the note which Sophia had written to her mother and cast his eye over the little room. Finally he placed the note in a prominent position on the centre table. As he did so he raised his head quickly.

Next moment he was ascending the stairs with much care. He tiptoed his way stealthily forward until he stood without the closed door of Mrs Wigger's bedroom. A smile flickered over his face as he bent forward to catch the fragmentary conversation which proceeded from within.

Peter straightened himself for a moment. He glanced downwards as though in response to a sudden intuition. Yes, the key happened to be on the outer side of its lock. His hand stole downwards. The temptation was almost irresistible.

A temptation which would be almost irresistible to another youth was altogether too much for Peter Wykeham.

He was quickly back in the parlour. The remnants of the fire, which Ruby Kettle had been commanded to kindle against the chill of evening, still smouldered. Peter stirred it into a little blaze and refreshed it with the note which Sophia had written to her mother.

Then he left the cottage and returned briskly to the *George and Dragon* inn.

'You haven't been long,' said Sophia gladly.

'No, I cut it short. Now, is Dann ready?'

'Yes, waiting. It will be lovely driving back to London with you, Peter. By the way, did you see Mother?'

'Oh, by the way, no, I didn't,' said Peter. 'She'd gone to her room. But I made it perfectly all right. I don't think she'll go on worrying so much about what happened last night now. Nor will Jones.'

'But nothing really *did* happen last night, did it?' asked Sophia with a thoughtful smile.

'Of course not,' replied Peter. 'Where's Dann?'

When Mr Bone arrived at Paddington his eyes wore a look of fascinated indulgence. He gripped his umbrella firmly by the middle, and was borne in a taxi to a small restaurant in the neighbourhood of Soho. He had dinner.

With his dinner he had two deep stoops of sparkling Lager beer. After his dinner he ordered a liqueur brandy. His eyes glistened with a strange light now. He had another liqueur brandy. He had three.

He paid his bill recklessly, looking past the *garçon* into the London night beyond the curtained doorway of the restaurant with a glassy smile. He seized his hat, coat and umbrella from the *garçon*, and rose.

He still gripped his umbrella by its middle portion. With his heavy moustache hanging over a savage grin, and his shoulders bent as though he were crouching for cover, he looked like some untamed cave-dweller of the Neolithic age, stalking forth into the night, seeking what he might devour.

He slung his coat over his left arm. Some object flew from the pocket and skidded, with a rattling noise which startled the diners, along the parquet floor of the restaurant. He took no notice. His eyes were piercing the prospect before him, bright with an enthusiasm which had lain dormant beneath those heavy lids for many a year.

As he pushed aside the curtain, a waiter rescued the object

which he had dropped from the skirts of a vexed female diner, and came running with Gallic cries to restore it to its owner. It was a hairbrush. Mr Bone nodded his acknowledgments with a little grunt, and struck forth into the night.

'Hallo, darling,' murmured Peter. 'I thought you were asleep.'

'I was,' said Sophia, nestling to him again inside the spacious limousine, which bore them smoothly homewards through the night.

'Cuddle down to me,' said Peter, 'and I will lull you.'

When Lady Bunter received Wemblow's despatch, and learnt that the young couple had met, had settled their differences, and had proceeded together to town, whence they hoped they might be allowed to visit her again at a more convenient season, she displayed her satisfaction at this latest victory over trouble by retiring to her bed and sleeping off her fatigue, in readiness for any trouble that might arise next day.

Mr Mock, too, was early asleep and was very shortly afterwards in bed.

Mr Goodie was, like many of the more exasperating of his race, an airly raiser. So he went to bed airly.

Sir Stirling told the Hacketts not to hurry on his account. So the Hacketts went to bed too.

'Poor little people,' said Margaret from the bed. 'I'm glad they have gone off happily together. Thank goodness Sophia came round. I only hope and trust that nothing more may come of my silliness.'

Hackett, standing at the window and looking out into the moonlight, turned with the gleam which was his smile.

'Come what may,' he said, 'nothing can change what we hold dearest, can it?'

'Nothing,' she whispered. 'But, oh, my dear, how lucky we

are. I don't think other husbands and wives can rely on each other as we do.'

He nodded gravely.

'Perhaps love is rare,' he said. 'Nothing can shake perfect trust, because trust perfected is truth. Love is truth.'

Margaret kissed her hand to him happily.

'It was really Pansy's fault,' she reflected.

Hackett's manner changed. He seemed, for the moment, almost apprehensive.

'By the way,' he asked, 'where is Pansy tonight?'

'Sleeping with the spaniel,' said Margaret.

THE END